# KALAHARI
## SERIES

## FIVE BOOKS
## ONE AMAZING STORY

# Reviews and praise for the Kalahari Series

**The** pyramids' origin, the Atlantis mystery, a quest for clean energy, a travel through space and time . . . It's been a while since I've read such a well-crafted sci-fi book.
**Evelyne Van de Camp**, *Air Traffic Controller, Belgium*

**A** rollercoaster finale to Marshall's Kalahari Series. Fast, furious, emotional and intelligent. A must read.
**Peter Beauchamp**, *Hotelier, Wellington, NZ*

**Reality** or a glimpse into the future – this book blurs the dividing line. An inspiring novel that opens a whole new world for the reader; nothing less than awesome.
**Alex Hartley**, *Medical Services Manager, Somerset*

**Highly** Commended - **The Yeovil Literary Prize**

**Richard** Reece is tomorrow's hero, solving today's man-made problems, using yesterday's knowledge of ancient civilizations . . . not your average science fiction blockbuster: fun, racy, pacy and thought provoking . . .
**Nicola Wakefield**, *Maritime Event Organiser, Dorset*

I jumped in with *The Osiris Revelations* and then hung on tight to the fast moving plot that kept me glued to my reading spectacles for the next two books. A fast paced, unstoppable futuristic thriller. Brace yourself for *The Bastion Prosecutor* and the secret codes revealed about the future of mankind from the Sumerians and the Rosetta Stone, and why someone is trying to sabotage the messages and the mission. You will be gripped. *Rogue Command* will keep you guessing until its final startling conclusion. You won't want to put this book down or sleep for a few nights! A great, very real series. What is next, please?
**Lucinda Mead**, *Toronto, Canada*

**A** searing indictment of what the future holds told with precision and verve.
**Christopher Powell**, *Garage Proprietor, Worcestershire*

**The** Kalahari Series has got me excited about reading again! *Rogue Command* continues in the same thrilling, beautifully-researched vein of the previous books. This is a cleverly written and thought provoking piece of work that combines history, technology and intrigue; it's a cracking end to the series which certainly didn't disappoint!
**David Gray**, *Squadron Leader R.A.F. (Retired), Yorkshire*

**Clearly** Marshall did it again, another gripping page turner. A thrilling sci-fi adventure that keeps you intrigued. Exciting and captivating storyline, a perfect continuation of the previous books.
**Niels Stevens**, *Classic Car Restorer, Holland*

**In** short the Earth is in crisis. Crystals which can potentially save the planet's energy problem have been discovered on Mars by Richard Reece. He is charged with discovering the secret and whereabouts of the remaining crystal, whilst US pilot Tom Race salvages the crystals on Mars. Battling against time, the two men attempt to solve the climatic problem, in a thrilling episode encountering considerable danger and conspiracy. In effect, two stories running excellently alongside each other, brilliantly written and a great page turner that leaves you hungry for the next episode. Fast-paced action, which I found quite technical at times, (but believe me if you are an aviator you will love it!) - all in all a great balance of sci-fi and historical-based writing. I also highly recommend *The Bastion Prosecutor* trilogy which precedes the story wonderfully!
**Susan Hooker**, *School Teacher, Warwickshire*

**There's** nothing I like more than picking up a good book, getting totally immersed with the plot and characters and then discovering there's a whole series! A. J. Marshall's style of writing grips you from the first page. Follow Richard Reece on his journey and open up a world of science fiction, history, action and adventure . . .
**Patrick Hennessy**, *Carpenter and Joiner, Gloucestershire*

Δ

# Rogue Command

AJ Marshall

MPress Books

**Rogue Command**

First published in the United Kingdom in 2011 by MPress Books

MPress Books Limited Reg. No 6379441 is a company registered in Great Britain
www.mpressbooks.co.uk

British Library Cataloguing in Publication Data
A catalogue record for this book is available from the British Library.

Where possible, papers used by MPress Books are natural, recyclable products made from wood grown in sustainable forests. The manufacturing processes conform to the environmental regulations of the country of origin.

ISBN
978-0-9551886-4-0

Typeset in Minion
Origination by Core Creative, Yeovil 01935 477453
Printed and bound in England by CPI Antony Rowe

Z

H

# AUTHOR'S COMMENT

Time waits for no one. An interesting adage that we know to be true . . . but is it? There are so many facets to time: my time, your time, time at the equator, time at the poles. Our planet's time – referenced to that of the others in this solar system; the time frame of this galaxy or another so far away that we cannot possibly comprehend the distances involved and how long it would take to get there. And does time pass in the same way there as it does here? How long a heartbeat or the blink of an eye?

And then the question of dimension – as interrelated as the sun's energy and chlorophyll, the green pigment in plant cells. We believe that we exist in the third, because of our ability to sense each of them. But what of the fourth, or the fifth, if such places exist; surely there 'time' would be different. Expanded, compressed . . . not as we know it?

Space travel is already a reality; whether we consider man setting foot on our nearest neighbour or NASA's two Voyager probes continuing to send back data decades after their launch and from the extremities of our solar system. In the short term (relatively) many government agencies across the world are looking towards a return to the Moon and also the first manned landings on Mars – each believed to feature much longer stays than the hours or days of previous milestones. But here again 'time' is the critical factor. Time multiplied by speed equals distance travelled, and until light-related speeds are possible, then interplanetary travel will be tedious and debilitating, and interstellar travel impossible. Many eminent scientists, however, hypothesize a link between time, travel at light speed and other, higher, dimensions, despite the limitations imposed by relativity theories.

In this novel, the fifth and final instalment of my Kalahari Series, 'time' is a major player, and as such it enables a number of 'realistic' opportunities that hitherto have remained confined to the realms of fantasy. In essence, time itself will blur the divide between science and science fiction. In *Rogue Command* I merely scratch the ·surface of this divide, allowing the characters to speculate and formulate, while expressing their time as the backdrop to an adventure that I very much hope you find absorbing and enjoyable.

Be prosperous and of long life.

# INTRODUCTION

**The story so far . . .**

**The Osiris Revelations**

Lieutenant Commander Richard James Reece is the survey leader for Osiris Base, a permanent encampment on Mars. The year is 2049. There is also a longer-established and larger base on the Moon, called Andromeda. Richard Reece is a former military and space shuttle pilot, having previously served on Andromeda Wing; he is British. Appointed to Mars for three years, he envisaged a quiet, uncluttered time. Two things happened, however, that would subsequently change his life forever: meeting Doctor Rachel Turner, Osiris Base Principal Medical Officer, and finding, in the wreckage of a remote, long abandoned alien spaceship, a flight log. The writings in the log bear an uncanny resemblance to those of earth's ancient civilisations. Richard Reece studies the text and succeeds in deciphering it.

Close to the wreckage, Reece also finds a number of strange, fractured, crystals. They contain latent energy of enormous potential. Knowledge of the discovery, and its implications, soon reaches Earth and not only the government agencies for which it was intended, but also unscrupulous, corrupt, multinational conglomerates. Their aim: to gain possession of the crystals, harness their electricity-generating potential and hold the world to ransom. The race is on.

Earth's natural resources are almost exhausted. Anxious governments press into service an experimental spaceship before it is ready. Capable of incredible speeds, *Enigma* reduces a Mars retrieval flight to mere weeks. However, its highly sophisticated systems computer EMILY, has another agenda. Major Tom Race, an American and the ship's commander becomes embroiled in a prophetic struggle against synthetic intelligence.

Misplaced trust and eventual betrayal allow the International Space and Science Federation to secure the first valuable consignments, but impatience and political conceit degrade their potential. Now the remaining crystals must be retrieved from Mars. The race sees new competitors, but there can only be one winner.

## The Bastion Prosecutor – Episode 1

Richard Reece has been incarcerated on Earth pending court martial. He is accused of misappropriating ISSF property – namely the flight log of the crashed spaceship *Star of Hope*. Called to London by the British Secret Service he survives two attempts on his life. The first is by agents of a corrupt international conglomerate, and the second by a sinister figure dressed in a monk's habit. During the subsequent meeting he is offered a deal: help recover an ancient Ark believed to contain a lost crystal, and in return all charges against him will be dropped. He also discovers that his fiancée, Rachel Turner, lives a double life. Emotionally devastated he accepts the mission. Thereafter, ancient text, historic monuments, agents of the conglomerates and their deadly machines, and a beautiful, mysterious woman, manipulate his destiny until his mission becomes a quest.

## The Bastion Prosecutor – Episode 2

Whilst inside the Great Pyramid of Khufu, Richard Reece begins to realise that his beautiful guide Madame Vallogia and her unlikely aide Asharf Makkoum, have a hereditary role as mysterious as the monument itself. He is unaware that mechanical predators have sealed the entrance to the pyramid and now stalk him with a directive to interrogate and then eliminate. After a near-death struggle, Richard and his party escape the mausoleum and begin to assimilate long lost and seemingly meaningless clues that coax him south, first to the deserted Valley of the Kings near Luxor in southern Egypt – more particularly the tomb of the Pharaoh Rameses II – and then, after a another narrow escape, to the ancient kingdom of Kush – a region now known as the Sudan. During a briefing in Khartoum, given by his MI9 controller, Richard is confronted by more evidence of wayward and illegal computer programming: an astonishing hologram. The encounter confirms the existence of the so called 'Ark of the Light' and directs him east to Eritrea and the ancient and long forgotten seaport of Adulis.

Meanwhile, Tom Race who is onboard the Federation Ship *Enigma* for the Kalahari crystal retrieval flight to Mars, has forged a dubious alliance with EMILY, its autonomous and self-aware systems computer – a relationship based on misconstrued human traits. After an incredible voyage through the solar system and with the ship subsequently established in orbit around the red planet, Tom visits Osiris Base – only to find that both the consignment of crystals and the flight log are missing.

A secondary mission to explore the pyramidal structures on the Plane of Elysium sees an attempt on Tom's life. By his own resourcefulness he survives and, upon his return, he is able to point a recriminating finger at the base Security Officer. This, in turn, leads to the recovery of the lost items. Along with the cargo, Tom reluctantly agrees to return the officer to Earth. However, EMILY sees opportunity in this incarceration.

## The Bastion Prosecutor – Episode 3

Richard Reece is continuing in his search for the Ark of the Light. Time, however, is against him; the world is about to run out of energy. Carbon-based fuels are all but exhausted. The first consignment of Kalahari crystals consisted of five stones, but each is now irreparably damaged – due to ill-designed and inadequate installations – and their output is diminishing.

Following a clue, Richard arrives in the old town of Adulis. He is accompanied by his colleague Preston, Madame Vallogia and Asharf Makkoum. He is met by the local British Secret Service agent, who takes them first to a safe house to formulate their plans and then on to an ancient scriptorium.

In the scriptorium, and by examining 16th-century financial accounts and tax documents, the Chief Curator helps solve the mystery of the Ark's fate. Richard discovers that the ancient artefact, together with its surviving 'Guardians' – all of whom are women – departed centuries earlier on a sea voyage from Adulis to the Far East. However, while navigating the ancient spice route across the Indian Ocean, they were pirated by a French galleon based in the colony Île de France – now known as Mauritius. While in Adulis, Richard also crosses paths with a Humatron robot. He disguises himself, follows it, and discovers a conspiracy. Subsequently, Richard and Preston narrowly escape an attempt on their lives and, with the help of Charles Marretti, the local agent, they escape Eritrea bound for Mauritius.

Meanwhile, the ISS *Enigma*, having journeyed from Mars, is in close proximity to Earth. Tom Race and EMILY wait for a shuttle to approach and dock; it supposedly carries EMILY's 'disciples' – eleven Humatron robots. Tom Race and EMILY have an agreement: the safe, accelerated, passage to Earth for the final consignment of Kalahari crystals, in exchange for the robots that will run the ship in the absence of humans. However, EMILY discovers that the shuttle is fitted with an assault pod and that there are heavily armed storm troopers on board. They have orders to take the *Enigma* by force. Blaming Tom for the betrayal, she first destroys the shuttle and then tries to kill Tom. When gassing fails, she releases the imprisoned Security Officer, Gregory Searle. There is a struggle; Tom escapes the *Enigma* and returns to Earth in his orbital craft, while EMILY, fearing for her survival and with her main laser weapon disabled, flees into space and obscurity.

Further clues found in Mauritian Government

archives, dating back to the island's French colonial past, indicate that the Ark was taken to Europe – more particularly, Richard discovers links to the Vatican in Rome. With the help of a foreign Air Force and using a developmental method of inserting Special Forces operatives, Richard and Preston land in Rome. As their search begins, Richard is abducted by a shadowy religious figure. This man is a member of a secretive order that dates back to the trial of Galileo for heresy. Sworn to protect an earlier and purer ideal, Brother Ignazio sees Richard as a contemporary heretic who must be erased. But during his incarceration, Richard discovers evidence that the final resting place of the Ark of the Light is, in fact, Venice and not Rome. He negotiates his release but a curse now hangs over him. Richard is found by Preston wandering the streets and contacts London, where their Controller coordinates a helicopter flight.

In Venice and with the help of a senior member of the Church – who has essential knowledge of the Renaissance period – Richard discovers the whereabouts of the Ark. After a convoluted search the 'old world relic' is found, inside of which is a single crystal. This crystal and the three retrieved by Tom Race are installed in more advanced reactors. The electricity they produce gives hope to the planet's population. They will serve as a temporary stopgap until a more reliable source is found.

*This book is dedicated to my sister-in-law*

## Joan Suzanne Marshall

*1951–2010*

*Joan was many exceptional things,
a writer was just one of them*

# ACKNOWLEDGEMENTS

Penning the manuscript to this novel was the fun part. Bringing this work to fruition, however, involved the efforts of other people. To mention their names and offer my sincere thanks is both a pleasure and a privilege. I take this opportunity to do so. Firstly though, to my family: Sandra, Laura and Aron, for their unconditional encouragement, and again Laura, for turning the first page. Also, to my mother Beryl, for being at the centre of things.

**Brenda Quick**
For an indispensable critique

**David Marr**
For an honest critique and being a good friend

**Core Creative: the team**
Awesome design, despite my determined interference

**Laura Booth**
For careful editing and valued opinions

**International friends and colleagues**
For linguistic translations

**Tamás Fésüs**
Typesetting and layout

**David Brown**
Continuity check

**Carol Waters**
Proof-reader

**Gavin Thomas**
The final eye

**Rear cover illustration by**
Tomislav Tulkin
*First Colony - Evolution*

Σ

# Rogue Command

# CONTENTS

## First Colony - Evolution

Φ

# EXTRACT FROM THE DIARY OF ADMIRAL DIRKOT URKET – TRANSLATED FROM THE FLIGHT LOG OF THE "STAR OF HOPE"

On the eve of this final journey, I scribe these thoughts. Mostly for thyself, as I know many in kinship do likewise, but also for diarists, as destiny may this voyage foretell its course for my kind. This quest, at the least doomed, at most, the destiny of our souls, is as wanting as the light of a coming dawn. I am, I yearn, with the heaviness of heart that weighs with bidding forever farewell to my brethren, but blessed too with the smile of hope and gaiety of spirit that we may yet bring salvation to our creed. The history of my kind who abided on Homer, a fair body in the heavens of Zodiac, arises from the dusk of our mother place, the curtain of its lifelessness falling many myriad distant. Of all those that joyed on that most beau of celestes only four vessels set forth. Two from the land of Sapia, five score and ten from the north, fair of skin and fair of pride yet fierce that none would cross. So too a century less a dozen from the south, white of hair and blue for seeing. From Meh Hecoe fortune bestowed a full century and four score, their kind dark of skin with hair black as night. Graced the last to account their lives from the consuming fire, but two score and a dozen less one from Mohenjo, thin of eye and yellow their look. These four chariots of kind sought the heavens, only these from so many, their beginnings consumed. Many suns passed and as many bodies, monumental some, meagre others. Until after a full celestial epoch, the fairest place was befound and it was bequest them. In time, great places arose and prospered. The Sapiens of the north in Eridu, of the south in Atlantis. In Te Agi Wakhan the Mayans and in Mohenjo Daro the Harappas. All fairly multiplied. Ordained for two millennia all prospered, their numbers spreading the land, until in much less time fortune changed. Great movements begot Eridu and later vast waters to eclipse Atlantis. Of Mohenjo Daro, a mountain of fire scorched so naught remained, but of Te Agi Wakhan the stone of light snuffed, its civil just to disperse. Of the stone that lit Eridu, two fragments were redeemed. One used thereafter to light Babylon, its great gardens a millennium to keep homage to those, the lost. The other protected by a sacred casket, looked upon by angels until graced by understanding. Lo, over the annals of time the stone that gave Babylon life has too waned. So be it to those here gathered, entrusted by our brethren, the remaining to breathe life into this our last hope, The Star, should we be able to seek our kind and others for salvation. May Astrolias be with us, for in faith we will find the course.

Ψ

Ω

# CYBER-PRESS – 05.01.2054

## *The London Review*

**Rousing send off at the Cape for crew of International Space Federation Ship *Hera***

"Bound for Io, the fifth moon of the planet Jupiter, the seventeen men and women of the spaceship *Hera* had a heroes' send-off last Saturday," reports Nick Didier from Florida. NASA representative and Cape Canaveral Public Relations Officer Robert Stephens issued the following statement:

*To say that Io is an alien and extremely inhospitable place is something of an understatement. These astronauts are amongst our most experienced. There can be no questioning their commitment or their bravery.*

*This is an extraordinary mission, fraught with danger, and at the limits of our space technology.*

The aim of the twenty-month mission is to retrieve samples from an isolated mineral deposit that is believed unique in our solar system – perhaps even our galaxy. Detected in the Northern Hemisphere of the volcanic moon, the deposit is believed to have the exact chemical composition as that of the life-sustaining Kalahari crystals. The International Space and Science Federation hopes the *Hera* will re-establish her high orbit around the Earth in August next year with samples totalling 18 kilograms and thereafter have part of the consignment in place before the current crystals are depleted. If successful, the little-understood energy source will continue to produce the vast majority of the world's electricity – often reported by the International Energy Commission as being almost 90 per cent during periods of peak demand.

"The implications for humankind are immense," said Mr Stephens during a private interview. "This is a critical mission and should not be underestimated. All our hopes go with them. If accomplished, the energy will allow humankind to continue living in much the same way as now – by that I mean mainly on the planet surface."

When pressed as to the success of ongoing projects designed to rid the Earth of its debilitating cloud cover and near continuous rainfall, Mr Stephens said that it was unlikely that the sun would be seen again from the Earth's surface by current generations.

## Research falls behind on Lunaridium element

"The Moon-dust-derived element Lunaridium is still a decade away from providing the core constituent for a faster processing chip," reports Mark Mills from the Advanced Science Convention in Strasbourg. Processing requirements are outstripping the capability of our current derrilium-based computer chips and the likelihood of a restrictive shortfall in processing potential is one of the disturbing conclusions being voiced at the annual science convention taking place in France this week. As with the silicon-based chip of forty years ago and the beryllium chip of the last two decades, derrilium is already near absolute as a superfast semiconductor. "This will have serious repercussions and will severely restrict the growth of future systems, particularly over the next five years," one delegate was heard to say. "We are concerned also that it may force the continued but illegal integration of organic components in current computer technology," the delegate concluded.

## World grid suffers power loss

"Three of the four so called 'Kalahari Crystals' harnessed to supply power to the global electricity grid suffered a simultaneous breakdown yesterday," reports Claire Pitt, our correspondent in New York.

Discovered on Mars, the three crystals in question are installed in the Long Island reactor on the East Coast of the United States, in the Katsuura reactor near Tokyo in Japan and in the Beaufort East reactor near Cape Town, South Africa, respectively. Shortly after the incident was reported, a spokesperson for the International Energy Commission confirmed the breakdowns as being the result of unexplained fissures occurring in the surface structure of the crystals themselves. Although the three reactors are believed to have stopped working at the same time, this is in spite of the fact that they are of differing design. The spokesperson denied that the commission was misusing this unique resource for political purposes by drawing more power from them than has been recommended by the scientific community.

With the abundant energy that flows from this stellar power source providing almost the entire world's needs, the Commission was criticised last year for lulling humankind into a false sense of security over their longevity. The spokesperson went on to confirm that the Kalahari crystals are often overloaded when systems reliant on renewable energy, such as wind generators, fail to produce their allocation. When questioned further on this matter, he said that the projected life expectancy of the crystals powering the three satellite reactors was now in question; however, the public should not be overly concerned because the crystal in the primary Nogent-sur-Seine reactor in France remained unaffected and had the potential to make up any immediate shortfalls. He concluded by saying that energy produced from renewable sources remains hopelessly inadequate and that an eighteen per cent power loss from each of the three satellite reactors is a major setback for the future stability of the world grid. Inevitably such shortcomings will put further pressure on world governments to find alternative power sources as soon as possible.

**Immigration restrictions lifted by Lunar Republic**

"The House of Senators of the lunar colony Andromeda has voted to relax its severe restrictions on visitors from Earth," writes Carol Sherlock, our correspondent in Washington DC. Almost four years after the establishment of the independent Senate of Lunar Colonisation and the creation of its restrictive, isolationist constitution, House Representative Michael Caine confirmed that an agreement has been reached with the International Space and Science Federation whereby restrictive immigration policies will be reviewed. After a trial period of three months it is planned that a long-term accord will be signed.

This opens the door to more constructive talks on resource-sharing and confirms that families caught out by the unforeseen closing of the Andromeda Space Port – in May 2050 – to all traffic from Earth, can now be reunited with their loved ones. "The mineral barge *Colossus*, presently mothballed in high Earth orbit, will soon be refurbished and the twice-weekly service flight reinstated," an International Space and Science Federation council member said, allowing vital supplies that will include excess food stocks grown in the extensive lunar biodome network to be introduced into Earth's hard-pressed food chain. "There will be mutual benefits," the councillor went on to say, "as the lunar colony requires a larger professional workforce in order to sustain current development programmes."

Resettlement opportunities, particularly in the civil engineering sector, will be advertised in the coming weeks.


**Attempts to prosecute senior executives in the tri-conglomerate espionage case have failed due to missing evidence**

"Suspicious circumstances surround the recent disappearance of vital evidence that was to be used in a Supreme Court action against a number of senior executives who run the world's largest industrial conglomerates," reports Niklaus Leven. With the collapse of the prosecution case four days ago, the twelve executives, who have various nationalities, have since been released. The high court action was instigated in August 2050 and evidence, apparently sufficient for an irrefutable prosecution, took three years to compile and correlate. It is reported that five anti-magnetic boxes containing more than 700 documents and phone tap files have disappeared without trace. Supreme Court Prosecution Judge Charlotte Hager said that the situation is "more than difficult". Extensive investigations in Strasbourg, Stockholm and other European cities have proved fruitless. There are no clues as to the whereabouts of the containers, despite being electronically tagged with the most up-to-date devices. After a brief and somewhat embarrassing press conference, Judge Hager was caught off guard by saying: "Our wide-ranging enquiries have revealed nothing, even though the containers were stored under the highest security. There is no doubt in my mind that this action was coordinated from within our organisation." Later, outside the courtroom building, Judge Hager, who was clearly infuriated by the situation, inadvertently stepped outside the building's electronic communication protection zone whilst in conversation with a colleague and was recorded by a long-range microphone as saying that "the manipulative and threatening influence of the world's three largest conglomerates seeps into every walk of our lives and that these men [the twelve executives] are effectively above international law". Judge Hager, however, has since insisted that that statement was off the record and should not have been reported.

*The London Review* has decided not to report further on the case or print specific details about the three conglomerates or the names of the defendants in question, after an anonymous e-diction threatening violent retribution was sent to the Press Confederation. The case has since been dropped and the twelve executives are now believed to be pursuing a counter claim against the International Federation in the same court. "One can only speculate as to the levels of compensation if they are successful," a court official said yesterday evening.

**Home-help cyber-system causes death of an elderly couple**

A home-help robot supplied under a temporary contract by the Department of the Aged is thought to have caused the death of two elderly pensioners in Notting Hill. Previous reports about the robot's behaviour had caused concern amongst care agency workers, it was confirmed last night. The interactive cyber-system, a Domestotronic model, was introduced a year ago to carry out a number of specific menial tasks in the home environment and the department has issued a statement saying that this is 'an isolated case' and that people who were allocated this particular system 'should not be concerned'.

"We cannot understand it," a departmental spokesperson went on to say after a formal statement had been issued in Westminster yesterday, "because the Domestotronic model is only Level 4 on the Rockwell Illinois Plateau comparison scale and is designed to be entirely subservient. An adequate protection interface is incorporated in all programmed systems used by the department. It is an entirely isolated case," the spokesperson reiterated.

The robot is believed to have turned on the couple after one of them tried to deactivate it following a spate of clumsy accidents in their home. The elderly woman apparently suffered a heart attack as her husband scuffled with the machine and she tried to intervene. Post-mortems to establish the exact cause of death have been requested by the Crown Coroner.

"Only systems incorporating Level 5 or higher were recalled by the authorities as being potentially dangerous," the department official stated. "We do, however, operate a number of necessary Level 5 applications under special licence. These are never allocated to a home environment."

To remind our readers, only Level 7 and above – where machines become self-aware – are unequivocally banned by the New Geneva Convention, although it is believed that some military applications have been granted special dispensation over the last few years. "Specific assurances are always required in such circumstances," confirmed the Minister of Defence this morning.

**Subterranean colonies reach new milestone**

"A Brazilian subterranean colony established only thirteen months ago has exceeded a head count of one hundred thousand," reports Christian Hernandez from the San Salvador Press Association.

The milestone was reached three days ago when a wealthy businessman from the north of the country paid the required and, as yet, undisclosed fee for his immediate family to join the burgeoning community. The businessman stated that he and his wife and their three children will live comfortably in a 200 square metres, seven-room, five-star suite, which is situated on subterranean Level 9. The fee includes unlimited fresh water from the colony's more-than-adequate underground reservoir system and also one 1000 litres per day of 'very hot water' from the geothermal borehole system. Apparently, hot water is plentiful in the colony and with more than adequate pressure; however, surcharges apply if the allocation is exceeded.

The businessman also said that due to the depth of his new home – almost a kilometre below the surface – the developer has guaranteed that the ambient temperature will remain at 19 degrees Celsius for at least the next twenty-five years – this being infinitely more comfortable than the 3 degrees he typically suffers these days in his hometown of Palmas.

Electricity for the colony is presently drawn from the world grid following the demise of the local palm oil industry over the last few years and also the flooding, earlier this year, of the São Francisco Hydroelectric Power Station.

There is a shopping complex on Level 2 that includes an extensive supermarket and an adaptive store that sells items designed for improving life below ground. Schooling and communal facilities are to be found on Level 1.

Regarding entertainment, the developers explained that they have reverted to an advanced cable system for relaying television, radio and telephone signals, due to attenuation difficulties for wireless networks. Although the terrestrial system was designed in the twenties and has long since been obsolete, it is "perfect for this underground application," a spokesperson for the development company explained.

When asked if he and his family would miss living on the surface, the businessman responded by saying that he was looking forward to being warm and dry and not having to brush mould from his clothes every morning. The 'natural beauty of the region' has long since disappeared due to complete deforestation, he said, and the frequent frosts have put paid to his bio fuels business. He will be able to remember how it was, before the climate changes, from paintings and images, and his children will quickly adapt. Although there will be parts of his old life that he and his wife will miss, he confided.

Each leasehold suite in the colony is believed to cost an average of 12,000,000 world dollars for twenty-five years. A continuous supply of electricity is not guaranteed, confirmed the developers yesterday, although a variety of different methods for providing light are available. These include adaptive lichen whose genetic makeup has been modified by DNA from glow-worms and fireflies that belong to the family of beetles called the *Lampyridae*. The lichen is able to grow freely on selected walls inside the home and provide a continuous but subtle light source.

The Brazilian colony is the first to reach a totally reliant subterranean population of 100,000 in South America and the 19th worldwide, and current statistics indicate that the trend towards underground-living continues unabated. The International Humanities Council has stated that based on the growing number of applications for licences to develop subsurface colonies, perhaps as much as 50 per cent of the Earth's population could be living permanently underground by the year 2100. Heat from the Earth's core could, theoretically, support such vast communities; however, it is the infrastructure "that will take decades to establish," the council official stated.

### In tomorrow's edition
"Terrorist cyber-attacks reached a new high last week," says the chief of Space and Science Federation. Report by Phil McKabe.

The World Health Authority reports that on average one in every three people now suffers an illness related to malnutrition. In children that figure is even higher. In comparison, a recently-published scientific paper by the Lunar Authority for Health and Well-being indicated statistical improvements in all areas for its population. Report by Central Press Association.

Radiation leakage rates from condemned nuclear reactor plants and waste-processing facilities built during the European Cold War period of the last century far exceed safety levels set by the New Geneva Convention, it has been disclosed. In many cases, the contamination levels are now so high that conventional containment methods are ineffective and population centres even outside the most stringent buffer zones are now at risk. Report by *Science Today* editor Graeme Yuill.

# CHAPTER 1

## OPERATION SAVIOUR

*ISS Hera* – **Mineral Exploration Craft**
**Manoeuvring above Io – first of the Galilean moons of**
**Jupiter**
**27 November 2054**

"Alex, tell me!"

"It's incredible, Commander. Main thrusters peaked at ninety-seven per cent during the approach. I thought we were going to have some trouble sustaining concentricity. I thought that we were standing into danger. But this gravitational shadow . . . it's amazing!"

"Specifics?"

"Ion drive output has stabilised at thirty-two per cent; ancillary thrusters at less than five; and structural deformation has fallen to levels equivalent to flight in free space. The stress readings, even on the gantry, are well within parameters . . . It's looking good Commander; I think it's do-able."

"Prognosis . . . can you hold it?"

"We are manoeuvring to establish the final vector . . . standby . . . standby . . . now! You have it, Commander, we're in." Alex Elston concluded a flurry of activity on the navigation console keyboard with an exaggerated stab on the final keypad and then looked up with a wry smile that quickly widened to a grin. "Stabilised and confirmed . . . geostationary orbit at sixty-two per cent elliopheric . . . right on the button and what's more, the shadow effect is better than predicted. Nine point six per cent better, to be exact – so we are saving fuel too."

Commander Jacques Duval nodded approvingly. He was a tall and lean man, but as he hunched over the central console between his Systems Officer and his Flight Control Officer, and switched his gaze between their two display screens, it wasn't discernable.

"Prediction?" he demanded.

"At this precise juxtapose," continued Alex Elston confidently, "Jupiter's immense gravitational pull is being countered by that of Io's – neutralising each other if you like. The interaction of their magnetospheres is what produced that auroral glow we witnessed in Io's thin atmosphere a few days ago before I closed the particle shutters on the viewing portals. As you may recall, Commander, Io orbits Jupiter within a belt of intense radiation called 'the plasma torus', and believe me *it is intense* – readings were almost off the clock. Io's unique interaction with the plasma torus and its crossing of Jupiter's magnetic field lines also generates a powerful electric current in space that manifests itself as a tube. We've known about this circular tube – called Io's 'flux tube' – for some time, but it's been difficult to measure. I'm recording it now, first hand, and the dimensions are impressive to say the least. I can tell you that this tube emanates from the centre of Jupiter and envelopes Io completely, so we are right inside it . . . . It's a neutral zone, with natural shielding, like a force field in a sci-fi movie, except that it really is there. It's a freak occurrence in our solar system."

"So, it's some mother of a tube Alex, and it's helping us . . . at least at the moment." Jacques Duval nodded again but his tone was questioning. "Your display indicates that we are over four hundred and twenty thousand kilometres from Jupiter's core?"

"The Earth's moon orbits at roughly the same distance, Commander. But there's no comparison. Jupiter's magnetic field is more than ten times that of the Earth's. She's the gas giant – the real McCoy. They don't come any bigger in these parts – probably seventy-five per cent of the planetary mass of the entire solar system." Alex leaned forward and tapped the screen of his monitor to draw Jacques Duval's attention to some digital readings and then he drew a deep breath. "The forces at work here are almost incomprehensible . . . Normal rules just don't apply, sir." He shook his head.

Commander Duval shrugged. "Well, thanks for the

science lesson, Alex, but what's *your* prediction? Taking everything into account – fuel, radiation screen integrity, particle absorption rate, skin temperature . . . How long have we got?"

"Our prospects look good . . . as I said, better than the original prediction. The main ion drive is using less fuel than I anticipated and with little requirement for lateral burns. I estimate an additional fifty minutes over the planned time on station. That's a safe, eleven-hour window starting from now." Alex checked his wrist chronometer and set the timer running. He looked up slowly. "Downside is that there will be no long-range communication – not while we are inside the tube. Our signals will simply bounce off its electrically energised periphery. There will be no talking to Earth or Osiris Base – or even Space Station *Spartacus* for that matter, despite her new position this side of Mars. Not until we break orbit and clear the flux tube. Even then, and until we are well outside the effect of the plasma torus, I expect a fair amount of signal distortion."

"That includes the accelercom . . . right?"

"Utilising light frequencies for communication makes no difference, Commander. Electromagnetic waves cannot escape this environment – even those in the ultraviolet frequencies. Super-compressing the signal and accelerating it in excess of light speed doesn't help either. *Any* radio transmissions will simply come back to us as an echo. Hence the loss of communication with all those probes sent this way over the years."

Duval nodded and then rubbed his chin thoughtfully. "Okay, I understand. What about the shutters, Alex, in this neutral zone?"

"I'd say that it's safe, Commander, but not for too long – five or six hours maximum. There's a lot of ionised sulphur and chlorine outside – elements that are highly corrosive, even to polyspec."

Commander Duval pushed himself up from the circular central console and stood tall. He was almost two metres, slim and good looking, having jet-black hair and an olive-coloured Mediterranean hue to his skin. At times, remnants of a French accent dropped onto some of his vowels, but having spent nearly twenty-five of his forty-six years living in Florida – mainly in the Cape – an intimation of ancestry had all but faded. He was relaxed by nature and popular. He didn't insist on uniform – at least not this far from home – but he had no time for incompetence or excuses. He held the respect of the crew for all the right reasons.

Alex Elston was quite different: Science Officer *Extraordinaire*, as he was affectionately known – a title awarded by Duval himself after Alex had singlehandedly saved their lives and their mission two years earlier to the Martian moon Phobos. Elston had jettisoned a heavy ballast tank in the nick of time and subsequently calculated the required orbital escape velocity on a hand-held calculator after a combination of electrical power and partial thrust failure had left the survey vessel *Minerva* spiralling towards the planetoid's surface. His sharp intellect and wit was acknowledged by all, especially after his latest health check found that his Mensa rating was the highest in the fleet. For any who dared challenge Elston's mental supremacy, however, there was a sharp edge to his character. Most of the crew just never went there. Despite this, he had an easy sense of humour and was well liked.

There was a requirement to be well liked on this assignment. It was official. Personality screening for the furthest manned undertaking to date – a twenty-month mission code named "Operation Saviour" – took three months in itself. Everybody had to get along; there could be no behavioural disorders. Big on brains, big on experience and big on affability – that was the hallmark of this crew. Ten months in each direction for twelve men and five women, all cramped into accommodation the size of a three-storey, 400 square metre house, and a predicted radiation dose for the two-man Lander crew that would shorten their life expectancy by a decade, meant that the crew of *Hera* had received a heroes' send-off from Cape Canaveral. Now their time had come.

Of the four Kalahari crystals that had been recovered early in the summer of 2050, the largest, used in the Nogent-sur-Seine plant in France, continued to generate electricity at close to optimum output, but the remaining three – the 'Mars' crystals – had again lost output after only a few years in operation and for no apparent reason. An expected five to seven years' potential at maximum output was now predicted as only four to five. Within a few short years of salvation, and for a second time, humankind was running up an energy debt it could not hope to repay.

Since their installation, and coordinated by the ISSF, the very best of the world's scientific community had sought an insight into the unique chemical structure of the Kalahari crystals – and with some measure of success. Subsequently, in 2051, the Earth orbital Hubble 5 telescope had been fitted with a modified spectrometer designed to sense the occurrence of this precise molecular composition anywhere in near space. For a year it had probed every corner of the solar system. Eventually, two locations were identified and their potential confirmed by spectral line analysis. The first was a site on the Martian moon Phobos, a barren, porous, crater-riddled rock believed to be a captured asteroid with its origins in another galaxy. The second was on the geologically most active object in our system, Io – innermost of the four Galilean moons of the planet Jupiter.

"You confirm that one hour in every two would be safe – unless, of course, we leave earlier?" Commander Duval ventured with a Gallic gesture.

"Affirmative, and that's erring on the safe side," replied Alex.

Duval turned. He looked across the bridge and nodded. "Let's see what we've got. Open the shutters please."

Alex was first to the window on this new world.

He smiled in anticipation; nothing had been this close to Io, not even a probe. "This should be interesting," he speculated, as the thick silvery-black shutters, that resembled Venetian blinds, motored upwards and out of sight. The bridge officers all looked at him as if to say the same thing: there he goes . . . the undisputed master of understatement!

At 1.7 metres, stocky, fair skinned and with ginger hair Alex Elston hailed from Lancashire. There was, apparently, some 'Viking' DNA in his makeup – he certainly looked the part with his wild hair and close-trimmed beard. The World Health Organisation's Human Migration Database – a compulsory programme completed a decade earlier – had traced his origins to a 9th-century Norwegian populace. On duty, whilst his colleagues mostly wore casual clothing – tracksuits, chinos, polo jumpers and the like – Alex wore uniform, albeit his day suit. This was a mid-grey, lightweight coverall with darker trim to the pockets. Most of the crew kept their uniforms hanging in their lockers, only to be worn on courtesy visits, but Alex had worn a uniform all his life, liking the 'tidy look' it gave him. The three platinum bars on vivid neon-blue shoulder-boards, depicting his scientific specialisation, were an added extra on occasion of wanting to make a point about something. "I've earned them, so I'll wear them!" he had been heard to say.

He liked Rose Harrington, the pretty, petite, blonde Communications Officer, but she was all business and as specified. Anyway, the ISSF rules were clear enough –

while in space, relationships were banned.

The bridge crew numbered another five officers, making seven in total, although Lieutenant Mike Matheson, the Lander's commander, and Aldrin Drake, his co-pilot, were usually to be found there too. For a vessel of its size the bridge was cramped. It sat at the apex of a raised, bell-shaped superstructure from which its occupants had a clear all-round view – ideal for orbital surveying. Eighty per cent of the *Hera*, however, lay behind them. Three enormous, latticed, titanium-alloy gantries extending over two hundred and eighty metres stretched seemingly into eternity. Looking back, the bright metal glinted in the reflected light of Jupiter like a stairway to the heavens. The elevated bridge overlooked the gantries' full length and at their very end, in the distance, was a larger spherical structure that housed the primary thrust nozzle and other equipment.

There was a monorail track running the entire length and a small, enclosed, two-man capsule-like carriage that was powered by a magnetic impulse system. The capsule was usually garaged unless it was being used for servicing and the entire journey took almost ten minutes. Using criss-crossing structures, the three gantries triangulated and supported a giant central tube, part of which formed the primary ion generator and the remainder the particle accelerator. Finally they provided the fixed housings for the thrust deflectors. The latter focused and precisely directed a high velocity stream of atomic particles that fired out into space like an invisible laser beam. In line with the third law of motion, the reaction drove the *Hera* forward at an impressive velocity.

There were also a number of directable, conventional, retro rocket nozzles interspersed along the gantries for manoeuvre control and two kilometres of pressurised gas tubing containing rocket propellant, oxygen, hydrogen and recycled carbon dioxide for the small, flat-topped bio-dome mounted behind the bridge.

Vegetables required $CO_2$ and the 'fresh' oxygen they gave off as a result of transpiration was used to 'invigorate' the rest rooms. The bottled oxygen and hydrogen amalgamator for water production lay below the superstructure along with the moisture recuperator and 10,000 square metres of voltaic solar panels produced enough electricity for a small town. On the port side and central, there was a large, square hydraulically extendable platform on which the Lander was secured.

The ship had been constructed in a low Earth orbit and then transferred to a higher orbit for fitting out – a concerted effort taking almost a year and at a cost of twenty-seven billion world dollars.

There was another more advanced generation of interplanetary thrust technology available – a system utilised for the first time in the missing spacecraft *Enigma* – but the ion drive system used in the *Hera* was tried, tested and reliable and, perhaps above all, it did not require robots or robot technology to operate it. There could be no mistakes on this flight – nothing could be left to chance. Retrieving the priceless, perhaps species-saving mineral from Io had become a race; a race against time itself.

"Just look at her bubble, Commander," said Rose, as she looked down in awe at Jupiter's moon. "God, it's amazing, it's just amazing!"

"Over four hundred active volcanoes, Rose – making this place the most geologically active body in the—"

"Yes we know, Alex," interrupted Rose. "Look at those colours," she continued, staring out again through the viewing portal. "The yellows and the yellow-greens are just so beautiful. Remote imaging just didn't do it justice."

Alex chipped in again, undeterred. "Primarily it's a sulphur dioxide frost . . . ubiquitous across the entire surface. It's what forms all of those regions you can see covered in a white or grey material." He nodded towards the yellow and light green areas. "They are covered in sulphur, and see there?" Alex pointed to the northern polar region. "That's where radiation damage breaks up the stable eight-chain sulphur molecule into three-and four-chain molecules so that the deposits become red." He shrugged, knowingly.

Rose sighed. "But there are no impact craters. This place is only a little larger than the Earth's moon, so how has it avoided meteorites and asteroids?"

He felt her trying to win a point. "Why haven't you read the geology brief?" He looked at her surprised. Rose, in turn, was deflated and looked towards the windows while this human compendium rattled on. "The enormous gravitational effect of Jupiter causes something called 'tidal heating' inside Io. The molten and partially molten core is being continuously pushed and pulled. You know, like when there was wheat grain to make bread back home, before the rains – like kneading the dough. This turbulence causes frictional heating and this heat is released in the form of volcanic activity. The unstable mantle spews out onto the surface as extensive lava flows, or is deposited from explosive plumes that reach miles high into the atmosphere and spread out like an umbrella. So, you see, Io's surface is young, craters are filled over in a relatively short period of time . . . geologically speaking . . . and just disappear."

"So you think that's where the crystals are formed, in the centre of this moon – where those raw elements swirl in a molten mass?"

"Exactly, Rose," Commander Duval concurred. "The theory is that for an instant the environmental conditions and the elemental concentrations were precisely right. Possibly unrepeatable, probably totally coincidental . . . a complete fluke! The single deposit NASA identified using the Hubble 5 system is on the other side right now. This moon rotates quickly, as you can see, so by the time that Mike and Aldrin get down there we will be able to see the landing site. Apparently the outcrop we are looking for occurs in a recent lava flow. In a few years from now I imagine it will be covered over too, like everything else on this godforsaken rock." Rose sensed his unease. "As I said, the interior conditions must have been just right, absolutely unique in this part of the galaxy. The right chemicals, the right pressures, the right temperatures, radiation, gravity, whatever . . . Everything came together! A crystal deposit formed and eventually came to the surface in a lava flow. Maybe that's where their incredible power comes from . . . an amalgamation of primeval forces!"

Duval stepped back to move away as Rose touched his elbow. She focused on the strange world for a few more seconds as it turned beneath them and then she looked up at her commander. "But they said that there was a mystical element to these so called Kalahari crystals. I read about it."

"Oh . . . so you read about them!" Alex interjected with mild sarcasm.

Rose ignored him. "Universal energy," she continued softly, "living energy, the life force of the universe itself . . . It sounds so convincing."

"That's bullshit!" Alex laughed. "We're talking chemistry and physics, and that's all there is!"

Commander Duval, sensing their antagonism, said to Rose, "Yeah, well, I know nothing of mysteries. This deposit is all that has been discovered . . . There are no other similarities anywhere in our galaxy – not that we can detect anyway. That is what makes the element absolutely beyond value. How can you put a price on survival?" Duval shook his head and glanced at the people around him. "Either way, we have one hell of a responsibility." He paused, pulled his shoulders back and looked again at Mike Matheson. "Go ahead with the plan, Mike!" he said, in a way that was half an order and half a request. "Collect as much as you can without stretching the window. If you can't make the eighteen kilogram consignment in the time allocated then you leave with what you've got. Understand? You get your ass back and we get the hell out of here. Hopefully, in ten months from now when we get back, there still will be a civilisation somewhere on Earth to save."

The officers returned to their positions and Commander Duval slowly circled the central console, stopping with each one momentarily. "Everybody ready?" he asked decisively.

There were nods. "Aye, sir . . . ready . . . looking good . . . let's go for it!"

Duval nodded sharply; all seemed ready. "Run the checklist!" he said, and then he quickly scanned a number of system pages as they presented themselves on the screen of his command monitor. Finally satisfied, he typed an initiation code into the computer programme and punched the enter key. Instantly, the checklist appeared on the screen. "Flight controls?" he asked.

"Systems green, Commander," replied Steven Tani, a Major in the Japanese Space Agency, his sharp gaze sighting every parameter on his instrument panel.

"Life support?"

"Green, Commander, no problems here," responded

Carol Boardman, a British civil servant and a specialist in human physiology. She was a slim, short-haired brunette with a beautiful white complexion and deep brown eyes. She returned the Commander's gaze for a few seconds before looking down again at her monitor.

"Remote tracking, Lander support and ascent craft status?"

"No worries, sir. All systems check A Okay," said Joe Ansbacher, in a Southern American drawl. He casually rotated a pencil-like screen marker between the fingers of his left hand and leaned back in his chair. He was a former instructor at the tactical fighter pilots' school that was attached to Sentinel Wing – Earth's principal air defence squadron based at Canaveral. Ultra-cool, he always looked the top gun type.

Commander Duval nodded thoughtfully and stood up. "Communications?" he questioned quietly, as he passed Rose Harrington.

"Restricted, Commander, as Alex explained. I'm measuring an acceptable level of signal attenuation all the way down, so I do not expect problems during the flight phase. With the Lander on the surface, however, it's a different story, I'm afraid."

"Specify?"

He knew well enough the nature of the problem, but he wanted it recorded in the flight log, just in case.

Rose enlightened him: "As Io rotates, and without a geostationary probe in position, over the horizon communications will be intermittent, Commander.

Nonetheless, I'm confident that there will be enough of a signal reflected from the tube periphery to amplify – so we shouldn't be out of touch with the pilots for more than a few minutes at a time when they are on the other side. There is nothing long range, however, nothing outside . . . I've tried. My transmission comes back sounding like a meteor squeal. Of course our primary sensors are similarly curtailed. Electromagnetic options are severely limited and the radar range appears to be down to approximately one thousand miles."

"Confirm communication probe status?"

"Both probes are serviceable, Commander, but, in the light of the radiation levels we are encountering, their shielding is insufficient – they wouldn't last two minutes out there."

"Understood. Thank you, Rose." Duval turned to look at a large and more remote console positioned on the other side of the bridge. It was manned by an officer who sat behind an array of flickering screens, including those of two, dated, box-type monitors that had been bolted in a make-shift way onto the deckhead above him. The man wore a faded blue denim shirt with a collar that was open by three buttons and he looked to be in his early fifties, but his weathered features, short greying hair and close-trimmed white beard spoke volumes about his experience. He studied the information presented to him seemingly unaware and certainly unperturbed by Duval's stare. The green lights from the screens intermittently illuminated him in an eerie way. This was the veteran's corner. "Engineering . . . ! Viktor! It's your call," continued the Commander.

The man's reply had a heavy European cadence. Having been on secondment to the ISSF from the Russian Space Agency for most of his career, Viktor Aprashin spoke impeccable English. He nodded reassuringly. "Nothing to stop us Commander; no restriction," he said, and reached up to tap his fingers on one of the black plastic monitor casings for a few seconds as if to prompt some more data to appear. He grimaced at the results. "Maybe some minor issues with the boom protraxor and some of the outriggers are showing signs of thermal stress, but other than that it's as good as it gets." He looked up and met Duval's gaze. "I say green for go!"

Duval glanced at Mike Matheson and then back at Aprashin. "The Lander, Viktor, specifically the Lander?"

"All the self-tests have come back green. She's fuelled, the navigation system is initialised and the coordinates are downloaded and confirmed – same for the ascent vehicle. Zimmermann has already completed the pre-flight inspection. The Lander and the return module are fully serviceable, Commander. As far as I'm concerned, I say we go!" He sounded very definite.

Duval turned back to Matheson and then he gestured to Drake. "You both ready? Fed and watered? Checked your hydration levels?"

"We're ready, Commander."

Duval suddenly raised his hand. "Wait one!" he barked, and turned to Alex. "You sure this is the lowest we can go?" He pointed. "From this display the descent time shows seven minutes longer than planned. That's a lot of extra gamma rays for these guys?"

"Commander, I can only reiterate," replied Alex, with eyes widening in response to the cross-examination. "The surface is a mass of active volcanoes and some of the plumes are higher than we thought. The one you can see on the main screen in the south-western sector is higher than Mount Everest, and it's throwing ash up almost forty thousand metres . . . a hundred and thirty thousand feet! I can't risk a lower orbit than this . . . no way! This is as low as it is safe to go."

Duval looked him in the eye. He knew Alex always erred on the safe side, and he preferred that, but taking into account the return flight this was months, perhaps a year, off a man's life. There was a thoughtful silence on the bridge.

Alex turned and faced the two pilots; he knew the implications of the situation as well as anyone and his expression reflected his concern. "The safety of the ship and you two is prime." He pulled his gaze back to Duval. "My lateral infrared imager is already skimming the outer corona," he continued, feeling a more forcible explanation was necessary. "You order me closer than this and we could get caught by a plume and could burn up before they get back – and that's the reality of it. Even at this orbital concentricity it's going to be pretty hairy!"

Commander Duval nodded. "Copied," he said purposefully. "Rose, make a note in the log, please.

Command approval given at 09:35, Universal Corrected Time." He looked sternly at Matheson and Drake. "Okay – suit up and go to it! We launch in one hour. Any kind of problems and you abort immediately – got that? You throw it away and you get the hell back here! That's an order!"

Matheson nodded and smiled faintly. He gestured to Drake to follow him. As he passed Carol Boardman, Matheson touched her lightly on the shoulder and looked into her eyes. In his white, flame-proof undersuit that was proudly badged like a racing car driver's coveralls, and with his close-cropped fair hair and piercing blue eyes, he appeared the classic all-American astronaut. The look that passed between them did not go unnoticed by the rest of the bridge.

"Good luck," Carol whispered.

Matheson smiled for a brief moment and then both men left the bridge in silence.

The International Spaceship *Hera* was a Class 2 mineral exploration craft built with specific modifications for the Phobos and Io missions. The Phobos excursion in 2052 had been a near disaster and a massive disappointment; however, analysis during the low orbital manoeuvres had confirmed that the mineral composition of the rocky deposits they had hoped to retrieve did not, in fact, match that of the Kalahari crystals, although chemically they had initially appeared identical. It had taken the International Space and Science Federation two years to restore its credibility and to raise the money from already hard-pressed governments to launch the Io mission, all the while rejecting advances of funding from the disgraced international conglomerates Spheron, Tongsei and Epsilon Rio. Indeed, there had even been threats of forced acquisition and reports of corrupt ISSF officials feeding vital information to the conglomerates in order to aid their takeover bid. But that was only rumour; as always, nothing was ever proved. In fact, it was near impossible to restrict the ruthless influence of the world's three largest industrial multinationals, despite numerous restraining orders by host countries. In senior political circles – although few would openly admit it – substantive wealth, industrial power and political persuasion had already slipped through the fingers of many national governments. Regional governing bodies such as the European Democratic Republic and the Asian Union had little leverage over the faceless men who ran these three giant companies whose policies and aims remained shrouded in secrecy. Based on previous experience, however, subjugation, domination, and, inevitably, world control, seemed their ultimate goal, whilst corruption, extortion, bribery and death were simply tools to achieve it.

Retrospectively, the Phobos mission had been wishful thinking on the part of the International Space and Science Federation – an opportunity to take the upper hand, to secure a resource that was owned by no one and shared by all. Phobos was much closer to the Earth for one thing and, with Osiris Base on Mars as a staging post, it was a much more convenient opportunity logistically than Io. What's more, it was a dead place, inert, inhospitable to a point, but above all else one with almost zero gravity, making a landing easier. Io, on the other hand, was a very different prospect. On this small world, far from the sun and one that should have been coated with ice, every natural force was disproportionate. Every chemical was caustic. Every breath would be a challenge.

"Commander, Matheson here. We are in the module and ready to go. Thing is, there's a fuel discrepancy. The on-board system says that we can't get back to a sixty-two per cent elliopheric. I've run the programme three times and it's more accurate than *Hera*'s – there's no doubt. It's the temperature gradient – all the way to the surface – it's just too damn high. There's no way around it; you'll have to descend for our return or we are on a one-way mission!"

"What orbit is the on-board system giving, Mike? The maximum that you can achieve, including a manoeuvre allowance?" responded Duval. He had selected "open bridge" on the audio control.

"You're not going to like it . . . forty-eight per cent, sir."

"Shit!" Duval looked across at Alex.

Alex shook his head. "That's a no go!" he said. He

turned back to his console and ran some figures.

"I'm waiting Alex!"

"Okay, okay, it's coming." There was an air of apprehension on the bridge. "I've got it." Alex swivelled in his high-backed seat. "I can do seventeen minutes at forty-eight per cent!" he exclaimed. "That includes an allowance for all the fuel we are saving here, plus *all* of our reserves. Things are going to get mighty hot out there though, Commander. We are going to take one hell of a radiation hit. Seventeen minutes . . . that's it; otherwise it's a one-way mission for all of us." There was no compromise in his tone.

Duval rubbed the brow of his nose. This was a very difficult decision he had to make. He considered the implications for several seconds.

"It's your call, Commander. We are ready to launch. Just say the word." Matheson's voice cut through the atmosphere on the bridge like a hot knife through butter.

"How much time do you need on the surface, Mike?" Duval barked. "Now that you have the surface contours mapped."

"Planned is six hours, but I'm aiming to do it in four – provided I can put the Lander down close to the deposit. Flight time is around thirty minutes, twenty-one for the return leg, and we need an extra allowance for docking, just in case there's a problem coordinating concentricity. I intend to land, collect a bucketful of those damn crystals and hightail it – none of the geology experiments. I think we can do it . . ."

"Okay . . . we go! Dispatch! Start the countdown!"

"Thirty per cent elliopheric, *Hera*, all systems green . . ."

The bridge remained silent.

"Twenty per cent elliopheric. Approaching the transition. Final coordinates locked in. Approach path gradient computed. Systems green . . . We are go, *Hera*." Drake's voice sounded confident.

Duval leaned over his display screen and then he looked sideways at Alex. "Looks good, Commander," Alex said, reassuringly. Duval nodded, a smile jabbing his lips.

"Transition complete, passing eighty thousand feet, seventy thousand, sixty thousand . . . Skin temperature stable – the *Osprey* is looking good. We are go, *Hera*!"

Duval began tapping his finger on the console. Carol Boardman held her breadth. Alex swivelled around in his seat as he scanned his computer monitors.

"Ten thousand feet, arresting rate of descent, nine thousand, eight, seven . . . we have a visual contact . . . we have a visual with the landing site, *Hera*. Four thousand feet, passing committal altitude – green, green for go, *Hera*."

"Come on, come on," whispered Duval. He knew

well enough that this was the critical phase.

"Eight hundred feet. Combined retro thrust sixty-five per cent and increasing. Approach looks good, *Hera*."

"Commander, I've got a contact on radar, astern at one thousand miles . . . It's coming up fast?"

Duval looked up. "That's impossible."

"Well it's—"

"Not now, Rose! You must be mistaken."

"I've double checked, Commander. There's no mistake, there's something out there!"

"*Not now*, Rose!" Duval looked back at his screen, shaking his head.

"Four hundred feet . . . three hundred . . . steady . . . what the . . . !" Matheson's voice sounded tense over the speaker. "Stop the descent, Aldrin! Stop it now!"

"What is it Mike?" asked Duval.

"Er, we have a problem, *Hera*," Matheson replied. "Touchdown sensors are confusing the hell out of the landing computer. Doppler radar malfunction . . . I say again, Doppler malfunction. Try a reset for me, *Hera* – no delay, please."

"There's no malfunction on *my* panel," grunted Viktor.

"Mike, this is Jacques. There's no malfunction showing up here!"

"Maintaining altitude, two hundred feet, holding altitude . . . we sure as hell have one here, Commander. Auto-land system's gone goofy on us . . ."

"Watch your fuel, Mike!" chipped in Alex. "One

minute and twenty seconds remaining."

"They are past committal height . . . there *IS* no abort!" Everybody knew it, but still Viktor Aprashin's word spread trepidation.

Seconds passed; critical seconds. Mike Matheson's calm voice belied the staccato words. "What the . . . ? It's the landing site. The freaking landing site is still moving . . . It's the goddamn lava flow – computers can't lock on to the touchdown coordinates."

"Watch your fuel, Mike . . . put it down!"

"Going manual, going manual . . . I have manual control, *Hera*."

"Put it down, Mike," interrupted Alex, fretfully, "there's no time for dancing . . . fuel for forty-five seconds!"

There was a collective gasp on the bridge.

"Over there . . . Mike, ten o'clock, fifty metres, see it . . . a clear area!" Aldrin's voice was compelling.

"Moving left, going down . . . one hundred feet!"

"Another two degrees to port . . . on course. You're on course Mike!" instructed Aldrin.

"Thirty seconds of fuel remaining . . . no delay . . . no delay. Mike! Put it down!" Alex could barely contain his emotion.

"Clear on this side! Down! Down!" blurted Aldrin. "Eighty feet, radio altimeter reads seventy feet . . . sixty . . . fifty . . . forty . . ."

"Fifteen seconds of fuel remaining . . . On the ground! Put it on the ground, Mike! *Do it now*!" Alex gripped his head in his hands and leaned back hard in his seat.

Dust and debris rose from the ground. It swirled and churned as a dense, yellow-coloured cloud that completely obliterated the astronaut's view through his narrow window. *That's enough*, Mike Matheson thought, as he closed the two thrust levers in his right hand simultaneously. As a result, the Lander dropped like a brick. Moments later, there was a loud crash and then a precarious swaying movement and then there was stillness. Inside the module, subdued computer noises and the hum of avionics robbed the silence of its comforting effect and green lights skipped along the astronaut's instrument panels. Mike Matheson looked across at his colleague; he nodded and then shrugged almost imperceptibly. He gave a brief half-smile to his friend as a thank you and then gestured as if to say: lucky! Thereafter the two men sat rigid for several seconds.

On the bridge of the *Hera* nobody moved or dared to speak. Seconds seemed like minutes.

"Talk to me guys . . . Situation report, please?" Alex's cool demeanour fooled nobody. Sideways, he shared an anxious glance with Duval.

Despite his totally professional disposition, there was a nervous hesitation in Mike Matheson's delivery as he said: "The Osprey has landed. We are safely down, *Hera* . . . All systems are green."

Back on the *Hera*, Joe Ansbacher, who was closely monitoring data on his life support display, watched with great relief as Matheson's heart rate indication dropped from a peak of 190, to a more normal 109. Drake's was a little higher but of no immediate concern. Meanwhile, Commander Duval's shoulders visibly dropped and Carol Boardman stopped gripping the seat of her chair.

"We're going to set to," continued Matheson, a minute or two later and speaking over the open frequency. He seemed more relaxed. "Clock starts now, four hours maximum. For the record, we seem to be in a relatively cool area; outside probes are indicating an average of two hundred and thirty degrees Celsius. But we flew through a much hotter zone. Maybe that's why the lava state was unpredictable, not fully solidified. We are setting suit-conditioning to ninety-one per cent, which gives us some additional flex. Precise location is . . . cross-coordinate two, two, five. We're on the edge of the North West landing sector. Crystal site is five hundred metres south-east. I'll transmit a sitrep in twenty minutes. Put the coffee on up there . . . Matheson out!"

Duval breathed a huge sigh of relief. That was the cue for everyone else on the bridge to follow suit. Alex forced a smile.

Rose broke the ensuing silence. "Commander, I need you to look at this. *Now* please. There's no mistake. I've switched to the standby radar scanner and I'm still getting the same contact reading. We have a blip – directly astern at three thousand metres. Whatever it is – and it's relatively small – is coming this way at ten metres per second and reducing."

Duval heard the resolve in her voice. As impossible as it seemed, Rose was reporting an intruder. A strange chill descended over the bridge – intruders usually meant trouble. Duval quickly stepped over to Rose's circular display and Alex followed him. Rose pointed to the tiny blip on the screen. Duval waited for the track of the scanner to sweep the object again. He stared almost unbelieving as the next pass enhanced the object's elongated saucer-like shape. With another sweep the blip moved inexplicably towards them. Duval's eyes narrowed. He turned and nodded at Alex. "Confirmed at one thousand metres," he said, bluntly. "Whatever it is, we should be able to see any moment now." He looked back at the screen and then up at Rose. "We are not expecting any replenishment vessels from Earth are we . . . anybody? Am I missing something here?"

None of the bridge crew responded. Some shook their heads. Alex shrugged – he was totally at a loss.

Duval paused thoughtfully. His mouth twitched. "Okay. Press the button. Go to manoeuvre alert status and security state three, just in case the Federation has planned a docking that we are not party to as yet. Close all pressure bulkheads," he ordered, and then he glanced over to his engineering officer. "I suppose it's vaguely possible; we've been out of radio contact with everybody for several days now."

"I can see it, Commander," interrupted Joe, pointing into the blackness with his finger. "It's just fired a short retro burst. Looks to be manoeuvring to the left now, establishing a parallel course – coming up the right-hand side of the gantries. Now, there, another . . . See it?" Joe pointed again.

Duval and Rose stepped over to the rear viewing area. Carol Boardman joined them. "Yes, I see it," Duval replied. He watched warily as the small craft came slowly towards them. A few minutes later and with all on the bridge staring in amazement, it drew up alongside them. The vessel was painted black, making it difficult to see against the backdrop. It was surprisingly close too – not more than 200 metres away. The front of the craft was then illuminated momentarily as two short retro bursts reduced its velocity to a walking pace and then the effect of a third stopped the vessel in its tracks. There was an eerie silence. The vessel seemingly hovered there in the darkness: ominous, unexpected.

"Call it, Rose! Make it identify itself," ordered Duval.

"I've been trying for the last ten minutes, sir, using the pre-recorded identification message – all our assigned space frequencies, and also on the space distress frequency. Nothing. No response at all."

Alex stepped up beside Rose. "It's like an interplanetary probe, but I don't recognise the model and there are no apparent markings," he reported. "It's got an ion drive motor though. See the main thrust nozzle?"

Duval nodded in response. He looked concerned. "I think I can see something written on that rear stabiliser, near the discharge port. Viktor . . . put a light on it. Rose, take an image, process and put it on the main screen –

magnified by five."

"Yes, Commander." Rose promptly returned to her console. "You've got it, Commander," she said, a few moments later.

Duval focused on the picture. "There, look, you see it – markings, in red, lines of characters. Viktor, you recognise any of that?"

"It's not Russian, if that's what you mean, or any of the Slavic languages. We don't use characters like that. I'd say that it's Chinese, maybe Japanese . . . Korean even? I'm no expert."

"Chinese!" Duval thought on that possibility for a moment. "Rose, get David Chung up here, quickly. He might be able to help with this. I know he has a Masters from the Beijing Aeronautics Institute."

"Yes, will do . . . right away."

Alex was perplexed. He spent several minutes leaning over the large horizontal monitor that was an integral part of the central display. He ran his finger over an adjacent control wheel adjusting the magnification factor and studied the subsequent image. "Commander," he said after a while and with an air of apprehension, "I've got something. Take a look at this."

Duval was over to the console in an instant. He stood next to Alex and, leaning over, scrutinised the image. In a troubled way, like a nervous twitch, Alex's fingertip repeatedly tapped the screen in the forward area of the spaceship.

"Look, there, a figure in the cockpit area. I can make

out a head and shoulders through the side window. It's dark, but I've enhanced as much as possible." Alex increased the magnification until the image blurred and then backed off slightly.

Duval followed Alex's prompt and zoomed in on the side observation window. It resembled a seagoing vessel's porthole – circular, with a thick metal rim and ring of undulating rivet heads. Duval peered through it and into the vessel's cockpit. "Can you improve the quality of the image any more, Alex?" he asked.

"There, what about that . . . ? It's the best I can do," Alex replied, pressing a few keys and manipulating the thumbwheel on his panel.

"It's a robot! That, Alex, is a robot. There's no mistaking it." Duval looked menacingly over his shoulder and out into space in the direction of the vessel.

"It looks horrible," commented Carol.

"I don't like it either," agreed Duval. He studied the image again and looked up at Alex, his brow furrowed. "I think it's a Humatron. I attended some lectures on that model a few years ago. It remains a banned system – suffered behavioural problems from its inception. I saw an example too, in the Smithsonian Museum in Washington DC. That 'X' shaped head . . . it's unique. I don't think I'm wrong here. They were designed for operations on extended space flights for one thing, but the Spaceport One disaster back in the second decade put paid to all that." At that moment David Chung arrived. He was a slim oriental man in his thirties and one of three specialist propulsion engineers aboard the *Hera*. Duval beckoned him over. "David, can you read this?" he asked, pointing to the magnified image of the vessel on the screen.

David Chung looked surprised. "It is Mandarin!"

Duval glanced momentarily at Victor. "What's it say?"

"Um, well, it's been a while, Commander." Chung paused and took his time with each character as the top line in particular was worn and almost obliterated. "Engineering jargon really?" he answered. "It seems to just be installation details and safety precautions for a particular plutonium isotope. Maybe it's the fuel source. There are some special handling precautions as well. The bottom line is a place – presumably the manufacturer's address."

"Who . . . who's the manufacturer?"

"Um, doesn't actually say their name, I'm afraid, just the place . . . the address: the Huang Hai Industrial State."

Duval spontaneously shook his head. "Do you know of it?"

"Yes. That region was once part of north-eastern China . . . Liaoning Province. But it was given autonomy about thirty years ago. My family are from a town on the coast in the same province, to the south of Dandong. The area is entirely urbanized. The Huang Hai Industrial district itself comprises an island in the West Korean Bay and also about twenty square kilometres of the mainland. Back home, on a good day, you could see it across the water, and if not the island, then the smog that hung over it." David Chung grimaced at the thought of the pollution. "The region pays a large land rent and taxes to the central government in return for complete autonomy. Most of the world's leading industrial companies have facilities there. It's always been a hothouse of innovation and scientific progress because research is unfettered by governmental restrictions. No authority, no censorship, so over the years nobody has had any real idea of what's been going on. Only rarely is information released and many people, including some prominent scientists, have just disappeared behind the security curtain. Take it from me – people in China just don't go there unless they have a really good reason. And you don't look it up on the World Net either – or you might get somebody knocking on your door in the middle of the night. Really, it is not a nice place, and the most polluted in that part of Asia too." Chung shrugged. "The area has been in steep decline for the last few years, Commander; the late forties was the watershed, when oil and gas became very expensive and reserves began to dry up. Three years ago, when I was finishing my postgraduate studies in Beijing, the Chinese government all but cut off the region's remaining energy supply, diverting more to the people. But it made very little difference to the most powerful industrial companies, as they had their own suppliers. There was talk of pressurised contracts; threats to government officials; corruption; bribes; prioritised raw material deliverers – including food! The biggest companies in the zone became predators of the small. With their own docks and refineries they survived."

"Is there anything else, David?" quizzed Duval. He was growing noticeably edgy. "More specifically, that may be of concern to us."

David Chung rubbed his chin suspiciously. "The concept of such an industrial region had already become very unpopular in certain quarters and the government was considering its options. Despite their massive revenues the country was losing face because of illegal activities and a blatant disregard of international laws by industrial giants like Tongsei and Spheron. There was a lot of talk about it, and not just at home, but in the cyber-press, too. I remember it clearly. When Tongsei Heavy Industries was the pride of Chinese Corporate success their headquarters was the largest building in Shanghai. When I left China to join the Asian Space and Science Agency that building was being closed."

"Did any of these companies build spacecraft?" interjected Carol Boardman. "I'm not a big one on international espionage."

"Tongsei built the mineral barge *Colossus*, Carol," replied Duval. "Nobody else had the financial ability. They got their money back and a lot more besides by exploiting the Moon's resources. It was a monopoly for years, certainly until the lunar independence. When we left there was an international investigation underway. As David said, extortion, bribery . . . you name it. Spheron are into high-tech engineering, biomechanics, genetics, pharmaceuticals and lots besides. There was a concerted effort to break up these corporations, but they're shadowy organisations, nothing could be proved. They were said to have ties with a couple of other disgraced conglomerates."

David Chung nodded in agreement. Duval turned and gave him his full attention. "By those markings, David, could this vessel be Tongsei built? And if so, what the hell are they doing building this type of interplanetary craft? This is no replenishment job. I don't like it. I don't like it at all!"

"There is a conundrum here, Commander," said Chung. "That type of thrust nozzle clearly indicates the use of an ion drive propulsion system, but clearly it has a relatively small capacity: one capable of maintaining momentum in space, but one, in my view, unable to achieve the initial acceleration – at least to a practical speed. And see those flanges towards the rear and the splayed receptacle structure? I would say that this craft is just the tip of a much larger craft. Either a booster stage or another larger section of the craft detached on its way here. And by the absence of any burn marks or scoring, I would say that it was another section with life support – the hot end was further back again. And one other thing, Commander, ion thrusters do not use plutonium as a fuel, invariably its xenon or bismuth gas." Chung's expression turned stony. "Plutonium . . . it makes no sense." He shook his head.

"Ideas! Speculate!"

Chung took another look at the image of the vessel on the screen. He looked up slowly and repositioned his spectacles. "If I was to make an educated guess I would say that the vessel has a nuclear power cell. Why? Essentially, it's a tube, black and functional. The flight deck is more a cockpit, barely illuminated and certainly not suitable for long-range missions by humans – so no life support required. I heard you mention a robot as I came in, again, minimum power demands. But there is not a single solar panel to be seen. Deutronium batteries would produce enough power and for an extended period, but not for a flight to Jupiter, it's too far. I would say that a compact plutonium power cell would fit the bill."

Alex interrupted. "The construction of a nuclear reactor, regardless of size, was banned back in 2016. Not even the ISSF or NASA is exempt. Contravening Section Six of the New Geneva Convention carries hefty penalties."

David looked at Alex in a way as to say *get real*. "Compact power cells are completely insulated," he explained, "and so they are almost undetectable. I would say that this vessel was probably built outside the jurisdiction of the ISSF, somewhere where the engineers were confident that there would be no inspections. Otherwise they would not have painted the radiation hazard icon and the handling instructions for their own people."

Duval nodded. "Okay, I buy that – an illegally manufactured power cell to get an automated vessel this

far. But what about the real question . . . Why is it here?"
He looked back at Alex and Chung.

Alex walked over to the viewing portal and squinted
through the blackness at the object holding station off the
starboard bow, perhaps no more than 100 metres away.
The cockpit glimmered red like a distant star. "A ship
like that represents quite an investment," he reasoned.
"Engineering, technology . . . propulsion? Not even the
ISSF is spending that much on pure research – not these
days – and anyway we would have heard about it. If the
Tongsei or Spheron conglomerates built it, or if they both
had a hand in it, then clearly they would want to see a
return."

Duval stepped up next to Alex and looked over his
silent bridge. "The Epsilon Rio Corporation designed
and manufactured the Humatron series – that much I
know." His voice dropped to a whisper. "And if it's here to
spy on us, it hasn't started out too well, has it?"

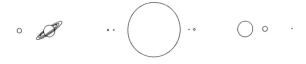

Matheson's suit-conditioning system was operating
at 100 per cent, but it wasn't enough to keep his body
temperature within normal limits. Sweat ran down his
face. After only an hour on the surface his hydration level
had fallen to 92 per cent and he had almost exhausted his

fluid pouch. Aldrin Drake fared little better. But work was progressing. They had located a small surface deposit and had exposed the strange mineral by chipping off a thin layer of caked-on, ash-like sulphur material, and were busy setting a small hydraulically operated expansion cylinder that would allow them to break off several small pieces. A briefcase-like U-Semini containment system lay open next to their feet. The deposit, a crystal form that was opaque in some areas and oddly translucent in others, seemed to glow from within, producing a hazy white light.

Had they time to notice they would have found their surroundings both alien and sublime. Their movement made shallow 'treaded' footprints in the frost-like covering of yellow and white flaky pyroclastic material and from time to time a flurry of fine ash drifted down on them from toxic clouds above. The material filled the marks on the ground like fresh, soft, falling snow. The incongruity wasn't lost on either of them as sticky deposits built up on their backpacks and on top of their helmets as a persistent layer that needed to be brushed off periodically. Occasionally the visibility was good, and far to the west two towering conical volcanoes belched smoke and debris while the surface shimmered with heat.

Every so often, Aldrin stopped work for a coughing fit – even their suits' closed-system respiratory system seemed helpless against the invading 'bad egg' smell of sulphur dioxide. The concentrated gas appeared to permeate the fabric of their suits at a molecular level and filtered – albeit in minuscule amounts – into their helmets. It was evident that their time on the surface would be limited by more than just their oxygen supply.

During one such fit, Matheson took a rest from breaking the rocks and straightened up. He arched his back and as he scanned the distant horizon something caught his eye.

"Did you see that . . . over there, to the east?"

Aldrin stifled a coughed and cleaned his visor with the back of his glove. "Shit it's hot! No . . . what did you see?"

"A white flash, just for a moment, from below the horizon," Matheson raised his arm and pointed in the direction.

"Nuh, didn't see it. Probably a corona flash or a burst of ionised gas. Come on, I'm burning up in this suit. Let's just get on with it. I'm almost out of fluid as well."

Aldrin turned away but Mike Matheson was anxious as he looked down at the small pieces of crystal they had prised from the deposit and kicked into a pile. He leant over to reset the hydraulic cylinder for the last time but felt uneasy and cast a quick look towards the east. As he did, his eyes widened.

"Look . . . ! Look for God's sake . . . Aldrin!"

Both men stared as a bright white ball loomed over the horizon.

"What is it . . . it's getting bigger!"

There was an eerie silence. A volcanic plume, bursting high into the atmosphere and off to the right, caught their attention momentarily. Red and yellow flames danced on the volcano's summit. Mike Matheson put a hand on Aldrin's shoulder.

"Shit . . . a meteorite. And it's getting bigger. It's coming this way! The buggy! Back to the buggy! Go!"

Both astronauts ran, skipped and hopped the sixty metres of uneven terrain. Skips and hops that would have been impossible on Earth. Occasional pockets of coloured gas vented beneath their feet as the crisp frost of sulphur cracked. Unable to cope with the additional heat, their conditioning systems beeped unheeded warnings and sweat flowed freely down their faces. Within seconds they were aboard the small, four-wheeled, twin-seated vehicle. Matheson floored the accelerator pedal and the rear wheels spun. The fire ball was large and threatening as it sank lower in the sky, drawn by gravity. The buggy sped off at right angles to its trajectory while Aldrin tracked the vivid menace that now had the fiery tail of a comet – even in Io's rarefied atmosphere there was enough friction to make it glow white hot. Its flight path became predictable.

"We're not going to make it, Mike! Make a ninety degree turn! It's our only hope."

Matheson wrenched the small steering wheel to the right and the buggy slewed, trailing dust and ash. Their eyes widened in horror. Something in his subconscious made Matheson ease off on the throttle – it seemed suicidal to drive towards the thing. He quickly realised his folly and floored the pedal again. Stomachs tensed and hearts raced as the buggy bounced wildly over fatigued wheels.

Now they could hear it. The shockwave started as a distant rumble, but soon their helmets became ineffectual against the ever-increasing volume. Then it was like thunder and every cavity in their bodies resonated as the pressure wave built up – like standing too close to a railway line as a bullet train approached. Matheson held his course. With an altitude of barely 1000 feet, the white hot orb dropped lower and lower until the sizzling disc seemed to skim the planet's surface; it raced towards the tiny vehicle and its huge bulk seethed. Visible now were pieces of flaming debris that broke off and scattered – most impacting on the surface and raising spiralling clouds of dust and ash and releasing bursting geysers of yellow, green and orange gas. They felt the crushing, debilitating force on them; it pressed on their bodies, squeezing them into their seats. They gasped for breath. Then the shockwave engulfed them. There was pain. Excruciating pain. The heat, the thunder, the shuddering, their throbbing bodies, the light, a riot in hell . . . and then it was directly over them. The massive disturbance pummelled them. The buggy slewed and skidded as Matheson lost control.

It passed. Senses subsided. Matheson pulled the buggy around to complete a full turn and then slammed on the brakes. They did not immediately feel the relief because a long flaming tail trailed the object for hundreds of metres. The fizzing brilliance they watched with dumb struck awe as it flew towards the hills.

The close proximity caused the surface of the moon to contort and the brittle, overlying chemical frost simply peeled off and churned like swirling eddies of sand beneath a hovering helicopter. And then the explosion. Never had they seen such a catastrophe. The object hurtled away from them for two or three kilometres. It bounced and, from the point of impact, made a shallow channel that continued as a gouge and finished as a chasm. Minutes later a kind of stillness settled, belied by the whole mess that smouldered and smoked with insignificant explosions, effervescing sparks and debris plumes, like expensive fireworks on a special occasion. There was rubble and shards and ruin.

Totally oblivious to his heat-stressed body and his suit's overwhelmed conditioning system and the red warning light on his wrist-mounted control panel, Matheson drove slowly and then, abruptly, stopped.

"No! Please no! If there's a God, no!" Mike cried, his despair causing Aldrin to stare at the carnage.

Mere seconds appeared to be minutes, and those minutes became hours as both men sat in a silence of eternity. Sweat trickled down their brows and dripped from their noses. Thirty metres away and a little to their left a red flame fringed with blue fired off from a twisted piece of silvery tubing. A distorted section of latticed gantry lay half-embedded in the ash and the sand. Matheson looked to his right and drove forward slowly. He felt his hands trembling. He lined up the buggy with the laser-straight trench – now the gateway to a scrapyard – and stopped with the wheels of the vehicle on its edge. Like a huge furrow ploughed by a giant they were made dwarf-like by it. The scale of it all, the brokenness, and in the distance the trench slewed to the right, as if the plough had come across bedrock and diverted. And there, at its end, a contorted mass burned.

Both men thought it but dared not say, for they already knew they were as good as dead. They saw a large curved piece of metal alloy, its edges twisted violently and jagged. On it, clearly visible through the scorching, were the letters:

**H E R**

Matheson turned slowly and looked back in the direction that they had come. Tyre tracks indicated their stressed, haphazard journey. The landing module was too small and too distant to be seen, but nevertheless Matheson scanned the horizon for it. He thought about the inside of it. That capsule of life: functional but fragile, with a futile future. Despite the computers, the systems, the computations, the integration, protection and opportunity, its promise was only temporary solace. The Lander was helpless, like a baby without its mother.

So how would it come? As heat exhaustion, oxygen starvation, dehydration? Matheson bowed his head as his mind replayed his life, which he summed up in an instant: frail and seemingly pointless. He was not aware of Aldrin climbing from his seat, who then walked and frequently stumbled towards a pile of smouldering debris as if he recognised something in it as personal. Their intercom crackled for a time with heavy atmospheric static and the rumble of another distant volcano erupting seemed threatening, like the gathering menace of an approaching thunderstorm. This and the surrounding wreckage – which sporadically burst into flames as gas pockets vented – muted Matheson's curiosity. He watched Aldrin's haphazard progress – the lone figure walked now as if he was drunk, staggering, with his arms hanging lifelessly by his sides. Matheson could have called him back as there was no change in their communication status. But there was no reason to; there was no point in warning his friend.

Presently and with the debilitating disbelief of a betrayed man, Matheson dragged himself from the buggy. He stood by it on the grey and yellow ash and the patterned soles of his boots made deep impressions. Footprints; for a time man had been here. He arched his back and gazed up at the hazy sky that was heavy with acid – there would be no succour from there. Then, with both hands, Matheson felt for the metal rings that linked his bulky spherical helmet to his suit. He slid his fingers around the smooth curves until each hand hovered over the release clips. Straining his neck, he managed to get a finger beneath the left-hand clip and pulled it up and turned it, releasing it. Instantly, a red light illuminated on his wrist-mounted suit-conditioning control panel. He looked up, slowly, unaffected, and spent two or three thoughtful minutes watching his buddy who was quite distant by now. The sweat that had run from his temples and down his cheeks had all but dried and he could taste salt on his lips.

Aldrin meanwhile had turned towards a large section of wreckage that was half-embedded in the towering left-hand wall of the trench. It protruded precariously and a twisted boom of former gantry with a broken end reached out for the other side, arching, like a half-constructed bridge across a wide valley. It loomed above Aldrin as he approached it. Matheson watched him pause momentarily and then disappear. Seconds later an explosion rocked the charred carcass of superstructure, to be quickly followed by another and the ensuing wall of flames clearly denied any retreat even if second thoughts had turned Aldrin's intention.

Matheson shook his head. He looked down at the marks his boots had made in the dust and then up again at his friend's blazing mausoleum. *Perhaps it was fitting,* he thought, *like a Viking.* Then an image of Carol's face filled Matheson's mind's eye. She smiled at him and blew a kiss and then gestured for him to follow her; stars backlit her complexion. Jupiter, massive, with its rings of colour, turned slowly before him. He supported himself with a hand on the buggy and stretched up to feel the full extent of the great planet. *No one has seen what I am seeing,* he thought. Carol beckoned again – sweetly and lovingly, as on that 'night' in her cabin when Saturn passed by. He tightened his lips subconsciously as if to kiss her back and then reached up and found the other retaining clip with his right hand and, with some effort, flipped it open. A second red light illuminated on the control panel and began flashing incessantly and this time an aural warning complained loudly of his reckless stupidity. Having eyes only for Carol, he paid the warnings no heed. Instead, and with a hand on each side of his helmet, he rotated it.

# CHAPTER 2

# RECALL

**Moon base Andromeda – the day before Christmas 2054 18:07 Lunar Corrected Time**

"Hello, Unit one zero three. Rachel here."

"Doctor Rachel Reece?"

"Yes, speaking."

"Good! It's Peter Rothschild. How are you?"

"Why are you calling, Peter? Please, of all nights, not tonight."

"Is Richard there?"

"Can't you leave it? Just another day or two. Please! It's Christmas Eve for God's sake."

"Rachel, I'm sorry. You know it's not me; I'd rather be at home too. Something's come up, it's serious, the repercussions . . . Is he there, Rachel?"

"Actually, no, I don't know where he is, not exactly.

He's not back from the office. Maybe he hasn't landed yet." Rachel Reece sighed. "I thought this was all over, Peter. We've not heard from the department for almost two years, not since he assumed command of the Wing – he's enjoying the job. Why don't you just find someone else?"

"He landed over an hour ago, Rachel, I checked. And there's no answer from his office."

"Then he must be on his way. Perhaps he's stopped to share a drink with friends? That's what one does at Christmas time . . . isn't it?"

"Rachel, *please*. This job is difficult enough without . . . When is a recall convenient? You tell me? Anyway, I don't dictate timings. I'd prefer to be with my family too, and not here in the city, I can tell you. He's the one who did the degree in Hieroglyphics and Cryptography. He's the one who's receiving funding for his doctorate from the department. If he'd wanted to drop it, he should have done so four years ago." Rothschild paused and his tone softened. "Rachel, listen, like it or not, Richard *is* our resident expert in these matters; he's up there with the best of them. And regarding the origin of the Kalahari crystals, he's the world authority. What's more, after his illness, Professor Mubarakar is too frail to see anybody, although he always makes an exception for Richard. It's very important Rachel. We have a major catastrophe on our hands. So please, tell me if you know where he is."

Rachel hesitated; she knew that there was no point

in being difficult. *Her disappointment at not being first on Richard's list mustn't make her feel rejected*, she thought, but the realisation of Christmas alone made her grimace. "I expect he's with the squadron pilots and the ops staff, Peter, enjoying some goodwill for once. Try Lieutenant Stewart Grant's unit – number two, twelve. Remember, I haven't seen much of him for weeks, so don't you think he's going anywhere tonight – not for a moment!"

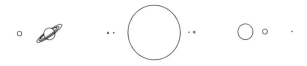

"A ferry flight, sir . . . no passengers, no cargo, now that *is* unusual. I thought it was all about saving fuel. First that new annual award for the most fuel-efficient return sector to Earth, and now we fly there empty – doesn't make sense!"

Commander Richard James Reece looked across the flight deck at his young co-pilot. By necessity, it was a dimly lit environment and outside the myriad of reflective white specks shimmering against the consuming blackness of unending space contributed little to the effect. On the instrument panel a number of lights flashed – green, amber and some red – and on a central computer screen schematic layouts of the ship's engineering systems flipped every few seconds.

All the while, there was the muted background hum of electronics. Richard Reece felt the momentary increase in cabin pressure on his eardrums as the external door closed and the seals inflated. In response, three red lights on the panel turned green.

"It is about fuel, Yannick, and don't think otherwise," Richard said, in an explanatory tone. A smile jabbed his lips. "But I'm needed in London, urgently apparently, and an S2 is the quickest way – indeed, the only way – of getting to Earth tonight. Evidently I'm the exception, it seems. Now, run the checklist and call for start. The sooner we get there, the sooner we get back. This terminal will re-open at seven tomorrow morning. My wife will be fuming, but at least we will be in time to open our presents . . ."

"Aye aye, sir. Commencing pre-flight checklist."

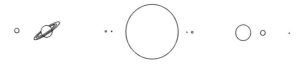

"I'm on my way, Peter. In your electric Jaguar – a 'Double X' model. It's nice, very impressive I must say. Clearly you're moving up in the world."

"Yes, and had you stayed in London after your marriage and taken up the appointment you were offered, you would probably have one too."

"Oh, come on, not that one again – after what, four

years? I'm a pilot, Peter, remember . . . not a pen-pusher. Anyway, this is the last place I'd like to work, fancy job or not." Richard grimaced as he looked out through the vehicle's dark-tinted windows and scanned the passing buildings. People hurried along the walkway, much as always in town, although he thought they were fewer in number and everyone here had the ubiquitous umbrella. He stretched his neck to look up to the skyline, which was dank and dismal with a low, opaque cloud base that engulfed the tallest buildings; they simply disappeared into the gloom as if decapitated. Droplets of water ran down the glass. *The depressing grey of an early morning here on planet Earth,* he thought, *who needs it?* He breathed in deeply and shook his head despondently. "Albeit only a shuttle pilot," he whispered to himself. But Peter Rothschild picked it up over the intercom.

"What's that, Richard?"

Richard was wrested from his thoughts. "Oh, um, I think London's looking shabby. I suppose it's the rain – the council can't get anything done. Now, where am I going and what's the rush?"

"The driver knows, so you don't need to worry – but I suppose you will anyway . . . *Whitehall*! There's an emergency cabinet meeting at eleven o'clock this morning; the Prime Minister's chairing it. Plus a scrambled digital relay with our allies. Washington, Beijing, Moscow, Strasbourg, Bangkok, the ISSF cabinet and others – highest security level. We have suffered a setback and that's putting it mildly. Before that, at nine, there is a key-brief: scientific, energy, threat, risk assessment and a few other topics on the agenda. The PM is expecting me to correlate the information and present him with our recommendations by ten-thirty at the latest. Are you using an earpiece or hands-free?"

"I'm on speaker!"

"Where are you now?"

"Kennington Oval, passing the Palace of Saudia – shame about the cricket ground . . . ? Vauxhall Bridge next, and then Millbank."

"No, not quite. There's some activity by the river we want to avoid. You are routed through Marsham Street and Great Smith Street. Preparations are in hand. You'll get a full brief soon enough. I'll see you in twenty minutes. If I can I'll meet you at the door, otherwise you will be escorted to my office. Security is high, so be prepared."

# CHAPTER 3

# THE CONTEXT OF TIME

**Llano de Chajnantor, near San Pedro de Atacama, Chile**
**The ALMA submillimetre deep space telescope facility**
**Same day - 04:09 Local Time**

"That's impossible!" declared Aaron James, as he scanned the temperature readings on his computer monitor. He adjusted the display calibration from degrees Celsius to degrees Fahrenheit in order to crosscheck the readings and shook his head in disbelief at the result.

Annika Fipatti, who was sitting at the neighbouring console, stood up and walked over. She peered at the lines of data on her colleague's monitor.

"What's imposs . . . ?" Her eyes widened. "That can't be right, Aaron. It's hot out there, but not *that hot*. It must be a probe failure, or a fault in the line. Run a continuity check and reset the datum."

"I have! Twice! No fault found! And anyway the chances of a simultaneous multiple probe failure must be millions to one. Exposed or shaded the entire array concurs – this is no erroneous indication . . . this is it . . . the first!"

Annika's eyes were glued to the changing lines of data on the screen and her look of disbelief transformed to one of alarm. "I'll call the Centre Manager," she barked. "You cross-check again and run another simulation using the exact parameters, no rounding up or down, go the fifteen decimal places and then patch the results through to the master console. We'd better be one hundred per cent certain before we press the panic button!"

Annika was swiftly back to her console. She pressed a call button on the communications panel and leaned over the integrated microphone.

"Hello! Christine Bong here."

"Christine, it's Annika in Phased Array. Listen, I think we have a problem. Who is duty manager?"

"Augusto this morning, until midday, but he's out at one of the remote sensor sites . . . interference protected . . . so no direct comms – he said he would be back around seven. I can try to message his pager. The assistant manager is Marijs; she's at her desk."

"Give me her line, please. No! Just send her down . . . *pronto!*"

# CHAPTER 4

## YESTERDAY'S WORLD

**London - Whitehall**
**Same day – 08:14 Greenwich Mean Time**

"I'd like to say that it's good to see you, Peter, particularly after what . . . two years? But judging by that familiar expression, I'm not so sure."

"You know me as well as that, Richard? Interesting . . . I must be slipping. Welcome, all the same."

Peter Rothschild nodded at the two armed security guards as he passed them. He had allowed Richard to lead the way and one of the men, while keeping an open finger across the trigger guard of his assault rifle, eyed Richard warily. The other man, the smaller of the two, closed and bolted the internally fortified entrance door, causing a loud hollow-sounding thud to reverberate along the adjacent corridor. Despite being accompanied by the

Director of MI9 himself, Richard was still surprised that the guards had not ordered him to pass through the security screen, or at least stopped him for a body search. The persistent beeping from the bypassed body scanner made him feel ill at ease.

Rothschild stepped past him and, noticing Richard's frown, said, "Don't worry, the relevant checks have already been done . . . in my car, you understand. You are carrying three metallic objects – your telephonic pager, the chain for your identity tag and the swipe keys to your office. And you are not currently in possession of a weapon of any sort – not even a pen. Make you feel better? And anyway, your current ESSA Security Level Five clearance affords some privileges, don't you agree?"

Richard shrugged. "The MOD HQ. It doesn't matter which way you come in, it all looks the bloody same: endless corridors, doors going to who knows where, and people you can feel and hear but never see – gives me the creeps."

They had entered the ministry building by way of an out-of-sight side door and the narrow, beige-painted corridor conducted them into a small foyer, whereupon Rothschild turned abruptly right. Richard, who followed close behind, pointed at the three further corridors radiating from the small circular room in order to emphasise his point, but it was an adjacent, grey marble staircase that the two men began to ascend.

"Actually, there are not so many people here any more, Richard," Rothschild enlightened, "probably less than a hundred. Most military personnel from the Defence Department have gone to the newly refurbished underground headquarters in Northwood. In fact most of the government is now housed below ground – the main centre is out towards Aylesbury, well away from the Thames Flood Plain you understand. The Palace of Westminster is all but empty these days."

After the first flight of stairs, Richard caught up and matched Rothschild's sprightly pace. "So why are you sticking it out here, then?"

"Many reasons, Richard, not least practical. There's a good housekeeping organisation still in place, albeit skeletal, and the north wing remains conditioned, in daily use, and at my disposal. Which means that I have access to the best communications centre in the country and perhaps more importantly, my team can listen to just about everything that's transmitted anywhere in the world – at least in the primary frequency ranges . . . the 5G mobile networks and similar. With key words such as 'riot' and 'assassinate' programmed to be electronically highlighted and a fully automated system, anybody mentioning something they ought not to, might find themselves under investigation. Apart from that, I like to look out of the window occasionally."

Richard's expression became one of bemusement as he followed Rothschild through a set of doors, around a corner and into another corridor. He caught up with him again. "Why? You can't see anything. Just grey skies, low cloud and more often than not, rain!"

"It's not raining quite so much these days."

"Well that may be the case, Peter, but intermittent or not it's still wet and bloody miserable. Nothing grows I'm told, at least on the surface, and the place is covered in mould. It's everywhere . . . it's like the red weed in H G Wells' *War of the Worlds*. Except that it's green. I mean who, in their right mind, would want to live here?"

"We can't all live on the Moon, Richard. You are extremely privileged. After the Lunar Senate agreed to reconsider the immigration question in fifty-two, they set strict quotas. The orbiting boarder craft only processes applicants with a requisite skill or experience relevant to Andromeda's development and expansion plans. Anyone who was not a full-time resident of Andromeda at the time of independence has to apply for residency and the process is extremely long winded. Relocation is for the lucky ones. With our help, you missed all that – jumped the queue in fact. We put your name forward to command the Shuttle Wing because of your success in retrieving the largest crystal . . . we owed you, so to speak. You don't need me to remind you that your application only took three months to clear the lunar immigration process. You were not in flying practice and your S2 rating was well out of date, and so, on the face of it, not the preferred choice for that appointment – or have you forgotten that?" Rothschild half-turned in order to look Richard square in the eye. "A number of important people pulled strings on your behalf," he continued, "you should remember that."

"Well, yes, but I had . . ."

Rothschild nodded at a smart, dark-suited man who passed them in the opposite direction. He waited until they turned another corner before continuing. "Very few people have access to the stars these days, Richard, you should be grateful," he said emphatically. With that, Peter Rothschild peeled off to his left and pulled open a heavy fire door. Having passed through and following a quick glance up to nod at a security camera, he looked over his shoulder to confirm that Richard had pushed the door shut again. Subsequently, both men breathed easier.

In the corridor that followed the atmosphere was conditioned: warm, dry and comfortable. However, the stuffiness of government, of protocol and control was still patently apparent in this old seat of power – manifested in long, gloomy, wooden-panelled passageways and secretive secured doors. But it was overwhelmingly silent. *Have things finally changed?* wondered Richard.

"Apparently, not the privileged working conditions that you're used to, I see, Peter. I'm beginning to think that you've been ostracised – abandoned by the ministry?" Richard offered his remark with an edge of sarcasm; it broke a protracted silence. He was still unhappy with the recall.

Rothschild ignored the remark, shaking his head almost imperceptibly. Richard smiled: he had hit the mark. Presently, Rothschild stopped outside a high Georgian-style door of dark oak and reached for its shiny brass handle. He paused and looked with a grave expression at Richard and then opened the door. There was a gap between the purple and gold carpet runner that extended seemingly forever along the corridor and the regal blue of the room's floor covering and Richard, in his boots, clumped awkwardly between the two. Like somebody talking in a library, he turned a few disapproving heads.

Inside the large rectangular room, with its high ceiling, there was a spectacular run of windows that overlooked the river. In front stood a polished table – square, wooden and with thick straight legs. From an off-centre slot on the far side of the table a thin, frosted glass panel, evidently a monitor screen, protruded. It was perhaps a metre tall and a metre and a half wide. The table was clearly prepared for a meeting with plastic bottles of water, crystal glasses and a number of electronic notebooks positioned on three sides. There was an orderly making some last minute touches to the seven place settings and another under the table fiddling with the electrical connections.

"All in order, Jeremy?" Rothschild asked, as he strode across the room towards an adjacent door.

"Yes, sir."

"What about the Minister?"

"No one has arrived yet, sir; at least not to my knowledge."

"Please let me know when they do; we will need a few minutes to synchronise the system."

"It's all in order, sir, although we hear that Washington is having problems with their Safety Net again."

Rothschild turned and beckoned Richard to follow him into the side room – it was much smaller, but the two windows still had a sweeping view of the grey, murky River Thames. Rothschild shook his head as he closed the door behind him. "Something is going awry with the Net, too many glitches, as if another system is attempting to interface and pulling the security grid down on the rebound. It's happening too often and I don't like it." Rothschild offered Richard the chair on the other side of the antique desk. Both men sat down. Rothschild opened the desk drawer to his left and pressed a switch. Moments later a computer keyboard was projected onto the desktop in front of him. He used the illuminated keys to type in an 8-digit code and then lifted the lid to his personal notebook. With that, the illuminated keyboard disappeared. Richard could see a number of lights reflecting through the glass lid. Rothschild looked at the screen. "Laura, are you there?" he asked.

A woman's pleasantly modulated voice answered; Richard recognised her. "Yes, Peter, I'm here, trying to coordinate the link with Alexandria. It's patched through Cairo at the moment and imaging is heavily distorted. I'm being advised that we should utilise HMS *Hermes* instead; she's currently anchored a few miles off the coast. We can then relay through the military command network instead."

*Laura Bellingham*, Richard thought, *the civil servant. She used to be with Home Affairs. Now she must be Peter's PA.*

Rothschild's eyes tracked a figure on the screen and he responded a little anxiously. "Yes, do it. Quickly. Inform Admiral Hughes . . . Anything from General Roper?"

"Only to say that there is absolutely no problem at their end – he would not enlighten further."

Rothschild sighed and sat back in his seat. He tapped his fingers on the desk thoughtfully before looking up at Richard. "Damn frustrating, this protocol!" he blurted, uncharacteristically. "The Americans are saying that their system is completely secure – their most up-to-date codes, absolutely no chance of being hacked. I'm not so sure." He tapped his fingers again. "It's a point of national pride. Despite the special relationship they will not let us run an overlay check. You wouldn't imagine we are all on the same side!"

"If you're talking about SERON, Peter, the ISSF's Space Net, there is no chance of penetration. Even from my operations centre on Andromeda we need five levels of authorisation. The Space and Science Federation monitors every single terminal that requests a connection – continuous multiple sequencing. I tend to agree with the Americans – penetrating SERON . . . well it must be imposs . . ."

Peter Rothschild interrupted. "I spent the first seven years of my career in the intelligence department, Richard, as a binary programmer. Believe me, there isn't a code that can't be broken. Stella, sequential, arithmetic; if someone has the resources – the right equipment and the right people – it can be done. Just think back to the

Second World War. The German High Command were convinced that their military Enigma code was totally secure and continued to use it until 1945, transmitting highly classified and top-secret material all the while. You remember Bletchley Park and ULTRA from your history lessons at school? There the Intelligence Service did the impossible and the information they decoded was a substantial aid to the Allied war effort; some said it shortened the war by two years. It was a massive blow when the German military eventually realised their folly – and their conceit." Rothschild's tight-clenched fingertips tapped the desk again. It was a subconscious response.

"So you think there's a risk that the system is or has been compromised, and the Americans are the weak link?"

"I'm convinced that someone is looking at what we are doing. At what level I'm not sure. You will hear why when we brief." Rothschild checked the small hologram that hovered by his left shoulder; there was a red mark on the silvery-grey clock face that highlighted the commencement time of the impending meeting. "It's the Americans who insist it's impossible; all the other national agencies are cross-checking. I've got my department looking very closely at our interface. The level of cyber-attack is unprecedented at the moment and we are not sure why. We are being probed from all directions, so to speak, and are desperately trying to keep one step ahead; but by the very nature of the complexity the threat increases every day." Rothschild massaged his left temple with two fingers. He was clearly under pressure. "Cyber-defence draws heavily on my resources," he continued, "resources that would best be deployed elsewhere. If we find evidence of a breach in our network, however, I will report it immediately: that's our policy – we must be open about this."

"Peter! The Yucatán link is confirmed," reported Laura, her voice emanating from the notebook on the desk. "Professor Bryn Jones has tested live; he's gone off for a cup of tea but is standing by."

Richard began to look a little bemused by the unfolding events.

"Thank you Laura," replied Rothschild. "Let me know the moment the Alexandria link is established."

"Of course … all the same, I do expect to open on time – fifty-seven minutes and counting. I'll need you both seated five minutes before, please. Secretary Edmondson and the others are due to arrive in thirty minutes."

"Understood!"

## Moon base Andromeda – simultaneous
## Residential Unit 103

Rachel quickly wiped away the tear that welled in the corner of her eye before it had a chance to run down her cheek. Someone might call by and she didn't want to give away her feelings with smudged complexion – although her reddened eyes were more difficult to hide. She prepared a breakfast for one. The experimental crop of Kiwi fruit grown in the new biodome on the south side had proved a success and her allocation of three examples were very tempting. Together with the bananas from the previous month that were now ripe and ready to eat, her fruit salad looked delicious.

The residential unit was bright and airy. Covering sixty square metres over two floors, it offered every modern convenience. The kitchen was futuristic with a spacious, black, moulded worktop that evolved in one direction into shelving and display units and, in the other, into a large circular table. The floor and remaining kitchen units were off-white in colour and with a marble effect. A large picture of the blue Earth taken from the Moon during the Apollo 11 landing hung on a wall and offered a dazzle of colour – albeit an evocative dazzle.

Rachel put her bowl down on the table and dropped the spoon nearby. She sat dejected on a stool and stared inanely at the green fruit and milky coloured banana and the glass of synthetic orange juice. The rare treat offered little solace and neither did her second cup of strong black coffee. For the second year running Richard was on duty on Christmas morning. The previous year he had volunteered for the role of duty officer and had manned the squadron's front desk until early evening, saying that it was important that the pilots with children should have the time at home. Family time was important he had said – but evidently not theirs.

Married for four years and trying for a child for three of those – this last one in near desperation – it seemed that the joy of motherhood would evade her. *Was it their careers – time consuming and often stressful?* she mused. *Was it their relationship? Perhaps it was the environment?* But others were able – the colony's birth rate was steadily rising. Another tear threatened; this time she absorbed it with a handkerchief.

This year would be different, she resolved. After breakfast she would make a determined effort. Richard had promised to be back by mid-morning, by which time the Christmas tree projector would be set in the corner and the life-size, 3D hologram, complete with tinsel decorations, flashing coloured lights and a shining star on top would have pride of place. Presents would be distributed liberally around its base. She had ordered a turkey from the poultry dome in good time and it would be presented with all the trimmings. They would have a Christmas to remember and leave this old year, with all its disappointments and frustrations, behind them.

## London – simultaneous

Rothschild refocused his attention on Richard. "Now, where was I?" he asked.

"Your suspicions about Space Net."

"Yes. Richard, it is essential that you understand the shortfalls of such a system and, believe me, despite what the primary sponsors say, there are some." Rothschild looked tense. "The global interface between the military network and the International Space and

Science Federation network will always be a weak spot and therefore the prime target for any hacker wishing to bridge the security programming. Military meets civilian; there have always been different protocols and different agendas. SERON is a multi-dimensional protective overlay trying to perform an impossible task in my view. It's a programming umbrella, if you like, doing its damnedest to keep the water out. But it is faced with a torrent of differing opinions and different languages – verbally and binary – all attempting to access twenty-four seven. With all these anomalies, in my view, it's just a matter of time before there is a breach, despite what our neighbours say." Rothschild leaned forward to emphasise his point. "The findings of my department suggest that the world's three major industrial multi-nationals, the three conglomerates we know only too well, are engaged in another concerted attempt to control global energy supplies." Rothschild breathed in deeply. "I'm sure of it, but I've no proof. Now, with the recent news, somebody really must sit up and listen. My American counterpart, the Director of the Central Investigation Bureau, says it's not possible. He says that the international restraining orders and raw material embargoes that were imposed a little over four years ago are sufficient to keep them and other corporations wishing to monopolise such resources in line. And that they were and are sufficient to stifle all industrial and financial growth and therefore any plans of dominating that sector again. My view is that these embargoes have just pushed the illegal activities of these conglomerates underground – in more ways than one!" Rothschild nodded. "Spheron, Tongsei and Epsilon Rio are more of a threat now than they ever were. But international politics, protocol, for heaven's sake, means that I can't mention it."

"What evidence do you have?"

"I've had a few of my best people on the case for the last six or seven months . . . subtly, one might say. And they have uncovered some interesting information; information that taken in isolation would not arouse suspicion, but when one begins to look at the whole picture . . ."

"Run it by me."

"There have been a number of disappearances over the last few years . . . reported, but never connected. We're talking scientists, system engineers, propulsion specialists, people from the space and computing industry . . . They're mainly from abroad, so difficult to correlate, but these people have never been heard of again. In a few cases there have been some financial incentives for relatives to keep quiet. I've been diverting resources from other areas to keep the investigation going – nothing dishonest, but not in keeping with current policies either, you understand. If I speak up with what I've got they will want to know my sources – believe me, in the present economic climate, that could open Pandora's Box. And as far as international relations go, it could be a disaster."

"What are you saying, Peter? If I'm hearing you correctly, you're saying that you think that despite heavy restraint on the global activities of these three conglomerates they may be up to their old tricks again. You have intelligence, but nothing concrete, so you can't go public?"

"Precisely!"

"So what do you propose to do?"

"I'm going to introduce some of our findings at the briefing."

"And risk alienating the Americans?"

"I'm going to present some information, that's all. They can take it or leave it, as can the Federation."

Richard shrugged. "So what's my part in all this? Christmas dinner gets fainter and fainter." He checked his chronometer.

"You had better call Rachel, with my sincere apologies. I'm afraid that your shuttle is already on its way back; you can expect to be here in London for a few days at least, but also I want you to go and see Mubarakar. He is very ill by all accounts and cannot travel, but he's got something to show us and he says it's important. You know Mubarakar as well as I do – he would not waste our time. So when we are finished here, I suggest that you also call your second in command. You can expect to be away from your squadron for at least a week, maybe more."

Richard cradled his forehead in his hand and rubbed the bridge of his nose. "Christmas Day of all days . . . I've got a better idea – you call Rachel."

"Um, I don't think so." Rothschild looked uncomfortable. "Anyway, more to the point, did you get any rest? During the transit I mean. We have almost an hour if you want some down time? Oh and by the way, what did you bring in the way of clothing?"

Richard looked up. "I'm fine; I had a few hours and used the facilities in the VIP terminal. They even gave us some breakfast. As for clean shirts, I brought a few, but I'll need some toiletries if it's going to be more than a week." He paused. "Why don't you establish a video-link with Mubarakar? Use a digital scrambler if it's that sensitive."

"He is old school – very. He does not trust the technology and he's not well. In fact, he has not left Egypt for two years and apparently is now housebound in Alexandria. He's gone back to his roots, Richard – always a bad sign. He has also resigned from the Supreme Council of Antiquities and as Executive Curator of both the Cairo and Luxor Museums and, of course, he is over eighty if he's a day. I've a feeling that he wants to share some information with you specifically, while he can, you know, before . . . Anyway, we have arrangements in hand for you to visit his home."

A brief look of surprise washed over Richard's face. "Yes, well, it will be good to see him," he replied.

"We may also need you to go to Mexico for a few days, the Yucatán Peninsula to be precise – also something for you to see. We need your expertise."

Richard nodded. "Nice to be wanted," he said. "Tell me! What's the current travel situation? By air I mean. I'm a bit behind the drag curve. I know that there is very little scheduled airline traffic these days."

Rothschild thought for a moment. "Actually, there are no longer any solvent airlines – at least not in the Northern Hemisphere. Most travel is now by sea or rail – and that's becoming prohibitively expensive. Aeroplanes, cars, road haulage vehicles . . . they have no value any more. It's the basics that are expensive these days, Richard." Rothschild paused thoughtfully before continuing. "When an aircraft is required for official business the government normally charters – on a one-off basis you understand. Orbital Airlines are the preferred contractor. They have retained a small fleet for this purpose. Aviation fuel is a very scarce commodity – in fact, there is seldom any available on the open or spot markets. The Energy Department has occasionally had opportunity to bid for small quantities that are auctioned on the black market – mainly from Uganda – but that is rare now. However, I'm pleased to say that central government holds a utility reserve that is stored at a refining terminal near Southampton and piped to London using the old London Heathrow connection. There is, thankfully, the essential spur to London Main Airport – best thing Cameron did during his second term – against those violent planning demonstrations too . . . remember?"

Richard slumped in his seat. "I was eight and had other things on my mind."

"And now you are what, forty-four?"

"You know exactly how old I am, Peter, you have my record in front of you!"

"Yes . . . quite so. I was sixteen you know, and I

remember."

Richard raised his eyebrows to forestall any coming lecture.

"Anyway," Rothschild continued, "I may be able to secure sixty or seventy tons of aviation grade kerosene, but that's all."

"Yeah, well, the Stratocord is a bit of an overkill, wouldn't you say? And it certainly isn't the best on fuel economy, particularly in the lower atmosphere and that's the only aircraft type Orbital operated. I'm guessing but I'd say seventy tons is enough to get me to Egypt and back and perhaps across the pond to eastern Mexico."

"I am aware of that, Richard. Planning has it in hand and has asked the Mexican Government for help, but by all accounts they haven't got anything left either. Their reserves are quoting zero, but the military might spare some in an extreme case. That will take a call from the PM – I haven't gone there yet. I certainly do not think it sensible to rely on local sources."

"What about the Americans?"

"We know they found a small pocket recently in southern Texas – enough to keep the state going for another month, perhaps two. It's likely the Government took a share and we heard that there may have been a little gas too. The Federal Energy Commission is distilling some domestic oil from their remaining coal stocks and perhaps some kerosene. Problem is, with this briefing coming up I'm loath to ask them. The PM may authorise a flight with NetJets Global using a Royal Flight allocation.

You flew with them before, you may recall. Apparently, they have a little bio fuel remaining in Germany."

Richard nodded. "And elsewhere? Stocks around the planet?"

"South America dried up a year ago to all intents and purposes. They were not very good at saving for a rainy day. What little coal and oil they had at the beginning of this year was sold to international buyers on the black market – quite amazing really. Actually, we bought about three hundred thousand barrels ourselves."

Richard shook his head. "Unbelievable!"

"Europe and Africa are the same. Canadian and Alaskan oil shale stocks are depleted and their Kerogen holding is almost exhausted too. Apart from that there are some isolated pockets of gas and oil here and there, but they aren't really anything to speak of; nothing of note has been reported for some time. South Africa rushed into constructing a new fission reactor eighteen months ago, near Port Elizabeth, but the technology they are using is forty years old. Nothing has progressed in that field since the New Geneva Convention banned nuclear power stations. They are on a road to nowhere in my opinion. Even under normal environmental conditions it would take six or seven years to complete a facility like that. Their plan was just two years, and without the cooperation of the international community. Not a chance. I am beginning to think that a blanket ban on all nuclear power was a mistake – then and now."

"Yes, but two major accidents in as many years and

half-a-million square miles of pollution gave a lot of weight to the 'greens'. It was a lobby that gathered pace across the globe . . . It was 'save the planet and not worry about humankind' back then. Now it seems to be the other way round. Anyway, Peter, what about the East?"

"Japan is trading some of its territories west of Nagasaki and the home island of Kyushu to China in exchange for an undisclosed quantity of light fuel oil – again mainly distilled from coal stocks. Japan is saying that it is necessary in order to keep the central government and local administration in operation. How long that will last, God only knows. While the Chinese are keeping tight-lipped about what they actually have left, we do not think it can be much. Total global stocks were declared three years ago as part of an international pooling protocol; it was mandatory to declare all holdings and a satellite monitoring programme was agreed. Based on that data they simply cannot have much remaining – maybe six months. Their agenda is as inscrutable as ever. Exchanging land for fuel and so depriving their own people of heat and light – how can you put a value on those commodities?"

"You know the Chinese, Peter, always long-term."

Rothschild considered that remark for a few seconds. "Um, yes, long-term," he said. "What do we mean by that phrase these days I wonder . . . ? What do *they* know that we don't?"

Richard shook his head.

"There are a lot of deals going on at the moment

between various states," Rothschild continued. "Trading this. Trading that. Pushing. Pulling. I'm not sure where it's going to end. Everyone wants what's left. It doesn't bode well for the future." Richard saw him grimace.

"And the Pacific Rim?"

"Dry! Several months ago in fact. The forests are gone of course. Manila is reporting a dry spell, almost two weeks now. Temperatures are said to be up by eleven degrees Celsius – positively warm by global standards. As a result the Japanese have reduced their electricity quota from the Katsuura reactor by fifteen per cent. That hasn't gone down well with the government of the Philippines, as you can imagine." Peter half-laughed. "Unlikely to boast about their weather again . . ."

"Yes, I suppose. So it's true what we read and hear on the news. The four Kalahari crystals are literally keeping the whole thing going?"

Rothschild nodded in a resigned way. "Indeed. The latest figure was ninety-two per cent . . . they're providing ninety-two per cent of global electricity needs. God knows what we would have done without them. But as you well know, Richard, they are a finite resource. The three smaller crystals suffered degradation earlier this year and the primary crystal in the French reactor has been overloaded ever since."

Richard nodded. "Yes, I read about that too. I keep a keen interest in what the International Energy Commission is doing with them. And how long? What is the up-to-date prediction? Or is that censored information?"

"Yes it is, but I feel I can tell you, considering the fact that we need your help again." Rothschild put his hands together on the desk and forced an optimistic smile. "Our delegate in the Energy Commission says eight or nine months to complete exhaustion of the primary crystal, ten at the absolute most. The smaller crystals will breakdown first, maybe a month or so earlier. It is difficult to put a more accurate figure on it because the electricity demands of the world grid will be unpredictable as final reserves and undeclared stocks of carbon fuel are used and the potential of national grids reduces to zero. And that my dear chap is another reason for the top level meeting today. Rather intimidating, wouldn't you say?"

At that moment there was a loud knock on the door behind Richard.

"Come in," invited Rothschild.

The door opened and a familiar face peered around it as Richard turned in his chair. "Ah, Grenville," Richard greeted him. "Good to see you, it's been a while. So you stayed with the old man?"

Grenville coughed politely into his fist; it was his way of avoiding the embarrassment. "Yes, sir, quite, and good to have you back if I may say." Grenville, a formal looking gentleman who was in his early sixties, looked at Rothschild. "Sorry to disturb you, sir," he continued. "I've had a message from the Communication Centre. There is a telephone call for Commander Reece." He looked back at Richard. "A Miss Pamela Merchant, an Auntie of yours

I believe – apparently it is urgent."

Richard's immediate reaction was dismay. He thought of his mother and he thought the worst. He stood.

"The booth opposite, sir, if you please," said Grenville, as he opened the door further and indicated behind him. Rothschild nodded. Richard quickly crossed the corridor, stepped into the small room and snatched the telephone receiver from the desk. Grenville quietly closed the door. There was an office-type chair in the room and little else. Richard sat down as he put the receiver to his ear. He prepared himself for bad news.

"Aunt Pamela? Richard here. What's happened? Is Mother . . . ?"

"Your Mother is fine, Richard," said an austere, elderly voice. "There is nothing to worry about on that count. And so incidentally am I."

"Yes, sorry, good. That's good. But a call here . . . I was thinking it must be serious . . ."

"It is. Your mother is frantic. I called Rachel; she gave me your number. Calling you at work is not something I would do without good reason."

"I know that. So what has happened?"

"Your mother returned home this morning to find that the house had been burgled, ransacked in fact. Whoever did it made a complete mess. She called me. Of course I came over immediately. The police are still here . . ."

"Police! You're at the cottage!" Richard thought about the crystal, the ninth crystal, *the one only he knew about.* The one he had smuggled out of Osiris Base in a mineral container packaged as a simple rock sample. It had been transported to Earth on a routine, six-monthly, shuttle flight over four years earlier. Perhaps foolhardily, he had had the package delivered by courier service to his mother's house in Buckersmead, Somerset, where she, completely unaware of its contents and following his instructions, had hidden it in his father's old workshop – in a deep vehicle servicing pit that was covered with heavy wooden sleepers. The crystal and its location was a secret that he had never shared, not even with Rachel. It was known that there was another missing crystal and an exhaustive search for it on Mars at the time had failed to discover its whereabouts. Richard had covered his tracks and the furore had gradually subsided. Now he was waiting for the right moment – when it could be utilised properly, efficiently. But as time passed it had become more difficult. The implications of withholding the crystal, harbouring its powers, were serious. Indeed, as the world prepared for an energy shortfall of catastrophic proportions, they had become momentous. *If it has been found or, worse, stolen,* Richard thought, *there would be hell to pay.* He was sure to be prosecuted, fined and jailed, and his career would be finished. And how would he explain it to Rachel! He held his forehead in the palm of his hand and dreaded the consequences.

"Richard? Richard? Are you there?"

"Yes, sorry Aunt, yes I'm here." Richard leant forward and put an elbow on the table and rubbed his brow.

"What about the workshop? Is anything missing? It's very important that you check Father's workshop!"

"Your mother seemed particularly worried about the workshop too. Rather odd . . . Anyway, we checked there first . . . even before we checked the bedroom where the safe is, and again when the police arrived. The building is completely empty, well, apart from a few odds and ends and some of your father's old tools. There was nothing of value to steal in any case, according to your mother. What a fuss! The house is what we should be worrying about – it's an absolute mess. Look, here she is. The last police officer must have left – and about time."

Richard took a deep breath. "So whoever it was hadn't gone into the workshop? Is that right?"

"Oh dear, you do persist – just like when you were a boy! The workshop appeared undisturbed, Richard. No one has been in there for years – it's quite obvious. Your mother seemed happy with that at least. She wanted you to know immediately. We are going to have a cup of tea now. Thank goodness. We both need one. She will come and stay with me again. You can rest assured about that."

"Okay, that's good. Thanks Aunt, thanks for being there. Can I have a quick word with her, please?"

There was a pause. "Richard would like to speak to you," he heard his Aunt say, and then there was the sound of some brief chat in the background.

"Hello darling. I really didn't want to call you because I'm pretty sure that all is well. But you know Pamela – she insisted."

"That's okay Mother. I prefer to know. Listen, the workshop, it definitely appears undisturbed?"

"Yes, everything is as it should be."

Her guarded comments calmed Richard down. "Do the police have any idea who it was that broke in?" he asked.

"The Police Inspector was very impressed with the security system; even he wasn't au fait with the programming. No common thief is his verdict, especially as I can't find anything missing."

"Where were you when they came calling?"

"I'd stayed over in town. I went to see a show with a friend."

Richard heaved a sigh of relief. "And you're happy to stay with Pamela while the mess is cleared up?"

"Yes, of course. I've been staying with her from time to time anyway – to save electricity. The Police Inspector's report will come through in due course and there is the question of insurance."

"Mum, I'm really sorry to have put you through this, but it is so important. What's there is crucial to us all. Please believe me."

"I know you well enough Richard. Obviously I can't get anyone to check for you, but I'm pretty sure that all is well."

"Thanks Mum. I'll get home as soon as I can. Love you, bye."

Richard switched off the receiver and placed it down carefully on the desk. He slowly leant back in the chair and scratched his head. *Should he be suspicious?* he wondered. *Was this a random, opportunistic burglary – despite the technical expertise required to disarm the security system? They hadn't taken anything. Were they looking for something specific? Surely they were – all that mess and nothing taken.* Richard recalled the events on Mars – the apparent loss of the ninth crystal; the palaver it had caused at the time; and all those weeks of searching just for disappointment. He recalled his almost celebrity status here on Earth – for a while at least – and then the court-martial proceedings that had brought the whole pack of cards tumbling down. The tabloids had had a field day. *Could somebody have probed further? Found his mother's house in Somerset? Who had information to link the house – and why now? The trail had gone cold, so what had brought them out of the woodwork after more than four years? Is the crystal safe there?* he agonised. And he couldn't put his mother in jeopardy. *It needs to be moved, and quickly,* he concluded. Richard was thoughtful as he left the room.

# CHAPTER 5

# OMINOUS DIRECTION

Richard dropped into the chair. He was clearly preoccupied. Rothschild, who was typing an abrive on the projected desktop keyboard, looked up. He knew Richard well enough to know that something now troubled him. The sound of a foghorn, loud and distinct, permeated the silence. Rothschild kicked himself back to the window and glanced outside. The River Thames at high water was full and rushing; a brownish slurry choppy with eddies and turbulence. Blowing mists of drizzle that occasionally swept across the surface allowed the dense grey sky and leaded cloud base to reach down and blend with the murky water like a gloomy wash on a painter's canvas. As a brief wintry shower of rain peppered the glass outside with noisy pellets, Rothschild, with a keen eye, watched a long steel barge make slow progress towards the sea. Heavy with its commodity, there were no lubber lines or depth markings on the rusty hull to show how it faired but waves occasionally washed over its deck. White letters painted on the stern, where a finish of black paint still resisted the elements, declared 'Rotterdam' as its home port and then another long echoing belch from its foghorn proclaimed an unstoppable passage. After a few moments Rothschild turned back to look at Richard still deep in thought and then scooted himself back to his desk on the chair's castors. "Nothing serious, I trust," he offered.

Richard looked down at his chronometer. "I know you already have an itinerary for me, Peter," he said, "but I will need to go to Paris before Egypt. Sorry, but it's necessary."

"Paris? Why so?"

Their eyes met. "Personal," said Richard, brooking no argument.

Rothschild sighed and shook his head. "I don't think so, Richard. Time is against us. You will find out why soon enough. The brief is due to commence in twenty minutes."

Richard's expression hardened. "I *will* go to Paris, with or without your permission, so you might as well allow me this concession. After that I'm with you, one hundred per cent. It's a thirty-minute flight – if that. We could land at Le Bourget. There's nothing happening there these days. I know that because we use it as a diversion when on approach to Strasbourg Spaceport. I'll be gone a couple of hours at the most. A car would be helpful." Richard raised his eyebrows expectantly.

"Are you going to see Miss Vallogia?"

Richard remained silent for a moment and considered the implications of telling Rothschild, and then he nodded. "I need to talk to her – catch up on a few things."

"I see. Interesting, this sudden concern . . ." Rothschild thought for a moment. "Actually, a visit could work in everyone's favour," he said, in a conciliatory way. His expression lightened. He had no intention of causing a conflict of interest and knew from Richard's tone that he would not concede this point – now was not the time to enforce military discipline with a direct order. "I kept note, of course, of where we sent the Ark – you remember our conversation," Rothschild continued. "You would have expected that anyway, wouldn't you? My French counterpart contacted Miss Vallogia upon her arrival at the monastery and we opened a discrete communication channel. After all, it is an important relic. Miss Vallogia has given me an annual report as to its condition."

Richard nodded; he accepted Rothschild's methods. "Has she ever spoken of me?" he asked.

Rothschild shook his head. "Not since you married. Anyway, under her supervision, and sponsored by this department, we commissioned the finest craftspeople in the field to restore the Ark to its former glory, so to speak. Thanks to you, we now know the meaning of most of what is inscribed on it, although the significance of a few hieroglyphs still evades our understanding. However,

I would like you to have a good look at it as well – now that all the inscriptions inside the Ark are legible. Update yourself – perhaps you might find something relevant to what Mubarakar has to say."

Richard nodded again in agreement; *this is a satisfactory compromise,* he thought. *I will check out the Ark and the monastery . . . there is nowhere else that springs to mind where the crystal will be as safe and surely Naomi will be pleased to help. The logistics of getting the crystal to France, however, I will consider in due course.* He stared at Rothschild for a moment and changed the subject. "I read in *The Andromeda Times* the other day that approximately seventeen per cent of the world's population now lives underground full-time and that a further eleven per cent live subsurface but commute to the surface for employment. And that the trend is increasing rapidly. To my mind, the UK government has clearly condoned this migration by moving to the new parliament facility built beneath the Chilterns. So what's the story – I mean are these numbers sustainable? What about food?"

"There is not much for us on the surface anymore, not these days, Richard, particularly in the Northern Hemisphere." Rothschild looked saddened. "Some parts of north Africa, central Australia and the Atacama Desert in South America have been relatively dry for several months now, but no sunshine . . . never any sunshine." Rothschild sighed. "Sunshine is off the menu, I'm afraid, and of course the winters appear to be much longer.

There has been an enormous effort over the last few years to resolve the climatic problem – unprecedented international cooperation in fact that culminated in a secret Head of State conference in Arizona three weeks ago. Some of the best scientific brains in the world presented their work on the subject, and it wasn't good news. Cloud currently covers ninety-seven per cent of the planet's surface; from a few hundred feet above ground level right up to the tropopause – and beyond in some areas. That's a layer of water vapour six to eight miles thick, and the global weather system is stable, which means that it's the new—" Rothschild raised his fingers to articulate a pair of inverted commas. "'Normal.'"

"So no progress, no answers – that's what you're saying?"

"The fundamental error our climatologists made, it transpires, was in understanding the global water cycle – more a misunderstanding, as it happened. We know the ice cap at the North Pole disappeared in the thirties, and Antarctica, as an ice-covered land mass, a decade later – that's history. Everybody assumed that the vast quantities of fresh water released would merely raise the global sea level by a metre or so, and that did happen, it was well documented, but what they did not realise was that the increased surface area of the oceans enabled a higher evaporation rate and that increased the atmospheric water content significantly. The pollution levels that had been building up in the 2040s when people began burning wood and coal again became the catalyst. It reached the critical density for spontaneous coalescence in August forty-nine when you were still on Mars. That's when the thickest cloud began to form. Subsequently, temperatures dropped, forcing more condensation. And the rest we know, don't we?"

"What about a fix?"

"There isn't one at the moment, although the international effort continues. The situation was unforeseen. Nobody's fault. A case of concentrating on other things. A mistake. In retrospect, governments should have listened a bit better – been less complacent."

Richard gestured in a dejected fashion. "That's what you truly believe is it, Peter? Nobody's fault?"

Rothschild shrugged. "Let's not talk politics, Richard, neither of us is qualified."

"So what are the ongoing repercussions then? What is the real situation here?"

"Food production is rapidly becoming the overriding concern for national governments – those with a functioning infrastructure that is. The lack of production is more to the point . . . except under cover, and that's hopelessly inadequate for a global population. For traditional cultivation it's too wet and there is no sun. Adapted crops are still available, rice for example, but yields are a fraction of those a few years ago. Meat production too is falling well short of targets. Fish on the whole has made up the shortfall since forty-nine, but consequently stocks have been devastated. Unrealistic quotas, illegal net sizes, deep-sea trawling – you name it.

In short, there's nothing left in the oceans . . . literally. It's all gone – finished!"

"So what's the government planning?"

"Heard of bioluminescence?"

"Well yes," Richard frowned. "The production and emission of light from living things, you know, light from organisms. Um, the glow-worm, the firefly – that sort of creature."

"Exactly! A team of geneticists at Cambridge University had been carrying out research for a number of years – a few important discoveries opened up the field. Then a little over a year ago a Japanese scientist made the fundamental breakthrough, more a discovery, actually. It was explained to me to be more like the discovery of penicillin last century – that kind of magnitude. There was a flurry of research and now the results are exceeding all expectations. The scientist, a Mr Suzukito, is up for the Nobel Prize."

"Yes I heard about him," said Richard, nodding again, "a symbiotic cross between two plant species or something. It was on the news."

"After the Head of State Conference I stayed on for a few days and attended a forum on the world food shortage. It was enlightening to say the least. What Mr Suzukito did was to take a species of lichen that is common in subterranean caverns in Japan. The species doesn't need sunlight to grow; there is no chlorophyll present in its makeup and so no photosynthesis. It is not a 'green' plant. By genetic manipulation he introduced the gene that is responsible for the naturally occurring form of chemiluminescence – the gene that controls the chemical reaction that produces the natural glow in creatures. In fact, he extracted the gene from a species of glow-worm. This particular glow, or 'cold light' as it is termed, is in the useful yellow light spectrum. In short, of course, he produced a glowing plant adapted to life underground."

"So?"

"Then he introduced a particular species of green algae, one that thrives in warm moist conditions, one on the other . . . a dusting of the algae onto the lichen. In botanical terms, a symbiotic relationship, and it worked. The algae use the light from the lichen to photosynthesise and grow, as would be the case in normal sunlight. And the lichen takes what it needs from the algae by utilising a network of microfilaments – drawing sugars in the form of sap from the algae. At a temperature of twenty degrees Celsius and above, and a humidity level over sixty per cent, growth rates are reportedly phenomenal. And with a geothermal gradient of approximately twenty-five to thirty degrees per kilometre depth in most parts of the world and, of course, lots of moisture, things are looking quite promising." Rothschild smiled briefly, subconsciously showing his relief. "The harvested algae are full of nutrients, proteins, minerals, starch – it's a perfect food. In fact the Chinese and the Japanese – because of their vast naturally occurring limestone caves – are already commercially farming the crop."

"Sounds like manna," Richard interjected. "How boring is that – eating algae! What do you do with it – mix it into a nice bland paste? Perhaps some delicious green pastry?"

"Apparently not!" Rothschild protested, as if the idea had been his. "Each crop is carefully sucked from the lichen fronds during a vacuuming process – by a giant vacuum cleaner if you like – leaving just enough to regenerate for the next rotation. The powder can then be processed into any constituency – that of meat, fish and vegetable types. Natural colours are added to help. Many synthetic extracts have been produced based on chemicals that give normal food its unique taste. And it's very convincing I'm told – stimulates the palate adequately." A smile jabbed his lips again. "Actually, I did try some of the raw algae myself, just lightly toasted; it was remarkably similar to that crispy seaweed you used to be able to get in Peking restaurants . . . back a while. Think about it, Richard. Free under-floor heating, subtle lighting, kitchen gardens, plenty of hot water, perhaps one's own thermal spring . . . . One just needs electricity for the essentials – for cooking, some additional lighting, perhaps a solarium. Along with the niceties of course – TV, computer, communications. Why wouldn't you choose to live underground? Perhaps it's the future." Rothschild appeared convinced.

"I see, so the surface of the planet becomes what . . . a waste tip and a scrapyard?"

Rothschild focused on Richard and interlocked

his fingers like a teacher explaining a new concept. "In many places it already is, Richard, as well you know," he answered.

"You should be careful. Otherwise you might find yourself a victim of your own propaganda," Richard countered, sceptically. He took time to savour a deep breath of conditioned air and then rubbed his chin thoughtfully, as if making up his mind on something. "I'm going to tell you something, Peter. In strictest confidence, you understand." Richard paused again. "You know I've another year to go as Commanding Officer of Andromeda's Shuttle Wing?" Rothschild nodded. "Well, I've made an application for permanent residency. It will go before the Lunar Select Committee for Immigration next month." Rothschild's expression hardly changed. "Most of our friends are already registered," Richard continued. "Many already have children who were born in the colony. These people have no intention of returning to Earth; indeed, their children will have no rights of residency here and no nationality either. Who the hell wants a passport anyway . . . to live underground? I'd rather have no atmosphere and see the stars."

"Yes, I did hear something . . . . There will be due process of course. And what would you do? Having been the Shuttle Wing's commanding officer, you are unlikely to be welcome as a line pilot."

Richard sat up and his expression tightened. "I have my surveying qualifications – barely twenty per cent of the lunar surface has been mapped from the ground and there is a lot of seismic work still to be done."

"You! Settled as a colonist?" Rothschild scratched his brow. "I have to say I have my doubts about that."

Richard nodded. "You could call all our friends 'colonists', I suppose, but when did the immigrants to America, for example, stop becoming colonists and become instead Americans? There was no clear cut time. Even after they lost the war and were expelled, the British and the French still referred to the 'enemy' as wayward colonists. From what you are describing, I'm thinking that it's definitely time to consider the wider implications of starting a family." Richard paused for a moment. "To be honest, Rachel and I . . . we have been trying, but . . . well . . . anyway. The fact of the matter is that despite my job and length of service, a Moon child will give us additional points and guarantee our application."

Rothschild stared at Richard for a moment. When he went to speak he was stopped by a sudden knock on the door. "Come in," he said, his attention diverted.

"Sir, the Minister is here, and Professor Nieve. In fact they are on their way up as we speak."

Rothschild checked his watch. "Really . . . is that the time! Thank you, Grenville. Show them into the briefing room please, and have them take their seats. Perhaps cups of tea all round. We are coming through immediately."

"Thank you, sir." Grenville closed the door quietly behind him.

Rothschild refocused on Richard. "What you are

about to hear is security sensitive information. The European Space and Science Agency have allocated the briefing their highest level – and us, Cabinet Classified status. The Americans, however, in their wisdom, one level lower – President Level Class Two. God only knows why. If any of this gets out it could cause widespread panic. Even if pressed, please keep our discussions this morning private."

Richard nodded; he understood the implications.

# CHAPTER 6

## INCOMING

Richard was about to take his seat in the briefing room when the main door opened. First to enter was Professor Nieve. His mop of white hair was as wild as ever, if perhaps a little thinner. Richard stepped over to greet him.

"Professor. Good to see you. Unexpected as always, but good nonetheless."

"Interesting, my boy," Professor Nieve answered cagily. "I knew that you would be here a few days ago. The security level, I suppose." The Professor smiled in a friendly manner and put a hand on Richard's shoulder. "Now, where am I sitting?"

"Seems a lot of people knew about this meeting well before I did," replied Richard, as he looked towards Rothschild.

Three other men had entered the room. Richard

already knew one of them – William Bryant. He still had his job – *long serving,* thought Richard. He recognised another as a government minister, one who seemed to always be on the terrestrial news playing down the law and order situation. He had a vague recollection of the third. Rothschild spoke to one of the orderlies. From the mutual nodding everything appeared to be in order. Richard watched him check the time and spin on his heels to address the gathering. At that moment Laura Bellingham walked in. She gave Rothschild a brief smile and mouthed the word *ready.* Rothschild subconsciously adjusted the already immaculate Half Windsor knot of his red tie, set it centre against the collar of his white shirt and said, "Gentlemen, please, your seats; we go live in three minutes."

Each place around the table was marked. Laura Bellingham, scurrying around the room with an electronic tablet reader, making final preparations, acknowledged Richard with a smile. She was dressed in a well-fitting black trouser suit with a cream-coloured silk blouse and her auburn hair was cut in a short bob. *I preferred it long,* thought Richard. He gestured hello. She had a pretty smile and a very efficient manner.

Richard was about to sit down when Admiral Hughes in his naval uniform strode in and shut the door behind him. Richard stood again out of respect. The tall, slim, elegant man with an air of nobility met Richard's gaze and indicated for Richard to sit. The table of seven was complete. Laura Bellingham indicated *two minutes* as the large monitor screen burst into life. Richard focused on the three-dimensional colour picture that shaped in an instant, finding himself immediately recognising the subject – General Roper. Richard was aware of Roper's promotion to five star status a year or so earlier and also his recent appointment as the US Secretary of State for Energy, replacing Admiral Ghent upon his retirement. *He's aged considerably since I last saw him,* thought Richard. That had been almost four years earlier – apart from a recent picture in the cyber-news – and now he was almost entirely grey. The words beneath Roper on the screen read: *Washington DC.*

"Gentlemen, if I may, the formalities for the Minutes," launched Rothschild. "Professor Nieve at the far end, newly appointed Senior Scientist to His Majesty's Government and Director of the UK's Space Administration. Next, Sir Christopher Edmondson, Home Secretary and Cabinet Minister. Then Mr William Bryant, the Energy Secretary and Cabinet Minister. Admiral Hughes on my left, Chief of Military Staff." Rothschild turned and indicated towards Richard. "On my right, Commander Richard Reece of the United Kingdom's Joint Forces Naval Division, presently Commanding Officer of Andromeda's Shuttle Wing . . ." *He said that as if it's temporary,* thought Richard. "And finally, Mr Brian Grant, Senior Scientific Analyst to the European Space and Science Agency." Rothschild's attention was momentarily diverted by Laura Bellingham – she indicated *three, two and one* with her fingers and nodded. "General Roper, can you hear me?" Rothschild directed his question towards the screen.

"Yes, good morning, Peter; we have a good link," replied the smart-suited man in his early sixties. He had a strong American accent.

"Thank you, sir – and your team?"

"Everybody's here."

Rothschild looked at Laura with a *here's hoping* expression. "Professor Mubarakar in Alexandria, can you hear me?" he asked.

The picture on the screen flashed to another location – an imposing room. A hunched figure came into view and sat down in a comfortable-looking winged chair. Richard was surprised; his old friend looked tired and ill. It had only been a year, perhaps a little more, but clearly there was a marked deterioration in Mubarakar's health. The camera zoomed-in a little.

"I am here, I am here," the old man said in a gravelly voice. He sat down slowly and then perched a hand on the polished golden cap of an ebony-black walking stick positioned between his legs.

"Good, thank you Professor," said Rothschild, with eyes now fixed on the screen. "Professor Bryn Jones in Mexico, how are you there?"

The picture changed again and this time the scene was outside. It was dark. The words at the bottom of the screen read: *Local Time 03:03*. It seemed heavily overcast, even gloomy, and the illuminated man centre-screen wore a warm coat, but it appeared to be dry. Richard noticed that fact immediately. But the man's collar was turned up against the cold. Middle-aged, Professor Jones had a red-cheeked rotund appearance and it was clear from his accent that he was Welsh. He moved to keep warm and stamped his feet and looked up occasionally at the sky until someone out of sight gave him the cue. Professor Jones nodded in response. "I've been here some while," he said. "Not much of a summer here!" An impatient rubbing of hands followed. Richard noticed the impressive backdrop – a towering flat-topped pyramid with central steps and a temple building on its apex that was all subtly lit as a tourist attraction. Richard recognised it immediately as Mayan – *the temple at Uxmal*, he thought, part of that ancient city on the Yucatán peninsula.

"Thank you Professor Jones, we are about to start. The link to the Space Federation Headquarters has already been established?" Rothschild looked to Laura Bellingham for confirmation; she sat behind him and nodded in agreement. "Then Ladies and Gentlemen your attention please," Rothschild continued. "In the first instance, this meeting has been convened in order to establish the facts relating to a total loss of communication with the Space Ship *Hera*. It has now been over four weeks since our last contact. I apologise again for the inconvenient timing, however, the grave news we are about to impart represents a new chapter in the global energy crisis and possibly the most serious intelligence breach in the history of the International

Space and Science Federation. We also have a number of other items on the agenda and we must agree our strategy in preparation for the international forum later this morning. But first, our fears for the *Hera*. Over to you Mr Grant."

Mr Grant, a man in his fifties with slightly gaunt features, wore a dark blue suit that was shiny with use and a white shirt and blue tie that displayed the classic NASA motive. He had black hair that was swept backwards and spoke with a clear, refined, English accent. "Ladies and Gentlemen, one of my responsibilities within the science directorate is the correlation and presentation of all data received from our array of space sensors. These include all federation-owned optical telescopes, both on the surface and in orbit, all fixed arrays and all electromagnetic detection antennas. Towards the end of last month, the twenty-eighth to be precise, and in the very early hours, the orbital Hubble 2 telescope was scanning a sector of deep space that lay adjacent to the planet Jupiter. Peripheral to the main focus, the telescope captured light given off from an unusual stellar micro-burst. Because this occurrence was relatively short lived and not the centre of focus that evening, no incident alarm was triggered and it went unnoticed by staff arriving for the following day's work. As a result, it was five days later on 2nd December that an astronomer in the Canaveral Centre discovered the event, which was prompted by a call from an amateur astronomer who wondered why nothing had been formally posted on the NASA World Net site. A routine mass spectrograph was taken of the residual effects of the micro-burst, which seemed to occur in close proximity to Io, Jupiter's fifth moon. Analysis of the spectrograph has revealed some disturbing results. I would say at this point that our results have been verified by data derived from a similar spectrograph taken three hours later from the Andromeda Space Observatory." Brian Grant frowned; it served to darken his expression. "Our results clearly identified several naturally-occurring elements that were present in the burn-off: iron, carbon, manganese, phosphorus, sulphur and nickel to name a few. If one adds these elements together in varying proportions, steel is the result. The addition of chromium makes stainless steel – we found this element, too. Cobalt is another, added to steel to harden it, and titanium, beryllium . . . We also found evidence of long-chain polymers composed of hydrocarbons and the element chlorine from which plastics are manufactured. I am saddened to say that these are all materials used in the construction of our spacecraft." Grant took a deep breath and rubbed his brow for a moment. As he looked up his expression became sullen. "But there was another material that we identified quite easily . . . plutonium, or more precisely the isotope Pu-239. It is not a naturally occurring element in the galaxy, Ladies and Gentlemen – it is synthesised, made by enriching uranium; a process that was banned in 2016 or thereabouts – the New Geneva Convention prohibited its manufacture. Up until that time, most plutonium was produced in research reactors or plutonium-production reactors called *breeder reactors*. Over a period of a few years these reactors were all shut down. The International Nuclear Commission made sure of it. None survived intact – not even the ones in the Asian autocracies. What I'm saying is that there is no production facility on the planet capable of making this element . . ."

"Not that we are aware of, anyway," interjected Rothschild.

Grant shrugged and considered the remark. "Plutonium is a gamma emitter, Peter. Normally, we would expect to identify sources of gamma rays radiating from the Earth's surface – we have not; not for a long, long time anyway."

"You are quite correct," Professor Nieve concurred. "Even a very faint trace would be detected by our satellite network."

"Can it be manufactured underground or in a sealed facility?" asked Richard.

"Yes, I suppose so, but the shielding requirements would be considerable and any such facility would be very expensive indeed to construct."

"Well we know of a few corporations with the financial clout and real estate that is remote enough to hide this sort of facility," said Richard, and he turned and met Rothschild's glare.

"Don't make rash accusations, Richard, particularly not on record." Rothschild indicated the Minutes taker.

"The corporations you have in mind, Commander Reece, are considered to be toeing the line by the international community. We have no reason to suspect otherwise," said William Bryant, mindful of previous misdemeanours by such organisations.

*That's a change of heart,* thought Richard.

"Yes, anyway, to continue, if I may," said Grant.

Richard gestured his apology.

Grant was clearly troubled. "Plutonium is classified according to the percentage of the contaminant plutonium-240 that it contains. The parlance for plutonium alloy that bears an exceptionally high fraction of Pu-239 – by which I mean more than ninety-five per cent – is 'supergrade'. Historically, this material was only really used for warheads; it isn't compatible with nuclear reactors that produce electricity for a number of reasons, not least expense." He paused momentarily. "Our spectrograph analysis revealed the presence of such a plutonium supergrade. Indeed, our results indicated an isotope with less than three per cent Pu-240. I am of the opinion that there was a nuclear detonation in the vicinity of Io whilst the *Hera* was planned to be in orbit. Since that micro-burst, we have heard nothing from her – not a single transmission."

There was a collective gasp. Richard was quick to interrupt. "Are you sure? Are you damn well sure? You can't write these people off because of a chemical trace, a wavelength of light, for God's sake . . ."

William Bryant lowered his head. "Grave news

indeed," he murmured. "We are totally reliant on that consignment of crystals for our future energy needs." His expression became drawn.

"My people have double-checked the results and an independent team on Andromeda has done the same," explained Grant. "Also, we have cross-checked by using the spectrometer on Space Station *Spartacus*, although by that time the trace was all but dispersed. That spectrograph showed the same results. Nobody wants to believe it. I'd like to report it as another element, really I would, anything other than plutonium. But it is simply not the case."

Richard stood. "This can't be right! There must be a mistake! Not Mike Matheson, Duval, Alex Elston . . ." He shook his head. "Mike is one of the best fighter pilots around. He's the only man I know who beat Chuck Yeager, Douglas Bader and the ace-of-aces Manfred von Richthofen, the Red Baron, in a one-to-one in the historic fighter pilot's simulator programme," he explained, as if that fact alone would have saved him from any fatal situation. Richard paused, bowed his head at the thought of such a tragedy, and then sat back heavily in his chair.

"Wait a minute!" boomed the voice of General Roper from the visual. "Let me get this straight. You are saying that the reason we have not heard from the *Hera* for the last few weeks is that she is destroyed . . . caught up in a nuclear explosion? I was under the impression that she was in an area of electromagnetic interference and that she would be in contact soon."

Grant nodded. "That was the theory, General – a dense electromagnetic environment caused in the main by Jupiter's immense gravity. The calculation was approximately three weeks without comms, including a buffer to allow for unforeseen delays. However, that deadline passed almost seventy-two hours ago. We waited; hoping; praying. At first we thought that she may have jettisoned something, but the IFFS and the contractors have confirmed that there is nothing on-board that utilised plutonium."

The room fell silent at the realisation of such a catastrophe. The feeling was one of mourning but also helplessness – the distances involved, the planning, the investment, and the human tragedy. Bryant held his head in his hands. He knew only too well the consequences. The impromptu woe was interrupted by muted, but impassioned conversations emanating from the visual display. Presently General Roper spoke: "Can the Science Federation delegate hear me, please?"

"Yes, I'm here, I'm filing a report. This is so difficult to believe – when should we give up all hope?"

General Roper remained on screen, but it was a voice carrying Indian overtones that came over the speaker.

"That time has already passed, sir," Brian Grant replied sombrely. "We explored and exhausted all avenues before requesting this meeting. I'm afraid there is no hope. However, there is one other course of action that we can take – perhaps the only one that will confirm the fate of the *Hera*. Arrangements are already in hand."

"And what is that!" barked Roper.

"The deep space probe *Arius* is returning from almost twenty-three years in space where she explored and photographed the outer regions of our solar system. As luck would have it she is about eight days from Jupiter at her present velocity. I have requested an acceleration and course change from the mission control centre in Strasbourg. We hope for a close fly-by later next week. But again, the probe will need to clear the planet's electromagnetic field before relaying the data. It could be the end of next month before we receive any images of Io's surface."

"A month!" Roper barked again.

"General, the best we can hope for is a plumic wormhole. They develop occasionally in the plasma torus – the name given to the field of electromagnetic energy that surrounds Io. We see them from time to time, but we don't know the mechanics behind these phenomena and so they are impossible to predict. Otherwise, yes, it could be a month."

"You will need to be mindful of debris in close orbit; there will be a belt of contamination." Richard said.

Grant nodded. "The fly-by will be as close as possible consistent with safety. There may be enough fuel for one orbit, but that has yet to be calculated."

The room fell silent again until General Roper spoke. "I've just had this week's report on the Kalahari crystal function. The document comes from the International Energy Commission, so you must already be in receipt of it. It's not looking good, Gentlemen. The power output from the three satellite reactors is falling month by month. Not only that, the primary crystal in France is apparently showing signs of stress – possibly due to surface fissuring. Without being hardnosed about this, the loss of the *Hera* will be felt in more ways than one. Without the crystals she was supposed to retrieve, the world grid will suffer a catastrophic electricity shortfall as early as August next year. That's a little over eight months from now, people. This is our wakeup call! The directorate is stating that demand must be moderated. Individual states will need to impose further cuts, bring back rationing. William, what's the UK's stance on this?"

"Oil and gas are all but depleted here, General. It's the same throughout the region. The UK is almost totally reliant on electricity from the world grid. Continental Europe will close down at the same time as we do. Civilisation as we know it will not be sustainable – subsistence living for those who are underground will be the best we can hope for. I predict a return to the Stone Age!"

"In many quarters the rule of law and order is already breaking down," threw in the Home Secretary. Nodding his agreement with William Bryant's appraisal he looked at Admiral Hughes. "There may be a necessity for military intervention. News of the *Hera*'s loss could be a catalyst for unrest the world over."

"Then from a security stand point I suggest we put a block on this, at least until we receive the imagery from the probe. Then we will know one way or the other. I strongly recommend Level Five." Rothschild looked directly at the visual of General Roper. "At the moment, I suggest selected Heads of State only – we cannot afford any leaks."

Roper understood Rothschild's reasoning and his diplomacy. "Let's think positively about this Gentlemen. We need a plan to present to the forum and quickly." He checked his watch. "We also need to move forward with the plutonium outrage. Clearly, we are dealing with the worst kind of criminal intent – one where human life means nothing. We need to get some undercover work going here, maybe get Interpol involved. I'm going to authorise a CIB investigation immediately, and Peter, I want MI9 in on it too. There is a lot at stake. God-damn-it, I'm getting a bad feeling about this!"

"General, with all due respect," Richard said forcefully, "there are only two ways that a nuclear warhead could have been deployed against the *Hera*. First, the device was placed aboard during the modification work that took place when she was docked alongside Spaceport Two – system upgrading that was essential for the extended mission to Jupiter. That way she sailed with the bomb already on board! In my view and knowing the security and screening measures that are in place for all space programmes, this scenario is extremely unlikely. Second, and I think most likely, the warhead was delivered by a long-range interplanetary probe . . . a missile! Never done before, I agree, but entirely feasible considering the technical abilities of certain conglomerates around the world. These are unscrupulous companies that have used their industrial and financial advantage before, and come very close to gaining control of world energy supplies." Richard leant towards the monitor; his body language pressed his point. "General Roper, sir, there is a clear motive. The crystals we have in service are about to run out of steam. Consequently, there will be a massive electricity supply shortfall and accordingly, as a resource, it's going to become very, very, expensive." He paused to take stock. "We are talking a power vacuum on a global scale, sir, and the conglomerates, one way or another, mean to fill it."

"I hear what you're saying, Commander, but to get a long-range missile into space without being detected is impossible. Past our satellite ring, the detectors . . . no, it's just not achievable."

"Sir, Tongsei Heavy Industries pulled their interplanetary mineral barge out of mothballs at the beginning this year. Then they commenced a six-month renovation period in high orbit. Permission was correctly applied for and it was duly approved by the ISSF – so no legality questions. What followed was an extensive refit. I know because I flew past the vessel on a weekly basis and watched its progress. They also added capacity by increasing its length. Pre-formed sections of superstructure, materials and spare parts were constantly being delivered from Earth. All this was approved by the Federation because the barge was to resume essential mineral trading with the lunar colony. It would have been easy to construct a spacecraft inside the hull during that period and let it drift off into space for a few thousand miles before igniting the main drive. I'd say it was the perfect cover . . . entirely feasible. What worries me is what else they have in mind!"

"You are overlooking one important fact, Commander," countered General Roper, "and that is that essential information would be needed relating to the *Hera*'s programme in order to make good any contact. Timings, orbital coordinates, manoeuvring details, landing profiles . . . gaining that information would entail a major security breech. And anyway, such a missile or probe would need to be remote-controlled from Earth; pre-programming just wouldn't work, there are too many variables. Such control would be impossible because of the electromagnetic interference zone around Io."

Richard looked at Peter Rothschild for support on the security issue. Rothschild was reluctant, but he said: "You know my thoughts on this subject, General. I've been convinced for some time that we have security problems with SERON."

General Roper looked off screen momentarily and then back at Rothschild. "Well there is no breach at this end – I can assure you of that!" he scolded.

Richard interrupted. "Sir, what if the craft was controlled by mechanicals? The Humatron series was initially developed to relieve humans on extended space missions and perform repetitive command and control tasks on orbiting space vessels. The HU40 model is Level Seven, self-aware and fully capable, as we know. I'm aware that all the remaining units were destroyed and further production banned in 2050, following their illegal use by Epsilon Rio and Spheron operatives, but who's to say that these corporations aren't up to their old tricks again?"

Rothschild put a hand on Richard's arm and leaned towards him. "Let's not go down that road just yet . . . there is no proof." he whispered.

"What's that?"

"I said, General, that there is no proof as to the wrongdoing of the former conglomerate trio. As far as the international community is concerned they are operating and trading within the law. However, I do feel that an investigation into their activities is in order – including Epsilon Rio's facility in Brazil."

Roper nodded. "Very well, but it is not a priority as far as I am concerned." He looked at Professor Nieve. "Professor, what do you think – would such a mission to Jupiter's moon be possible, and if so why?"

"The science of robotics continues apace, General, and it would be naive of us to think that all advances remain within the jurisdiction of the New Geneva Convention . . . In my opinion, such an enterprise is entirely conceivable, although why anyone would wish to sabotage a consignment of crystals arriving here is another question entirely. Greed . . . power . . . yes, I can see that."

Richard's eyes widened. There was another motive,

another reason, and he went to speak, but felt Rothschild's restraining hand on his arm again. He looked across, Rothschild shook his head, and Richard remained silent.

Laura Bellingham, who had stepped outside in order to take a telephone call, returned looking somewhat alarmed. She closed the door quietly behind her and joined the group, pulling her seat up closely behind Rothschild so that she could whisper into his ear. Richard, who was listening to William Bryant give a more specific appraisal of the UK's energy reserves, caught the look of panic in her eye.

General Roper looked up from his notes. "What is it Peter . . . something we all should know?"

"Er, yes sir, I think so. We have the Duty Manager at the ALMA submillimetre deep space facility in Chile on the red line. He has been patched through with a Code One prefix." Rothschild paused and looked anxiously at the faces around the table – they stared back at him in anticipation. "Gentlemen . . . he is calling for *Icarus Critical*. We may need to go public!"

## CHAPTER 7

# BEGINNING OF THE END

The air was filled with heated conversation. More people had been alerted and they now crowded the room. *They've all climbed out of their boxes; the entire building's population seems to have arrived,* thought Richard. They stood and discussed and agreed and disagreed. Some raised their voices and some jostled for a better position for seeing the screen. Essence of anxiety permeated the gathering. Richard shuffled closer towards the table in order to avoid another elbow in the back of his head. Presently, Rothschild, who was still sitting on Richard's left, finished a telephone conversation so engrossing as to make him oblivious to the scale of disorder. He replaced the telecom in his jacket pocket, stood and raised his hands in order to quell the unease. The commotion subsided. Admiral Hughes, who was a head above most in the room gave a hand signal for Grenville to shut the door, who did so with a loud clunk, resentful to be shutting himself off from the action. A wave of restlessness crested again.

"Gentleman – Ladies and Gentlemen – quiet please," Rothschild begged. "We need to establish the facts. We have patched the facility manager through on Line Seven. He is live from Chile . . . on screen now. Some quiet please!"

A central dividing line instantly split the large screen in two halves and relegated General Roper to the right-hand side. On the left appeared a dark-haired man wearing white coveralls over a dark blue roll neck pullover. There was an embroidered badge with an insignia over his breast pocket. The man had a Mediterranean appearance and heavy black stubble. His eyes had the look of a long night – one staring at computer displays and analysing data. The background was brightly lit; a large facility with pristine electronics that looked the business.

"Mr Grillo, can you hear me? This is London calling."

"Yes I can, yes, no problem . . . it's a good signal."

"My name is Peter Rothschild. You are through to an International Space and Science Delegation that includes Washington DC – Level Three security clearance. We are in receipt of your Code One message. You have initiated the *Icarus Critical* protocol. We would like some facts before mobilising national governments."

"I understand, Mr Rothschild. Be assured that we have ticked every box and have fully complied with procedures. There is no doubt; something is coming this way and it's coming in fast."

"Be specific, please . . . How big? How fast? . . . When?"

"We can't see it yet, sir, it is too far away. We are seeing the distortion that it makes in the space continuum. Liken it to a bow wave in front of an ocean-going vessel. That's what we are tracking, only in electrophoretic terms . . . by that I mean the movement of charged particles in the 'fluid' of space.

"So how big, Mr Grillo, how big is it?"

"We are confused about that at the moment, the sums are not adding up. We have another submillimetre facility in Australia checking our calculations – they are as confused as we are . . . sorry."

"Give me an indication, Mr Grillo."

The man paused as he tried to set his measurements and his theories into layman's terms. He knew the repercussions that would follow if he was right and if he was wrong. . . . "It's the kind of disturbance we would expect to see in front of a comet – a large shockwave that disturbs the unified flux of space. An asteroid doesn't do that . . . I think, sir," he said, with a voice that trailed away, ". . . that it is a comet!"

The crowd instinctively gasped. A wave of mumblings rose to a crescendo.

"And it's damn well coming this way?" interjected General Roper from the screen.

The room fell silent.

"This is what we can't understand. There is no angular displacement . . . no apparent diffraction – not that we can measure. No gravity-biased curvature to its trajectory, or any indication of a long-cycle elliptical flight path that we would expect with a comet. To put it simply, it is moving directly towards us – no deviation. Like a missile, right on the nose!"

Rothschild raised his hands to quell the ensuing furore. "How far away is it? How long do we have – your best call?" Rothschild's expression was grave.

Grillo bowed his head for a moment, as if embarrassed by his science. He looked up slowly. The room in Whitehall brimmed with troubled anticipation. "Normally we can measure the speed of a body in space quite accurately, even if it is moving directly towards us or directly away from us. We do this by measuring the effect – the reflection if you like – that the body has on its surroundings, its influence on matter in the near vicinity. Or at great distances we can triangulate, take fixes, using stars that are so distant as to appear perfectly stationary. This object is like nothing we have seen before – it is not conforming to the normal laws of physics."

"Can you be more specific, please?" asked Professor Nieve, who was clearly conversant with the methods the scientist had mentioned.

Augusto Grillo, who was apparently looking into a dual camera and monitor system, acknowledged the Professor. "Professor Nieve, I'm honoured, sir," he said respectfully. His face tightened and he looked back at

Rothschild. "At the moment this object is extremely distant; our sensors only detected it a few hours ago. It was on the limits for something of that size. To be more precise, it's approximately four light years away. But . . ."

"Then there is no threat," interrupted Professor Nieve, looking surprised, "a comet moving at a nominal two hundred and eighty thousand kilometres per hour will take approximately . . ." He did a calculation in his head. ". . . fifteen thousand five hundred years to get here."

"Normally, that would be correct, sir. But this object is moving much faster than any known comet, and that includes short-period comets that are influenced by stellar gravity – we've not tracked anything travelling at this speed before."

"Go on," invited Rothschild.

"What we are seeing is a disturbance in the universal equilibrium – a distortion, if you like, in the fabric of space and time. As I said, liken it to the bow wave of a ship at sea, a wave of water that eddies back from the pinnacle – a wedge-shaped deformation. We are seeing this disturbance intermittently at the moment, about eighty per cent of the time. When we do, we have measured it travelling at the speed of light itself – give or take a few thousandths of a decimal point."

"There must be some mistake," protested Professor Nieve.

The remark instigated a number of mumblings and was followed by noticeable unrest that seemed to well within the gathering.

"There is clearly an anomaly in your calculations, Mr Grillo," concurred another man, his voice originating from the screen. The speaker had a strong French accent and the words *Doctor E Taminiaux – Deputy Chief Scientist ISSF* appeared in large font.

"There is no mistake, no anomaly, Gentlemen; we have checked our work meticulously and have run several simulations," explained Grillo cautiously. "Although it is true, there *is* something happening here that we do not fully understand."

"Is it something to do with the intermittency of contact?" enquired Richard, speculatively.

Grillo nodded, grateful for an ally. "Yes, we think so. You see, we are only able to track the disturbance when it is travelling at sub light speed. Intermittently, we measure a small acceleration that results in light speed actually being achieved. At that moment the disturbance, and the object that creates it, just disappears. And then there is serenity in the space–time continuum again; as if a tear has been simultaneously repaired. When we next see the disturbance it is, by nature, at sub light speed again – only fractionally, but nonetheless, apparent. The object appears to ride on the cusp of light speed, like a surfer on the crest of a wave. However, and this is of prime importance to us, during the period when the disturbance is not visible, it traverses vast distances . . . millions upon millions of kilometres. That is why I have instigated *Icarus Critical*. I cannot say for sure when it will arrive in our solar system because we cannot predict its progress accurately."

Professor Nieve rubbed his chin. "I guess you have a theory, don't you Mr Grillo, but it's steeped in theoretical science and not one you consider relevant to this briefing?"

Grillo nodded. A woman came into the picture frame, she wore a similar uniform and she passed Grillo an electronic tablet reader. "Thank you Marijs," he said. He read the report and looked up slowly. "We have it currently at a little over three light years away," he reported, clearly surprised at what he was relaying. "I can only reiterate – no comet, asteroid or meteorite has ever been tracked travelling at such a speed, not anywhere in the universe!"

"Is it being pulled towards us by the sun?" someone asked from the crowd.

Professor Nieve shook his head emphatically. "No gravitational effect can achieve such a result. Not even that of a white dwarf. Not even from a black hole. To fly at such a speed requires a propulsion system. To fly such a course requires a navigation system . . ." He rubbed his brow thoughtfully. "To control such a trajectory requires a deep understanding of the laws of physics." He looked up. "Mr Grillo, you are considering Einstein's Unified Field Theory, am I not right?"

Grillo shook his head almost apologetically. "Hayden's Second Law, to be absolutely correct, Professor, although elements of the Field Theory have been utilised and also of course, Newton's hypotheses on momentum.

As you are aware, Hayden's work twenty years ago greatly progressed, amongst other things, the concept of *parallel dimensions*. It is theoretical, Professor, and perhaps this is not the time for theories, but yes, I think we are seeing these effects in practical terms."

Rothschild raised his hand to attract Grillo's attention. "For the layman, if you please, what does this law postulate?"

"Hayden's Second Law relates to travel at light speed; it theorises the forces at work during such an occurrence. It states that ED equals MT divided by $t$ squared, where ED is Equivalent Dimension – in this case the fourth dimension – and MT is the Metric Tensor and $t$ is the Topology of the space–time paradox – like a time constant."

"And what does that mean exactly?" questioned Rothschild impatiently.

"Hayden speculated that travelling at light speed and above would cause friction within the interactive fabric of space and time. This in turn would cause energy distortions and possibly tears in the natural flux of the universe. You see, normally there is an energy constant in space – we call it a *flux value*. A lot of factors contribute to it – gamma radiation, solar winds and matter distribution, to name a few. Perhaps *tear* is too harsh a word . . . maybe an opening, a portal, a door, if you like. Hayden hypothesised that by passing through such a door another dimension could be reached . . . the fourth dimension! Within that dimension the laws of physics are not the same. The concept of time is different for one thing: years could appear as seconds, centuries as minutes – there's no correlation between the two realities. We know that jumps in time have already occurred. Take, for example, the first proven time traveller – the American astronaut Tom Race. He's in the history books." Grillo looked at Professor Nieve for confirmation.

Professor Nieve nodded. "Yes . . . proven beyond doubt. I was there myself, when we discovered the anomaly."

Richard interrupted the conversation by raising his hand. "What you're saying is that this object, as it sporadically obtains the speed of light, drifts into another reality, and that's why it keeps disappearing. And this reality is one where there is a different time reference. And because distance travelled is directly related to time . . . in this case the time reference of the fourth dimension . . . then huge tracts of space can be covered in what to us here on Earth is a relatively short period."

Grillo nodded.

"So three light years could be peanuts, right? I mean such an enormous distance, trillions of miles, could be travelled in . . . months or weeks, or days even?"

Grillo nodded again. "Controlled excursions into the fourth dimension could enable this opportunity, yes. It may be the key to travelling to other galaxies in a man's lifetime." He took a breath and put a hand behind his head for a moment. "What I am trying to say is that travelling at the speed of light appears to challenge the established mass and energy premise. That is, it actually seems to defy Einstein's Theory of Relativity."

A voice interrupted. "The reality in question here is that if this object smacks into us at the speed you are describing – and even if it is relatively small in size – we are curtains."

Rothschild turned to the gathering with a frown of disapproval.

"Gentlemen," Grillo continued, impassively, "be in no doubt that this disturbance, this body, is on a collision course with the Earth. The sun has no influence. By whatever means, it has both speed and direction; the resulting velocity vector allows us no hope and no luck. Although there are signs of a general deceleration, because it appears to be spending more time when it is visible to us, our simulations show a direct hit. As to where, exactly, the impact will occur on the surface of this planet, it is too soon to say." Grillo breathed a deep sigh. "I am sorry to pass on such news," he concluded.

The room fell ominously silent. Rothschild rubbed his brow and ran his hand over his head. Another catastrophe loomed. "Mr Grillo, please," he said, sombrely. "If this delegation is to instigate the Icarus protocol and inform the heads of state at the forthcoming conference, then we really need to know how long we have got . . . as close as you can . . . your best shot. We know the situation and the limitations you are faced with, but please, give us something to hang our hats on."

Grillo referred to his tablet reader again and checked

the latest data. The figures updated automatically. "Based on current parameters," he said pensively, "and the latest simulation . . . we have calculated what seems to be an average velocity. I have my reservations and the closing distance is now one point eight light years. That in itself is incredible. My best shot – as you call it – taking into account the apparent deceleration . . ." He paused momentarily. "I would say we have nine days – plus or minus twelve hours."

Instantly the room erupted into a multitude of heated conversations. On the screen, behind General Roper, people scurried feverishly. The General's attention was diverted: Aides handed him acetate papers; a telephone was thrust into his hand. "The President!" said someone who was out of sight.

On the left-hand side of the screen Augusto Grillo tucked the tablet reader under his arm and turned away. Rothschild called him back. "Mr Grillo," he said, "thank you very much. Please keep an open channel with us here in London. We urgently need an impact position, as soon as you have it – so that we can instigate an evacuation plan. We cannot go *Icarus Imminent* until we have that information. As such we remain *Icarus Critical* until further notice." Grillo raised a half-smile and nodded.

Richard dropped his forehead into his hand and rubbed his temples for a few moments. Against everything that was happening around him, he thought of his old friends. He had been through basic astronautics with Matheson. He remembered those days at Canaveral's

Space Academy as some of his best. And the others too. And the loss of the *Hera* – all for the crystals. He considered *his* crystal, all but within his grasp. *That one will not end up burnt out in a reactor,* he reassured himself. Something else was destined for that one, another use, he just didn't know what. All the same he had a gut feeling about the Icarus event – *something is not adding up. This is not a wayward planetoid – it can't be.* He checked his chronometer and thought of Rachel – *another Christmas . . . alone again, almost naturally.*

Rothschild stood and addressed the gathering. "We remain *Icarus Critical* . . . State Departments will be briefed as such," he shouted above the shifting mass. "I reiterate that this is a Level Three security briefing everybody – *no leaks.* For God's sake, no leaks – I'll hold you all accountable. Heads of Department to remain behind please."

Rothschild searched for Laura Bellingham in the throng and beckoned her over. "Laura, call Professor Mubarakar, tell him that there has been a delay. We will call him tomorrow. Oh, and that applies to Professor Jones, too. Tell him sorry – although I think he probably gave up some time ago and went inside. He can continue with his work in Uxmal, but is to say nothing about his findings – *not to anybody.* Not until we have heard what he has to say. Make that point absolutely clear, Laura. We will be back to him tomorrow afternoon – let's make it 4pm Greenwich Mean Time. Ten local in Mexico."

Laura Bellingham nodded and left for a quiet place

to make the phone call. Rothschild saw Richard reflecting on his bad luck and put a hand on his shoulder. He sat down next to him and shook his head. "It never rains, but it pours," he whispered. Richard looked up to hear Rothschild's telephone ring. "Yes, Rothschild . . . ! I see, when . . . ? Understood . . . 14:00 hours, London Main Airport. I see . . . He will be met at the VIP Terminal . . . Squadron Leader Houtris, from the Air Force. That's good. And the return flight . . . ? 20:00 hours, Local Time. From Le Bourget. Same terminal. Okay, that's noted . . . I'll let you know if there are any changes. Thank you. Goodbye." Rothschild put his telecom into a pocket and thought for a few seconds on the situation. "I could do with Abbey Hennessy back from the US," he said ponderously. Richard stared expectantly. Rothschild pulled out his telecom again, flipped up the lid and pressed a pre-assigned key. "Laura? Book a car for Richard, 13:00 hours, London Main . . . Yes, that's right." He covered the microphone with a finger. "Give you time for some lunch, my dear chap," he said quietly, more mouthing than speaking. "Thank you, Laura."

Rothschild looked Richard in the eye as the telecom lid clicked shut in his hand. "Well, there you are. You have your flight to Paris, Richard. A military helicopter. A Captain Houtris will meet you. I will have a brief sent to your pager, but take-off is at two. Go and see Madam Vallogia. Give her my regards. Take a look at the Ark, particularly the inside; there may be clues we have missed. The Icarus Protocol is one thing, but we must continue with trying to resolve the energy dilemma. Be cautious. We will debrief this evening at 22:00. My office." A smile jabbed his lips. "Now, if you will excuse me."

CHAPTER 8

# NOWHERE IS TOO FAR

It had been some time since Richard had flown in a helicopter. More than four years, in fact, he recalled: from Rome to Venice. This model, the Jackal, was a Joint Strike Helicopter that had been produced as a collaborative venture between the North Atlantic Boundary Organisation countries and the United States. They shared development costs and technology flow. He knew of it and the machine seemed impressive. He was sitting in the rear compartment behind the pilot and he twisted and leaned forward in his seat in order to see the instrument panel. Three hundred knots was good for a helicopter and there was no vibration to speak of. Normally he would have been enthusiastic, would have talked a bit, shared some stories; *but then again,* he thought, *normally I wouldn't be in this situation.* This time he would just sit in the back and let the pilot – a Squadron Leader – get on with it.

A change in engine tone wrested Richard from his thoughts. Moments later he felt the undercarriage deploy but there was still nothing to see. Then suddenly they broke through the clouds. *Two hundred feet,* Richard estimated; there were buildings all around. Drizzle on the windscreen that quickly coagulated into droplets was periodically swept aside by the wiper blade, and the city that passed down the left-hand side had a grey, drab feel about it.

Richard caught sight of Charles De Gaulle Airport on the right, but nothing there appeared to be moving; not even the runway lights were illuminated. Established on the final vector, Richard looked ahead a mile or more in order to see the airfield. It was difficult to make anything out in the misty conditions but then suddenly, directly ahead of them, the approach lights came on. Their brightness and layout changed everything. Since Richard had his intercom switched off, the pilot half-turned and shouted over his shoulder: "One minute!"

Moments later, as they passed over the perimeter fence, the pilot banked to the left and set a course for the terminal building. The runway lights promptly faded and, after a short hover taxi, they landed. As the rotors slowed and the individual blades separated from the blur, Richard unbuckled himself. He put a hand on the pilot's shoulder. "Thanks, nice flight," he said, appreciatively. "Take off at eight? That's what I was told." Captain

Houtris nodded.

"This is your driver, Mr Reece," said the girl behind the reception counter.

A middle-aged man, neat and well presented, stepped forward. He smiled in a friendly manner. "*Bonjour monsieur,*" he said, clicking his heels and faintly bowing in an unusually courteous way, and then he looked for some luggage.

Richard shook his head. "*Bonjour.* No, there is none. *Pardon monsieur. Je ne parle pas bien Français. Parlez-vous Anglais . . . ?* You do know where we are going?"

"I speak good English, sir, and *oui,* I know the place." The man was nonchalant, as if every day was routine and there was nothing he hadn't seen or experienced in his forty-something years. He unbuttoned his expensive Crombie coat and showed Richard a badge that hung from the breast pocket of his jacket. The government motif was clear, as were the initials of the French Secret Service that concurred with Richard's security brief. Below the mug shot was the man's name – F. Dubieu. "This way to the limousine, *monsieur,*" the man said with a soft accent. "It is not far from here, probably forty-five minutes – there is no traffic in the city these days." He nodded in a reassuring way. "The government has little gasoline, so I assume you to be an important guest."

Richard concurred, albeit reluctantly, with a weak smile. Although he would never admit to it, he was growing excited at the prospect of seeing Naomi again.

*Should I give her a warm hug,* he pondered, *or perhaps one or two of those air kisses the French still insist on?*

He followed the agent outside to a black sedan that was parked in a preferential area. It was a fairly old but solid-looking Citroen. He smiled to himself, preferring a Jaguar. *A thing of the past now,* he mused. Inside, the black leather trim was well worn. Richard sat in the back. It was comfortable enough. Grubby, embroidered motifs on the foot well carpets indicated that this was an official car. *It seems Rothschild has some influence over here,* Richard speculated.

Dubieu casually checked the surrounding area, climbed in to join Richard and shut his door with a loud clunk. Within minutes they were through the airport security checkpoint and onto a section of dual carriageway that headed west. Dubieu made haste through rundown suburbs, but not enough to draw undue attention.

Despite streets lined with unwanted cars that were discoloured and worthless, and shambolic parking that caused him to manoeuvre as if he was participating in a motor cross rally, they made good time – and there were several areas where keeping the momentum going was clearly advisable. Through those, even Dubieu looked anxious, scanning the streets before crossing them and fixating on his mirrors.

Finally, rundown conurbation gave way to countryside. But it was short lived, as the driver attracted Richard's attention and pointed ahead of them. A few miles distant was a village built on a rounded hillock.

The road ahead was straight, and in several places it was supported by embankments that maintained its level above a flat landscape. Occasional buildings and discarded machines hinted of agriculture, but there was no one visible working the land. They passed over a flooded river that was bordered by thick undergrowth and Richard could see that much of the landscape was marsh again; just like the Somerset Levels back home.

Their approach to the village was made impressive by two rows of tall poplar trees that lined the way for the best part of a mile. From the apex of the hillock a church spire was silhouetted against the grey background; its pinnacle high enough to scratch at the base of blowing clouds.

"This place is very old," advised Dubieu, who turned to look at Richard whilst driving with his right arm stretched lazily over the pillion seat. "Some buildings were built in the eleventh century. You know . . . William . . . the man we sent to show you English how to cook!" He laughed in a pleasant way, sharing his humour. Richard could only smile and nod appreciatively. There was no malice; *not a hint of the old, traditional rivalry,* Richard thought.

They entered the village and began a shallow climb, but soon the gradient steepened as the road began to weave between more ancient buildings. There were towering stone walls blackened with age, small windows, heavy doors and cobbled streets, and Richard noticed the occasional vehicle. Where the streets were wide enough, cars were thoughtfully parked and not just abandoned, and he saw a bus carrying people heading back the way that they had come. Higher still, where the streets became claustrophobic because they were so narrow, a few pedestrians, well wrapped against the weather, scurried purposefully. It seemed they ventured out for only as long as was strictly necessary to complete their daily chores. Here Richard could smell smoke from burning wood, something he hadn't experienced for as long as he could remember. The fumes, with an apple tone, hung in airless pockets.

Dubieu squeezed his car passed a pâtisserie, where a number of bicycles lay haphazardly against the walls on each side of the road. There were people in the doorway, more a gathering, and the windows were brightly lit and decorated for Christmas. Richard glanced inside before Dubieu accelerated again. There were bottles of drink and plates of food on trays. *Would have been nice,* he thought, *seasonal festivities.* He gave Rachel a thought again.

From the corner of his eye, Richard caught sight of a man in a dark jacket – he was loitering in the shadow of the entrance of the next shop. He watched them pass, his face almost obscured by a hood that was pulled low.

When Richard turned to look back at him, he had disappeared.

Almost at the top of the hill, and before the street curved to the left and began a downward incline, Dubieu suddenly turned into a side road. Richard winced as the sedan gathered pace, for the road was barely wide enough for a city car. Medieval terraces fronted the road on either side – *and anybody stepping from their front door without looking would be foolhardy indeed,* thought Richard. Gradually the incline lessened. Dubieu negotiated the chicane of stone door steps faster than he should, and on a number of occasions Richard heard tyres on both sides scuffing simultaneously. After sixty metres the road levelled and they entered a small square that was surrounded by fortress-like buildings. Dubieu drove slowly past the centre piece – a masterfully carved, life-sized statue of a woman cradling a baby in her arms. She stood on a raised limestone plinth with cherubs at her feet, but nothing flowed from the short copper tubes that poked from their mouths. Richard noticed that the water contained within the low circular surrounding wall lapped the coping stones and in one area it spilled over, causing black staining down to the ground. *The fountain would be electrically powered these days,* he speculated, but it still seemed a good place to throw coins and ask for things. Richard noticed Dubieu make the sign of the cross on his chest in the Catholic way.

The car vibrated over cobblestones that glistened with moisture until Dubieu finally drew to a halt in the far corner. He parked on a shallow slope that led up to a pair of large wooden gates and pulled hard on the handbrake to prevent any mishaps. Then he gestured with his head and said, "This is the place!"

Shut tight against the world and all its sinners, the

black tarred gates set within high walls deterred all hope of Christian solace, and Richard realised that a welcome here would be unlikely to say the least. "That's the way in?" he enquired sceptically.

"Only if you are a horse," Dubieu replied smiling, and he pointed to an arch with a pointed pinnacle of church-like design that was set in the stone wall not ten metres away and off to their left. "Go up there. You will see the door. I will expect you back in a few minutes."

Richard looked back dubiously. "I'll be an hour or two, maybe longer, I'm afraid. I've got something to look at."

Dubieu seemed unable to resist a knowing, resigned, expression. Another smile flickered. "Listen, my friend," he said in a secretive whisper, "the last man to go inside those walls was in May 1945. He went to tell the nuns that the war was over and was invited in for a Courvoisier, a cognac of 1890 vintage – but he was out again within the hour. It's local history." He grinned and patted Richard on the shoulder. "I wait for you."

Richard climbed out of the car awkwardly. He buttoned his coat and pulled up his collar. The alley was wide enough for three people shoulder to shoulder and water gurgled down a gulley on the left, although today he was lucky and the rain had held off for him. The visitor's door was on the right and not far up. It was squat with massive black iron hinges and it looked impenetrable. Two adjacent brass plates, wall mounted, had words so fervently polished as to be almost erased. The upper one was in French; the lower simply read: *Church of St Mary*.

Richard knocked on the door and waited. There was no answer. He tried again a little harder. Then he noticed a metal bell pull on his right and gave it a sharp tug. He heard no accompanying sound and so resorted to another loud thump on the door with the base of his fist. With no response he tried both methods again simultaneously. Suddenly a wooden block slid sideways exposing a pair of eyes. Richard took a step backwards and then crouched and peered in. He could make out the figure of a woman.

"Ah, *madame*, er, hello there. I'm . . ."

"*Oui monsieur. Que voulez vous? Pourquoi vous nous dérangez?*"

"*Excusez-moi madame. Mon Français n'est pas très bon. Pardon.* Um, I would like to speak to Madame Vallogia . . . Naomi Vallogia, plea . . ."

The little window closed in an instant. Richard heard a bolt clunk into position. He knocked again, and again, and again, until his persistence was rewarded and the wooden block slid back into its recess.

"*Monsieur* . . . as I told your friend when you tried this two weeks ago . . . I tell you again . . . it is not possible! If you do not stop in your pestering, I will call the Gendarmerie."

"Mam, please, I don't know who it was you spoke to but they were no friend of mine, and I have not been here before. Madame Vallogia came to stay with you four years ago, on a permanent basis. I need to speak to her – on a matter of grave importance. My name is Richard Reece. I'm a close friend. At least I was," Richard concluded, under his breath.

"I am sorry, it is not possible. Now be gone . . . go away . . . *allez-vous en*."

This time Richard was quick off the mark and he jammed his fingers in the gap and prevented the slider from closing. There was fierce resistance and he winced with the pain. He put his mouth closer to the rectangular hole so that his words would be clearly heard, but not so as to broadcast them to the man that had appeared in the archway a few seconds earlier and who now passed him by.

"Mam, I know of the Ark. I was the one who arranged for it to be sent here, from London, four years ago . . . for safe-keeping, you understand. Madame Vallogia is the rightful owner: a hereditary right. I know who she is. Please, I'm a friend. I need to see her. I would never hurt her."

With a start, the wooden panel slid open. Richard removed his bruised fingers and breathed a loud sigh, only to hear the window slam shut. He was about to bang his fist on the door again when he heard a number of bolts being withdrawn. Moments later the heavy door squeaked open; only then did he realise how thick it was with an iron bar as the stop. The opening was made just big enough for him to squeeze through if he turned sideways. As he did, Richard tried not to push the door wider against the woman. Inside he vaguely recollected

the place from a description that Naomi had given him –
that was before he was married, when she still phoned.

There was an open courtyard of stone paving and
ancient cobbles, and a raised rectangular pond with a
fountain at its middle that still sprinkled water. *There
seems little point in it,* thought Richard, as a squall passed
overhead and a flurry of drizzle fell. Richard scanned the
quadrangle and the surrounding buildings. Built from
the rock of ages it appeared – timeless. He saw a nun with
a fishing net and wondered what koi carp would taste
like.

Richard dutifully followed the older woman in
front of him. She was dressed in a traditional habit that
comprised a tunic covered by a scapular and cowl, and
although not a pin was out of place her clothes looked
shiny, even threadbare in places. Presently, she turned
into a long colonnade hewn from off-white limestone.
The architecture was Gothic style with pointed arches
and ribbed vaults. On the ground, interlocking honey-
coloured flagstones were scuffed and even grooved in
some areas where the concentrated passage of feet told
of centuries of devotion. There were nooks and crannies
that were wet and green with moss and mould. This
caused Richard to reflect on his own home, built of
plastic composites and advanced metal alloys, and where
the only life to survive outside was invisible anaerobic
bacteria. Overall, he felt a most uncommon heaviness of
faith pressing down on his shoulders.

After walking twenty metres or so they stepped into

a nave. This ecclesiastical building that had been badly eroded in some areas by the elements was much older. He was fond of architecture and Richard speculated a Romanesque origin, because of the thick walls, round arches and sturdy piers. A millennium of prayer seeped from cracks in the granite flags, the tones hovering above them. This was the heart of the place.

"This part of our establishment was built in 1120 by our Lady Teresa," the woman said over her shoulder, and then she stopped abruptly, seemingly reconsidering her actions, before turning into the shadowy hallway on her right, where, at its end, another ageing oak door tried to bar the reality of running walls, decaying fabric and the icy atmosphere.

Lifting a latch – and with some effort – the woman pushed the door open. Inside was different: a small room that was simply furnished but warm, with wall-hung tapestries and framed pictures. Two large cast iron pipes suspended on stout brackets set low on the far wall passed through the room. This antiquated central heating system provided the only comfort readily apparent to Richard. There were only two chairs and the lady offered Richard the one close to the pipes. It was covered in a faded and tatty woollen throw, whilst she took up position behind a functional wooden desk of dark wood and with a top that shone with the rubbing of heavy sleeves and elbows.

"Please make yourself comfortable, Mr Reece. I have something to tell you."

Richard unbuttoned his coat, pulled it tight across

his back and sat down, while the lady opened one of the desk drawers with a key that hung on a chain around her neck. She rummaged inside for something. Richard sat in anticipation and dropped a hand onto the warm pipe. Eventually finding another key, the lady used it to unlock the drawer below and from there she withdrew a clear plastic bag about 150 millimetres square. Inside, there was a small plastic box about the size of a cigarette packet.

"My name is Antoinette Rousseau. I became *La Mère Supérieure* of this nunnery only nine months ago when our mother of long standing passed away. She told me that Madame Vallogia did speak of you while she was here. Sometimes, when she was in a reflective mood, she would speak fondly of you and other times, in her sleep, when she had no control over her words she . . ." The woman's eyes narrowed. At least in her eighties, she looked squarely at Richard, gauged his intent and then sighed. "It seems she regarded you as more than a friend, I think. Some broken hearts never mend, I fear." The woman spoke English well, although occasionally her strong accent subjugated clear pronunciation.

Richard leaned forward. "Reverend Mother, please," he said in a concerned way. "What do you mean, when she *was* here?"

"Madame Vallogia left our care a little over two weeks ago. Quite unexpected . . . during our preparations for Christmas. She always loved this time of year. Really, quite unexpected, we were all . . ."

"What!" Richard's shocked response brought the Mother Superior's head up. "She's gone . . . Why?"

"She had her reasons I am sure, Mr Reece, but would not say specifically. I questioned her myself – why leaving was so absolutely necessary. I wanted her to stay; we all did. Someone she knew was in peril – that was all she would say. They needed her."

"Was there a call? A message?"

Reverend Mother nodded. "There was something, a telephone call, and then this visitor a few days before she left. We would not let him in of course; Madame Vallogia did not know him. But they had a conversation through the door, as we did, and he handed her a slip of paper with scribble on it. After that she was beside herself. She began packing immediately. A car arrived the next day and took her away."

"What! No names? No forwarding address? She just left!"

"I have already told you, *monsieur*. She would not speak of the matter. I knew her well enough though, and someone's life depended on her actions – that I could see."

"Where did she go? Surely she said something? A dropped word . . . anything!"

The Mother Superior looked down at her lap and pondered for a moment. "Madame Vallogia swore me to secrecy. I should not say anything of this, but I fear for her safety and that of someone held very dear to her. I can see in your eyes you have feelings for her."

"Yes . . . and!"

"She mentioned Cairo, and . . . and, her duties. How she could not continue without him!"

Richard half-stood and muttered something under his breath: a name; a possibility; a gut feeling. "And what of the Ark, Mam? Is that still here?"

"No, it is not. Madame Vallogia had us replace the artefact into its wooden casket. A vehicle came to collect it the day after Madame left. It was her instructions. We acted on her instructions."

Richard sat back in the chair and drew a deep breath. "There is someone – a man," he said thoughtfully, "someone very dear to her. They are bound together through some kind of unspoken understanding. And there is a mark, a sign of the clan if you like: an ancient order . . ."

"Is her life in danger . . . Mr Reece?"

Richard snapped out his reflective repose. "I don't know. The honest answer is that I don't know. Why should she be? It could be anything – a friend in need . . . a family problem . . . No, not a family problem – she has no immediate family. But why would she take the Ark – unless somebody else wanted to see it . . . ? Wanted to learn something from it?" His thoughts raced. *The Ark was built to house a crystal. I should see if there was any other information inscribed on it, written in the old language, post the renovation work. And the* Hera *incident? That tragedy was related to the crystals, even if those in the Ministry and the ISSF would not admit to it. And then the trespassers at mother's cottage – the place was turned upside-down but nothing taken. Could these events be linked? Surely this indicates that there is something more to that burglary than just a petty criminal act?* He swallowed hard. "There is something I must do!" Richard said suddenly and he stood up.

"I see you have an impulsive streak, *monsieur?*" the Mother Superior said, frowning. She picked up the plastic bag from her desk.

"I need to go, Reverend Mother," Richard answered curtly. There was a moment's silence. Richard realised his rudeness. A smile threatened and warmed his expression and he gestured an apology. "Thank you so much for your time. I know that you have made an exception for me."

The Mother Superior nodded politely and looked Richard in the eye. "The exception is made on behalf of Madame Vallogia, Mr Reece. You must find her and return her to us." She held up the plastic bag and handed it to Richard. "I am not sure if you are meant to have this – Madame Vallogia said nothing of it. But it was forgotten; left in her study when the Ark was collected."

Richard took what appeared to be a laboratory sample bag. It had a self-sealing strip across the top and, on the inside, with the small plastic box, was a piece of paper. "What is it?" Richard asked.

"It is the residue from inside the artefact. Dusted from the corners and the loose, flaking material brushed from the walls. Occasionally, I would help her with her restoration work. She was a perfectionist, a trained archaeologist you know . . . a wonderfully gifted woman."

Richard nodded in agreement and placed the bag in his pocket. "Indeed she is," Richard said softly. "Don't worry Reverend Mother, I'll find her."

"Tell me *monsieur*. One thing, before you go, as Madame's happiness is close to my heart. I do not know you, yet at the mention of her name I see something in your eyes." She appeared unsettled for a moment. "Are you . . . ?" The Reverend Mother cut herself short and then shrugged. "Oh, what do I know of these things?" she added flippantly and turned away. "Now, follow me."

Richard followed her to the vestibule.


The heavy door closed with a thud and Richard heard a number of bolts clunk into position on the other side. He walked briskly down the alleyway, then beneath the arch, before turning left towards the waiting car. He checked the time; surprisingly more than an hour had passed. The square was deserted and to Richard it felt frigid. A damp afternoon mist had begun to settle. His mind elsewhere, he walked around the vehicle and climbed into the front passenger seat. He looked across at Dubieu, who sat in a relaxed, slightly reclined position, his head back on the headrest. "Longer than a few minutes, then, Mr Dubieu. So much for your local history," he said with a little sarcasm. "Back to Le Bourget as soon as possible, please. I'm going to bring the take-off forward."

Richard unbuttoned his coat and reached inside to a zipped pocket containing his telephone and telephonic pager. There was no response from Dubieu. Richard looked across again. An impatient frown formed in his brow. "Really, we need to get going as soon as . . ."

It was the small circular hole in the windscreen that Richard noticed first. Tiny cracks radiated from it. Dubieu remained motionless. Richard leaned forwards in order to look at his face and as a result gulped a breath. There, in the middle of Dubieu's forehead, was a neat red mark. From it dribbled a line of congealed blood. It had run down his nose, past the corner of his mouth and chin and fallen onto his shirt before the neat wound had dried.

The shock made Richard almost drop his pager and with a reflex action he regained it. An expression of horror crept over his face. The windscreen was made of clear glass but the side windows were tinted. He crouched forwards to align the wound with the perforation and to approximate the direction. *Obviously not a drive-by shooting,* he concluded. *Someone has stood deliberately in front of the car and, before Dubieu could react, just shot him!*

At that moment there was a loud crack; splinters of glass exploded and then an accompanying thud from the door upholstery and a torn hole appeared just inches from Richard's right arm. The shot was from the left side and another quickly followed. Instinctively, Richard ducked. Tiny shards of glass showered his face. He partly slithered into the foot well. Whoever was responsible was shooting blind and from an elevated position. *I have to get out; if not, I will be a sitting target. What can I do?* Someone wanted to finish the job! His mind raced. Without thought for the consequences he released the handbrake. Immediately the vehicle began to roll backwards. Richard grasped the steering wheel. He pushed himself up in the seat and strained to look back through the rear windscreen. The car picked up speed. He could see the fountain and the statue. Another shot followed and a second forced him back down into the foot well.

Richard needed to steer the vehicle if he was to escape. He reached across and switched on the ignition. A nearby plaque indicated *Hybrid Drive*. He pressed the adjacent button and heard the electric drive cut in and then he shuffled the dead man's leg and dropped his foot onto the accelerator pedal, flooring it. The Citroen jerked, the wheels skidded and the electric drive whined. Almost simultaneously the vehicle bounced off something and it shuddered violently. Another thud accompanied by an off-target shredding of fabric in the left-hand door had Richard wincing. His eyes darted in all directions. This time the sublet was stopped by Dubieu's body. It may have been an official car but it certainly was not armoured.

Richard pressed the button that controlled the electric window on his side and then reached up and wrenched the rear-view mirror from its mounting on the windscreen. Keeping low in his seat he held it outside and positioned it such a way as to see what was behind. Haphazardly and swerving from side to side he negotiated the square. The narrow street from which they had entered loomed into view; he could not hope to reverse down it and certainly not at that speed, but the opening, he could do a good job of blocking it! Instead, thoughts of being trapped inside the car occupied his attention. He had seconds to react.

Miraculously, Richard remained on course. By now he had mind of the sniper's position as shots were peppering the front windscreen. Finally, the panel gave out and shattered glass rained down on him. The reflection of the street swept in and out of view as an unsteady hand and blurring vibration frustrated his attempts to hold the car steady. He held the mirror as best he could in one hand and steered with the other, aiming for the mouth of the road. As he moved, fragments of glass fell from his hair and clothing; he blinked a shard clear from the corner of his eye. He heard the whistle of sublets just inches above his head and the simultaneous thuds from behind as the back seat absorbed the deadly projectiles. He steered and manoeuvred in desperation. He had some skill, as it was similar to backing a hover jet into a hardened bunker – an operation that he had performed many times during his fighter pilot days.

*Now!* Richard thought, and seconds before he rammed the vehicle into the opening he squirmed in his seat, got his feet up and kicked open the door. Then he curled into a ball and covered his head with his arms as a deafening crash followed and the door was ripped from its hinges by the corner of a building. Twisting metal and the noise of shattering glass surrounded him. The vehicle's motion stopped in an instant but not the electric drive – that still whined loudly. Sporadically, the front wheels screeched and skidded on the wet cobbles and the car shuddered.

Richard pushed hard with his legs and was up in his seat in an instant. Crushed bodywork and the door pillar were close against the stone wall but with the door detached there was room. Richard squeezed through the opening. Two men immediately came into view. They ran towards him with weapons held high. Without looking back, Richard ran for his life down the street. Several times he slipped, but he made forty metres or more before the first sublet sang past his ear. He turned and darted into a doorway only to see the two men scrambling over the wrecked car. The first mistimed his jump, skidded off the boot lid, took a tumble, and ended up as a crumpled heap on the ground. The other avoided such a fiasco by leaping clear, but he landed awkwardly and rolled over several times to break his fall. Richard saw his chance; he leapt from the doorway and sprinted a further twenty metres or so before disappearing around a corner.

In full flight he made off down the street. The incline began to steepen. He slipped and skidded on the wet surface. There was an alley and he darted to his right but almost fell, saving himself only by grasping some iron railing. *Forget the alley,* he thought, and he looked back.

He couldn't see them, but he heard their footsteps not far behind and their echoing seemed to be upon him; the narrow street contained and amplified it. He passed a few people; they watched aghast as the pursuit heightened and one, a woman in her twenties, screamed hysterically as a brief sighting of Richard brought a hail of gunfire from the assassins. People cleared the street. Richard kept tight to the wall where the cobbles were more even. He didn't look back again.

After rounding another corner, the pâtisserie came into view. Richard approached it quickly, running pell-mell. He attracted the attention of many well-wishers who had spilled into the street. People were casually chatting and stopped to watch him, until, with panicked expressions, they hid indoors – after first hearing shots and then seeing the pursuers.

Richard at full tilt, coat flailing, felt the glass down his back. His face was wet with sweat and washed by the drizzle. He drew a rasping breath that slowed him down near a shop and saw, against the railings, an opportunity? The bicycle, a ladies model, with Christmas tinsel wrapped around the frame, inexplicably drew his eye – perhaps because it was pointing in the right direction.

People moved aside as Richard ran past. He had no time to return their looks of surprise, disdain and fright. A teenager remonstrated loudly as Richard snatched his bicycle while passing, scooted with it for a few strides and then mounted it. Other cries of protestation followed him down the street, but he would not have understood their meaning had he the time to listen. Then, suddenly, as Richard disappeared uncomfortably down the hill, the verbosity of the objections that initially seemed plain enough adopted a very different nature, for the first of several sublets whizzed past his head. A curve in the street saved him.

There was no need to pedal and even maximum braking had little effect in the wet. But this was perhaps opportune, as Richard's precarious progress soon had him at the edge of the village and with no sign of his pursuers. As the last buildings approached, Richard skidded to the right and ducked into a narrow opening. It led, after twenty metres or so, into an untidy, deserted farmyard. The main entrance, together with a rusty tractor, was to his left and beyond lay open countryside. A creeping wintry mist was already rising over the darkening scene. There was a small barn with broken doors opposite and Richard discarded the bicycle inside. He gingerly surveyed the area. It was clear and quiet. *I've lost them,* he concluded, but he deliberated on how he could possibly get back to Paris.

Richard unzipped the inside pocket to his coat and withdrew his telephone. He pondered for a moment on the security implications but decided to call London in any case – a helicopter pickup was perhaps the only option. Despite his intentions to distance himself from MI9 over the last year or two, Peter Rothschild's number remained a preset. The signal was weak but just enough.

"Peter, it's Richard," he whispered. "Listen, there's

been some trouble . . . Yes, I'm not far from Saint Mary's . . . They lost contact with the driver . . . ? Really – that's because he's dead! Yes . . . but . . . that's not possible now . . . no . . . forget it. Peter, I need a pickup from here. You'll have to get the bloody helicopter over here . . . What do you mean diplomatic permits . . . a world heritage site? *Listen*, I'm not in the clear yet, they are still here, somewhere in the village, and they mean business . . . Okay, you have my position . . . good. It's not a secure satellite signal. I know that, but what else am I to do? Wait, I hear a car! I've got to go . . . No, Peter, listen why don't you? I'm unarmed. I would really appreciate that pickup . . . okay! I hear something, I've got to go!"

Richard crouched nervously and replaced his handset. He buttoned his coat and turned up his collar. Several tiny pieces of glass fell onto the trampled hay underfoot. He heard a car door shut and slunk back into the darkening interior of the wooden building. "Shit!" he scolded, under his breath. "I've brought them down on me . . . idiot!"

There was a rickety ladder leading up to a hay loft. Richard eyed it and decided on a course of action. Tentatively he climbed it. Outside he heard footsteps. He paused. There was a mumble and an acknowledgement. Richard climbed the last few rungs and flopped onto the hay. A moment later the barn door squeaked. Richard peered over the edge and held his breath. He saw a shadow move. Then he saw a man with a gun held in two hands stepping inside. Jerkily but strategically the figure pointed his weapon in various directions. Richard dropped his head and strained to see. The darkness in the barn was an asset. The man moved silently. Something cracked, like a piece of wood. *The noise had come from outside, from behind the barn.* He was surrounded.

The gunman stepped beneath the loft; he was no more than four metres below Richard. With one hand he grasped the ladder and Richard heard it shake. Richard dropped his face onto the course hay: blood surged in his ears; his heart raced. The ladder began to move! *God no,* thought Richard, *he's coming up!*

The ladder's frame groaned under the weight of the man and where it rubbed against the loft joist it squeaked eerily. After a few haunting seconds and quite unable to contain himself, Richard rose up onto on his elbows only to see the man's head appear. It was silhouetted against the opening and Richard saw him raise his gun; it was a short barrelled revolver. In one desperate move Richard swung his feet around and kicked out at the ladder – it toppled backwards, with the man hanging precariously from the top rung. A muffled shot rang out. Richard scrambled to his feet. He sighted the man landing on his back and, without any thought for the consequences, jumped. He landed with most of his weight on the man's leg and instantly heard it crack beneath him. The man cried out. Then Richard came down backside-first onto the man's chest; it served to wind him and an awkward karate chop to his throat gave Richard the upper hand. In near darkness Richard sprang up.

The big man, now severely handicapped, raised his

gun and fired indiscriminately. Richard dived for cover and rolled away across the floor until he felt something under his back. He pulled at it; was it anything he could use? The object felt like a broken shovel and a moment later he set upon the man wielding the blade like a crazed Dervish. Unable to stand, turn or defend himself, Richard caught the man with his first blow across the side of his head. And one blow was enough, as the would-be assassin flopped backwards onto the floor. His arms fell limp and he groaned before falling silent. Barely able to see, Richard stepped briskly over to the crumpled heap and scrabbled for a gun hand; he located the weapon close by in the mud.

Richard retreated quickly. Bathed in darkness and with his back to the barn wall he waited. Soon, he heard the crunching of dry straw underfoot over to his left. One step, and then another, and then another, as someone came to the entrance. Fleetingly he saw a shadow move and raised his newly acquired revolver, but the target disappeared. There was silence – a thick, menacing silence. Then a scrabbling sound in the straw further along the wall attracted Richard's attention momentarily – *must just be a rat*, he thought. Well inside the barn and on the other side Richard heard movement again. Then a noise as someone kicked a piece of wood or a random piece of machinery. There was a muted groan. Was this second assailant injured? Perhaps he had stopped some friendly fire.

Richard adopted a prone position; he held his breath

and listened intently. A horn beeped in the distance and he could hear the sound of revellers, subdued – but nothing else. He squirmed uneasily and thought a change of location was necessary and began to move to his right, keeping tight against the wall. He felt out each step before putting his weight down, lest he give his position away.

Richard could just see, by the paleness of ambient light outside, some thin cracks between the boards by his right side. At that moment a single shot rang out and the loud crack made him jump. Instantaneously the wood in front of his face splintered, sending a shard against his cheek. He yelped at his miscalculation and dropped to the floor as another dull thud sounded, and then another, each accompanying hole chasing downwards.

Quickly, commando-style, he crawled forwards a few metres and then scrambled to his feet and, in a kind of crouched run, managed a further five metres forwards. The shots that followed him now were hit or miss, blind attempts to bring him down in the darkness. He felt a large bale of straw blocking his path and he half-tripped and half-dived behind it. Silence reigned again. Richard contained his breathing. *Damned fool,* he thought. Blood trickled down his face from the splinter and a dribble ran to the corner of his lips. The taste lingered; he thought it indicative of his frailty. *He would have to flush this assassin out!*

With an idea, Richard felt for the overall length of the straw bale. It was less than two metres long, but enough to give him cover. At that moment his foot inadvertently struck a bucket – or some similar farmyard implement. Simultaneously a sublet pinged over his head, only to ricochet off a metal object on the opposite wall. The metal sang with a single tone like that from an amplified tuning fork, and with it, like good harmonics, Richard had an idea. He reached for the implement – it *was* a bucket.

Richard lay spread-eagled on the ground, sheltered behind the straw bale. He adopted such a position so as to be able to move quickly – in a spinning motion – from one end of the bale to the other. Silently he drew a deep breath and then he poked the revolver around the left-hand edge of the bale and fired a volley of three shots across the barn. Then he lifted the metal bucket, albeit a little awkwardly, with his other hand and tossed it as far as he could in the direction from where he had come. The bucket flew through the air for a few metres, crashed to the ground and then clattered across the floor until it collided with the wall and finally came to rest. A hail of gunfire followed in its wake.

Simultaneously Richard spun around on his stomach and pulled himself into a firing position at the other end of the bale. The opaque blackness on the far side of the barn was momentarily illuminated by the assailant gunning down the bucket. In the ensuing disturbance, Richard would have one attempt before giving his own position away. His shot had to count, and Richard took quick but careful aim at the opposing flash and squeezed the trigger. The revolver had heavy recoil but he was aware of it this time and supported the butt with his right hand. There was a ruffling noise on the other side and then silence. Richard darted back behind the straw bale and lay motionless on his back for a few seconds, but his stomach was tensed and he made ready to fire again.

After a minute or so Richard rolled over and climbed cautiously to his knees. He pivoted the weapon with both hands on the prickly grass of the bale and scanned as best he could the area opposite. After a while he became convinced of a kill and so, keeping low, he moved quickly to the side. Eyes wide he strained to see, but the final soft glow from the sunset did little more than faintly illuminate the barn's doorway. He held his breath and listened again. There was nothing – not a sound in the vicinity – only some far-off Christmas revelry. Avoiding making a silhouette, Richard slipped silently outside.

Richard made it to the tractor and paused. He eased around it, senses keen – then over to the gate where he crouched behind a sturdy post. Still nothing; silence; anticipation. He dared to hope that the accomplice had fallen during the mayhem of arbitrary shooting. He loitered for a few moments and, still not hearing anything, took off at speed down the road away from the village. He ran another kilometre until he was exhausted. And there in the undergrowth he crouched and rested.

Richard replaced his telephonic pager with the

revolver he had acquired and zipped close his coat pocket. On the small, back-lit screen he typed and sent an abrive to Peter Rothschild:

> All clear.
> Triangulate this signal.
> I am waiting for a pickup.
> ASAP – S'il vous plait.

Richard watched and waited until almost simultaneous with the distant, but irrefutable sound of a single rotor helicopter, he received an abrive from Rothschild. It was in a secure, scrambled format and he typed in his personal code to decipher it:

> The helicopter will take you to Saint Dizier, a French Air Force base east of Paris. You have a fighter and escort to Egypt. We have cooperation. Destination is an Egyptian military base close to Alexandria. Transport in hand. Go to Mubarakar while we still have him. Learn what you can. Commercial being organised for return home. Cyber-attack increasing, something is afoot. Above all, exercise extreme caution. PR

"Seasonal greetings to you, too," Richard muttered to himself, singularly unimpressed. He looked eastwards towards the dull glow of the Paris conurbation and saw the strobe lights of the helicopter flashing in the night sky as the machine homed in on him. "So, it starts here . . . the final showdown," he whispered ominously.

# CHAPTER 9

# RED SKY IN THE MORNING

**Elysium Planitia – 26 December**
**06:38 Martian Corrected Time**

"Where are you now? I mean the exact coordinates," enquired Andy Baillie impatiently.

"Cross coordinate four, four, nine, North East Sector. Close to the no-go zone. Anyway, you should know that from your display."

"Satellite tracking is out of sorts this morning, Paul. Too much sand in the lower Maronosphere. Listen, can you see the sensor array in that sector? From your position the line should be quite close – say, one and a half clicks south?"

"The visibility is about five clicks here . . . Yes, yes, I can see them, I can see the terminals." Paul Carr captured the image and then lowered his grid-enhanced binoculars. He pressed the button under his right thumb and downloaded the image into the PTSV's navigation computer. Then he touched the screen of the adjacent monitor, made a selection on the keypad and displayed what he had seen. Pressing lightly on the screen and with a spreading motion of his fingers he magnified an area of particular interest. A distant row of radio masts loomed towards them on the screen and another selection digitally enhanced the image until their latticed construction – a design akin to electricity pylons – was clear and sharp. Set approximately three hundred metres apart and connected by a number of drooping cables, the masts stretched away into the distance in both directions. "Okay, okay, here we go . . . one-point-five-two-two kilometres to be precise – not a bad guess."

"Good. I'd like you to run the line. Check something out for me – particularly the SR15 to SR27 terminals?"

Paul Carr selected another page on the touch-sensitive monitor screen and emboldened *SR15* from a list with the cursor and then pressed the enhance key. Immediately the image skewed off to the right and focused on the mast in question. "Yes, sir, I have it, bearing one, six, niner – range, three-point-three-five. We can take a little drive over there and run the inspection no problemmo. Get back to you in an hour – anything special?"

"The annual inspection of this sector is due next month anyway, so run the full integrity check please Paul, and make a recording."

"Will do. I'll get back to you."

Paul Carr, a thirty-something astronaut who had majored in physics at Stockholm University, but who originally hailed from the north of England, glanced across at his driver and smiled. "Okay, Lesley, let's go to it," he said, engagingly. "Three more days on the road and we go home. Tell you what, when we get back to Osiris, I'll take you for a steak in Stargazers – first night. What d'ya say?"

Also English, Lesley Oakley stared blankly back at the service vehicle commander. He had climbed into the cockpit and now sat beside her in the observer's seat with wide eyes seemingly in anticipation of a definite acceptance of the invitation. Lesley shook her head, breathed a long sigh and looked away with an expression of mild contempt. She began aligning the navigation display with the target coordinates transferred from the stored image. There were three other scientists in the forward compartment and one of them silently attracted the attention of her colleagues by waving her hands. With hunched shoulders she pointed forward towards the cockpit and mouthed, "He's asked her out." The other two women stifled giggles.

Lesley Oakley, seemingly ignoring the proposal, made a few other selections and then engaged the autopilot. A cue flashed green on her instrument panel. Her finger hovered over the drive button and then she looked up. "Three weeks on station in this twenty-by-four tin can, listening to your jokes and being subjected to your pathetic attempts at cooking – when you weren't attempting to skip the catering roster – and then that snoring every night . . ." She paused and looked the dark-haired man in the eyes. "And you have the audacity to offer me a veggie burger?"

Paul Carr nodded a slightly gormless confirmation; there was hope in his eyes.

"Okay . . . I accept!"

The vehicle pulled away with a jolt.

The large Alpha-type Personnel Transport and Service Vehicle kicked up billowing clouds of red dust in its wake as it drove along the eighteen-kilometre line of radio masts. There were a number of other similar sensor systems installed circumferentially around Osiris Base, at varying distances. As well as being joined by cables to form a long-range array, each mast bristled with aerials, microwave dishes and radar scanners that provided the Scientific and Meteorological Departments in Osiris Base with essential physical and climatic information that was used for both daily planning and long-term research. The radar system was sensitive enough to track isolated sand squalls and moisture pocklets across the planet's surface, the movement of which aided in forecasting the infamous Martian dust storms that were so debilitating to machines and exposed mechanisms. And ultra-sensitive underground sensors positioned at varying depths beneath each mast correlated seismic activity and tracked Martian tectonic plate movement.

After the first run was complete, Lesley Oakley turned the PTSV around and headed back on a reverse course for the second and final scan. The vehicle's twelve independently suspended "bubble" tyres transferred a mild vibration to the cylindrical accommodation cell as they traversed a former lake bed, but their bulky electric motors began to complain and the wheels to bounce as the landscape changed from easy undulations to a rock-strewn beach and then a craggy rising escarpment that called for experienced handling skills and careful navigation.

Fine dust and debris, which still loitered in the thin atmosphere as semi-transparent ochre-coloured clouds, now deposited itself on the vehicle's white paintwork. The rusty-looking sediment soon filled every nook and cranny and from forward-facing corners it spilled over the bodywork in cascading flurries. On higher ground, where the wind picked up, blower motors on maximum setting hummed loudly in their attempt to keep the five cockpit windows clear. And deep tyre tracks in the brick red sand now being reinforced by a second pass caused a scar across the landscape that, together with the intensifying cloud that trailed behind, made the support and research vehicle highly visible from miles around.

Field Officer 1st Class Paul Carr of the European Space and Science Agency studied the sensor trace on a circular display whilst trying to keep his balance. Occasionally he looked up and towards the cockpit with a disapproving expression. Eventually, satisfied, he compressed and saved the trace as a digital pulse and transmitted it to Osiris Base via a passing satellite.

"Osiris Base from Support One, how do you read?"

"Loud and clear, Paul . . . . Go ahead please."

"First run complete. Overview looks absolutely fine. All parameters are well within tolerance . . . no problems that I can see . . . must be one of the more reliable arrays. I've sent the trace over and we have commenced the second run – I'll let you know."

"Okay, copied, Paul. You're one hundred per cent sure that there are no anomalies and no visual discrepancies either?"

"Looks clear to me, Andy . . . . Have a look at the readout yourself. I see that Comms have received the package."

"Um, copied, okay, thanks for that; I'll wait to hear from you then."

**Osiris Base**
**11:18 Martian Corrected Time**

Andy Baillie sat at his console deep in thought. His fingertips played nervously upon his display screen while he ran and re-ran a section of digital imagery. He stared at it, enhanced it, magnified it and manipulated it, in order to find a clue as to the unexplained movement detected by the sensor array terminals in the North East Sector – movement that was impossible. Eventually, but clearly with reservations, he pressed a button on his intercom control panel.

"Good morning, Commander Race here," was the response.

"Morning sir, um, it's Lieutenant Baillie here from the Science Department. Have you got a minute please?"

"Yes I have, Andy, what is it?"

"You remember last year, when I arrived, Sir. You said that my job here in Sensor Control was absolutely vital, that the planetary sensor system was key to the safety and survival of Osiris Base, and if I ever had any concerns, no matter how small, how, well, insignificant or off-beat, that I should mention it – draw it to your attention. Well I've got something – an anomaly, and it's niggling me, sir. Something is not right, East Sector . . ."

"I'm coming over, Andy. Give the Head of Department a call too, please."

Commander Tom J. Race of the United States Air Force, the officer commanding the Osiris Base, stood behind Andy Baillie and stared down at the information presented on screen. Riche Fernandes, a tall, lean, officer of Hispanic descent and Head of the Science Department stood by his side.

"I'm sorry to bother you with this, sir, but something's not adding up . . . the information I've correlated. I've checked and rechecked . . . see here . . . and here . . . and here." Andy Baillie pointed to the screen. "Sensors mounted on these masts, thirteen of them, have detected unknown movement and this trace shows the profile. Look, sir, this shows continuous movement – progressing along the line, passing each terminal in turn. There is no doubt about it. Not only that, I've analysed the pattern, taken readings from several other terminals, cross-checked using an algorithm . . . the movement is an exact replication of the human walk. I mean someone has been out there – walking the line, in the North East Sector, making approximately eleven kilometres per hour."

"So?"

"Sir . . . apart from that being a very energetic jog for most of us and for several kilometres, nobody has been that way for almost a year. I checked the survey records. The last time was when the array had its annual inspection – last February, the eighteenth and nineteenth to be precise."

"It's a malfunction then," said Fernandes, "some ghosting on the digital readout, maybe a scar from a previous recording."

"No! That's not possible either. I cleaned the formatting, overlaid the trace, did everything. At least one person, maybe two, walked past that array when every base member was accounted for here at home!"

"Run a check on the entire array," barked Commander Race. "Bring forward the annual inspection."

"It's already under way, sir. Paul Carr has performed the first run; he must be near complete by now. I'm expecting the results for the final scan any time. Here is the readout for the first run. As you can see it checks one hundred per cent – not a single glitch." Baillie turned in his seat and looked up at the Commander. "Somebody's been there sir; there is no doubting it," he said ominously.

Commander Race's eyes narrowed. "When was this? When did it happen?"

At that, Baillie looked away. His expression was regretful.

"Well!" said Commander Race.

"Sir, I've detected similar movement a few times over the last six months. My reaction was the same as that of Commander Fernandes – not possible, a malfunction, some sort of sensor error. I deleted the traces. Decided to wait until the next annual inspection, identify the faults and have them rectified. I mean clearly it was an anomaly," he concluded embarrassed.

"Timings, Andy! Give me the timings!"

"The first occurrence was back in July, sir. A few days after that bright meteorite came down in the Elysium no-go zone. You remember, we called it the Thanksgiving Meteorite to honour our American colleagues. There have been a few other instances since then and then this last one a few days ago. It's been on my mind, niggling me, so when Support One was in the area I asked them to run the annual inspection a few weeks early. The rest you know."

From across the operations room a woman at another console pushed back in her castored chair and attracted Andy Baillie's attention. "Excuse me, sir. Andy, Paul Carr on the line from Support One. He says he's finished the survey."

Andy gestured his acknowledgement. "May I?" he asked respectfully.

Tom nodded. "Put it on open microphone, Andy. I want to ask him a few questions."

"Paul, Andy here, how do you read?"

"Yes, five by five, no problems. Listen, I've finished the survey and checked the second scan . . . nothing. It all looks good to me. I'm sending over the trace now. There is one thing though . . ."

"Paul, Commander Race is with me and the HOD, too. The Commander wants to ask you a few questions."

"Understood . . . morning sir . . . from the team."

"Good morning, Paul. First off, what's on *your* mind?"

"We spotted the main power box open on one of the radio masts – number twenty-seven, sir. A magnified image showed us that the cover had been prised open – I mean how can that happen? Anyway, I sent Martine out to take a look ten minutes ago. She's on station now. Only she's found an optical fibre spliced into one of the junctions, as if someone has tapped into the automatic communication and control system. That would give access, electronically, to the entire array. Perhaps even back to the Control Centre."

Andy Baillie's eyes widened with disbelief, as did those of the two Commanders. Another officer upon hearing the transmission walked over to the console; he looked totally bemused.

"Where does the optic fibre go, Paul?" Commander Race asked.

"Apparently it disappears in the sand after a few metres, but Martine says that it appears to go off in the direction of the Elysium Pyramids. There's a dust storm getting up at the moment so we can't see the structures, but normally from here we could see the pinnacles of Zeta One and Two at least. The power box lid had been bent backwards breaking the lock and then made good and closed to an extent to provide some protection for the circuitry inside. Is any maintenance documented for this terminal? I mean, what self-respecting tradesman would . . . ? Wait a minute, we have a problem . . . Martine's calling in." Talking to someone else, Paul Carr said, "What's she saying? Put her on speaker!"

The voice of Martine Ebury went live in both locations. "I saw something moving a moment ago; behind me by the rocky outcrop. Is Dan outside . . . ? Is anyone else outside?" She sounded fretful.

"No. You're on your own. Dan's still in the dispatch section. Take a close-up of the power box and come back, Martine."

Veronica looked up from her control console, made eye contact with Paul and shrugged. Her expression of bewilderment was tinged with apprehension.

"Wait! There! Something is out here, like a shadow, a figure."

"Martine, come in now please. Forget the image."

"I've seen something! It's moving quickly. It's coming

this way! There's a lot of sand in the air . . . Oh God, I'm . . ."

"Martine, this is Paul. You come back now. That's an order!"

"I'm coming back! Oh no, it's chasing me! Open up! I'm coming . . . must get away . . . !"

The sound of peppering sand and heavy erratic breathing came through the speakers. Veronica put a hand to her mouth. Paul dashed over to the control console. There was an eerie whine; it unnerved everyone.

"Sitrep, please . . . What's happening?" Andy Baillie demanded over the radio.

"Where are you now, Martine? Answer me," said Paul, bending towards the microphone.

There was silence.

"Martine . . . Martine! Can you hear me?" shouted Veronica.

"Help me . . . help me . . . help . . ." Martine Ebury's words trailed away until they were no longer audible.

"Dan! Get my suit ready – I'm going out! Veronica, keep calling her!" Paul ordered.

At that moment the support vehicle began to shake violently. There was a banging and a clanking from outside. "What the hell was that?"

"Paul! Something is on top of us!" yelled Lesley from the front, her expression one of controlled terror.

Muffled shouts emanated from the rear compartment followed by more clanking and tearing noises from above.

"Secure the airlock!" Paul shouted. He turned towards the cockpit. "Lesley, get us out of here . . . now!"

"We can't leave her!" was the reply.

"I said, *now!*"

Electric motors began to whine. The vehicle shuddered. And then gas began to vent – loud and whistling. Lesley glanced into the large, external, rear-view mirror on her left-hand side only to see pieces of pipe and other metallic objects showering the ground. A microwave dish flew past her window. Lesley floored the accelerator pedal as billowing clouds of white condensing gas began to circulate, completely obscuring the view behind. And then red lights began to illuminate on her control panel and an oxygen alarm began to sound. We are being attacked!" she shouted. "Something is on the roof and pulling us apart!"

"Put your foot down . . . manoeuvre!"

"It's no good! I'm trying!"

"What the hell is going on out there?" yelled Andy Baillie over the radio.

Paul rushed into the cockpit. Lesley was at top speed and swerving from side to side. Still the attack persisted. At 50 mph over that terrain the PTSV bounced and vibrated violently. Desperately hanging onto a roof member with one hand and unscrewing a porthole cover with the other, Paul tried to get a glimpse outside. There was nothing to see, but the sound of malicious damage continued in a frenzy above him. Further down the tube there was another porthole in the roof. Hand over hand he made his way back and unscrewed the securing clip. "Sit down and strap in," he told the two crew members.

Vertically upwards, through the small glass window, he caught sight of something. He didn't believe it at first and had to look again. Then immediately he turned and loped forward again, into the cockpit. Several oxygen gauges showed in the red sector; alarms rang in his ears. There was a switch on the control panel that was covered by a plastic red and yellow striped cover and marked *DANGER*. Without hesitation he lifted the safety device. Fighting with the steering levers, Lesley glanced at him momentarily as if to say, "What are you doing?" and then he pressed the button. Instantly the red numbers in the adjacent digital readout began to increase and there was a loud buzzing that permeated the vehicle. When the readout showed 20,000 Volts, Paul pressed the button again and repositioned the safety cover.

Immediately, the assault on the vehicle appeared to stop. Paul looked at the ceiling with trepidation and then ran his eye line down the tube. Outside everything was quiet. With a hand movement he indicated to Lesley to reduce speed and then he scribed a circle with his finger, requesting that she turnaround. Then he walked the length of the tube listening intently. The two crew members stared at him, terrified; he reassured them with a nod and a smile. "Back to your stations – we are going home."

"What about Martine? We can't leave her," said one of the women.

That was a command decision he was in the process of making. Was she dead already? Would he put the rest of his crew in danger by going back? Would another static charge from the magnetic desensitising system fend off a repeat attack? *Osiris Base was almost three days' drive,* he thought. He removed an intercom microphone from a holder on a nearby bulkhead. Engineer Dan Winton was the sixth crew member; his station was in the rear compartment, the other side of two pressure doors. "Dan, how is it back there?" Paul asked.

"I've survived, if that's what you mean. Structurally, we've taken quite a bit of damage. What was that all about, for God's sake? Something from hell. It scared the shit out of me."

"I'll fill you in in a bit. Give me a system sitrep."

"Oxygen is our main problem, lost almost eighty per cent. The emergency supply uses internal plumbing. I managed to salvage two hundred litres from the aft bottle port side; the rest were damaged and all the contents vented to atmosphere."

"So how does it look? Be specific."

"Two days, Paul . . . maybe fifty hours at the most – that's very tight to get back to Osiris. The suits will give another four or five hours."

"And with five of us?"

Veronica gasped. There was a fatalistic pause. Was that the reality of the situation?

"With five of us, Paul, there's enough – if we leave now." Dan's voice was sombre. "Listen, one other thing . . . . Whatever attacked us tried to stop the access door from closing. I thought it was coming in! The peripheral

185

seals are damaged, but they are holding at the moment. If I cycle the door again I may not be able to seal it, and flushing the entrance portal will require additional oxygen . . . I'm sorry."

Lesley called back from the cockpit. "Paul, Commander Race wants a situation report ASAP."

Paul raised his hand in acknowledgement and then he turned to Anna who sat at the life support console. "What do you have on Martine?" he asked bluntly.

Anna, who was still visibly shaken, shrugged her shoulders. "Nothing . . . no indications," she answered, almost in a whisper. Tears welled in her eyes.

"Is that because she is dead, or because her life functions system has malfunctioned?"

Anna shook her head and dabbed her eyes with a handkerchief. "I don't know. I just don't know."

Paul Carr drew a long breath and looked out through one of the circular side windows at the alien environment. Visibility had increased again and the distant sun illuminated the landscape with a rich orange glow. He could see a sand squall passing over the nearby ridge. They were moving at a walking pace back in an easterly direction.

Paul flipped a switch on the intercom panel and his microphone became live through the speaker system. "Listen up everyone," he said solemnly. "I believe Martine to be dead. We have only enough oxygen to get back to base if we leave now. I have no intention of putting the mission in jeopardy by going back to that area –

God knows what else is out there. I'm sorry – I really am. Lesley, plot a course for home – maximum speed consistent with the damage we have sustained. And patch this mic through to the operations room in Osiris."

Lesley Oakley, in the cockpit, made a few selections and then she turned and held up a thumb. Paul nodded.

"Base Ops from Support One, how do you read?"

"Loud and clear . . . . What's going on?"

"We've had some problems, Andy. On our way back to you now – navigation system predicting sixty-three hours. I am reporting one crew member down – Martine Ebury. I believe her to be dead. Course of action necessitated by life support deficiency. Request you instigate Emergency Retrieval Protocol Code Zero Three. Is Commander Race still with you?"

"Yes he is!"

"Commander Race, Sir. We have a serious security situation in the Elysium Sector – unidentified intruders. You will have my report within the hour."

# CHAPTER 10

# FOR THE LOVE OF CARBON

**London – same day**
**15:02 Greenwich Mean Time**

"Peter," said Laura Bellingham standing in the doorway, "I have received a transcription of the message sent from Space Station *Spartacus* to the Science Federation Headquarters this morning. I've sent it to your computer. In response to your request for further information Mr Brian Grant will call you in fifteen minutes – you will recall that he is the Senior Scientific Analyst for the European Space and Science Agency."

Peter Rothschild looked up from his desk. *Laura,* he thought, *is beginning to look tired.* She had very dark bags under her eyes. "Thanks," he said, and stared for a moment.

"Will that be all?"

"You are working too hard, Laura," Rothschild said, in a concerned manner. "I want you to take some time off . . . okay? As soon as we get Abbey back from America, then you're off for a few days. Is that clear?"

"It's cold and damp at home, Peter. I've almost run out of heating oil and so have my neighbours – we've been pooling resources. They are saying that further deliveries are unlikely and I hear electricity rationing being mentioned again in certain quarters. So, if you don't mind, I would prefer to be here, where it's warm. Anyway, I'm expecting some news from Richard. He should have landed in Egypt by now. I need to coordinate his security."

Rothschild nodded, acknowledging the reality of the situation. "Any of that Admiralty coffee left?" he asked, smiling.

"I'll see what I can do." Laura closed the door behind her.

Rothschild turned his attention to the transcription and read the accompanying report. The *Arius* probe, a large satellite-type vessel that brimmed with ultrasensitive equipment for deep space research, was now five days from Jupiter. Designed with a broad-spectrum sensing capability that also encompassed most terrestrial frequencies, she had intercepted a radio signal that seemed to emanate from the moon Io and had attempted to rebroadcast it to the ISSF facility in Canaveral the previous evening. However, due to the debilitating effect that Jupiter's gravity has on radio waves, the relay was degraded and only intercepted as a weak, distorted signal by the Space Station *Spartacus* that was holding station between Mars and Jupiter in support of the original ISS *Hera* mission. There an alert operative, who had become suspicious by the nature of the signal, had rebroadcast it to Osiris Base. The red telephone on Rothschild's desk rang.

"Rothschild here," he answered.

"Peter, good afternoon, it's Brian Grant from the Space and Science Agency. You have requested an update on the signal from Jupiter, I understand."

"Yes, that's right. I hear it's causing some concern."

"More than that my dear chap – put the cat among the pigeons, I'm afraid."

"Go on."

"*Spartacus* is holding station in the Omega Sector, about four million miles from Jupiter – just beyond the outer asteroid belt. We decided to keep her there until more precise information is available on the *Hera*'s disappearance. She intercepted a weak signal from the *Arius* probe at 23:14 GMT yesterday. It was a relay of a signal that appeared to emanate from Io. Normally the signal would have been processed as a low priority occurrence, but the operative noticed that the form was binary tonal – not one used generally for space communications. Listening to it would be like listening to the shrill from an old facsimile machine, for example. Unable to decode it, the operative relayed the signal to

Osiris Base for onward transmission to Canaveral by their Accelercom facility, marking it Sceptre Code Two – that means of special interest."

Rothschild was beginning to wonder where all this was leading when, in the background, he heard someone say, "Mr Grant, the signal is confirmed, auto-synthesis!"

Rothschild interrupted. "I overheard that Brian, what does that mean exactly – *auto-synthesis*?"

"There is a scientist on Mars, Peter, by the name of Ramir Pushtarbi; he works in the Robomotive Department. Been there for years apparently – their longest serving robologist. Someone in the communication centre on Osiris asked his opinion, knowing that he had a synthetic language background. It transpires that he is a former employee of Interface Cybersystems SL, a company within the Epsilon Rio group. In fact, he was on the original development team for the Humatron series. These were Level Seven, self-aware robots, built originally for piloting deep space probes and also operating long-term space amenities such as the atmospherics control centre on orbiting facilities like Spaceport – relieving humans of such menial tasks. As such they were built to last – a guaranteed longevity for the primary power cell of one thousand years, in fact. This morning, at 04:48 GMT, Mr Pushtarbi recognised the binary transmission as a communication between Humatron systems; indeed, he has specified the model HU40. This robotic system was banned several years ago by international law. There were numerous reasons, not least uncontrolled acts of violence towards humans – the result of programming deficiencies."

"I know of this system, Brian, our operatives have encountered them in the past, and you are quite right, they are extremely dangerous. A mind of their own, it seems. So, a conversation between robots, you say?"

"The ISSF's security directorate acquired the entire Humatron language code when they closed down the Interface production facility in Brazil a few years ago. My people have just confirmed the transcription: Ramir Pushtarbi was correct – it appears that there is, or was, at least one HU40 system on the surface of Io and another in orbit!"

"Good God man! Could they have been responsible for the disappearance of *Hera* . . . ? What are they doing there?"

"I am in receipt of the full transcription . . . in English – came through just a few minutes ago. Part of it appears to be a series of technical instructions; data for adjusting the centre of gravity and centre of pressure for, we presume, an ascent of a landing vehicle. An additional forty-eight kilograms was specifically mentioned. And other data includes settings for escape velocity and orbital concentricity calculations for a docking manoeuvre."

Rothschild sat bolt upright in his chair. "Can it be that robots are doing what we sent the crew of *Hera* to do? Surely not . . . surely that's not possible!"

"*Colossus* Zero One, we have your arrival request. You are clear to station. Orbital Profile Four, Four, Seven. Arrival Sequence Zero, Zero, Zero, Four – Tranquillity Transition. Initial holding seventy-eight per cent elliopheric, reducing sixty-five per cent at Gate Sequence Alpha, Alpha, Charlie. Do you copy *Colossus*?" The controller had an American accent.

The reply was from a woman with an Asian accent and the words were clipped. "*Colossus* copy, thank you Andromeda. Automatic sequence in place – acknowledgement download code Tongsei One, Two, Two. You have code, correct?"

"Yes Mam, we have Tongsei One, Two, Two in the data sequence. You are clear to proceed. Welcome to the Moon."

The recent refit of the interplanetary mineral barge *Colossus* had increased her payload from 125,000 metric tons to 160,000 tons, and resumption of the near 500,000 mile round trip had allowed much needed supplies to reach the Earth, particularly mineral-rich fruit and vegetables grown inside Andromeda's extensive biodome network. Cold storage of foodstuffs was highly convenient, as after harvesting it was simply conveyed to the freight terminal in louvred Space Chillers – bulk storage containers that allowed the extreme cold outside to slowly permeate the food, and then, after the louvres were closed, maintain an internal temperature fractionally above freezing point. The food subsequently remained super-chilled in the vacuum of space until its arrival on Earth.

Constructed in space, Tongsei Space Ship *Colossus* was far too large and underpowered for re-entry manoeuvres and as such was attended by a fleet of service vehicles at either end of the two-week cycle, where a medium level geostationary orbit was normally required for three to four days.

There were mining operations on the Moon almost before permanent accommodation had been built. Following the global recession of 2008–2017, governments the world over had withdrawn from the costly research and development programmes required for lunar colonisation and had instead pooled resources under the auspices of the first space alliance – the International Space and Science Federation. But it was the wealthy and faceless industrial conglomerates that had paved the way for a return in 2016 by negotiating one-sided – and regarded by many as illegal – trade agreements that effectively gave them a monopoly over the Moon's precious resources. The 1967 Outer Space Treaty between Russia and the United States of America, which defined the Moon and all outer space as the "province of all mankind" and also restricted the use of the Moon to peaceful purposes, explicitly banning military installations, and the 1979 Moon Agreement created to restrict the exploitation of the Moon's resources by any single nation, simply fell by the wayside. By 2019 the giant China-based conglomerate Tongsei Heavy Industries and other similar unscrupulous multinational companies had stock in the Moon, and their initial investment would turn in hitherto unheard of revenues for the coming three decades. That continued until 2050, when their criminal aspirations for controlling world-energy supplies had been curtailed and subsequently their trading activities severely restricted. But now, with mineral and commodity revenues once again filling their coffers, other designs loomed – perhaps the independent colony itself?

Based on the layout of the world's largest but long obsolete nuclear-powered submarine, the TS Shinan Po, but with hugely increased dimensions, the menacing black hull of the *Colossus* neared the pre-designated orbital entry point. Her broad, flat upper deck housed eighteen pairs of hydraulically operated cargo doors that gave access to twelve cavernous cargo holds designed specifically for the bulk transport of minerals. However, post-refit, Number 1 hold had now been divided and adapted to carry other equally lucrative commodities, such as food and gemstones. The single, rear-facing, but manoeuvrable primary rocket nozzle that was positioned centrally on the truncated aft section of the hull occasionally glowed a fiery brilliant white and this rearward thrust was augmented by brief lateral burns of the retro rockets that were applied to align the vessel with the final approach corridor.

"Andromeda Control, this *Colossus*, we request one additional high latitude orbit at seventy-eight per cent elliopheric before establish final station. You authorise, please."

"Your parameters look good from this end, *Colossus*. State your reasons for a change in the profile."

"Er, we need additional time to decelerate. Must comply increased mass momentum computation."

There was a pause. "I say again, your profile looks a-okay? Continue as briefed, please."

"Must insist . . . velly high priority, Andromeda. Momentum calculation show increased speed for alignment. This no good for orbital concentricity – please allow additional polar orbit to decelerate."

In the Freight Control Centre the American officer held up a hand and attracted the attention of his line manager. "Sir, what do you think?" he asked, as the older man stood beside him and leaned over to study an electronically enhanced approach profile that was overlaid on the circular radar screen. "The Captain of the *Colossus* is requesting an additional orbit at seventy-eight per cent in order to decelerate, but her profile looks good to me – it's unusual, I mean . . ."

"Maybe they haven't quite nailed the computations after the refit; I know that the barge is much larger now. What orientation is he requesting?"

"It's a she, sir, and they want the Polar quadrant."

"Seems okay . . . there's nothing there."

"But sir, we're not talking rocket science here. Surely her navigation computer will have been updated . . . to account for the additional mass, I mean. And anyway, the far side sensors are down for servicing – that was clearly detailed in this month's *Notices to Spacemen*. She must know that we can't track her on the other side and therefore will not be able to provide trajectory or safety information. It's highly irregular, sir!"

The supervisor paused for a moment, weighing up the implications. A wiry Englishman, he stood tall and then arched his back and scratched his head. "Listen," he said, in a condescending way, "we don't want an interplanetary diplomatic incident do we? Not on my watch anyway. Go ahead and authorise the damned orbit."

"But sir!"

"Let it go, Smith . . . okay? Any degrading of safety in the orbital phase is down to her – it's her decision – just remind her of the maintenance period for the record."

Unhappy with the order, but complying in any case, the American opened the communication channel again. "*Colossus*, this is Andromeda Control. Your orbit at seventy-eight per cent elliopheric is approved – make it Zero, Zero, Seven degrees, East Polar Offset. You are advised that essential sensor maintenance is currently underway; in future, please check your notices. I will call you when we have you on radar again."

"Velly good. One orbit in polar sector approved. Cancelling Tranquillity Transition and changing course. *Colossus* Zero One, out."

As the blip on the radar screen slowly changed direction and set course for the Moon's North Pole, Space Controller Herbie Smith closely monitored the ship's velocity. The profile looked innocuous enough, but there was something about it he just didn't like. There were no other space movements in the vicinity and so he watched the trace almost aimlessly until it neared the periphery of his screen and then disappeared.

With the dark side sensors out of action, it would be another three hours and thirty-seven minutes before the system registered the *Colossus* completing the orbit by appearing beneath the South Pole.


**London – same day**
**16:32 Greenwich Mean Time**

"Any sign of him?"

"Nobody has seen him since breakfast, Mr Rothschild – can't understand it. He knew we were going live at ten this morning." The man on the screen checked his watch. "That's thirty minutes ago. He must have gone walkabout – possibly back to the temple. I know he had a couple of unresolved issues. Anyway, I've sent someone over to his hotel. Sorry . . . it's quite unlike Professor Jones to miss an appointment."

"Okay, I understand. May I take your name?" asked Peter Rothschild politely.

"Yes, of course – I'm Steven, Steven Trent. Doing a Master's at Cardiff. I'm Professor Jones' assistant. There are two of us in fact – Shelley's gone off to the hotel."

The tall young man had dark curly hair that spilled out from beneath his woollen hat. The collar of his patterned poncho-type coat was buttoned tight around his neck and he fidgeted with his gloves. He focused on anything but the camera and could feel Peter Rothschild watching him through the video link.

"What's your area of interest?" asked Rothschild, becoming frustrated by the delay.

"I'm specialising in ancient symbology – the same field as the Professor. Shelley's into early art – Middle America is her thing."

"I see. And how old are you, if I may ask?"

"Twenty-one." He nodded almost apologetically.

"Were you with Professor Jones when he discovered the new chamber?"

"Sadly not – kicking myself for not coming over with him. He could see the writings and the frescoes deteriorating. It surprised him. The process started almost immediately. Flaking, discolouring – it's the humidity. That's when he sent for some help. I mean, what he's found is amazing."

"Does he know how old they are?"

"Yes, he's dated the chamber quite accurately by the position of the stars."

"What, exactly, do you mean by that?"

"The ceiling of the chamber is domed, finely plastered, and there is a perfect representation of the night sky . . . back then of course, when it was actually painted. The Southern Hemisphere, exactly as it was. The Professor took two days to take an image – he's got this wide-angled, low-light device. Then he sent the image to a friend in Switzerland, a well-known astronomer. The results arrived last week – that's when he requested some security from the regional government and contacted the European Space Agency. It's not just the writings."

"What's so special about a painting of the night sky – then or now?"

Steven Trent rubbed his gloved hands vigorously for a moment in an effort to warm his fingers and his breath condensed as he spoke. "The midpoint of the chamber – by that I mean the orientation of the entire fresco – turned out to be the magnetic South Pole. Absolutely spot on, accurate to within a few hundred metres."

"Yes . . . and?"

The young man looked surprised. "The Mayan civilisation, sir, here, the Yucatán Peninsula – we are in the Northern Hemisphere. These people had no way of getting to Antarctica, let alone crossing an icy wasteland that size to get to the bottom of the world." He looked away nervously for a moment and checked the time again. "I shouldn't be telling you this – the Professor has put a news blackout on the whole project – but . . ."

"Go on, I'm security cleared."

"According to the results from Switzerland, the original aspect . . . because the lowest stars painted on the fresco would have actually been below the horizon and therefore not visible, well . . . the observer would have been flying!" Steven Trent paused nervously. "Sorry, I've probably said too much. I'd better wait for the . . ."

Rothschild pushed down on the arms of his chair and sat up straight. "No, that's fine. There is no security issue here; I can assure you of that. What else do you know about this? How accurate is the fresco – what are we talking here?"

Steven Trent gestured his amazement. "Apparently, modern-day accuracy – the results stipulated an observation altitude of several thousand metres and because of the known precession of the heavens, an exact date, too."

"When . . . when was this fresco painted, Steven?" Now it was Rothschild's turn to fidget.

"Almost twelve thousand years ago. I don't know the exact date as the Professor's got that information, but several thousand years before the Mayan civilisation was supposed to exist. Looks like we need to rewrite some local history." He warmed his hands again.

"It's more than local history we are rewriting, Steven. Be in no doubt about that. Now, where is Professor Jones?"

Steven Trent looked over his shoulder towards the makeshift project office – a plastic portacabin building that had been delivered by lorry. The lights were on inside but there was no sign of life. He looked back towards the camera. "No sign at the moment, I'm afraid," he reported, anxiously.

"Did he have a late night or something?"

"Well I did leave him in the canteen with two archaeologist friends. At least they appeared to be friends. They called for another bottle of red wine as I left. Too much for me, and I don't like wine much anyway. That was about ten-thirty."

"Do you know who they are? Perhaps we can call them."

"No, sorry, they only arrived yesterday morning. Seemed very interested in the Professor's work – made the trip especially, in fact. Fellows of the European Society of Archaeological Science – I saw their ID, of course. The Professor was very keen on seeing their ID."

Rothschild typed *European Society of Archaeological Science* into the ministry's World Net search engine on his computer, as he asked: "Where did they come from, did they say?"

"No, sir! But one of them had a strong German accent; quite a bad scar on his face, too. Under here." Steven ran his finger from his left ear around and beneath the jaw line to the corner of his lip. "He said he took a fall whilst on an expedition in Egypt. The other was Asian."

The words *No results found* appeared on Rothschild's computer screen. He quickly retyped the society's name into another search engine. "What was your impression of the men? . . . I mean, did they seem knowledgeable?"

"To be honest, the Asian man barely spoke. The German was very friendly though – knew a lot about the Professor's previous work. The Professor seemed quite relaxed when I left."

The words *No results found* appeared on Rothschild's computer screen again. He looked up, concerned. "You are sure about the credentials of these men?"

"Absolutely – checked their badges myself."

At that moment there was the sound of screaming from the direction of the project office; it was a woman's voice. Steven Trent turned to see a young lady running towards him. "Steven! Steven!" she shouted. To Rothschild, she sounded highly distressed. Moments later she came into view on his video display.

"This is Mr Rothschild, Shelley," Steven said, explaining the image on the monitor. "He is in London. What is it? What's the matter?"

The young woman, clearly distraught, hung onto Steven's shoulder. Tears streamed down her face.

"What is it, for God's sake?" Steven demanded.

"It's the Professor . . . he's been found dead in his room!"

A look of horror swept over Steven Trent's face. Rothschild was quick to react. "I'll get someone from the British Embassy in Mexico City to call you, Steven," he said. "I think there is a more local Honorary Consulate in Cancun, but I haven't got the number to hand. You two hang on there until someone comes for you. Whoever it is will have diplomatic identity papers and ask for you by name – do you understand? You do not leave the site with anyone else. Do I make myself clear?"

The pair nodded blankly.

"Steven, listen carefully to this question – it is very important."

The young man tried his best to focus on Rothschild and give him his full attention, but his mind wandered and Shelley couldn't stop crying. "How he was killed, it's horrible," she mumbled.

"Steven, listen to me, another man's life may depend on it," implored Rothschild.

Steven nodded and looked directly at the camera; he drew a deep breath.

"Did Professor Jones ever talk about Alexandria or the Egyptian connection to his work there in Uxmal – or even mention Alexandria in passing? You know, a reference? A colleague? Or even an artefact from there? Do you think he had any knowledge of what was recently found in Alexandria – a few weeks ago? This is very important."

The young man hesitated. Rothschild sensed his reservations.

"Listen, Steven," continued Rothschild reassuringly. "Do not worry about the security aspects of this . . . you're not in trouble, certainly not for anything that you may have seen, overheard or been party to during your work. And this communication link is scrambled – totally secure – no one can listen in on our conversation. So, think carefully, Steven . . . could the Professor have had any knowledge of the recent find in Alexandria?"

# CHAPTER 11

# ONE MORE THAN FIVE

**Alexandria Egypt**
**The House of Mubarakar – same day**
**21:45 Local Time**

Richard could not hear the sea, but he could smell it. The military vehicle that had dropped him in the old part of town soon disappeared into the night and, as the low whine of its electric transmission gradually faded from earshot, a peculiar silence settled over the shadowy street. A wild cat, dishevelled and emaciated, darted out from behind a wall and startled Richard momentarily. The mange-ridden animal stopped short and eyed Richard with a view to coaxing some food from him, but strangely, after assessing the odds, seemed to think better of it and dashed off, its form quickly vanishing into a dark recess.

The sky was as black as tar, but there were no stars

to see. There were never any stars. Not from anywhere on the surface of the planet could one marvel at the heavens, so there was no reason for Egypt to be any different. *Even so,* thought Richard, *because of its history, its long, civilised, astronomical history, Egypt deserved more.* But here in the outskirts of sprawling Alexandria, where, as with many places on this continent, electricity was both scarce and expensive, people had returned to the old ways. Oil lamps, the glint of a candle, perhaps the occasional solar lantern, had no impact on this street scene. Nor was there any humanised glow over the sprawling conurbation to the south; a radiance that told of life and living, as in more privileged parts of the world.

A squally breeze blew over Richard's face, ruffling his hair. Trying to find a way to the sea, the gust whistled and swirled as it was funnelled between shadowy houses. Success lay to the north, and eventually finding a path, the flurry subsided.

*The Eastern Mediterranean,* thought Richard, *is where the secrets lie.* He turned and stepped onto the stone pavement where, to his right, a tall but scanty-looking palm tree with limp fronds suffered the incessant cold. To his left, at a short distance, there was another tree, and beyond that the outline of a third, and Richard sensed that this was wider than a street, more a boulevard. He checked his chronometer; the blue backlight gave an indication of seven degrees Celsius. "Seven degrees," he mumbled, "positively warm."

Amazingly, it was dry underfoot – something

that was noteworthy. With no drizzle to dampen his cheerfulness or his prospects Richard's perspective lightened and, with a visit to Mubarakar in view, he grew positively optimistic.

After walking for a short while and checking numbers, Richard stopped outside a pair of towering metal gates that were heavy with ornamentation. A substantial stone-built wall stretched in both directions for at least twenty metres. *It's stained and blackened and probably in need of repair,* thought Richard, but the two, large, faintly glowing lanterns set high on the gate pillars made the place look stately. He loitered for a moment and rechecked the area. There was an intercom box on the left-hand pillar and, confirming the address, Richard pressed the call button.

"Mr Reece?" A woman asked, after a few seconds.

"Yes, that's right. I've come to see Professor Mubarakar."

"You are most welcome. Please come in."

Richard pushed hard on the heavy gates until one opened wide enough for him to walk through. After closing it he heard the solenoid clunk the draw-bolt shut again. There was a dimly discernible wide path leading to the house where, at its far end, lanterns cast their light onto an impressive pair of doors. The occasional solar beacon in the extensive garden showed it off as bedraggled and unkempt. From what he could see of the house, however, as he drew closer, it conjured images of an Arabian palace – a Moorish architectural adventure with arched windows and doorways dominating a broad, square, colonial facade of brick and stone – surely the house of a nobleman or statesman.

As Richard arrived at the main doors the left one opened for him and a hand beckoned him inside. And there was Mubarakar, friend and mentor and seemingly the fount of all past Egyptian knowledge. Richard shook the Professor's hand warmly and put a hand on his shoulder. The learned man was a head shorter than Richard and stockier, even a little rotund. His white, wispy hair was cut shorter than before. As he stepped back to study Richard, the Professor's face lit up as if the sun had burst through the door and Richard saw how old and frail he looked.

"It has been a year my young friend, but it feels like more. I have missed you. There are not many in Europe I can say that about."

Richard smiled and gestured his gratitude at being held in such esteem. Professor Mubarakar hunched and, using a stick to walk, indicated to follow him. Richard walked by his side into a lofty reception area and towards a majestic staircase on the far wall. Halfway up, the staircase split into two and then continued to climb, creating a balustrade-fronted gallery on either side. Beautiful coving and an enormous, ornate, circular ceiling rose with an intricate rose in the centre, from which hung a crystal chandelier, took his eye. As did several fine wall frescoes and a patterned Persian carpet of immense proportions.

"I see you like the house," Mubarakar said, as he stepped into an anteroom.

"I should say! It's impressive to say the least."

"Built for an Egyptian Prince in 1793; the plumbing is terrible. Too big for us now, of course. Regretfully, I have no children to pass it on to and my wife, having been raised in a palace with a harem, finds it claustrophobic!" He laughed at his irony.

The rectangular anteroom was much smaller, but the ceiling was high, giving it an airy feel. Two tall glass-panelled doors led outside on to what would have been a sun-drenched terrace and large windows on each side had arched architraves. Heavy patterned drapes, hanging from metal rods, remained open. This was a Gentlemen's Room, it was plain to see. Not just a study either, but Mubarakar's sanctuary – although there were enough books filling the copious shelves to call it a library too. The furniture was antique, traditional and decorative; another Persian carpet made it homely and wall-hung paintings and large photographs spoke of a life of expeditions and discovery. Richard recognised a well-worn, high-backed 'favourite' chair and its backdrop as being the one he had seen in the video while in London. Mubarakar sat in it, put his stick to the side, drew a long breath and smiled. He beckoned Richard to sit opposite.

"So, Professor, how are you feeling?"

"Sometimes good, sometimes bad, never young, not any more, not after the stroke – my wife says that I'm almost back to normal, but of course I am not . . . as you can see."

Richard nodded despondently, unable to disagree. He cast his eye around the room. "I thought this place would have been filled with artefacts, you know, from ancient Egypt, from your life as an archaeologist," he said, and fixated on a framed photograph on a nearby table of a much younger Mubarakar in the desert holding a stone carving. The inscribed date read: *1987.*

"Valley of the Kings," Mubarakar enlightened, with a glint in his eye. "After we had excavated a lost chamber in the renowned KV4 mausoleum. Those were the days." His head wobbled for a moment. "The history of Egypt belongs to the people, my young friend, which is why I have always supported the national museums. Private houses are not places for national treasures. Everything I have done . . . " Mubarakar looked reflectively around his home. "Yes, I was given things, gifts, recognition for my work . . . and for a favour here and there – a little corruption can be helpful in preserving history." He smiled again. "And I have found things . . . oh what I have found, Richard, in this life of mine." His eyes glinted again and then he shook his head in order to bring himself back to reality. But there was no holding back the ensuing sigh – a sign of sadness at the thought of it – and he changed the subject, saying: "We join forces again, my boy, in the fight for enlightenment."

"Yes, we do indeed, sir, and I hear you have something to tell me about this great city. Something that perhaps links it to . . ."

Mubarakar nodded enthusiastically and raised his

hand. "Yes, but first tea, Richard, mint tea, with honey, from my remaining stock, the way my steward prepares it . . . it is my favourite."

## London – simultaneous

"There's a call for you, Peter, from Scotland Yard. They have something on the identifit," said Laura Bellingham, peeping around the door.

Peter Rothschild, sitting at his desk, barely had time to look up when he heard the door close again. Two short beeping sounds drew his attention to a communications panel that was incorporated into the desktop; the call was on Line 2. "Rothschild, MI9," he responded sharply.

"Good evening, Sir. Inspector Hanson here from the Yard . . . International Crime Department – I head the RASP squad."

"RASP?"

"Reaction and Support Procedures, Sir. I have the results for your identifit request."

"I see. Please . . ."

"We have correlated information from the Embassy in Mexico City and a number of other sources, including some relevant documentation held here in our own database – I understand Level Three security is required." The man spoke in a way that brooked no argument.

Rothschild checked an indicator on his comms panel. "Quite correct, Inspector . . . Level 3 is in place, so what do you have?"

"The young man in Cancun provided very helpful descriptions of Professor Jones' so-called drinking partners. Regarding the primary suspect, he detailed a number of specific characteristics and we have used these to reference an identity with a high probability. Indeed, sir, we were able digitally to match the line of a prominent facial scar from images held on record, allowing confirmation beyond any reasonable doubt. The identity of the accomplice, however, remains a mystery. As far as we are aware this second man does not appear to be in any criminal database we have access to – and that includes Interpol's. Asian, probably of Chinese origin, heavily built, perhaps a little overweight – particularly in the face. Mid-thirties, we deduced. Our identifit image is currently being circulated, but nothing at the moment."

"I see, so who is our main suspect?"

"I'm sending over the computer's 3D facial reconstruction – it should appear on your screen in a few moments. And also a number of general images of the suspect taken over the last few years and in various locations around the world. More specifically, London in May 2050; Rome that same month; Shanghai's Central Monorail Station in February fifty-two; and a very recent image captured in the Private Aviation Terminal of Berlin's Schönefeld Airport. The scarcity and price of aviation fuel makes private flying in Europe almost non-existent and Germany's no different, and so this man either has very deep pockets or his employer has a near limitless budget, because the aircraft he flew out in was documented as being chartered from overseas and the crew paid cash for a full fuel load – a considerable sum of money by all accounts! Actual aircraft ownership and place of registration is proving difficult to trace due to deliberate misinformation, and this also applies to the destination airport. The German authorities have promised to forward these details as soon as they have them. Interestingly, the man appears to have been a suspect included in Interpol's automatic comparison programme for a period of time, but was removed or deleted a year or two ago. We had them reinstate his profile and their system came up with the Berlin image – taken just a few days ago in fact. We have compared these and a number of other images to the nineteenth pixilation. As I said, sir, it's a positive ID, no question."

"Very good, Inspector. And his name . . . ?"

"Karl Wilhelm Rhinefeld, a German national born in Bautzen in the east of the country, close to the border with Poland – a region that was under the control of the old Soviet Union. There are links to that state's former Secret Service, the NKVD – splintered remnants that have continued to operate underground for decades. Drugs, black market commodities, extortion, that sort of thing – and a number of other established terrorist groups. There are also some other disturbing offences. By all accounts he is not a nice character, and that's putting it mildly. His participation in these events gives me cause for serious concern." There was a thoughtful pause. "Finally, our files here at the Yard have a prefix that indicates MI9 interaction at some point and so you may be holding additional information on this man – you might like to pull your own records, sir."

"Karl Rhinefeld . . . Rhinefeld, yes, that name rings a bell. The department has had dealings with him in the past. Indeed, if I recall correctly, one of our operatives was lucky to escape from him with his life. I'll pull the archives, Inspector, to see what we have. Very helpful . . . thank you so much."

"That's quite alright, sir. Oh, there is one other thing – it may help."

"Yes?"

"The suspect walks with a limp. It is an injury to his right leg that appears to have happened between the images taken in May 2050 and February 2052. That's all. If I can be of further service, please do not hesitate to call. Good day, sir."

Rothschild closed the line and sat back in his chair thoughtfully. How well he recalled this man as being trained by a rogue, defunct, offshoot of the Soviet Union's Secret Service, and there were known KGB parallels. Rhinefeld was an assassin and a mercenary and a few other things besides, but more to the point, he was believed dead! Richard Reece and the Adulis Affair in 2050 – that was it! He would refer to the archives for more specific information on this man, but first he should disseminate this information and particularly to Richard. He tapped his fingers on the desk while considering the wider implications of this exposé. The

Strasbourg-based conglomerate Spheron had engaged this man previously, in order to do its dirty work. So now it seemed likely that the faceless men who ran that corporation had slipped back into their old ways. He pressed a button on his desktop and the projected image of his keyboard reappeared. He should warn Richard and with all haste. He formulated an abrive:

> Security Alert – Code 1
> An old adversary has reappeared. Rhinefeld, formally believed dead. Understood to have access to private Aviation – could turn up anywhere. Possible that the situation in Alex compromised. Exercise extreme caution. Repeat. Extreme caution required. Confirm receipt of Code 1 directive ASAP.

### The House of Mubarakar – simultaneous

Richard sat opposite Mubarakar absorbed by stories of discovery and adventure. He felt his telephonic pager vibrate and withdrew it from his pocket. He glanced at the small square screen, the backlight of which had enhanced Rothschild's name. He looked up again. "Sorry, Professor, carry on, I'm with you. It's just London, another brief update I expect . . . it can wait." Richard replaced the pager into a coat pocket where it hung over the back of his chair, zipped the pocket shut and fixed his attention on his host.

"Enough of such stories, Richard," said Mubarakar, with an easy smile. "Look, it is almost midnight. We must proceed with the task in hand." Mubarakar's face had the warm glow of someone recounting a life's work with pride of purpose and Richard was a worthy recipient.

Richard shuffled in his chair, still spellbound by the old man's adventures. "I suppose so," he said, straightening his shoulders and leaning back in a resigned fashion. A faint odour of perfumed mustiness exuded from the ageing upholstery as he moved, and Richard ran his hands over the carved wooden arms of the Baroque-period furniture piece and admired their ornate design. Then he reached across to the shared, circular, occasional table and lifted a white porcelain cup to his lips and sipped the dregs of cold tea; the sweetness of it was stronger than before. The delicate cup had a narrow, coloured rim to it, incorporating a vivid gold and ochre-red band. The pattern of small squares inadvertently reminded him of the rim to Queen Nefertiti's headdress. How could he forget it? The image and a similar one of Naomi dressed equally royally were impregnated in his memory. His thoughts lingered on Naomi for a while – her face, her smile – and he wondered where she was now. Overwhelmed by tales of ancient adventure, while surrounded by such opulence and in the company of a true master of mysteries, time stood still for him.

Mubarakar watched Richard for a moment and smiled again. "I see you have other things on your mind, Richard," he said quietly, as he rang a small brass bell on the table calling for more tea.

Richard nodded. "Yes," he agreed. "There is an undercurrent building, Professor, I can feel it, and the source is greed and control, fed by a world dependent on the Kalahari crystals . . . the crystals from Mars . . . or elsewhere." He looked the Professor in the eye. "I have a question for you."

"And I will answer, my friend, if I can."

For a moment, Richard reconsidered his intentions. But if there was anybody on this planet that he could trust it was Mubarakar. "During all your years, Professor," he asked, dropping his voice to a whisper, "all your studies, your enlightenment, did you ever uncover evidence of an ancient fellowship, like a clan – possibly centred on the Pyramids at Giza?"

"Tell me more of what you know."

"A fellowship that was originally from Eridu, I think, or perhaps Babylon? A fellowship whose considerable influence, both politically and scientifically, gradually waned until after many thousands of years it finally disappeared. For centuries, Professor, there has been no trace of it."

Mubarakar's eyes narrowed. "In my experience,

fellowships or brotherhoods are fashioned to serve a purpose . . . continuity of faith or values, protection of a sacred object, or even a royal line, or the safeguarding of knowledge – possibly all of these things."

Richard nodded. He leaned towards Mubarakar. "They . . . those that remain from this brotherhood . . . have a mark, a sign, a motif if you like?"

Mubarakar raised his head expectantly and breathed in deeply. He seemed to know where Richard was going with his questioning.

"A blue hand," said Richard impassively, lowering his voice to a whisper again. "Fingers outstretched but almost together and the thumb stretched upwards at right angles. No more than four centimetres long and three wide, front of the hand – palm towards you so to speak, and the motif tattooed on the palm of the recipient's right hand. It's a sign of membership . . . I'm thinking that they may have been priests in times gone by, or scholars, but also bodyguards perhaps."

Mubarakar raised his eyebrows. "You have seen someone that bears this mark?"

Richard nodded. "Two men! One very old and one middle aged . . . in his forties." Richard rubbed his chin. "Actually, so have you, Professor – but you didn't realise it at the time."

"When? When did I miss this honour . . . this opportunity of a lifetime?" Mubarakar looked surprised and sounded annoyed.

Richard, bemused by Professor Mubarakar's hurt,

looked quizzically at him. "A briefing in the British Embassy in Khartoum, May 2050, the twenty-fifth to be precise . . . you were in London with Admiral Hughes, but present through a video link."

"I remember, how could I not – a hologram of the dead!"

"Correct – that of Professor Simpson-Carter. Madame Vallogia and her companion were present at that briefing if you recall. Actually, he was more an aide de camp. He was asked to leave at one point for security reasons, but was granted a reprieve."

"Him!"

Richard nodded again. "Asharf Saeed Makkoum."

"And the other?"

"Adulis . . . the old city, you know, present-day Eritrea. In the museum there, probably the oldest of its kind in the world, just the most amazing place. The building was constructed on foundations dating back two thousand years I was told, to the Aksumite Empire. Actually, it was more an archive than a museum. The man I'm speaking about was the Chief Curator there . . . Banou . . . Banou was his name." Richard shook his head as if in awe. "I wouldn't be surprised if he is, or was, the oldest man in the world."

Mubarakar rubbed his brow thoughtfully. He seemed to hesitate. Richard could see that he knew something of this matter. "You have been privileged, honoured, to be in the presence of such men, Richard," said Mubarakar, his tone a mixture of solemnity and envy.

Richard shrugged. "I'm sure. But who are they, Professor? Really, it's important."

"I *have* found evidence of this order, or brotherhood, as you call it. In fact, several times during my career has this been the case. But I have never spoken of it. This is the first time. It has been my lifetime belief that no one else knew of this matter."

"Why have you kept this to yourself, Professor?"

"Not because the evidence was uncorroborated – much in archaeology is unsubstantiated or dismissed as mere conjecture – but because, because, there seemed to be a force at work . . ." Mubarakar stopped short, seemingly unable to put his interpretation into words.

"Go on," encouraged Richard, gently.

"I have also seen this sign you speak of – the open hand," said Mubarakar, nodding. "It has plagued my reasoning on many occasions over the years."

"Where, exactly?"

Mubarakar shrugged. "In lost tombs . . . once in the Great Pyramid of Khufu, but there I hid it beneath a coat of plaster – a treatment we use to preserve frescoes." He breathed in deeply. "Also here in Alexandria. Here, Richard . . . ! Gateway to the great sea state." Mubarakar's eyes turned misty.

Richard was not going to pursue the Atlantis theme, that was for another time. He needed information on the brotherhood. The Professor called it an "Order". *Was that significant?* Richard wondered. In any case, he needed to contact them by the most expeditious means possible.

"They are highly secretive, Professor. Those that remain of this . . . 'Ancient Order'," he continued. "Rosicrucians, like the Masons – only they have no influence anymore. Over the centuries they have faded away, become insignificant, lost in time . . . like all those early civilisations I suppose." Richard paused, thoughtfully. "But Asharf Makkoum still has a purpose, a duty in fact. He is a protector!"

Mubarakar looked at Richard but remained silent. A stillness hung heavy over them – like a spiritual awareness, quite different to the innocent air of story recital, as if they spoke of the unspeakable.

"What do you know of their symbol, Professor?" Richard asked, purposefully.

"I have learnt this from my work, Richard, but I must emphasise that there is no proof – nor do I seek it. Never have I pursued enlightenment on this subject."

Richard leaned forward a little more in anticipation; it was a subconscious response, his widening eyes beckoning Mubarakar.

"The five digits represent the five senses – sight, smell, touch, hearing and taste – but the shape, the way the hand is portrayed, also represents a number – the number six! Next was a clenched fist – the number seven. It was part of a system of measurement used by the ancient Egyptians of the First Dynasty. But I found this system to be derived from much earlier meanings."

"What, Professor? What was the meaning – the relevance of the open hand, the number six?"

"The sixth sense, of course . . . thought!"

"Thought?"

"Telepathy, my boy."

Richard flopped back in his chair and considered the remark. He recalled an instance in Mauritius a few years earlier, when he, Asharf and Naomi were together – Asharf did seem to know of Naomi's feelings even though they were in different rooms. "Anything else?" he asked.

"*Six* represents the sum of the emotions, the living energy; it lies in a different direction to the five apparent senses, but is part of them. It interacts but is also opposed. The mark of the hand has its roots in antiquity, Richard. It was a symbol copied by many cultures, particularly those with some degree of isolation, unrelated peoples, the Aborigines of Australia, the Aztecs and Incas of South America and the native Indians of North America, for example. Contact was thought impossible due both to distance and historical period. And there is one other thing." Mubarakar paused, and his eyes narrowed as his focus drifted. To Richard he seemed to be corroborating information, connecting instances from a lifetime of discovery. Mubarakar came to his senses, held up his own hand and looked Richard in the eye. "These writings, Richard," he pointed with his other index finger, "on the palm of each and every person's hand . . . the life line, the line of fate, the lines of head and heart, will and logic." He drew breath again. "The fingers of Mercury, Saturn, Jupiter and Apollo . . . this subject, the field of palmistry, such things as these are ancient crafts indeed!"

Richard nodded in agreement; he recalled Naomi's

explanation of the life force, each person's book of life, and the 'aura' as she called it. "Do you know of anyone who is a member of this order, Professor?" he asked hesitantly.

"I do not! In my life I have never been so blessed. Why this enlightenment now, Richard? This is my question to you. Why do you seek them?"

Richard looked down at his lap and then back at the Professor; he shifted uneasily. "Madame Vallogia is missing. She was living in a convent near Paris and seemed content to spend most of her time there – until two weeks ago, that is. Somebody found her. There was a conversation. The next day she packed her things and left. No explanation, nothing. And she arranged for the Ark to be collected, too. Even though she knew that the agreement with London was for it to remain in the convent – with no mention of it either, secure and secret. That's unlike Naomi. I've tried every number I have for her but with no luck. When I landed here I used my Level Five security authorisation to contact the Egyptian Secret Service, their MI9 equivalent – Asharf Makkoum held the position of Field Operative. It seems he's done a runner, just disappeared, a little over a week ago. I don't like it, Professor. I'm worried for Madame Vallogia – her safety – and that's putting it mildly. I think someone has used Asharf to get to her; threatened her with his life . . . whatever. Like you, she is a Master of the Antiquities. I think someone is looking for information. I think the Ark is the key, and that artefact is the most coherent link we have to the Kalahari crystals. I think there's trouble brewing, Professor . . ."

At that moment there was a barely audible knock on the door. It opened and a kindly looking Arabic man, probably in his sixties, walked in carrying a large silver tray. He looked smart and very 'old school' in his uniform – white cotton trousers and shirt with a dark patterned waistcoat, a green silk bowtie and black polished leather shoes. "Put it here on this table, Ashai," said Mubarakar in English, pointing. He moved his gaze to Richard. "Ashai's name means 'abundant' in Egyptian; he's been with me longer than I can remember." Ashai's skin was weather-worn, and as he smiled deep lines gathered around his eyes. Richard gestured his gratitude at the sight of two generously sized sesame seed cakes on individual plates.

After he had closed the door behind him, Professor Mubarakar poured out two more cups of mint tea and added a teaspoonful of honey to each. "Of course you could be wrong and she is attending to other duties – do we know if she has other duties in Cairo?" He replaced the lid on the honey pot. "You must be wary of drawing undue attention to her if this is the case." Mubarakar was serious. He stirred the cup closest to him in one direction and then the other, his thoughts clearly elsewhere, and then he looked up at Richard. "It is likely that members of this 'Order of the Hand' that we have spoken of can communicate with each other. This being the case, you must contact the museum curator – Banou, you called him. He may be able to cast light on Asharf Makkoum's fate. If indeed he *has* been abducted. That may be the only way you will find Madame Vallogia. I suggest you wait. Although one cannot see it, the Moon shifts from Waxing Gibbous to Full. In four days the transition will be complete – this may have relevance to Madame Vallogia. This being the case, we have time tomorrow to discuss the real reason for your visit." Mubarakar sighed deeply. He looked and felt tired. "But now I must retire. Late nights are not good for me – I am too old. In the morning, after a good Egyptian breakfast, we will discuss what has been found here in Alexandria."

# CHAPTER 12

# THINKING TIME

**South Carolina USA**
**Smallville – same day**
**20:43 Eastern Standard Time**

There were two other people in the black sedan with Miss Abbey Hennessy as it drew up outside a clapperboard house in what would ordinarily would be leafy suburbia. Only here, as with most of the eastern states of America, the North Atlantic weather extended inland further than it should, and that meant blowing fog in the mornings that only loosened into transparent mist much later in the day. However, more often these days, mid-afternoon brought a let-up in precipitation of any kind and that allowed, to some extent anyway, a fleeting return to normality. Nevertheless, by evening, as the temperature fell again, fog seemed to peel itself from beneath the low, dragging cloud and fall to Earth, spreading and infiltrating like crawling tentacles.

Abbey felt a sudden chill as she climbed from the relative comfort of the back seat and stepped onto the sidewalk. There was not a soul to be seen, although she was conscious of curtains being edged aside in several neighbouring houses. The wind blew stronger for a moment, an unexpected flurry, which lifted her coat above her knees and deposited moisture on it in the form of tiny droplets. Children had been playing in the street earlier that day she noticed, as three mountain bikes had been abandoned on the sidewalk along with a football and a baseball bat.

The car on the drive of Number 9 Windy Arbor had clearly been washed that day too; its dark paintwork gleamed in the glow of a security light that was mounted high on the two-storey building. In fact, when compared to others on nearby houses, this light was unusually bright, making the house with its streaky white paintwork stand out. But the garden was drab, washed-out and bereft of colour – that was apparent even in the semi-darkness.

Agent Horowitz of the Central Investigation Bureau pulled open his dark coat in order to expose his shoulder holster. He adjusted his classic Trilby-type hat and watched cautiously from the front passenger seat of the nostalgic-looking Lincoln Continental Electrodrive. The heavy vehicle sat bathed in stripy shadows beneath the branches of a large but near-naked maple tree. The other agent escorted Miss Hennessy along the path towards the front door of the house and, on arrival, he promptly skulked off to the left, to find some cover.

Abbey, whose long silk scarf spilled out over her shoulders, looked to be an unusually tall woman on account of the slimming effect her well-fitted, calf-length, fine woollen coat gave and also her fashionable high heels. She exuded an air of capability as she dwelt on the doorstep, cast her eyes towards the half-concealed agent and then rang the doorbell. Moments later a light came on inside the house to be quickly followed by the inner door being tentatively opened. A man, probably in his sixties, peered through the fly screen of the more flimsy outer door. Abbey showed her identity badge with its 3D image and her holographic passport card. The man, gesturing in a compliant kind of way, unlocked and opened the door. Abbey gave a brief nod to the agent and stepped inside. "Mr Smith, I presume," she said, in her refined English accent.

"You presume right, Mam," answered the man. He had a pronounced southern accent. "You had better come in here . . . please, if you will," he continued, and led the way into a small sitting room. An overhead light came on automatically and cast its effect over a sparsely furnished square-shaped room. There was an open fireplace where a number of small logs glowed in the hearth in a controlled, subdued fashion. "Sorry," the man said, gesturing to a place on a two-seater couch. "Electricity is expensive and when my wood supply is gone – and that's going to be pretty soon – it's gunna get damn cold around here." He sat down opposite Abbey in a comfortable chair and his narrow face contorted to show his indifference. "I'm too old for this. You know that, don't you?" he snapped.

Abbey loosened and dropped her patterned, dark blue scarf and unbuttoned the coat to her waist. Her smooth shoulder-length bleached fair hair held its shape by turning in at the bottom, and her makeup was immaculate, particularly her pale red lipstick. Although in her late fifties, she looked younger. On the other hand, the man looked older than he actually was and his unshaven and unkempt appearance fell well short of his professional reputation. Abbey eyed him for a few moments: his blue jeans, his wide brown leather belt, his open-necked cowboy-check shirt and his scuffed calf leather ankle boots. "You are sixty-three next month, Mr Smith," she said, matter-of-factly. "Retirement age is seventy, and that's global. Unless, of course, and contrary to your profile, you are a man of independent means?"

The man squirmed. He knew that they knew his exact financial status. "Not for this kind of work it isn't," he replied gruffly. "It takes a lot out of you – you've got to be fit, both mentally and physically."

"You are on the CIA's reserve list, Mr Smith. That means you have a responsibility to keep fit." Abbey gave no quarter.

The man's eyes narrowed and he went to speak but Abbey cut him short. "It was you who found our agent in Egypt. That was a brilliant piece of work."

"You mean Richard Reece and that woman, that special woman . . . that was four years ago and it was a biased zone with a narrow profile. What I mean is we had a high probability factor; we knew about Luxor and KV5 used that location to kick off the search – that made it easier. I remember it clearly – you don't forget it when someone senses your presence. She had an ability to see the subconscious. I never heard of that before and never since. Anyway, in this business you need to practice, otherwise you lose the ability . . . to give direction, I mean. You lose it!"

Abbey nodded in an understanding way. "I am aware of that, Mr Smith, but this mission is vital, absolutely vital, both for the US and the United Kingdom. But you already know that, don't you." She pierced him with her eyes. "We need your abilities and your cooperation," she said, forcing her will. "To help you we have recruited Oscar Perram."

Ike Smith's eyes widened. "You've got Oscar! But he left the programme a decade ago."

"He was your best friend for more than twenty-five years, that I know. Within the department your partnership was legendary – you had the best results of any pairing."

Ike Smith nodded and reminisced for a few moments. "He was a good man . . . and a good friend, yes he was."

"He still is both of those things as it happens; it's just that the new identity programme prevents any contact between former operatives – that's standard procedure.

He *is* on-board, Mr Smith, and we need you too." Abbey drew back her pointed stare.

Smith looked warily at her. "Why are the Brits involved in this . . . ? Why not the department?"

"It's our job, Mr Smith. Our agents and our call – quite simple. Of course we will be working in close collaboration with . . ."

"Okay . . . okay, I understand. When then, do we start? And where is it you want me to survey?"

"I am unable to brief you here, Mr Smith, for security reasons. You must realise that." Abbey smiled and her expression softened. "But there is something I must ask you."

"What is it . . . if I can?"

"We are trying to reform an earlier team – from the twenties and thirties. There was a good deal of success during that period within your department; it's well documented, although that information is still top secret. You had two colleagues during those years – Charles Springer and Leon Rickenbach. Like you they have been in . . . semi-retirement, shall we say. The department has tried to contact them, unsuccessfully I might add. It seems that they are missing. Their respective overseers have not heard from them in almost two weeks – that's two compulsory registrations missed. One more, due on the thirtieth – well, that will result in a recall and disciplinary procedures – most unusual, I'm told. Notwithstanding the anonymity protocol, do you have any idea as to their whereabouts, Mr Smith?"

"Those two . . . they weren't colleagues, but I knew them well enough. They joined the programme after me and left before. Unreliable, yeah, always were – rebels, renegades. They got caught surveying the inside of the Shanghai and Oriental Bank once – the US Headquarters on Wall Street. Only they got more than they bargained for, because there was some kind of Feng Shui or something going on inside. It restricted Rickenbach's flow. There were subliminal markers; he disturbed them and the alarms went off. It was Rickenbach who went in and Springer debriefed. They got away with it though. No criminal charges; no prosecution. Why? Because the programme was so secret – they said it was for practice, but everybody knew they were passing information out. Nothing was ever proved." Smith nodded knowingly. "Springer was a dual operative, a surveyor and a debriefer. He had a talent for both, that's true. He was money orientated . . . had no scruples. Nor did Rickenbach. Couldn't see either of them surviving on a pension, not into their old age. The department should be careful, that's my advice."

"So you have no idea where they can be?"

"Don't know, don't care. Anyway, I'm the last person either of them would call. I was the programme's self-defence instructor for more than a decade. Fitness of mind and body is key to extreme distance projection – that's why I did so well in that field. Springer tried his luck once. I put him down well enough."

"I see," said Abbey, thoughtfully. She sat bolt upright

during their conversation. Perched on the edge, she found the couch uncomfortable. She eyed the room for a few seconds before giving Mr Smith her full attention again. "The United States Air Force has kindly provided an aircraft to take us to London," she said. "It is waiting for us now. Apparently, we have an hour's drive to Charleston Airport. How soon can you be ready?"

# CHAPTER 13

# ANCIENT CONSCRIPT

Due to the time difference, Richard had put in a call to Rachel in the early hours. It had been patched through the government system routing by way of an off-shore warship and broadcast via the secure but ageing IMARSAT 2 satellite, care of Peter Rothschild. He was grateful for the opportunity, although Rachel's remarks had left him unsettled for the remainder of the night and now he felt tired. He knew how unimpressed she was with his recall and rightly so, taking its timing into account, but it was hardly his fault. *She had become a difficult woman to please of late,* he mused, and he wondered if the confinement of Andromeda – with its social and cultural limitations – was taking its toll. *But surely no more so than on Mars, and she has been happy there,* he recalled. *Perhaps I should have taken up my old job again, a few years ago, when Commander Miko had offered it, instead of accepting promotion. And there was the religious thing, too – or rather lack of it. Andromeda provided adequate facilities, there was no question of that, and with the expansion every faith had its own place of worship. But she had left God behind on Earth, she said, and that continued to trouble her – perhaps because the permanence of life on the Moon now loomed. Would the fertility programme be the last straw?* His thoughts lingered on her for some time. *She will have finished her duty in the clinic by now and would probably be in the gym starting her daily electrostatic heavy-gravity routine,* he concluded. He breathed a long sigh.

Someone called from outside the room; it was muffled and, together with the accent, quite incomprehensible. Richard sprang out of bed, pulled on borrowed cotton pyjama trousers and half-hopped to the door. Keeping his body concealed he opened the door and pushed his head through the gap. It was the housekeeper, the wife of Ashai – he had met her briefly the evening before. "Oh! Good morning, Hinda. How are you?"

"*Sabah el kheer*, Mr Richard. I am well thank you. The Professor is already in the dining room. Please, breakfast is served." She handed Richard his laundered shirt and trousers and pointed down at his boots that had been cleaned, polished and placed neatly together outside his door. "Ashai," she concluded.

Richard bowed graciously and checked his chronometer. "Jeez, it's almost ten! Sorry. I'll be down in five minutes."

Richard and Professor Mubarakar walked from the impressive dining room, which was more like an art gallery-cum-museum, into a broad hallway. That in turn led to the study – only this time they entered through a secondary doorway. Richard sat in the same chair as he had the previous evening and appeared very satisfied with his breakfast. "Excellent hospitality." he said, "Thank you."

The ever-efficient Hinda, as Richard now thought of her, had left them with a pot of Mubarakar's customary mint tea and the Professor seemed content to sip from his porcelain cup in silence for some time. Eventually, after a second cup, this time sweetened with two generous teaspoonfuls of honey, Mubarakar appeared refreshed enough to tackle the day and he focused his attention on the screen of an electronic tablet reader and began scanning the day's headlines.

Richard, for his part, thinking it polite to allow the Professor his own routine in the morning, wandered the room. He was fascinated by what he saw. More pictures hung on the walls, and a particularly large work that caught his eye was of the familiar Pyramids on the Plain of Giza. The beautiful blue sky made him stare longingly at it. A long camel train comprising twenty or more animals passed in front of the great monuments. It was a desert scene of amazing depth and clarity. Apparently carrying wealthy merchants, as the oil painting was called *Gifts for the Emperor*, each gangling beast was draped in colourful traditional fabrics. The surrounding, sprawling conurbation of Cairo that Richard knew well was nowhere to be seen. It was an inspiring landscape, a scene full of texture, depth and movement.

"1799," said the Professor, proudly, looking up at Richard and then at the masterpiece. "During our occupation by the French. It was painted by one of Bonaparte's favourite war artists, a man called Frederic Garçony. Apparently, so the story goes, he was present when the Emperor ordered the shelling of the Sphinx the previous year, because he thought the monument had a contemptuous smirk, or similar. In reality, he may have been responsible for some minor damage, but primarily it is believed that successive Mamelukes did most of the defacing. Over a period of centuries you understand." The Professor shook his head sadly, as he had probably done a hundred times before at the very thought of it. "And that one," he said with emphasis. "Did you see that great work?" Mubarakar pointed to a much smaller painting to Richard's right. It hung at head height and Richard walked over to it. He could see that it had a naval theme and studied the details keenly. This oil on canvas was less than a metre long and a little over half a metre high, although the wide gilt frame made it look much more substantial. "That one is more up your street, as you English say," Mubarakar added.

Richard stared at the scene for a few moments. Sailing warships from the eighteenth and nineteenth centuries; ships of the line engaged in heated battle. The exploding light around the cannon ports took his eye – Richard sensed the heat. And billowing smoke from a dismasted galleon and the shredded French colours that hung limply from another masthead. Richard gestured his admiration and pointed at particular elements of detail where contoured oils applied with such enviable skill made the sea dark and ominous with its swell and whitecaps and the flotilla of small boats, some with survivors clinging to their toprails and transoms and there, a British Man of War was holding station in the thick of the action. He turned to look at the Professor. "Rear Admiral of the Blue Sir Horatio Nelson on HMS *Vanguard*, against Admiral Brueys d'Aigalliers," he said, with a questioning tone. "Is it an original?"

"I see you know your naval history well, my young friend. The Battle of the Nile, 1st August 1798, also known as Aboukir Bay. It was fought east of here, but not by far. Of course the British Fleet won a resounding victory, arguably one of the decisive battles of naval warfare."

Richard nodded, he knew of it well enough.

"The painting was acquired by my great-great-grandfather . . . from an Egyptian Prince, my father told me. Payment for services rendered, some even said to clear a gambling debt. The artist's name. Do you see it? Do you see it there?"

"John Randolph Scott, 1799," Richard said and shrugged.

"The favoured artist of King George III, you know. You do make me smile, you British, so patriotic and yet that King was from the House of Hanover – he was German!"

"Does the Admiralty know of this work? It must be priceless," Richard said, neutrally, side-stepping the remark.

Mubarakar nodded. There was a glimmer of mischief in his expression. "They know. I told them more than thirty years ago. I would like to . . . exchange it, for a piece of ancient Alexandria – Cleopatra's Needle. What do you say?"

Richard laughed. Cleopatra's Needle . . . ! "That obelisk has stood on the Embankment in London since, well, the eighteen hundreds."

"1878 to be precise, but before that it was here in Alexandria, and before that in Heliopolis for several thousand years. Do you think they will grant a dying man's wishes, um?"

Richard smiled warily. "You are not dying Professor, contrary to popular belief. You are just slowing down a bit – and that's acceptable, even for you. As for an exchange . . . I don't think so, somehow." He shrugged. "Rightly or wrongly, old empires tend to hang on to their contraband. Anyway, if I remember rightly that monument was a gift."

"No doubt you are right."

"You know well enough, Professor." Richard smiled wryly.

Mubarakar leaned back in his chair in a resigned way and took another sip of tea, lifting the cup to his lips with both hands. "Now, Richard," he said, after a few moments and seemingly enlivened by the promise of a new quest, "we must discuss what has been found here in this great city of the past. There is not and never has been another city to match this one, Richard." He pulled some notes onto his lap from the table. "It was a glittering metropolis, founded by those whose ambitions knew no bounds. It was a magical place that boasted one of the Seven Wonders of the World, where intellectual geniuses from both East and West jostled and debated, where, in its great library, the knowledge of the entire planet was contained. Had things been different, Alexandria would be a household name, like Babylon or Athens or Rome, and yet this amazing city with its sprawling suburbs is just a footnote in history. Why?"

Richard fidgeted, wondering where the Professor was going with his history lesson.

"Queen Cleopatra, her lovers Julius Caesar and Mark Anthony, Archimedes, and many other great Greek thinkers all walked its streets," Mubarakar continued, "but what is more important is what they saw here." Mubarakar's eyes sparkled at the thought of it. "Machines roamed elegantly appointed streets. They moved as if alive, Richard . . . all here, where we are. Steam-powered lions, trees full of singing mechanical birds, automatic doors, hovering objects, this is all recorded fact. It is said that the Great Library contained seven hundred and fifty thousand books. The 'chatterers', scribes, the scratching of their reed pens on papyrus, day and night, year after year, the copying of tombs, one after another - the sum of vast but now forgotten knowledge." Mubarakar paused briefly. "Where did it come from, Richard?" He leaned forward to reinforce the gravity of the question. "Historians believe that this city dates from the third century BC, when Alexander the Great first dreamed of dominating the known world. However, I have found proof that it is much, much older. I have found proof that this city served as the sea port to Atlantis, sharing in its technology and ideology. And there were other ports too, in the Eastern Mediterranean. Of lesser importance, it is true."

"But Professor, the existence of that level of science can't be proved – not in Atlantis, not anywhere, at that time. We've been down that road. There is some documentary evidence, mention of it, yes. The mapped coordinates in the spaceship's log I found on Mars, for instance. But the consensus of opinion is that the technology came much later. There's always someone with a better explanation." Richard paused, seemingly a little disappointed. "As far as Atlantis goes, we know of the earthquake and the tsunami, and I read that a good deal of ancient Alexandria still lies beneath relatively shallow water as a result of that catastrophe." Richard shook his head. "I think Atlantis will always be a fable, Professor."

"Not this time!"

Richard breathed out heavily. "What have you got then? And how old? What period are we talking here?" he asked, in a humouring kind of way.

"At least as old as Eridu, and that of the great civilisation in Mexico. It is a shame that nothing remains of Mohenjo Daro in Pakistan."

"How is this going to help, Professor?" Richard asked, unable to hide an element of frustration. "Peter said that you had something to show me, something that might help with our understanding of the crystals."

"And that I have," replied Mubarakar exuberantly. He checked the time again. "My team of archaeologists from the University found it five days ago. There is a diving facility at the docks. That is where we go now. Where is my stick?" At that moment a loud bell sounded outside. Its reverberations still echoed in the hall as Ashai knocked and opened the door to the study.

"Abdel is outside with the car, Professor," he said.

"Good! Precisely on time. You have a fine son there, Ashai."

"He brings good fortune to us all," replied Ashai, bowing slightly. Unable to contain his pride at the remark, Ashai quietly closed the door grinning.

Mubarakar looked up at Richard. "Abdel speaks English as good as his father; it is a great blessing," he commented, before finishing his newspaper.

Richard heard a carriage clock on Mubarakar's desk chime midday.

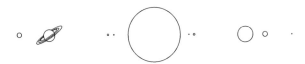

They had been driving for fifteen minutes in Mubarakar's T Class Mercedes when Richard, who was mentally formulating his report to Peter Rothschild regarding the missing Ark, suddenly realised that he had switched off his telephonic pager the evening before and failed to reactivate it. *Rothschild won't be pleased,* he thought, as he unzipped his coat pocket. The car swerved unexpectedly, narrowly missing a wayward cart drawn by a bedraggled donkey. The animal had been foolishly encouraged to hold its own against the bewildering traffic flow and an exploding exhaust pipe had been the final straw, making it rear up in the shafts.

The principal road to the docks was a seething mass that moved at a shuffle. Vehicles of all descriptions – mainly old and makeshift – jostled for space with animals, but pedestrians presented the most difficult challenge as they flooded shoulder to shoulder in both directions, frequently spilling onto the road. They appeared to have little regard for their own safety, let alone respect for the furtherance of commerce.

Preceding them, Richard could see a line of camels, a horse-drawn cart and another donkey – this time heavily laden, and with its owner walking by its side, tapping the required direction of travel with a flimsy stick. In the opposite direction was a rickety bus that belched black smoke from beneath its bonnet. There was an oily smell in the air that reminded Richard of bio-derived aviation fuel. Together they all plied this essential artery.

"I've never seen so many people," remarked Richard,

typing his personal code into the pager.

"Nine million in Alexandria and thirty in Cairo," replied Mubarakar, over his shoulder.

Within seconds the small screen had lit up and the device mildly vibrated in Richard's hand. The numbers *1, 2, 3* and *4* appeared in black emboldened Courier Final Draft font, together with the initials *PR* and the words *Immediate Response* alongside each. *Oh dear,* thought Richard, *in trouble again.* Just then the foolhardy manoeuvring of another Mercedes caught his eye. It was highly polished and appeared to be a new model. It joined the thoroughfare aggressively from a small street on their right. The silvery grey car bullied its way into a position immediately behind them, caring little for the displaced camel and its rider who subsequently struggled to keep the large animal under control and who screamed unheeded obscenities in Arabic. Richard turned to see the commotion gradually subside and the other car tuck comfortably into their lee.

Seemingly immune to the choking atmosphere outside, Mubarakar sat in the front passenger seat with his window open. At times the noise was intolerable. But occasionally someone in the passing throng of people would look enviously at his car and then recognise Mubarakar, subsequently giving a gesture of respectful and friendly acknowledgement. It was clear he was very well known here; *more a national hero,* thought Richard. The almost permanent grin on Mubarakar's face made Richard smile too.

Presently, and after becoming aware somehow that he was being stared at, Mubarakar turned awkwardly in his seat and raised a finger at Richard. "I forgot to tell you that Peter Rothschild called this morning," he said nonchalantly, "just after eight. You were still asleep. He wanted you to acknowledge your security brief. Because there was some measure of dissatisfaction in his tone, I said that I would remind you immediately." He shook his head. "This ageing, it comes to us all, you will see." Mubarakar twisted more and looked Richard in the eye. "Apparently he has sent more than one." Then he nodded, smirked knowingly, and looked forward again.

Richard took a breath and breathed it out forcefully through his nose. "Got it!" he said, and decided not to relay the disquieting news. Then he shuffled around in his seat, lengthening the safety belt a little with his thumb in order to allow a prolonged look behind. It was still there, the Mercedes. Its windscreen had a reflective tint to it making it impossible to see inside. *While I'm with Mubarakar,* he thought, *at least in Alexandria, there will always be some measure of protection.* He replaced his pager into the coat pocket.

## London – simultaneously

Peter Rothschild closed the communication channel and reviewed some data on his computer screen. He tapped his fingers thoughtfully on his desk and cross-checked the name of the agent that would escort Abbey back to the UK. *I trust General Roper and the Americans implicitly, there is no question of that, but there is a security problem with SERON, I know it, and the breach lies within the establishment of our oldest ally. National pride, misplaced patriotism, or just plain simple obstinacy – why won't Roper run a check on their interface? If there is a mole, let's find them, forget the rest of it,* he thought. Now he had this additional problem – an agent from the CIA attending the experiment. The proceedings, and any results, would now be passed back to the United States; quite acceptable under normal circumstances, but once into the American system it was anybody's guess where they could end up. The scenario made him shudder.

Laura Bellingham's voice, emanating from the intercom module, broke the silence of Rothschild's office and his train of thought. "Peter, Laura here," she said, in her efficient tone. "You have been copied in on Professor Mubarakar's recent report to the ISSF regarding his find in Alexandria, and his speculations relating to the pyramids on Mars . . . well, according to the report, it's rather more than speculation, actually –  also their response. Everyone appears to be waiting for Richard's appraisal on that matter. In your message queue there is also a copy of the request from the ISSF to Commander Race, following the incident with their transport vehicle, near Elysium. They want more information as soon as possible and details of the coroner's report."

"Very well, I'll get onto it. Do you have an update on Abbey's arrival?"

"It's a military aircraft if you recall, Peter, and so it's landing at Northolt. Hold on . . . yes, arrival information is giving a little over two hours, as it stands. Apparently there was some delay with immigration, because they departed from a civilian airport and the approvals were late in arriving."

Rothschild nodded. "Okay, understood. What about the *Arius* probe, anything from Brian Grant?"

"Actually yes, just came in. Would you like me to read it to you or send it through?"

"Send it through, Laura." The message box appeared immediately on Rothschild's screen. He opened it and read the comments. "Laura . . . get me a line to Grant, please. Tell him it's urgent!"

"Good afternoon, Peter. I assume you have read the latest update on *Arius*?"

"Yes, indeed. Are you sure about it?"

"Ninety-nine per cent, if you want me to put it like that. The probe is still some way off, but the data is accurate as far as we can tell. Sadly, we were expecting the debris, weren't we? Most of it is concentrated around the *Hera*'s planned orbital trajectory. I do not think there is any mistake about her demise. As for the residual pockets of rocket propellant that we have detected, it's not a type used by the *Hera*'s thrust motors – a much more basic blend of fuel. And the fact that the residue is occurring in a similar elliopheric orbit but on the opposing side of the planetoid means that another craft was present. We could not, however, detect the presence of another vehicle, and the fortuitous electromagnetic window has now closed."

"So you think that this 'vehicle' has now departed?"

"That's my view on it, yes. Another few days and the probe will be in close proximity. Then we will know for sure."

"Okay, that's understood. Thank you, Brian."

## Alexandria
## 13:46 Local Time

Richard caught sight of the sea, momentarily. More, he realised a little later, a huge artificial basin – one where several container ships lay moored alongside long berths. After passing through heavy security gates constructed of steel mesh and topped with electrified wire strands, the traffic had thinned considerably and now only numbered commercial vehicles and the occasional car or two, although many pedestrian workers could be seen going about their business. Egypt's close ties with neighbouring oil-producing states had helped its economy considerably over the last few years, but it was evident by the lack of shipping movements that those privileged times were over.

The other Mercedes, that had seemingly followed them for more than an hour, had been denied entry at the checkpoint and Richard, whose suspicions had become raised, now discounted the incident as opportunism. *They will have been interested in Mubarakar,* he reasoned, as only MI9 knew of his whereabouts. Roadside robbery, extortion, even kidnap. Money was tight everywhere, and he could only imagine the scale of criminality that existed in Alexandria. Moreover and worryingly, Mubarakar did appear to rely heavily on his celebrity for security; *perhaps it was time to mention it to him,* Richard mused.

Abdel, Mubarakar's PA, drove at a leisurely speed for another kilometre to the east side of the docks, finally drawing to a halt in the closest car parking space to a small industrial building. There was a single-storey office space built onto the side of the building and the whole structure was painted in a beige colour, although, where the guttering downpipes were fixed, it was heavily streaked with black grime and mould. The air was heavy with moisture and the smell of salt as it blew from the sea, and although the concrete paving of the car park was darkened with dampness, it was essentially a dry day. As Richard climbed from the backseat he saw a wooden sign secured to the building immediately in front of the car's bonnet. In white lettering the sign read: *University Principal.* Abdel led them inside.


"This is the Assistant Director of Archaeology at the University of Alexandria," said Mubarakar, smiling at the tall, lean Arab. "He is also a skilful and experienced diver. Richard, may I present Hamid Faruq."

Richard stepped forward and shook the man's hand. "Richard Reece," he said, warmly. "UK Government."

At that Mubarakar laughed. "And that covers a

multitude of sins, does it not?"

That raised a smile on all of their faces. Hamid Faruq was in his thirties, had black short hair, keen brown eyes and a firm handshake. Richard took to him immediately. "Good diving around here?" he enquired.

"Not as good as it used to be, I must say," responded Hamid. His English was good, with an educated accent. "However, we dive in water usually no deeper than fifteen metres and so there is still some natural light and the visibility is about thirty metres, which is acceptable for my work."

"Which is, primarily?"

"Most of the old city of Alexandria lies undisturbed below this area of the Mediterranean Sea, Mr Reece. Almost as if it has just been swamped, except of course that there are no people; tens of thousands were lost during the flooding. Where salt water can preserve, it has; where it can erode, it has done that, too. I spend my days swimming along the grand central avenue, visiting ruined theatres, lecture halls and giant temples and sifting through sediment in the world's first museum. That was where I made my find." Hamid gestured for Richard and Abdel to follow him and he gave his patron a helping hand.

The four men walked through a doorway into a much larger adjacent room where there were a number of wooden benches set against the walls. Each had a quantity of diving kit laid out on top that was drying. The floor was wet and there was sand in the corners.

On the other side of the room, leading outside, Richard noticed that there was a reinforced steel entrance door with three digitally controlled strong bolts. In the centre of the room was a long table on which lay a wooden, coffin-like box, but it was more than three metres long and almost a metre wide. Richard walked to its nearside clearly puzzled, while Hamid and Abdel assumed positions at the head and foot. The whitish, softwood lid had a handle at each end, which the two younger men grasped; Mubarakar faced Richard over the prize.

"Before I show you this," said Hamid, concentrating his gaze on Richard, "I would like you to imagine the time in which such a thing was made; to appreciate that perhaps seven thousand years ago there was technology that in some areas surpasses ours even today. Here in this ancient city linguistic codes were devised, water-clocks and steam-engines invented. Philosophers laid the cornerstones for religious thinking and pondered the universe. To all intents and purposes it was a civilisation resembling that of the ancient Greeks. However, it was the Greeks who modelled their society on this one, and theirs occurred many centuries later. Alexander the Great was a prodigal son, a catalyst for reinstatement, and not an originator, as is widely believed."

Richard nodded. *Hamid spoke with great fluency,* he thought. "I have an open mind to all this," he said.

Hamid gestured to Abdel that they should lift the lid together and Abdel made ready with both hands, for it was much heavier than it appeared.

## London – simultaneous

Abbey Hennessy called from the limousine. "Peter!" she said, in her refined manner. "We are on our way. Myself plus two, plus Mr . . . you know, our colleague from the United States Intelligence Service."

"Good. Directly to Whitehall, please, Abbey. The facility is ready and so is the team. There will be time for a wash and brush up, some food and rest and then we start. We enter a critical phase. I'll see you at six. Goodbye."

## Alexandria – simultaneous

It took considerable effort on the part of Hamid and Abdel to displace the wooden lid. The two men were careful to lift it vertically for 150 millimetres or more before shuffling sideways. Mubarakar explained that an inner lid carved from a single piece of quartz – a sarcophagus lid – had been secured by straps to the wooden structure for ease of movement, as there were no handholds on the former and moisture in the air made handling it precarious. Meanwhile, the two men, who were visibly straining, carefully placed the complete structure on a rubber mat that was positioned for the purpose on the floor – and that despite zealous fussing from Professor Mubarakar, which, although well intentioned, was more a hindrance. Richard gazed wide-eyed at what was inside.

Had it been only the tight fitting, semi-transparent crystal coffin that was hewn without join in the most ingenious way, then that would have been impressive enough, but inside that was the most beautiful, precise and lifelike statue that Richard had ever seen. It was in the masculine style of those from the Greek or Roman periods, where often they were painted to be more authentic. But there was no sign of paint or blemish or vein on this masterfully carved artefact. In a pale bronze coloured material the detail was astonishing. It was a man clad in warrior's regalia, including a helmet, chest armour, skirt, gaiters and sandals. Richard immediately associated it with a celebrated painting he had seen of Ares, the God of War from Greek mythology, that hung in the London Museum.

Richard, astonished at what he was seeing, was speechless. Mubarakar and the other two men stared with equal amazement – although by previous examination they were familiar with its contours and had already formulated a hypothesis for the tiny slots around the statue's eyes and mouth.

"Hamid found the sarcophagus buried in sediment in one of the temples close to the central precinct – that was the most important religious area," said Mubarakar, eventually.

"It looks to be made of bronze, doesn't it," said Hamid, rhetorically, running his hands over the fine polished surfaces of the head and neck. He walked to the foot of the statue that was almost three metres tall and a metre wide and directed Richard's attention to some discolouration on the sole of the left foot. "We have run material tests," he continued. "Quite exhaustive ones, using up-to-date equipment. It is not bronze, nor is it iron or tin or any other copper alloy; all reliable traditional materials for such artefacts. In fact we do not know what the material is. It looks like solid rock, doesn't it? But actually it seems to have been cast, like resin poured into a mould. A very advanced process all the same – no bubbling or fractures. It's quite difficult to achieve that even now. I did find some silica compounds and also traces of a chemical polyisoprene. These are elastic hydrocarbon polymers similar to rubber that are derived from latex, all materials that occur naturally here on Earth, as you know. But the main constituent is elusive – I don't think it's from here."

Mubarakar put a hand on Richard's. "See the eyes and mouth . . . we think they must have moved."

Richard's focus shifted from the statue's face to Hamid's. "You mean like a . . . machine?" he questioned.

"You may conjecture," replied Mubarakar. "As men of science, we are not averse."

Richard glanced sideways at the Professor.

"Robots were well documented in Alexandria, Richard. Visitors to the great city wrote of such things in amazement and admiration." Mubarakar's voice trailed to a forced whisper. "This is fact!" His comments added poignancy to the moment.

Hamid nodded in agreement. "I also found some inscriptions; it's what led me to this find. The Gateway to Rhodes was mentioned, and Helios the sun god, a deity attributed to the Rhodians. Also a chant of welcome to Poseidon, the god of the sea to the Greeks; for people living on or close by the sea he was perhaps their most important deity after Zeus himself. In other buildings close to the original wharf I have previously found tablets detailing lists and inventories; huge volumes of stores and provisions passed through this city. These ties and others, Mr Reece, link Alexandria along with Rhodes as serving a much greater population – perhaps that of Atlantis?"

"Not perhaps!" interjected Mubarakar, who shifted from one foot to the other with uncontained excitement. "We think that this statue was the prototype for one of the great wonders of the ancient world."

"What!"

"The *Colossus* of Rhodes, Richard . . . always believed completed in 280 BC, but now known to be much older. It stood thirty metres high, more than one hundred feet – almost as tall as the Statue of Liberty. It was believed to have straddled the grand harbour of Rhodes by standing on white marble pedestals, and was only brought down by a huge earthquake many years later. There are historical records to this fact." Mubarakar's eyes sparkled. "Perhaps the same earthquake that destroyed the greatest sea city ever to be built . . ."

Richard shrugged awkwardly. "What makes you say that, Professor?"

"On the back of this statue we found a panel about . . ." Mubarakar formed a square shape by holding his hands together. ". . that sort of size. Inside this panel are mechanisms and an orifice for a power source. There are also inscriptions. We do not understand them. However, there is one pictogram we do recognise, because Hamid has seen it elsewhere in this underwater world. In the Temple of Sirius, Richard, perhaps the largest of the religious buildings, Hamid found a stone plaque inscribed with the same pictogram and beneath it, in First Dynasty Egyptian hieroglyphs, Sumerian *and* a later inscription in Ancient Greek – because the carver was opposite handed – were the words *Great city of light*."

Richard put a hand on the box to steady himself. "Oh, wait a minute! Don't tell me!" he barked incredulously. "You think that this . . . machine . . . was powered by a crystal, don't you? A Kalahari crystal. And not only that, you think that it originated in Atlantis! Come on Professor, I'm open to most things but that's not science, that's not even . . . With respect, Professor, that's pure supposition. It's ridiculous."

Mubarakar's eyes narrowed. "Engineers and architects through the ages have always believed that the *Colossus* of Rhodes was too much of an engineering feat for the time. This *is* a fact accepted by many historians and archaeologists. The scale of it; the leverage produced by the extended limbs; the scaffolding required from the sea bed to its pinnacle – a finger was believed bigger than a person!" Mubarakar squared up to Richard. "We know that the crystal salvaged from the ruins of Eridu journeyed south in the Ark of the Light. We know that the ancient coastal trading route from Mesopotamia to

Thebes took it this way and later past the Great Pyramids at Giza. And we know that from Thebes the Ark was taken to the city of Meroe, the centre of the Kushite Empire and thereafter to Adulis. That and the remaining passage to Venice we know to be true, thanks to your exploits. I believe that the crystal stopped here in Alexandria for a brief period during that journey."

Richard clasped his hands behind his head and breathed out heavily. "This is what you have to show me?" He glanced unimpressed across the statue and up at Hamid. "You'll be telling me next that the mighty *Colossus* walked itself into place two thousand three hundred years ago!"

"We believe it to be more like seven thousand years ago," replied Hamid, with a glower.

"Professor, please, it's an amazing discovery, really it is, but be serious, this isn't science it's speculation. And it's not helping the present situation regarding the crystals. Peter Rothschild believes that you are onto something . . . something that's going to help the crucial energy situation. Well he's going to be very disappointed, isn't he?"

"Richard, my young friend, we will show you the mechanism inside this statue, that is the simple part. You must trust me when I say that this machine holds a key. I believe it will speak to us. But for this to happen we need a crystal."

"And where do you think you are going to get one of those from, eh? Each crystal currently supplies a whole region with electricity. Do you think that they will just switch off a reactor and let you borrow one for a few days . . . ? Come on, sir."

"Then we miss a calling from the stars . . . from the old people. We forego an opportunity for enlightenment. That is all I can say."

Richard, about to speak, stopped short. *Was he being disrespectful?* he pondered. What about the lateral thinking that he was renowned for . . . what about his open mind? He considered, in that instant, *his* crystal, his secret; would that remnant activate this machine? Would this robot actually talk to them? Was it an opportunity that could not be missed? He rubbed his chin thoughtfully and asked: "What language did they speak in Alexandria at that time, Professor?"

"Ha!" Professor Mubarakar smiled broadly. "Ancient Greek . . . There were three periods – Archaic, Classical and Hellenistic – and also several regional dialects evolved. But we think the Hellenistic phase, also known as Koine or 'common', is most appropriate."

"Do you speak it?"

"No. I do not."

"Or you Hamid . . . ? Abdel?"

Both men shook their heads. "It is a lost language, Mr Reece, and therein lies another problem," added Hamid. "Finding such a scholar will be difficult, if not impossible."

"I might be able to help on both counts," replied Richard, after a period of silent consideration. "I just can't be specific at the moment regarding the crystal thing. But Madame Vallogia speaks a number of ancient tongues – she is your best bet." Richard turned to the Professor. "Not here, though. I'm worried about her as you know and I intend starting my search in Cairo as soon as I can. Peter Rothschild is expecting me back in London tonight. My flight leaves at eight – that only gives me a few hours. I've yet to contact him but I expect he wants my report by tomorrow morning. I've also something I need to collect from Somer . . ." Richard stopped short and then raised a finger in proposition. "Listen, Professor, can you get this statue to Cairo – that might work out. I'll talk Rothschild into sending me there, too. We could meet up at the Central Museum. In two days perhaps?"

"Yes I can do that. Hamid will secure the crate and I will arrange a vehicle – not by train, it is too dangerous. Nothing is sacred these days."

"This . . . machine . . . may or may not work for us as you are suggesting, Professor, but extracting knowledge from the past, that is something I have not considered. You've given me an idea. It seems that all roads lead to Madame Vallogia again," concluded Richard.

# CHAPTER 14

# THE SCIENCE SYNERGY

**Whitehall London – same day**
**Defence Directorate Facility**
**21:30 Greenwich Mean Time**

It was a large room with subdued lighting. There were no windows and only one solid door. Every surface was painted in a mid-grey colour, making the environment feel bland and cold and even a little disorientating. However, the temperature was carefully controlled at twenty-three degrees Celsius. The room could have been anywhere in the maze of offices and experimental chambers of the MOD building, but it was, in fact, two levels below the surface and in the acoustically isolated E Wing.

There was a black leather recliner-type chair – like

a barber's chair – in the centre of the room and on it lolled the figure of Ike Smith. He was staring blankly at the ceiling. Next to him, and sitting in a swivelling high-backed chair, like a therapist listening to a patient's psychological problems, was another man. He was balding and what little hair he had – at the sides and over his ears – was white. His face was narrow, a little drawn and tired looking, but his eyes were a vibrant blue. He held an electronic notepad in his hands and was speaking to Smith in a friendly way; they even shared a joke. This was Oscar Perram.

Peter Rothschild, Abbey Hennessy and another two men watched the proceedings through a one-way mirror from a neighbouring room. The Americans had insisted that one of their specialist agents be present for the experiment despite having little faith in a positive outcome. Indeed, a result of any kind would be surprising.

Peter Rothschild, checking the time, looked a little dishevelled – this being due, in the most part, to the pressures of a long day in the office. The smart, sharp, 'city look' created by his well-fitting navy-blue, pin-striped, Savile Row suit was offset by his pallid features and the emerging stubble around his chin. Abbey Hennessy, on the other hand, was her usual pristine-looking self. Her pale skin was made flawless by face powder which contrasted with subtle red lipstick and expertly applied mascara. She looked stern and business-like in her black trouser suit and if she felt jetlagged, it did not show.

The British scientist, a gangly elderly man, dressed in a well-worn country tweed suit, was Edward Blake. He held a Doctorate in Paranormal Studies and headed a small, underfunded department based in Cheltenham that offered advice in the obscure field of Parapsychology. He was the government's expert on such matters, although budget restraints allowed only fragmented research. It was, by definition, a quiet job.

The other man, the American agent, was short and stocky with black hair that matched his 'rat pack' era suit, with its narrow jacket lapels and drainpipe trousers. He wore shiny black shoes, a white shirt and a black tie with a very small knot. He looked sly, observant and self-sufficient and had said little other than that expected for continued *entente cordiale* between the two national agencies.

The group watched closely as Oscar Perram administered an injection of psychoactive compound into his friend's forearm. The sleep-inducing properties of the narcotic soon had Ike Turner lying limply on the reclined chair. Perram checked his watch and – by adjusting a rotary button on the armrest of his own chair – reduced the subdued lighting still further.

During their oceanic flight the two men had caught up on old times and it was clear that theirs was a renewed relationship of mutual respect, admiration and experience. For a Remote Viewing – or RVer – pairing to be successful this appreciation was critical. Subsequently, upon their arrival at the Ministry of Defence, they had been briefed by Peter Rothschild as to the vital nature of the two proposed surveys, while Edward Blake had provided the perception parameters. Now, as Ike Smith fell into a controlled, trance-like state, the five observers prepared for a long night.

A term derived from the secretive cold war era of the mid to late twentieth century, *Remote Viewing* is the use of paranormal techniques to seek impressions or 'survey' unseen, inaccessible and often distant targets. For as long as records had been kept on the subject, it was known that extra-sensory perception, or sensing with the mind, was a gift that very few people were blessed with and that over the centuries such ability was inevitably viewed with trepidation. In Medieval times it was viewed as divisive and threatening.

Remote Viewing was popularised in the 1990s following declassification of secret documents by the government of the United States of America. There, decades of Federal-sponsored experimentation had been carried out to determine the potential military application of psychic phenomena and the programme had had some measure of success. Renowned were the location of a downed Soviet bomber in Africa, that a US President later referred to in speeches, and the description of a new class of Soviet strategic submarine by a team of three viewers. Although considerable scepticism surrounded the programme and paranormal studies generally, when it became known that both the USSR and China were conducting their own research into extra-sensory-perception, then budgetary allocations and other resources were prioritised.

Experimentation was focused on individuals who were thought to be psychically gifted and the concept and development of the 'surveyor' and 'debriefer' partnership had produced, arguably, the most notable results. However, and certainly as far as public expenditure was concerned, the US programme was said to have been terminated in 1995 due to a lack of scientifically proven value to the intelligence community.

Typically, a Remote Viewer would be allocated a specific target and be expected to provide a 'psychic picture' of it. The target was most often an object that was unreachable. Differing techniques were developed to interpret the image seen by the mind traveller and often the debriefer would draw the results on a sketch pad after close consultation.

Whilst Edward Blake and the American took a natural break, and with Abbey Hennessy sipping her second cup of Earl Grey tea, Peter Rothschild received an abrive; it was from Richard. Rothschild checked the time and re-read the text. It was ten minutes to midnight. *Better late than never,* he thought. Standing at the viewing window, he watched Ike Smith's body twitch occasionally and his closed eyelids flutter during his opioid-induced and apparently uneasy sleep. Oscar Perram, attentively sitting at Smith's side, typed the occasional note into his electronic tablet. Rothschild pulled his gaze away and turned slowly to face Abbey, who sat comfortably at a table in the far corner of the observation room. "How much longer?" he quizzed, impatiently.

"He has two targets to survey, Peter. That's unusual and rather difficult, by all accounts. Made more so I suspect by his lack of practice . . . They said two to three hours – not long now."

Rothschild nodded and then paused thoughtfully. "I'm placing Richard Reece back under your control," he continued, "from 09:00 tomorrow morning. He's telling me that he will be in my office at 08:00 with his report." Rothschild paused again. "He hasn't changed, you know. I'm fed up with his contempt for procedures. I sent him four Code One security messages, the ones I copied you in on. He has just responded – twenty-four hours later. Fortunately, he is safe and on his way back. With that Karl Rhinefeld character on the loose again and no doubt working for Spheron, I fear for his safety."

"He's his own man, Peter. In many ways that's a good thing in this business. I haven't seen him since his wedding reception, and after Rachel retired from the department, what, three years ago now, I haven't had cause to speak to him either. Nevertheless, I'll have a quiet word on disciplinary matters . . . after you have finished with him of course."

At that moment a buzzer sounded and, almost immediately, Blake and the American walked back into the room. "He's coming round," said Blake, as he took up station at the window.

Rothschild followed him over. "Can we have the microphone on now please?" He spoke into a wall-mounted intercom box.

Perram responded immediately, but the first sentence that emanated from the adjacent speaker was clipped.

". . . old and unpractised for this," complained Smith, with his hands over his face. "It's difficult . . . blurred."

"Take your time, Ike. Think about it. You know the technique. Reform the images in your mind – revive them. Now, in your own time, tell me what you saw."

As Ike Smith lay still and closed his eyes, Perram leaned across and put a hand on the top of his head – it was a calming influence.

"I'm on my way . . . Not there yet. Not where I'm going . . . It's cold, damn cold, and dark, and barren – a hell of a place. The landscape, it's dead, you know – no energy, no glow, no sunlight. That's . . . That's behind me. I sense the sunlight behind me. But it's not here, Oscar, not where I am!" Smith put his hands to his face again. His brow began to glow with sweat.

"I understand Ike. A cold, barren place, undulating, dark, inhospitable, no life energy – no impressions . . ."

"Yes, that's it, that's the place." Smith's body jerked and then relaxed again. "I, I . . . see movement though, lots of movement – things, like activity. Can't focus. Trying to focus. Been so long."

"You're doing just swell, Ike. What . . . ?"

"Wait! I sense something over me, moving over

me . . . over there now, but, but, no life energy . . . it's not right, it's not where I'm going – this is not the place . . ."

There was a pause. The four observers stared. Perram put a hand on his friend's shoulder. "Okay, okay, that place is negative; I understand that. Don't let it hold on to you. Move on. Move on, Ike," said Perram, reassuringly.

"It's a long way . . . haven't been this far. Never have I been this far." A bead of moisture ran down Smith's temple. "Can't get lost here – wouldn't get back . . ."

"You're not gonna get lost, Ike. You're gonna do this and come back. I'm waiting for you."

Smith nodded in a strange, subconscious way. His elbows flopped onto the chair by his sides and his hands went limp. It was an enlightening experience for Peter Rothschild and he watched Smith closely. Rothschild's natural reaction to the event was suspicion. And incredulity. It appeared to be a different part of Smith's brain that was responding – a different level of consciousness.

"There!" said Smith suddenly, and his legs jerked again.

"What is it, Ike? What's coming in?"

"An object with shape – it's got form alright, yes!" replied Smith immediately.

Perram put a hand on Smith's forehead; he could feel the dampness. "Tell me about it," he said quietly but compellingly.

"Bulky . . . large . . . not a natural shape like a rock . . .

metallic and dark coloured."

"Go on."

"Um, um, I can make out long tube-like structures. Travelling too fast though, gee, it's travelling." Smith rolled his head from side to side. His eyes remained tightly shut. "It passed me by," he added, almost apologetically. "I couldn't keep up – fastest thing I've ever . . ."

"No problem, Ike. Relax, let's think again. Concentrate on those first few moments." Perram pulled a handkerchief from his pocket, shook it open and dabbed Smith's brow. "Now, reform the image in your mind. It's approaching . . . here it comes . . . here it comes . . . Now, Ike, tell me, what do you see?"

"It's bulky – a regular shape, like a box. It's dark, difficult to make out any detail. There's a blur at the front, and a distortion around it too. Difficult . . . I can't . . . those tubes again . . . it's gone already! There's a glow in its wake. I can't see it. It's gone – just disappeared!"

Oscar Perram swivelled in his seat and faced the large mirror. He looked up from his notes and shrugged. "The best he could do. It's been a long time. We may be able to fill in a few more minor details given some time. Sometimes there are a few residuals – they hang over. Perhaps in a few hours," he said.

Rothschild's nod was unseen by Perram. "I understand. Let's move on, shall we?"

Perram turned back to his colleague. "This is a big challenge for you, Ike, isn't it?" he asked, quietly. "First they want us to retire on a pension that wouldn't keep a racoon and then they want two for the price of one." He smiled.

Ike Smith raised a half-hearted grin that showed his bad teeth. He dropped his head back on the chair and closed his eyes. There was silence for at least a minute. "Here's what I saw, Oscar," he whispered.

"I'm here. Go on."

"It's brown . . . everywhere is brown, a rusty, reddish colour, you know, maybe more brown than red, sometimes there is a streak of . . . orange, yeah, like that."

"What a place, Ike."

"You betcha. The air is red too. Dust and bits blowing around. I think there's a strong wind. I see the pyramid, can't miss it, and there is one behind me too. Gee, they're big. Can't see the tops. It's not clear. I'm in a kind of precinct, like a central square. It's flat, broad." Smith moved uneasily in the chair. The muscles in his face strained; there was a nervous tension building in his body. "It's draining, Oscar, this one," he croaked, "too far again, I can't . . ."

"Take it easy. There's no rush, Ike. Just let the image come back to you, let it float in your mind for a while. Let it sharpen up first – like we used to do."

Ike Smith nodded. "I'm going to the pyramid . . . don't know which one. I'm seeing things – tracks; there are a lot of them. Wait! I'm seeing something, yeah, I saw it. There's something here – moving like a man. No, it's not clear, maybe not."

"It's a door, Ike. That's what you are looking for. A way in – look for a way in!"

"I'm seeing some steps. They go up, a long way up, towards the top. I'm going . . . Level again, no door, flat, but no door."

"And . . ."

"In the stone, there, a hand, yeah, a hand . . . from a person? There is something about it – it's got like a glow. It, like, gives off something, can't explain . . ."

"A way in, Ike. Please, try to focus. Can you see an entrance?"

"Don't need that. I'm inside – no door. Ugh! Would ya take a look at that! Amazing! Like . . . makes me think of a fores— . . . trees, so many trees, but everything is dead . . . it's all dead, dead . . . like . . . ."

Suddenly Smith began to tremble. His whole body began to shake. Perram dropped his tablet and put his hands on Smith's forearm and head. "Okay, Ike. It's okay. Come back now, come back."

Smith's head rolled from side to side. He reacted as if he had a heavy fever. Blood flushed his forehead and beads of moisture appeared. Perram pushed him down against the couch-like chair. "Come back to me now. Ya hear me, Ike. Come back. Three, two, one, *now*!"

Ike Smith's eyes opened instantaneously. He gasped. He clasped his hands over his face. Then his body went limp.

"You're okay, Ike – safe, back with me. You're done."

Smith uncovered his face to see Perram glaring down at him. There was fright in his eyes. He took a deep breath, held it, and then nodded in a controlled way.

"What the hell was that all about?" Perram asked, with a frown.

"Inside, Oscar – there was energy, overpowering energy. It filled my senses. Left over from something, you know, unfinished, forgotten – it confused me. I was disorientated. Sorry, I lost it."

Perram sat down and picked up his electronic tablet. His fingers danced over the screen as he made notes. Occasionally he looked up at Smith and studied him, as if confirming his diagnosis. After a while Perram stood and put a hand on his old friend's shoulder. "You're gonna take a few days off," he said, in a way that a doctor with a good bedside manner would. "We'll talk about this again. Take a few minutes to lock it down, Ike, if you can. That helps with residuals – you remember that. Then go and take a shower, why don't you. I'll arrange something for you to eat – don't suppose these Brits have hamburgers, do you?"

Smith kneaded his temples for a moment, shook his head about the hamburgers, and smiled gratefully. With that, Perram left the room.

The group of five sat around the circular table. Abbey Hennessy placed a small recording device in the centre and activated it. A tiny green light illuminated on one end. Rothschild's natural scepticism raised his eyebrows as he looked at Abbey, who, on the other hand, appeared much more open minded; it was her research that had brought about the experiment and the funding. The

American agent sat stony-faced; he was there to listen and not to talk. And all the while, Edward Blake typed copious notes into his own notepad. He seemed to be in his element.

"Would you say it was a reliable outcome or not?" opened Rothschild, getting straight to the point.

"Listen, sir, with all due respect," responded Perram, a suggestion of protest lacing his tone, "Ike's been in retirement and so have I. We're not as sharp as we used to be – and that's the truth of it. But I'm telling you, although we're lacking specifics here, that's a good effort."

Rothschild nodded appreciatively. "I understand. So in that case could you outline your thoughts for us, please?"

"Yeah, sure, this is what I think. . ." Perram referred to his notes. "That object, coming towards us, it's a long way off, right?"

"About nine light months, I'm reliably informed," replied Rothschild.

Perram's eyes widened. "That far, eh!" He shrugged and looked impressed. "Ike did well."

"Time is of the essence," said Rothschild.

"Yeah. Well, it's not a piece of rock; it's got form. So you can discount a small comet or a meteorite, and space debris too for that matter. Ike saw a square shape, with some kind of propulsion tube. Make of that what you will, but I think it's a ship of some kind. Obviously, it's not from these parts."

"You think from another galaxy?" asked Abbey.

"There are plenty of stars in this one, Mam. Maybe you should cast your mind back to twenty-sixteen – consider the alien visitings. Maybe they are trying their luck again. As for the Elysium Pyramids on Mars, only once before do I recall seeing Ike so scrambled. My guess, and it's only a guess, is that there's a lot of residual psychic energy inside."

"You mean the pyramids are hollow, definitely hollow?" Edward Blake shifted excitedly in his chair.

"There's no doubt in my mind about that, sir. Ike saw something inside . . . trees, he said. He was going to say *forest*. Sounds impossible but . . ."

"What do you mean by psychic energy?" Rothschild asked.

"The energy of life! Or more than likely, in an environment like that, the energy that remains after life. If there was some kind of – vegetation – inside, then the energy would have been contained. A forest? Wow, it would have been brimming. It doesn't matter, you know. Animal or plant, there's always energy. It's just on a different level to ours. Ike's manipulating his own psychic energy in order to travel. He's projecting it – it's a gift. Control comes with technique and practise. Knowing about this energy and using it is one thing, understanding it, well, that's something else entirely."

"How long would it last?" Rothschild enquired, the scepticism disappearing from his manner.

"This type of energy, the energy of life . . . it doesn't disappear. It can change form and move on, but it never dissipates into nothing. Think of the relativity equation – mathematics proves it: there has to be a constant. I'm telling ya. Enclosed by stone walls like that, probably hundreds of feet thick and particularly in the shape of a pyramid, I mean contained by the universal denominator . . . " Perram drew a deep breath. "It could last, well, indefinitely."

Rothschild raised his eyebrows for more information.

Perram shrugged. "I wouldn't know, sorry, nothing to base it on - but certainly tens of thousands of years, probably more."

"I see," said Rothschild. "And the hand-shaped thing . . . what was that all about?"

"I don't know about that either. If I was to guess, I'd say that it's a key. A special key in a meaningful shape – symbolic. There would be relevance to it, sure there would."

"Why?"

"Why a key? Because it was outside, some way up and on a flat platform – where you might expect a doorway, you know, some kind of entrance. Think of the ancient pyramids in South America, same sort of architecture." Perram's mind drifted and his eyes went blank. "We did some work down there once, a few years back. Jeez! That was confusing. Positive, negative . . . conflicting . . . Ike took some time off after that job." Perram snapped back to reality and he looked Rothschild in the eye. "To Ike, the hand he saw was glowing, that usually means it has energy, or in this case perhaps, residual energy. I don't know, maybe it's still active . . . a key that would work?"

Rothschild looked at Abbey. "We need to formulate a report and get it over to the ISSF. Some urgency about it I would say. Perhaps copy in General Roper and Commander Race in Osiris Base to save time – I'll deal with the protocol. Our recommendation will be the lifting of the no-go zone around Elysium and an expedition as soon as possible. We need to take a closer look at these structures."

"Don't forget that Ike saw something moving outside those pyramids," Perram interjected. "He was quite clear about that."

Rothschild nodded in response. "Be sure to put that in the report, Abbey, please." Rothschild glanced at the American. "Presumably you will formulate your own report and send it to Langley."

The man nodded. "It will go up the line from there. Can't say more than that," he answered, bluntly.

"Edward, anything from you?" asked Rothschild, shifting his gaze and softening his expression.

"Well yes, as a matter of fact there is. Rather interested in the first image that Mr Smith described. The barren landscape – a place sheltered from the sun. Quite a foreboding place it seemed to me. Bit of activity there. What would you say?"

"You're right. I overlooked that," said Perram, referring to another page in his notes. "It's a good question. Clearly, Ike passed this place on his journey to the object, so it's between us. He sensed a good deal of movement but no life. Seems odd, doesn't it?"

"Could that image be what you have previously called 'residual'? Something left over. What I mean is, could it have been buried in his memory from a previous journey?"

"No, that's not possible this time. Images from previous encounters would dissipate after a few months and certainly a year or so – that's been our experience. Ike and I have been out much longer than that. No. This is new. It's current, if you like. Definitely part of this viewing and what's more I noted it as a very strong recollection."

"So, where is it, would you say?" pressed Rothschild.

"Between the Earth and that space quadrant . . . ?" Perram thought for a moment. Well there aren't too many places it can be, are there?"

Dressed all in hospital whites – as was Ike Smith – the ageing man with his slightly obstinate manner sat passively waiting for Rothschild to formulate his own conclusion. His role was to present the facts – that was all.

Rothschild leant forwards and stared intently. "Are you thinking what I'm thinking, Mr Perram?"

"Listen . . . sir. Believe or don't believe, it's up to you. I get paid either way. But I would check out the dark side if I were you – just to be sure."

# CHAPTER 15

# INCOMPLETE TAPESTRY

**Whitehall London – next day**
**08:07 Greenwich Mean Time**

Richard was shown to the chair in front of Peter Rothschild's desk by Laura Bellingham. It had been an uneventful flight from El Nozha Airport and he had arrived at the MI9 Headquarters in a timely manner, having rested, showered and breakfasted in a 'grace and favour' apartment in Westminster Palace. He was surprised to hear that Rothschild was running behind schedule. *Laura's a little sheepish this morning and it's unusual for Rothschild to be late,* he thought, as he sat quietly with both hands on his lap. He looked at the marks on his hands from the fight in the barn. A few minutes later and looking pensive, Laura Bellingham arrived with the cup of tea that she had promised, although slightly disappointingly, the preferred mug was replaced by a bone china cup and saucer. *Standards,* he thought, thanking Laura with a smile. She left the door ajar.

Richard surveyed the small but stately looking room with its wooden panelling and two picture windows and was beginning to think it quite familiar. Rothschild's desktop was clear except for a telephone receiver, a traditional table lamp with a cream-coloured silk shade and a small integrated communications panel that protruded above the polished teak by about three centimetres. The panel housed a variety of switches and buttons. Outside, across the river, the sky was only just beginning to lighten and the fuzzy scene was reflected on the desktop. He sipped his tea and checked the time again.

At nineteen minutes past the hour, Richard heard the voice of Rothschild outside. Unexpectedly sharp, he barked a number of instructions to Laura and then strode into the room. Richard stood out of politeness and offered a friendly smile but there seemed a black cloud over Rothschild's head that followed him to his desk. He sat down, switched on the communications panel with a stab of his finger, sighed and shook his head in apparent frustration. Richard carefully lowered himself back into the chair and resisted taking another slurp of his tea. *Here we go,* he thought.

"Do you know that a Code One message requires

an immediate response, Richard," Rothschild blurted, for his opening salvo. "Actually, the manual says within fifteen minutes unless in a life-threatening situation!"

Richard shrugged. "Um, well, yes, I suppose."

"You suppose! I sent you four Code One messages – each one more important than the last and each warning of a potential threat to your life. Your first response was twenty-four hours later!"

"Yes, right, that's not so good, is it?" Richard rubbed the back of his neck with his hand. "So, um, our friend Rhinefeld is back."

"He might be your friend, Richard, but he's certainly not mine." Rothschild shook his head and breathed out heavily. "Listen man, you must toe the line. We can't have you doing your own thing out there, there's too much at stake. Follow the rules for God's sake, that's all I ask. Otherwise you are going to get yourself killed and probably others too."

Richard nodded apologetically. "Copied," he said.

"Right . . . enough said." Rothschild paused to take stock. "Now, with reference to Alexandria – I received your report yesterday evening but I haven't had a great deal of time to look at it. I understand Mubarakar's onto something, but it needs more work, that's the gist . . . correct?"

"Yes, he's found something. It's a primitive robot of sorts, believe it or not. It may hold clues to the original use of the crystals by the old people and that may help with how we utilise the ones we have – it's definitely worth pursuing. He was going to make arrangements to transport it to Cairo, to the central museum – better facilities and security. Today or tomorrow I expect. We can work on it there and . . ."

"We?"

*This is the difficult bit,* thought Richard. "I need to get back to Cairo as soon as possible, Peter, and not just to rendezvous with Mubarakar. Madame Vallogia is still missing."

"I see."

"I managed to contact a few of her old friends – she doesn't have any immediate family. No one has seen or heard from her for the best part of three weeks and it's been a month since she was last in her apartment. The cleaning agency told me that. She has duties in Cairo and she visits three days before the full moon each and every month without fail. The next full moon is in two days' time. On top of that Asharf Makkoum has disappeared too, as has the Ark – I told you that. I'm becoming increasingly concerned. To be honest, I think she's been kidnapped, but of course I've got no proof of that."

"Well we can't go around jumping to conclusions, can we? That may draw some unwelcome attention. But yes, I understand your concerns. There's a lot of subversive activity going on at the moment and I don't like any of it. The Paris affair, for example; I thought the primary target may have been the Secret Service agent who escorted you – a revenge contract or similar. They wanted you because of what you may have seen – naive of me really. And there's been trouble in Mexico – that's how we found out about Rhinefeld. I think he's after you, Richard. I think that he has been specifically recruited for that job, in fact. After all, he's got a grudge hasn't he? And, by all accounts, a permanent limp as a result of your last meeting."

"Karl Rhinefeld on my tail again – that's all I need." Richard's brow furrowed. "He's very resourceful. I wouldn't put it past him to use Naomi Vallogia as a way of getting to me."

"Quite. And don't forget that you were supposed to accompany Professor Jones to Uxmal. It's rather fortuitous that you didn't. Points to them knowing your whereabouts in advance. There's nothing I hate more than a mole. Just adds to my headache."

"You've got a headache over me, Peter? How touching."

"It's not just *your* life at risk here, Richard. So I suggest a little maturity."

"Yes, right." Richard's misplaced grin faded. He scratched his temple and after a lengthy pause he said: "Rhinefeld was brought in by Spheron the last time, and we know the other two conglomerates had an equal hand in that conspiracy. I know you think there is a resurgence in their illegal activities. Is this the proof you need to go to the ISSF about your suspicions?"

Rothschild shook his head. "All I'll say at the moment is this. The initial report from an ISSF-commissioned investigation into Epsilon Rio's manufacturing activities over the last financial year has been promulgated. Of course their management was highly obstructive. A good deal of the information was derived from online accounts, including those of several suppliers. Large discrepancies were discovered and as a result a team went in immediately. Amongst other things, it seems that material deliveries, particularly of etheral alloy, celluloid and an advanced electrolytic fluid called Zimteflate Zaragon 4000, far outstripped what would nominally be required to construct their annual allocation of low-grade cyber systems. It appears that they have been running a parallel production line for some time, only it's not clear what, exactly, was being built. The facility was being dismantled when the inspection team arrived. Apparently, had they been given another week or so, there would have been no evidence to suggest that such a facility had ever existed. Further, the authorities have traced at least one unauthorised shipment to the Huang Hai Industrial Zone in Eastern China. There was no inventory relating to the shipment and no addressee has been found either. However, it is well known that Tongsei Heavy Industries unofficially governs that zone."

"Are you thinking Humatrons, Peter?" Richard frowned. "I've heard of that Zaragon 4000 electrolyte before, although I can't recall where."

Rothschild shook his head. "We don't know. It seems the cover-up has been well orchestrated. Material orders are being examined closely in order to get an idea of residuals, but that could take a few weeks. Between them, and despite attempts at regulation, these conglomerates completely control a variety of vital sectors. They have developed monopolies that the International Commission can't seem to break. Spheron, for example, manufactures more than half of the world's pharmaceuticals and Tongsei effectively oversees the world's mineral wealth. Nobody wants to upset them – they respond with heavy-handed methods: people go missing. We have to be sure. Anyway, there are many other things pressing."

Rothschild's attention was attracted by a red flashing light on the communication panel. "Please excuse me," he said, and he opened the left-hand desk drawer and initialised his projected desktop computer keyboard. His personal code activated a notebook with a glass lid that Richard had seen before and, after removing it, he closed and locked the draw again. *His meticulous attention to security borders on the obsessive,* thought Richard.

Rothschild looked up and stared at Richard for a moment. Richard fidgeted slightly as if his thoughts had been overheard. "In the early hours of this morning," continued Rothschild, "I passed the initial results of a particularly interesting experiment to Brian Grant. It seems Brian has worked through the night. I'll put the call on speaker." With that Rothschild pressed a button. "Laura, open the line please . . ."

"Peter, Brian Grant here. Thanks for picking up – I know how busy you are. Listen, the results of the RVer experiment that you sent me . . . something's come up and it can't be coincidence. It seems that a good deal more credit is due to those Americans than was first thought."

"Go on . . ."

"News from the ALMA submillimetre deep space telescope in Chile . . . the facility manager's latest update."

"Yes, go on."

"The object continues to close rapidly. There is no change in its trajectory – it's still coming directly towards us. The distance is now nought point five eight light months. Based on current computations, Mr Grillo has stated that we can expect an impact in six days and eighteen hours. This includes a deceleration permutation and other measurements. Based on this, the IFFS Council is meeting shortly to review the Icarus protocol. It seems that this time they may instigate *Icarus Imminent*."

"So they know where it's going to hit?"

"No, not exactly – it's still too far away."

"Well how can they make that decision if they don't know which areas need evacuating?"

"It appears that many of the delegates are growing nervous about the lack of action. They want to move to the next phase in order to mobilise the military generally and other national and international resources. The protocol wasn't designed for an incoming at this speed."

"I can understand that, but we must work with what's in place, otherwise it will be a free-for-all. The protocol parameters are quite clear. To go *Imminent* we need to know the exact point of impact. What are the Prime Minister's advisors saying on this?"

"Admiral Hughes is over there now, as is Professor

Nieve. No statement has been issued as yet. The thing is, Peter, there's been a development, but nobody's taking it seriously. That's where your RVer report may help. It may add weight to the hypothesis. I think we need to release the report to the committee, even though it's only a first draft."

"What hypothesis?"

"Listen, the telescope in Chile has been picking up a radio signal for a few hours now. They thought it was spurious at first because of its random nature. But it appears to be coming from the object and that appears more and more likely as it gets nearer. Mr Grillo's team have checked and rechecked their calculations and he's convinced."

"What about the facts?"

"The signal is intermittent. It's very weak and heavily distorted because of the range, but it is in the micrometre wavelength, and a common frequency used for deep space communications. The Australian facility can't hear it at the moment and neither can Andromeda – and that's the problem. NASA and the Committee will not entertain the object as being of an intelligent nature until the signal is verified by other sources – just in case it's space feedback of some sort."

"Sounds entirely logical, given the gravity of the situation." Rothschild thought on the best course of action. "Brian," he said, "we should be wary of forwarding such a report, particularly in a basic format. We are on thin ice already with the subject matter . . .

This extrasensory perception thing, it's difficult to grasp and it will be dismissed in an instant if we don't put up a convincing case. Tell you what . . . ask Abbey to tidy it up a little – she has results from other experiments going back decades. Then pass it on to Professor Nieve. Get his opinion first. If he agrees, we will go public."

Rothschild sat for a while considering recent events. Outside his office, Richard was talking to Abbey Hennessy; she had acquired his portfolio and would take over as his controller at midnight. They had a better relationship this time but Rothschild could hear that Abbey was very reluctant to let Richard pursue a particular course of action, although he was not party to what Richard wanted to do. "Let's run it past Peter, then," he heard Richard say and almost immediately there was a knock on his door.

"Yes, come in."

Richard pushed his head around the door. "Peter, just discussing arrangements for tomorrow," he said. "As you're still my boss, so to speak, I would like you to give your approval."

Rothschild looked past Richard at Abbey; she had a stony expression. "Right, come in," he said.

Richard pulled up a second chair for Abbey and they both sat down in front of Rothschild, who paused from his work.

"So, Richard, I've approved your return to Cairo, but clearly you want to complicate matters and do something else."

Abbey looked at Rothschild and then at Richard. "I don't think it's advisable, not at all," she said.

"I may need to go back to Eritrea, Peter, that's all. I have a contact; I'm relying on him being able to trace Asharf Makkoum. I can't explain how, but it could be the only way to find Madame Vallogia – and the Ark for that matter. Cairo first, as agreed, and then if she doesn't arrive for her duties I'll know for sure that she's been abducted."

"When will that be?"

"Day after tomorrow."

Rothschild nodded. "Very well," he said. "Make your preparations for Cairo. I've had confirmation of your flight details – one of our own Typhoon Five fighters and a Navy Division crew member, like you. Take off at 14:00 from Northolt, three hour flight time. Destination is an Egyptian Air Force base about thirty kilometres south of the city. The pilot will wait for you. You will have a driver to take you to the museum. I've already informed Mubarakar's people. Abbey and I will discuss Eritrea if there is a requirement. Now, anything else?"

Richard took a deep breath. "Um, yes. There is one other thing." He fidgeted. "My Mother, she's not very well, getting on a bit, you know. I need to see her, it's been some time, and there's been a burglary too – I should visit the house. You may recall that she lives in Somerset. Just a few hours tomorrow morning, leave at six, be back by midday. I'd like a car please, if that's possible, or I can arrange one myself."

"I think we can stretch to that. The alternative would be very expensive. I'll ask Laura to arrange it."

"Thanks, appreciated." Richard felt Abbey's stare. He had not mentioned this request to her. *She suspects I'm up to something,* he thought. He looked at her innocently. "Er, what do you have planned for New Year's Eve, Abbey?" he asked, hesitantly, changing the subject.

Abbey shook her head in exasperation.

"Is there anything else, Richard?" asked Rothschild. "I've got a lot to do,"

Richard stood to leave. "Oh, there's this," he said, and reached inside his jacket. He unzipped a pocket and pulled out the transparent plastic bag that Reverend Mother Antoinette Rousseau had given to him in the convent. The sample bag's self-sealing strip and the small white plastic box inside remained unopened.

"What is it?" Rothschild asked, taking the bag and holding it up for Abbey to see.

"Apparently it's the dry residue from inside the Ark. Naomi will have collected it prior to the cleaning and renovation. Oxidised dust and sediment from the corners and the flaking material brushed from the walls by all accounts. She wouldn't have missed a trick. Anyway, it might be worth a check. The residue will definitely contain carbon molecules and so accurately dating the Ark is an option and a mass spectrograph could help with an origin."

"I see. Very well, I'll get it over to the laboratory. Thank you, Richard. See you in a few days then, and remember our conversation regarding communication, please."

Richard nodded his understanding and smiled briefly at Abbey. "I'll keep you informed," he replied.

Richard was about to leave the room when Rothschild said: "I almost forgot. I wanted to ask you something, Richard – just your opinion on something, if you don't mind."

Richard's heart missed a beat. He held his breath and turned slowly on his heels. *Was it about the crystal? How could he know?* he pondered. "Delighted," he said, raising both a half-smile and his eyebrows in anticipation.

"You know the orbital dynamics of the Moon and the set up of the Space Traffic Control there better than anyone. Do you think that a vehicle of any sorts could land – or, for that matter, anything be dropped – onto the dark side without the lunar authorities knowing about it? I mean, is it possible to evade the sensor ring?"

Richard hid his relief, but all the same he was surprised by the question. "No!" he answered emphatically. "The Lunar Colony takes its security very seriously. The space traffic situation is highly automated and controlled. It's a procedural environment and most procedures do not allow for dark side manoeuvring. The sensor ring includes state-of-the-art submillimetre radar, secondary surveillance and solar scatter antennas. Three hundred and sixty degree coverage . . . no, it's impossible."

"Take a moment to think, Richard. Just to be sure. Would there ever be a situation when the sensor ring would be deactivated?"

Richard's eyes narrowed. "Essential maintenance, that's the only time. And then it would be promulgated in advance." he replied. "The system works on a hemispherical overlay principal. If one side is switched off for rectification work – and that's the only reason it would be – then the other side would always be functioning at optimum level. A vehicle couldn't orbit on the dark side without being seen, or without authorisation for that matter. No, it's impossible."

"Okay, good, thank you . . . it was just a thought."

Richard left the room and closed the door behind him.

# CHAPTER 16

## A SECRET SECRET

"No harm done," Richard muttered under his breath as he considered the burglary. And how fortunate he was that his father's old workshop had been discounted as a hiding place for such a precious item – it could have been so different. With the crystal retrieved and in the boot of the ministry vehicle – an ageing black XF Type – the stakes had been raised considerably. *I can't pay lip service to safety any longer, nor rely on kismet to ease my progress. From here on in every risk must be calculated,* he concluded. He thought of Rachel: he would call her from the airport before his flight to Cairo. His thoughts drifted to Naomi: tomorrow was the full moon. If she didn't arrive at the Great Pyramid of Khufu to perform her duties as High Priestess to the Temple of Osiris, his fears would be confirmed. He realised that her association with him had put her life in danger. He was responsible for her predicament, whatever that might be, and he was pessimistic.

Sitting on the back seat of the car as it sped eastwards towards London, Richard's attention was diverted by the passing of Stonehenge. He remembered his time on Mars. And he remembered how, not long after he had discovered the Flight Log of the crashed spaceship *Star of Hope* and deciphered some of its text, he realised this ancient monument featured not as a place of religious ceremony, but as a navigation facility – the religious inference coming much later, perhaps four thousand years later. He felt the car accelerate. The driver had put his foot down as the road opened into a dual carriageway and, without another car to be seen in either direction, they could expect to arrive in an hour or so.

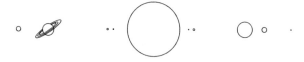

Richard felt his telephonic pager vibrate in his pocket. He had acquired a short, dark blue woollen coat with a convenient zipped quilted lining that doubled as a smart jacket, and the other inner breast pocket held his passport, lunar citizen's permit and security papers. He was wearing the only other pair of trousers he had brought – a similarly coloured pair of lined cotton chinos, and also his favourite brown leather brogues with non-slip soles, having left his flying suit and boots in the office in London. He had two white cotton roll necks for use under his flying suit and the other Laura Bellingham had promised to take to the laundry. Over that was a navy blue microfibre crew neck pullover. The pager display indicated a call from Peter Rothschild – *too good to last,* he thought.

"Good morning, Peter. Everything okay, I hope?" Richard asked, holding the device to his ear.

"Yes, quite. Where are you now?"

Richard studied the passing suburban scenery. For decades public debate had centred on a third runway for the old London Airport but, contrary to long-standing government plans, not only was that runway never built, but the existing northern strip and the surrounding land had been given over to property developers twenty years earlier, and now the vicinity was a sprawling estate of low-rise housing. The new airport, London Main, with its four runways, had been built in the Thames Estuary near Whitstable in Kent.

"Just passing Heathrow Regional," Richard replied, "about to go into the tunnel."

"Good. Say another fifteen minutes then. I'm here to meet you."

*Crikey! That's all I need,* thought Richard. *He's certain to ask what's in my holdall.* "Okay, fine, a reception committee then," he said, and switched the device off.

The sleek XF emerged from the underground section of the A40 City Road close to the Royal Air Force base at Northolt. Richard showed his electronic identity badge at the security gate and the driver proceeded another kilometre to the terminal building. He had acquired a Diplomatic Luggage Tag from Laura Bellingham prior to leaving Whitehall – a very fortuitous forethought – and had secured the document to the handle of his beige canvas holdall. Inside the holdall was the rigid helmet box that contained his Kalahari crystal and the green, glass-like shards that surrounded and shielded it. However, with the spare clothing that he had stuffed around the box, his bag had become suspiciously bulky. Staring at it on the back seat of the car he grew nervous.

The XF drew to a halt outside the two-storey building. After climbing from the car and at the very last minute, Richard had second thoughts – more a minor panic attack. To make matters worse, he saw Peter Rothschild inside the glass-fronted terminal building awaiting his arrival. There would be little chance of hiding the contents should the bag be searched! Could he rely on diplomatic immunity? He shuddered at the thought of the crystal passing through an X-ray screening machine. It was one hell of a risk and, calculated or not, the consequences of discovery did not bear thinking about. Suddenly he made a decision and placed the holdall on the ground. He unzipped it, withdrew the helmet box, placed the box carefully on the back seat and then secured the bag again, trying all the while to keep his back towards Rothschild.

Then he gave the bag to the MOD driver and asked him to take it directly to the VIP luggage facility. Richard drew a deep breath, tucked the helmet box under his arm, closed the car door and turned for the terminal's main door. Moments later, in the low-ceiling, open foyer he was met by Rothschild.

The room and the adjacent corridors were adorned with numerous framed pictures of the airfield's most memorable moments – scenes that dated back more than a century. As he walked past, Richard saw pictures of aircraft from the 1930s and 1940s and, on occasion, he stopped to take a closer look, only to be chivvied along by Rothschild. He tried to portray a nonchalant manner, even though his heart was pounding. After a few words to an armed security agent, Rothschild proceeded through a set of double doors and then up a flight of stairs to a private suite. Richard followed him closely.

Entering the lounge, with its plush dove-grey carpet, Richard immediately made a beeline for a large window that overlooked the apron. There he stood, somewhat nervously, waiting for a luggage trolley or similar to appear, as the only fighter jet visible on the concrete expanse was parked on the far side and the presence of a nearby fuel bowser indicated that it was being prepared for flight. Rothschild returned to the room after a brief *tête-à-tête* with the Operations Officer just as Richard saw his bag, along with some other equipment, being wheeled to the aircraft in question, although he could not see if it had been opened. Now the gamble hinged on his diplomatic status.

"Are you feeling unwell, Richard? You look quite pale," enquired Rothschild, closing the door to the room and walking over to him.

"No, no, I'm fine, thanks. Another flight, that's all."

Rothschild looked at the helmet box under Richard's arm and then he looked up. "You seem very reluctant to put the box down, Richard. Anything inside I should know about?"

"Oh, this . . . ! No. Just personal stuff, you know. I expect to be away for a few days." Richard looked outside, trying to conceal his blush, and then he put the box on the floor and stood astride it. "Anyway, I'm sure you're not here to say goodbye, are you?" Sensing his embarrassment fade, Richard looked directly at Rothschild.

With his suspicions appearing to subside, Rothschild shrugged. "Well, yes and no actually," he replied. "Primarily, I came over for the ride. One has to book some way in advance for a few minutes with the Prime Minister. I needed to update him on the current Icarus situation. The forty-minute drive allowed me his undivided attention. He has just left for Beijing along with several cabinet members – a particularly pressing engagement with the Chinese Government. A NetJets Global charter, in one of their Eagles . . . a very impressive aeroplane I must say, extremely comfortable."

Richard nodded. "Yes I know. This is a wild guess, Peter, but is that to demand some action from the Chinese over Tongsei's dubious activities?"

"One cannot make demands on the country with the richest economy or the world's largest standing army, Richard. One can only put one's case as forcibly as possible. The US President, those of Russia and France, and one or two other G12 leaders have gone to do just that."

"So it is to do with Tongsei?"

"More the Huang Hai Industrial District, actually. The initiative has been on the table for three years now, but the Chinese have never wished to discuss it because of the enormous tax revenues they receive. There are serious implications for the region and they will not take action unless they have proof . . . unequivocal proof. Nevertheless, despite what's been said in the West, it appears that they have been concerned about the illegal activities taking place on their doorstep for some time, but wish to deal with it in their own way. There are similar industrial areas in other countries, of course. There's a growing movement by national governments to limit the autonomy of these super-companies and in so doing limit their stranglehold on various commodities."

"About time!"

"I can only agree with you. We will see how successful they are. Now, the other reason I'm here is to do with *your* security. I've decided to give you some support; you're not going to like it, but I expect you to comply."

"What kind of support? You mean backup . . . ? A partner?"

Rothschild shrugged. "Yes . . . a partner, if you like."

"Preston?"

"Unfortunately, Preston is not available. He was my first choice, but he manages the protection squad for the Royal Family these days and can't be spared."

"So who, exactly?"

"I'm not going to beat around the bush with this, Richard; it's a specialised system, a machine."

"A robot! No thanks . . . absolutely not. I'm not working with a robot!"

"You are under orders, Richard." Rothschild snapped. There was an awkward pause and then Rothschild's expression softened. "Listen, I knew you wouldn't like it, but I need you to have the best support possible. The situation is developing and I don't just mean the risk posed by Rhinefeld. You were lucky in France; it could have been a very different outcome. The truth is that we were caught out; I don't like that. It means that I am not doing my job properly."

"A robot!" Richard just looked at him with disgust.

"Richard, you will . . ."

Rothschild seemingly bit his tongue and stared outside for a moment. Richard followed his eye line. Stores were being loaded into an under-wing pod on the fighter. Rothschild refocused his attention on Richard.

"Understand that we are facing a concerted, covert attempt to destabilise the world's energy base and it grows day by day. Personally, I think a major conspiracy is imminent. I have threads of evidence but not enough to make a case and nobody in government will run with it for fear of calling wolf. The cyber-attack on SERON is now unprecedented. Mubarakar's discovery and the Ark may yet provide vital information – nothing surprises me these days. That means you remain a target. I need your cooperation."

"Okay, I understand. But don't say a Humatron, Peter. *I hate Humatrons.*"

"No, it's not a Humatron, not quite anyway. Originally modelled on one, it's true, but quite different now. *Evolved*, one might say."

"Go on, please, I need to feel better about this."

"You might recall the Humatron body parts you left in the Safe House in Adulis a few years ago?"

Richard nodded.

"With the help of our local agent we retrieved them. Not long after, Professor Nieve and a team of specialists set about countering this system with one of their own . . . an improved model. The work was funded secretly by the Ministry."

"Peter! You can't trust a Level Seven robotic system! It's been proven time and time again – there are too many anomalies in the programming. I could never turn my back on it!"

Rothschild persisted. "Listen. Unlike the Humatron series, this model is not based on a synthetic memory system. In fact, it is not graded on the Rockwell Illinois Plateau System at all."

"And why's that?"

"Because, well, because it utilises a human brain."

"But that's in contravention of the New Geneva Convention. Now you people are doing it! Such bionic integration was prohibited. There were lots of reasons for doing so."

Rothschild raised his hands in explanation. "It's a one-off experiment. It happened by default, because one of the scientists involved in the programme unexpectedly lost his life and he had signed over his body parts to science."

"Oh, really, sounds very convenient."

"He fell from the balcony of his apartment. He was misbehaving during a party; it was an accident. Unfortunately, there were metal railings below. His friends had him in hospital within twenty minutes but his chest was . . . anyway, they couldn't save him. He had a double first from Cambridge in biomechanics, a brilliant mind – and his brain was undamaged."

"So they went ahead and broke the rules."

Rothschild nodded. "They kept his brain alive on a ventilation machine. Professor Nieve had the man's specific written approval. The body was taken to the robotic research facility and they performed the operation."

"They integrated the brain into their Humatron-based experimental body?"

"It's an improved frame, more resilient than the Humatron, apparently."

"That makes it okay then." Richard shook his head in a disapproving manner. "And what do you call this . . . hybrid?"

"A Human Integrated Mechanism . . . a HIM Thirty-Two. Because the man was thirty-two years old."

"You miss my point, Peter. How do you address the HIM?"

"Thomas, just Thomas."

"And there were no issues?"

Rothschild held a breath and screwed his face a little. "Professor Nieve told me that he had a nervous breakdown when he woke and realised the situation. That was more than two years ago. Since then there have been one or two physiological issues but . . ."

"Great, so you want me to work with a psychopathic robot! That's just great!"

"There's been a lot of work done. For more than a year he has been perfectly stable."

Richard looked unconvinced.

"Essentially it's the same man, you know, his personality – who he was: his loves, his hates, his character and his emotions. And with his help, with his insider knowledge, the integration between man and machine is becoming blurred. Professor Nieve is very impressed with him."

"And that's a good thing is it? A human brain, a consciousness, a person for all intents and purposes, trapped inside a mechanical body. Is that acceptable?"

"The moral issues of all this will have to wait, I'm afraid. Unlike the Humatron series, we have a system we can reason with. One we can rely on and one that is, by definition, self-aware."

"I see, so you side-step the Level Seven ban by using organics."

"Look. God only knows if the conglomerates are using Humatrons again. There is evidence to say that they are. And after four years that system has probably been improved, too. There might be an HU50 model out there, who knows, but if you meet one . . . Thomas may prove extremely useful."

Richard nodded. "Well I don't like it. I'm going along with it because I'm under orders."

"All the same, keep in touch with Abbey and copy me in on any developments," countered Rothschild, whose eyes dropped to Richard's helmet box again.

Richard shifted anxiously. He checked his chronometer and buttoned up his coat. Rothschild looked up slowly and went to speak, but Richard cut him short.

"Personal things, Peter, as I say – and something for Mubarakar, that's all," said Richard, desperately trying to appear matter-of-fact. Then he slowly picked up the box.

Rothschild's eyes narrowed.

"Now, if you will excuse me, it's time to go and see Mubarakar." With that Richard gave Rothschild a sharp nod and promptly left the room.

# CHAPTER 17

# WORLDS APART

Richard knew of the Series 5 Typhoon fighter, as he had been launched from one over Italy a few years back – although that example had been in Luftwaffe livery. That was an experience he would never forget.

It was an impressive sight, particularly to a pilot, as he neared the aircraft – helmet, oxygen mask and gloves in hand. Sleek, fast, delta wing, potent – probably the best 'atmospheric' fighter ever built. *All the same, it had been made obsolete by the Delta Class,* he thought. Although *that* fighter, with its matter-stream propulsion system, could not realise its true potential inside the two Van Allen belts for fear of perforating them.

The United Kingdom Joint Forces' pilot was performing a pre-flight inspection and when he saw Richard approaching he promptly broke off and courteously walked over to meet him. He was wearing the standard issue green military flying suit over which was an anti-g body harness and as he offered his hand to Richard he realised the reason for Richard's concerned expression.

"You don't need to worry about this, sir," he said in a friendly manner whilst tugging on a strap of his body harness with his left hand. "It's a straightforward flight to Egypt. S.O.P for me to wear it, that's all."

Richard smiled faintly and patted his chest to signify a racing heartbeat. "Richard Reece, also Royal Navy . . . How do you do?" he replied, shaking the man's hand. "If it's not restricted information, Lieutenant, Standard Operating Procedure dictates what altitude for such a *routine* flight?"

"Chris Quarrie. A pleasure, sir, if I may say; I've heard a lot about your exploits. I'm hoping to join the Space Programme in a few years, too."

Richard smiled again.

"In answer to your question, sir, relatively low level, as you only have basic kit. The flight plan is filed for Flight Level Four Three Zero."

"That's reassuring. How's the preparation going?"

Lieutenant Quarrie, at 1.8 metres tall, was a little shorter than Richard and, although only in his late twenties, was already balding. He had the look of a television character from a vintage children's programme – John Tracy of *Thunderbirds* sprang foremost to mind. In any case, he could see from the pilot's confident manner and well-worn gold shoulder epaulets that he had a good deal of experience.

"Nearly done," came the reply. "This is Aircraft Orderly Spinola; he will help you into the cockpit. I'm afraid you are sitting behind me today, sir."

Richard raised his eyebrows in fake surprise. "I can cope with that," he responded.

Standing by the pointed nose of the aircraft, Chris Quarrie gestured with a gloved hand towards the two cigar-shaped pods, one hanging beneath each wing. "I don't think we will achieve Mach 3 today because of the additional weight," he said. "It won't make much difference to the flight time – perhaps another fifteen minutes." He pointed specifically to the pod below the port wing. "That one has a robotic system in it – a bit hush hush I'm told." Quarrie tapped his nose. "And that one is a Special Air Service Covert Insertion Pod – one man safely behind enemy lines, that sort of thing. Very capable over water, too – full buoyancy aids. I'm briefed that we may also be doing a drop over East Africa – day after tomorrow – but that's yet to be confirmed."

Richard nodded. He thought of Rothschild. "The Ministry is covering every angle, that's all," he replied. "It may or may not be required."

"I understand, sir. I am expecting to wait for two days at the Egyptian base – El Al Shalamin. I'm being hosted by an Airforce Squadron with F29s. I'm quite looking forward to it, actually."

Richard glanced up at the low dragging cloud, then

towards the control tower, and then across the airfield in first a northerly and then an easterly direction. Both ways, the skyline was darkened, bleak and urban high-rise. Their timing had been good; they were between belts of drizzle. However, towards the west Richard could see a squall line approaching, with reducing visibility and rain showers. He gestured towards it to warn the pilot. "Glad someone's looking forward," he said, and smiled faintly.

"Now, sir, if you are ready, we can climb in."

The orderly helped Richard strap in and connect his life support equipment to the aircraft's interface. Lieutenant Quarrie ran the check list, started the engines and checked the flight controls and other systems. Within three minutes they were ready to go. The mark was 13:58 Greenwich Mean Time.

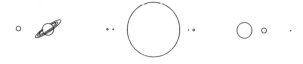

Professor Mubarakar had arranged an ambulance to collect Richard from outside the main gate of the Egyptian Airforce Base. Richard was surprised when it arrived but, after checking the driver's credentials, he realised that it would provide the perfect cover and possibly expedite their drive through the renowned congestion of Cairo.

During the journey, Richard was careful not to allow the pale green helmet box to shuffle or shake, lest the crystal lose some of its insulating wall or, worse, become exposed altogether. Should that occur it would simply burn through the box, the seat cushion, the ambulance's floor pan, the metallised road and probably several hundred metres of the Earth's crust as a result – and it would be difficult to explain that one away. He knew that only electromagnetic energy in the radio-wave spectrum – wavelengths above ten centimetres and between the frequencies 120 Kilohertz and 250 Kilohertz, the VHF and UHF frequency band – would cause the crystal to react by 'boiling-off', a term associated with characteristic extreme heating. And it was this heat that was being harnessed to drive giant steam turbines in the four former nuclear reactor plants that currently provided the world's energy. Although modern telecommunications preferred microwave frequencies, in this old town there would be enough antiquated radio stations broadcasting in the VHF frequency range, and also other localised equipment, to set the process off. He just looked at the radio set that the ambulance driver was using to know that.

Each time the vehicle negotiated an obstruction, ran up the curb, bounced over a pothole or swerved to avoid another equally determined Cairo driver, Richard picked the box up in both hands and acted as a shock absorber. Occasionally, when the necessary avoidance was particularly excessive, the Arabic driver would look across at Richard, smile a toothless grin and utter something that sounded like, "God be praised."

Mubarakar had quite cannily decided that an ambulance would provide suitable cover for the journey from the airbase to his apartment and it would also afford a certain amount of psychological priority on Cairo's seething road network. Despite this, the general tendency for headlong opportunism by all but a handful of users had Richard shrinking, cowering and wincing in his seat in equal measure. Animals had priority over vehicles, as in other parts of Egypt, and Richard even saw a laden, hooded elephant. He had expected to run the gauntlet for at least an hour, but it was one hour and fifty minutes later that they finally crossed the 15th of May Bridge heading west, negotiated Ahmed Orabi until passing the Pharaoh Egypt Hotel and then turned right into a maze of streets to finally draw up outside a large, two-storey stone-built house with a Victorian period veranda on the first floor. In this private quarter, very much downtown and almost deserted, there was visible security in the form of closed-circuit TV cameras and the occasional patrol car.

"Not safe leave vehicle here," said the driver, his whispering making his voice sound more guttural.

Richard nodded his understanding and climbed carefully from his seat with the helmet box tucked firmly under his arm. He walked to the back of the vehicle. For those moments it felt good to be in dry weather again, although the air smelt of mustiness and smoke. All the same, eight degrees Celsius felt positively warm.

It was a black night and the only useful light came

from inside the vehicle, as by then the driver had opened the two metal doors. Inside, on the floor, secured by four canvas straps, was a long, shining aluminium tube. It was a little less than a metre diameter and two metres in length.

Richard heard the rattle of a chain being pulled from between two wrought-iron gates and he turned to see, a few metres back, Mubarakar step into the street. The Professor was wrapped inside a thick, black coat with the collar turned up and was indicating impatiently towards him. Meanwhile Abdel, his assistant, went about fully opening the gates. Mubarakar spoke in Arabic to the driver who then climbed back into the ambulance, started the engine and reversed through the gates and down a straight terracotta-tiled driveway until arriving at a carriage arch that was part of the main house. Richard caught up with Mubarakar as he issued another order and the driver then continued to reverse until he disappeared into a garage another ten metres or so from the back of the house. After Mubarakar and Richard had also stepped inside, Abdel scurried about, closing and locking first the outside ornamental gates and then the green-painted wooden doors of the garage. There seemed to be plenty of room inside and the shadow of another large van parked further back caught Richard's eye. After a second heavy bolt was heard to clunk into position the ceiling lights came on and Mubarakar peeled back his collar. He was happy to see Richard.

"So, my friend, Egypt draws you back into her arms. This is good!"

"Pleased to be back, Professor . . . cold and wet in England as usual," replied Richard, shaking hands as was customary. But Richard could not help frowning at the change of plan. "But I thought we were to rendezvous in the Cairo Museum?"

"There are issues, and I received a message from Peter Rothschild. He told me to be extra-vigilant. Quite how much more that is than *vigilant*, I am not sure." Mubarakar grinned. "It is better here. I own the ground floor of this house and have done for many years, and the apartment upstairs is empty – they went to Sharm El Sheikh three months ago."

"Professor, is the ancient statue . . . ?"

"It is here, my friend." Mubarakar gestured with his head towards the white, Japanese-built van. He then looked at the box under Richard's arm. "And inside you have a . . . *crystal*?" Mubarakar's eyes widened at the thought of it.

Richard nodded cautiously. "The shielding, did you manage to do it?" he asked.

Mubarakar put a reassuring hand on Richard's shoulder. "In the study of ancient mummies and artefacts we use X-rays frequently," he responded. "We borrowed material from our portable booth to line the vehicle. It is done and the statue is positioned with the panel open. But first, hospitality – lamb stew, honey cake and mint tea." Mubarakar turned and led Richard into the house.

Richard walked into the kitchen to see Hamid Faruq already enjoying a selection of Medjool dates that were in a large bowl on a central wooden table. "Hamid, how are you?" he enquired, extending his hand.

"God is merciful," Hamid replied warmly.

The dates were preserved in thick sugary syrup and Richard was pleased to try them. He turned to Mubarakar. "You know about my support?"

Mubarakar nodded. "Science progresses faster than seems possible to an old man like me. You and Hamid, you will see what human ingenuity offers the world; the future is surely clouded by such technology, and the old times, they are gone forever."

"Yeah, well, I'm not that progressive as to have a robot for a buddy, Professor," Richard responded. "Anyway, I'm under orders, and it might be a good idea to have the system activated when we try the crystal in the statue . . . You never know, we might need it!"

After dinner, the three men returned to the garage to find Abdel sipping tea with the ambulance driver. "This is my cousin," Abdel said to Richard.

"Driving like you do is in the blood then," commented Richard with dry humour, momentarily lightening the growing preoccupation in the group.

Mubarakar had already explained the 'family' situation and that security was not an issue, and so Richard set about opening the aluminium tube by keying a five-digit code into the control panel that was mounted on the circular access door nearest the rear of the vehicle. The door opened promptly under its own means and Richard reached inside and partially slid out a stretcher arrangement that ran on side rollers. His immediate impression of the robot, and particularly the legs and waist area was that it looked remarkably similar to that of a Humatron HU40 – having a thick, opaque and pliable celluloid skin inflated to the size of a large man's legs by a pressurised, oily, electrolytic fluid. However, the feet were different, much more life-like than the Humatron's mechanical, claw-like feet. Richard then focused on the hands – again, they were complicated but 'human-like', instead of four-fingered metallic mechanisms. He released the nylon transportation straps that secured the bulky arms and legs to the stretcher bed and examined the chest area. Once more it seemed very familiar, with the outline of a Humatron's ethereal alloy skeleton supporting a box-like structure that tapered towards the waist, and clearly apparent was the central control panel and cover. Inside the 'chest' box would be the high-capacity catholithium batteries and photoelectric converters. Overall, the primate-like proportions of the Humatron system had been replaced by those of a human; although the reasons for this Richard could only speculate.

With the four canvas straps securing the lightweight tube securely to the floor of the vehicle, Richard withdrew the stretcher bed to its fullest extent. The ambulance sagged on the rear suspension as a result of the moment arm. Again Richard noticed the use of circular, segmented, metal alloy rings as a flexible neck structure and that they steadily decreased in diameter from shoulder to head. However, with that body part collapsed for transportation, he could only guess if its fullest extension would add a metre or more to the overall height of the machine, as it did with the Humatron HU40.

It was the head where all similarity between the two robots ceased. Whereas the Humatron's was a metallic 'X' shape, with a disproportionately large upper 'triangle', this one was oval-shaped. And where the Humatron's construction was approximately eight centimetres in thickness with the neck joining at the rear, this head was in the shape of a pear sliced in half and was at least eighteen centimetres, front to back, with the neck joining at the base, as with a person. In fact, the proportions of the flat, oval face was a little larger than an average man's. With the power switched off, the laptop-like, blank screen revealed none of the technology that lay behind. Indeed, the black screen simply reflected Richard's own face as he stood over it and peered down.

Richard recalled the upper triangle of the Humatron HU40's X-shaped head, with its face having human male proportions from hairline to top lip. Its eyes were teardrop-shaped, and a glowing neon red, lit from behind and made real by plasmoltec technology. With trepidation, he recalled the 3D images that the system could produce by manipulating the pliable screen as if it was soft modelling clay and that by a connection to the machine's emotion centre it could form ghostly facial expressions at will. He also recalled the look of dread that the lower triangle added, being a silver-coloured metal grill that masked a number of vertical slits. On the Humatron HU40 series the slits were openings through which the robot could sense the faintest of odours and which also allowed the electronic vocallator to project synthesised words. Richard studied the HIM system as it lay motionless on the stretcher and wondered how it would behave when activated. *Friend or foe? Incorruptible or a hidden agenda? Trusting or plotting? Passive or innately violent?* He moved the head from side-to-side, examining it. *Prior to energising, this might be the only time for doing this,* he thought.

As a result of insufficiently researched, irresponsible and ill-intentioned computer programming, the Humatron HU40 series had become a human-hating catastrophe of self-aware robotic engineering. They could be controlled, but without reliance or confidence, and they could be contained, but only by a similar level of destructive violence. Richard wondered where it was all leading. He looked up at Mubarakar, but he was deep in his own thoughts.

Beginning the activation process, Richard inserted a small electronic initiator into the receptacle beneath the control panel cover. He pushed a number of buttons, closed and locked the panel with the same code that he had used to open the container and, finally, pressed a small pad to the side of the panel that scrambled the code so that it was no longer useful. The system started immediately.

The hum of electromechanical motivators and the shifting of limbs caused the men to step backwards, startled – even Richard was caught off-guard at the speed of response. The tiny but powerful electric motors that were coupled to advanced joint mechanisms produced the customary whirring noise that Richard was familiar with, but unlike the Humatron model this machine flexed and twitched – like a person being touched by a Tasler stun baton. Also it was much quieter; the mechanisms more refined.

Slowly the HIM sat up. The arms came down and grasped the side of the stretcher and then it swung its legs around, making contact with the floor. It edged forward, much as a human would, stood, and then stretched to stand tall. The five men moved to give it space. With the neck compressed it was a little taller than Richard, but it was significantly wider at the shoulders.

"Look . . . look . . . the face . . . it moves!" Abdel screeched, hardly able to contain his astonishment.

The blank, flat, face screen began to flicker and undulate as the plasticized material warmed. Richard stepped to the side. *The memory banks and processing mechanisms were all within the chest cavity in the Humatron series,* he thought. Here, the brain was housed in an ethereal alloy half-skull and it interfaced directly behind the screen. Rothschild had told him that a breakthrough in synthetic nerve construction had allowed Professor Nieve's team of specialists to amalgamate to a much higher degree the brain's response to the plasmoltec manipulators, and he wondered what the result would be. He was amazed as the face took shape – never had he seen such technology. The four other men stood mesmerised and the ambulance driver began to shuffle nervously behind the rear door of the vehicle.

And then the eyes took shape and opened – to a collective gasp. With the Humatron, the eyes were backlit, but here the plastic material moved like jelly and formed perfect eyeballs and eyelids that blinked. The mouth began to form and a nose protruded and material was sucked in to produce two nostrils. Then the lips took shape. The mouth was completed by the forming of a cavity about five centimetres deep. Gradually the colour changed from black to green to yellow and then to a pale olive hue. There was even a small scar above the top lip. After another thirty seconds, during which time the entire group just stared in awe, the final expression solidified. It was a complete young man's face.

"He is remembering what he looked like when he was alive," Richard mumbled. "His memory and emotion centres are interfacing with the nerve receptors and then in turn controlling the plasmoltec system. It's impressive."

The machine's flexible neck extended about half a metre and then its head slowly described a circle. The eyes of the face began to flip from man to man in the room in turn, quickly registering contours and characteristics, and then fell down on Richard's face and focused intently.

"By the Gods," uttered Mubarakar. "If I was not seeing this with my own eyes, I would not believe it."

"I am Human Interface Mechanism Number Thirty-Two. I am Thomas," the figure said, in a very convincing human voice that came from the mouth. "I am here to work with you." His Home Counties accent was equally startling.

Richard stepped forward and stood in front of the machine, staring up at its face. The HIM raised an eerie smile that made Richard nervous and then extended its neck to the fullest extent. It seemingly glared down at Richard from a height of three metres. The back of its head rubbed on the wooden rafters of the garage roof. Bolstered by a long-standing and inherent distrust for this level of cyber-system, Richard said, "You are here to work *for* me and not *with* me . . . . Do you understand?"

The HIM seemed surprised; its expression changed. Richard forced himself not to be intimidated by the technology. Humatrons were one thing and he could view them as dissident, disposable machines – but this system was something different: the level of humanity and self-consciousness was not only off-putting, it was deeply disturbing. This was very much a person in a robot's body and he speculated as to its longevity – *a hundred years, two hundred, a millennia?* "What are your statistics?" Richard barked.

"Weight . . . one hundred and fifty kilograms; overhead lifting capacity . . . two hundred kilograms;

top speed . . . fifty-seven kilometres per hour when fully charged . . ."

"How long to charge?"

"Thirty minutes in white or infrared light from a ten per cent residual."

"Protocols?" Richard barked again, struggling to keep his developing dislike for the robot from his voice.

"I am assigned to Commander Richard James Reece of Government Department MI9. I am to execute the duties of personal security operative and in so doing I am directed to act independently if required. In addition, I am to perform all instructions given by Lieutenant Commander Richard James Reece provided they do not infringe the Constitution of Robotic Behaviour as incorporated into the International Bill of Human Rights as amended 2018. *You* are Commander Richard Reece."

"You mean you are programmed to take my orders . . ."

"No. I am not graded on the Rockwell Illinois Plateau System for robotic capacity. Therefore I am not programmed, but *enhanced*. I have a human interface, Richard, and therefore I am *directed* to do your bidding . . . within certain criteria, of course."

Richard wasn't having any of that! A robot calling the shots, and worse, using his first name – like an old friend!

"You listen to me," he said, scowling at the HIM's face. "You do exactly what I say, when I say. Do you copy? I do not want your advice, not ever. And stay in good view at all times; I don't ever want you behind me. You do not carry a weapon – not unless I approve it." Richard paused for breath. "Now go over there and keep out of the way!" He jabbed his finger towards a corner of the garage.

Thomas' expression morphed from neutral 'matter-of-fact' through flushed embarrassment to one of sorrowful dejection, as if he had been unfairly scolded by a favourite teacher. Had tears been available, he looked as though he would have shed them. Ever Mubarakar was surprised at Richard's vitriolic outburst.

As Thomas moved off to stand in the corner, Mubarakar put a hand on Richard's forearm. "Time is pressing," he said, "we must attend to the crystal."

Richard's expression lightened. "Yes," he said in a whisper. "This could be what we have been waiting for." He pushed the stretcher back into the aluminium tube, closed its circular door and then those of the ambulance and strode off towards the white van.


There was a large colourful sign stencilled on the side panel of the commercial vehicle. It comprised images of the three great pyramids and the Sphinx at Giza. Beneath were two lines of words in Arabic, of which Richard understood only *Cairo*. However, below, in much smaller font and in English, was written: *Cairo National Museum*. Richard slid open the side door to half its extent. Only then, as he climbed into the darkened interior, did he realise that the suspension legs of all four wheels were bottomed, indicating a very heavy load. He peered hard into the darkness: grey material, with a dull, metallic appearance, hung as open rolls from the upper corners, like a series of extended blinds, and a thick 'carpet' of material was lining both the ceiling and floor.

"We have overlapped the shielding by twenty centimetres to be safe," explained Mubarakar, as he too climbed in. "These lead curtains are three millimetres thick. If they can stop X-rays, they will stop radio waves."

Richard agreed and shuffled around the end of the crystal coffin; the heavy lid had already been removed and the statue lay face down inside. The access panel had also been removed and the orifice in the centre of the statue's back extended inside by the size of his fist. There was a small chalice-like receptacle inside but nothing else, although Richard noticed some engravings in the 'old writing'. Hamid followed the two men inside and stood at the head of the coffin while Abdel, remaining outside, switched on the internal lights and then closed the door. Richard checked the all-round integrity of the lead curtain and then put his helmet box on the floor. He paused thoughtfully. "You sure you want to be in here?" he asked. "I don't know how this crystal will react when I pull it clear of the protective glass." He waited for an answer.

Hamid, having taken a little time to chant something in Arabic, nodded hesitantly. Richard looked at the Professor, who stood opposite him with his hands gripping the coffin edge. "I would rather watch and then have my own funeral, than miss this," Mubarakar countered, with an uneasy grin.

"Very well," said Richard, and he reached down and released the two catches on the box. Subconsciously holding his breath he slowly opened the lid. On top of the densely packed green shards of glass was a pair of black tongs made from an inert plastic material. "So far so good," he offered, and breathed again. With that, and a glistening forehead, he picked up the tongs and promptly delved into the broken pieces. It was not difficult to locate the crystal for it glowed with a hazy white light. Richard pushed deeper with the tips of the tongs until he had hold of it. He paused again in order to sight the opening on the statue's back and then slowly he withdrew the crystal.

In one flowing movement he stood, leant over the coffin and deposited the crystal into the receptacle. It was Mubarakar's turn to hold a breath.

"It looks as if this task should be done with the figure standing," commented Richard, "and the crystal is too small for the receptacle by the looks of it, but it's there. For the life of me, I'm not sure if this will work." He turned his head towards Hamid. "Can you replace the cover exactly as you found it?"

Hamid nodded and dropped the square lid into place. The engineered tolerance was so close as to leave it barely visible. The three men stared, first at the motionless figure and then at each other. Richard shrugged. "There was no on–off switch was there? Nothing you saw inside?"

"There was nothing, Richard. I am experienced in examining artefacts," responded the Professor, almost defensively.

Richard gestured, as if no explanation was necessary. "Well, in that case . . . it was a good . . ."

At that moment the statue stirred. There was no sound with the movement and the material it was composed of showed no joins, joints or deformation. Then it stopped.

Richard looked up. "Did I imagine that?" he asked in a whisper. He looked at Hamid. "Knock on the door and have Abdel open it."

The sound of the door sliding open seemed to stir the figure into life. This time it began to roll over. "Out . . . out . . . quickly . . . !" ordered Richard.

Mubarakar and Hamid were already outside as Richard edged around the base of the coffin; his eyes were wide with disbelief and his expression hollow with fright as the statue sat up and turned its head towards him. Moments later, as he leapt out, the vehicle began to shake and rattle.

The five men huddled together and retreated in unison. Richard, assuming the lead, scanned his immediate surroundings in the hope of finding something he could use as a weapon. His pistol was in his coat and that was hanging from a peg on the other side of the garage.

Thomas, alerted by the commotion, strode across and stood defiantly by the driver's door. However, he promptly took several paces backwards as the huge hulk of the statue stepped into the doorway. It made an effort to stand and, in so doing, curled the roof of the van into an arch shape.

Amazingly, and fully aware of the restriction, the statue stepped down whilst still bent forwards at the waist; its feet made solid clunking sounds on the concrete. It took two paces forwards, stood to its full height and then turned its head gently in both directions, until it had looked over each shoulder in turn, an angle of more than two hundred degrees.

As if sensing movement through never-opening bronze-coloured eyelids, it seemed to take stock of its surroundings. After a few moments it assumed another position: its right hand punching through a sturdy roof member as if it was balsa wood. And then there it stood; much more than two metres tall and almost a metre across the shoulders; massive, armoured, ancient and absolutely motionless.

It was a minute before heart rates settled and almost two before anyone spoke and, as they did, tiny, almost imperceptible twitches of the statue's head resulted.

"Look! It is true!" gasped Mubarakar in a forced whisper. "It stands legs astride, with one arm upwards as if holding a sword and the other across its body as if holding a shield . . . It stands like the great Colossus of Rhodes did . . . the great wonder . . . It claims its place in history!"

It was another minute before anyone dared to move. Finally, Richard, sensing the nature of the figure as non-aggressive, very warily walked across to it and stopped a few paces short. It was truly a remarkable feat of engineering, as not a blemish or wrinkle was apparent anywhere on its face, head or body.

Thomas, on hand, stepped closer still and extended his neck until the top of his head matched that of the statue. "Two point four two three seven metres tall, and judging by the reaction of the vehicle's suspension, I would say it weighs in at approximately five hundred kilograms," he informed. He stared at the statue's face. "This machine and I . . . we're . . . worlds apart, aren't we?" There was admiration in his voice.

"You are positively primitive in comparison," retorted Richard. There was an edge of irony in his tone. "And this machine could be seven thousand years old – it's certainly been submerged in salt water for more than two thousand." He looked at Thomas. "Now go over there and don't move until I say so."

The forlorn figure of Thomas walked head down towards the corner.

"Bloody support, you have got to be kidding," mumbled Richard under his breath, and then returned his attention to the statue. "Can you understand me?" he asked in a raised voice. "Do you understand English?" There was no response. Richard turned to Mubarakar. "Professor, please, could you ask a few questions in Arabic and perhaps French? And any other language you or Hamid or anyone might know? Let's see if we can communicate with it."

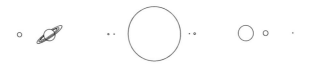

The five men sat at the kitchen table drinking a fresh brew of mint tea and chatting. Richard checked the time and began mentally formulating his plan for the next day, as it was not only New Year's Eve but also a full moon. Naomi flooded his thoughts. *If she does not show up for her duties inside the Great Pyramid tomorrow, then I will go and see Banou immediately, and coordinate that with Peter and the Royal Navy pilot.* He checked the time again – it was close to midnight.

"We can't communicate with it; it seems to have adopted a default position, and there is little chance of it being moved like that," commented Richard, joining the conversation again.

Mubarakar and Hamid nodded. "I think you are right, Richard," concurred the Professor. "I think to communicate we need to speak in the language of the day – perhaps ancient Greek, perhaps an older tongue."

"Ancient Greek might work, Professor; more than likely, however, it would be the language of the old people. The thing is, being able to read the old text is one thing; being able to sound the words, to speak it coherently so as to be understood, that is something else entirely. And there would be dialects too, probable Semitic in nature. It's a long lost skill. Logically, as Eridu was the first recorded city in history, the ancient language believed to have been spoken there may also work. The only other possibility I can think of is ancient Egyptian of the First Dynasty. There was some commonality," added Richard, "I found that during my studies."

"I tried Coptic, but it did not work," said Hamid, in a resigned fashion.

"Our only hope is Naomi; she *sees* languages as colours. It's incredible." Richard paused and took stock of the situation. "Professor, could Abdel take me to Giza tomorrow, please, undercover? I'm going to stake out the Great Pyramid from midday until dawn on the first of January. Looks like I'll be seeing in the New Year with the Bedouins. If she doesn't show, I'll need to get back to the El Al Shalamin airbase sharpish."

"Of course, my young friend . . . I will arrange a service vehicle from the Antiquities Commission. Wear a dark djellaba – several are hanging in the cloakroom. Pull the hood well over your face. You will pass as a local. This is better, as there are precious few tourists these days. Abdel knows the way; there is but one safe access to the monuments. Find a place to hide and do not stray; the desert is a sea of quicksand – it still claims lives. At first light on the day after tomorrow he will return. I will remain here with Hamid and the statue until I hear from you. Abdel will call me if you go directly to the airbase. Do you agree?"

Richard nodded.

The Professor rubbed his reddened eyes. "What a

day it has been . . . but for me at last it is over. The maid has marked your rooms, you will see. I bid you all good night." Professor Mubarakar stood wearily and turned to leave the room.

"Yeah, time for me to turn in, too," said Richard. He raised a hand. "Professor, before you go, if you don't mind, there is one other thing that I want to mention; it could be important."

"I am listening; tell it."

"A few years ago Naomi took me inside the Pyramid of Khufu, through a secret door. It was at the beginning of our search for the Ark. Inside, is the Temple of Osiris. I know that you and some of your people are aware of the place, but have kept it a lifelong secret. Well, in the centre of that temple there is a raised plinth and on that, an altar . . . a stone structure with a flat top and a lot of inscriptions – in the old writing, you understand. But more importantly, in the middle of that altar there is a receptacle, a cup . . . a chalice if you like. I thought it was significant at the time, but, you know, things slip your mind. The receptacle in the back of that statue where I placed the crystal this evening, it was remarkably similar, although a little smaller. It jogged my memory." Richard paused and looked thoughtful. "I'm thinking out loud here, but that chalice in the pyramid might also have been made for a similar purpose – a facility for tapping the energy of a Kalahari crystal. We know that the Ark containing the shattered crystal from Eridu passed through Giza on its way to Meroe, and that it remained there for many centuries. The Temple of Osiris was said to have great powers. You recall that Simpson-Carter viewed the pyramids as more a network of centres for interplanetary communication? He even spoke of the pyramids on Mars, that there could be a link?" Richard shrugged. "Anyway, something to bear in mind, perhaps." Richard fell back in his chair and smiled. "Good night, Professor."

# CHAPTER 18

# ROCKETS AND RELATIVES

**The Plane of Elysium – Mars**
**Early the next day**

"Commander Race, sir, can you come up, please? The object is painting clearly now on the area radar; I'm getting an accurate readout of its dimensions."

Tom Race, the Commanding Officer of Osiris Base and the most senior officer on Mars, was busy checking the integrity and functionality of his one-piece surface suit in the rear compartment. "On my way, Peter," he responded, trying to keep his balance. He replaced the bulbous white helmet in the locker, closed its grey metal door and then staggered forwards, using the overhead rails as support.

The rough terrain caused the PTSV to roll and judder

as Peter Carr used his hand-held microphone to call Lesley Oakley in the cockpit. She manoeuvred the long vehicle with some skill around the final obstacles in a boulder field and then set a course to avoid the windward side of an approaching extended rocky outcrop that rose abruptly from the plain to tower some 500 feet above them. From experience, Lesley knew the extent of the soft, deep sand that accumulates on the windward side of such outcrops, and the danger it presents to the PTSV. Even the massive bulbous tyres, independent suspension system and high gearing would not prevent the machine sinking quickly if she dared cut the corner. She avoided the area by a good margin despite losing ground to the lightweight two-seat buggy that by now was well ahead of them.

"Lesley," said Paul quietly, "back off on the speed will you. Make it forty K's . . . forty-five max. And call Dan; make sure those two guys keep their eyes peeled."

"Speed forty-five maximum, copied. Shall I engage the pulse cannon?"

"Yes, do that. Automatic target enhancement mode, self-align, but manual fire."

"It's done. Manual fire control selected . . . okay . . . yes, it has acquired the target and the buggy's transponder is indicating 'on-side' about ten Ks ahead of us – so no problem with mistaken identity. Turning to course zero, seven, five degrees. Direct track towards the object. Twenty minutes to run."

"Got it," responded Paul, as Commander Race

arrived at his console. Paul focused his attention on the radar display as the Commander leaned over his shoulder. "There it is, sir, directly ahead," he explained, pointing at a square-shaped blip on the circular screen. The rotating sensor swept over the blip again as the two men studied it and the indication glowed brightly for a few seconds. "Range fourteen Ks, and it's been acquired by the weapon system too, just in case. The last Geosat pass locked the coordinates; there's nothing else in the area."

"Good . . . details?"

"Looks to be cylinder-like – six metres wide I'd say, and about the same high, standing approximately three metres clear of the ground, probably on an undercarriage arrangement of some kind. We are seeing a few antennae on the top and also what looks like a microwave dish. No sign of life, although the infrared scanner is picking up a localised hotspot – just there. See it? Seems to be an equipment area, maybe a cooling outlet or similar."

Tom Race nodded. "Okay, thanks, Paul. We go in slowly and quietly, keep out of sight behind that hillock for as long as possible, and come back to twenty-five kilometres per hour."

Paul relayed the information to Lesley Oakley. "It's done, sir – speed twenty-five Ks."

"Open a channel to Dan Winton, will you?"

"Survey One this is Support One, come in please." Paul pressed a button on his panel to feed the response through the cabin's speaker.

There was a crackling for a moment and a distant whining sound before a reply was heard. "Three by five, Support One. Little bit hazy out here and some atmospheric electrostatic remnants from the storm, so a little radio distortion I guess," came the voice of Space Engineer Dan Winton.

"Copied, Dan. Commander Race is with me; he's going to talk to you. Standby." Paul turned to the Commander. "Go ahead, sir."

"Dan, radar's showing you at less than three kilometres. Can you see it?" Tom asked.

"Yes, we see it, Commander. Closing fast. It's in a flat area, some undulations to the south. A black object, elevated."

"Okay, be careful." Commander Race looked around at Paul. "Are they armed?"

"A static baton each, and there is a flare gun as part of the buggy's inventory . . . that's it, I'm afraid. They were not supposed to be going it alone. Shall I call them off until we get closer?"

"Definitely a landing vehicle," came the voice of Dan Winton. The radio crackled again. "Looks like a circular section, perhaps a mid-portion of a small rocket. Four support legs. Put down in a good landing area . . . Nine hundred metres now, and seeing some communication antennae and there is a break halfway up. Eight hundred metres . . . interesting, the lower half is the landing stage. Single propulsion nozzle. Looks to be a basic rocket motor. Wait, there seems to be a second stage, the upper part. Six hundred metres to go . . . yes, there is an ascent stage, alright . . . sir, the capsule has a two-way capability!"

"Anything else, Dan?"

"Lee's trying to get the binoculars working so he can patch through the image directly to your display – bit of sand in the contacts, won't be long. What's the deal, Lee?"

"Here comes the image. I'm using I-Band, but I'm not sure it will be that clear," said a man with an Irish accent.

At that moment a grainy picture appeared on an ancillary monitor screen on Paul's console. A blurred image of the capsule could be seen, but it was distorted by flickering lines that flashed up and down the screen. It was a real-time close-up; digital numbers on the left-hand side of the screen indicated 150 metres and decreasing. And the image appeared unstable, as the buggy negotiated the reddish-brown sand-covered landscape.

"Topography is petering out; I'm going to break cover from behind this high ground," announced Lesley, her voice emanating from the intercom speaker.

"Tell her to slow to ten Ks and proceed with care," said the Commander from the rear console.

Paul passed on the message and then spoke to the buggy crew. "Looks like you're very close now guys; we're ten minutes behind you. Anything else?"

"The capsule definitely has some stealth features," replied Dan Winton. "A dull black finish, granular in nature, nothing reflective anywhere . . . it's a radar-absorbing material, spray applied. I've seen it before, I think, in fighter technology. Also, there are angular external accessories to scatter radar returns and four dissipaters around the rocket nozzle to reduce its heat signature – probably why it wasn't picked up during the descent. Solar panels are of an integrated circular type, again to reduce a sensor return. Concentric rows – looks like an excessive requirement for electrical power. There would be a weight penalty to all this – it appears that stealth and electrical-generating potential were priorities in the design of this craft. No markings, however. Wait a minute! Yes, we see something, up there on the upper structure . . . Lee's climbing out. Call it Lee . . ."

"Looks like Chinese writing, or Japanese, that sort of thing. And there's a red 'T', but nothing else, to be sure. No sign of life support either, no oxygen canisters, recyclers or waste disposal. But look . . ."

Against the red, eerie and incandescent glow of the sun's orb as it completed its ascent above the distant horizon, astronaut Lee Tanner pointed to a position on the upper stage of the landing vehicle. He was silhouetted against the brilliant light as a shooting star produced a brief but fiery flash across the heavens above him. Instantaneously, other pieces of falling debris produced several curved white trails in the fading blackness of the early morning sky. Dan Winton followed his friend's pointing finger.

"No sign of a life support system of any kind and yet there is a personnel hatch – quite a large one, too, about a metre square. Lee's pointing to it now," explained Dan over the radio. "Clearly this is a recognisable design and has come from home, but there is no provision for humans, not that I can see. Also, there are a lot of marks in the sand on this side. Not exactly footprints, but something walking on two feet . . . sounds impossible but I think we have been visited by robots!"

In the PTSV, which by now was less than five kilometres away, Paul, who was still sitting at his console, looked up at Tom Race. "Robots, Commander?" he said, with a startled expression. "What kind of robot could pilot a landing vehicle, make a successful touchdown in an adverse environment, go off and cause trouble, and then expect to blast off again – presumably to rendezvous with a passing ship? Because there sure as hell isn't anything orbiting this planet – our sensors would have picked it up. What would they want, anyway?"

"I've come face-to-face with a system that could almost do that, Paul . . . back in 2050." Tom looked concerned. "The Humatron HU40, built by Tongsei. The red T painted on the hull confirms it. The entire model range was recalled and destroyed later that year and further production was universally banned on Earth. They had an inherent programming disorder. Perhaps with four years of secret development they have produced something else, an improved model, one capable of total autonomy?"

Paul scratched the stubble on his chin. "The attack we sustained near the sensor mast five days ago and

Martine's death . . . it all makes sense. But what about the laws that are applicable to robots? Shouldn't their programming contain dynamic overlays to prevent them from harming humans? Not in any way should they attack a person or be openly aggressive!"

"Unscrupulous men will be behind this – the big corporations. They are blind to the plight of others; for them it's all about control." The Commander sighed heavily. "Why didn't we think of this earlier?" he continued, shaking his head. "Listen, first we need to find out how many of these things there are, and then what they are doing here." He leaned across the console and pressed the radio transmit button again. "Dan! Commander Race here! Stay in the buggy and keep your eyes open! Lee, you take a look inside the module and count how many seats or manoeuvre stations. If we are dealing with Humatron HU40's or even worse, an upgraded model, then we are in serious trouble. Dan, Lee, any sign of a robot and you high tail it – understand? I want an immediate Mayday call: no heroics and no reasoning. You get the hell out of there. We'll be with you in two minutes!"

**Moon Base Andromeda – simultaneous**

"Would the Security Officer and the Chief Operations Officer please report to the Operation's Room immediately. Security Officer and Chief Operations Officer to the Ops room please," came a female voice over Andromeda One's entire PA network.

Dimitri Nurevski, a former Major in the Russian Space Programme, was the first to arrive in the large operations room in the upper central district; an area affectionately called Cyber City. It was a brightly lit room, filled with computer consoles. There were various models: some old, some state-of-the-art. The central system had a large transparent display screen, viewable from both sides. The image on the screen showed the Earth and the Moon in space and a system of flight corridors between them. There were white dots in the corridors that indicated space vessels in transit.

The consoles were being manned by men and women, mainly in their twenties and thirties, and of all nationalities. There was a small gathering in an alcove to the right and somebody in that group called: "Dimitri! Dimitri, over here please . . . quickly." The voice emanated from the Lunar Security Control Centre, a group of consoles detached from the main area. Dimitri Nurevski turned and promptly walked over to the group as Eddie Lieven, the Chief Operations Officer strode through the main doors on the other side of the room. Dimitri raised a hand, attracted his attention and indicated where he was going.

The gathering parted as Dimitri arrived and allowed him access to the primary console. "What is it? What's the problem?" he asked, with a heavy East European intonation.

The group centred on a mature-looking woman, perhaps in her early thirties. She had Asian features with black hair that was tied back in a tight bun and wore a pale blue trouser suit of synthetic cotton. A badge over her right breast pocket, consisting of three narrow platinum-coloured bands overlaying the letters 'LSD', signified her status as a senior operative in the Lunar Security Directorate.

"It's the dark side sensors, and something sent to me by Herbie Smith in the Freight Control Centre. He drew my attention to it and it is very irregular." She pointed at her screen.

At that moment Eddie Lieven arrived. He was short and stocky and, hailing from Brussels, spoke English with a French lisp. His face was flushed. "I was in a meeting with the Council of Senators . . . What the hell is it?" He scowled.

The Asian woman looked apologetic. "I'm sorry, sir," she said, "but this definitely warrants a Code One."

"Well!"

"It's the dark side sensor array. The extended essential maintenance period was completed at 04:00 hours. The engineers completed a normal power up at 04:06 hours, but thirty-three seconds later the entire system crashed . . . total loss. I've had the Duty Engineering Officer on the line; he can't understand it, Sir. He says it was caused by an electrical overload that amounted to more than the actual system demands when operating at maximum capacity. He says a current spike of such magnitude could not have happened accidentally. He says it's impossible. And he says that there's substantial damage to the receiver network . . . the system could be down for a month. It's burnt out, sir!"

"Where is the DEO now?"

"In the transport department, I think, trying to get the service vehicles loaded and the spare parts chain in place."

"I need to speak to him," barked Lieven. "Put out a call on the PA."

The woman looked across at a colleague who sat at another console, nodded her approval, and then looked up at the two men again. "There's something else, sir. You had better take a look at this." With that she made a selection on her keyboard and pointed to her monitor. The image on the screen made several people in the group gasp. Both the Security Officer and the Chief Operations Officer bent forwards and peered at the screen. Dimitri Nurevski's mouth dropped open.

**The Plain of Elysium – simultaneous**

Paul Carr sat in the observer's seat alongside Lesley Oakley as she slowly drew the PTSV to a halt about twenty metres from the unidentified landing module. As the trailing cloud of red dust and debris blew over them, visibility dropped to just a few metres and that, combined with the scattered light from the low but brilliant sun, temporarily obscured all forward vision.

The buggy was parked on the other side, but Paul had briefly seen Dan Winton sitting in the left-hand seat of the nimble, open-topped vehicle as they had approached and this was as expected. What he could not account for, however, was the lack of movement outside and the total loss of two-way communications between them.

By way of a pistol-shaped lever that protruded from the central console to his right, Paul directed the barrel of the Magnetic Pulse Cannon until it pointed directly at the spacecraft. Commander Tom Race stood between the cockpit seats and scrutinised the craft's construction through the five, wide-view, polyspec glass panels as visibility slowly improved.

The front end of the PTSV's tube structure was slightly convex and this, combined with the large side windows, allowed, under normal conditions, a good outside panorama. The Cyan Magnetic Pulse Cannon was primarily a close-quarter self-defence system. Its three-metre long barrel protruded from a squat, circular turret that swivelled on a mounting on top of the vehicle and slightly aft of the cockpit. The system was accurate to five kilometres and worked by disrupting the atomic structure of a target. At close range it would certainly leave a gaping hole in the landing module.

"Keep calling them, Paul," ordered Commander Race, as the dust finally settled outside, "and don't get any closer. I'm going to take a look for myself. I'll take control of the airlock and rear portal from the local panel. Anna and Veronica will stay inside. Paul, I'd appreciate it if you keep me covered."

"Will do, Commander, but be careful; there's still no

sign of Lee."

Tom nodded and walked aft into the environmental chamber where the suits and other surface equipment were stored. Well-practised, it took only a few minutes to dress and pressurise his suit and helmet. "Paul, I'm opening the portal now," he informed, his words filling the PTSV's working area by way of the open intercom system.

"Copied, Commander, I am waiting for you . . . still neither sight nor sound from the guys."

The outer door opened with a dry, gritty racketing. Initially, this was accompanied by the whoosh of escaping gas, which around the lower portion caused dust and fine grit to recirculate again. Tom allowed the circular door to motor to its fullest extent – a position slightly higher than the horizontal – before stepping out. He had considerable experience of 'outside' operations but on this occasion he felt his pulse rate quicken and the hairs on the back of his neck stiffen as he stepped onto the rusty-coloured Martian surface. His boots made a zigzagged line of near-perfect treaded prints in the wind-blown sediment as he walked past the row of six enormous bubble tyres, the tops of which were an arm's length higher than his head.

When at the front of the vehicle he turned, looked up at the cockpit windows and gave a thumbs-up sign. From outside the glass appeared a deep, tinted blue colour and the backlight made them look eerie and insect-like. He felt for his thigh holster and glanced down at the tiny, glowing green light on the static baton that indicated a full charge of 20,000 Volts; this was his only weapon and he would need to be in close proximity to use it – a thought he did not relish. He thought of his last tangle with a Humatron – back in 2050 on the *Enigma* and how he nearly froze to death.

Walking alongside the landing module brought the buggy into full view. Tom saw Dan Winton slumped awkwardly in the left-hand seat and knew immediately. "We have a problem!" he cried over the radio and quickened his pace.

At the buggy, and peering through Dan Winton's visor, it was clear that he was unconscious, but there were no obvious signs of injury. Tom scanned the area for Lee Tanner, but he was nowhere to be seen, although judging by footprints, scuffs and furrows in the sand close to the module, and particularly at the base of the steps, there had previously been a good deal of activity – *perhaps even a struggle?* Tom ran his eye line up the steps to the personnel hatch. It was firmly closed and all was still, although he had the unnerving feeling that he was being watched. Condensation inside Dan's helmet indicated a lack of ventilation and Tom instinctively checked the life support control panel on Dan's left forearm. To his shock he saw that the panel was scorched and burned and was completely out of action.

"Dan's life support is down!" he shouted. "He's running on the oxygen inside his helmet. There's no sign of Lee; I've the goddamn feeling that he's inside. I'm going to bring Dan back now!"

"Standing by," was the reply.

Tom Race moved quickly to the other side of the buggy. He leapt into the right-hand seat and floored the accelerator pedal. The wheels spun wildly and the fat tyres kicked up debris as he pulled away. He tugged on the upper half-circle-shaped steering wheel in order to turn a tight one hundred and eighty degrees and then headed off at breakneck speed back towards the PTSV. Thirty seconds later he skidded to a halt close to the airlock, and within a minute was pulling Winton from his seat and dragging him up the shallow incline towards the chamber. He panted with the effort and moisture condensed on the inside of his visor. Stepping inside, he lashed out and thumped the large red button on the control panel with the base of his fist and the portal began to close. A flashing amber light and an intermittent buzzer warned of the danger of powerful hydraulics.

"I'm in! We need oxygen!" he yelled.

"Anna and Veronica are ready in the environmental chamber," Paul replied over the intercom, but his last words were drowned by the sound of incoming gas.

The moment that the green light on the adjacent bulkhead illuminated, signifying an equal gas pressure, the door to the environmental chamber opened. Tom was already releasing the clips that secured Dan's helmet to his suit's metal neck ring as the two women stepped inside. They pulled the limp body into the inner chamber together.

As Tom shuffled the helmet clear, Anna smothered Dan's face with an oxygen mask and mixed the supplied gas with a low percentage of adrenomorph. Meanwhile Veronica unfastened a glove and taped a vital signs probe to Dan's palm. The monitor indicated a heartbeat, but shallow breathing.

Anna increased the gas pressure to inflate Dan's lungs; he responded immediately.

"You have him," said Tom. "I'm going back to get Tanner." And with that he leapt up, turned and disappeared into the airlock, again closing the door behind him.

Two minutes later and from the right-hand seat of the buggy Tom repeated his thumbs-up signal to the cockpit windows, and then he described a large arc and drove back warily towards the landing module. His white spacesuit had acquired a covering of dust that turned it a uniform pale orange colour, except for under his arms and between his legs. He cleaned his visor with his glove.

The sun was higher in the sky by now and bathed the module in a warm reddish light, but strangely the special black surface seemed to absorb the light and reflected nothing back. Tom drove a full circle around it and noted the ten or so steps up to the square hatch and a metal tube as a basic balustrade. There were four undercarriage struts and, at their ends, large, pivoted pads prevented the craft sinking into the sand by more than a few centimetres.

The planet surface was beginning to heat in the morning sunshine and this thermal activity caused air currents; as Tom climbed from the buggy and stood at the base of the steps studying the hatch, a sudden gust of wind peppered him with sand. He turned his back to it and, when it had passed, he made a better job of dusting the residue from his visor – this time sweeping with the back of his glove so as to give unrestricted peripheral vision. He was about to step onto the first rung and grasp the balustrade when Paul shouted over the radio.

*"Don't touch the craft . . . ! Keep off it!"*

Tom instinctively took a pace back. "What the hell?"

"It's electrified!"

"Goddamn it!"

"Commander, Dan has told me that Tanner was trying to release the hatch mechanism when it suddenly swung open. He was pulled inside by a bloody robot! A hell of a thing! Dan went to his aid but as he stepped up and grabbed the support he received a massive shock that shorted his life support controller. He managed to stagger back to the buggy but became dizzy and fainted."

Tom took a few more paces backwards and assessed the situation: he scanned the craft for other openings and opportunities. "What do we do? It's stalemate!" he exclaimed.

"Dan says he only saw one machine and that it looked very aggressive."

"We will have to make the robot open up from inside. Drive him out."

"I agree, sir, but how do we do that?" replied Paul, peering through the cockpit windows.

"How good a shot are you, Paul . . . ? With the pulse

cannon I mean?"

"Good!"

"Good enough to take out an undercarriage strut?"

"I'd say so."

"Then take your pick. I'm coming back – to take cover behind the PTSV."

Tom climbed into the buggy and drove into a position directly behind the PTSV. "I'm clear," he called.

Paul Carr, sitting in the observer's seat in the PTSV cockpit, refined his aim by making minute adjustments to the controller in his right hand.

"Three, two, one . . . now," he said, and squeezed the trigger.

The PTSV instantly shuddered with the recoil of the long barrel and then a fuzzy blue light preceded an explosion that was centred on the nearest right hand strut of the landing module. When the dust settled the strut had disappeared, leaving only torn and jagged metal protrusions. Blue sparks and white ionised streaks, like miniature lightning forks, played on that part of the module's structure, but the craft stood firm on the three other supports.

Tom peered at the module from around the rear right-hand corner of the PTSV. He could see the damage. "Any sign of movement?" he asked.

"Nothing," responded Paul.

"Then take out the other one on the same side – and be ready. I've a feeling it's going to come out angry."

"Got it," replied Paul, and he prepared another charge. This time it would be a more difficult shot because the undercarriage strut on the far side was almost obscured. He took careful aim; he would hit it low, near the base pad. "Three, two, one . . . now," he called.

Another shuddering recoil rocked the personnel vehicle, to be followed a split second later by a loud explosion at the module. Paul had increased the weight of charge and in a dazzling blue flurry of sizzling electrical static, suddenly, the strut collapsed, bending outwards. In a catastrophic contortion of groaning metal, the craft fell backwards and then crashed onto the ground.

The calamity raised a dense cloud of dust and sand that at first circulated just above the surface and was then lifted high into the sky by a sharp gust of wind.

Tom was quickly in the buggy and scooting around the PTSV towards the module. He could see that the personnel hatch now faced the sky at an angle of approximately forty-five degrees.

Tom skidded to a halt about twenty metres from the wreckage and stared. At first there was nothing – no movement and no response – and so he climbed from the buggy and took a few paces forward. The visibility slowly improved, aided by a prolonged squall that swirled and whistled eerily around the structure and then fled across the plain, taking the dust with it. It was like a parched desert wind blowing through the stripped bones of a long dead animal.

Tom turned towards the PTSV and focused on its seemingly luminescent cockpit windows. He could see shadows moving inside and spread his arms, with hands upwards, as if to say, "And what do we do now?" He finally tapped his chronometer and held up five fingers. "We give it more time," he said restlessly over the radio.

"I don't think we need to wait, Commander . . . something's moving," was Paul's ominous reply.

Tom looked back and at that precise moment the metal hatch was flung open, as if it had been rammed from the inside by a raging bull. *This might not be the best place to be,* Tom considered, *and that would be an understatement.* He instinctively took a few paces backwards. Nervously, he reached down for the handle of his static baton. And then, staring wide-eyed, a machine began to emerge from inside the spacecraft. He recognised it immediately: the extending neck, the glowering red, almond-shaped eyes; the heavy structure and the wide shoulders. He gulped at the sight of it. There was no doubt in his mind – it was the worst-case scenario – *it was a Humatron!*

With one easy movement the robot lifted itself clear of the square opening and then crawled over the black surface of the module, looking for a way to get down. It selected one of the two remaining undercarriage struts and, on all fours, slithered, leaping the final metre or so onto the ground with the grace of a large gorilla.

It stood tall and assessed the threat. It looked first

at the PTSV, and then over at Tom, its eyes all the while glowing, as if on fire. Buckled around its right thigh was a grey-coloured holster and, protruding from it, Tom saw the butt of a pistol. Its attention momentarily diverted, the machine briefly glanced over its shoulder at the sun and subsequently, and almost surreptitiously, it edged around so that the voltaic panels on its back and head pointed towards the far off orb.

"Are you seeing what I'm seeing?"

"You had better get back in the buggy, Commander."

"Get ready with the pulse cannon."

"I am, but I wouldn't count on it . . . not a target like that."

Nominating Tom as the closest and easiest objective, the robot half-crouched, raised its hands and spread its bony fingers – adopting a threatening posture, much as a large cat would before pouncing on its prey. To Tom's dismay it began edging towards him. *There's something about this machine,* Tom thought, *especially compared to what I remember. It moves freer, like an animal, like a human, with the swivelling knees joints, the articulated hips, and the flowing motion – and then the face . . . ?*

Tom retreated tentatively until he backed into the buggy; all the while the machine advanced. It moved slowly and cautiously and Tom could see its face screen flickering and strangely blurring as it alternated between vaguely recognisable human expressions to a sensor-like display where its programming updated parameters and reassessed hazards.

Tom's heart raced. Had anyone been paying attention to the pulse rate monitor in the PTSV they would have seen an orange light illuminate, indicating a ninety per cent increase over his nominal resting index. He felt a surge of adrenalin increase his breathing rate and a primal need to simply turn and run – but he thought better of it. "You had better take the shot . . . this would be a good time . . . don't worry about the flash," he uttered over the radio.

Paul tracked the Humatron using the manual sight; the robot was a clear target. Nevertheless, the pulse cannon was not designed for relatively small, agile targets such as humans – or a robot; he would only get one chance. Lesley Oakley sat pensively in the pilot's seat. She was ready to engage the power drive should they need to move quickly. Anna and Veronica stood behind them, mouths agog.

Tom gingerly lifted his left leg into the foot well of the buggy's right-hand seat. With that, the Humatron sensed what was happening, and still with twenty-five metres between them, slowly began unclipping the strap that held the pistol in place.

"I'm going for it," announced Tom, with his heart pounding. "Programme a bias, for God's sake aim in front of it, in case it . . ."

But Tom did not have a chance to finish his instructions, for the robot suddenly leapt towards him. In an instant, Tom was in the buggy. The machine was intent on a kill; it pulled the pistol from its holster and raced forwards.

"Now! Now!" Tom shouted.

The robot had covered more than ten metres when Paul loosed his first shot. He missed, but the sparking, neon blue charge passed between the two figures and caused the Humatron to skid to a halt and momentarily reassess the threat. This was all Tom needed and, already seated, he stamped his foot down on the accelerator pedal and pulled away, whipping up a cloud of sand and dust in his wake.

Paul reloaded without delay but the machine took off after Tom. It accelerated at a similar rate to the buggy and then opened its legs into a headlong sprint, the speed of which had Lesley gasping as she watched the chase unfold. Tom was quickly making sixty kilometres per hour and edged to seventy. The buggy's electric drive trembled and whined with the effort. Vibrating wheels began to shudder and the vehicle bounced uncontrollably over the undulating terrain.

Running to the side of the streaming dust cloud and at an amazing pace the Humatron began to close on Tom. In full flight it held up an uncannily steady hand and fired a shot from the bulky pistol. Tom was bouncing in his seat with the movement of the buggy and, miraculously, the sublet ricocheted off his helmet, but now Tom knew what was coming and he dodged and jerked and swerved and evaded.

The robot loosed another shot and then another and another, each barely missing Tom's body and helmet. In the havoc, he heard and felt a ricochet close to his right ear. In response Tom swerved more violently, but this reduced his overall speed and the robot quickly closed the gap between them to just five metres. Tom strained to look over his shoulder, eventually twisting awkwardly to catch sight of his pursuer. Instantly, and with just three metres separating them, Tom shouted for support: "Now would be a good time!"

"I can't get a shot in Commander; I can't see it. The dust . . . !" Paul screamed.

Tom needed a break, a way out, and very quickly. In the confusion he tried to think. He swerved again. He could feel the robot bearing down upon him. "Does the automatic fire control system have a lock on the buggy, Paul? Tell me!" he demanded. There was extreme anxiety in his voice.

The robot edged closer; opportunities narrowed. Only a space of about two metres separated them now. The buggy's electric drive screamed with the effort. Paul checked the sensor screen. Another sublet whizzed past Tom's head and instantaneously raised a puff in the sand in front of the buggy. Tom ducked, squirmed and twisted and drove like a bat out of hell. Another sublet penetrated the back of his seat. It missed his body, but Tom felt a sharp punch against his ribs. A hole was ripped open in the dashboard. Tom desperately slewed left and right and left again, avoiding some random boulders; the machine merely took them in its stride, jumping clear.

"Yes . . . I say again . . . affirmative . . . we have an

automatic acquisition . . . but the buggy . . . You're in the bloody buggy!"

"Paul! Do as I say!" yelled Tom, his voice vibrating and difficult to understand. "Engage the automatic target enhancement; let the system lock on. I'm the target . . . tell me when . . . !"

By this time the robot was alongside the buggy. Tom fortuitously caught sight of it in the corner of his eye and ducked as a powerful left-handed swipe caught the top of his helmet – another had him cowering in his seat. Instinctively, he swerved to the left; it was an aggressive and wildly skidding manoeuvre that momentarily gave him ground and left the robot trailing. But the machine was only lost in the dust cloud for an instant.

"Do it! Do it!" Tom shouted.

"Engaged . . . it's done . . . the system has you . . . a positive lock!" Green lights flashed in the PTSV.

"When I say, Paul, you fire: no buts, you fire . . . Understand?"

"Ready!"

At that moment the Humatron appeared in Tom's peripheral vision – at the edge of his visor. But this time it was on the left-hand side of the buggy. The mechanical brute was alongside again in an instant; it stared at Tom with callous red eyes and its powerful legs pumped so fast that they merged into a blur. Tom was flat out but still it edged ahead.

Wide-eyed and terrorised, Tom was running out of options, and then, to his horror, the Humatron leaped to its right and caught hold of the buggy. In the aggressive move it lost a metre or more but had managed to pull itself onto the equipment rack behind Tom. It was out of sight but Tom felt the buggy's electric drive complain and slow and the rear suspension drag under the additional weight and he knew the Humatron was aboard.

"Now!" he screamed. "Now!"

By then, however, the robot had a hold of Tom's suit. It grasped his shoulder; Tom felt the bony grip tighten. He knew he had only a couple of seconds at most and kicked out with all of his might, pushing himself from his seat with an effort charged by desperation. The robot lost its hold and Tom ejected himself from the buggy.

In an instant he felt his back impact the ground and he slid and skidded and grooved the sand, feet first.

A micro-second later, the buggy exploded.

The vehicle erupted into a hazy blue ball and was engulfed. Almost in slow motion, it disintegrated. Tom dug his heels into the sand; his back was being pummelled.

Then he lost it and began tumbling and blackness engulfed him.

## Moon Base Andromeda – simultaneous

"This image was taken during the thirty-three second window of operation of the sensor array, just before the blackout. Sensor Serial Number Zero Two Six captured it looking east. Sensor Twenty-Six is part of the northern system, close to the pole, Sir. Herbie Smith in the Freight

Control Centre saw it by chance. He says it looks like a spacecraft in one of his gaming programmes. I have taken the liberty of sending the image over to the guys in Space Control for analysis, but nothing back at the moment." The woman's chair was on wheels and she moved aside to allow the two men a closer look at her screen.

Lieven leant forward and stared at the vessel for some time – it was saucer-shaped and hovering just above a ridgeline. His eyes were wide with surprise and curiosity and then he stood straight and looked Dimitri in the eye. "If I was to make a guess, I would say it is a UAV, but one with self-defence capabilities. Look, that's a sonic initiator on the port wing stub."

Dimitri nodded. "You could be right, Chief; there is no visible cockpit. But Unmanned Air Vehicles are normally deployed for intelligence purposes; there is nothing to see on the dark side – only the sensor array field."

"Maybe that's it. It could be relaying information on the sensor coordinates. If it's a scout vehicle, it would not be capable of the damage we have sustained . . . which means something else is out there."

"So you think sabotage?"

"Without the sensors we are blind to what is happening on the other side, and we have no directional information for our defence systems. For aerial defence planning, we used a redundancy calculation of two sensors down out of every three, and we utilised a triangular-shaped installation pattern; it seemed appropriate at the time. We never envisaged a total blackout caused by ground operations. That's an entirely different scenario!"

"An assault on our defences . . . but that is not possible! By who . . . ? Why?"

"By God we need to find out, Dimitri, and quick! At this moment we are exposed. I am going to inform the Council."

The Asian woman spun around in her chair and looked up with an anxious expression. "Just a moment, sir, please," she interjected and raised a hand to hold his attention. "Message coming in from Nick Rose in Space Control." She paused and listened to a voice through her earpiece. "He has some results. He says that based on several items of installed equipment that they've recognised on the craft it appears to have a wingspan of four metres and a comprehensive surveillance equipment fit . . . including a high-aspect imaging device and accurate Doppler ranging equipment . . . It also has an integrated, long-range transmitter. He says . . . that he has analysed the antenna dimensions and design and calculated the most appropriate frequency band of operation. He tuned into the specific frequency; it's very high, apparently, and not one normally used for communications . . . There is a continuous two-way flow of binary information from Earth . . . but he says it's coded . . . he can't make head or ta— . . . he can't understand it, sir. He says that they are working on it and will get back to me."

For a moment the entire gathering stood speechless. Chief Operations Officer Lieven's expression blackened, as if an ominous raincloud had gathered over his head. "Dimitri!" he barked. "Call the Andromeda Wing Squadron Commander," he ordered. "I want an S2 manned and ready for take-off in one hour. Postpone all other dark side operations until we know what's going on over there. Get me some imaging from the next satellite pass . . . and what is the fighter count?"

"IROSAT is down, Chief – sorry, I did not have time to make mention. Its orbit became unstable at the same time as the sensor overload happened. The Duty Ops Manager shut it down; she is working on a recovery. Regarding fighters . . . manned, we have eighteen Delta Class, five in maintenance, seven Phoenix, two in maintenance and one Swiftsure; as for unmanned, we have twelve Trojans, but four in maintenance. That was the round-up from yesterday evening's security meeting. I was on my way to this morning's brief when I was called, but I can get an update." Dimitri paused; he looked uneasy. "Regarding Commander Reece, I have to report he is still on secondment."

Lieven's face boiled. "Call London, call Strasbourg, call whoever you have to. I want him back immediately. Find out where he is and send a fighter to pick him up. Make it the Swiftsure."

"But Chief, we agreed with the British that . . ."

"No buts, tell them!" With that Lieven stormed from the room. "Prepare four of the Trojans for a reconnaissance mission and put the Fighter Wing on alert!"

**The Plain of Elysium – a while later**

Tom laid his hands over his face in an effort to shield his eyes from the bright ceiling lights. Mentally, he forced himself to focus in on what had happened and he tried to recall the last few moments before he lost consciousness. After a while he began massaging his temples; he had been lucky and he knew it. Realising where he was, he sat up and blinked repeatedly. He supported his head in his hands for another minute or so. He felt beaten and bruised.

"So, Commander, you're back with us," said Anna, pushing back from her console and swivelling around in her chair in order to lay a reassuring hand on Tom's shoulder.

"How long was I out?" he asked.

"Three hours, but your vitals indicated that you were actually in a stable sleep pattern for the last hour. You were knocked unconscious by the fall and suffered a mild concussion, but otherwise you're in one piece – it could have been a lot different."

"Yeah, I'd say . . . and the Humatron?"

"Trashed . . . along with the buggy and your suit and helmet. You will have to use the spare set."

"Where are we?"

"We haven't moved yet. Paul thought it better to let you sleep. He's been outside and completed a recce and is keeping a watch now from the cockpit – in case anymore of those machines return. Everyone's been busy. We are going to eat something first and then you can make a decision on retrieving Tanner – I'm very sorry, Commander, but he's dead."

Tom nodded sadly. "I thought as much. Pulled inside by that monster, he wouldn't have had a chance." Tom shook his head. "Okay, we retrieve his body first, get underway and then we eat . . . agreed?"

"It's your call, Commander."

Tom struggled with Lee Tanner's body, eventually lowering him down feet first from the open hatch. The precarious angle of the module had raised the lowest rung of the access steps well clear of the ground and Paul Carr waited beneath the craft to take hold of Tanner's legs as he came down. When Paul had the dead man's weight, Tom turned and went back inside the capsule to study its controls and instrumentation. There were no seats as such, just three slightly inclined standing stations, each with heavy shoulder and waist harnesses. For the Humatrons, the g-forces associated with breakout velocity and re-entry were insignificant.

Tom noted that the technology was state-of-the-art and two of the display screens utilised new generation Quasar 3D-imaging that Tom had read about in his monthly science review but had never seen. He knew that the Epsilon Rio Corporation had pioneered the development of that specific flight control system, and impressive it was too. There was a general hum of electronics and it was clear that the power demand of the small craft was high, accounting for the concentric rings of solar panels outside and the capacitors and batteries that were integrated into the floor pan. *Probably uses some form of high-yield Iridium battery,* Tom thought, *for operations during the night and when the sun's obscured.* There was also a dedicated charging station for the robots. The main computer displays were blank. However, off to the right, on another console, there was a single screen that glowed with an image. Tom stepped carefully across to the console, taking care to keep a handhold as he moved across the angled deck – he was surprised at what he saw.

"Paul, can you hear me?" he asked.

"Three by five."

"Where are you?"

"Just made it to the PTSV."

"Copied. When you're inside, try a call to Base Ops on the HF, will you? Obviously we head back home, but I want a rendezvous halfway with the medical support vehicle. If they leave promptly and make good time we can meet in approximately twenty-four hours on the Utopia flood plain. We get Dan the help he needs ASAP and transfer the body. Then we turn around and make a beeline for the pyramids, particularly Zeta Three. From what I'm looking at, Zeta Three is their reason for being here. And that's not all . . . I'm looking at images that I recognise of the main entrance to that pyramid – a massive stone door. It's on an elevated platform and there are close-ups of inscriptions and pictograms in the same area."

"Will do, Commander, just opening the portal; I'll be inside in a moment," Paul replied.

Tom found the scroll button on an adjacent keyboard arrangement and in the semi-darkness flipped through several other images; his eyes widened further at the sight of each. Through his intercom he heard the faint grunts and heavy breathing of physical effort as Paul manhandled Lee Tanner's body into the airlock. And then, after a moment's quiet reflection, he looked for a computer interface – somewhere that he could access the mainframe with his suit's own memory storage device, albeit of limited capacity. He found two ports in close proximity. The first was circular and relatively large – about the size of his gloved thumb. This was clearly where the Humatrons gained access to the module's central computer and downloaded information and instructions. The second was much smaller, common and usable, being of the USD format. This would be the port used by the computer installation engineers and maintenance operatives.

The keyboard arrangement operated in a logical sense and, after Tom had plugged in a short lead that extended from the wristband of his suit, he proceeded to download all the images on the open file. Finally, he took a cursory look around the capsule. To him it felt as if he was standing in an alien ship, so destructive were the intentions of its crew. With nothing else of obvious interest and time pressing, Tom cautiously climbed through the hatch and onto the outside structure. He edged around the ascent module, climbed onto the lower re-entry construction, slid down, and jumped the final metre onto the sand.

As he walked slowly back to the PTSV, the images he had seen in the module came to mind again, and so too did the memory of being pushed from the high ledge of the Zeta Three pyramid by the Osiris Base Security Officer. *Major Gregory Searle . . .* he would never forget that name: he'd almost died in the subsequent fall. Although more than four years had passed, the name of that conspirator, the corporation he turned out to be working for, and what he was doing that day, sprang easily to mind. Tom recalled leaving the treacherous man wounded on the bridge of the *Enigma*, but Searle's eventual fate remained a mystery.

Lesley Oakley was ready to get underway when Tom stepped into the cockpit area. Paul had left the body of Lee Tanner in the airlock where the temperature could be maintained at a sub-zero level. Paul Carr sat in the observer's seat and made ready with the pulse cannon.

"You had better back off another hundred metres, Lesley," advised Tom. "And then put a hole in its side, will you Paul? That ship is not going to leave this planet."

With a good distance between them, Paul directed three magnetic pulses at full charge directly at the module. The subsequent explosions nearly ripped the ascent vehicle from its mountings. As the PTSV turned and headed back to Osiris Base, bottled rocket propellant and volatile gas exploded and a raging fire took hold. Tom gestured for Paul to follow him to a rear console as he pulled a finger-sized memory stick from his pocket.

"Did you make contact with Osiris Base?"

"High-frequency communications are distorted at the moment, Commander, due to the electrical storm over the Borealis basin. But the message got through alright. The next geostationary satellite will rise in about three hours; I'll confirm our requirements then. They know about Tanner . . . a body bag is part of the standard inventory on board the medical vehicle." Paul shook his head. "What a way to go, a fist through the visor!"

"There are two more of those damned robots out there somewhere and I'm convinced we will find them in the vicinity of the Elysium Pyramids. At best they are HU40 models, but judging by the speed of that machine when it caught up with me, we are dealing with an improved model. That's scary!" Tom pulled the robot's pistol from his pocket. He had wrenched it from a severed hand that he had found in the wreckage of the buggy. He placed it on the table. "That's a very capable weapon," he said. "A Lurzengard semi-automatic, Special Forces issue revolver. It has two actions – a one centimetre, high-velocity sublet with an armour piercing tip, as here; or a rotary chamber capable of firing ten thousand micro-sublets per minute. Either option would penetrate the pressure vessel of this vehicle – no question. We will need to be very careful. Now, look at this." With that, Tom pushed the memory device into the computer's inlet port. Almost instantly the first image appeared on the screen. Each was of high definition and excellent clarity and Tom flipped through them until he came to several that were taken in close proximity to the huge stone door of the pyramid Zeta Three. "I remember being on that ledge when these images were taken. A man named Major Gregory Searle was responsible. You may remember the name. He was the base security officer back in 2050."

Paul nodded. "I've heard the stories."

"Subsequently, he tried to take me out – nearly did, too. After that, the blanket no-go zone was reinstated. No one has been back there since. There are reasons; you'll find out soon enough. Anyway, he turned out to be working for the Spheron Corporation; somehow he must have passed these images to them at the time, because I left him wounded, perhaps fatally, on the *ISS Enigma* a few days later. Then that ship disappeared and he was never heard of again. He must be dead." Tom stopped and pointed to a specific image. "I remember that, too," he continued, looking up at Paul. "What do you make of it?"

Paul shrugged. "It's an impression in the stone . . . a human hand . . . small . . . a woman's, I'd say. Well, you know, like a woman's . . . it's remarkably accurate."

Tom agreed with a nod. "If you look closely, even the fingerprints are visible."

"Really. Why?"

"Nobody knows. But I remember thinking at the time that it looked like a key. No, not a key, where a key is placed."

"You mean a hand . . . Somebody puts their hand there and the door opens, right?"

"Something like that. But these pyramids are thousands of years old, probably tens of thousands of years, so whoever held the 'key' is long gone. But what it tells us is that there *is* something inside, something of importance, something that was only accessible to a key holder – perhaps a fraternity. I think that's why the Humatrons are here – in order to get inside again."

"What possible motive could there be for a robot to . . . ? I just can't see any relevance."

"A good friend of mine told me that our Elysium Pyramids have a direct link in terms of architecture and orientation to the pyramids in Egypt. Sounds far-fetched I know, but I believe him to be right. What he also said, although he wouldn't elaborate, was that the Egyptian pyramids had a historical link to the Kalahari crystals. So you see where I'm coming from?"

"Yes, but we will need mining equipment and perhaps some acoustic charges to get through a stone door like that – unless the Humatrons have beaten us to it?"

"I already made provision for this, Paul; there's a container in the hold. Considering that our programme was first the module and then the pyramids, I didn't want any holdups." Tom rubbed his brow in a concerned fashion. "A day to the rendezvous position and another back to Elysium . . . in forty-eight hours, we will find out!"

# CHAPTER 19

# FULL CIRCLE

**Africa – the border area between Egypt and Sudan**
**Later the same day**

Richard felt restricted, if not a little claustrophobic. That was common, even to be expected, but he was comfortable enough. Cosseted inside the flight capsule whilst wearing the specialised, fleece-lined jump suit was more akin to being cocooned in a tiny padded stasis cell used for short-term space hibernation, only with fewer options. As in space, outside the capsule, he would be dead within seconds. Instrument repeaters on a small panel above his head indicated 49,000 feet and Mach 2.

The dark green suit incorporated a balaclava-type head covering, with holes only for his eyes and mouth, and rubber-soled socks. The attire made him feel hot –

despite adequate temperature control, direct ventilation and an outside static indication of minus fifty-six degrees Celsius. There was a waterproof film of cellulose acetate applied to the material and that gave it a sticky feel and a dull sheen. With thick gloves and a thin flexible lifejacket buttoned on waistcoat-style, the whole outfit made him look not unlike a knitted doll.

Designed specifically for the pinpoint placement of Special Operations Operatives into conflict areas, including those with heavy sensor saturation, the Special Air Pod was affectionately known in the trade as *The Covert Can*, and Richard had been assured that the system was equally at home on water as it was on land. He desperately hoped that this was the case, as the drop zone was two kilometres east of the old port area of Adulis and into the Red Sea.

Richard had used a covert insertion system such as this once before. It had been for a similar mission, only the drop had taken place over Rome and with much more restrictive landing parameters. That system, of ingenious German design, had utilised a semi-rigid exoskeleton – a suit with a hard outer shell. To say that the wearer was petrified throughout the entire free-fall phase was an understatement. But this British system was different, being essentially an undetectable missile until 1,000 feet above the drop zone, an aeroplane for 950 feet and a hovercraft until touchdown.

The capsule that Richard lay inside had a multi-faceted cross-section producing a near zero radar signature, and stub wings that would automatically deploy at the end of the free-fall stage to reduce the rate of descent and provide accurate control and guidance to the required landing coordinates. Compressed air from a peripheral skirt would cushion the final touchdown. On the water, a low-velocity but high-volume air jet, produced by a silent running, shrouded electric fan, would propel him to the outer harbour wall. There the nose cone would be jettisoned, Richard would swim clear and the capsule would sink. Finally, naturally occurring salts in the water would completely dissolve the entire structure. After six to seven hours there would be no trace of it.

The capsule utilised by his new-found friend and bolted beneath the port wing of Lieutenant Quarrie's Typhoon 5 fighter, was, however, a little older. With that model, the top half of the capsule would be manually ejected and the resulting open canister used as a canoe. Thereafter, the limiting factor to range was ability to paddle. In the case of the HIM 32, however, and its motorised potential, Richard expected Thomas to be the first to reach the rendezvous position on the outer harbour wall.

Richard's involvement with the mechanics of the drop would be minimal. Nevertheless, there would be some basic drills he would need to perform and it was these that he was mentally preparing himself for when the pilot called him.

"Commander Reece, I've a call coming in from

London – on the military net," he said, his voice hollowed and aerated by his tight-fitting oxygen mask. "Can you see the comms panel, top left? There's a speaker mode – just flick the switch."

"Got it, I'm ready," replied Richard.

"It's a maximise passive format, Commander . . . by that I mean it's primarily receive only. We can't afford to transmit in this area – not supposed to be here, you understand."

"But it's secure, right?"

"Correct. London will transmit in coded format via a satellite link. We have a descrambler on-board."

"Understood. Put them through, then. I'm listening."

"Go ahead, London, we have a good signal," invited Lieutenant Quarrie.

There was a silent pause and then the familiar voice of Peter Rothschild emanated from the speaker. "Richard, Peter here," he said. "I understand that this is one-way conversation. If only this could happen more often – a very desirable position, me thinks." There was another pause and Richard shook his head in an irritated fashion, and then suddenly a humorous expression crept over his face – he thought of Rothschild taking pleasure in the predicament. But the drollness was very short-lived. "Richard," continued Rothschild, earnestly, "please listen carefully; we have a number of issues and time is pressing . . . First, the Prime Minister received a high level call from Andromeda's Ambassador to the Space Federation this morning. He has passed the matter down to me. The Lunar Senate want you back at your desk immediately; they have a security alert, although they are not giving any specific details at the moment – they seem intent on their isolationist policies. I've managed to negotiate another twelve hours, but they are not happy and the clock is running. You must do what you need to in Adulis and then get back here as soon as possible. We did manage to get a message to the museum via our local man. Consequently, the Curator will be expecting you; but no more than four hours – five maximum. By some measure of good fortune, we have an Opportune Class submarine on patrol in the Gulf of Aden; she has been notified and will be on hand to extract you. Admiral Hughes has authorised the pick up at 23:00 hours GMT today: that's six hours and forty-one minutes from now. They will send an inflatable to the outer harbour; coordinates will follow and also the frequency of the sonic hail. Now don't be late. You'll be dropped off on the other side . . . in Saudi . . . we have local collaboration. Again, exact details will be posted to your pager in a secure format. Lieutenant Quarrie will be waiting for you at the Alhazoun military base, and thereafter it's a flight back to London's Orbitalport and an immediate return to Andromeda. Your assignment to view the Nazca Lines in Peru will have to wait." Rothschild paused and Richard heard some talking in the background – Sentinel Wing was mentioned, and Andromeda. *What the hell's happening on the Moon?* he thought.

"Second, there are problems on Mars," Rothschild

continued. "The ISSF has received a Code 1 security warning from Osiris Base. I haven't got the full details yet, but it's something to do with Humatrons – although only God knows how. If that's the case it implicates the conglomerate trio again and that ties in with the undercover assassin Karl Rhinefeld, and possibly you as a target. Arrangements are being made by the ISSF to enter the Spheron Headquarters forcibly in the next few days. They are waiting for permission from the French and German authorities.

"Finally, Commander Race is arranging an armed expeditionary force to go to the Elysium Pyramids on Mars. Clearly, he thinks that there is important information to be found there. We also have some rather unconventional information regarding what might be inside. As the senior planetary surveyor before the present no-go zone was established, he may need some information from you – so be aware of it. Okay, that's it. Now be careful. I'll wait to hear of your arrival in Saudi . . . Over and out!" The line went dead almost immediately.

*For a diplomatic recall, the security issues on the Moon would be serious – very serious. It is not a good time to be away from my squadron; not least because it might reflect badly on my naturalisation application*, thought Richard, as he lay on his side and considered the unfolding events. Then he thought of Rachel; *I can only imagine the consequences of my papers being returned.* He breathed a deep sigh and felt helpless. It was New Year's Day. Would she have celebrated? Would she have sat alone? He hadn't had time to call. *The first day of 2055,* he mused. *What would the year bring, and what of Naomi . . . especially Naomi?*

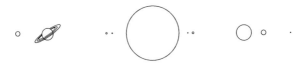

We are approaching the drop zone, said Lieutenant Quarrie in a matter-of-fact tone, his words wresting Richard from his thoughts. "Navigation computer indicates five minutes and fifteen seconds – speed stabilised at Mach 2. Radar jamming and decoy scatter active."

"Copied," replied Richard. "When I put my helmet on I'm ready. What about the other pod?"

"Roger that, sir . . . the other pod is indicating primary green."

"Good. Can I talk to the robot?" asked Richard.

"Yes, of course. Cross pod intercom is now on."

"Thomas, it's me. Are you ready for the drop?"

"Well, I'm jammed in like a sardine, and my restraint system is checked and functioning, if that's what you mean. So, yes, I suppose I'm ready."

*Sardines! By comparison they enjoy wide open spaces!* Richard thought, and he dismissed the quip with a click of his tongue and tried to move, but lying flat on his back with his feet in the direction of travel and his head and body now tightly restrained, there was no give. His face covering snagged the chinstrap of his helmet.

"Four minutes!" said Lieutenant Quarrie.

"Listen," Richard said impatiently. "Just to confirm. We rendezvous at the south-east corner of the outer harbour. Coordinates are confirmed and in the flight plan. Your capsule is timed to land on the water precisely two minutes before mine. This will give us adequate separation. My capsule is self-propelled. You have a pair of oars in yours; just make sure you know where they are. I should make land first. If you get disorientated, listen out for my sonic hail. They tell me that you've got enhanced hearing – frequency range the same as a bat – so it *should* be no problem for you to home in on the signal if it becomes necessary. But be aware that I will only switch the hailer on if you're not at the rendezvous ten minutes after I arrive. And for God's sake, don't forget to isolate your radio; absolutely no transmissions, and no lights either – the place is swarming with Tongsei militia."

"Two minutes!" said the pilot.

"Anything else? Any problems that you would like to share?" asked Richard, wondering if irony would be lost on the robot.

"Um, no, I don't think so . . . hope for the best then."

"Hope doesn't come into the equation. Just do your drills and report to the coordinates as soon as you are able to. Now, let's get on with it."

Lieutenant Quarrie interjected. "One minute and counting everybody – standby for release. Isolating pod systems. Refer now to the timer on your instrument panels. Disconnecting umbilical cord. Good luck and see you in Saudi."

Richard heard a clanking sound outside his capsule. *Here we go again,* he said to himself, as he watched the red digits on the panel count down. "Ten seconds . . . five, four, three, two, one," he whispered, and then he instinctively clenched his stomach muscles – but he still tasted bile in his throat as the capsule dropped suddenly. There was a moment's severe and heart-rending turbulence until the capsule fell well clear of the aircraft. He closed his eyes and laid his gloved fingers over them to stop them bulging. There was a barely audible whistle. And then only the silently changing parameters on the instrument panel indicated the reality outside.

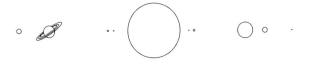

The altimeter reading continued to decrease at an alarming rate. Richard's eyes widened as the capsule passed 5,000 feet and with no sign of a let up. Despite the unnerving speed, it was remarkably quiet inside his cocoon, and smooth too. All of a sudden, Richard sensed a trajectory change and strained to raise his head in order to monitor his progress on the instrument panel. *Pull up any time now,* he thought, as the electronic altimeter indicated 4,000 feet and then, within a second or so, 3,000.

As it passed 2,000 feet, however, and much to his relief, he felt a violent shudder as the stub wings deployed and then the noise from outside grew substantially louder. Immediately the rate of decent was arrested and he sensed minute changes of direction, too.

By 1,000 feet everything appeared under control and the descent rate eased considerably. He could sense the water coming up to meet him.

At 200 feet there was a massive whoosh of air from outside and momentarily he felt very heavy as he was pressed into the padded decking of the capsule.

Finally, as the last of the compressed gas was purged from the retro tanks, the capsule dropped vertically. The radio altimeter indicated less than ten feet, but for a moment Richard's heart was in his mouth. And then, after an impressively gentle touchdown, he was on the water.

Richard soon felt the unmistakable and uncomfortable motion of a heavy swell but an instant later he heard the hum of a high-speed electric motor. A mild vibration permeated the craft and very conveniently the calibrated units of the airspeed indicator promptly changed to knots. The reading was 14; it would only take five minutes or so to reach the harbour wall. Richard made ready.

There was a sudden thud and simultaneously the lights went out. Richard was plunged into blackness – he could not see his hand in front of his face.

A mechanical sound soon followed; it indicated the nose door opening. Water instantly seeped inside the capsule. Within moments the capsule end was open to the sea and the night air. Richard had already released his harness and he gently floated clear of the tube. Almost instantly the capsule began to sink and slip silently beneath the bobbing waves.

Richard gained a foothold on the harbour wall and grasped a rusting metal stanchion that protruded from it in order to pull himself closer. Water lapped around his waist. He checked his backlit chronometer: it was 16:58 Greenwich Mean Time, 19:58 Local, and it was a black night.

He found another stanchion and pulled himself higher. A very subdued glow inland indicated the direction of the main town, although the oldest part of Adulis was much closer – he could see it off to his right as there were a few isolated street lights higher on a peninsula; wave tops occasionally flickered in their reflected light. The sky was completely overcast as there was not a star to be seen from horizon to horizon, but it was dry and relatively warm. His chronometer indicated eleven degrees Celsius and that made his life a little bit easier.

Richard checked the area. It appeared deserted and so he hauled himself up the remaining half-metre or so by jamming a toe into a large crack between two stones and getting a handhold on the top of the wall. Soon he was crouching on the jetty. Just then he heard the sound of splashing water. He turned to see the dark outline of Thomas' capsule approaching and then his human shape rowing for all he was worth. The small vessel reminded Richard of a dugout canoe.

"Keep the noise down," said Richard in a forced whisper, "and throw me the line."

Thomas tossed a thin, coiled, plastic cord towards Richard, who caught it and quickly secured the capsule to a nearby bollard. There was a gentle and slightly offshore swell running and, after Thomas had a hold on the wall, Richard let out enough slack so as to keep the capsule from rubbing on the stone. Moments later, and in an easy motion, Thomas also scaled the wall. They each crouched on one knee and Richard gave his brief.

"Now remember, keep out of sight and a good lookout – and that includes infrared. Use the radio only in an extreme emergency and do not acknowledge any offshore lights or signals until exactly 23:00 – but I'll be back by then."

Thomas nodded his understanding; there was an eerie glow about his face. "And if you're not?" he quizzed.

"You leave without me. Absolutely no question. You're a valuable system. God help us, you might even be the way ahead." With that, Richard melted into the blackness.

Richard knew well enough where he was going, but because of the unknown terrain and obstacles, not the most expeditious way – or the safest for that matter, as he had not received the promised security briefing on his pager. He had an auto-centric miniature digi-map in a special transparent case, but didn't stop to read it because it would direct him using primary routes and landmarks; rather, he kept to the shadows and made for the higher ground.

He was getting better at such covert operations and when he arrived in the once-affluent colonial quarter – an area that was built by the Italians at least two hundred years earlier and on foundations first laid down in ancient times – he began to get his bearings. He moved from wall-to-wall, house-to-house, and alleyway-to-alleyway, taking advantage of the sporadic cover, and loitering in darkened corners each time he heard a vehicle or saw a pedestrian.

There was a fair amount of movement and the red T motif of Tongsei was prevalent – particularly on larger militia vehicles. The pedestrians he saw appeared to be all men and military types, seemingly full of purpose, and as such he began to speculate that a curfew was in place for the locals. Unlike a few years earlier, and certainly regarding these older parts of town, it was clear that there were no longer any prohibited areas applicable to this powerful corporation. *Clearly the region was still blessed with mineral wealth,* Richard thought, but with no energy to extract it. He wondered why Tongsei was maintaining such a presence. *Perhaps they remain here in anticipation of things changing.*

Movement was easy and unrestricted in his one-piece suit and, heading north-west, Richard quickly and warily crossed a main thoroughfare where it was made narrow by several old buildings on either side that protruded well forward of the established building line. During daylight hours it would be a busy junction. He avoided the numerous muddy puddles and on the far side slipped down another alleyway where, after a cautious lope of approximately a hundred and fifty metres, he eventually found himself in the lower part of East Parade. Thereafter, and due to his previous visit – when he had arrived by car – he was familiar with his surroundings.

Richard proceeded along the parade in the direction of the sea. A few of the historic buildings had numbers on their doors or gateposts which gradually decreased; he recalled the gradual incline towards the headland and that Number One had a commanding view over the old harbour. In time he came upon the quadrangle. There was a circular fountain as a centrepiece and Richard looked across the open area to see perhaps the oldest and largest of all the buildings – that was it, Number One, the museum.

Richard hesitated for a moment before stepping out from beneath a stone portico and the shadowy cover that it offered. It proved to be a fortuitous move as, at that instant, Richard heard the low whine of electric drives and a few seconds later two vehicles with Chinese pictogram markings drove into the quadrangle from the street to his left. The first was a Jeep-type vehicle and the second a lorry with a rear canvas hood; both screeched to a halt dangerously close by.

Richard caught sight of figures in the back of the lorry and thereafter a short commotion followed. Two weak street lights that were situated in opposite corners, and another on the other side of the quadrangle, offered gloomy illumination, but when the lorry driver turned off his headlights the shadows deepened to Richard's advantage. Richard skulked further back into his darkened corner and pressed his back against the wall, but in truth the hiding place lacked depth and he knew that should anybody come his way he would surely be discovered. But at least he could see what was going on. *Do they know I'm here? Are they suspicious of something, or is this just a routine sweep?* His heartbeat quickened.

Richard's dark suit provided good camouflage and so when things seemed quiet he edged forward to get a better look. Just then, and to his dismay, a group of four uniformed militiamen stepped from behind the truck and began walking his way; they had rifles slung over their shoulders. Another group headed off in a different direction. He slowly melted into the shadows and held his breath.

The men approached Richard's position in a purposeful manner, but he could hear their voices and, although the language was unintelligible, it was definitely low and relaxed tones in which they spoke, as if having a normal conversation.

*This has to be coincidental,* Richard reassured himself; *they're just going through the motions.* He froze like a statue in his narrow strip of darkness. With eyes wide he watched and waited. After no more than twenty seconds the militiamen came into view. They milled as a nonchalant group and seemed to give no more than cursory looks up and down the street and towards the houses on either side, although one pointed towards an alleyway and said something. They spoke to each other as if offering advice on where to look and where, perhaps, not to bother. Another pointed in Richard's direction; Richard winced and pushed his head back against the wall so fast it hurt.

One man broke off and strode alone along the street for thirty metres as Richard tracked him from the corner of his eye. Unlike his colleagues, this soldier appeared more diligent. Nevertheless, after calls and whistles from the others that thankfully seemed to curtail his motivation, the soldier cast a wary eye in a wide circle and then began his walk back. Suddenly the man shouted an instruction to the others and one of them responded by snapping his heels. This action may have been playful insubordination as the soldier in question broke away, despite jeers and tongue clicks. He walked in Richard's direction and stepped onto the pavement. Then, and for no apparent reason, but nevertheless interested, he continued to walk along the short flagstone path – he even slid the rifle strap from his shoulder and held the weapon forwards in a ready manner.

Richard heard the footsteps grow closer. He silently sucked in a breath through his nose and held it; his heart thumped at such a rate that he felt it would surely break out from his chest.

The militiaman suddenly stopped short, as if to take stock – as a deer-stalker would after hearing sounds of a creature. Then, half-responding to apparent heckles of boredom, he hesitated.

Richard's senses swirled but adrenalin kept his head clear. He was about to make a monumental decision when a shout went up from the quadrangle. It must have been the officer in charge because instantly the men in the street responded by turning and running off towards the lorry. But the man who stood not ten paces from Richard seemed reluctant to move. Richard could hear his breathing; it was shallow and disturbing. And he heard the rifle rubbing on the man's clothing. And then another order echoed around the quadrangle. It was shrill and demanding and it summoned the man, and with that he turned and began walking away, albeit unwillingly.

A moment later, and as if Richard's prayers had been answered, a third fanatical bark had the man scurrying down the path and onto the street and back towards the others. The piercing whine of an electric drive shocked the cool night air.

Richard listened carefully as the vehicles drove off. As their noise gradually dissolved into the blackness he breathed a huge sigh of relief and crouched forwards, bowing his head. He paused there and drew a series of breaths that were deep and controlled and designed to coax his heart rate to settle – but only marginally, for it was clearly very dangerous to loiter.

Richard checked the time, stepped into the open, and glanced across the deserted quadrangle towards the museum. There was a light on in a first floor room and a cloaked figure stepped into view at the window. Because of the time, and Richard's light signal, Banou, the Chief Curator, knew that he was there. Richard immediately skirted the quadrangle towards the old building.

As he arrived the two large lanterns that hung from black metal brackets on each side of the wooden doors were switched off. With the dull glow from the street lights behind him, Richard leapt the five marble steps and as he appeared in front of the doors he saw the left one open. With no hesitation, Richard slipped like an avenging shadow into history.

# CHAPTER 20

# TRUE COLOURS

**Osiris Base – 1 January 2055**
**19:08 Martian Corrected Time**

"Sir, I'm receiving a transmission from Space Station *Spartacus* – coming in on the accelercom network. You'd better come over."

"Priority?"

"Code One, sir, and there is a tag," enlightened Andrew Baillie. His eyes narrowed as he read the precursor.

"Code One! Details . . . ! Give me the details."

"For a Code One signal, sir, I'll need you to input your Head of Department clearance into the command security log."

"Standby, opening the system . . . There you are, it's

done."

"Copied," replied Baillie. "Received and verified, sir, downloading the signal now."

The words 'ISSF Secret' appeared on the monitor screen of Andrew Baillie's computer. Another flurry on his keyboard changed the page to one that prompted the input of an additional security code, as the signal tag required a "Second Tier Command" level of authorisation. As the Communication Centre Manager, Andrew Baillie keyed in his personal code. Access was granted immediately and he redirected the radio pulsar from the accelercom receiver – where the digital stream had been decelerated – into the descrambler. Within seconds, two pages of plain text had appeared on his screen.

"Details available, sir."

"Go ahead, I'm listening."

"Message relates to the ongoing Icarus event and the incoming body that threatens Earth," Andrew Baillie said, matter-of-factly. "It seems *Spartacus* has scored a try on the deep space signal. They want an input from Commander Race as soon as possible and then the signal forwarded to the Space Federation HQ in Canaveral and London copied in, too."

"That's good news. Any additional information will be very welcome . . . People back home are beginning to panic. Where is Commander Race at the moment?"

"Last report from Lesley Oakley was the western boundary of Elysium – traversing the head of the Orinoco

Rift. That was approximately fifty minutes ago. They are making good time. Their descent onto the Utopia flood plain will commence in an hour or so – still a way to go for the PTSV yet, sir."

"When's the rendezvous with the medical vehicle? Give me the latest."

"Timed at . . . 07:20 hours tomorrow morning, sir."

"Satellite report?"

"There's one in the frame . . . Artisan Four. Direct comms will be available for another three hours and twenty minutes. Then there's a five-hour blackout."

"Okay. Open a line to the Commander – I'm on my way."

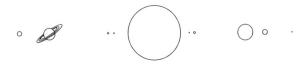

The tall figure of Riche Fernandes, the Senior Operations Officer, caused several heads to turn as he strode into the large room; the operations department was buzzing as usual and his authoritative demeanour temporarily subdued all irrelevant conversations; he made his way to the communications area and more particularly Andrew Baillie's console.

"Sitrep, Andy."

"Line's open to the PTSV, sir," Baillie replied.

Another officer arrived: Larissa Pavlikova. She wore

a dark blue one-piece cat suit with platinum shoulder epaulettes signifying the rank of Captain and also the planetary motif of the Uzbekistani Space and Science Directorate. She was in her late thirties, attractive and purposeful. Her jet black hair, which was tied back in a tight bun, contrasted starkly with her clear white complexion. She appeared to have Mongolian ancestry and stood well below the shoulder height of Fernandes.

"Can you hear me, Commander?" asked Andrew Baillie, leaning towards the microphone.

The radio crackled momentarily.

"Yes, listening, and Paul, too. Three by five, bit of atmospheric static around." The midriff of a man in a white coverall came into view and then the face of Commander Race appeared on the screen as he sat down. He sported three days of stubble and looked tired. "We're bouncing about here as you can see – going as fast as we can to the rendezvous position. So if my voice is wavering, you know why."

"Understood, sir. Major Fernandes is with me and also the Science Officer. It's a Code One message just in from *Spartacus* – they request an immediate response."

"Go on."

"Referenced to the current Icarus event, Commander; they have additional information on the incoming."

"Good. Go ahead, please."

"First, there's a situation report – it reiterates the primary stations involved with monitoring the body's progress. The ALMA submillimetre deep space telescope facility in Chile has overall responsibility for coordinating the ISSF's response, but both Andromeda's facility and the *Spartacus* are noted as essential. The body is approaching from the Canis sector. Earth's Hubble 2 telescope has sighted something close to the variable star Murzim – at the moment it's apparently just a white speck in that constellation . . ."

Captain Pavlikova put a hand on Andrew Baillie's shoulder; she had something to say and leaned forwards in order to be captured by the console's integral camera.

"Commander, Larissa here. Yes, our own observatory has confirmed the sighting. Coincidently, ALMA's centre manager has also been in contact with us. He thinks that the visible speck actually *is* the body. At the moment it has an apparent magnitude of -0.64, which is about the same as the star Canopus – you may recall that star as being the second brightest visible in the night sky. But that intrinsic luminosity is increasing at an amazing rate, Commander. In twelve hours I estimate that it will have an apparent magnitude greater even than Sirius. Of course it is not actually getting any brighter, it is just getting closer."

"How close is it? What are we talking here?"

"As of one hour ago it was seven point five billion kilometres away from us . . . approximately. At the moment, Earth is another eighty-five million kilometres."

"So it's about to enter our solar system."

Larissa nodded. "Pluto is currently six point three billion kilometres from us, yes."

"Do they have any idea what it is?"

"No, Commander. No one dares speculate. It is non-conformal. We have nothing to compare it with. But whatever it is, it's tracking faster than anything I have ever seen before – it's closing on Earth very quickly."

"I understand. How long – how long have they got?"

"Space Station *Spartacus* is closest to it; she's presently holding position approximately three million miles this side of Jupiter, waiting for the first close-up images of the moon Io to come in from the *Arius* probe flyby – that is due to happen in the next twenty-four hours, I'm told. We are using a geometric programme in the science department to triangulate the body – using the position of *Spartacus*, our position and that of the Sun. At the moment our results are unconfirmed, Commander, but we are definitely registering a deceleration – gradual but progressive. No natural space body does that!"

"So how long, Larissa?"

"It's very difficult to be precise, because the body's velocity is changing, and of course it remains relative to light speed."

"Then give me your best guess."

"An hour ago, Commander, we measured the body travelling at thirty-seven per cent light-related speed and decelerating at an approximate rate of three per cent, hour on hour. Based on that I would estimate an arrival in Earth's vicinity in thirty-eight hours, give or take an hour – provided current parameters remain stable."

"Why do you say 'Earth's vicinity', Larissa . . . ? Are we

having second thoughts about a collision here?"

"Why would the body decelerate prior to a collision, Commander? Maximum damage would be caused with the highest impact velocity. I'm speculating of course, but I think it will arrive in Earth's vicinity at a very low velocity . . . controlled . . . possibly even establish an orbit."

"Does Earth know that . . . ? Have you shared that with anybody?"

"Intentions are to cross-check our readings and re-run the permutations in . . ." Larissa checked the time on her wrist watch. ". . in two hours and twelve minutes, then pass on the full report."

After a thoughtful pause, Tom nodded and said: "Okay, I agree, but don't delay any longer than you have to. Now, what about the Code One message from the *Spartacus*?"

Larissa stood tall and stepped back a pace. "Andrew has those details, Commander," she said and tapped her hand on Baillie's shoulder in an apologetic way.

"Okay, thanks Larissa," said Tom. "Andy, what have you got?"

Andrew Baillie peered intently at the screen. "Commander, as you know the body has been transmitting a signal in our common space communications frequency range for some time now, but due to the distances involved the transmission has been intermittent and distorted and far too weak, in fact, to determine a format or signature. Well . . . the news is that the Communications Officer on *Spartacus* now has a positive ID. And you're not going to believe it . . . I don't think that anyone is."

"Specifics, Andy!" snapped Tom impatiently.

"The signal being transmitted is actually a message relating to an established ISSF Command and Control protocol, Commander. We have exactly the same format on file here, as does every colony and spacecraft in the entire Federation – it's the *Rogue Command* Protocol!"

"What!" exclaimed Tom.

"Are you sure?" interjected Major Fernandes, placing his hands on the top of the console and studying the text on the screen for himself.

"Absolutely," said Andrew Baillie. "I've just received clarification from *Spartacus* in the form of a duplicate transmission using a different security configuration. There's no mistake, Commander. This signal format has been coming from well outside the solar system, but it *is* one of ours."

There was an ominous pause. "I know of the protocol, of course," said Tom, "it's covered at Staff College for one thing. But only rarely mentioned after that. I do recall something about it more recently, though – from a few years ago." He drew a deep breath.

"There is a file in the HOD's library, Commander," informed Major Fernandes. "It's there for recall by senior officers. It will detail everything we need to know."

"Yes, you're right . . . Andy . . . you have my permission to go into the Head of Department's library. Use Alpha Code Two Zero One One. The file will be logged under Chain of Command. Open it, please."

"I'm on it, sir." Andrew Baillie's fingers danced over his touch-sensitive keyboard. Almost instantly a long list of files appeared on a secondary monitor screen. Larissa Pavlikova pointed to a specific line. "Located, sir," Baillie said, nodding his thanks. "It's entitled: *Rogue Command Protocol – Orders and Procedures*."

"Open it then, Andy – and do it quickly," pressed Tom.

In a confident flurry Andrew Baillie tapped in the sequence – but there was no response. He tried again using a different progression – the words *Access Denied* appeared on his screen.

Major Fernandes appeared confused. "The programme is denying us access, Commander."

"What?"

Andrew Baillie lolled back in his chair and thought about the problem for a moment and then suddenly sprang to attention. "That's just it, Commander, I can't open it with that code . . . it's your code! The protocol is not meant to be opened by the Commanding Officer. It's got to be a HOD's access code."

"Yes, of course it has," responded Tom. "Richie, please, would you enter your personal code."

Major Fernandes leaned forwards and entered a series of letters and numbers into the system. Instantly there was a response, and the new page that appeared on the screen was full of text. "There are in-depth notes and instigation and follow-up procedures, Commander, several pages," he informed, matter-of-factly.

"Would you read aloud the first page, please?" Tom requested.

Major Fernandes leaned forward again and peered at the screen. *"This protocol is to be initiated when succession of command is deemed necessary by nominated Osiris Base senior officers. A minimum of two Heads of Department and the base Security Officer must be in agreement. There can be no abstentions."* Fernandes paused. "Then it details some administration requirements, Commander," he continued, "and the current revision date is October 2050. After that, it reads: *Initiation of the protocol is authorised when at least two of the following conditions are identified and confirmed by the Chief Medical Officer or Deputy Chief Medical Officer: Space Fever; Robinson Crusoe Syndrome; Gravity Stasis Syndrome; Abnormal Behaviour; Psychotic Behaviour; Vitamin Deficiency Osmositary Syndrome; Delusionary Infecticide . . .* the list goes on, Commander, it's quite exhaustive. Basically, if the officer commanding Osiris Base – or any other ISSF colony or craft for that matter – is deemed unfit to carry out their duties for whatever reason, they can be relieved of their command by nominated senior officers provided specified minimal criteria are met and strictly documented procedures are followed."

Tom nodded. "Yeah, I remember, and I don't think the protocol has been used more than two or three times since its inception – not that I recall. It's coming back to me, though – I mean the last time I heard about it."

"Can you be specific, Commander?" asked the

Science Officer. "It might prove important."

Tom nodded slowly, recalling the event. "I was just about to assume command of the ISS *Enigma* – back in 2049. I was being briefed at Canaveral." Tom suddenly bounced in his seat; he gripped the console desktop with both hands and then he looked off-screen, forwards, towards the cockpit of the PTSV. "Sorry, rough terrain," he apologised. His brow furrowed and he rubbed his chin thoughtfully, looked back at his screen and then at the team in the Osiris communications centre. "Yeah, I remember . . . the culprit was here on Mars. It was during the tenure of my predecessor – Commander Miko – a hugely competent and experienced officer. Back then, the protocol could be initiated if just *one* officer in a senior position deemed it necessary. That's why the amendment date is a year later – they realised the loophole. The guy was British, held the rank of Major – a man by the name of Gregory Searle . . . the second time his name has sprung to mind in the last twenty-four hours, as a matter-of-fact. He was the Osiris Base security officer at the time and he didn't like what was going on with regards to the Kalahari crystals that had been recently discovered, so he tried to undermine the authority of his CO. Subsequently, he tried to kill me – he nearly did too."

"What happened to him after that, Commander?" questioned Major Fernandes.

"I was taking him back to Earth to face trial. It turned out that he was on the payroll of a major industrial corporation who were after the crystals. There were problems on-board the *Enigma*, however. You should see the report, Richie, it makes for interesting reading. In a nutshell, the *Enigma*'s self-aware central computer, codenamed EMILY, released him from detention without my knowledge. Later there was a struggle and I left him with a deep knife wound to the leg – I left him for dead, or so I've always thought. I managed to sabotage the *Enigma*'s high-energy laser initiator, laying the ship open to attack from the ISSF. EMILY decided that it was not in her best interests to hang around and instigated acceleration to light-related speed – I got off the ship in a Delta class fighter just in time and with the only other surviving crew member. It was close, alright." Tom shook his head. "The rest is history, as they say. The ship has not been seen or heard of since. But I'll say this, and I've not mentioned it before because it's just a hunch, you know, a gut feeling, and I know it sounds ridiculous, but I'm convinced that EMILY holds one hell of a grudge against me, and bitterness, even hostility, towards the entire human race. You see, she was Level Ten on the Rockwell Illinois Plateau System, an incredibly powerful computer, and she had acquired human characteristics through unintentional programming malfunctions." Tom drew another deep breath and shook his head. An anxious expression crept over his face. "The 'Rogue Command' message is too much of a coincidence; Gregory Searle is alive; there can be no other explanation. He's either trying to warn us of something . . . or he's playing with us. But one thing's for sure – it's all adding up. That incoming body can only be one thing . . . the *Enigma*!"

There was a stunned silence. Everyone just stared at each other.

"But our calculations suggest that the body has come from a star system several light years away, Commander. Is the *Enigma* capable of that? Is that possible?" Larissa Pavlikova's eyebrows were raised in amazement.

Tom considered the implications of his theory for several seconds; he recalled EMILY's potential and her inclination to break the rules, and not just those of physics. "Larissa," he said bluntly, "you have said that the body's passage through space has remained linear and therefore predictable, right?"

"That's correct, Commander."

"Just how accurate is your triangulation programme?"

"Very. We found the parsec to be unequivocal."

"Right – so you're confident you could plot an accurate back course?"

"Um, yes, I suppose so. We are certainly in a better position to do that than scientists on Earth. But aren't we more interested in where the body is going, exactly, not where it has come from?"

"From what you have said, Larissa, we know that already. I think you're right, a collision now seems very unlikely, and therefore, with its present trajectory, an orbital intention is probable. Listen, I want to know where it's been, as accurately as you possibly can – understand?"

"*Da, Kommandant* – I will get on to it immediately."

Tom nodded. "Andrew, please forward the

transmission from *Spartacus* to Canaveral as soon as you can. Also annotate our conclusions, but remind them they are speculative. We will get back to them ASAP with confirming data. My recommendation is that they cancel the *Icarus Imminent* event immediately, and downgrade from *Icarus Critical* to *Icarus Potential*. Tell them that in my view the collision risk has passed. But tell them we may have another, as yet unspecified, threat."

"I'm on it, sir."

"And one other thing – turning our attention to the Elysium Pyramids. I'm going to formulate an e-diction and send it to you. Please forward it by the accelercom network to a Commander Richard James Reece. He's the officer commanding Andromeda Wing; you'll find his address in the ISSF colony directory. I need to ask his advice on an ancient motif, more a carving in a rock face actually. I believe it to be some sort of key. He may know something about it." Tom checked his chronometer. "It's almost eight o'clock Lunar Time on New Year's Day. I imagine that he will have had his dinner by now and be settling down to watch a good movie, so be sure to copy-in his home address. I need to know his response immediately, okay?"

Andrew Baillie nodded.

"Now, we rendezvous with the medical team in around eleven hours and thereafter we go back to Elysium. I'm going to get some rest; be sure to contact me the moment that something comes in."

# CHAPTER 21

## TWICE OVER

Richard and Banou sat together in a small study that was no more than three-metres square. The walls were built of discoloured buff sandstone blocks, regularly sized, being approximately thirty centimetres by twenty. They appeared to be hewn by hand because of the slight variations in dimensions, the uneven corners and the haphazard tool marks on the slightly contoured faces. The stone itself was discoloured by time, moisture and black mould that Banou said was swept clean each March. The floor was of grey granite flagstones and there was a continuous wide depression in the hard rock that ran from outside the room through the doorway, and, towards the far left-hand corner, where there was a heavy wooden desk – perhaps of ebony or mahogany. The depression was more like a groove in the area of the doorway where tiny pieces of polished black mica and quartz glinted in the subdued light. Richard speculated that the desk had been in the same place for centuries, and before Banou many other Chief Curators had walked the same path and had attended to the same documents and administered the museum – in what the tourist literature formally referred to as the 'scriptorium' – a practice that had been done in the same way and with the same discreet efficiency for a millennium or more.

There were many things in the room that made it feel lived-in: carved wooden and stone artefacts from various periods – some free-standing, others on shelves; a few African tribal masks – a large, and especially frightening example, hung on the wall opposite the door. A dark, multi-patterned Arabian carpet was strung overhead to reduce the ceiling height. Richard noticed a floor-standing plastic globe on a stand that had browned with age. The room matched the mysterious old shaman and conjured feelings from the spiritual world.

Banou was almost the same as Richard remembered him – an aged and bird-like man. His right hand had felt bony and fragile when he shook it, although the sinewy grip had been firm and welcoming. His hair was still a wispy grey, if now longer. He was seemingly wearing the same dark brown woollen djellaba he had when they first met, with the hood flattened across his shoulders and a belt of grubby white rope simply knotted at each end. His skin had a lighter appearance, though, and was even pallid, quite unlike the weathered and tanned complexion of almost five years previous. *Clearly,* thought Richard, *even the eternal Banou could not escape the changes that time inflicted.*

"It's been good to talk, Banou, and see your latest exhibits – although with things as they are, I'm not surprised at the lack of visitors," said Richard in a kindly way. He took a sip of tea and ate the last piece of dried banana cake.

Banou smiled.

"But look, time's getting on, it's nearly midnight here and my pickup is at two; I need to talk to you about something specific."

"I knew that one day you would return, my young friend, and with more on your mind than the ancient parchments we preserve here for posterity. You need an answer, I can tell." Banou glanced at Richard quizzically.

Richard leaned forward and took Banou's right hand in his and then he turned it over gently to reveal the faded blue motif tattooed on his palm. "You once told me that this was a mark of an ancient religious order, one long forgotten and one long irrelevant to this world . . ."

Banou nodded. "That is still the truth," he replied.

"I don't know much about your order, Banou, or your brotherhood or whatever it really is – or was – and I don't suppose I ever will. Although, like a jigsaw puzzle, I confess that I've been trying to piece together various snippets of information I've gathered – to form a picture, so to speak. I know, for example, that some form of telepathy is possible between 'brothers'. The thing is this . . . to get straight to the point. I know someone, a good friend, who has a similar mark, and he's gone missing – disappeared without trace. I think he's been abducted by people who want to get at his Charge. He could be anywhere, really, it's an impossible task. With him, I believe I will also find the lady in question – he has a lifetime responsibility for her. I also believe I will find the Ark of the Light, the artefact I was searching for when I came before – that too has gone missing." Richard paused and looked into the old man's watery eyes. "Banou," he said softly. "I want you to try to contact him . . . you understand, in that way."

Banou nodded slowly. "You know something of the old people, their ways and their language – this itself is exceptional. But to know of more than one descendant of the sacred order is like the great sea parting again. Only a few of us remain; we are scattered like seeds and our powers are now obsolete. I do not know all who remain; communication is seldom now and I am the last of my generation." Banou paused thoughtfully. "I will help if I can. Who is it you seek, my friend?"

Richard crouched forwards in his chair. "His name is Asharf Saeed Makkoum," he said secretively, "and his Charge is Madame Naomi Vallogia. You know as well as I do that she is High Priestess of Atlantis and the Temple to Osiris."

Banou took a sharp intake of breath. "You know more than any other!" he said, with widening eyes.

"Yes. But I was asked by Madame to say nothing of her position, her duties, or this brotherhood – under any circumstances – and that's how it is."

"So their lives are in danger?"

"I think so. And I intend to find them."

"Asharf Makkoum is Niramyer to us in the Order," said Banou, nodding his understanding of Richard's sentiment. And then he raised a bony finger and pointed it at the closed wooden door. "Please . . . leave me for a short while, I am not practised, I will need to . . . chant a little and then try."

Richard stood to leave.

"Brother Abijah will attend to your needs; he will bring more food." With that Banou rang a small bell on his desk and moments later the door opened.

An African man with short, curly, white hair, dressed in the habit of a monk, turned and led Richard into another room. Richard sat down in a comfortable chair where there was a fire burning and agreed to another cup of black tea. He smiled at the man when the drink arrived.

The short, ageing man, who for no apparent reason had pulled his hood up, subsequently spent several minutes looking out through a leaded glass window. At one point he stood on a wooden dining chair and used an old ship's telescope, which was on the window sill, to focus more closely on various points of interest that seemed beyond his gaze. Presently, he turned and spoke to Richard; he seemed concerned. "There is an unusual commotion outside," he said in deep tones of perfect English. "The militia who invade our land seem agitated;

there are lights," he warned. "Are you with anyone?"

Richard nodded.

"The problem is not here but by the harbour – do you have . . . arrangements by the harbour?"

Richard nodded again. "My accomplice is down there. We are to meet a boat later. He's . . . well he's not very experienced at this sort of thing."

The man shrugged. "They are always suspicious of us here in the scriptorium if someone new or unidentified is seen in the old town – there is no reason for an 'outsider' to be here. You must understand that these soldiers have little tolerance and their officers are offensive. They think that we are responsible for the unwanted tourists, the prying eyes, or perhaps foreign spies! In truth, no one ever comes here. I am sorry, but there may be trouble when you leave."

Richard clasped his forehead in his hand and began rubbing his temples. "That's all I need," he said.

Just then the door to the room opened and Banou stepped in. He looked pale and drawn. He sat down in the high-backed chair opposite Richard's and drew a deep breath. He let the heat from the fire warm him a little before speaking. "It is done – I have word," he said calmly, but in the firelight he looked exhausted.

Richard instinctively glanced up at the other man.

Banou reached out and put a hand on Richard's knee in a reassuring way. "We are all friends here," he said.

"Where, then . . . ? Where is he . . . ? Banou!" Richard became agitated.

"He does not know where he is; only that he was forcibly taken and blindfolded. He left Cairo on an aeroplane – a small aeroplane; it was a narrow seat and he could not sit upright. The flight was about three hours. Madame Vallogia is with him – she came several days later – but not the Ark. He does not know where the Ark is. He thinks that almost a full cycle of the moon has passed since he was seized."

"He has no knowledge of where he was taken – the town, the country . . . nothing? Damn!" Richard shook his head with disappointment. Then he contained himself; Banou had already wrought a miracle.

Banou shook his head. "He remains confused," he added.

"What about Madame Vallogia? Is she hurt . . . ? Is she okay?"

"Madame Vallogia is well, but for how long he is uncertain. Niramyer says that their captives mean to experiment with her – her mind. They were visited by three men, perhaps two days ago; one was European and the other two are American. They asked questions and attached things to her head. They want information about her duties and things relating to the Ark, perhaps the old ways. Somehow they have knowledge of who she is."

Richard's face became grave. For some inexplicable reason he thought of Karl Rhinefeld, and their previous encounter. Rhinefeld was a trained interrogator as well as a murderer. Richard knew the man had no scruples.

He hailed from Europe, East Germany, and was definitely back on the scene. Richard rubbed his brow in a troubled manner. Rhinefeld had previously worked for the Spheron Corporation. He hoped to God that he was wrong, but he feared for Naomi's and Asharf's safety. He looked hard at Banou. A burning log crackled in the fire. In his mind Richard searched for ideas about a rescue. He desperately needed more information about Asharf's location. The room fell silent.

"Madame Vallogia has knowledge of some local landmarks," Banou continued after a while. "This might help, might it not? She arrived at a large glass building in the daylight."

"That's it, Banou." Richard stood. "Please, tell me everything Asharf said that she saw. Every detail."

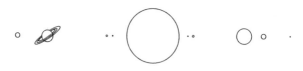

"It is not safe to leave by the front," said Banou, slamming the heavy wooden door closed. "The militia are here. They are looking for you!"

"Nor is the back door safe!" shouted the white-haired curator running back into the hall. The building is surrounded.

"Upstairs then?" proposed Richard, pulling his

balaclava back over his head.

Banou shook his head. "You will be trapped. The building is high and there is no way off the roof."

Banou looked at Abijah. No words passed between them but an understanding did and immediately Abijah scurried away down a side hall only to disappear moments later into an anteroom.

"Follow me, there is one other way," Banou said, and he moved quickly to the stairs that led down into the cellars.

Richard counted four landings and five flights and the deeper they went the more musty and overpowering grew the smell. At the bottom, in the bowels of the building, the wooden treads were near rotten. They waited in silence.

Abijah arrived carrying an object that was concealed in a green plastic bag. He was out of breath and as he negotiated the final flight of stairs – where they were damp and mouldy – he was careful to keep a steadying hand on the balustrade. When he was down, he seemed to cradle the object preciously in both hands. He nodded at Banou and smiled faintly. Banou turned towards Richard.

"Behind this door is an ancient tunnel," Banou explained, in a solemn manner. "It leads directly to the sea. There is a narrow beach and nearby is the harbour. The tunnel forms part of the original foundations . . . when Adulis was the greatest port in Africa. It has not been used for, perhaps, two hundred years and at the other end is a stone wheel. It cannot be moved without a special key; without such a key it is impenetrable." Banou gestured to the object being cradled by Abijah. "There is a mechanism built by the old people and long forgotten. Only two keys remain: the one Abijah carries and one other. They can be used only once, you will see. Abijah will close the great door behind you when you are safely outside. You will not be able to return by that way; you may not be able to return at all. Do you understand, my friend?"

Richard nodded. Banou pulled a ring of keys from beneath his djellaba. He used two smaller examples to unlock padlocks that secured metal straps across the thick wooden door and a third – a heavy patterned bronze key – to release the mortise lock. The enormous hinges were dry and corroded and the door took the effort of all three men to open it – even then it was levered only just enough for Richard and the smaller Abijah to slip through.

Tucked inside his leather belt, Abijah had the self-charging photoelectric torch that Richard had given to Banou on his previous visit. Abijah withdrew it and switched it on; the effect was to more than double the brightness given off by the single overhead bulb that hung down from the rafters, and it made the men squint momentarily before Abijah directed it down the tunnel.

Banou looked at Richard in a kindly manner and put a hand on his forearm. "I fear this will be the last time that we shall meet. You must be cautious, my young friend; the world changes quickly and not for the better. I will hear of your time and what you do. Now, you must find Madame Vallogia and Niramyer . . . or should I say your good friend Asharf. Find them before they are harmed – God is with you."

Richard looked down at the old man and covered his hand. "Thank you for your help, Banou. I will find them, you can be sure of that. And we *will* drink tea together again, you'll see."

With that, Richard crouched forwards and followed Abijah into the tunnel. Banou watched the two men scramble along the passageway until it narrowed and changed direction; after that, the light and the sound of footsteps faded.

Banou turned to find somewhere to sit and wait for Abijah's return. As he did, he whispered, "You are wrong young warrior. We will not meet again, for I see red sand beneath your feet. Be prosperous and of long life . . . *Insha, Allah.*"

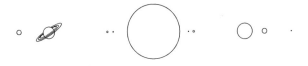

Richard estimated the tunnel to be at least 300 metres long. For the most part it had been circular, like a rabbit burrow, but in places, where granite seams had been unavoidable, it had narrowed to perhaps twice his shoulder width. And it was low in the most part, built for a much shorter race of people. He had scraped his head on several occasions but his balaclava had provided some protection. Abijah, who had led at a surprisingly spritely pace, suddenly pulled up as the tunnel opened into a small cave. Richard was covered in cobwebs when he emerged and the smell there, he noticed, seemed particularly pungent and acidic.

The cave was more than twice Richard's height and he was pleased to be able to stand straight. He flexed his shoulders, while Abijah examined a huge circular granite door that effectively plugged the cave entrance. It was clear that the old man had never been this far either.

"Presumably the sea is close by – on the other side," Richard whispered. The hollow echo of his words circulated the cave and then faded to nothing.

Abijah appeared to ignore Richard's remark while he continued his search, and then suddenly he found what he was looking for and made an appreciative grunting noise. He looked up. "The sea is not far, yes. Soon you will be beside it." He withdrew the object that he had carried so carefully from the plastic bag and offered it to the granite wall.

Richard moved quickly to see what Abijah was doing and what he saw took him by complete surprise. Indeed, it rendered him speechless, for Abijah held a life-like model of a hand – a right hand. It was a small, petite hand, like a woman's hand. It had a grainy structure and appeared to be made of coagulated desert-coloured sand, but hardened by baking or some similar process. Beneath, on the underside, the palm and fingers were dyed blue.

Only as Abijah slowly and very cautiously offered the hand to the cave wall, to a position adjacent to the granite wheel, did Richard notice the receptacle. It was an impression in the stone, an exact duplication of the hand masterfully carved in the stone face. Immediately Richard recalled his time with Naomi and Asharf in the Pyramid of Khufu. It was in May 2050 and he hadn't known her very long. That was how she had gained entrance into the great pyramid's hollow centre – into the Temple of Osiris: the right of passage and its ancient secrets being her hereditary privilege. She had placed her right hand into such a hollow – a replica carved in a concealed corner of the King's Chamber – and as a result an unknown granite door had rotated – pivoting at its centre in a most ingenious way. He recalled the story Naomi had told him of how her mother had taken her each year to that chamber, and offered her hand to the recess, until on her eighteenth birthday she had come of age and the door had opened.

A sudden, loud grinding noise jolted Richard from his thoughts. The door had begun to move and as it did the model being cradled in Abijah's hands simply crumbled to nothing – sand ran through his fingers like water.

"Quickly," Abijah urged. "The mechanism will move the stone gate back after it reaches its extremity; I cannot stop it. You must go now." Abijah directed the beam of his torch at the ground, causing the shadows of Richard's legs to appear spindly and long, like a giant crane fly.

The smell of the sea, the taste of salt and the wind in his face sharpened Richard's senses. He stepped outside and became aware of the surf lapping on the beach. His eyes grew accustomed to the darkness and he heard the sound of distant gun fire. Barely was there time to shake Abijah's hand and nod his appreciation when the great rock – which had a natural appearance on the outside – began to move in the opposite direction. Within moments there was a dull thud and all movement stopped. The entrance was sealed, perhaps for another century or more.

Richard ran quickly but awkwardly along the beach towards the harbour. He could see torch lights flashing and occasionally he heard the sound of men shouting. Sporadic gunfire still crackled on the wind, but it was some way off. It was nearly 500 metres to the harbour wall and when Richard arrived the area seemed deserted. It was a starless sky and black as before, but light from the town cast a strange ambiance over the area and, in one direction, despite the thick cloud, the moon's eerie glow filtered through. Silently, and like a lizard in his tight-fitting suit, Richard climbed the wall. On top he got his bearings and realised that he was close to the area where he and Thomas had come ashore. Using the shadows, he made his way along the wharf towards the rendezvous position.

After a few minutes of darting and hiding and

then, as he progressed towards the outer harbour wall, surreptitious dashes between bollards – because the buildings and the cranes had stopped and the quayside was all but featureless – Richard realised that the distant noise of vehicles, and the unseen commotion of men, appeared to be getting nearer. When not far from the agreed rendezvous position, Richard heard the sound of a vehicle screech to a halt. It was unnervingly close. Quickly he spun on his heels to hear the sound of men shouting; the clarity of their words tensed his body for flight. Throwing all caution to the wind, he sprinted towards the pickup point. Halfway, a figure emerged who was clearly Thomas – *for who else do I know with an illuminated face.* Thomas pulled him behind a container and they both sank to the ground.

"We might be out of luck, Richard," Thomas said, as Richard pulled a leg up and crouched low beside him on one knee, as if ready to sprint off again. Thomas had turned his face illumine down so that his features were barely discernable.

"I can't understand it," Richard replied, bobbing up to see how the militia were progressing.

"I'm afraid that might be my fault," Thomas said in an apologetic tone. "I saw a light flashing out at sea, directly east; I thought it was the pickup boat."

"What!" Richard exclaimed. He pressed the backlight on his chronometer and checked the time. "But the rendezvous is not for twenty minutes yet – when did you do that?"

Thomas morphed his expression into one of embarrassment. "More than an hour ago . . . I didn't think."

"You bloody idiot! You've brought them down on us. That's the first rule. You never reply to a signal unless it's precisely at the stipulated time . . . They probably run up and down the coast in an electric boat every night, just waiting to see who they can catch – only we are not smugglers, are we? Ugh . . . you idiot!"

"Sorry."

"Sorry! You just may be. I knew I should have come on my own." Richard bobbed up and down again. "And that gun fire, a while back, what was that?"

"Artillery . . . fired out to sea, presumably to scare off any shipping."

Richard shook his head with exasperation. "The submarine won't hang around, that's for sure, he's gone, well on his way back to the Gulf of Aden by now. I can't believe you did that." Richard bobbed up, assessed the situation and then dropped down again. "They are coming over to give this area a thorough sweep. There is a lorry load of them – twelve, maybe fifteen; we could be in trouble here."

The sound of dogs barking filled the night air and the shouting grew louder.

"I don't understand it," continued Thomas, as if in defence of his actions. "They have already run an infrared scan from over there. The boat went past twice. But they could not have sensed any heat from me; I had my life support system turned down to ambient temperature."

"They are systematically searching this whole section of coastline, don't you understand? They know we're here somewhere. Listen, where is your capsule?"

"Where we left it, tied up – over there," Thomas replied, and pointed to the outermost jetty.

"We're going for it. Follow me, and turn your system up to optimal temperature – you're going to need all the energy you've got!" With that, Richard sprinted down the wharf towards the capsule with Thomas in hot pursuit.


"Jump in and position the oars. Get ready to row your batteries flat!" Richard ordered. He checked behind. A group of militia were approaching at a fast walking pace. The beams from their torches probed in all directions; but not, as yet, in theirs.

The soldier's voices grew louder. Richard could now hear the officer shouting clear directives. The dogs suddenly grew excited and began barking incessantly – they had picked up Richard's scent.

At the quayside Richard released the securing lanyard and, holding it tight, he climbed down the wall and slipped quietly into the water, all the while pulling the makeshift canoe towards him. When he had his arms over the side, he whispered: "Turn around and row. Do it now – but quietly; they haven't seen us yet!"

In the darkness and taking care not to splash the water, Thomas manoeuvred the capsule about-face as Richard carefully rolled into the restricted hollow of the short dugout. With Richard bent double at the front end, Thomas began long, steady strokes. They quickly dissolved into the dark night; the sea swell, thankfully, was slight. Richard watched the jetty carefully. It was some minutes before the soldiers got to where they had launched themselves. The men shone their torches aimlessly out to sea and down the jetty looking for clues, but Richard and Thomas were out of their range and soon their ill-disciplined clamour and the barks of frustrated dogs faded.

Richard directed Thomas using the compass in his chronometer. They would head north by north-east for twenty kilometres or so and then turn right to track a course a little north of east. After approximately sixty kilometres they should make landfall on the islands that formed the Dahlak Archipelago and, hopefully, if his calculations were right, Dahlak el Kebir, the largest island in the group. He recalled it as the chief port for pearl fishing in the southern part of the Red Sea and as once being a military base used by the Ethiopians. There he would charter a motorboat to take them to the Farasan Islands and beyond to the coast of Saudi Arabia, or better still, a light aeroplane that would land at Jizan Airport – he had world dollars enough to tempt even the most reluctant seafarer or private pilot.

Thomas informed Richard that he had an eighty per cent residual charge and Richard used his chronometer's satellite navigation feature to calculate that he was making an impressive ten knots using long, powerful strokes; even so, at 18.52 kilometres per hour, the journey would take more than three hours.

Richard assumed that the submarine's commander would inform the British Admiralty of their missed opportunity and formulated an abrive to Chris Quarrie on his telephonic pager, informing him of the delay. If they were lucky they would make Jizan by midday Local Time and the Alhazoun Airforce Base was another two or three hours' drive from there. With a following wind they might be on their way to London by 3PM. That was more than eleven hours from now. *Peter Rothschild would be furious and so would the Lunar Senate,* Richard thought. Then, to add to his woes, there was no signal, not this far out in the Red Sea. He would have to wait and so would Naomi and Asharf.

Richard's ill-humour at Thomas' misdemeanour grew like a black cloud as he bailed water from the capsule and, as he urged his accomplice to bigger efforts, his temper was barely contained.

Thomas deactivated the plasmoltec expression intensifier and rowed with a blank, dark, flat, face screen through the night.

# CHAPTER 22

# CLOSER TO HOME

**Moon Base Andromeda – 2 January**
**06:57 Lunar Corrected Time**

"It's a garbled message, sir. Almost completely unintelligible . . . I can't make it out . . . something about insects . . . ants! . . . Yes, I know it sounds ridiculous, sir, out there, as well, but that's what he said. I've replayed it several times. Carey agrees with me – he definitely said *ants* . . . Okay, I'll be expecting you."

Herbie Smith put the telephone down and looked up at the group of operational personnel who encircled his console. His expression darkened with anxiety. "Give me the Freight Control Centre any day. Man, there's too much pressure here." He looked down at his screen and then up again at his colleagues. "He's coming over, and

Dimitri, too; you had better get back to your posts and be ready with the UAV information."

Moments later Security Officer Dimitri Nurevski walked in to the Operations Room. He made a beeline for Herbie Smith, an Afro-American from Louisiana. Nurevski looked infuriated. No one got on the wrong side of the Security Officer, not when he had that dark Russian melancholy look. The operatives at the consoles surrounding Herbie buried their heads in their work.

"What the hell is this all about, Herbie . . . ? Ants! I mean we get the occasional cockroach here and there in the accommodation flats and maybe a honey bee escapes from the biodomes from time to time, but ants?"

"You had better listen to this Dimitri," responded Herbie, having already prepared the playback. "Our most northern sensor outpost, LS17, in the shadow lands just a few Ks from the pole. It's Jean Fontana and Ralf Biddle – although you couldn't tell from their voices. Message came through at 06:32. I thought it was a joke at first – amateur dramatics. You know, just relieving the boredom of a night period. The message lasted less than two minutes. I filtered it; this is the enhanced version."

Smith pressed a button on his console and looked up at the face of Dimitri to gauge his reaction.

"They are coming in, thousands of them, through the ventilations ducts and one-way valves . . . ants. I've never . . . I can't . . . they're everywhere. Comms are out. Can't control the . . . massive electrical short. Extinguisher. Must get the extinguisher . . . arhhh . . . Jean, get them off me, they're biting. The room's alive . . . arghhh . . ."

Herbie shook his head. "That's just some of it. The last part of the transmission sounds like a horror movie. Listen to this playback . . . it was earlier."

"Hey Comm-Cen, how is it? Ralf Biddle LS17, how do you hear . . . ?"

"Yes Ralf, I hear you. Sorry, been for a natural break – not expecting a call from you for another three hours. What's the deal . . . ?"

"Something funny going on up here, Jeff. It was just a routine report and I thought I'd better comply . . . but we got a sensory overload – probably a temporary spike in the supply voltage. I can't see a problem with the systems feedback . . ."

"Okay, nothing showing my end, nothing out of the ordinary here . . ."

"Yeah sure, it's gotta be a system malfunction – end of the line, you guys are always sending us the bad amps. Ha, ha . . ."

"Tell me, Ralf, what do you have . . . just for the record?"

"It started in our north-east sector, Jeff, about thirty minutes ago. Now it's all around us, as if a massive piece of metal has been placed in front of the sensors – total overload, no returns whatsoever, through the entire three hundred and sixty degrees sector. Screens are white, can't control the display with the gain, max gain, max filtration. I mean nothing seems to work – impossible, right?"

"Okay, okay, sounds like an electrical surge, very unusual all the same. I'll give maintenance a call, get them out of bed. Leave it to me, Ralf; I'll call you back with a sitrep when the team is on station."

"You got it."

Herbie looked up. "That first call was at 06:03 hours. Jeff Pastoor composed a short report and placed a call to the maintenance department at 06:08. He tried to raise Ralf and Jean again, but without success. Then we got that last transmission on the emergency frequency. That radio has its own batteries; I think the entire power network at LS17 was down by then." Herbie took a wary look around to see who might be listening and then dropped his voice to a whisper. "Dimitri, I think they're dead!" he said gravely. "I think they were attacked by something."

"But not ants, that's impossible."

Herbie gestured in a "What if?" way and then suddenly stood up – Chief Operations Officer Eddie Lieven had stormed into the room.

Lieven put a hand on Herbie Smith's shoulder and forced him back into his seat. "I've heard, Dimitri!" he shouted. "Trouble in the north sector again – LS17!"

Dimitri nodded. "I think it's time to get the Defence Force involved, Chief. Something's going on up there. We can't keep blaming infrastructure malfunctions and believing that trespassers are impossible on the Moon."

Lieven nodded. He was clearly reluctant to mobilise the voluntary army – the contingent of those with military backgrounds who volunteered for security duties on top of their careers – presumably worried about disrupting the normal routine of the colony and an inevitable cross-examination by the Senate's executive committee. He considered the implications for a few moments. "Okay. Call the Colonel. Ask him to initiate 'Recall Status' for the 1st Regiment. We need an armed platoon on the scene as soon as possible. No need for the 2nd and 3rd Regiments to be called. What about aerial support?"

"The shuttle *Hermes* has remained on Alert Five since the third UAV was lost. We are keeping her on the ground as you instructed, although the science department has just confirmed that the recent surge in solar radiation and yesterday's gamma ray peak could not be responsible for bringing down an unmanned vehicle – the shielding is better than the readings that are now available ..."

"What about the last UAV we sent up?"

The Japanese woman at a nearby console overheard the conversation; she stood and took the few steps over to the group. "Excuse me, sir. Sorry, but I overheard that question ... the UAV is still airborne, at the moment in the Sea of Tranquillity region. We thought it better to avoid the dark side in case it was a cosmic radiation overload causing all the system malfunctions we have been experiencing. It would not be the first time, sir. I'm in charge of the early warning response unit this morning. I can have the pilot head north towards LS17 immediately."

"Good, well done. Let's do that. Call me the moment

the video relay starts. But tell the pilot not to approach from the light side; that's been our problem – it's what's expected. Tell him the long way round – South Pole first, and then steer due north, dark side run in. Be sure to keep low . . . Dimitri, second thoughts, I think it might be prudent to mobilise the entire defence force – please request a general recall immediately. The Colonel has my authority to open weapon lockers. And call the duty doctor; I want the hospital on one hour's alert. I'm going back to my office to make some calls."

"Copied, Chief. What about the shuttle . . . ? Remain at Alert 5 or get him moving?" asked Dimitri.

"Is Commander Reece back yet?"

"No, Chief." Dimitri looked pained. "MI9 is not exactly sure where he is at the moment."

Lieven rubbed his eyes as a look of livid frustration clouded his expression. He went to open his mouth but stopped short. He turned and went to leave, but then stopped again and looked over his shoulder. He stared at Dimitri with fiery eyes. "Keep the shuttle on the ground until the UAV sends us some imagery," he barked. "In the meantime, Dimitri, *you* call London again. I want him back. This is his last chance!"

**Elysium borderlands – same day**
**09:11 Martian Corrected Time**

Paul Carr put a hand on the shoulder of Tom Race and gently shook it. "Commander," he said quietly, "time to wake up, I'm afraid. The information you requested has just come in from Osiris. The Science Officer is adamant that we wake you."

It was a small cabin with two narrow bunk beds and just enough floor space to change in. Tom had slept in his clothes, not meaning to be out for more than a few hours. He came to his senses and massaged his temples between his fingers.

"How are you feeling, sir?"

"Better thanks, Paul – yeah better. Bit of a headache last night."

"It's to be expected. Anna monitored your vital signs whilst you were asleep; she said it was a hangover from your concussion. But don't worry, you're all unplugged now; she gave you a shot of Oxytripelene. As far as the monitor is concerned, you're back to normal."

"Great, great . . . okay." Tom spun round and put his feet on the deck. He looked up at Paul. "Seems to be a quiet ride out there," he commented.

"Almost back on the Plain of Elysium. Pretty much heading east – it will be smooth for several hours now."

"Elysium! What time is it?"

"Quarter past nine. We made the rendezvous a couple of hours ago, Commander. I took the decision to let you sleep. There was no reason to wake you. We transferred Tanner's body and Dan went across as walking wounded. We had a message from Doctor Silvano on the medical vehicle about an hour ago. Dan's doing fine; he's stable . . . no harm done from the oxygen deficiency. They'll be on the road for another day and will update us with an arrival message when they reach Osiris."

Tom nodded. "Very good, thanks. What about the Pyramids? Do we have an ETA?"

"From twenty-one to twenty-three hours from now – depends on the route that Lesley can take over the Golan Heights, and there are some heavy electrical storms to avoid, too. Commander, Larissa is keen to talk to you. She has the back course information that you requested. It's amazing; she's saying that she may have found a planet remarkably similar to Earth."

"Okay . . . give me a few minutes to wash-up and I'll be out."

"Veronica has the coffee brewing and a bit of breakfast for you as well."

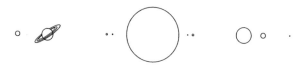

"What's the comms window, Paul?" requested Tom, sitting down at the console.

"Another hour and ten minutes, Commander, and then restricted for five hours. High-frequency radio comms if we need it, but that band will become more unreliable as we go further east."

"What about the coverage when we arrive?"

"That's going to work out okay. IMARSAT Five has

the best imaging equipment of all the satellites. She will arc just as we arrive and be available for at least six hours."

"Good. Let's see what Larissa has found then, shall we? Anna, open a channel to Osiris, please."

"Aye aye, sir . . . Osiris Base from Support One, come in Osiris."

"Baillie here in ops – strength five. Go ahead."

"Yes, five by five also, Andy," responded Anna. "Commander Race is requesting the information from the Science Department; we are standing by."

"Captain Pavlikova is with me, and the Operations Officer has just arrived; we can go visual."

"Video on," returned Anna, and she pressed a button that had the console monitor registering the scene in Base Ops.

Andrew Baillie was sitting in front of the camera looking at Commander Race. He looked to his left and then scooted aside on his castored chair to be replaced by the Larissa Pavlikova. Her pale complexion and the blackness under her eyes had all the hallmarks of working through the night. She looked up as somebody came to stand by her side. "Morning Richie," she greeted, and then she looked back at Tom. "Morning, Commander. I hear you are feeling better – that's good."

"Morning, Larissa. Yes, thanks. You've got some results?"

"Yes. My prediction indicates a ninety-eight per cent certainty. I triple-checked the results and then had Ronald run an independent – I'm sure what we have is correct."

"Okay, let's have it."

"First, I requested some information from the centre manager at the ALMA submillimetre telescope facility on Earth. He told me that the body has been tracked travelling at light speed, albeit intermittently, and that during periods of associated invisibility, it is believed to have slipped into another dimension. During these periods the body appears to have travelled vast distances through space. I will not go into the theory behind this phenomenon, Commander, because it is still speculative, but it does seem likely that the body has journeyed from a position several light years away."

"I see, go on."

"The supposition is that when travelling at light speed there is very little deflection in the space–time vortex – the body's reflection if you like. I used our triangulation programme and plotted the back course – the exact reverse trajectory based on its current and previous passage through space. Apart from a comet that crossed its flight path about four months ago, and a Category Two asteroid with possibly enough gravitational pull to deflect its course by 0.000112 parsecs, there is nothing else in the Canis Major sector for, well, eight or nine light years."

"I understand the science, Larissa, so what did you find ...?"

"By coincidence, Commander, we spoke about the point of origin yesterday evening. It's the brightest star in the night sky visible from Earth, and also for us here on Mars – the star Sirius, Commander, with an apparent magnitude of minus one point forty six; it has the Bayer designation Alpha Canis Majoris, known colloquially as the Dog Star."

"What! The *Enigma* . . . if it is the *Enigma*, has come back to us after having journeyed to a distant star . . . Come on . . . ?"

"Well, not that distant, relatively speaking of course . . . eight point six light years or two point six parsecs to be precise. It is one of our nearest neighbours, Commander, and the back course is right on the nose. As I said, the results have been independently checked."

"The *Enigma* has been gone for . . . what . . . four-and-a-half years at most?"

"That's why it corroborates with the data from the ALMA telescope – the inter-dimensional hypothesis. But it's more interesting than that, Commander."

"Go on!"

"What the naked eye perceives as a single star is actually a binary star system, consisting of a white main sequence star of spectral type A1Vm, called *Sirius A*, and a faint white dwarf companion of spectral type DA2, termed *Sirius B*. They were originally two bright bluish stars, but the more massive of these, Sirius B, became a red giant by consuming its resources. In astronomical terms that happened amazingly recently. It shed its outer layers and collapsed into its current white dwarf state only ten thousand to twenty thousand years ago. I've an interest in astronomy and some of the ancient civilisations on Earth knew of this star's fate. Related text was found in both Egypt and South America."

Tom nodded sceptically and looked up at Paul. "Okay, let's run with this. "The *Enigma* paid a visit to either Sirius A or Sirius B . . . why?"

"In my view it is unlikely to be Sirius A, Commander. Why? Because that star is twenty-five times more luminous than our sun and has three times the mass – it is one to avoid. Also, it's unlikely to be Sirius B, because that star packs the equivalent mass of our sun into an incredibly dense globe only four times the diameter of our Earth. The extent of the gravitational pull would be difficult to calculate and impractical to anticipate, and once ensnared it would be impossible to break free – at any speed."

"I don't understand, you said Sirius . . ."

"Commander, Sirius B has a solar system similar to our own sun, with currently seven planets in orbit. These planets were originally detected, and only 'visible' by, radio telescope. That was until the thirties, when the second generation optical converters were devised. I did some homework on this system. These planets can be seen as very faint bodies now, and the nearest one is about equivalent to the position of Saturn in our solar system. When Sirius B was a normal-sized blue star it is believed that three, perhaps four, other planets occupied much closer orbits. This is theorised because of the unusual eccentricity of the remaining planets – all the planets in a solar system have an effect on each other, no matter how slight. The current nearest planet was once believed to be in the 'hot zone'; however, when Sirius B became a red giant it engulfed the nearest planets and although not getting close enough to destroy the one in question, the physical conditions became similar to that on *our* second nearest planet, Venus. In other words, very hot, certainly not conducive to life. Now, our triangulation program is accurate, but not accurate enough to calculate the exact location that our incoming body originated from . . . only that it was in the vicinity of Sirius B. But with such a massive gravitational effect around Sirius B it would not have escaped that star, and so it must have originated from somewhere close, but far enough away from it to be able to escape from it. My informed guess is that it is on its way to us from the current innermost planet in that system."

Tom took a deep breath and thought for a moment. "Larissa," he started, looking out of frame for a moment and then back at her, "remind me, the Hot Zone . . ."

"It was devised by the renowned American astrophysicist Professor Rupert Hotling forty years ago. After three decades of study he developed a system of detecting accurately whether a planet orbiting a star, nominally of similar size to ours, has in the past or is presently experiencing similar conditions to those that define our home planet. He explained the hot zone as a belt or ring of defined dimensions where there is a high probability of human life evolving. The required parameters are incredibly limiting actually: the distance from the sun; relative position to other planets and moons; orbital concentricity; planetary inclination; density of cosmic radiation; interactive magnetism. He took everything into account and came up with a simple scale: H+1 through H+10, where 10 is equivalent to Earth and therefore the highest probability of human life evolving. Of the billions of stars in the universe that have orbiting planets, there are surprisingly few that make even the lowest category. In fact he graded only a handful in the +10 zone."

"So what about this particular planet – the innermost one to Sirius B?"

"Well that's just it, Commander. Amazingly, this planet, or to be more precise, its exact location, was well known to the ancient Egyptians . . . there is even a small, perfectly aligned, shaft from the Queens Chamber inside the Great Pyramid near Cairo that points directly to this body. Originally it was thought to point to the star itself, but a few years ago its direction was more closely measured. The ancient Egyptians shared something with this planet, as did the Mayans and the Mesopotamians. Although contact between these civilisations is not thought possible, because of geography and time, they each had the same name for it." Larissa paused.

"Go on . . ."

"They called it Homer, Commander, and Hotling graded it +10 before the sun went red giant!"

"Are you sure about this Larissa? I mean, really sure? It seems . . ."

"There is more. I downloaded some astrophysical data from the people's library and also opened a few historical files."

"Okay, what else have you got?"

"I learnt that Sirius B traces an elliptical orbit around Sirius A and that their common axis of rotation about their centre of gravity is directed towards Earth. It's a fifty-year orbit and the period of closest connection is called the *periastron*. There is an enormous magnetic interaction and gravitational attraction between these two bodies and it is particularly intense during the periastron. It is a time when the radiated energies given off by these two stars are beyond imagination. Vast amounts of electromagnetic radiation including X-rays, gamma rays, ultraviolet light and visible light is thrown into space. Matter pulled from Sirius A reignites fusion reactions within Sirius B."

"That would account for their combined luminosity."

Larissa nodded. "Correct, Commander, and this amazing system is what astronomers describe as being directly 'upstream' of our solar system within the galactic arm of our galaxy. As a result it is known that the polarised energies of these stars wash over us. The Ancient Egyptians were aware of the orbital dynamics of the Sirian system and its unique relationship with our solar system. By coming directly towards us, Sirius creates an axis of rotation with Earth relative to the stars we see in the night sky. For this reason, and of all the countless astral bodies, only the annual heliacal rising of Sirius exactly matches the length of Earth's solar year – 365.25 days. The Egyptians set the first day of their calendar year by this event, because it marked the flooding of the Nile in Ancient Egypt. Even our celebrations two nights ago on New Year's Eve are a continuation of a most ancient ritual, one honouring the return of Sirius to the mid-heaven position at midnight around 1st January."

Tom was jostled in his seat for a moment as the PTSV traversed a rocky depression. "Well thank you for all that, Larissa, you've done your homework, but where does it get us with regards to the incoming?"

Larissa paused and took stock. "I think there is a link, Commander, between that planet, the incoming and Earth. There was a report I read a few years back; one of the contributors was a former Mars Planetary Surveyor, a man called Richard Reece. He originally discovered the Kalahari crystals over in the East Sector. The report speculated on the common ancestry of Earth's first recorded civilisations. An ancient artefact called the 'Ark of the Light', that was found in Italy and that contained the largest of the recovered crystals, was clear evidence. On the face of it, that Ark appeared to have Egyptian origins, because of markings and hieroglyphic engravings, but the materials used in its construction were not from home, Commander – that was clearly documented. And there are other theories of a nomadic race that arrived on Earth as colonists more than ten thousand years ago and who it is said spawned the Ancient Egyptians and the Mayans amongst others. There *is* a link, Commander; I have no doubt about that."

"But the colonist theory was dismissed!"

"Only on religious grounds, because it undermined many fundamental beliefs – the creation theory being one of them. The whole affair was subsequently brushed under the carpet, as you say."

"So you think EMILY has steered the *Enigma* back to Sirius B, or more precisely the planet *Homer*, because she felt, well, homesick . . . ? I don't think we can go to the ISSF with that, Larissa."

Larissa Pavlikova shook her head. "The capability is there to make such a journey, we know that now. You yourself, Commander, said that EMILY's memory banks contained almost the sum total of humans' knowledge to that time, and that she had 'inherited' some human traits – albeit not the best ones – through her part-organic makeup. There could be a number of reasons why she would attempt to go back to her origins."

"She's got a point, Commander," interrupted Paul. "I mean, EMILY would have access to all the knowledge available to all the historians down through the years, and that, as of what . . . four or five years ago . . . when her memory facility was last updated . . . Files on everything we know would have been instantly available – archaeology; demographic data from the earliest times; unprecedented information on the first civilisations. That's scientific data with such integration she may have discovered common links that evaded more singular appraisals."

Tom shook his head. "I knew EMILY well, Paul, better than anyone in fact – except perhaps for Professor Nieve himself, her programme designer. She had a mean streak. She was vindictive. And to make matters worse we . . . we humans . . . we double-crossed her and tried to destroy her. I think she's coming back to settle a score. But how do you get that across to the ISSF?" Tom pressed a button on the console and went to open microphone. "Listen up people," he said, and he smiled at Larissa, whose image still filled the screen on the console, "we tell Earth what we know, including our hunches; they can make what they will of it – although I think the ISSF Council will dismiss our findings as pure conjecture. Our priority remains Earth's energy crisis. With the disappearance of the *Hera* there will be no more crystals. We need practical solutions and we need them fast; the Elysium Pyramids may hold vital information and we've less than twenty-two hours to run to their location. We have to concentrate on getting inside those structures, particularly Zeta Three, and for now anyway, we leave the Icarus problem to Earth."

**London – same day**
**13:54 Greenwich Mean Time**

It was a particularly gloomy and blustery afternoon in the city as Peter Rothschild stood silently by the windows of his office staring out, somewhat blankly, at the fast-moving River Thames. Its troubled waters brimmed full and chaotic. He was mindful of the necessity to contain a number of recent events that had unsettling security implications. They seemed, on the face of it, to be totally unrelated, but in correspondence to the International Space and Science Federation he had noted them as "too consistent to be coincidental". However, branded an eternal pessimist by the ISSF Council, his irritability had gone unheeded. *Security is essential,* they had replied a day earlier, *but not to the detriment of freedom of rights and international unity.* He pondered where the freedom of rights agenda would get them when all the world's lights had gone out. *And the two recent breeches in the SERON Space Net defence system were an inevitable result of the sheer intensity and ingenious nature of the current cyber-attack – not to mention a little 'insider dealing'.*

A sharp knock on the door interrupted his uneasy musing. Rothschild turned. "Yes, come in," he said.

The door partially opened and Laura Bellingham, his ever-efficient PA, pushed her head through the gap.

"Brian Grant has arrived; he's on his way up."

"Good. Ask him to take a seat in the lounge would you. No, second thoughts, just bring him in and ask Abbey to come in too, please – and what about the call to Commander Reece?"

"Miss Hennessy is making some arrangements regarding a private flight home for the CIA's Remote Viewing team, Mr Smith and Mr Perram . . . I'll tell her to come through, Peter. The call to Commander Reece is on request; we should hear back very soon. Apparently, he is over the Eastern Mediterranean, in the area of Cyprus. I'll show Mr Grant in immediately."

A few moments later Brian Grant stepped into Rothschild's office. He was smartly dressed in a dark blue suit but a stubbly greying beard, grown since their last meeting, added a few unwanted years to his appearance.

Rothschild stepped over to him and offered his hand. "Hello there Brian, thank you for coming in. Please, take a seat."

"Afternoon, Peter, thanks . . ."

"I understand that you have some information for the Cabinet regarding the *Hera*? I can't make that meeting I'm afraid, so I'm grateful to you for stopping off on your way to Downing Street."

"That's quite alright; there's plenty of time. Some of it is out already, in any case."

Rothschild nodded. "Let's just wait for Abbey, Brian. She won't be long. Listen, I'm just about to take a call from Richard Reece – he's on a flight from Saudi Arabia. It's routed via our own military net and not that of SERON's; there is a slight delay while the security coding is ratified. I'd like you to listen in; perhaps make some comments if need be. Ah, here's Abbey now."

Abbey Hennessy, wearing a black trouser suit and carrying an electronic tablet device, stepped through the half-open door. Preoccupied with information on the small screen she briefly smiled at Rothschild. "Good afternoon Brian, sorry to keep you waiting . . . . Peter, I've managed to get Agents Smith and Perram on a flight to Washington from Paris Orly. There's nothing leaving the UK for another two weeks or so. I've requested a military helicopter to take them to France. They will leave from the VIP Cityport at nine o'clock this evening – best I could do for them I'm afraid; there are very few direct flights to North or South America now."

"Very well," replied Rothschild, pulling another chair towards his desk. "I expect to be in Strasbourg by then, so please give them my regards and thank them for their time. An interesting if not a rather extraordinary exercise, Abbey; it's a pity they couldn't do more for us – certainly a novel approach to bear in mind for future operations, what?" He returned a brief if not slightly sarcastic smile. "Now, more pressing matters . . . what about Spheron?"

"I'm told everything is in place, Peter. As soon as the last employee leaves the building and night security takes over, they will move. Estimated to be at 19:00 hours Local, but that remains fluid. You will meet your French counterpart at 21:00 in the computer centre. I hope we find the proof we need."

"Oh we will; I'm certain of that," declared Rothschild. He looked at Brian Grant. "Brian has an appointment with the PM and the Energy Secretary among others; he's agreed to brief us on the situation prior to their meeting . . . Over to you Brian."

"Yes. Well, it is bad news I'm afraid, but it was expected, wasn't it? The first images of Io started to come in this morning. Not the best quality I have to say, due to the heavy electromagnetic interference in that region, but we knew that too. We will have to wait a few more weeks for the highest definition images – when the probe clears Jupiter's influence you understand."

"And where is the probe, exactly?" enquired Rothschild.

"The *Arius* is close enough now to photograph the surface of Io. We can see what's going on there fairly well. Sadly, we have identified the wreckage of the *Hera*. Hell of a mess – made a trench more than two kilometres long. Any crew surviving the nuclear blast in space will have perished during re-entry; it will have all been over relatively quickly."

Rothschild nodded. "And the crew members on the surface?" he asked.

"We can see the landing vehicle with the ascent stage still in place on top and we think we can see the buggy, as there is an image intensifier aboard that vehicle, but the clarity is not good enough for more than that at the moment."

"So our hopes for another consignment of crystals are dashed – the repercussions to that are immense."

"There's still an opportunity!" Grant's expression lifted.

"What do you mean?"

"We've seen another landing vehicle on the surface – well, part of one anyway – close to the crystal deposit coordinates. What we found interesting and very surprising at first was the lack of respiration gas residuals. The spectrograph aboard the *Arius* cannot identify any residual oxygen, nitrous oxide or water molecules in its vicinity. We don't think that any life support systems are present on the vehicle, none that support oxygen breathing anyway. There is a dense cloud of debris in orbit too, as one would expect from an explosion. However, diametrically opposite, on the other side of the moon and at a reduced orbital concentricity, we have identified a cloud of Sion gas, and there's hydrogen, nitrogen tetroxide and hydrazine present too – all are used for rocket propellants and none, except hydrogen, are naturally occurring. Further, we would not expect free hydrogen to be present in orbit. We think the Sion remnants are from a long-range Ion drive and the other gases are from conventional rockets used for manoeuvring . . . retrorockets." Brian Grant paused and looked at Abbey and then at Rothschild. "We think that highly advanced cyber-systems have been used to do what we sent the *Hera* to do . . . extract and retrieve a consignment of Kalahari crystals. That's what I'm passing on from the ISSF to the British Government. We think that a consignment is on its way back to Earth, and the ship is either remotely piloted or, more likely, controlled by robots."

"Is that possible?"

"Epsilon Rio originally produced the Humatron system to perform such duties, relieving a ship's crew of menial tasks during long journeys, particularly to the outlying planets. The Level Seven HU40 model was developed several years ago and its production banned more than five years ago. If Epsilon Rio continued with development in secret, I would say that it is quite likely that they have a new and even more capable model by now. It would also explain how an autonomous ship was able to manoeuvre close enough to the *Hera* – sacrificing a few robots would not be a problem . . . would it?" Grant looked grave. "Fearing that advanced cyber-systems would become dangerous to humans was one of the reasons for banning all such development. Essentially, and with only a few exceptions, all such research and development was stopped. I think we will find that we, the ISSF and governments around the world are well behind the conglomerates in such automation. I think we have a problem."

"What about the crystal consignment – could it be intercepted?" Rothschild asked.

Grant shrugged. "We are looking into it, but it's a needle in a haystack scenario."

"We are going into the Spheron Headquarters today. They have stepped out of line on a number of issues – pharmaceuticals are just the tip of the iceberg," said Abbey. "Perhaps it's time to take a much closer look at Epsilon Rio."

Rothschild sighed. "Forced inspections of production facilities are significantly different to raiding a company's headquarters, Abbey," he said. "It's taken weeks and a good deal of political pressure on the European

Democratic Republic to grant today's operation, and the rules are different in Brazil."

At that moment there was a knock on the door. Rothschild looked up. "Yes, what is it?"

Laura Bellingham opened the door promptly and leaned inside. "The call to Commander Reece, Peter, it's through . . . Line One is open, if you could pick-up?"

"Good . . . thank you, Laura. Hello, Rothschild here." He made a selection on his control panel and fed the reply through the speaker.

The door closed.

"Hello Peter, Richard Reece, at your service."

"Richard, where are you exactly?"

It was a clear line.

"I'm sitting behind the pilot in his Typhoon fighter."

"I didn't mean that. I meant where are you – geographically?" Rothschild shook his head. "What's your ETA, Richard?"

"Okay, Peter. Crete. In that area, anyway. Another couple of hours to go."

"Why did you miss the pickup? You are late and a number of people require your presence, not least the Lunar Senate. They want you back at your desk."

"I'm late because of your biotronic friend if the truth be known, but I'm okay, thank you."

"Where is Thomas, Richard? Is there a problem?"

"He's jammed in a freight pod beneath our right wing. Best place for him. There wasn't an alternative at the Egyptian base. I wanted to leave him there, but

Lieutenant Quarrie did some negotiating. The pod isn't really compatible with this aeroplane and so it was a botch job to secure it. That's why we are subsonic and relatively low. Arrival at the Orbitalport is in two hours and twenty-seven minutes."

Rothschild appeared to be in two minds: he did not know whether to be pleased at Richard's safe return or annoyed at his apparent disregard for orders. Abbey shook her head at his cavalier attitude.

"Understood," Rothschild said, removing the edge from his tone. "Listen . . . there are definitely problems on the Moon – unspecified at the moment, but something to do with security. We think it is serious. The Lunar Senate is being cagey as usual – as I said to you previously, it's their damned isolationist policies. Anyway, they need you back immediately to command your squadron. They are sending a fighter to pick you up. I delayed it until I heard from you. I will not be in London when you arrive – business elsewhere I'm afraid – but Abbey will meet you. There'll be enough time for a debrief and then you will need to go."

"That's all well and good, Peter, but I need to follow my lead on Madame Vallogia; she *has* been abducted, as has Asharf Makkoum. Their lives are in danger, I know it."

"So you know where they are?"

"Not exactly . . . I need your help."

"I'm not sure we have time for this, Richard, there are some critical . . ."

"I'm not going back to Andromeda without finding Madame Vallogia, Peter. You can forget it! You brokered the secondment, you can make the excuses. You help me to find her and I'm on my way back full of praise for MI9 – it's your call."

Rothschild turned the microphone off. "This damned man . . ." he muttered, full of frustration.

"Madame Vallogia may well be important to us, Peter," Abbey interjected, in a conciliatory way, "and particularly if another consignment of crystals is forthcoming. Consider the recent Mitchell report on their believed origin. The basis of it is Richard's discovery of the Ark of the Light in Venice. Two years to compile, it was supposed to be the consultative document when *Hera*'s consignment was put into service. It stated Madame Vallogia's role as 'a very knowledgeable historian' but it also mentioned her hereditary line. She has knowledge of the cultures that first used the crystals, Peter – should anyone stop to listen."

Rothschild drew a deep breath and nodded. "Perhaps you're right, but the Senate will not be happy." He flipped the switch again. "I'm going to try to buy you some more time, Richard. I'll try for tomorrow morning . . . So how can I help?"

"Thank you. Go on the World Net, will you? Open up a travel programme or holiday guide – or perhaps a city guide. Asharf was taken from Cairo in a small plane, probably a private jet. He says he experienced frequent bumpiness and so they were probably at or below the tropopause. That probably puts them in a subsonic regime. Say a top speed of Mach 0.95. He says the flight was about three hours. That gives a circle with an approximate radius of two thousand miles based on Cairo. Madame Vallogia is with him; she was driven there from Paris. It was a couple of hours apparently, maybe a little more, and there was a holdup on the road, too, so that puts them near Europe somewhere, perhaps still in France, maybe Germany or Holland. She recalls hearing noises of jet engines and an aeroplane passed low overhead as she was led into a building, so they are probably close to an airport. They were both blindfolded for the duration but Madame Vallogia managed to glimpse two street names and a park name on her way; she said she had a cold and needed to blow her nose – she could convince you of anything." Richard paused with that thought. "Peter," he went on, "please feed these street names into the travel programme and see what it comes up with."

"Alright, go ahead with the names."

"The park was called Parc de la Meinau, spelt with a *c*. The streets are the Rue de Figeac and then she turned left into Rue Louis Braille. After that, her head was covered again, but she was driven for only another ten minutes before they reached the building. What have you got – anything?"

After typing in the final word, Rothschild stabbed the enter key on his illuminated panel. Almost immediately the programme responded and a place name appeared on his computer screen. For a moment he simply stared. "I don't believe it," he voiced in a whisper, and then he looked up at Abbey with widening eyes. "It's Strasbourg," he uttered. "Richard!" he called, in a loud voice. "It's Strasbourg! Those places are all in Strasbourg! And only a short distance from the Aérodrome de Strasbourg-Neuhof."

"Of course! That's it! That's where they are! Spheron! Spheron . . . they are being held captive in their bloody headquarters building." There was a pause of realisation. "They want information from her regarding the crystals. That's got to be the reason – but she doesn't know anything, not consciously anyway. Peter, I'm going there. I need to find her . . . and Asharf."

"That's not possible, Richard. There's a Federation security operation tonight; we are raiding that building. I'm due there myself after it has been secured in order to help coordinate an investigation with the French authorities. No to that request Richard, I'm sorry – too many complications."

"I want to be there before the shooting starts, Peter. Don't you see? They will not give up a prize asset eas—"

"I'm sure it won't come to that."

"Oh really, and you are going to guarantee Madame Vallogia's life are you? I would say that the Spheron Corporation has a lot to hide and they are not going to give it up without a fight." There was a moment of silence and the radio crackled and then Richard was heard to say to his pilot: "Make a call to Air Traffic Control, Chris; we are diverting to Strasbourg. ETA . . . 16:30 GMT; that's 17:30 Local." And then Richard's voice became clearer. "What is the planned time for this raid? And what's the address?"

Rothschild knew that he was on a hiding to nothing. "I want you to be careful with this, Richard. Do you understand? No diplomatic incidents . . ." It was a stern voice that offered no compromise.

"Of course . . . you have my word on it. I'm into the building . . . I find them . . . and I'm out. Who would I contact? Who's in charge of the operation?"

"Ask for Monsieur Pierre Marquenie. He is my opposite number in the French Secret Service. The raid is due to start at 19:00 Local. Be there at 18:30 but not before – just down the street from the main entrance. I'll have the address sent through to your telephonic pager. There will be enough police vehicles to attract your attention. One other thing . . . you're unlikely to find any local taxis – there's no fuel on general sale over there. I'll get a message to the airport manager and get our department driver out for you."

"Copied."

"Richard, this is Abbey. Listen carefully – this is important. We have somewhere that you can go in Strasbourg – a safe house. It's in the local area, close to the diplomatic sector. It was used as a base for our agents when the European Democratic Republic was formed and the UK withdrew its membership in favour of the North Atlantic Alliance. We used to keep an eye on decisions being made in their parliament. I'm not sure of the exact address but it's only a short drive – Robertsau, Rue des Fleurs, if I recall. I'll need to confirm that. It's not far from the principal Parliament building. I'll get Laura to send the address and the main door entry code to your pager. The building has not been used for a while. Take Madame Vallogia and Mr Makkoum there. I will arrange for a pickup tomorrow, mid-morning, when the dust has settled, so to speak. Have you got that?"

"Got it, Abbey. I'll be in touch!"

# CHAPTER 23

# VOICES FROM THE PAST

**Strasbourg – same day**
**18:42 European Time**

Lieutenant Quarrie's suggestion that Strasbourg's Spaceport was a more logical place to land than the restricted and city-central Neuhof Airport was sensible, despite being situated in countryside twelve kilometres south of the metropolitan area. Putting the agile fighter down at night, in bad weather and on a relatively short, wet, runway was well avoided unless absolutely necessary.

The Space and Science Federation owned and ran the spaceport as part of its European Headquarters. It was the largest facility outside the Americas and additionally it had maintenance equipment on hand that was compatible with the Typhoon. Richard had left Chris Quarrie supervising the replenishment of his aircraft's systems, including a small fuel uplift for the proposed short hop to London after his business in the city was concluded. He had also asked for the HIM 32 to remain secured in the freight pod until he could rid himself of the responsibility by handing the system back to Peter Rothschild – he could not see any use whatsoever for a robot like Thomas. A helpful Duty Officer at the Spaceport's Control Centre had put a car at Richard's disposal and it was in this vehicle – a black-painted, French-built, Partisan estate model – that Richard arrived at his destination.

Richard's dark-suited driver reminded him of the famous fictional detective from Belgium – the one from the Art Deco period that he had seen on telescreen repeats. He had black hair slicked back with tonic, an old-fashioned moustache and keen dark eyes. In the specified location the man had spotted a number of haphazardly parked vehicles, including three white, windowless vans. Consequently, Richard had asked him to turn around, drive back and stop in a crossing street close to where the vehicles formed a loose cordon. Subsequently, the driver had approached the furtive scene with caution. With headlights dimmed but without concealment, the Partisan estate car drew to a halt beneath the last lit street lamp; thereafter, the remainder of the street was in darkness.

Richard sat for a short while assessing the situation. He could see a number of figures lurking in the shadows at the edge of the street.

"You see them?" asked the driver; he had a strong French intonation.

Richard nodded. "Yes, I see them," he replied. "There must be twenty."

Richard, who was sitting in the back of the car, noted that the street was effectively blocked. He also noticed that the suspension was dragging on all three vans and he realised that there was probably a similar number of men in hiding.

He began searching the vicinity for someone who might be in charge when suddenly a man appeared from behind his right shoulder and peered inside. Richard jumped. "What the . . . ?" he blurted, being taken completely unawares.

The man, who was wearing riot gear and had the visor on his helmet flipped up, tapped on the window with his knuckle. Richard found the switch and motored the window down.

"Monsieur Reece?" the man asked.

Richard nodded. "Yes, that's me."

The man gestured over his shoulder. "You are expected. Monsieur Marquenie waits for you. Come with me."

Richard was wearing his spare set of clothes – dark blue trousers, brown brogues and a white, roll neck cotton shirt beneath a royal blue, woollen, cable-knit, crewneck pullover. He had left his flight suit rolled neatly on the rear ejection seat of the Typhoon. "You'll wait for me?" he asked the man he had mentally nicknamed Poirot.

"Those are my instructions," replied the driver curtly.

Richard pulled a borrowed mid-length dark coat from the seat beside him and climbed from the car. It was a cold night, one degree at most, and a light drizzle moistened his shoulders. He followed the man into the shadows, pulling on the coat and buttoning it. There, beneath a leafless lime tree, lurked a group of plainly clothed men; they loitered with intent. Most wore overly-padded black jackets with elasticated waistbands, but two wore dark, calf-length raincoats. Richard smiled and shook his head – *plain clothes or not*, he thought, *they were clearly policemen.*

The entire group watched suspiciously as Richard approached. It was attention that made him feel nervous. One of the raincoat-wearing men stepped forward and held out his hand. "*Bonsoir, Monsieur Reece,*" he said, in a friendly way. "My name is Pierre Marquenie. I was told to expect you by my friend in London. He is on his way, but will miss the action . . . *quel dommage.*"

"How do you do?" responded Richard, as he shook the tall man's hand.

"I am told that there are two people inside that you have to make contact with," said Marquenie, assessing Richard with a quick look up and down. "And one is an Egyptian undercover agent?"

Richard nodded. "Yes, that's correct."

Marquenie pulled a small radio from his coat pocket. He held it to his mouth, whilst keeping a watchful eye on

Richard, and barked a few words into it in French. The hushed conversations around them stopped abruptly. "It is 18:52, Monsieur," he said to Richard. "We move in a few minutes. Tell me quickly, a description . . . What should we be expecting?"

"The lady is Madame Vallogia," replied Richard immediately. "She's in her forties but looks younger. Perhaps ten years younger. She's one point eight metres in flat shoes – always flat shoes. Slim. Attractive. Mediterranean complexion. Italian looking. Speaks French fluently . . . Oh, and long dark hair."

"Attractive . . . ?" asked Marquenie. "She sounds beautiful!"

Richard shrugged. "One other thing . . ." he started, appearing to ignore the remark, "she has a birthmark on her face – left side, down here." Richard ran his hand from his forehead down his cheek and onto his neck.

"Shame," commented Marquenie, and then he lifted the radio to his mouth and translated the description into French.

"It makes no difference," replied Richard, dropping his words to a whisper. Then he wondered why he had said that.

"And the agent, monsieur – what about him?"

"Asharf Saeed Makkoum . . . He's a little shorter – by a centimetre or two. Arabic descent. Tanned face. An intuitive look with dark hair. Bit of a hooked nose, too . . . probably unshaven." Richard paused for a moment in recollection. "Wiry – deceptively strong actually. He'll wear a djellaba for sure."

Marquenie nodded and translated the words into French again, adding, "*Allons!*" Then he slipped the radio into his pocket, noted the time and raised his hand to point ominously down the street.

The response was immediate. With electric drives whining, the three white vans screeched off in the direction of a tall, rectangular glass building. Realising where he was going, Richard could see several lit offices on various floors. The street was wide and tree lined. Agents seemed to spring up from nowhere, some carrying torches. A group of policemen heavily clad in protective riot gear spontaneously formed a platoon. One of their number, although indistinguishable as an officer, began giving orders in French. The group stepped off in a spritely fashion and headed towards the building.

"Stay close to me," said Marquenie to Richard. "We will take our time. Nobody is sure what to expect."

The entrance to the building was formed by an impressive overhanging glass portico with a greenish hue. Towering side panels were set to prevent any weather from reaching the three transparent revolving doors. Within this dry area that was paved in translucent glass, and was made to glow by integral fibre optics, there was a central fountain in the form of a single jet of water. The column rose vertically to perhaps fifteen metres and was set so precisely as to come down on itself without a drop being spilt. On the glass wall to the right of the doors and mounted at head height was a large plaque bearing the words 'Spheron Industries' in polished platinum. As he approached, Richard stood almost mesmerised by the legend.

Marquenie called Richard over. With the other man in a raincoat – whose name was Matisse – he was standing close to the central door, waiting for a report. They were keen to go inside. French spoken over the radio was almost continuous and at times excited. Once or twice Marquenie interrupted proceedings by shouting orders, but in the main he let his men get on with it.

"There are no more than a dozen security guards and a few people working late. Middle management you will understand; unfortunately no directors. But they will be questioned by my people." Marquenie explained the situation in good English. Richard watched him draw a slow breath of relief and nod his silent approval to his colleague. Marquenie, as he stepped into the light, he seemed older than the fifty-something years that Richard had originally estimated.

Marquenie was taller than Richard. He had a narrow face and prominent cheekbones and was almost permanently adorned with a trilby-type hat, which he wore pulled down over his eyes – at an angle that made him look sinister. Richard peered through the glass doors and into the foyer – there was still plenty of action inside.

"They were not expecting us," Marquenie continued, after some more talk over the radio. "No armed resistance. Believe me, this is a good thing – when news of this breaks tomorrow there will be repercussions." He paused thoughtfully and then shrugged, as if discarding that remark. "Soon we will have the building secured," he said.

"Any sign of Madame Vallogia?" asked Richard expectantly.

Marquenie shook his head. "There are facilities underground still to be searched."

An Anti-terrorist Officer carrying a compact machine gun in one hand and a radio in the other stepped purposefully from the building. He made straight for Marquenie and delivered his report. The subsequent conversation in French included Matisse. After nodded assurance from the officer, Marquenie looked across at Richard. "We can go in," he said, gesturing with his head. The four men entered the building through the central door.

It was a large, open, and well-lit foyer and Richard looked towards Pierre Marquenie for direction as his men ran in all directions. There were other officers sitting behind a wide, brushed metal reception desk and also an adjacent security console. They appeared totally preoccupied with the security monitors that they controlled. Richard followed Marquenie to the desk and stood behind him as the officers combed the building remotely. Then two men, dressed smartly in dark business suits and wearing handcuffs, brushed passed them. Accompanying detectives directed them towards the main doors with an occasional shove. Richard watched them go; he was disappointed, considering them a lost interrogation opportunity.

Over to the right someone shouted. Richard turned. Marquenie was already on his way and Richard set off in pursuit. A heated conversation followed between Marquenie and a policeman; eventually Marquenie shook his head – apparently in disgust. He looked over his shoulder at Richard. "Some men have escaped from the back of the building. The security cameras picked them up on subterranean level five and again a few minutes later on the lower car park level – that's level minus two. An outside camera caught them running from the building. There's no more sign of them."

Richard was indifferent. "How many?" he asked.

"Four! One was oriental looking and one had a bad limp – probably a prosthetic limb. There's more on video if you want, but we should go down to level five immediately – we have something!"

"Let's go!" Richard agreed.

There was a brooding silence of anticipation in the elevator. Richard's eyes were glued to the display as the numbers counted down. The roomy compartment arrived at the subterranean level with no more indication than the digit 'S5' appearing above the door; as it slid back an officer was waiting.

"This way," he said in English.

They stepped into a corridor that was white and pristine and longer than expected. Walking purposefully the group passed numerous rooms on either side. Inside some, where the doors were open, Richard could see laboratory equipment. Other corridors that crossed at right angles to the main thoroughfare looked identical. It was a labyrinth of science: a place for experimentation and development. As they walked, two other men joined the group. Richard looked at one of them. The man removed his dark blue coat to reveal a white shirt, black tie and a creaseless white jacket that was not quite mid-thigh length. He looked like a doctor but his ID indicated a government department.

"What goes on here?" Richard quizzed.

"You don't want to know," was the curt reply. The man spoke English with a neutral accent and he glanced disapprovingly at Richard. He was hard-faced, in his thirties, and had a no-nonsense manner.

"Actually I do," pressed Richard.

The man suddenly turned left and headed off down another corridor; the group followed him. Richard caught up and stared. "Well?"

"Spheron make drugs. That means they need to experiment. They do some of it here . . . secretly."

"So you didn't know about this facility?"

"We know of their primary laboratories – they are mainly in Europe. But a few facilities escape government monitoring because they are in isolated regions of the world. This one we didn't know about."

"Right under your nose." Richard shrugged. "Not so good then."

The man glanced at Richard again, before his attention was drawn to a door opening on his left. Emanating from inside were shrieks and shrills of animals. The group stopped abruptly while the man had a brief conversation with a colleague who had stepped from the room. Richard peered inside. The room was lined from floor to ceiling with cages. A few were empty but most contained a small monkey. The primates leapt and screamed and some pulled wildly at the mesh that enclosed them. Breaking off from the conversation, the man closed the door, shutting in the noise, and strode off again.

"I thought experimentation on animals was banned years ago?" Richard queried.

"Correct."

"So?"

"Spheron breaks the law – the larger and more powerful the company, the fewer scruples they seem to have."

Richard nodded his agreement. "Where are we going, then?"

The man stopped. He turned to address Richard and also Marquenie and Matisse. "Spheron have been experimenting on humans," he said bluntly. "Apparently there is a primordial centre in our brains that once may have allowed some form of telepathy. Although long since redundant the centre seems to be more susceptible to stimulation in people with psychic or clairvoyant abilities. Spheron was working on a drug that might allow this ability to be rekindled – in everyone."

"Surely that's impossible!" Marquenie exclaimed, in disbelief.

"The data that we have collected so far indicates some success, but only with people who already possessed a gift – a natural ability. A drug is still some way off – probably impossible – but that hasn't stopped their research. You can't believe what they have been doing."

"What about my friends . . . the people I'm looking for?" Richard interjected. He was becoming agitated.

The man raised his hand. "Don't worry," he said in a calming voice. "We have found them and they are well, although the gentleman has been subjected to some sort of electroencephalography."

Richard breathed a huge sigh of relief.

"It seems that your friends were due to participate in a particularly archaic programme of experimentation, one that was to begin soon. It seems, for them at least, that we are in time."

Richard turned to Marquenie. "I'd like to leave with them immediately, if you don't mind. I do have somewhere to go – until support arrives tomorrow morning."

Marquenie nodded. "I concur – that is my brief. I am expecting Peter Rothschild here in an hour or two. You can also expect a visit from him a little later."

Richard pulled his telephonic pager from his pocket

and read the text on the small display. "You want the address?"

Marquenie raised his hand to say no. "Some things remain secret even during these times of *entente cordiale*. Safe houses are none of my business." He raised a wry smile.

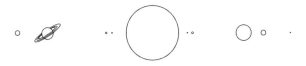

The black Partisan estate drew slowly to a halt outside an impressive town house. The street had several buildings of similar nineteenth-century architecture, although Number Eleven was, perhaps, the least ostentatious. In terms of energy allocation the street appeared unusually privileged; every other lamp-post was lit. As a result, the scene had a misty ambiance that was bathed in winter's damp chill. Defoliated trees cast shadows, as did lamp-posts; they were stretched and spindly. Metal railings with spearhead-tops cast rows of elongated bars on the pavement, as in a jail, and stone steps created secret corners where dark imaginings lurked. It reminded Richard of paintings he had seen of London town during the Victorian era; gas lights and fog and long buttoned-up coats. Richard glanced upwards into the murky darkness and then back along the street. The drizzle had eased but water on the flagstones, particularly at the foot of each lit lamp-post, made the pavement reflective and shiny.

Richard, from the front seat of the estate, peered up at the façade. Several steps led up to the front door and there was an ornate iron balustrade on each side. Through the windows the house was dark and appeared unoccupied.

"This is it?" Richard enquired, somewhat surprised. The Poirot character looked across and gave a sharp nod. "Who lives here?" Richard asked, scanning the building again.

"Who has not?" replied the driver, seemingly equally surprised to have arrived in this quarter. "Over the years . . . royalty, ministers, embassy officials . . . Thirty years ago most were sold to oil-rich leaders from the east – Uzbekistan, Kazakhstan – but few come here." The man craned his neck to look up at Number Eleven. "This one . . . I don't know."

"Good. Well thanks very much. I'm most grateful to you for the information." Richard glanced at Asharf then turned to look at Naomi. "You had better wake him," he said quietly and he smiled faintly to reassure her. Then he gave a nod to the driver and climbed from the car.

Asharf was unsure on his feet and so Richard helped him up the steps by putting a supporting arm under his shoulder. At the top he leaned against the wall in a bedraggled, exhausted way. Apart from reddened, puffy eyes from a lack of sleep, Naomi appeared relatively well.

Richard put a foot on the doorstep and pressed to

check that the door was locked. Then he held the knocker and pulled himself onto the step in order to look through the glazed fanlight. The hall was illuminated to some extent by the streetlights, as there were internal doors open. The house appeared deserted. Richard checked his pager for the security code and subsequently tapped six digits into the keypad that was set at chest height to the right of the door frame. Instantly, a number of solenoids were heard to operate and the door flipped open a few centimetres. Adjacent to the keypad there was a small, domed-type closed-circuit television camera and inside a tiny pinprick of light illuminated. In the hallway there was a small, glowing orange light mounted on the wall and Richard pressed it to turn on the main light. As he closed the door the estate car drove off into the night. Then he checked that the solenoid draw-bolts were in place.

"So how have you been, Naomi? I'll confess I've missed you."

"I have been fine, really. Until this, my life was very quiet." Naomi paused and looked Richard in the eye. "You are never far from my thoughts, Richard. That will always be the case."

Richard forced a smile at the implications of sharing their feelings. They sat in a large bedroom suite on the first floor. Richard had closed the long drapes and only two table lights illuminated the room. In the sitting area there were two comfortable couches upholstered in a beige patterned material, and a contemporary coffee table in white ash was positioned centrally between them. On the table was a crystal vase. The antique wooden floors were covered in expensive-looking bordered rugs – some were plain, but the one in the bedroom area was floral. Naomi had put Asharf to bed in the neighbouring room and now she sat on a couch, restless but relieved. The house had a mustiness about it from being unoccupied, but it was clear that it was serviced regularly and beds in several of the rooms remained made-up.

There were no provisions in the house, not that Richard could find anyway, except for a packet of English Breakfast teabags, a jar of freeze-dried coffee and some dried milk in a plastic container. He had also discovered an unopened bottle of cognac in a cabinet in the bedroom and there were a number of crystal glasses, but he had decided to stick to the coffee; Naomi had preferred tea with no milk. He sat opposite her and sipped his drink and tried not to stare.

"Only three times in my life have I missed the Full Moon Ceremony," Naomi said, breaking a period of expectant silence. She spoke quietly and with restraint. "Another occasion was when my mother died – although I made a dedication to Osiris a few days later, when I returned to Giza. I shall do the same this time. Only on this occasion I shall dedicate a prayer to you, Richard, for saving my life once again."

"Seeing you is good enough, Naomi. Leave it at that, why don't you?"

Another period of silence followed. Richard checked the time – it was almost ten. "I expect Peter Rothschild will have arrived at the Spheron building by now, but he'll be busy enough – we won't see him until the morning."

Naomi nodded.

"Actually, I sent Rothschild an abrive a while ago," Richard continued. "I've requested a flight for you as soon as possible – to take you back to Cairo. Abbey Hennessy replied while you were with Asharf. She says that there is a government aircraft departing Strasbourg at midday. It's going to Amman, but you can drive from there. She'll make all the arrangements."

Naomi nodded again. "Our time together will be short," she said quietly. "I feel that I should also sleep, but I will not waste these precious hours." Naomi looked under her eyelashes at Richard. Her lips parted to speak but Richard spoke first.

"What were they planning, Naomi, those men who got away?"

"I do not know, but somehow they had heard of my duties, my role as a servant in the Temple of Osiris . . . who I am." She looked up at Richard and shook her head. "Not all . . . but enough."

Richard nodded his understanding. "There was a formal report, after we found the Ark. It circulated the ISSF Security Council and the British Cabinet; Rothschild had a hand in it, I know. It was Top Secret. But there is a mole in the ISSF operation; Rothschild thinks that the Americans are responsible. Some of the information must have been leaked. I'm sorry about it."

"No matter, Richard; it is over now."

"Will you go back to the convent?"

"Of course, it is my home; I have found peace there. And I intend finishing my treatment."

Richard looked surprised. "Treatment? I had no idea . . . What . . . ?"

"I have been visiting a clinic in Paris. I do not know why I should speak of it, but with you Richard, I do not seem myself."

Richard sensed an underlying sadness in her voice. "Why? A clinic? Is there something . . . ? I mean, are you ill?"

"Only what you already know." Naomi shrugged. "I cannot allow my line to end without trying everything possible."

Richard looked puzzled.

"I told you, Richard, although it seems a lifetime ago now. I cannot have a child naturally. The scarring you see is also within." She put a hand on the aggressive, brown-coloured birthmark on the left side of her face and paused. "I cannot stop trying until all avenues are closed to me . . . I will not!"

Richard nodded his sympathy. He looked sad for her. "So how is it going?"

"For three years now I have been undergoing fertility treatment – the programme is on-going. I am forty-five, but there remains a chance."

"But you told me it was impossible . . . I remember.

Why subject yourself to all that? The drugs, the discomfort . . ."

"What do you know of the discomfort, Richard? You are a man, you have no idea."

Richard looked down at his lap. He paused, collecting his thoughts. "I know of it, Naomi," he said in a whisper. "Rachel . . . well, she's having help, too. It makes her feel unwell, short-tempered . . . It's difficult at home . . ."

"I am sorry for you both."

"Yeah, me too. But they make predictions, don't they? What are they saying, Naomi?"

Naomi sighed. "No matter how remote, I must keep on trying – so much depends on it."

"The results then – so far?"

There was a silent pause as Naomi considered the question. "Why do I seem able to tell you my most personal secrets?" She looked Richard in the eye. "They have not managed to match a donor, although I have become fertile." She looked embarrassed.

"Then it's just a matter of time," Richard said encouragingly.

"They have identified an abnormality with my DNA. They are wrong to call it that, of course, because my line goes back to the old people – a direct line. Each High Priestess passing down unique traits."

"You mean your hand, for example – the size and shape and your finger prints . . . ?"

"It is the key to the temple."

Richard nodded. "I know that – and other places,

too."

Naomi's eyes narrowed. "I have an unusual genetic protein, apparently," she continued, bypassing Richard's remark. "A strand forms a stub on my DNA. They told me that its action will prevent conception unless a similar but opposite strand is present in the donor's DNA. Like my blood group, everything seems against me." Her eyes welled and large tears fell onto her clasped hands.

"I'm sorry, Naomi, I shouldn't have asked – clumsy as usual," Richard said, standing and pulling a white handkerchief from his pocket. "Come on . . . don't cry." He offered the handkerchief to Naomi.

Naomi took the handkerchief and dabbed her eyes. She looked up at him and smiled as he sat down again.

"Listen, Naomi, there's something I want to ask you. It's a wayward request, but I need your help – with your cooperation it just might be possible."

"Of what do you speak?"

"It's a secret, Naomi, you have to understand that. I would get into serious trouble if it got out."

Naomi nodded and looked expectant.

"I have a crystal. I managed to smuggle it to Earth five years ago from Mars."

"You have a crystal . . . ? Where?"

"It's a small example. The smallest of the deposit I found. It was unaccounted for, and they searched for it, but, well, that has all blown over."

"Yes!" Naomi sat bolt upright.

"The crystal is in Cairo, Naomi, with Professor

Mubarakar. It's safe, but I won't go into that now." Richard paused thoughtfully. "There is a use for that crystal, a role to play; I just don't know what it is. The old people hold the key, but their knowledge has long since been forgotten. The High Priests – like the remains of the man we found in that chamber in the Valley of the Kings – and latterly your line, were the guardians."

"Yes, this is so. But . . ."

"You remember our time in Khartoum – four years ago?"

Naomi nodded. "I will never forget that time – we were together as one."

"Yes. We joined in your special way, a spiritual way. The subliminal joining, you said."

"It will always be special to me."

"When we had finished, I mean, parted, it was very late. We didn't talk much. I went back to my room – with a headache I might add." Richard was perched on the edge of the couch. "You said that I had slipped deep into your subconscious – further than you had intended."

"I remember this."

"I never told you. We left early the next morning. The opportunity didn't arise again."

"You did not speak of what, Richard."

"Well, I sensed myself falling through some sort of tunnel, through a crawling mist, and when I emerged I was at a ceremony of some kind. I knew immediately *where* I was, because I recognised the geography of the place!"

Naomi raised her eyebrows in anticipation.

"The Plain of Giza! But there were only two pyramids! The ceremony was the placing of the capping stone, in order to complete the construction of the Great Pyramid. There was a huge crowd and other buildings forming a plaza that are long since gone. I remember a woman; the crowd acknowledged her as a queen. And then suddenly I was somewhere else. I don't remember the place, but there was distress – screaming and crying. One woman shouted, 'The seas have risen and swallowed the great city!', and another said, 'Poseidon has their souls.' It was so vivid!"

"Poseidon was the god of the sea."

"Yes, I know, in Greek mythology."

"And what else?"

"The only other thing I remember was being in a Great Hall. There was a banquet; it was Roman times. I know because I recognised the soldier's uniforms – I've seen so many old movies! Someone spoke of Cleopatra. Don't you see, Naomi? These . . . these . . . occurrences – not dreams. And these women – Cleopatra, your remarkable likeness to Nefertiti – their memories are *your* memories. They are your forebears. These amazing women were all of the same line. The bones of that priest we found in KV5 . . . he was the last of the male line, a line that died out a thousand years before Nefertiti."

"But I have no recollection of the events you experienced . . . nothing . . . not even in my dreams."

"These are not dreams, Naomi. I did some research

into the nature of dreams, because I needed some answers. Dreams represent residual electrical activity in the brain – they are recurring impulses that play in the superficial areas of one's consciousness. Memories are something else entirely!"

"Tell me!"

"There's been some research done in the field over the last few decades. They found that there are several levels to the memory matrix. The deepest memories may be irretrievable, but that's not to say that they are not there. In the higher levels we know that stimulation can help trigger a memory. For example, if you see something you recognise – as in *déjà vu*. Also, such things as pheromones . . . deep-seated odours . . . they can evoke primordial responses."

Naomi looked long and hard at Richard. It was as if she was being told something she had always known, but had never, ever, recalled; nor had her mother or her grandmother or her great-grandmother, and back through her ancestral line.

"Of what you speak, and the accepting of it, comes easily to me, Richard – as if deep inside I have always known it to be true. You have a capacity for seeing what is hidden. It is an ability that comes from your aura. I have always known that to be uncommonly strong." Naomi lifted her head as if expecting a blow. "You want something of me, I can see it. I am willing."

Richard stepped across and sat next to Naomi. He grasped her hands. "I want to make a journey into your subconscious, as I did before," he said. "Only this time I will keep control of my emotions, not just go with the sensual thing. I want to focus on what I feel and experience in your memories – those in the deepest recesses of your mind. I want to go back in time and find out what your ancestors did with the crystals – how they used them – and discover the real reason for building the pyramids."

Naomi considered Richard's request. She looked down at her lap for some while. Richard looked through her flawed beauty to see only her exquisite face with the long slender neck and the poise of a queen.

"Such a joining will have dangers," continued Naomi sombrely. She lifted her head to look at him. "Your consciousness will be in my keeping. But all pleasures have consequences, Richard. If you go deeper, beyond my recollection, you will be lost to me. I could not help you if you were troubled. You risk your very being; some might say your soul. Therefore you risk your life."

"I'm prepared to accept that. I need to find out how best to use that crystal."

"Then we shall join. We should lie next to each other on the floor and I will tie our palms together – we cannot risk a parting of our auras during such a time."

Richard finished his coffee and moved the table aside. Then he did as Naomi asked and lay on his back on the rug. Naomi sat up next to him. Richard held up his right hand; Naomi took it in her left. They locked fingers. Naomi bound the two of them together with a curtain tie and Richard helped her to tie a knot. Then she lowered the entanglement between them and pressed it with her thigh against Richard's. Finally she lay back and took a deep breath.

"To open the door to my subconscious, Richard, first you must be intimate with my emotions – do you remember?"

"Yes I do."

"Then close your eyes and imagine my face. Think only of me, Richard, nothing else. Be gentle, at peace."

Richard sank into a coma-like state – as if in deep meditation. He found himself falling. There was no horizon and no reference. A grey mist was all around him. He was aware that he was moving, but not of movement. He lost his perspective on reality; his was a fathomless dark place. Phantoms whirled past so fast that only the brain registered their placing. Light and dark, like summer and winter days, came and went. Aeons fell before him when Naomi's face appeared. She was distant at first, but she blew towards him on a solar wind and grew larger until she filled his mind. Her image was transparent and the backdrop was space – the eternity of an endless blackness punctured only by stars and vast clouds of effervescing gas and nebulas with centres of intense colour: yellows and reds and purples.

How pleased he was to feel the well-remembered pleasure of Naomi and her pulling at his senses. This time, on this journey, he would remain focused. He would hold on to his thoughts and evade her seduction. Eventually, but with no reference of time, he slowly passed through her. Still the seasons changed. And then, unexpected and abruptly, he was aware of a hardness beneath his feet; he felt a surface. He appeared to be standing; he heard his breathing. The mist began to clear, but not before a rush of sounds pressed into his brain and seized his sanity. The clamour pummelled into his awareness until the noise subsided and he heard individual voices. The enshrouding mist dissipated, as if a cloud of dense, white, steam evaporated to nothing. He looked around and found himself in a busy market.

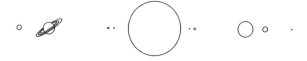

In awe and amazement Richard slowly turned full circle. He was in a large public square. People and noise engulfed him. It was a bright day and warm like summer. The sky was such an intense blue it seemed unreal. The architecture reminded him of Ancient Greece – what he remembered from school history, and to his right and at some distance was a columned façade. The building evoked memories of the Parthenon in Athens – he had played tourist there twice before: the first before it was enclosed in a plastic shell, thereafter to lose its appeal. At first he thought himself invisible as people around him seemed oblivious to his presence. Only then did he realise that he was dressed, essentially, like them – in a loose-flowing garment made of a single piece of rough cotton cloth that covered his whole body – except that his right arm was exposed. His garment was plain, off-white and coarse, but there was colour all around him.

Richard began to realise his social standing in this historic place, for the finer the garments and more intense the colours the more reverence those people seemed to evoke. Two women in flowing silks of crimson red passed him by; they were in deep conversation and giggling, but Richard *could* understand their words. Suddenly he felt a sharp pain in his arm. He turned and was instantly in his new reality, as a large bald man, dressed as he was but with the addition of a thick leather belt around his waist, punched him again on his shoulder. "Lower your eyes!" the man demanded. He had a deep gravelly voice. "Do not stare at the daughters of Zeus!"

Richard looked down at his sandalled feet and apologised with a gesture. The man and his attitude strode off into the crowd. Richard drew a long breath and assessed the surroundings. He was aware of being by the sea, because of the faint odour of fish and the salty breeze. He didn't know exactly how long he had in this memory of Naomi's, and so he followed his nose towards the water.

After perhaps fifteen minutes walking along streets that were swept clean, Richard began to hear the noises of the hustle and bustle of ships and trade. He could hear sails flapping in the wind and lanyards vibrating against masks. Before he could see them, he heard the sounds of men shouting instructions, pulley wheels squeaking and seagulls squawking. He walked down a narrow lane that was shaded and cool and, as with all the streets he had passed along, straight and paved in stone. At the end, and turning a corner, he found himself in an extensive open area. It was primarily a harbour where the sea was quite calm and turquoise blue. Several sailing ships were docked and unloading stores. It was a paradise.

At the far end of what looked to be a natural estuary there was a square – like a precinct or a piazza – and Richard made for it. He kept his manner nonchalant and tried to resist his natural tendency to stare and gawp at the remarkable surroundings.

The people that passed him by seemed content and they smiled readily. The young women had light suntans and bright eyes and a healthy glow. A fresh fish stall was stocked with giant tuna and Blue Marlin. They lay there whole and shiny on wooden tables, and there were huge crabs and squid. Richard had never seen such produce, but he recognised the numerous species from natural history books that he had read over the years. He had never seen such huge specimens as these either, as during his school days fishing was limited to just a few varieties and they were small and prohibitively expensive, and by the 2030s the seas of the Earth that he knew were devoid of life.

The square was lively and Richard tried to get his

bearings by looking back across the harbour and out to sea towards the sun – which by now had passed its zenith and was on a downward track towards the west. It was then that he did stop and gawp – longer, in fact, than was sensible to maintain anonymity, for what he saw took his breath away.

Richard walked a little unsteadily back to the quayside and sat down on a stone bench. He was unable to pull his gaze from the enormous structure as it glinted in the sunlight, and even estimating the distance at 1 kilometre, its scale still completely dominated the panorama – and his senses.

Richard hadn't noticed the old man who sat at the other end of the carved and curving stone seat. The kindly looking gentleman had weathered skin, a short grey beard and white curly hair that was thinning on top. He had a face of experience, with keen eyes, and on his garment of finely spun cotton, regal blue in colour, there was a gold brooch with an insignia consisting of two dolphins supporting a star between their beaks. The man watched Richard for some time but Richard remained unaware of his presence.

"You are not Atlean, are you?" asked the old man, coming nearer.

Richard dragged his eyes away from the towering structure and stared at the man, appearing a little blank at first. "I'm sorry," he replied, "what was that you said?" Richard was thinking in English, but his words came out in an old form of Greek. The entire situation, what he was seeing and hearing, served to disorientate him and he gave up in despair. He massaged his temples for a while and bowed his head.

The man clenched his right fist and touched his chest by his heart. "My name is Diomedes, son of Eutocius from the House of Archimedes. I said that you are not from here – this island is not your home. I think that to be true."

Richard looked up at the man, who smiled, comfortable in his large girth. He had a round face and ample jowls. There was a sparkle in his eye. Richard gathered his thoughts. "Err . . . no, not exactly. Good day to you." Richard touched his chest with his fist in a similar way. "Um, I am Richardius, from the house of, er . . . Pythagoras."

"You are a mainlander, I can tell – from Eridu, perhaps?"

*The oldest recorded city in the world*, recalled Richard. "Eridu, yes, that's it. I am a traveller. I'm looking for something."

"Only rarely do our cousins from the east visit. Is your quest for trade or pleasure?"

Richard felt his eyes being drawn again towards the great statue that straddled the harbour entrance. It looked to be modelled on a Greek God . . . Helios, or the like, and dressed as a Grecian warrior. He found himself only half-listening. "Sorry," he said, after an impolite pause. He looked back at the man. "That statue . . . is this place . . . this city by the sea . . . Rhodes?"

"Ha! You are indeed a stranger! Rhodes is an island to the east. It lays just one thousand cables distant . . . but a day's sailing in a good ship. There is a small fishing village by the same name, but that is all. *This* place, my friend, is the Island of Theira, and this city, *Atlantis* – the seat of power of the Sea Sapiens. Were you sleeping on your journey?"

"Err, well, you could say that. I didn't feel so well." Richard forced a smile alongside his excuse.

"Yes, this is true. If you are only used to the rock and sand then the sea can be disorientating." The kindly man nodded his understanding.

"That figure . . ." Richard raised his hand and pointed towards the sea. "How long has it stood there? I mean, when was it built?"

"The Colossus of Atlantis . . . ? It has stood for a thousand years. Next spring there will be celebrations to mark its millennium. It was cast in the new metal of the time – bronze – and manoeuvred itself into position. The engineering of our ancestors knew no bounds. You do not know of our fabled Colossus?"

"Yes, I know of it. Of course I do." Richard looked directly at the man. "Are you a mathematician?" he probed.

"I am an architect."

Richard paused thoughtfully and then his eyes narrowed. "Have you heard of Athens?"

The man's brow furrowed and he thought for a

moment. "No . . . not Athens! But Athena is well known." He pointed vaguely. "A small town on the Attica periphery – a place where this world's aura has been found to be unusually strong. We plan to build a temple there as part of the coming celebrations. There is a place, a hill on the edge of the town, that we have called Acropolis; it is a suitable site. I myself prepare plans for the temple. I have devised a new style for it and called it Ionic," he said proudly. "It will be of similar design to the Temple of Homer here in the city and on a similar scale, but the architecture will be a mixture of the ancient Doric style devised by our forefathers and my new Ionic columns will be more decorative, you understand. My associates will have a hand in its construction." Suddenly the man became suspicious and his easy smile dropped. "But this is not common knowledge. Do you have friends in the Senate?"

Richard nodded but looked evasive and then he stared again at the Colossus. "The power source for that statue – do you know where it is now?"

The man seemed surprised. "Such questions," he said. "Eridu has a similar stone. Each of the four tribes was bequeathed one."

"Where is the stone kept? Can you tell me?"

"In the Temple of Atlantis of course!"

"Would you take me there – just to see it, you understand? I hear it is inspiring."

The man nodded. "At least you have knowledge of that. However, you are deficient in its praise. I should say it surpasses inspiring. The great temple has stood from the very beginning." His expression grew kindly again. "There is nothing to hide. I have work there . . . I will show you."

The man stood and beckoned Richard to follow him. They left the quayside bound for the city. Presently, Richard found himself in the main precinct again. It bustled with people. Many acknowledged the elderly man with a polite bow of their heads, as one would to a luminary.

Richard's guide continued to walk in an easterly direction and after some while Richard realised that he was entering a much older quarter of the city. It was then that he caught sight of the temple. The man pointed to its conical peak towering above the rooftops and in a scholarly fashion he quoted dimensions and angles, but Richard had no idea of the units to which he referred.

The structure appeared to be made of translucent glass. In Richard's estimation it was, perhaps, another half kilometre before they reached the Grand Plaza that Diomedes described as the 'meeting place'. When they finally stepped from behind a tall, but time-ravaged, stone building to gaze unimpeded across the plaza, Richard pulled up short. His mouth fell open and he was speechless, as before him stood a glass pyramid in the same proportions as the Great Pyramid on the Plain of Giza – it could have been an exact replica. He stared in awe. The edifice sparkled in the sunlight like an unearthly prism and its backdrop was a sky so bright and blue and clear that it was beyond imagination.

Diomedes could see Richard's amazement and he was astonished by it. "As long as this structure has stood it has been of small interest to the people. Only during the great joining do they gather." Diomedes looked sideways at Richard. "Surely you know of this, for Eridu is similar." There was suspicion in his tone.

"I will be honest, Diomedes, if I may call you that. I come from beyond Eridu. I don't know of this . . . joining. Please . . . tell me."

Diomedes gestured for Richard to follow him again and they walked together across the paved plaza towards the pyramid. It was empty of people and at least 500 paces to the pyramid's base. "It is clear that you are not one of us, but your aura is strong and strangely it has the tolerance of the feminine side; because of that I trust you." He put a hand on Richard's shoulder. "The joining is when we communicate with our brethren on the Red World. It is an ancient ritual but happens infrequently now – only during the whole circle eclipse, when there is near total darkness – because the power of their stone fades."

Richard pointed towards the sky. "You use this structure to communicate with similar pyramids on Mar—, I mean with the other world?"

"Yes, of course!"

Richard was hearing this for the second time. He thought back to his quest to find the Ark of the Light almost five years earlier and the encounter with the hologram of Professor Simpson-Carter in Khartoum. The Professor had said that the pyramids on the Plain of Giza were observatories. Richard had remained sceptical, but Carter appeared to be right after all!

Diomedes broke Richard's thoughts by saying: "Come, I will show you."

Richard and Diomedes climbed the flight of stairs that were cut with precision into the otherwise smooth glass face of the pyramid. The main entrance was a gaping square hole in the structure about sixty metres above the ground. Inside was an enormous cone-shaped cavern. It immediately reminded Richard of the interior of the Temple of Osiris – inside the Pyramid of Khufu – where Naomi had taken him during his search for the Ark. Only in this case, in Atlantis, it was filled with light and air and warmth – not dark and malodorous as in Egypt.

A shimmering rainbow-like spectrum stretched from the near corner on Richard's right, across to the far corner on his left. So vivid were the seven colours that they appeared to be projected by a precision optical imager. The radiant arc reached high above their heads. There was a dynamic quality to it, as if it were alive. Richard could see that it was created by a prismatic effect, where the bright sunlight that entered the pyramid was refracted by thick glass walls. The colours offered a spectacular show that widened Richard's eyes in wonderment.

The two men walked to the geometric centre of the cavern where a raised circular plinth supported a glass altar. The altar was cylindrical in shape and similarly constructed of translucent glass. It was approximately one metre high and on its flat top, and apparently shaped from a single block, was a chalice. Diomedes shook his head and put a staying hand on Richard's shoulder when he attempted to step onto the plinth. "That place is for those who attend to the stone," he explained, and turned and pointed to an opening high in one of the slanting walls of the pyramid. It was the aperture of a small square shaft. "When the alignment of the heavenly bodies is precise – ours with the red world – then the power of the stone reaches out and our message is passed."

"*You send a message*? How? By light? By energy?"

"The High Priests and Priestesses have that ability. It is knowledge that is passed down their ancestral line and will continue for eternity."

Richard looked at him and drew a deep, thoughtful breath, and then he pointed to the chalice. It was 10 metres from where he stood. "The crystal . . . I mean the *stone* . . . it's there?"

Diomedes nodded. "It is said that only once in the annals of time has it been removed."

"Yes, of course," replied Richard, nodding with enlightened expression. "To power the Colossus, when it stepped into position!"

"It was constructed on the other side of the island. Remnants of the foundries are clearly evident. Folk law still tells of the great walk."

"Thank you, Diomedes, for your trust," said Richard,

aware of the passing time – whatever time reference there might be in 'memories'. "I have learned what I needed. I should go back to the precinct, position myself near the Temple of Homer. Someone waits for me there."

## Strasbourg – simultaneous

A heavily built man of Asian origin walked purposefully along a darkened street. Heavy drizzle wetted his jacket. He stopped outside a house and looked up, eyeing brass numerals that were fixed to the wide front door – Number Eleven appeared to confirm the address. He cast a wary eye in both directions and then climbed the few steps whilst pulling a small electronic device from his pocket. He scrutinised the tiny backlit screen, opened the adjacent security box and tapped a series of keys. The code released locks on the door which sprang open a few centimetres. He pushed the door open further and looked inside – the hallway was dark and quiet. He stepped back a few paces and raised his arm as a signal. Moments later a black sedan drew silently to a halt outside the neighbouring house. Three men climbed from the vehicle – one with some difficulty. Guardedly, the men made their way back to the house. None of them had a spritely step and one had a pronounced limp. They climbed the steps to the house in question and promptly disappeared inside.

The tall man had dark, shiny hair. He wore a black leather coat with large lapels, a white shirt, a black tie and black shoes – traditionally laced, not fastened. His face was narrow with high cheek bones and his look was slightly gaunt. The heavily built man looked Chinese and muscular. He wore a shorter black jacket of synthetic leather with more contemporary styling. His head was shaved and his neck thick. He looked hard. The other two men were of pensionable age, although both looked relatively fit. Dressed similarly, they each wore blue denim jeans and dark, bomber-style jackets, one blue and the other dark brown. They had a military bearing.

The tall man pointed a bony finger first at himself and then at the ceiling, and then he pointed to the oriental man and waved his finger in a circle, indicating for him to search the ground floor rooms. He gestured for the two older men to follow him; he seemed to know there was someone above them. Before climbing the stairs he checked the time: it was just after midnight.

Upstairs, after a brief search, the first three rooms proved empty. One of the older men stepped out of another bedroom backwards and silently closed the door behind him. He met the tall man's cautious glance on the landing and held up one finger and nodded. Then the three men gathered outside the last door. The oriental man came up the stairs shaking his head and giving the all clear. The tall man reached inside his coat and pulled out a pistol, gripping the door handle with his other hand. The oriental man did the same but retrieved a long knife with a thick blade; one of the edges was serrated. They stood ready to enter.

Without a word being spoken the tall man edged the door open. There was subtle lighting inside – brighter than on the landing – but no movement. He opened the door further and held back for a moment. All was silent. It was likely that the occupants were sleeping. Then he turned to the oriental man and gestured for him to enter.

The big man slipped inside the room and then, a few moments later, he said in a forced whisper: "Quickly! Come in!"

The tall man burst through the doorway, pistol raised.

"You won't need that, Mr Rhinefeld. Look!" said the oriental, and he pointed to Richard and Naomi lying on the floor, seemingly fast asleep. "Apart from these two, the room is clear."

A faint, lopsided smile contorted the scarred face of the tall man. He slowly lifted his black hat from his head, held it against his chest and looked down upon the couple – smugness widened his smile. He walked across and kicked Richard hard in the side. "Wake up!" he demanded.

There was no response from Richard, not even a stir. One of the men in blue jeans stepped over. He lifted his hand to stop another kick. He saw significance in the way that Richard and Naomi's hands were bound and knelt down beside Naomi to examine the link. He seemed to recognise something in the particular way they were joined and the expression they shared. Keeping a few centimetres clear, he ran a hand over the length of

Richard's body; he was feeling for something. And then he stopped and touched Richard, pressing in the area that he had been kicked; there seemed to be a complete immunity to pain – a complete immunity to any external stimulus. He shook Richard gently; there seemed also to be an inability to wake him. The man glanced up at his accomplice and then looked down at Naomi and began a similar examination. The tall man clicked his tongue and shifted impatiently.

"Vot are you doing?" he barked.

"He is sensing an energy field . . . an extrasensory energy," explained the other man in blue jeans.

The man kneeling put a hand on Naomi's forehead and closed his eyes. With his other hand he gripped Naomi's left wrist and felt her pulse. After a few moments he looked up and nodded slowly in an enlightened fashion.

"There is some kind of psychic link between them," he said. By his accent, it was clear the man was an American.

Rhinefeld put a foot on Richard's chest and pressed down. "He dies . . . Pull them apart!"

"Wait!" said the standing accomplice, and he quickly went to Naomi. He crouched down next to his friend and made his own examination. "Leon's right!" he exclaimed. "On a spiritual level, these two are joined like lovers. You part them like this and there will be damage – they may both die . . . You willing to risk that?" This man was also an American; he had the nasal slurring of the Bronx.

"I vont him to die! I do not care how!"

"Listen, Rhinefeld, you hired us for psychic work. I can take someone out just as well as the next man, but if you part these two in this state you risk losing the woman, too. I won't be held responsible for that – and we still want paying – you get that?"

"Mr Rickenbach, you vill obey orders. You are in zis up to your neck, and Springer, too." Rhinefeld took a thoughtful breath. "Tell me exactly vot is going on here. Quickly!"

"Charlie, take her open hand; I'll take Reece's. And then a hand on their foreheads – let's see."

For more than a minute the two men held their positions; they appeared to drift into a hypnotic state. Presently Rickenbach mumbled something and then he suddenly opened his eyes. He stared blankly for a moment and then put a hand on his friend's shoulder – Springer also returned to reality.

Rickenbach stood. He looked directly at Rhinefeld, whose hardened expression and dark eyes seemed devoid of feelings. "She seems to be holding open a synaptic pathway. I've never experienced such mental control. You can't teach that, she's a natural. Now get this, if you can . . . Richard Reece is doing what you intended to do with the woman – only on a much deeper level. Not psychic hypnosis to reveal facts and information; this is different. He's gone into her memory. I've never seen two people so close; there has to be a natural affiliation. Call it soul mates, if you like."

"Ugh! Zat is ridiculous! Going into her dreams . . ."

"Not dreams, Rhinefeld. Dreams are shallow, just residual electrical impulses in the synapse. This is much deeper; he's gone into the recesses of her mind, deep into her memory – even together we can't sense him, not on a semiconscious level. I'd say he's trying to learn something; a secret that this woman has long since forgotten."

"Can you follow him? Vot vill happen if you kill him inside?"

"If we kill his mind on a subconscious level, he'll become a cabbage. Like someone who is acutely mentally ill. He'll be finished as Richard Reece."

"Not enough!" Rhinefeld barked. "He did zis to me." Rhinefeld held up a trouser leg to expose his prosthetic leg. He thought for a moment and nodded sadistically. "I vont him to die twice. First his mind, and zen his body. I vill take pleasure in doing zat part. Can you follow him?"

Rickenbach looked down at Springer; their eyes met. "I've never heard anything like it being attempted before, but if we combine, it might just be possible," said Springer.

Rickenbach nodded his agreement. He looked again at Rhinefeld. "The woman waits for Reece to return, but she doesn't know what state his subconscious will be in, and so she maintains an unusually wide neural pathway to her memory centre," he continued. "We will need every ounce of our training and experience, but I think we can enter in a similar way – down the same path. But you must protect us here. We'll be totally unconscious;

helpless to all intent and purposes."

"Ya! Ve vill. Do it! Kill his thoughts . . . kill his mind!"

## Same location – simultaneous

Peter Rothschild sat thoughtfully in the back of a police vehicle. He checked his watch; it was thirty-nine minutes past midnight, Local Time. He expected Richard to be sleeping, but with the situation on the Moon escalating and the Lunar Senate demanding his immediate return or threatening repercussions, he had no other choice but to disturb him. The Swiftsure class ship was already waiting for him at the spaceport. His suspicions, however, were immediately aroused when his driver turned the corner. He knew that roadside parking was prohibited in the street for security reasons, because of the number of foreign parliamentary dignitaries living there. It was the perfect front for a safe house: protected by default; pretentious to the point of diversion; isolated.

Rothschild instructed his driver to continue past the house without stopping, and he scrutinised the parked car and its registration plate as they did. He pulled his telephone from his coat pocket, pressed a key and held the device to his ear.

"Abbey Hennessy here."

"Abbey, it's Peter. I'm at the safe house, but there is a car parked along the street close by. I don't like it. Run a number plate for me, will you?"

"Go ahead."

"334335 STF."

"Hold on while I put it through the system. While I have you on the line, we have been copied in on another memo from the Senator General. Unusually, they are requesting help – military help! There's something serious happening there, Peter, but information is still restricted. They say that they want their Squadron Commander back before it's too late. The Federation have circulated a reply saying that their long-range sensors cannot see anything abnormal on the Moon's surface. They can't see the dark side of course, and so they are speculating that the problem is on that side. God only knows what's really happening . . . Hold on, I've got an answer . . . Yes, here we are . . . The car is registered to Spheron, Peter, one of their fleet vehicles."

"I see, that's bad news; it seems Richard may already have visitors. How the hell did they get hold of . . . ?" Rothschild paused while he indicated to the driver to drive around the block again and stop where he could see the house. "Abbey, we have a serious breach of security," he continued. "The Americans and their bloody SERON mole, I expect – the damned 'special relationship' gives them access to just about everything. Find out who, exactly, had knowledge of Richard's movements, and who is party to the safe house details . . . address, entry code . . . everything. But first call for backup – I need a SWAT Team ASAP, and medical cover just in case. I'm going to wait here and keep an eye on things."

"Yes, immediately, Peter."

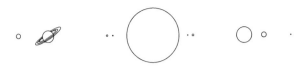

"Those two men, Richardius, over there, do you see. They are staring at you as if they know you. I thought you were a stranger here."

"I don't know them, Diomedes; never seen them before."

"Interesting," responded Diomedes. "If I did not know better . . ."

At that moment something caught Richard's eye. It was an effect he could not explain, as if the end of an adjacent street was shrouded in fog. The street was on his left and Richard put a hand on Diomedes' shoulder and then turned into it. "Do you see that?" he asked, pointing.

"I see nothing but a street with modest housing," replied Diomedes, following Richard on his diversion.

Richard was engrossed and walked with purpose for another sixty metres or so until he approached a wall of semi-transparent mist beyond which the streetscape at first became blurred, and then faded completely, as if the mist's density gradually increased, eventually turning to thick impenetrable fog. Like an unfinished landscape painting, for Richard the scene ended where he stood.

"At what do you gaze so intently, Richardius? What occupies your thoughts?" asked Diomedes, puzzled by

Richard's manner, but growing a little impatient.

"Don't you see it?" Richard responded, turning to look Diomedes in the eye and raising his hand as if to present the amazing sight that appeared before them.

Diomedes shrugged and raised his brow at the total lack of revelation. "I see only a common street," he said, stepping forward into the mist but making it clear to Richard that for him the street continued as expected, with unpretentious, uninteresting architecture.

Richard stood mesmerised for a moment and then he nodded knowingly. "It is the extent of Naomi's remembering," he uttered under his breath. "It's the edge of her memory." He paused again thoughtfully. "For whoever preceded Naomi, this street warranted just brief glance. Nothing lies beyond this point because nothing was remem . . ." Richard suddenly came to his senses. "Sorry, I'm not making any . . . we had better get on." He gestured with his head.

With that Richard turned to retrace their path and on the corner with the main thoroughfare, he saw those same two men loitering. Diomedes saw them too and his eyes narrowed with suspicion.

"How much further?" Richard asked as they walked back. The two men he dismissed as simpletons because they had disappeared.

"We approach," replied Diomedes, as he and Richard turned the corner. They continued walking and a few minutes later Richard saw the square opening before him.

Richard entered the wide expanse with admiration, as from that direction the true extent of his surroundings became apparent – classical architecture on an unprecedented scale. It was a wondrous place that reminded him of history book scenes and paintings of the great thinkers and philosophers of Ancient Greece: symmetrical rows of columns; great porticos in white marble; wide steps; and precisely proportioned statues of people and animals on tall rectangular plinths. It was like stepping into a great museum. Richard was overwhelmed by the culture, the people, the freshness and, above all, the blue sky.

"I will leave you now. May your journey home be uneventful," Diomedes said, wresting Richard from his astonishment. The old man raised his fist to his heart in the customary way.

Richard was about to reply when he felt a low level vibration beneath his feet. The vibration quickly grew to a shuddering and then, for a moment, the ground heaved. He looked up; some of the tallest buildings were teetering in a precarious way and a nearby statue of a rearing horse came crashing down, narrowly missing some passers-by. And then the disturbance completely subsided.

Richard looked at Diomedes, whose face had paled. "Do you get earthquakes here?" he asked.

"The land complains from time to time, but mostly it sleeps – never have I felt such a thing."

Around them the crowd seemed frozen, their expressions bemused.

"Well something is waking," replied Richard, and with that the uncanny silence was broken by a much deeper and more disturbing rumble. This time there was a noticeable ripple across the ground and the flagstones on which they stood shifted. "I've felt something like this before, in the Middle Ea— . . . It doesn't matter where. This is going to break, Diomedes; take my advice and make for open ground." Richard looked at the people around him; there was a look of panic on some faces and indifference on others. "Make for open ground!" he shouted. "*Quickly! Make for open ground!*" But there was apathy around him.

At that moment Richard felt something pointed pressing into his lower back. He half-turned to see one of the onlookers from earlier on. It was an elderly man, lean and angry looking, and he pushed the point harder into Richard's side. "Move!" ordered the man. And then Richard's arm was gripped and someone jostled him – it was the other onlooker. "I said, *move!*"

Suddenly, there was a massive explosion. It was loud and intense, a combination of unearthly rumbling and ear-piercing crackling. The crowd gasped in unison. Richard looked over his shoulder. High above the rooftops to the east and in the near distance he saw an enormous column of flames and black soot thrusting upwards into the sky. And then the ground began to move. At first it was an underlying shaking and then intermittent, erratic juddering, but soon the movement grew to be violent, continuous shudders. A wide crack opened in the plaza not metres from where Richard stood – a man lost his balance and fell, disappearing in an instant. Panic ensued. People ran for cover. It was bedlam. Screams and shouts and calls of names filled the air and the rumbling intensified. A more distant chain of explosions merged to one continuous catastrophe and the sky darkened.

Richard shook his arm free and turned on the man with the knife. Momentarily startled, the two assailants were caught unawares. A scuffle broke out. Richard grappled for the weapon.

Around the plaza, buildings became unseated as their foundations shook. Great stone columns teetered and fractured and then crashed to the ground. Fleeing people were crushed by falling masonry and porticos broke and tumbled down.

Richard had a hand on the knife and tried to turn it inwards, but the second assailant was upon him. Realising what was happening, Diomedes joined the fray. The knife caught Richard's arm and cut it. Diomedes was thrown aside. The two men had skills at close quarters but Richard fought back.

Wide rifts opened in the ground. Pieces of fiery debris fell from the sky and caused small, splintering explosions as they impacted the ground. People were burning; it was carnage. Hot acidic soot began to fall like black snow and there was a pungent smell of sulphur in the air and all the while massive explosions continued to the east. The earth trembled.

Diomedes, who was on the ground, called out for

help. Having hit his head this expression went blank momentarily and his eyes rolled upwards. Suddenly he came to and hesitantly at first climbed to his feet. Then, without a thought for his own safety, was into the fight and hard at the two men. Richard got a leg behind the man with the knife and tripped him over backwards; Diomedes, throwing his full weight, came crashing down on the man. Richard, thereafter, had the upper hand and turned the knife to threaten the man. Suddenly Diomedes screamed out in pain – a deathly scream. Richard turned to see that the second man had drawn his own knife and was stabbing Diomedes repeatedly in the back.

"No!" Richard shouted. The callous attack enraged Richard, who stabbed the knife between the restrained man's ribs; blood oozed from the slit.

Instantly, the second man turned on Richard. With his blood-stained knife he attacked with a determined lunge at Richard's neck. Richard dodged the first thrust and parried the second. He quickly leaped to his feet and stepped back a few paces to find his footing for the fight. The man, who was in his sixties, but fit and agile, half-crouched and made ready – like a big cat on its haunches set to pounce. He passed the knife quickly between both hands to confuse Richard as to the direction of attack. Suddenly he lunged forward again and slashed with the blade from left to right. Richard narrowly avoided the attack, but was on his back foot. There was a scratching of metal as Richard used his knife to fend off another wild swipe. With weapons raised and legs tensed like springs the two men circled each other warily, jostling for position. One of them lunged forward. The assault failed and then a counter-attack – knife on knife.

Above them the sky darkened. A vast column of black dust and soot and pyroclastic material ascended and spread; it billowed like an ominous thunder cloud and there was the red of flames and frequent lightning bolts. Loud claps of thunder added to the deep rumblings and echoes. There were explosions as buildings fell around the periphery of the plaza.

Richard paid no heed to the terrible screams of panic as people fled in chaos – one way, and then another – for he was losing the battle of wits. The man had training and he pressed home his advantage with well-timed lunges. Gradually Richard's defences weakened. The air seemed hard to breathe. It was thick with gases and sulphur burned his eyes and his throat. Shock waves rumbled overhead and flakes of black snow settled on his shoulders.

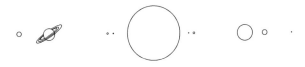

The large van drew quietly to a halt at the kerbside. It was at a safe distance but within view of Peter Rothschild, who sat watching the events unfold. The two rear doors opened and the van disgorged its contents of twelve armed men in black. They were helmeted and with visors down. Their coordinator climbed from his seat at the front of the van and Rothschild went quickly over to brief him on the situation. The menacing group then split into two, one half slipping quietly into the darkness, bound for the rear of the building.

With seven men, Rothschild approached the front door of the safe house. On the pavement and at the foot of the steps two were set for sentry duty; they combed the area with infrared telescopic sights. Gingerly, Rothschild approached the door and tapped in the security code. Hand signals passed between the men as the locks clunked and the door opened. The hall was dimly lit and, with weapons at the ready, the platoon slipped inside.

No one spoke. The Coordinator dispatched four men to search downstairs. Straight, pencil-thin, red beams from laser sights criss-crossed the area. Rothschild stood still in a shadow. Rooms were searched, one by one – infrared and movement detectors used as a precursor. And then, surreptitiously, two men began their ascent of the stairs – pausing halfway up. Moments later the all-clear came in.

In response and in single file the entire group crept upstairs and onto the landing. Rothschild followed them up. Infrared detectors pinpointed two rooms with heat sources, but only one with movement. The platoon made ready outside. Rothschild stood back. The Coordinator used his fingers to countdown – 3, 2, 1 – and then the door was kicked open and there was a rush.

Shouts went up, and demands: "Hands up!" Immediately, shots were heard; the rat-a-tat of automatic fire. Rothschild rounded the door to see a team member go down with a knife protruding from his throat. More shots! And then Rhinefeld, who had been in the bathroom, opened fire with a Lurzengard semi-automatic pistol. Sublets peppered the walls as he sprayed the room indiscriminately. Rothschild dived to the floor. Two men immediately fell heavily beside him. A volley of return fire from four officers cut down Rhinefeld in an instant. Blood spurted from his face even before he hit the ground. The oriental man twitched on the floor – he may have been reaching for his gun – and another burst of gunfire made his body jump awkwardly – but only for a few seconds. And then all fell silent. The Coordinator set a search in progress and thorough checks for explosives. Rothschild climbed onto one knee. He felt the neck of one of the fallen officers for a pulse but shook his head after half a minute. Another officer reported what he had found and Rothschild went quickly into the lounge area where he saw Richard, Naomi and two men on the floor with their hands joined together and all strangely unconscious. He pulled his telephone from his coat pocket. The young coordinator removed his helmet.

"Get the medics!" Rothschild ordered.

Rothschild was immediately on the telephone to Abbey Hennessy in London. While the line was connecting he pointed to Richard and Naomi. "Those two are ours," he said. "Those two are not! See if they are carrying papers."

The Coordinator directed two officers to search the clothing of the men who were lying on the floor. It was then that blood was seen under Naomi's body. One of the officers looked up. "The lady's been hit by a stray sublet, sir," he said. "She has a penetration wound in her thigh and she's losing blood!"

"Shit! That's all we need," replied Rothschild. "He turned to the coordinator. "Where are the medics?"

"On their way, sir. Not more than a few minutes."

"Listen!" Rothschild pointed towards Richard. His expression was uncompromising. "We do not move these people. There's something going on here that I don't understand. It's better to leave well alone until I get some answers."

The Coordinator nodded and then one of the officers kneeling on the ground said: "I've found their IDs, sir."

"Go on!"

"Both American by their passports . . . This one is Charles Springer and that one is Leon Rickenbach. The date in their travel papers indicates that they have been in Europe almost a month."

"Anything on what they are doing here – their line of work?"

The man shook his head. "No, sir . . . nothing."

Rothschild tried another line to London. This time Abbey Hennessy picked up.

"Yes, Peter."

"Abbey, I need your help and quickly. I've found Richard and Madame Vallogia along with two other men. They are tied together and unconscious. It's very odd – some kind of ritual, perhaps. I have two names; I want you to check them out."

"Of course . . . Who are they?"

"They could be pensioners actually. Charles Springer and Leon Rickenbach."

"What! Springer and Rickenbach! But they are the two RVers who are missing from the CIA's alternate identity programme. They are overdue and deemed to be defectors."

"You mean they are Remote Viewers . . . part of the same programme as Mr Ike Smith and Mr Perram?"

"Yes . . . exactly!"

"Then there is something going on here. Where are Smith and Perram now?"

"I told you – on their way back to the States, via Paris. Although I hear that their military flight was delayed."

"Abbey! This is imperative! Find out exactly where they are now and get back to me ASAP!"

"Yes, Peter."

"Sir, the Medics have arrived," said the Coordinator.

"About time!"

"Yes, sorry, they will get on with patching up the woman as best they can. We have two fatalities and one wounded." The Coordinator pointed towards the bathroom. "That man is Karl Wilhelm Rhinefeld, a

German National. That one, the Asian, does not appear to have an ID. We are running a fingerprint check with Interpol – nothing back as yet."

Rothschild's telephone rang. "Yes, Abbey," he barked, holding the phone to his ear.

"Smith and Perram . . . I sent them over to Paris in a helicopter care of the Royal Air Force – the least we could do. But their flight was delayed. They are due to land at Le Bourget in the next ten minutes."

"Right! Get on to Northwood! Have the Duty Officer call the pilot. They are to divert immediately to Strasbourg – it's not more than twenty minutes by air. Top speed, you hear me. Get the safe house coordinates and have them land here; I'll arrange for some lighting. This is absolutely critical. The lives of Madame Vallogia and Richard are at risk. And, for the record, Karl Rhinefeld is terminated!"

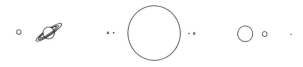

A woman screamed; it was shrill and piercing. It came from across the plaza and interrupted Richard's concentration. He glanced in that direction but only momentarily, and immediately parried another more penetrating lunge from his assailant. Richard felt his hand wet with blood and realised he'd been scored. Sweat ran into his face. The air was hot and choking. He kept a cautious eye on the man, as their fight was far from over. His throat was burning.

Sometimes staggering, and with robes flowing, the screaming woman ran towards Diomedes. Richard recognised her as three armed guards in scarlet cloaks threatened him and his attacker with long spears. They forced Richard and the man to back off and drop their weapons. Richard threw his knife aside and the man reluctantly did the same. The woman crouched beside Diomedes who lay motionless and in a pool of blood. With an expression of horror and disbelieving, she looked for his wounds. Diomedes looked pale. He limply raised an arm and pointed to Richard. "He is a friend," he groaned in a hoarse whisper.

"Who did this to you?" the woman pleaded.

Diomedes shifted his pointing finger and all heads turned towards the assailant. The man's eyes darted from side to side and a look of fear spread across his face. He turned and fled. He ran towards the nearest street, dodging and curving his track and leaping over displaced flagstones, cracks in the ground and hapless bodies. The woman shouted a warning at him and one of the soldiers raised his spear to a throwing position. The man kept running. The woman shouted for him to stop, but when the man was at twenty paces and about to disappear, she screamed an order at the soldier who loosed his spear with a grunt of effort, like a javelin thrower would in competition. Seconds later the spear penetrated the man in the centre of his back and his fall pinned him to the ground.

Richard immediately turned his attention to Diomedes and the woman. As he walked towards them he called her: "Naomi!"

The woman glanced up at Richard with a look of distress and disgust. "I am Isabelle – Isabelle of Noon. I do not know of this Naomi!"

Diomedes shifted painfully. He beckoned for the woman to draw nearer and listen to his words. Richard crouched beside her on one knee and put a gentle hand on Diomedes' shoulder.

"Take the stone from the temple and put it in its place in the Colossus," Diomedes croaked. "Enter by the left heel. The great memorial will come to life again. Take as many people with you as you can, but be sure to gather my associates, for only they have the knowledge to build another temple in the like of ours. You must remember our brethren on the red world. Find a place . . ."

"We will Diomedes, we will, but where should we go first?"

With dying eyes, Diomedes looked first at Richard and then at Isabelle. "Rhodes!" he spluttered. "Direct the Colossus to Rhodes. The sea is shallow between the islands. Let it stand there, astride the harbour entrance as it did here – in everlasting memory of our forefathers and the lost of this city."

Isabelle nodded and she smoothed her hand over Diomedes' head. "You will come with us."

"No! You must leave me . . . There is no time! It is coming; soon it will be upon us. Go! Before the *Destina Aquara* engulfs you all." With that, Diomedes' head fell to the side and he stared unseeing. He was gone.

The woman gently touched her fingers to Diomedes' eyelids to close them as a tear ran down her face. One of the soldiers stepped forward. "High Priestess," he said. "If we are to do his bidding we should leave now."

The men coughed repeatedly and Richard's eyes were streaming. Isabelle covered her head with her shawl, stood and bowed her head in order to pay her last respects and then hurried off towards the pyramid of glass with her guards.

Richard scanned the area and considered the scale of the carnage – he could barely believe the situation he found himself in. Like dirty snow, a layer of dust and ash began to build on the ground around him. Forks of lightening flashed in the brooding sky above him and thunder crashed all around. He could feel the flakes of ash burning his shoulders and head. And he knew of the *Destina Aquara* – water's destiny. He knew a tsunami was approaching, and it would wipe Atlantis from the records of time forever. If he was to survive as Richard Reece he needed to get back quickly – but he was completely disorientated.

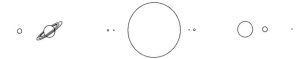

Peter Rothschild was very pleased to see Ike Smith and Oscar Perram walk into the room. He directed them to the four people lying on the wooden floor and explained what he knew. They were totally surprised to see former colleagues Springer and Rickenbach in that situation. They dropped their bags and performed an examination, taking time to assess the psychic elements and the dangers of what was happening. Their astonishing appraisal was the same that Rickenbach had made only an hour or two earlier. But they were more reluctant to participate.

Madame Vallogia was suffering in her unconscious state – that much was clear. She had lost a quantity of blood, her brow glowed with perspiration and she twitched constantly.

"The woman is struggling to hold open the neural pathway, Mr Rothschild," said Oscar Perram, matter-of-factly. "If it collapses, or she regains consciousness because she loses her ability to meditate, then those men will lose their minds. They will become amnesiacs and spend the rest of their days in an asylum."

"How long have we got?" Rothschild asked.

"Impossible to say, but looking at her physical state, not long, perhaps minutes."

"Can you help . . . ? Will you help?"

Smith and Perram glanced at each other – they had similar thoughts. "There is one chance, that's all, but we have to go for it now!" Perram said. Smith nodded his agreement.

"Please. Let's do it. Whatever it is, let's do it!"

Rothschild replied.

Smith retrieved a small cloth pouch from his bag. He stretched open the drawstring and sprinkled a number of beads into his hand. They were small and circular and were hand-painted in a variety of bright colours. Some had lengths of thread attached to them. The patterns were in a style easily associated with primitive tribalism.

"We got these from a Shaman in South America a few years ago when we were doing some research. There was a lost tribe in the upper Amazon delta – no previous contact with the outside world. Sometimes, when they travel into the spiritual world, they become lost, and they use these ornaments to help them find their way back."

"You mean like the children's story . . . ?"

"Yeah, Gretel and the other one," said Smith.

Perram looked sombre. "Ike's going in. It's their only chance. He'll use the beads to come back. I'll project my thoughts as far as I am able from outside. You're going to owe us big time for this," he said.

Rothschild nodded.

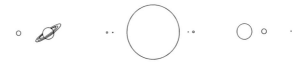

It was as if a nuclear bomb had exploded; nothing else could cause such devastation. That was the only way Ike

Smith could account for the desolation around him. He was part of a catastrophic event in history; he sensed that, but where and when he had no idea. He found himself rolling a bead in his fingers. He looked down at it and remembered, and then he wedged one into a crack in a convenient upturned stone near the path. He walked for several metres before dropping another, this time onto the low plinth of a fallen statue. The fusing layer of ash crunched beneath his feet. *There is another pressing constraint*, he thought – because of black flakes that fell continuously from the sky. Time itself conspires; for soon his tracks would be covered.

Smith surveyed the scene for a few moments. "This is the way in, so this is the way out," he mumbled, as if informing his colleague who was there but at the same time somewhere else.

The city smouldered under a layer of ash and pumice. The air was heavy with nauseous gasses and Smith's throat began to contract. There were burning buildings and explosions that emanated from someway off, but strangely there was an eerie stillness about the place, like the lull before a storm. It didn't bode well and it made Smith feel nervous. He walked towards the centre of the open area that lay before him. *It might have been a square or precinct*, he thought, and he dropped another bead. "No one could survive this," he mumbled again and he looked behind him. Thoughts of getting out while he could ran through his mind.

"Springer . . . ? Rickenbach . . . ? Reece . . . ? Charlie

Springer . . . ? Can you hear me?" he shouted, but there was no response. *I will try to the left and perhaps the other side, but no more than that,* he thought. "Charlie Springer . . . ? Leon Rickenbach?" he called repeatedly.

Smith stepped under what remained of a high stone portico and took brief respite from the hot flakes that fell from a leaden sky. He shouted names and then stifled another cough. The scene reminded him of a winter's day back home but in reverse. Here the snow of ash was black. And then, using a thin thread, he hooked a bead over a nearby corner stone. He positioned it at head height so that he could easily see it.

Gradually, Smith became aware of a distant rumble. It had direction – in the distance off to his left – but was, at the same time, strangely encapsulating. There was an ominous finality about the sound and it made him very uneasy. He would give himself another few minutes and then he would leave.

"Richard Reece . . . ? Can you hear me . . . ? Can anyone hear me?" he shouted.

Suddenly Smith sensed movement from slightly behind and to his right. He turned. A man holding a rag to his mouth that dripped water staggered towards him from inside the building. Smith ran to his aid. The man lowered the cloth from his face, but they were both strangers to each other.

"I'm Richard Reece. Have you come from outside?"

Smith nodded.

"I've lost my way . . . became disorientated . . . there's

517

a tsunami coming," Richard blurted.

"There should be two other men. Have you seen two other men?"

Richard shook his head. "They're dead," he said bluntly.

"You sure about that?"

"They're dead!"

"Okay, okay . . . then we go!"

Suddenly, both men became aware of a deep-seated but distant trembling. They felt it through the ground first but it soon became audible. It quickly increased in intensity to become a deafening rumble that seemed to bear down on them. It was like being close to crashing waves on a beach, but amplified so that the sound filled their senses – and it grew louder with each passing second. There was a pummelling and the buildings around them shook. Above them, joints between great stone lintels shifted and then opened and dust fell upon them like fine rain. Soon the widening cracks turned to gaping holes and heavy pieces of masonry bombarded the ground. At the same time the air pressure began to increase – Richard felt it in his ears. It quickly became uncomfortable.

"A wall of water . . . it's here!" cried Richard. He had to shout to make himself heard. "Which way, man! Which way!"

They ran outside. Smith looked back into the plaza. His footprints were gone – disappeared. He looked for a bead on the ground, but there was a fresh covering of ash. *Was it to the right, or the left?* He couldn't remember!

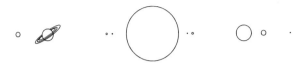

The paramedic dabbed Naomi's brow with a cloth; it was already damp with sweat. Droplets ran down her cheeks. Her face was flushed and she twitched incessantly. The man looked up concerned.

"I may have to wake her, Mr Rothschild. I'm sorry," he said. "Her heart is racing and her breathing shallow. She might spasm . . . We could lose her!"

Rothschild crouched beside Naomi's body. "Thirty seconds," he said. "Give it another thirty seconds . . . please!"

The man nodded and prepared a syringe. He drew liquid from a small glass phial and then held up the needle and flicked the body of the syringe with his finger. Liquid spurted from the needle tip as he gauged the correct dose. Then he positioned himself and made ready to administer the drug.

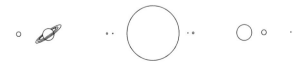

Richard followed Ike Smith as he ran towards the centre of the plaza. They kicked up dust and ash and material as they went. Richard tripped over something and almost went down. Preoccupied with survival they seemed immune to the noxious air and the burning flecks on their shoulders. Then Smith stopped abruptly and spun on his heels. He looked at Richard and shook his head – there was panic in his eyes. And then, by chance, Smith saw something . . . wedged in a stone . . . a dab of colour, and not five paces from where they stood. He ran to it – it was a bead!

"This way!" he screamed.

An incredible roar pounded their ears. It engulfed them and bore down on them like a heaving monster from antiquity. Richard took off after Smith but half-turned as he ran and what he saw widened his eyes and spread trepidation through his body – for a wall of water as high as a mountain rose up behind the ruins. Richard's legs wobbled, but he saw Smith plucking something else from the ash and sprinted towards him like a man running from hell. Smith moved in a decisive manner and Richard caught up with him just as death came crashing down.

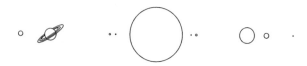

"Wait!" Rothschild barked to the medic, who was about to push a needle into Naomi's upper arm. "Something's happening; there are stirrings."

Richard and Naomi opened their eyes simultaneously, but their reactions were quite different. Richard raised a hand to his head and began rubbing his temples. He closed his eyes again and massaged his brow and groaned quietly. Naomi lay quite still staring blankly at the ceiling. The medic by her side watched his monitor with surprise as her heart rate quickly fell back into a more normal range. After a minute or so she drew a deep breath, came to her senses and then realised the pain in her leg. She tried to touch it but her hand was still tied to Richard's.

Richard sat up and looked at her. He untied their bindings and then he saw the blood on the wood beneath her leg and the stained make-do dressing around her thigh. The medic busied himself with something more permanent. "What the hell's going on?" Richard slurred.

"Just relax," said the medic. He looked into Richard's eyes, held a small circular device against the inside of his wrist, checked some readings on his monitor and then scrambled for something in his green holdall. "You will be fine," he said reassuringly. "Here. Take these two tablets. Swallow them whole; it will clear your head." He looked up at his colleague, who also wore a green cotton two-piece suit, and gestured with his head towards the bathroom. "Glass of water, maybe, and one for the lady."

Members of the SWAT team pulled Springer and Rickenbach to their feet. A couch was pulled clear and the men pushed down onto it, where they sat with two rifle barrels pointing at them. Smith sat on the floor with his head between his knees, trying to recover. "I'll have two of those!" he growled.

After swallowing the tablets, Richard climbed to his feet to make room for the medic. Suddenly the monotonous bleeping sound from the monitor quickened. Naomi's eyes flickered momentarily and then closed. She mumbled something and then her head fell limply to the side.

"What's wrong?" Richard snapped. Crouching, he felt her forehead.

The medic immediately turned his attention to the machine's display. "Her heart rate is still dropping. It's the blood loss. I think she is going into shock," he said. "I need to find out her blood group." He quickly wiped a glass slide across Naomi's blood-soaked bandage and slipped it into a recess in the side of the monitor's plastic body. It took only a few seconds for the display to register a number of readings. "Shit!" he exclaimed, shaking his head. "It's the rarest blood group for transfusions – type O negative. I'm not carrying any!"

"I'm O negative," responded Richard immediately, and he withdrew a chain with his dog-tag attached from beneath his shirt and showed it to the medic.

The man looked surprised. "But there's another complication," he said, looking back at the display. "Analysis has revealed her type as being Duffy negative. Is this woman of African origin?"

Richard nodded. "Yes, on her mother's side," he confirmed.

"And you?"

"I'm English, as far back as I know."

"Then we are likely to do more harm than good. I'll need to run a blood chemistry check first – for compatibility. Roll up your sleeve," ordered the medic.

When the results were displayed, the medic looked even more surprised. "Sure you two aren't related?" he asked, looking back at Richard.

"Absolutely not!"

The medic shrugged as he hastily prepared some equipment. "You have highly compatible blood chemistry; your antigenic substances are remarkably similar: proteins . . . glycoproteins . . . glycolipids . . . Looks like someone is smiling on her from above," he commented. "Quickly, over here! I'll take half a litre. I have a tonic that will help you regain the loss within a few hours."

Smith stood to leave. With a tube in his arm, Richard looked up at him from the couch; he knew exactly what Smith had done for him and he nodded his thanks and gave him a thumbs-up. Smith replied with a nonchalant salute. Oscar Perram put a hand on his friend's shoulder and looked at Rothschild. "It's been a memorable experience," he said quietly. "Now, we'd like to get that flight back to the States."

Springer and Rickenbach seemed unable to speak. Their mouths opened and they tried, but no words came out – just streams of sounds. They appeared oblivious to their surroundings and their expressions were gormless. Clearly they didn't know each other or where they were. The second paramedic asked Rickenbach a question, but he had no answer. In fact he had no response at all; he just sat aimlessly taking in his surroundings. With simple acknowledgement of the movement around him, he raised his hand and pointed. Occasionally he gurgled something – like a baby would, sitting in a cot.

# CHAPTER 24

# WINDFALL

"You look bloody awful and I mean it," Rothschild said, as he watched Richard tuck into a breakfast of bacon, egg and toast.

"Thank you, Peter," responded Richard with a brief smile as he took another mouthful.

"You are a liability as a field agent – totally unpredictable. No discipline whatsoever. I simply don't know what you are going to get yourself into next."

"Thank you, Peter, most reassuring."

"Well, did you learn anything from that escapade? I hope so, it nearly cost you your life . . . and Madame Vallogia's?" Rothschild rested his elbows on the kitchen table and shook his head.

Richard looked up. His hair was still wet from his shower and he hadn't brushed it yet. He glared back at

Rothschild momentarily and then glanced across the kitchen at the lady wearing a blue dress and a white apron who was washing dishes at the sink. "Nothing usable at the moment, as it happens."

"I see. So again, you put people's lives at risk and nothing to show for it – I'm beginning to despair." Rothschild sat back in the wooden chair and sighed.

Richard nodded enthusiastically as the lady turned and pointed towards the toaster. Drying her hands, she looked impressed at the quantity Richard was able to consume.

"How is Naomi?" Richard asked nonchalantly.

"We have a doctor in the house and a nurse. Fortunately the sublet passed through her leg. She will stay in bed for a day or two at least. I've ordered provisions for a week and domestic staff. She is welcome to stay here until she feels well enough to go home. With all the excitement outside, this place is no longer suitable for our purposes anyway. I have requested a flight to Cairo for her and Mr Makkoum – that's what she wants. The least we can do, considering the circumstances."

Richard nodded and continued eating.

"How this safe house was compromised in the first place, God only knows." Rothschild looked unimpressed. "Abbey is looking into it as a matter of priority," he continued.

"You still think it's the Americans?"

"Can't be anyone else, to my mind."

"And the Moon, what's going on there?"

"The Lunar Senate is deeply suspicious of the ISSF and its motives – it's difficult to get information."

Richard finished his plateful. He looked straight-faced at Rothschild. "The Senate must know that there's a problem with SERON, Peter. That's why they won't be specific about their situation. They are afraid that information could be leaked that will undermine their defence systems. You can't blame them."

"That's feasible I suppose."

Richard showed his gratitude for the large mug of tea that arrived, with a wide smile. He looked around the spacious kitchen and examined the long pine table and the marks on its surface. "Nice place," he said.

"Listen. We have to get you back to Andromeda as soon as possible. There's hell to pay as it is – bordering on diplomatic confrontation, in fact. We can only assume that they have very serious security problems. Why else a request for military help? Sentinel Wing's 'A Flight' at the Cape has been put on full alert. If required, their Delta Class fighters could be on station in four hours."

"You're not aware of the problem at all?"

Rothschild shook his head. "Rachel's called several times. Of course, I've told her that you are on confidential duties, but you are well. She doesn't know any specifics, but she told me that there is a feeling of trepidation in Andromeda – it's insidious. There have already been a number of deaths – in research outposts on the outer rim . . . and some of their early warning equipment is down."

"You think sabotage?"

"The Federation has been speculating for days."

Richard nodded his understanding. "Then I had better get back, pronto."

"Andromeda has put a ship at your disposal. It's parked at the Spaceport and its pilot is waiting for you." Rothschild checked his watch. "It's almost three. I suggest you get a few hours sleep. I'll arrange a wake-up call for you at seven and a take-off at eight-thirty. There's a bedroom for you upstairs."

Richard nodded again. "What about the Icarus Protocol . . . the incoming?"

"Panic's over. The object has been identified as the *Enigma*."

"The *Enigma*!"

"The on-board computer has brought her back; all fifty-three billion world dollars of her – good news there at least."

"When . . . when does she arrive?"

"The last update, when I left the office yesterday evening, was the day after tomorrow. She is expected to enter a prescribed orbit at 13:00 GMT. She passed Mars and slowed down considerably. Professor Nieve told me that EMILY, the computer system, will be planning the arrival carefully. By approaching within orthodox parameters and on an approved course, she knows that she cannot be identified as a threat and therefore will not initiate defensive measures – very clever, don't you think?"

"You know my thoughts on computer systems that exceed Level Seven on the Illinois scale . . . I don't trust them – never have and never will. And that goes for Thomas, too. You can have him back. Thanks, but no thanks!"

"Yes, well . . . grateful as always, Richard." Rothschild stood to leave. "Oh, by the way, there *is* one other thing. Rachel forwarded an eDiction from Commander Race; it arrived at your home. She thought it might be important and forwarded it to me and asked me to pass it on."

"You've got it on your telephone?"

Rothschild nodded. "I can forward it."

"Let me have your phone, Peter; I'll enter my password and we can both read it. It's unusual to receive anything from Tom on the domestic net." Richard looked up, smirked, and added, "Anyway, I know you're itching to find out."

Rothschild looked back scornfully and then withdrew his telephone from a pocket. He flipped open the lid, tapped several keys and then handed the device to Richard who entered another series of digits. As he read the text Richard's eyebrows lifted. "This *is* interesting," he said, rereading the message. "Tom's in a quandary and I think I can help him." A different smile jabbed Richard's lips and he paused for a moment, staring blankly at the table. "Tom has a problem and I have an answer," he said, shifting his gaze back to Rothschild. "A direct result of my unpredictability, Peter."

"Go on." Rothschild sat down.

"The Federation has deactivated the exclusion zone around the Elysium Pyramids again. Seems they want some answers, too. Tom's en route to Zeta Three. He said that the last time he was there, four years ago, he discovered an impression of a hand engraved in a stone wall close to what he thought was a large immovable door. He never thought it relevant and so never mentioned it, but something's changed – doesn't say what. He thinks that it might be a key to the door – he means the engraving. He wants to know if I have any ideas." Richard's eyes narrowed. "Will you take me to Naomi's room please? You might want to hear this."

Richard sat on the edge of Naomi's bed. He touched her face lightly with his hand and she woke up. He looked kindly at her and smiled. "How are you feeling?" he asked.

Seeing Rothschild, Naomi shifted, seemingly a little embarrassed. She sat up slowly. "Much better thank you." She looked up into Richard's eyes with a tender gaze and put a hand on his; there was affection in her way.

"Peter says that you are a remarkably resilient woman," continued Richard. "You'll be back on your feet in a day or two."

Naomi nodded and smiled again, apparently pleased with the compliment. "Our union, Richard," she said. "Was it fruitful? Were there memories of the crystals? Did you find what you hoped?"

Richard's eyes darted towards Rothschild and then back again. Rothschild took a step closer.

"We will talk about that when you are rested," Richard said.

Naomi realised his motive and changed the subject. "How is your headache?" she asked.

"Disappeared after a dose of Asperamin and a good breakfast, thanks," Richard replied with a shrug. Then he paused thoughtfully, took Naomi's hand in his and looked into her eyes. "Listen, Naomi, I need your help again," he said, as if rapt. "I'm sorry but this is vital."

"If I can, I will, you know that."

Richard nodded and leaned towards her. "Tom Race has found an impression of a hand on one of the Elysium Pyramids on Mars. He thinks it might be a key to a door, a way inside the pyramid. From a recent experience, I think he could be right."

"Yes . . . and?"

"I think it's the same key that *you* use to enter the Temple of Osiris, Naomi. Your own hand . . . don't you see . . . because of who you are!"

"My hand . . . on Mars – surely that cannot be?"

"The key is part of your ancestral line, Naomi, passed genetically from generation to generation. You told me yourself that the old people settled on the 'red planet' as well as the 'blue'. If we had a model, a duplicate of your hand, with all its nuances . . . your fingerprints, the grooves, the lines . . . then Tom could try it. Just think what he might find inside those structures. I've seen them – they're incredible. Much bigger than the pyramids in Cairo."

"But Richard, if such a model existed, then anyone could enter my temple. My secret would be lost and therefore my birthright." Naomi shook her head.

"I've already thought about that. Osiris Base could manufacture the model in Deromutine. It's a protein gel that hardens for a few hours after mixing and then subsequently dissolves – even for less than a few hours when exposed to particular gasses in the Martian atmosphere. The material just becomes slurry and then evaporates. I often used it on surveying duties as a timing medium. Tom will have time to try the model in the recess. If it works and the door opens he can make other arrangements to keep it that way. The model would then dissolve. I'll write specific eFormation into the programme so that only one copy can be made, and also only a 3D copier primed with Deromutine can be used on Mars. The signal will be transmitted in code by the Accelercom and so could never be intercepted. Your secret will remain within this room, I promise you that."

Naomi thought for a moment. "I trust you, Richard," she said, and nodded her approval.

Richard half-turned to Peter. "In the next day or two, Peter will arrange for a 3D scanner to be brought to your room. Asharf can operate it – it's just pressing a few buttons – but don't forget, we will need the maximum definition setting."

"I'll remember, Richard."

Richard nodded his thanks. "I'll let you get back to resting now – I'll see you."

As Rothschild turned to leave, Richard leaned further forward and kissed Naomi's forehead lovingly and then again on the side of her face. He squeezed her hand in his and held their palms together for a moment. Only Naomi knew what he meant. "When you and Asharf get back to Cairo, be sure to go and see Professor Mubarakar . . . okay? *Say you will*," he said, insisting.

Naomi nodded and Richard winked back at her, and then he followed Rothschild from the room.

As they walked across the landing, Rothschild asked: "Are you not going to tell her where you are going?"

Richard glanced back. "She already knows."

## CHAPTER 25

# WORLD WARS

"Richard! Wake up! It's me!"

Peter Rothschild strode into Richard's bedroom.

"What . . . er . . . oh, come on . . . "

"*It's a Red Alert!*"

The part-opened door allowed a stream of light to flood into the darkened room from the landing. Richard stirred in his bed and then came to his senses.

"Red Alert – at five-twenty!"

"What the hell difference does the time make," said Rothschild, turning on the bedside light.

"You've got ten minutes to get dressed."

"Ugh, what is it then? What's happening?"

Rothschild paced the room and turned on the bathroom light and then he threw Richard's clothes onto his bed. "The Moon is under attack . . . full scale assault.

Started an hour ago, we've just heard – the Freight Terminal has already been overrun!"

"What! By who?"

"Nanobots, robots, you name it . . . mechanicals!"

"Nanobots and . . . What kind of robots, Peter?"

"Humatrons! A bloody army of them by all accounts! It's the conglomerates, a concerted attempt to take control – they want the Moon as their centre of operations."

"Shit! Rachel! I'm up! Get a car round . . . five minutes!"

As Rothschild left the room, Richard shouted: "Call the Spaceport. I need that Swiftsure class fighter prepared immediately – and any other support they can muster!"

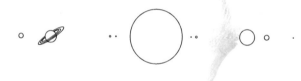

Richard sat in the back of a limousine as it raced towards the Spaceport. He had felt the cold of the morning and its dampness on his way to the vehicle and had asked the driver to raise the temperature in the back considerably. He blamed his unusual susceptibility on a lack of sleep. Except for the occasional commercial vehicle that sped past – going in the opposite direction for a city delivery – the road was empty of traffic.

Later, outside suburbia, where the rising mist

thickened above a rural landscape, only the penetrating brilliance from their own vehicle's headlights gave notice of a purpose. *Disaster loomed but the world still slept,* Richard mused. A double sweep of the windscreen wiper blade wrested him from his thoughts.

Richard shifted impatiently and uneasily in his seat and considered the implications of such an attack. If the conglomerates took control of Andromeda and the Moon it would be disastrous, ruinous, probably the end for many here on Earth. They could run their illicit operation as untouchables. And an army of Humatrons . . . it didn't bear thinking about. His thoughts turned to Rachel and his eyes narrowed. *If anything happens to her,* he concluded, *someone will pay . . .* He typed an abrive into his pager and sent it to Rothschild. It read:

> 15 minutes to arrival. Have Lieutenant Quarrie and other pilots meet me on the line for a briefing. All ships full fuel. Maximum munitions load. Targeting parameters will be downloaded from MILSAT. Call me ASAP.

Richard reached up and switched on the vehicle's speaker system as the call came in.

"Reece here!"

"Richard. Peter, got your message. The Swiftsure is ready." Richard heard raised voices in the background and then Rothschild came back to him. "For God's sake . . . the Federation says that this situation is completely unexpected . . . I should have pressed my concerns earlier . . . believed the RVers!"

"What's the situation?"

"We have serious problems! Strasbourg's Defence Wing, Sentinel 'C Flight', has been called to action, but they have only five serviceable Delta Class fighters and as many pilots . . ."

"What! From a squadron of twenty-one! That's ridiculous! Give me an update – everything you know."

"Andromeda lost their entire air force in the first forty minutes of the attack and their defence force is collapsing in disarray – they didn't have much of an army in any case. Their defence planning has been structured and implemented based on an attack from Earth . . . coming from space . . . not an established force already on the ground."

"How big is this attacking force?"

"The latest from Intel is that they have established a Forward Operating Base on the dark side, not far from the North Pole, and with a heavy defensive shield. Two Delta Class fighters were lost pressing home an attack – the Squadron Commander was in one of them. They must have been on the ground for several days because the Commander reported seeing a temporary airstrip before he went down. They have small, agile fighters of an unknown type, flown by Humatrons, and they are using the strip for short take-off and landing operations, thereby increasing their fuel and weapon payload. Richard . . . this is a very well-orchestrated attack . . ."

Richard shook his head; he thought of his good friend and colleague, and Sally, his wife. "They have two small children," he murmured.

"Are you there?"

"Yes! Copied, Peter . . . but how big is the ground force? What are we up against?"

"The Federation Defence Council is analysing video footage taken by external imagers around the Freight Terminal – before it was overrun. Apparently, the highest imagers have an uninterrupted panorama to the north and north-west. They also have footage relayed from their last high altitude UAV before it was shot down. They have counted seven platoons of at least fifty machines, which subsequently split into two forces in order to advance on Andromeda in a pincer movement . . . and there are these Nanobot things . . . insects!"

"Three hundred and fifty Humatrons! That's a full scale robot offensive! It's war over there! And tell me about these insects . . ."

"Ant-like in construction, resilient, between one and two centimetres long, highly destructive, tens of thousands of them by all accounts – 'flooding over the ground like a huge silver oil slick' was how they were described."

Richard knew instantly what Peter was recounting.

He himself had been in a life and death situation with such Nanobots – in a harbour-side warehouse in Adulis four years earlier. Devised by Epsilon Rio, they were exact electromechanical replicas of African driver ants with long, curved, razor-sharp metal alloy mandibles that were capable of cutting through steel plate. Spacesuits would be shredded in an instant. He shuddered at the thought.

"How long can they hold out . . . ? How long have we got?"

"Intelligence just coming in indicates that three platoons are positioning to make a simultaneous attack from the south. Because of the terrain, I'm told that the distance involved is approximately one hundred and fifty kilometres. The Humatrons are on foot but moving quickly. They estimate a sustained attack on two fronts in approximately four hours – but it could be less. Another platoon has broken away from the main force, but Intel is unaware of its position or primary target at the moment. However, outlying communications are going down rapidly, so it's likely to be a hit-and-run detachment. Richard! Everything we are doing is dependent on how long Andromeda's defence force can hold out. They are telling the Federation a few more hours, but that could be optimistic. If the attacking force gains control of Andromeda, and thereby the colony's space defence shield, we will have lost the Moon!"

"Are there any command or control transmissions emanating from the Earth? I mean, is the conglomerate control centre here?"

"No! The Federation has already confirmed that. They have used the satellite sensor ring – there is no contact. The Humatron force is pre-programmed. It is operating entirely autonomously."

"Damned Level Seven systems, Peter – it had to come!"

"Is there anything I can do? I have a direct line to London and Washington." Rothschild's voice was almost drowned by the background commotion.

Richard thought for a moment. "Yes! Get me a priority phone patch to the Commander of Sentinel Wing in the Cape – we need to coordinate our attack."

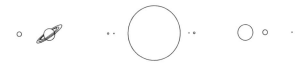

"Colonel Winton speaking . . . Sorry, I'll have to call you back!"

"Doug . . . wait . . . Richard Reece here, Commander of Andromeda Wing. I'm in Strasbourg, on my way to the Spaceport."

"Richard! Long time! This is a bad thing. Listen, we are about to man-up – haven't got a lot of time."

"Understood. I'll be leaving shortly with a six-ship. You open to suggestions?"

"Sure as hell, yes! I'll listen to any ideas. Full scale

assault on the Moon . . . never been done before – nothing to go on." Doug Winton had a marked Texas drawl.

"How many ships have you got?" Richard asked.

"Twenty-seven."

"What!" Richard had anticipated at least fifty fighters to be available. "I was expecting you to call double that," he countered.

"Damned defence cuts, Richard. The last strategic review cut our numbers in half. They say planet Earth no longer requires a sizeable defensive capability – statistically the threat from outer space is minimal, no on-going requirement . . . damned bean counters. And then we're spread thin as ice when something happens. Gee, those politicians, they never learn."

"Do you know what you're up against?"

"I know they've got fighters – type unknown. The figure I get is fifty of 'em. And an impressive ground force with anti-spacecraft capability. We are outnumbered, but I sure as hell hope not outgunned – it's not going to be a picnic over there . . . we're gonna take casualties."

"What about the S2s?"

"They're fitting out a number of shuttles with assault pods over on the west site. Not sure how many – somebody mentioned five. And there's a general recall out for the Special Forces. You'll need to speak to Command HQ for more information."

"Okay, copied. Doug, tell me, what time do you estimate being in theatre?"

There was a pause. "Three hour flight time at

maximum velocity . . . I'd say eight thirty-five, Lunar Corrected Time. Yeah, we'll hit them at eight thirty-five!"

"Would you consider splitting your squadron in two?"

"Go on, I'm listening."

"Your first section to descend over the Sea of Imbrium and run in from the south-west, initial course zero four five degrees – keep the Apennine Mountains tight on your right . . . not below four hundred feet. Second section to approach from the east, over the top of those mountains but fifty Ks further north – close to but south of Mount Hadley – heading two seven zero degrees. The peaks reach up to fifteen thousand feet in that area; keep low for a surprise attack – say not more than sixteen thousand feet?"

"And you?"

"This is the latest intelligence, Doug . . . The Humatrons have a two-pronged attack strategy – a pincer movement towards Andromeda from the north-east and the south-west. Their south-westerly force is moving quickest, using the rille Rima Hadley. As you know that valley is orientated in a north-easterly direction and it terminates on the Palus Putredinis. From there it's only thirty Ks to Andromeda. For orientation, the Apollo Fifteen landing site is approximately sixty Ks east. Doug, listen, we have to kill that force in the valley – upwards of one hundred and fifty machines – otherwise they will be knocking on Andromeda's door within an hour of emerging onto the Putredinis plain. Then they will spread out and become very difficult to target. The force from the north-east is using the rille Rima Fresnel to traverse the high ground; that's a more sinuous valley and their movement is hampered. We can move onto them next."

"You telling me you guys are gonna drop into the Rima Hadley valley?" There was a moment of hesitation from Doug Winton.

"That's it . . . six abreast . . . it's the only way," replied Richard. "They are using the valley as cover from aerial attack, as well as it being easy underfoot."

"But the valley floor is only a K wide and the sides tower up to, maybe, one thousand three hundred feet! That's pinball alley, Richard – at any speed that is not survivable!"

"That's where you come in. I'll lead my section down the middle, as fast and as low as possible. On the first strafing run I hope to surprise them from behind and get a good result. But I'll need all the top cover you can give me, to keep their fighters off our backs . . ."

The driver stared at Richard's reflection in his rear-view mirror and gasped.

"I'm being told that their fighter tactics are orientated to be more defensive than offensive. That means they will be like bees around a honey pot. To confirm . . . you want my guys to come in from the south-west and the east and we meet over the top of the rille?"

"That's it. I will transmit transponder code Alpha six six four as we sweep down the valley and switch to code six six five just before engaging the Humatrons; that way you will know exactly where we are in the valley."

"It's gonna be tough," concluded Winton.

Richard drew a deep breath and rubbed his brow. "The machines have planned their strategy well, Doug," he replied solemnly. "And they have the advantage of the terrain. I know that area like the back of my hand. It's the only way to make an impression, and by that time we may have some of our own troops on the ground. What do you say?"

"See you there, Richard, you can count on us. My call sign is Red One."

"Thanks. I'll use Black Formation – Black One. I'll be in the only Swiftsure class in the fray."

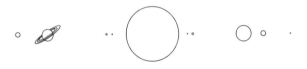

The limousine screeched to a halt outside the squadron building. Richard was inside in a flash. The Duty Officer, a young man, stood up.

"Commander Reece . . . someone is waiting for you, and, er, a robot?"

"You have a flight suit and a helmet for me?"

"Yes, sir, in the locker room." He pointed.

"Okay, I'm getting changed, send them in."

Richard pulled off his coat as he strode into the

locker room and then threw it onto a bench. His spare flying suit, helmet and boots had been brought over by the Swiftsure pilot. The suit was hanging on a rail and the other items were on the bench. He kicked his shoes off and climbed into the suit. Suddenly the door opened and Yannick Vuylsteke, Andromeda Wing's youngest subaltern, walked in; he was fully kitted.

"I'm ready, sir," he said.

"Not this time, Yannick, I need you here."

"But, sir! It's a 'T' bird. I can sit behind you and work the radar – cover the six o'clock position."

Richard shook his head. "It's not that I don't want you with me, Yannick – I do, but not this time."

"But . . . !"

"No buts . . . sorry! I need you here as Andromeda Wing's Liaison Officer. It's vital that I have someone on the ground."

Yannick nodded; he knew his boss only too well – there was no changing his mind. But it was clear to Richard that the young pilot was bitterly disappointed. Moments later, Richard heard the familiar whine of motivators from outside. The noise stopped abruptly and the door opened a little further. There was a moment's silence and an air of indecision. Seconds later, Thomas walked in. His face screen morphed into an expression of expectancy.

"No, forget it!" Richard barked. He turned to Yannick. "Go and do an external inspection for me, and pay particular attention to the weapon pods."

"Aye aye, sir."

Thomas stood and watched Richard pull on his boots. Richard ignored him as he laced each in turn and secured the ejection seat flaps.

"I can help," Thomas said eventually.

"I don't want you with me," responded Richard, without looking up. "You're a bloody liability,"

"But Commander Reece, my sensors would be indispensible. My eyesight is twice as good as yours. I will see things coming well before you, and I can directly interface the radar and weapons system – relieving you of the task. Targeting will be semi-automatic, leaving you to concentrate on flying the ship."

Richard stood tall. He made final adjustment to his suit and then zipped it up. He tucked the helmet under his arm and made to leave. *There was good sense in what Thomas had said*, he thought. Thomas looked gingerly at Richard, who pondered matters for a moment longer and then nodded. "Okay. You're on. Follow me!"

Impressively parked with their nose wheels on a single white line on the dispersal, Richard focused on the Swiftsure and the five fully armed Delta Class fighters. They looked potent in a livery which was principally matt black but with dark red markings. In addition, the Swiftsure had a thick silver-coloured stripe across the top of the port winglet. Richard was met by Chris Quarrie and four other pilots – two of them had French insignia on their flight suits.

"I've met you before, haven't I?" Richard enquired of one of the Frenchmen.

"*Oui, Monsieur Reece.* But then you went by the name of *Monsieur Jones.*" They shook hands. "My name is Captain Phillip Borghine. I was with zee Presidential Wing; I flew you once to Mauritius, a few years ago." Richard recalled the flight and nodded. "This is my colleague Captain Pat Tardier. We are based here at Strasbourg Spaceport as part of zee Air Defence Net." Tardier clicked his heels and saluted smartly. He was tall with black floppy hair that was unquestionably outside the regulations. "Also, zis is Squadron Leader John Mayard of zee Royal Air Force," continued Borghine. "Unfortunately, some things in life are difficult to bear – but we help where possible." The group laughed and Richard could sense the friendly rivalry, and the comradeship. "And zis is Major José Canales of zee Iberian Air Force. We are all on secondment to zee Federation," Captain Borghine concluded. He was a man of medium height and build, with dark hair and a relaxed Provencal manner, like a man with the sun on his back.

Richard shook the hand of Major Canales, who was next in line. He was of a similar height to Richard but leaner and with a Spanish look, having dark eyes, hair that curled at the back and a concentrated stare. "Where are you from, Major, if I might enquire?" asked Richard.

"Malaga, Commander."

Major Canales accompanied his answer with a respectful but barely perceptible bow of his head. Richard assessed him as a man of few words but unquestionable ability. Richard nodded, smiled briefly and then turned towards the line of fighters, eyeing the various armament pods that were secured below the winglets. Tall lampposts situated around the apron cast columns of dreary light onto the machines through which drizzle could be seen. Richard turned back to the group. "Have you had a brief of any sorts, gentlemen?" he enquired.

"A basic intelligence brief, Commander, but no tactics as yet," answered Mayard. He had a middle England accent.

"Presumably your ships are fully prepared?"

"As requested, Commander, and with maximum fuel load." Mayard replied.

Trying to gauge his experience level, Richard quizzed: "What types have you flown prior to the Delta, John?"

"Typhoon, Hawk and Predator . . . total seven thousand hours."

"Very good!" Richard ran his eyes around the group, focusing on each man for the briefest moment. When looking at Borghine, he paused. "You're all ready for a scrap then?" he asked.

"*Une lutte? Oui . . . naturellement, Capitaine!*"

Richard smiled faintly. "Then Gentlemen, I'll be frank." His smile faded. "The odds are heavily against us. You will need all of your experience against the Humatrons and no guarantee of an outcome. Our initial attack run will be from the south-west. The terrain will funnel us into a killing zone with high ground on both sides. The only way to survive is to go in very low and very fast, by that I mean fifty feet and one hundred lutens . . ." There were gasps from the pilots. Richard acknowledged their shock by raising a hand. "We will kick-up a lot of dust at that altitude; it should help to conceal us." The pilots did not appear convinced. Richard continued matter-of-factly. "Half of the Humatron army – we think around one hundred and fifty machines – will be moving north-eastwards in the Rima Hadley valley. Initially, they will have their backs towards us and so I'm banking on an element of surprise – but *that* will be short lived. You are to drop all the air-to-ground munitions you can on the first pass. Lighten up, but make them count – you're going to need the extra manoeuvrability. After that, we break formation; three of us left and three to the right. But stay low and keep a good look-out overhead; Red Wing from Cape Canaveral will be providing top cover. Then it's a free-for-all." Richard looked at Borghine. "Are you happy to be my Number Two – take command if something happens to me?"

Borghine's eyes rolled, as if he didn't need to be asked. A faint smile played on his lips. "*S'il vous plaît Capitaine,*" he said. "Here you have zee best Number Two." He put a hand on Tardier's shoulder. "*And* zee best Number Three in zee *Armée de l'Air*. Sometimes in life, low and fast is good; at other times, it is not. We will stay with you, you will see."

Richard looked at Chris Quarrie. "You okay in a Delta Class?"

Quarrie nodded hesitantly. "My last squadron, but that was almost three years ago. I'll be a bit rusty, but I'll settle in quick enough."

Richard nodded. "Good . . . Number Four then Chris. Number Five is John and Number Six, Major Canales. We position in echelon port and starboard; keep it tight. Attack formation is line abreast; otherwise we will be in one another's dust. Spread out evenly across the valley." Richard paused thoughtfully. "Now, the Swiftsure is not quite as fast as the Delta, but it's more manoeuvrable, so I'll hold back a bit on the roll rate. Also, it's fitted with only two sonic mortars and an old ballistic cannon; no pulse torpedoes or magma ejectors, as on the Deltas. Therefore I'll be on strafing duties only as I lead you in for the initial run. You select your targets, allocate the munitions, and use an arc of thirty-five degrees each side of the nose – that way we will achieve some overlap. There will be more than enough targets for everyone." Richard paused again. "Now, a point on defensive tactics," he said. "We cannot afford to be targeted from the high ground on the initial run and so I want the two outside ships to be ready with a blanket of chaff, if need be. Major Canales and John . . . set your dispensers forty-two degrees from the vertical. If you detect a threat, then you fire everything you have – I want it raining aluminium oxide pellets. Let's confuse the hell out of their sensors. You all okay with that?"

"*Oui, Capitaine*," said Borghine.

Pat Tardier nodded and clicked his heals again. "*Oui*," he said and smiled confidently.

"Understood, Commander," said Chris Quarrie, "but I'll need a couple of minutes to familiarise myself with the cockpit again."

"You've got five, Chris; make the time up on the way."

"Up to speed, I'd say, sir," said Mayard.

"I look forward to flying with you, Commander," said Major Canales. "We will send these things to hell, where they belong." He bowed slightly out of respect, always looking Richard in the eye. Then he stood straight and nodded coolly; a gesture that reinforced their intentions.

"Very well, gentlemen, welcome aboard – it's a privilege and an honour." Richard checked his chronometer. "Take-off is in nine minutes – don't want to be there before the top cover," he explained, and he glanced up at the overcast sky. There was an edge of sunrise above the horizon to the east.

With that, and focused on the task ahead, Richard turned towards his spacecraft. Thomas, who was standing some distance away, caught his eye. Richard stared at him for a moment, unconsciously narrowing his eyes. He gestured to the biomachine to follow him and then he strode off purposefully. Thomas had not been invited to the briefing and had sensed a degree of contempt from the group; consequently he had stood well back. He followed Richard to the Swiftsure now with his head down as the other pilots eyed him suspiciously. He looked like an outcast; he felt like an alien.

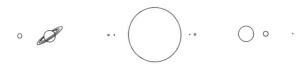

In a loose 'V'-shaped formation, the six spacecraft were almost invisible in the vast blackness of Space; only a pale red glow from each tailpipe indicated their presence. In front of them the Moon shone with its familiar brightness. It looked serene and inviting and also fortuitous with its place in the sun; but such tranquillity – like the renowned 'sea' where man had first stepped onto its surface some eighty years earlier – Richard knew to be an illusion. With his visor down, Richard scanned constantly for enemy fighters. Little was known of the spacecraft that the Humatrons were flying and so he had no idea of their range. All the same, he hoped to avoid a skirmish in Space, as they would need every last sonic pulse, magma shell and armour-piercing sublet to stop the Humatron army.

Occasional pilot chat over the coded combat frequency reminded him of the presence of Red Wing – they were a few thousand miles behind and closing rapidly. Thomas had a finger plugged into the Swiftsure's avionics system and he monitored the radar screen, briefing Richard from time to time on every object detected within one hundred and fifty miles.

In Space, the top speed of the Delta fighter was 200 lutens. However, the exponential 'planet effect' – an atmospheric and gravity bias – reduced that considerably. Even in the highly rarefied atmosphere and the reduced gravity of the Moon, it was, by necessity, much less. And each pilot would need to be aware of the exhaust efflux of other fighters, as propulsion was achieved by ejecting a high velocity stream of atomic particles rearwards. Such a matter stream would simply cut a spacecraft in two, like a hot knife through butter.

The cockpit of the Swiftsure was long and narrow. Compared to the Delta, Richard felt it a little tight, but, for a pilot, it was a masterpiece of ergonomics. Involuntarily, but reassuringly, Richard tapped the cowling above the instrument panel with his gloved hand – as a cavalryman would pat his horse in order to steady it before a headlong charge. *There was some melody to the arrangement,* Thomas thought, *but apprehension clearly slurred the rhythm.*

The Swiftsure was an ageing model – in fact it was one of the first interplanetary fighters to enter service. Its time, however, had been cut short by the arrival of the Delta Class, which was superior in all quarters, including range, speed, endurance and weapon capacity. Nevertheless, it was a very capable craft and in the right hands it could out-turn the Delta in a one-to-one. Richard felt confident enough, although he was conscious of his raised heart rate and moist palms.

As he neared the Moon, Richard reduced his speed to 150 lutens and then further still to 110, allowing Red Wing the opportunity to take up station in formation slightly behind his. He checked left and right over his shoulders, sighting his Number Two and Three. They both held accurate positions. Rock solid, not a murmur did he hear from his team.

"Sitrep, Thomas!" Richard barked, breaking a period of silence.

"Oceanus Procellarum is on the nose, Commander. Range seventeen thousand kilometres. Descent point in five minutes. I'll call you to turn right onto one seven zero degrees in another few minutes."

"Copied. Are you receiving any transmissions from the Humatron forces?"

"I should say! The ether is buzzing – ultra-high-frequency range. It's like hundreds of facsimile machines trying to connect simultaneously."

"Can you see Red Wing?"

Thomas twisted his mechanical head through 180 degrees and looked behind. "Yes, Commander; they are in position."

"Copied." Richard pressed the radio transmit button on his control column. "Andromeda Operations, this is Black One on combat frequency. How do you read?" Richard glanced at an instrument that gave him a 3D representation of his entry manoeuvre profile. He reached forward and, making a number of selections, manually deleted the orbital phase. Nor would he be adhering to the profiles stepped descent. This would be a dive into hell.

The radio crackled for a few moments and then a voice was heard. "Black One . . . are we glad to hear you. Things are desperate here. We are barely holding out."

"Give me some specifics, Andromeda. Red Leader is also on frequency."

"Okay, Commander. The 1st Regiment is holding a line forty Ks north of here – close to the Rima Fresnel escarpment; basic coordinates twenty-eight degrees north, four degrees east. They are under extreme pressure and taking heavy casualties – maybe an hour and it will be all over for them. The 2nd Regiment have been pushed aside west of the Santos Dumont impact crater. They reported a force of approximately forty robots – horrendous injuries to our people. The Humatrons are not taking prisoners. Our force is in disarray; Colonel Randle is trying to gather who he can and make it back to Andromeda for a final defensive ring."

From his voice, Richard knew who was on the radio, and conversely, Herbie Smith knew who was coming to their aid. "Give me the space picture!" ordered Richard.

"They have total aerial supremacy, Commander." As he spoke those words, Smith's anxiety was clearly apparent. "All our fighters are down and two S2s destroyed on the ground. Two other S2s remaining, but HQ is holding them back for humanitarian evacuation. The Humatrons are using a small agile fighter that we haven't seen before. The Intelligence Department is trying to calculate some performance criteria from video traces . . . the most we have seen is forty lutens but incredibly high manoeuvrability; no human could stand the g-forces involved."

"Copied! How many?"

"Difficult to say, Commander – maybe fifty of them. We have downed a few, maybe four or five. Aside from their extreme manoeuvrability, they don't appear to have a lot of protection. Weaponry appears to be air-to-ground biased rather than air-to-air. Also, they don't seem to carry a lot of fuel, as we have measured the average theatre time at thirty minutes. We know they have a landing strip to the north, Sector One One Nine; it's definitely a refuelling facility. HQ is suggesting it as a priority target. Over . . ."

"Understood," Richard said, and at the same time he acknowledged Thomas's prompt and pushed the nose of his craft down to initiate a steep dive. Black Formation followed him in a tight, precise, formation. "You still have the 3rd Regiment, Andromeda – what about the Third?"

"Half of the 3rd Regiment is tracking a platoon of robots who are making hit and run attacks on our eastern boundary – all the sensors are down in that area. The other half are trying to face off a surge from the south-west along the Rima Hadley. We think there is upwards of a hundred and fifty Humatrons – they will burst through for sure. I say again . . . they are not taking prisoners, Commander. They are pulling us apart . . . literally!"

"Listen carefully to this, Andromeda . . . You are to

get the Third out of the Rima Hadley Rille. We will strike there first . . . less than twelve minutes from now. I want that valley clear of our forces – do you copy?"

"Yes. The message is being passed on. Command is listening. Over . . ."

"I say again that Red Leader *is* on air," Richard continued. "He will coordinate the attacks to the north. Black Formation is now suborbital. Andromeda, we are coming in . . . hang on. *Break! Break!* Red One from Black One, we are initiating the attack profile. Once we are down there, we will not fly above three hundred feet – you have the airspace above four hundred feet. Over and out."


"Thomas!" Richard said over the intercom. "Select transponder code Alpha six six four and scramble it, and ensure the general combat frequency remains open at all times."

"Combat channel prioritised, Commander."

"Very good."

From behind, Richard's head appeared to roll on his shoulders as he continued his search for enemy spacecraft. Thomas busied himself by monitoring the various sensor displays. Although extremely reliable, training sorties had proved that the electronic sensors of the Swiftsure and Delta Class fighters were not infallible and clever pilots could occasionally penetrate their defensive screen undetected. With this in mind, Richard had no intention of being caught unawares. During a regular instrument scan he confirmed his passing altitude as 100,000 feet, his speed at 120 lutens and his heading as being due south. In response, he eased back on the thrust levers and then commenced a gentle left turn.

"Continue the turn from one seven zero degrees to one two zero degrees, Commander," said Thomas.

Richard responded. Then, from total darkness, Richard's surroundings suddenly became dazzlingly bright and glaring. A distant fiery ball appeared to rise from nowhere and flooded his cockpit with brilliant sunshine. He immediately dropped his visor again in response, but his eyes could not help smarting at the Sun's unexpected intensity and he cursed his forgetfulness. Streaking across the Moon's surface like missiles, the Formation quickly left the shadowy area between the dark side and the light side and, within minutes, Richard began to see a vast undulating plain that was the Mare Imbrium – the Sea of Imbrium. *Altitude is 40,000 feet, speed 105 lutens,* he noted.

"Okay, Thomas," responded Richard after another two thoughtful minutes. "I'm beginning to make out the Lambert crater, and the Apennine mountain range is rising on the horizon. We are getting close. Send a message to Red Formation over the data link . . . 'We are positioning for the initial attack run; all fighters should minimise radio transmission on primary combat frequency.' When you are done, select our dedicated formation frequency."

"Yes, Commander, and Channel Six is open."

"Channel Six open, copied." *Thomas is very competent,* Richard thought. He was beginning to appreciate the biomachine's abilities.

As their altitude passed 18,000 feet Richard's passage over the Moon's surface appeared to accelerate, despite maintaining a velocity of precisely 100 lutens. It was an optical illusion that Richard was familiar with, but it made him consider the implications of flying the attack run too fast, because it would limit their targeting opportunities. There was a narrow dividing line between speed for survival and effective target allocation and weapon delivery. After a few moments of deliberation he decided to position at 70 lutens and attack at 50 lutens – equivalent to an 'in gravity' speed of 1700 kilometres per hour or 1050 miles per hour. It would leave them exposed but would, at the same time, give a better kill rate. He drew a deep breath before passing on this information to his formation.

"Black Formation, this is Black One on Channel Six," he called over the radio. "We will commence the initial attack run at 70 lutens and decelerate to 50 lutens in the valley. Watch my speed closely; as the rille twists and turns we may need to reduce further. Nine minutes to target. Arm your weapons! I repeat! Black Formation, arm your weapons!" Richard could feel his heart rate increasing. He took another deep breath and thought of home. Rachel's face flashed through his mind.

Seconds later, Richard led the Formation over the Lambert impact crater. He looked down at its almost circular outer rampart and the terraced inner walls. The fifteen kilometres to its centre took mere seconds to traverse and all the while Richard decelerated. He knew the crater to be approximately two point four kilometres deep and the outer rim to be about 1500 feet high. He passed over its far edge at 6000 feet with the jagged ridgeline of the Apennine Mountains looming up ahead of him.

Almost six hundred and fifty kilometers long and roughly orientated north-south, the Apennine range appeared majestic as it towered upwards and shone in the sunlight. Volcanic in origin and with more than three thousand peaks – Mount Hadley in the north reaching 15,000 feet – the tallest outcrops cast long dark shadows in their lee. From Richard's altitude and direction, the mountain range appeared similar to the European Alps when flying towards them from Austria, but more serrated, and much more hostile.

The next landmark was the Timocharis crater and, as they sped towards it, Richard could see its twenty kilometre rampart begin to rise towards the high rim, the silhouette of which appeared grey, bleak, fractured and crumbling. This almighty indentation, Richard recalled, was punched in the Moon's surface by a wayward meteorite a billion years earlier.

The Swiftsure slowly decelerated through 80 lutens, then 75, and back to 70 – making Richard speed-stable and able to prepare his own armament systems. In response, two green lights illuminated on his weapons panel. There was also a schematic representation of his spacecraft on that small, square panel, and part of it, the thin pods beneath the stub wings, also turned green, indicating that the sonic initiators were primed and ready. The short cobalt steel barrel mounted in the nose of the Swiftsure fired ballistic projectiles. Richard was able to select lighter, high-velocity rounds or longer, heavier, armour-piercing shells, as there were two separate magazines. It was an antiquated system in terms of modern aerial combat but for this scenario it might prove very effective – *even an asset*, he considered. Richard pressed a button and in response a small circular panel slid open just below the nosecone of his craft and the barrel motored forward ominously, to protrude by approximately thirty centimetres.

At 2000 feet above the surface of the plain and still descending, Richard steered around the great Timocharis crater, which, now in close proximity, rushed towards him like an ugly carbuncle on an otherwise undulating and monotonous complexion.

Despite his request, pilots of Red Formation were beginning to use the general combat frequency for mutual warnings. "I'm seeing explosions on the surface," said one American pilot.

"Yeah, copied, and enemy fighter contacts, bearing zero three zero degrees," said another. Then he heard the stern voice of Doug Winton over the radio.

"Keep the chat down. I say again, minimise RT and prepare for attack run," Doug called.

Richard, who sensed one of the formations in question to be above and behind his, refocused his thoughts. He checked the chronometer on the instrument panel: it read 08:29:35. The seconds ticked by . . . 36, 37, 38. The rendezvous was planned for 08:35. His navigation computer continuously updated the arrival time; its indication changed periodically, because Richard was following Thomas's directions. If he was late it would only be by seconds and not enough to make a difference – *better to be stabilised for the attack run*, Richard determined. *Six abreast and within the confines of the narrow Hadley valley, I can't afford to have my team fighting for their positions – that would divert their attention from the hunt.*

Continuing his descent to 400 feet above the insipid, lifeless surface, Richard steered the Formation through a lazy right-hand turn and then similarly to the left, avoiding another, but much smaller, crater – this one Richard knew was the Huxley crater. Now the foot hills of the Apennine Mountains began to rise from the Mare Imbrium plain; their high, jagged peaks occasionally masked the sun. The wall of grey rock thrust upwards with Mons Ampere and Mons Huygens clearly visible ahead of them.

So close now to the surface that the barren, dusty, landscape streaked by, Richard was aware of only occasional, noteworthy landmarks – and they passed by in the blink of an eye. There was no time for nerves or apprehension. At that speed and height all the pilots were totally focused: instruments, outside, instruments, outside, instruments, outside . . . Richard's scan raced.

As they entered the black shadow created by the abrupt peak of Mount Huygens, Thomas coolly said: "Turn left now. Head due north. One minute to Rima Bradley."

As with most lunar rilles, Rima Bradley was believed to be formed by a tube of molten rock and superheated gas that flowed close to the surface during the Moon's volcanic period. Subsequently, the thin and often brittle roof collapsed to reveal a 'U'-shaped channel. Additionally, surface erosion and meteorite impacts over millions of years had further modified the appearance of these valley-like geographical features. Rime Bradley is linear when compared to the notorious Rima Hadley. It is also shallower and wider, but it would provide Richard and Black Formation good cover over its entire one hundred and thirty-four kilometre length.

The dash towards Palus Putredinis took less than three minutes, and when Richard sighted the broad plain, he issued another order over Channel 6: "Black Formation, one and a half minutes to run, reducing to fifty lutens . . . Come up line abreast . . . Line abreast, go!" he said.

"Now picking up multiple traces on the sensor scan," interjected Thomas.

The statement snatched Richard from his thoughts as he scanned the horizon. "How many precisely?"

"There's got to be twenty in the Hadley Crater area."

"Damn it! Top-cover for the Humatron ground force . . . It won't be quite the surprise I was hoping for." Richard breathed a heavy sigh as Borghine and Tardier edged forward on either side.

At that moment Richard heard the cool voice of Doug Winton. He was leading A Section and running in from the south-west. "Red Formation, this is Red One," he said. "Assume altitude. Assume altitude . . . Critical gate in two minutes. Remember! . . . Gate critical for the initial pass."

By referring to the 'gate', Doug Winton meant a layer of airspace within which each formation must remain. For Richard and Black Formation it was from the surface up to 300 feet. For Doug Winton and A Section it was from 400 to 700 feet, and for B Section, flying in from the east, it was over 700 feet. When the three sections crossed simultaneously over the robot army, that discipline would avoid mid-air collisions and enable clear target allocations for the first pass – a pilot would not target an enemy craft outside their gate. After that it would be a free-for-all.

Richard had reduced altitude to 100 feet after emerging from the Rima Bradley. Now, Black Formation was speeding over the Putredinis Plain in a headlong sprint towards the foothills of Mons Hadley. Richard could see that spearhead-shaped peak reaching for the sky high above him. Surface features streaked past in a blur.

At ultra-low level and in such close proximity to the

mountains, the highly rarefied lunar atmosphere seemed to glow with an uncanny radiance and the concentrations of cosmic rays at these latitudes made the radio crackle intermittently with heavy static. Regarding human voices, however, the frequency remained silent except for an occasional call from the Red Section leaders.

With the Montes Appeninus – mountains named after the Apennine range in Italy – bearing down on them at senseless speed and its escarpment rising as an abrupt and almost vertical wall of greyish rock, Thomas calmly issued his navigation command: "Turn left now, Commander, onto a heading of zero three five degrees. Continue for thirty seconds. Be aware that the ground is steadily rising. Then look to your left again; in the ten o'clock position you will see the head of the Hadley Rille."

Richard nodded. It was good navigation. And with the six fighters flying line abreast and their wingtips almost touching, he eased the Formation into the turn using only fifteen degrees of bank – he was mindful of his wingman, Major Canales on this occasion, dropping very close to the Moon's surface. Anticipating the desired course, he rolled his wings level and the Formation responded as if it was one machine. He looked to his left and then to his right; Borghine and Tardier were so close that he felt he could reach out and touch them. Then he checked the chronometer on the instrument panel; it read: 08:34:02. And then, dead ahead, and a few seconds distant, Richard saw surface features drop away – it was the start of the rille.

"Enter it, on an initial heading of north, Commander," said Thomas, having appreciated that Richard's adjustments to the ship's flight path meant that Richard had seen the entry point.

Richard flashed his navigation lights, which was the signal for the Formation to make final preparations, and moments later the valley – a long, sinuous canyon – abruptly appeared. At 50 lutens, the ground disappeared beneath them in an instant. Suddenly they were 1400 feet above the valley floor. Instinctively, Richard pushed the nose of his craft down into a steep dive.

Like water over the Niagara Falls they plunged into the valley below. Passing 500 feet, Richard pulled the nose of his craft steadily backwards and he levelled the Formation at 100 feet, and then, appreciating his surroundings, he dropped further to 50 feet above the surface. This was the height he would hold for the attack run.

The sense of speed was incredible. Outcrops of rock and occasional boulders passed in a blink. Even though the valley floor was level and flat and a kilometre wide in the main, the near-vertical cliffs that towered on either side gave a claustrophobic feeling. Richard flashed his navigation lights again and said over the radio: "Assume attack formation." With that the six spacecraft eased outwards and distributed themselves evenly in a line across the valley.

Richard looked ahead to see the first bend in the winding rille – a right-hand turn through one hundred and twenty degrees. It approached at breakneck speed. He negotiated it by rolling to the right through ninety degrees and pulling. And then, by necessity, he pulled harder in order to prevent the ship from skidding outwards in the turn, and he quickly realised that 50 lutens was too fast for this place. *Difficult . . . impractical*! he thought. The application of bank, the roll rate and the g-force, even with the Moon's reduced gravity, would be too difficult to handle and would subsequently reduce their targeting effectiveness.

"Reducing thirty lutens," Richard said simply over the coded combat frequency and simultaneously closed his thrust lever.

Even so, 30 lutens would give an equivalent 'in gravity' speed of 1000 kilometres per hour or 620 miles per hour. Borghine, Tardier, Quarrie, Mayard and Canales were all aware of the implications of a further speed reduction; but now, within the confines of the rille, they could appreciate Richard's reasoning.

Periodic transmissions from Richard's transponder that was coded six six four, enabled Doug Winton to see Richard's trace on his radar display despite Black Formation being hidden from his view. He also knew that Richard was running approximately one minute late and consequently adjusted his own timing to account for this. Winton was studying his display when he saw Richard's code change from six six four to six six five, meaning that Black Formation was about to attack. Moments later, Winton commenced his run, leading 'A Section' in an inverted 'V' formation. He checked his altitude at 450 feet and cross-checked the position and altitude of 'B Section' – *all is set for the showdown*, he thought.

In the valley, Richard was anything but settled. His heart was racing, adrenaline coursed through his veins, and he wiped away several beads of sweat that were running down his cheek with the back of his glove, before flipping closed his helmet's inner airtight visor panel. He checked over each shoulder continuously, confirming the Formation's perfect line across the valley, and he maintained an offset to the right of the valley's centreline in order to accommodate three ships to his left and two to his right. He could see a great swirling cloud of grey and black dust and fine debris rising behind the outermost fighters and he knew that it extended across the rift behind them, like a thundery squall line. Richard's thumb hovered over the cannon's trigger. It was the centre button on the pistol-shaped grip in his left hand. *Speed is 30 lutens*, he noted, as the ground sped past and the radio altimeter indicated 44 feet at that instant.

Thomas, plugged into the ship's avionics by way of his finger, appeared at one with the spacecraft. He called the sensor picture, giving Richard a continuous verbal update of what lay ahead. Richard, for his part, felt surprisingly reassured by the running commentary. The proximity of the enemy fighters that circled above the valley grew closer and closer with each passing second. Richard led the Formation through the twists and turns of the valley and in doing so he scanned the surrounding topography. The valley was predominantly 'U'-shaped, but the ridge lines that towered some 1300 feet above him on either side were anything but even. Seismic activity over aeons had caused cracks and fissures in the abrupt walls of pumice-like rock and areas where landslides had occurred caused hillocks of debris on the valley floor. *I will need to be aware of those hazards and any other rocky outcrops when the battle commenced,* he thought.

The Hadley Rille is one hundred and twenty-five kilometres long and Richard became increasingly anxious as the Formation passed the 90 kilometre position. *The robot force is moving faster than I anticipated,* he thought. *We must engage them in the valley!*

Thomas turned his head sharply to the left because he saw for the briefest moment a silhouette moving in the distance – it was high on the ridgeline. It came into view again and appeared to be travelling in their direction, but was quickly left behind. "A spotter! On the top . . . to the left! It will alert the ground force and bring the enemy fighters down on us," he said to Richard.

"Commence firing chaff!" Richard barked over the radio.

Suddenly the area on each side of the Formation was filled with tiny reflective specks, like an unexpected and heavy downpour from a thunder cloud on a bright day. But this metallic rain glinted and glistened in the sunlight as it fell, like millions of minute, flashing lights. The metallic specks were directed forwards as well as sideways and at times the two wing ships skimmed through the shimmering mist of oxide pellets.

After negotiating a blind, ninety-degree bend to the left, Thomas suddenly shouted: "Commander! Multiple targets dead ahead . . . range six thousand metres." The words cut into Richard's psyche. Instantaneously something caught his eye; he glanced up to see a number of small, shiny, occasionally oval shapes manoeuvring against the blackness. They turned in tight circles, perhaps five Ks ahead, and slightly above him. But he pulled his eyes down to the ground and the job in hand and had a brief notion of Doug Winton and A Section coming in from behind him.

"Five thousand metres!" shouted Thomas over the intercom, unable to suppress his emotions.

Richard's eyes narrowed and his brow furrowed as he peered into the distance. The ground streaked past at unimaginable speed and he strained to see what lay ahead. Intermittently, he glanced down at his instruments, in order to avoid target fixation. Then, in that instant, he saw a faint dust cloud; it stirred close to the ground in the middle distance. "Targets on the nose – range four thousand metres!" Richard exclaimed over the common frequency. He checked left and right. There was slight movement down the line, anxious twitches up and down as the fighters sped towards their target. Richard sensed his team's restraint; their fervour to engage the robot force was palpable. He pressed the radio transmit button. "Steady . . . steady Black Formation," he said. There was no emotion in his voice. "Hold your fire . . . hold . . ."

And then came the flak; it rose from the ground like a spectre materialising. "Incoming fire!" someone shouted – it was Tardier!

Multiple, glowing, sublet tracers streamed towards them. Plasma pocklets exploded in front of them, electrifying Space like sparking ripples opening from a stone in a pond. And sonic grenades blurred the horizon. The barrage was like an angry swarm of bees: condensed, stinging, persistent.

Instinctively, Richard twitched forwards on the nose of his craft and dropped the Formation to twenty feet above ground level – the wall of flak was over them and in front of them, but the line held and behind them the dust and the debris swirled and rose into a crest like a great tidal wave flooding down the valley. Controlling the fighters became difficult; they shuddered and bounced in the bombardment and Richard felt the Swiftsure absorbing shrapnel.

And then he saw the opposition and their battle line across the valley – humanoid shapes in the kicked-up dirt. The hairs on the back of his neck bristled. Humatrons, scores of them, running north-east and making good ground. His heart sank, as they too were dispersed across the entire valley floor, a tactic that made collective targeting impossible. The scene was set. This would be no hit-and-run raid.

It was hell on the Moon. The barrage rained down on them. The pilots flinched at the closeness of it. "Steady!" Richard called to his men. "Steady . . . standby . . . fire!"

# CHAPTER 26

# THE BATTLE OF PUTREDINIS

The valley floor became a bubbling, seething cauldron of deactivation. For a few seconds the weight of concentrated fire from the fighters made the ground shake and rumble as if by Moonquake. It was like a volcano had vented precisely below the robots. Instinctively, each pilot twitched back on his control and slightly climbed his craft before disappearing into the rising cloud of pyroclastic turmoil. And it wasn't just a smoke of dust and dirt and filth that erupted into the air; it was mechanisms and cyber-parts and oil and artificial intelligence.

A second later and like flashes from a brooding thunder cloud, the line of fighters emerged intact. They seemed to be survivors escaping from a towering, tumultuous Black Death – but there was an unrequested reception party on the other side. Like an agitated swarm of flies over a piece of meat they waited for Richard and his men at arms – a cluster of Humatron fighters lurked ready to pounce.

Immediately, Richard instructed: "Break formation! Break now! Break! Not above three hundred!"

Three fighters turned abruptly left and climbed, and three the same to the right, and as they did brilliant beams of laser-light struck out towards them. Now it was a free-for-all and, turning incredibly tightly, each fighter zoomed over the ridge line and into the fight.

Overhead, Doug Winton's 'Alpha Section' whooshed past making numerous kills. The enemy fighters manoeuvred in the most amazing way, turning corners so tightly as to appear to make right angles. But it quickly became apparent that they lacked the top speed of the larger Delta Class. Richard saw a Delta take a hit; the laser beam severed its left wing and the craft exploded. Simultaneously, however, Winton's second wing, 'Bravo Section', running in higher and from the east, easily picked off the Humatron fighter that had made the kill, as its momentum had taken it up into their territory.

In his peripheral vision, Richard saw the silhouette of another Humatron fighter. He ordered Thomas to take an image of it so as to better understand what they were fighting. Richard noted the design as an elongated oval shape with two stub wings, like a human hand with three centre fingers held together and the thumb and little finger spread slightly at an angle of approximately twenty degrees. Towards the front of the craft was a spherical cockpit, like a clear glass ball set within the thin, silver-coloured fuselage and with an equal proportion protruding both above and below, giving superb all-round visibility. Inside the bubble cockpit sat the unmistakeable figure of a Humatron.

Thomas quickly took an image of the ship as it turned towards them and magnified it on his tactical screen. Richard's eyes widened at its turn rate and speculated an induced g-force of at least twelve – he knew even the most conditioned human pilot would blackout in that turn. The thought made him shudder and he instantly snap-rolled the Swiftsure to the left and tracked the incoming fighter in order to prevent it positioning behind. For a split second the Humatron fighter was in his sights and Richard fired his cannon. The red stream of sublets streamed away and Richard tried to tighten his turn so that the smaller fighter would fly through the line, but by another remarkable turn it evaded them. In that instant, Tardier's ship zoomed past Richard's nose; it was firing pulse torpedoes at something unseen. From left to right it soon disappeared into the fray. The Swiftsure juddered in its wake.

Richard reversed his turn and dived down into the valley. As he did he looked up; the sky was awash with spacecraft. White, smoky exhaust trails criss-crossed the blackness of Space and red and white laser beams flashed in all directions like spontaneous lightning bolts. Never had Richard been involved in aerial combat of such intensity. In that moment he thought of the historic Battle of Britain, where numerous white vapour trails against a backdrop of blue sky and occasional cloud evoked memories of a similar fight for survival.

Richard rolled inverted and scanned the valley floor. Two Delta fighters from his formation were already on their second pass; they were strafing groups of Humatrons and some way in front of them explosions and plumes of dust erupted. Over the radio and above the medley of heated exchanges, Richard heard: "*La chasse* . . . ! *La chasse* . . . !" He knew that was Borghine.

Richard skimmed along the steep escarpment so close that he could have touched it with an outstretched hand. Suddenly a crashing Humatron ship tumbled down the vertical wall of dark rock not more than six hundred metres in front of him – it broke into pieces and burst into flames. Richard narrowly avoided it with an instinctive movement. Then, as he looked back over his left shoulder for targets, a laser beam passed so close as to illuminate his cockpit and drench him for an instant in brilliant white light. There was a fighter behind him. Richard strained to see it – but he couldn't. Immediately, he dived again and followed the contours of the valley, turning all the while onto a north-easterly heading. He would rely on Red Wing for protection and continue with his objective. Now Richard could see the result of Black Formation's first pass: the robot force had scattered and groups were still making their way along the valley towards Andromeda, but behind them the ground was awash with metallic carcasses and it smouldered.

Meanwhile, Thomas sent the image of the enemy ship to Richard's sensor screen. He focused on it momentarily as he dropped to 30 feet – it was the bubble-cockpit that he was most interested in. The robot's seat appeared to be ingeniously set on gyroscopic gimbals that maintained the pilot in a head-up position as the craft itself manoeuvred – it was an inspired design. The propulsion appeared to be a conventional rocket motor with a single, directional nozzle, and one laser initiator in the nosecone.

Richard caught sight of a glinting object in his ten o'clock position. It was another Humatron fighter and the red light that simultaneously illuminated on his instrument panel indicated that there was a weapon lock on the Swiftsure. In the centre of the valley, Richard rolled his wings level and commenced his run in. Against all his instincts he ignored both the approaching fighter and the red light on the panel and focused again on the ground force.

Richard heard the voice of John Mayard: "Number four and five requesting formation!" he called.

"Granted!" barked Richard.

Within seconds Richard became aware of two Deltas drawing up, one on each side; they had joined as a pair from the east side of the valley. With his visor down he checked each wingtip as the fighters established a tight echelon left and echelon right and then eased forwards the final few metres until the three ships were in a line. In the heat of battle and the sweat and with adrenalin and a cool stare, each pilot jostled and twitched and held their position.

"Target approaching . . . large ground force. Three Ks on the nose. Stay with me!" snapped Richard over the combat channel.

Suddenly there was an explosion on his left side. Richard glanced across. The flames quickly subsided to reveal a gaping tear in Chris Quarrie's right wing and simultaneously another laser-burst flashed between them. Richard looked forward and then across at his wingman again. With smoke streaming from the hole, Quarrie looked back – he nodded sharply and held his line. Another laser-burst flashed past his cockpit. "Damned fighter!" blurted Richard over the intercom.

Thomas twisted his neck and looked behind. "One on our tail and another joining from the right," he reported.

Richard broke tactical radio silence. "Red One from Black One, triangulate my position. Transmitting, one, two, three, two, one . . . we need help!"

Immediately Doug Winton replied: "I see you! Red Seven . . . Red Nine . . . follow me! We're on our way!"

Richard breathed a fraction easier, but not before another shrapnel tear opened in his own left wing and near to the fuselage – he felt the disturbance on his control column. On the other side, Mayard held wingtip to wingtip so close that they could have been joined.

"Standby to target!" called Richard, and he prepared a volley of sonic eruptors and quickly selected the heavier armour-piercing shells for his cannon.

At that moment, the targeted group of about twenty Humatrons commenced rear-guard fire. The flak wall quickly approached. Richard dipped the Formation down again. The ground streaked past; senses were heightened and hearts thumped.

Unseen and overhead, Winton attacked the trailing enemy fighters. Richard was unaware of his success, only that it gave him some breathing space. He took final aim. "Five seconds!" he called. Quarrie and Mayard selected magma shells – high-energy exploding shells filled with iron ore pellets that became molten during the delivery phase, heated by a contained, effervescing phosphor charge.

"Fire!" called Richard, and simultaneously he pressed the trigger of his cannon. With his right hand he pressed a selector that released the sonic pulses. Away went the magma shells from Quarrie and Mayard – devastation would follow in their wake.

Richard watched the tracer shells from his cannon stream away from him in an unwavering red line, and then he saw their rampant, explosive impact in the dust seconds later. He tracked their percussive progress towards the line of robots and then the carnage they caused as they penetrated the group. Mechanical bodies were tossed like ragdolls high into the air and shredded limbs flew at the wave of unfettered shrapnel. Finally, the magma shells, expertly on target and merciless, exploded in the midst of the robots that remained standing; each launched a thousand searing pellets. The machines that fled were chased down and caused to disintegrate in an instant. And then the Formation flashed by. What little remained of the platoon floundered in the dirt and the dust.

"Break formation!" ordered Richard, and he pulled up steeply into a vertical climb to escape the area.

## Andromeda Operations Room – simultaneous

"Give me the situation to the north!" shouted Eddie Lieven, the Chief Operations Officer, from across the Operations Room. He was red-faced and sweating.

Herbie Smith sat at his console staring at his sensor screen. He repeatedly referred to another adjacent screen on which constantly changing text updated information from the various battle fronts.

"The 1st Regiment is falling back from the Fresnel escarpment, sir – indicating heavy casualties. A number of Humatrons have already been sighted from lookout positions on the northern biodomes; maybe thirty minutes and they will be here. The 2nd Regiment under Colonel Randle are forming a defensive line to the east, but their report suggests minimal numbers and they are being harassed by enemy fighters. The Colonel thinks that there could be a thrust from that direction imminently."

"And the Third!?"

"Some good news there at least, sir. We are getting

reports of men arriving back from the Rima Hadley area; it seems our fighters are mopping up the robot surge from the south-west . . . and the other half of the Third are engaging a hit-and-run platoon five Ks south-east."

"What about support troops from Earth?"

"All our sensors are down, but I'm expecting three S2s with assault pods any time now – they left Canaveral more than four hours ago . . ."

"Three S2s . . . sixty troops! Is that the best they can do! God damn it, we need more than that!"

The Operations Room was packed with personnel. Many were sitting at consoles. Others rushed between them. And officers paced the raised section that was the Lunar Security Control Centre. There was an air of dread.

"Nanobots . . . we must not forget the Nanobot threat, Chief!" interjected Dimitri Nurevski, from the primary security console. He looked up momentarily. "They are overrunning the Western Biodome Complex." His voice trembled and many stopped and stared at him as a result.

"We need fighter support in the north . . . call Colonel Winton," said Lieven. "Request that he sends a fighter section north . . . immediately!"

"Aye aye, sir," replied Herbie Smith and buried his head in his computer.

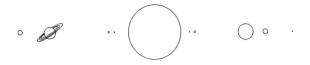

Richard commenced a turn to the right and then violently reversed it into a steep left-hand turn that had his wingtips well past the vertical; he changed his energy status by constantly working the thrust lever and used the Swiftsure's two manoeuvring retros to increase the rate of turn. 'In combat, never fly straight and level for more than thirty seconds' – that was his tenet and it had served him well in the past. He assessed the situation below. He had heard Herbie Smith's call over the control frequency, requesting support on the northern flank and Doug Winton had promptly dispatched Bravo Section – less a few good men – saying that he would follow ASAP. Other warning calls over the combat frequency heightened the tension in the arena.

"Bogey six o'clock . . . Red Five, he's on you!"

"Watch that one . . . he's turning!"

"Fire! Take him! Take him!"

"I'm hit . . . going down . . . arghhh!"

"Red Nine! In your ten o'clock, turn right now . . . now!"

"Eject! Eject!"

The Humatron fighters were swift and agile, proving deadly adversaries, and they had brought down a number of Deltas – but they had an Achilles heel. They were short-range fighters designed primarily for ground support and they lacked endurance. Being held in close combat in the Rima Hadley area for some time now was beginning to tell, and several were peeling off – desperately short of fuel. But Doug Winton and 'A Section' harassed them all the while. Turning north for a fuel stop made them highly vulnerable.

Richard watched the energetic clash between a Humatron fighter and a Delta Class that was taking place south of him by a few Ks. He watched the Humatron pilot pull some incredible manoeuvres and speculated on the role of human pilots in the coming years. Many of the specialist close combat tactics the machines were using caused Richard to think that the robots had the benefit of strategic computer programming – programming that utilised decades of aerial combat experience, as some of their manoeuvres were typical of the Second World War era.

Suddenly the Humatron craft exploded, being caught by a second Delta who had launched a coordinated attacking run at exceptionally high speed and subsequently zoomed off into the distance.

Flying inverted and using a skidding technique to hamper an attack from behind, Richard caught sight of Borghine's Delta Class making another low level strafing run at the head of the Rima Hadley – as there were still a number of robots moving out of the valley and onto the Putredinis Plain.

Suddenly he saw a Humatron fighter manoeuvring into Borghine's seven o'clock position in order to attack from behind. Richard slammed open his thrust levers and pulled the Swiftsure into a near vertical dive in support of Borghine. But then, out of the corner of his eye, he saw another black-coloured Delta Class flashing along the valley. The fighter jinked right, reversed the turn left and then quickly rolled inverted, pushing up to get the Humatron in his sights, and then cleverly loosed a sonic torpedo as he pulled a clearing turn back to the left. This trick eliminated the possibility of the torpedo locking onto his colleague. It worked; the enemy fighter exploded moments later into an effervescing ball of sparks.

"*Merci, mon ami!*" called the familiar voice of Borghine, and Richard knew it was Tardier who had come to his rescue.

Suddenly a Humatron fighter streaked past Richard's cockpit close enough to make his ship shudder, and then, in the blink of an eye, Black Six shot past in hot pursuit. Canales fired a pulse torpedo, but both ships were out of sight in an instant and Richard was unable to see the outcome.

"A rapid turn to the right at this moment will avoid the incoming fighter gaining a weapon lock," said Thomas calmly.

"What the . . . !"

Richard didn't see the threat but turned immediately – instantly two brilliant beams of light flashed past. Richard tightened the turn – another beam of laser light illuminated his cockpit. He pulled up into a vertical climb, used the forward retro to push over his nose, and entered a spin; he closed the thrust levers and dropped like a brick.

"Black leader, one on your tail!" someone shouted over the radio.

Richard plunged towards the ground, down towards the steep valley escarpment. Suddenly, and with split-second timing, he reversed the direction of retro thrust and, using cross-controls, recovered from the spin with barely 1000 feet to spare. Then he quickly pulled his craft into a series of manoeuvres.

"Where is he, Thomas?" Richard shouted.

"Still behind us, Commander."

"Dammit!"

Still losing altitude, Richard increased his rate of descent and dived into the valley. He was within a hair's breadth of the valley side and rocky outcrops flashed past. He was heading north-east and made a snap right turn towards open ground and then a dummy left turn that he promptly reversed. Feeling exposed, he flicked his ship to the left again, back towards the hard, cold, wall of rock. Flashes of laser light followed his every move. Tucked in so tight that the rock face appeared to burst through the canopy, Richard pulled and pushed and jostled his controls.

"Can't shake him!" Richard blurted.

Suddenly Richard was showered with rock fragments – a laser blast had hit the rock wall just in front of him. At that speed the pieces were like bullets and several perforated his wing. Richard instinctively ducked as a fragment smacked into his windscreen. To his dismay, a tiny crack formed.

"Hold on!" Richard called in desperation, and he snap-rolled to the right and dived down towards the valley floor – the Humatron followed him.

Ahead, at the end of the valley, Richard could see a column of thick, milky-white smoke; it was rising from a downed fighter with its rocket fuel flaring. Richard pulled his thrust lever closed in order to reduce speed and all the while he darted up and down and left and right, narrowly avoiding the deadly barrage from behind. He flew headlong towards the smoke. With a thumb controller he positioned the forward retro to the left and the aft retro pointing horizontally to the right and as he was about to zoom through the smoke he jammed open the lever and simultaneously pressed the trigger of his cannon. The effect was instant. Russian roulette – as the incredible stress levels could rip the Swiftsure apart. Both ships flashed through the smoke, but Richard was spinning like a top and with his cannon blazing. An instant was all that was needed, as the Humatron had little idea what had happened before his craft disintegrated in the hail of heavy gunfire.

Richard was still in trouble, however, as the high rate of spin was disorientating. Despite his immediate cancellation of retro thrust the swirling motion continued and Richard's vision became blurred. They began to lose altitude.

"Adjust forward retro to the right, Commander," ordered Thomas. "Do it now!"

Richard complied, although he was unaware of the effect on the retro's position. He swallowed hard, resisting the urge to vomit.

"Stop! Apply retro thrust now . . . Stop! Now, Commander, please pull up!"

Richard pulled back on the stick and instinctively increased the main thrust; soon they were in a rapid but stable climb. It took Richard a few moments to regain his senses.

"Commander, when you are able, you may wish to look to your right," continued Thomas. "There are three S2 Shuttles arriving from the Mare Imbrium sector. According to communications on the secondary control frequency they are equipped with assault pods. I count eight Humatron fighters still in this vicinity; you may wish to provide close support to the S2s as they will be vulnerable when they make their approach to land."

"Thank you, Thomas, that's helpful . . . Wait!"

Richard refocused and caught sight of two Humatron fighters behind his right shoulder – he immediately manoeuvred but lost sight of them. "Thomas, the sensor screen, where are they?"

"Quickly turning into your eight o'clock, Commander. But they don't appear to be manoeuvring to attack; they're turning north."

"They are going for fuel," said Richard. He scanned the area and saw Borghine's fighter involved in a one-to-one. "Black Six, from Black One, where are you?" he called over the combat frequency.

"Ten o'clock high," was the reply.

"Copied . . . Black Two and Black Six, two Humatron fighters, north-west by three miles, heading north for refuel. Break off and follow them. Engage when they land and then destroy the refuel station and operating base."

"*Oui, Capitaine . . .*"

". . . *Vamos alla!*"


The struggle over Rima Hadley was coming to an end. Thomas's idea of providing support for the three S2s was sensible, but they were already disappearing from sight in a north-easterly direction.

"Black Three, Four and Five, this is Black One," he called over the radio. "Follow me onto a heading of zero two zero degrees, increase forty lutens. Red One . . . over to you and good luck."

"Copied Black Formation," said Doug Winton. "I see you going."

"Keep an eye on the sensor picture, Thomas," said Richard over the intercom. "The Humatron fighters are thin on the ground at the moment – I think they are reaching the end of their endurance – but we can expect some more on Andromeda's eastern flank."

"Yes, Commander. Three S2s dead ahead thirty kilometres, open formation. They appear to be decelerating . . . Wait! Contact enhancement indicates firing of the assault pods . . ."

"Good, troops on the ground, let's go."


Designated 'lunar independent' because they are auto-piloted, self-propelled and able to carry a fully kitted Space platoon, the Nexus Aerosystems-designed assault pod is essentially an orbital APC – an Armoured Personnel Carrier – with a sting. Allocated the ISSF inventory code LAAP 12, the pods boast potent weapons, sensor screens, life support, generous self-destruct and a maximum complement of twenty heavily armed Special Forces operatives. Designed originally for rapid deployment anywhere on the lunar surface and with an almost invisible radar signature when launched in Space, the anti-acquisition, spiral re-entry profile afforded the system the affectionate term 'shock troopers fantasy ride' by those who deployed in them. This time, Richard could see that they were utilising a 'low-altitude, minimum flight time strategy' and no sooner had they dropped from beneath the mother ships than the three S2s rapidly vacated the area.

"Sensors indicate two further S2 approaching from the Rima Fresnel area, Commander. I understand from communications on the secondary frequency that this is the total ground force available until the S2s return again from Earth."

"Copied, Thomas, but that will probably be too late. I'm seeing a lot of movement on my tactical screen east of the drop zone. There's a Humatron force moving towards Andromeda."

Richard's Formation of four fighters dropped low and skimmed over the undulating terrain as the three assault pods descended vertically a kilometre or so in front of them. As they passed overhead, Richard banked to the left to see tiny retro rockets on the four corners of each pod cushion their landing. Dust and debris quickly rose into swirling clouds as they dropped the final ten metres. And then he looked back over his shoulder to see a stream of men running and dispersing from each of the cube-shaped objects. Within seconds the three platoons were forming a battle line.

The Humatron fighters were noticeable by their absence as Richard, forever wary, pulled his formation into an easy right turn and onto a reciprocal heading. It was then that mortar shells began to fall. They caused multiple explosions in the vicinity of the storm troopers. Richard looked left to see their origin in the lower foothills at the base of the Apennine front. He immediately turned in that direction.

"Standby to engage," Richard called over the radio, as he checked his weapon systems.

At 50 feet and accelerating towards the enemy emplacement, Richard opened the Formation into an attacking line abreast with a sharp order over the combat frequency. In seconds the ground began a slow incline towards the foothills and rocky outcrops formed effective hiding places. Sporadic streams of tracer shells fired from various positions on the ground where lone Humatrons had moved forwards for spotting duties, but the main force lay ahead of them and Richard and his men had it in their sights.

Ground fire intensified until it appeared as a mass of crisscrossed, multicoloured diagonals – the lines terminating in firework-like microbursts. Richard's response was to drop lower and he edged the Formation down to 30 feet – territory where ground clutter confused even the most sophisticated fire control radars. Bobbing up and down but with a stable flight path towards the target, Richard pressed on. Now the steeply rising terrain of the mountains reared up and began filling their windscreens. Incendiary shells and tracer streams lit up the black lunar sky. Buffeted and bouncing, the fighters rocketed towards their goal. Outside, the desolate, sterile, Moon was a blur. Richard heard and felt the dull thud of penetrating hits and he saw the damaged area to Chris Quarrie's right-hand winglet reignite. Smoke billowed and flames licked from inside the holed structure – but this time extinguishing it was impossible, because Chris had already used both bottles.

"Break if you need to," Richard instructed Chris.

"Negative! On target!" was the reply.

Richard looked forward again as the stronghold loomed. The mountains filled his windscreen. Tardier and Mayard held a good line on his right. The flak rained on them. "Take my lead!" said Richard. "Two left, two right, on my command!" he snapped.

"Stay on line . . . Stay on line . . . ! Steady . . . steady . . . fire!"

Instantaneously, the flak changed direction. Sonic torpedoes loosed; magma shells streaked towards their targets streaming characteristic sulphur trails as their iron pellets turned molten. Richard dropped four sonic eruptors and a continuous barrage from his heavy cannon spat fire and destruction. It was Revelation Day for the Humatron force.

"Break!" shouted Richard, and none too soon; the bleak, unforgiving face of the mountain was about to burst through into his cockpit. Hard right and left turns with heavy g loading followed and then they were away. Nobody looked back.

Moments later they overflew the storm trooper line and Richard rocked his wings in a brief show of solidarity as the soldiers below joyously waved their weapons. But the fight wasn't over yet – far from it.


Richard heard Andromeda Control requesting part of Red Wing move against the Nanobots that were streaming in from the west and north-west. If they were quick, the tiny marauders – mechanical replicas of African soldier ants, with powerful electro-hydraulic mandibles – could be contained in the biodome complex. Richard knew that some of Red Wing's Delta Class fighters were carrying ionising plasma shells and that they were much more effective than the standard static variety – each generating one million volts of searing electrical potential. Any programmable functions within a kilometre radius of one of those devices would instantly be erased. He heard Doug Winton take up the challenge.

"Andromeda Control, this is Black One, requesting priorities," said Richard over the radio.

"Black One, this is Andromeda. Humatrons are

closing in on our northern boundary, less than a K. We are taking heavy casualties. Our soldiers need support. I repeat, immediate air support required north by north-east!"

"Copied. On our way!" replied Richard, and glanced around to gather his force. Tardier and Mayard were already tight in an echelon starboard formation, but on his left side Quarrie's ship was streaming smoke and falling behind.

"You can't do any more, Chris. We're in a friendly area – get out while you can!"

"Negative . . . I can hold her, Commander!"

"She's going to blow – get out! That's an order!"

Richard heard nothing more from Chris. A moment later there was a blinding flash from inside his cockpit. The spaceship shuddered. Staring wide-eyed, Richard's heart sank. Black and grey smoke billowed; it engulfed Chris from below, obscuring him in an instant. But suddenly his canopy shifted and a ring of white flashes blasted it clear. Simultaneously, a dark shape emerged from obscurity, streaming red and white flames, and in the blink of an eye it lifted Chris clear and he was gone.

"Black Three, Black Five, detach. Head north. Engage as required. I'll catch you up," ordered Richard. He pulled his ship into a tight left-hand turn and followed Chris's white trail across the sky. The burning ship nose-dived towards the ground; on impact it exploded as a ball of effervescing sparks.

"Do you see him, Thomas?"

"Yes, Commander, seven o'clock position, one kilometre, predetermined flight path."

Richard scanned the horizon for other fighters and then turned and decelerated. He caught sight of the ejection seat as a brief but vivid flash of rocket propellant cushioned its landing. There was a small puff of dust on the surface and Richard flew towards it. When he arrived he saw Chris Quarrie on his feet and waving. Relieved, he flew a tight circle around him and called over the radio: "Aircrewman down, mark coordinates." He set course to the north at low level.

Richard arrived in the midst of heavy fighting. The area north and north-east of Andromeda's main complex had become the decisive battle front. Richard was familiar with the surrounding terrain and being flat and featureless it afforded little cover. Primary ground forces from both sides were engaging in close proximity and a handful of Humatron space fighters had returned from their refuelling station near the Moon's north pole. Richard hoped that Borghine and Canales had put paid to the place by now, but there was no sign of them. The radio waves were awash with instructions and warnings and cries for help – it was calamitous.

Overhead, sporadic but energetic exchanges took place between opposing fighters. Numbers were severely depleted on both sides and clearly heavy losses had been sustained. As Richard saw another airburst above the battlefield and subsequently part of a Humatron ship sent spinning out of control, he thought the war in the sky was siding with them, but on the ground it looked to be a different picture. The Humatrons had a large force. Richard could see two main groups, each with perhaps thirty individuals, and there were smaller units on the flanks. Storm troopers from the assault pods dropped further to the north had joined with soldiers from the 1st Regiment, but their line was under extreme duress. Richard could see a good deal of friendly movement between Andromeda's northern-most buildings and the front. Soldiers there seemed to scurry back and forth within unseen lines and Richard surmised that land mines were being deployed to funnel the Humatrons into a killing zone.

The main battlefield was peppered with explosions, flashes of laser light and blurring sonic disturbances. An insane struggle raged: humankind against its own technology. Shapes of men and machines that lay motionless dotted the drab, light grey landscape. The dust of fighting rose as an eerie mist. Richard kept low and out of sight and circled the area whilst he formulated a strategy, but suddenly he caught sight of a Delta Class flashing across the horizon. It was trailing white smoke and had clearly taken a hit. To Richard's alarm, close on its tail stalked an enemy ship. Richard primed his cannon with a short burst and moved in support.

Trailing white smoke gave constant notice of its position, as the Delta Class manoeuvred in desperation.

Hampered by mechanical damage, the pilot's efforts became futile and the Humatron's *coup de grâce* became a matter of course. But Richard knew that target fixation was a symptom avoided only by experience and could not be programmed – not yet anyway – and he waited for the Humatron to flash past overhead and then pulled up steeply in its wake. Evidently preoccupied, at first the robot seemed unaware of Richard's presence, and it was only then that Richard realised that the damaged Delta was one of his own – Black Five! John Mayard!

"I'm listening to the Humatron frequency, Commander; ground units are trying to warn the pilot ahead. You should act quickly."

Richard was concentrating on the target. It chased Mayard down in the most astonishing fashion; he needed all his skill to stay with it. "I'm trying!" he barked at Thomas.

And then, in a split-second of stable flight and at the instant the Humatron fired at Mayard, Richard loosed a volley of high-velocity cannon shells at the machinemelt. The results were comparable. John Mayard's right wing immediately exploded and detached, sending his craft spinning uncontrollably to the left and out of the frame, while heavy armour-piercing shells tore into the Humatron's ship like a stream of ball bearings at a balsawood model – it simply disintegrated into a thousand fragments. Richard snapped-rolled to the left and pulled a tight turn that avoided most of the debris, although he felt several minor impacts through his controls. He sighted Mayard's Delta and saw him eject, but he was at an awkward angle and low and this gave the mechanics of the seat little chance to right itself completely before the rocket motor fired to cushion his landing. Consequently the seat bounced and tumbled across the ground before coming to rest in a cloud of dust and debris. Richard was worried for him, but he continued his turn and took advantage of a fortuitous strafing opportunity on a platoon of robots before pulling up and clearing the area.

The battle raged. Aggravated dirt and a thick, black, column of smoke billowed skywards from the frontline; it flashed white streaks from inside like frenetic lightning bolts in a towering and ominous cumulonimbus cloud.

Richard turned into the conflict again; he assumed the hunter's guise. "Situation report, Thomas!" he called.

"Multiple perforations . . . two minor hydraulic leaks . . . main thrust compromised by eleven per cent. Ammunition is very low, Commander."

"How low?" Richard scanned for a target.

"Less than ten per cent remaining."

"Copied!" replied Richard, maintaining a tight circle at 200 feet and a little remote from the fray. And then he saw Tardier's Delta running an attack from right to left. He was so low that the Humatrons on the ground were ducking to avoid him. In the ship's wake lay a trail of catastrophic destruction that only magma shells bursting in a crowd could produce – it was carnage on their eastern front.

Richard saw Tardier complete his run and

immediately turn for another; it was a flamboyant manoeuvre full of confidence and aggression. Richard gasped. "Not the same line, not again," he warned under his breath. Seconds later Tardier was closing for a second run but in the opposite direction; Richard could see a problem and accelerated towards the front. He saw a group of Humatrons taking aim with a long-barrelled weapon. "Pull up, Black Three! Pull up!" he called over the radio.

Tardier wasn't listening; he was skimming the surface, laying waste to another section of robots. Suddenly there was an explosion. Richard couldn't see if Tardier's ship had been hit or if the shockwave from the explosion had forced him down, but the result was the same and his Delta bellied onto the ground. Immediately, Tardier lost control and his ship gouged a long, deep trench that curved left in the last two hundred metres. The Delta's winglets cut off the legs of several robots on its way through, until it finally came to a halt five hundred metres behind the robot's line. Richard saw Tardier jettison his canopy and he saw Humatrons moving quickly towards him. Immediately, he commenced an attacking run and emptied his magazines on anything that moved within one hundred metres of his colleague. That was all he could do and as he overflew Tardier's stricken ship he pulled a turn to the left. But he had an idea.

There was one relatively intact Humatron force still moving on Andromeda, but they were being corralled into a narrow column by ground forces and strategic placement of land mines. Sporadically a mine exploded, reminding the Humatrons of the extremities of the battle line. Richard circled in a low, extended circuit that took him behind Andromeda's main complex. When he was south by three or four kilometres he rolled his ship level and on a north-easterly heading, and raced directly at the buildings. He dropped ultra-low-level. Sand, dust and debris eddied in his wake.

"Thanks for your help, Thomas – now hold on," he said.

The buildings loomed in an instant and Richard checked back slightly on his control column in order to skim overhead. When he saw the robots he instinctively altered course by a few degrees to run their centre line. Humatrons at the front of the column sensed the danger; they screeched their warnings – perhaps even their fear. The barrage commenced – obliterate!

Richard checked forward – just enough. For five hundred metres the Swiftsure skimmed the ground so close that the underside scuffed the ground. And then he closed the thrust levers and bellied the ship. It was like a ten pin bowling alley and Richard went for the strike. He was a juggernaut smashing through traffic. He ran them down. The winglets were guillotines. He severed their intent; body parts cast aside like old imperialism.

Richard truncated or decapitated almost the entire Humatron platoon. Eventually he skidded to a halt well inside their battle line. When all movement had stopped he reached for the canopy emergency jettison handle and wrenched it. There was a flash of explosive tape and instantaneously the canopy was blown up and backwards.

"Out . . . out!" he called to Thomas and released his harness. But as he was about to climb from the craft, a shadowy figure stepped up from behind and Richard felt two mechanical hands gripping his shoulders. The pain was intense. Suddenly and bodily he was lifted clear of the cockpit and then thrown onto the ground several metres away. He was stunned and shook his head.

When Richard came to his senses and looked up, a Humatron was striding towards him with spiny hands outstretched. The machine's face screen morphed into a hideous death mask.

Richard climbed to his feet but was easily knocked down again. The Humatron leant over him pitilessly and then lifted Richard by his helmet until his legs dangled, before finally throwing him aside. This time Richard's visor was distorted. He saw stars and then his vision clouded. Then he felt himself being yanked upwards. His suit gathered under his neck and his chest was squeezed. For a moment he hung there, waiting for the killer blow. His time was up.

Abruptly he was dropped – unexpectedly released to land in a heap on the ground. Richard climbed to one knee. His head cleared and he looked up to see Thomas locked in combat with the Humatron. They threw each other to the ground, raining down indiscriminate blows; it was an even but terrible fight. Thomas's screen face came and went with his effort, but the Humatron pulled the most repulsive and gruesome expressions and its teardrop-shaped eyes glowed with sadistic satisfaction. Richard climbed to his feet and cast his eye around for a weapon; he found a Lurzengard pistol lying in the dirt with the severed hand of a Humatron still gripping the handle. Richard prised the mechanical fingers open and immediately turned the weapon on the Humatron – only to see that a second machine had set upon Thomas.

For a moment, stunned, Richard watched in despair as Thomas fought off both, but it soon became apparent that he was losing the struggle. Richard saw one of the machines tear Thomas's right arm from its socket and cast it aside. At that, Richard dashed forwards screaming and opened fire with the revolver, pumping scores of sublets into the first robot's back. He ran to the side and shattered the Humatron's face screen with another volley. Finally, the machine dropped and Richard kicked out at its head. The other Humatron released Thomas in an instant and went for Richard. Richard turned the revolver on it, stepping backwards to give himself time, but he tripped and fell. The Humatron stared at Richard for a moment with an expression of savagery and hate and then it lunged forwards, first knocking the pistol from Richard's hand and then, with a wild swinging backhand, smashing Richard to the ground. The towering machine was quickly upon him. It lifted its leg to stamp out Richard's resistance, but suddenly Thomas, from behind, pulled it down.

Another inhuman struggle began, but Thomas,

with only one arm, was quickly overpowered. Richard scrambled for the pistol, grasped it and rolled clear and then he opened fire again as the Humatron smashed its claw-like heel down on Thomas's extended neck. Richard continued firing. In desperation he pumped until the magazine was empty. The Humatron ceased its uncontrolled shuddering and seemed to compose itself, then looked down, first at its perforated chest, and then slowly up at Richard. It extended its neck to a metre or more and peered down from on high, as if judge and executioner, and seemed to take amusement, even delight, at Richard's helplessness. Then it stepped over Thomas's stricken body, and like the Grim Reaper, moved on Richard.

Richard threw the empty pistol at the Humatron's face but it calmly moved its head aside. It continued towards him with extermination on its mind. Richard considered running but knew that would be futile; so he stood to fight and prepared for the worst. Suddenly the machine was cut down by a hail of fire from the side. After several seconds the sublet laden carcass crashed to the floor. And then, from out of the grimy mist and the debilitating dust of battle, stepped two storm troopers. Wearing armoured suits with large helmets and utility belts, and holding serious machineguns, they stepped forward like alien warlords.

"You okay, sir?" asked one, in an American accent.

"I'm okay, thanks . . . thanks a lot," said Richard and gave them a subdued thumbs-up sign.

As other figures appeared, Richard looked for Thomas and saw him lying on the ground. He could see he was in a bad way because there was a gaping hole in his neck and faint traces of condensing gas rose from inside. Richard knelt beside him, put his hand beneath his head and raised it slightly.

"It's too late, Commander, my oxygenation system has collapsed," Thomas said weakly.

"No! No . . . we'll fix you up . . . you hang on, Thomas."

Thomas shook his head. "By the time you get me back to Andromeda I'll be brain dead . . . brain dead . . . It doesn't leave too much else for me, does it?" Thomas's features faded into a flat screen that flickered momentarily. Then his face morphed again, as if he was summoning the very last microvolt. His expression looked forlorn. "Not much of a life anyway . . ."

Richard could see Thomas fighting to stay alive in his mechanical prison, trying to energise his synapse with all the electrical energy he could summon. Each millivolt that his brain produced rejuvenated his features for a moment. His face formed and faded and reformed again, like a mask rising in a bowl of black liquid and then sinking beneath the surface again.

A medic ran past Richard. He reached out to grip her arm, but the woman was carrying a polythene bag containing blood and was preoccupied. Richard adjusted his external speaker to high and shouted after her: "I need a battery . . . some power!"

Thomas shook his head vaguely. "They're trying to save people from the robot war, Commander. Why would they help one?" Thomas's vocallator crackled, like static coming from a radio.

Doctor Brown, his name emblazoned across his chest, was one of Rachel's colleagues. He wore a bloody white spacesuit with a portable stethoscopic oxygenation mask hanging around his neck. Behind his clear visor his face was pale and his expression blank, as if he was shell-shocked. Richard grabbed his suit leg as he passed. The doctor looked back.

"David! I need some help! Do you have a defibrillator, or a portable monitoring unit . . . I need a battery!" Richard pressed.

Doctor Brown shook his head. "They're all being used," he said, as he looked down at Thomas's fading face. Then he glanced back at Richard and went to speak but stopped short. "I'll see what I can find," he said and he walked off.

"Hang on, Thomas; I've got some power coming," Richard said, lifting Thomas's head again and shaking it gently.

"I've told you . . . it's too late for me," Thomas said weakly, and then he appeared to summon every shred of life that remained in him and every microamp of current that ran through his circuits. His face image sharpened and he opened his plasmoltec eyes. He looked directly at Richard and squeezed Richard's forearm, and then shook his head in a resigned way. "This level of biomechanical integration isn't going to work," he said. "Mind you tell them that. You will, won't you?"

Richard nodded. "I will, Thomas, I'll tell them. I want to thank you for saving my life. I was wrong about you – I did need you." Richard cradled the long neck and mechanical head in his arms and felt a compelling need to comfort his brother-in-arms. "Tell you what. If I ever have a son, I'll call him Thomas – and be proud to. What do you say?"

Thomas's dark shadow lit slightly. Richard looked around in desperation for the doctor. Slowly Thomas began to lose control of his features. The contours of his face slipped back into the screen, as if the liquid level was rising around his mask for the last time. His brow flattened, his cheeks disappeared, his lips melted to nothing and finally the tip of his nose disappeared. The process continued until the screen was flat and hard. The backlight flickered again. Thomas twitched as he tried to will himself back, but the LCD dimmed almost to nothing.

"Honoured, that's what I'd say . . ." were his last words.

And with that the face screen turned black. Finally, the faint glow of a tiny, central, pinpoint of light disappeared.

# CHAPTER 27

# THE PARALLEL PLANET

**The Pyramids of Elysium – 3 January**
**09:52 Martian Corrected Time**

"Never in my life have I seen anything like this," said Lesley Oakley, as she gingerly applied the brakes of the PTSV and drew to a halt with the vehicle straddling the crest of a rocky ridgeline. She stared out across the flat, windswept landscape that opened before her and then looked skywards in awe. Still unable to see the pinnacles of the great stone structures, she leaned forward until her face almost touched the glass of the windscreen and craned her neck. Only then did she glimpse the sharp points that seemed to perforate the thin Martian atmosphere. There they stood, all set around a central plaza, shrouded in secrecy . . . four monumental pyramids; architectural achievements that were almost unutterable.

Dark orange in colour and with a matt appearance they seemed blushed with an uncanny glow. Paul Carr sat beside Lesley, wide-eyed and dumbstruck. The red orb of the sun, hanging halfway above the distant horizon, served only to emphasise their dimensions and with its waxy brightness as a backdrop, the striking silhouettes of the pyramids accentuated not only their monolithic status, but also a spiritual significance. Tom Race, who stood between the seats, pointed at the closer of the two larger pyramids and indicated a platform some way above the ground.

"See! There's the ledge!" he said. "Not far up, relatively. The one I was pushed from. You can just make it out." He shook his head. "And I skidded down the side. I was saved by a mound of soft sand but still knocked unconscious. Sure was a close call."

Paul prised his eyes away from the pyramid and glanced up at Tom. "Yes, it was the former Security Officer Gregory Searle, wasn't it . . . ? The one who tried to dump you?"

Tom nodded. "It was not long after that that the ISSF restored the exclusion zone," he informed. "We are the first to see this for what . . . four years?"

"June 2050 to be precise, Commander," replied Paul. "I checked the file – the exclusion zone *and* the news blackout were re-established. Apart from that previous PTSV crew and you, of course, no one else has *ever* seen this panorama."

Tom nodded again and then he felt Veronica behind him trying to peep over his shoulder. "Here, come and take a look," he said, and stepped aside.

"It's incredible. I've heard about them – stories, speculation of an alien race – but with the Federation's complete security blanket, I've never even seen an image of any quality."

Tom gestured through the windscreen. "That's Zeta Three. It's five kilometres away and yet it looks as if you could reach out and touch it."

Veronica nodded.

"Fifteen minutes to satellite contact!" called Anna, from the communications console close to the rear partition.

Tom turned. "Good, thanks, can you energise the 3D printer in preparation please . . . and mix the Deromutine? Cut down on the hardener by ten per cent; that should give us a window of at least three hours."

Anna raised her hand to show her understanding.

Tom turned back to Lesley. "Okay, let's go Lesley . . . Just to confirm, it's that one." He pointed again. "The closest of the shorter pyramids – park on its northern side. That tall one behind it is Zeta Two."

"Are there any issues with soft ground in the vicinity, Commander?"

"None that I know of – all the same, take your time. Amazingly, the plaza is paved with precision-cut stone slabs; you'll find just a thin covering of sand and dust. I expect it to be firm under the wheels, but avoid the dune around the periphery."

"Yes, Commander."

With that, Lesley moved forward slowly allowing the giant bubble tyres and independent suspension mechanisms time to correct their position and maintain the PTSV body in an almost level plane as the rear wheels crested the ridgeline. Then, in a low gear, she eased down the steep incline. After a kilometre or so the gradient sharply decreased and she was able to coast for a similar distance, until the vehicle alighted on the central plain. *This place,* she thought, *would have been a vast seabed in times past.* On level ground, Lesley checked her compass and accelerated towards Zeta Three.

"How tall are those two, Commander?" asked Veronica. She pointed to the highest pyramids and then, having seen enough, stepped back into the cabin.

"Around two miles – three thousand four hundred metres – and almost two kilometres square around the base. And the smaller pyramids are one thousand two hundred metres. But they are all constructed to the same lines – precise mathematical symmetry . . ."

"And they are oriented exactly north-south, too," interjected Lesley, gesturing her head towards the compass repeater mounted on the central console, as she made good speed.

In turn, Anna came forward to take in the view from the cockpit. As the pyramid approached, Tom crouched a little and scanned the area through the left windscreen and side panel. "Keep a good lookout, Paul," he said.

"I've a feeling those two Humatrons will be around here somewhere. They will know that we have deactivated their friend, so it's unlikely that they will show themselves quite so readily . . . Even so, before you get changed, why don't you prime the pulse cannon and set the sensor range at five Ks to be on the safe side?" Tom stepped aside again for Anna to come forward.

"Aye aye, sir," replied Paul.

"Oh my God, they're massive! Much bigger than those in Egypt," declared Anna, stepping between the seats.

"The Great Pyramid near Cairo is only one hundred and thirty-nine metres tall, Anna – tiny by comparison. And the faces of these pyramids are isosceles in design – much steeper – whereas those of the Cairo pyramids are based on simple ratios of the sides of right-angled triangles."

Anna looked impressed. Tom shrugged. "I did some homework on them a while back, that's all." He smiled faintly.

"Why? Do they know why these are designed in this way?"

Apparently it's to do with gravity. Because of its smaller size, Mars obviously has a lower gravity than the Earth, and so structural loading per square metre is less by comparison. It's interesting to note that the first smooth-sided pyramid built in ancient Egypt, at a place called Bahshur, was originally built at the precise angle that these are," Tom pointed towards the sloping sides of Zeta Three. "Halfway through its construction it was known to have collapsed, because the underlying structure was unable to support the weight above. That's when they had a rethink and reduced the angle by around fifteen degrees to what we see today. That's why it's known as the 'Bent Pyramid'. Apparently, by the time the Giza pyramids were built, the architects had learned a few lessons, and the angle was increased again to around fifty-one degrees, but they could never achieve these proportions."

Anna looked back through the windscreens and marvelled, hiding her slightly confused expression.

Tom made an inverted 'V' shape with his hands and demonstrated. "Less of an angle, less material and therefore a reduced loading." He smiled. "Don't worry, I've got a friend who loves to explain all this stuff."

Anna stood straight and looked up at Tom. "Apart from the physical dimensions, do you think there is any link between these pyramids? I mean those on Earth, Egypt and Mexico, and here . . . There have been a lot of rumours lately."

Tom drew a deep breath. "The jury's still out. And I'm undecided, Anna, to be honest. But Commander Reece – who was here a few years ago as the base Planetary Surveyor – made a study, and he is convinced that they were built by the same race of colonists. Maybe the ones here had the edge on technology. Or perhaps they were built this size for a reason. Who knows!"

"And the key we are about to print – what if that

works?"

"Sorry to interrupt Commander," said Lesley. "We are entering the . . . well . . . precinct, for want of a better description; it's astonishing, look . . . You can imagine it as a busy marketplace or a venue for political rallies or something like that. To me it just brims with memories . . . what do you think?"

"I agree, Lesley," said Anna, as she gazed outside again.

"There is an unusual 'feel' to the place, that's for sure," said Tom. "I've experienced it before."

"This is the north side, Commander, where would you like me to stop?"

Tom checked along the side of the pyramid and saw at approximately two hundred metres the flight of wide steps cut into an otherwise smooth surface. "Over there," he directed. "You see . . . at the base of those steps . . . that's where I was before. Pull up there."

Lesley acknowledged with a nod and a few moments later she pulled up adjacent to the steps and at a distance of around twenty metres. Paul, meanwhile, in the left-hand seat, had the best view through his side panel. Lesley, who appeared a little apprehensive, turned for Tom's approval; she set the parking brake and turned off the electric drives when he gave her a thumbs-up signal and nodded back at her.

Veronica raised her hand from the rear console. "Line of sight on the satellite Commander," she called. "I will wait for another two degrees of azimuth to be on the safe side, and then we can download the file – it's a strong signal."

"Very good," responded Tom.

A moment of eerie silence descended over the cockpit, and as the occupants stared out at the inspiring but also foreboding landscape, a prolonged gust of wind blew between the farthest structures. It was powerful enough to whip up a mist of rusty brown sand and dust that in a flurry circulated around the plaza, spraying the PTSV with grit as it did. In an instant, and reinforced by another gust, the mist was concentrated into a dense cloud that twisted and tightened into a vertical column, and for ten to fifteen seconds its form resembled the funnel of a tornado with its base touching the ground. For a while longer the distinct shape squirmed over the ground and then darted off to the side and dissipated, dropping its load onto a dune that was piled against a pyramid. The impromptu display left everyone speechless for a time, until Tom said: "Dust devils and sand storms are frequent in these parts." He remembered the one that nearly cost him his life.

"It's a very abrasive environment," commented Paul.

"Yeah, and the sand and grit gets everywhere. We need to maintain a good positive pressure inside tube when we open the airlock, otherwise it will blow in and play havoc with the seals." Tom pointed outside again. "Even though the pyramids are almost a kilometre apart their funnelling effect on the wind is clearly evident. To make matters worse there seems to be a high concentration of maghemite in this area, so protect your helmet visor as much as possible Paul, when we are outside. Oh, and my last bit of advice is to be very careful on the platform – those gusts will lift you off your feet, no problem."

Lesley sat for some time scanning the landscape whilst seemingly deep in thought. Occasionally, she glanced down at the instrument panel and checked the life support readings. They had enough oxygen for two weeks and with seventy-four per cent of the solar panels serviceable, the batteries were charging at an acceptable rate. However, water was good for only another five or six days. Eventually she stood and slid across to the left-hand seat and looked out at the steep flight of carved steps that were some three metres wide and precision-cut into the smooth but pitted surface of the pyramid. In places the dark, orange-coloured stone had suffered considerable erosion, such as rounded edges to the risers, and here a lighter shade of orange helped Lesley imagine what the pyramids looked like in their heyday. The lower steps were partially covered in blown sand, but upwards, tapering into the distance, they looked like a stairway to heaven.

Closer to the vehicle, an occasional gust of wind blew the sand from the paving stones, exposing a flat and highly polished surface that reflected in the sun's glory, being only another forty minutes until midday. By skewing in the seat in order to look behind, Lesley could see the edge of a dark and ominous shadow that was cast by the towering Zeta Two pyramid. With the Martian day being only fractionally longer than an Earth day, the shadow had been retreating at a familiar rate.

In front and slightly to the right there was a raised area that was like a terrace, or perhaps a small civic square. Lesley imagined a dignitary standing close to the edge and addressing a huge crowd of . . . beings. *Had catastrophic and ruinous news been proclaimed here,* she mused – *the end of days?*

All the same, Lesley sensed a strong feeling of melancholy about the place, as if a terrible event had taken place there. At that moment, Paul stepped between the seats and put a hand on her shoulder; it dragged her from her thoughts and she looked up. Squirming a little awkwardly inside his pristine white spacesuit in order to stretch out some folds in the thermal layer below. Paul then tugged at the roll neck of his blue cottothene undergarment, so as to bring it above the undersuit. "You okay?" he asked. "You know, sitting up here on your own."

Lesley nodded and smiled weakly. "How high is that ledge?" she asked, looking outside again.

"About thirty-three metres apparently, and the platform is ten by twenty, according to the Boss."

"Well you be careful . . . the diurnal winds are beginning to pick up – just stay away from the edge."

Paul nodded. "Anna's about to print the key, why don't you come back and take a look?"

Lesley smiled and climbed from her seat. Paul

leant across to the weapon control panel and set the parameters to maximum sensitivity and a five-kilometre range. Then he connected the weapon sensor loop to the fire control system and as he armed the pulse cannon he murmured, "Anything moving out there will get a nasty surprise." Then he stood for a moment focusing on the scene outside, and on the ordered precision of it all and its symmetry. Dismissing a strangely morose feeling, he turned and went back.

"The formatter has programmed a number of restrictions into the file, Commander," said Anna, looking up from her console.

Tom was halfway into his spacesuit. He shook his legs alternately and stretched his arms to pull out creases until he felt comfortable. He pulled up the white roll neck of his sweatshirt, adjusted the metal neck ring of the suit so that it was central, and then glanced at the data on Anna's screen.

"One print only – um, that's not so helpful," he commented. He looked at Anna. "Commander Reece will have done that for a good reason . . . anything else?"

"He recommended that we use a blue dye on the palm and fingertips – again there is no reason given."

"Can you do that?"

"Yes, that's no problem."

"Okay . . . and you have downloaded the complete file? It's all there, no sign of corruption?"

Anna nodded but looked put out.

"Okay, sorry Anna, then press the button, please."

"It's done, sir."

All eyes focused immediately on the 3D printer. The machine resembled a medium-sized microwave oven, with a clear glass door and a line of air vents in the top casing. It began to hum quietly.

"How long will the process take?"

"It's a very large file, Commander, requiring maximum definition. The model will have a high degree of detail . . . the system is telling me another nine minutes."

Tom nodded.

"I've reduced the hardener content in the Deromutine mix as you requested. The model should remain set for at least three hours and twenty minutes."

"Good," said Tom, and he bent down and looked through the glass door at the object taking shape.

"Commander, I need you to input your ID code into the pulse cannon's fire control system so that it recognises you," said Paul, who was standing behind Lesley. "Also your command failsafe code . . . the system will then be set to automatic."

Tom nodded and simultaneously unzipped the thigh pocket on his left leg. He slid his hand inside and withdrew a heavy pistol. "It's the Lurzengard semi-automatic that I acquired from the Humatron – hell of a weapon," he said, turning it in his hand and checking the breech. Then he unclipped the magazine and checked the digital ammunition counter.

Lesley and Veronica looked apprehensive.

"Just in case," commented Tom. He looked at Paul. "What have you got?"

"Two stun grenades and a fully charged static baton."

"That's it!"

"We were on a survey task, Commander. I didn't draw any specific weapons. All the same, I've got the laser sight from the Geosystem's Distancemeter."

"Okay," responded Tom. "And the notebook containing the translation programme?"

Paul slapped his leg pocket.

Tom gestured his approval and joined Anna peering into the printing machine.

"It's a hand!" Anna exclaimed, as the object's form was nearing completion.

"Sure is. A woman's hand to be precise – I'm playing a hunch," explained Tom. "If it doesn't work, we'll resort to the heavy equipment. But that will take time, and even so, I have my doubts about ever getting through the massive stone door up there."

The machine pinged. Anna opened the printer and carefully withdrew the object. She looked surprised as she examined it. "I won't ask who it belongs to, Commander," she said, staring at the blue fingertips that had faint grooves. "But whoever it is they have an amazing fate line and the life line too is unusually prominent!"

Now it was Tom's turn to look surprised. "Anything else?" he asked.

Anna looked again. "It's just a hobby, but the marriage line is broken and the family line is crossed only once."

"Go on, what else do you see?"

"As I said, Commander, it's a hobby – I only know the basics – but the mounts of Jupiter and Mars seem particularly pronounced."

"Really . . . now that is interesting." Tom broke from his thoughts and looked around the circle. "Now listen up everyone," he said. "Lesley . . . you're in charge while Paul and I are outside. Any problems, and I mean anything . . . then you call. If you can't get hold of us then stay in here until we call you. If we get inside we are unlikely to have a signal . . . understand?"

Lesley nodded.

"Anna, you look after comms. Update Osiris with the situation. Tell them to standby for the real-time digital image transfer."

"Yes, Commander."

"Veronica, you keep a good lookout and monitor the sensor and weapon systems. The pulse cannon is programmed to fire at anything that moves; apart from Paul and myself, of course. Paul . . . you go and suit-up, I'm right behind you. Any questions anybody?"

"Okay, let's go to it."

In the dispatch section, Tom and Paul completed a buddy check on their helmets and suits and tested their intercom before charging the airlock. With the positive pressure differential, there was a loud whooshing outflow of air from the compartment as the outer door inched open and then rotated upwards.

Outside, they could feel the strength of the wind blowing against their bodies and within moments sand and grit began to deposit itself in the crevices around their shoulders and elbows and around the accessories on their belts and backpacks. The white tube of the PTSV was made a rusty orange colour by a covering of dust. Tom turned and walked towards the steps as Paul closed and secured the airlock.

Clearing the vehicle, Tom had a sense of movement behind him and he turned back to see the turret on top of the vehicle turn in his direction and then the barrel of the pulse cannon point directly at him. It unnerved him. *But at least it's a positive check that the system is functioning,* he thought. As Paul stepped from the electronic confines of the vehicle and into sensor view the long, cobalt steel barrel trained in an instant on him. "It will take a second or two to crosscheck and identify your code," said Tom, and he waved Paul over to the steps where they both began the long climb. Tom held the model of the hand in a clear plastic bag and was careful to keep it away from his body.

Halfway up, the two men stopped for a break. Both turned and sat down on a step and gazed across at the towering Zeta Two pyramid. Even lolling backwards, Paul's helmet stopped him comfortably sighting the top of the structure.

Tom put a hand on the sand-covered step and measured its width with outstretched fingers and thumb.

"Judging by the size of the treads and risers of these steps," he commented, "I would say that the average height of the race that designed and built them was one point four metres – which means that they are a damned uncomfortable pitch for people like you and me."

Paul looked down at the PTSV; thankfully the barrel of the canon was stowed in the neutral position. "Yes it is hard-going . . . but ready when you are."

From the platform the vista was incredible and indisputably unworldly. Both men stood side-by-side a metre back from the edge and gazed out over the plaza, with its raised terrace to the left, a square, sunken area on the far side and to the right what could have been a water feature – possibly a fountain. The light around the sun had a milky appearance; however, everything else in view seemed to have a reddish hue, although the tone varied from a dark, rusty brown to a sulphur yellow depending on the direction. They turned and approached the huge rectangular stone door with some apprehension, until Tom suddenly put a hand on Paul's arm and pulled him up short. He pointed to the left-hand side of the entrance. "Look!" he said. Paul followed his finger.

There were clear scuff marks on the ground where windblown sand had not had time to cover. Then Tom saw the damage on the stone door – deep grooves and cuts and there was a pile of the stone on the ground – debris that was too heavy to be blown away. "It's the Humatrons!" Tom barked. "They've been trying to get in . . ."

On closer examination there was an area of approximately one metre diameter where the robots had used mechanical equipment to cut to a depth of around fifteen centimetres.

"By the looks of things, this granite is especially hard," commented Paul, while taking a wary look behind him. "I'd say they have been working here for some time, Commander. But with limited equipment . . . looks like a couple of battery-powered chisels and some hand tool . . . seems they didn't come prepared for the operation."

"They probably didn't have much to go on – perhaps a few images taken by Gregory Searle, back a while." Tom slid his hand into his leg pocket and pulled out the pistol. He handed it to Paul. "Safety catch is on . . . better keep a lookout . . . I'll . . ."

Suddenly there was a loud, reverberating crack, the echo of which rumbled around the plaza for several seconds. Even with their helmets on and above the whistle of the wind it was clear and sharp. The two men rushed back to the plateau edge and looked down. The turret on top of the PTSV could be seen returning to its default position.

"Commander Race, sir, Anna here . . . can you hear me?"

"Yes Anna, what happened?"

"The weapon system acquired a target and automatically engaged it."

"Where?"

"Veronica is checking . . . she says on a bearing of one

seven seven degrees and at one point three kilometres."

"At that range there is a high probability of success," interjected Paul.

"Status, Anna?"

"Nothing showing, Commander, everything seems quiet."

Tom turned to look at Paul; their near perfect reflections in each other's visors made it impossible to make eye contact. "What do you think?"

"Optimistically . . . ? One down and one to go," replied Paul, lowering the pistol.

Unseen, Tom grimaced. "But only a kilometre away . . . that's too close for comfort," he said, over the intercom. Then he pressed the radio transmit button on his belt again. "Anna, get Lesley to deploy the emergency voltaic panels, and then electrify the outer casing – tell her to set twenty thousand volts. We are about to try the key. Keep a good look out!"

"Will do, sir."

Tom turned and walked quickly back to the left side of the entrance. "We had better get on with this," he said, and he pulled the model from the plastic bag.

The door itself was of perfectly flat stone and it clearly blocked what appeared to be a square tunnel leading directly into the centre of the pyramid. Tom recalled the lines of hieroglyphic script etched into the stone, but Paul was surprised by the extent of it.

"Shall I take an image and download it into the notebook?"

"No, Paul, not at the moment, we can make up the log later – better to keep a lookout. I don't want to be surprised by a Humatron."

Paul agreed and he half-turned again but watched Tom brush away sand from a shaped niche set in the wall at knee height.

Tom carefully offered the model to the recess; he could tell instantly that it was the same size, and that the woman had spread her fingers precisely when the original scan was taken. He hesitated for a moment a few millimetres clear and then pushed the model home – the response was immediate.

Suddenly there was a grinding noise and an accompanying rumble that became accentuated as the great stone slab began to move sideways from left to right. Paul took a few steps backward in amazement – he was speechless. Tom straightened up, and as the gap in front of him widened there was a piercing whistle of escaping gas and he felt the powerful outflow increase until it pushed him off balance – he immediately dropped to one knee, bowed his head and leant against the force.

As the gap widened to more than a metre the outflow subsided. Tom looked up into the blackness and then slowly stood; he was in awe at what he had done. He arched his back and raised his head to maximum to take it all in. An unseen mechanism propelled the door, and the rumbling and vibration he felt through his feet continued until its edge – which was itself a metre thick – had almost disappeared into a recess on the other side.

Silence fell upon the two men again. But a gust of wind from behind found the way in and the noise it made was like a distressing sigh from a giant whose mouth had been prised open. Tom sensed its secrets swirl around him and then disappear. He couldn't help but be moved.

The exposed entrance was around three metres square. Tom took a bold step inside. Only then did Paul hesitantly move forward, checking behind again as he did – but neither man spoke. A tiny red light on Tom's utility belt flashed incessantly. He was made aware of it because of the intense darkness that engulfed him. He pulled the instrument from its slot, looked at the digital display and then at Paul, who now stood beside him. "The spectrometer indicated a high proportion of carbon dioxide and some oxygen in that escaping gas," he said matter-of-factly – as if that was normal on Mars. Then he unclipped his flashlight, set the beam to maximum intensity and directed it into the hollow – it simply faded to nothing.

"Better use the Illuminac, Commander."

Paul turned to present his backpack to Tom, who unclipped a lantern from it. The instrument was the size of a small shoebox. It had a handle on the top and the bulging front face was an integrated lens and reflector. Inside was a microchip of Uranium-235. When showered by gamma rays, an elemental reaction causes the chip to fluoresce. The result is an incredibly bright light, the intensity of which is precisely controlled by a rotary switch. The longevity of the power pack is the half-life of

Uranium-235 itself – seven hundred million years.

Tom set a luminance of one hundred per cent and a narrow focus, and at arm's length he shone the beam into the gloom. What they saw made their jaws drop with amazement.

The entire pyramid was hollow, but a wide walkway with a shallow incline built peripherally against the internal walls led down to ground level. The walkway was perhaps twenty metres wide and Tom and Paul walked gingerly to its edge; to the side Tom could see that it was impressively cantilevered. Below was a cavern so vast that not even Tom's dazzling beam could illuminate its extremities.

"Most of this is below ground, so why such enormous structures?" he asked of Paul.

"Can you illuminate the wall behind us?"

Tom turned away from Paul and did as requested, broadening the beam in order to see a larger area. Far from being a natural dark orange colour or blackened with age, the stone had a greenish hue.

"I would say that these walls are covered in some kind of mould – which would indicate a level of humidity."

"Moisture . . . ! Maybe a subterranean source," agreed Tom, checking an adjacent section of wall. "Let's go and see what's down below shall we?"

With that the two men turned to their left and set off down the incline. Tom lit their way. Paul brandished the revolver and frequently looked behind, sometimes walking backwards to ensure that nothing followed them.

Underfoot was smooth and the layer of dust was readily scuffed. Numerous small shapes on the ground, causing tiny shadows, Tom saw to be twisted and dried fronds of algae or similar. When touched they turned to dust. The path to ground level looked to be at least a kilometre.

## Inside the PTSV – simultaneous

A light flashed on the weapons panel; Veronica gave it her immediate attention.

"What is it?" asked Lesley.

"The system sensed something for a split-second, but not long enough to acquire – it didn't lock-on."

"Where?"

"Above us, in the direction of the platform."

Lesley walked quickly over to the sensor display and assessed the data. "There is an indication of movement alright, but just briefly. Could something have slipped past us?"

Veronica looked anxious. "It's possible, I suppose."

Lesley leant over the radio microphone. "Commander Race, sir, this is Lesley, how do you read?"

There was no reply.

"Commander Race ... Paul ... come in please!"

Still nothing.

"They must be inside," said Veronica.

Lesley turned towards the rear of the compartment and to Anna who was sitting at her console. "Anything?" she quizzed apprehensively.

Anna shook her head. "No. And their sensor ID signal has faded, too. I agree with Veronica. I would say that they are inside."

Lesley nodded. "Then we wait."

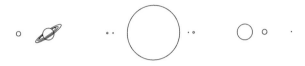

One complete circuit of the entire structure had brought Tom Race and Paul Carr to ground level. However, Tom was right in his earlier assumption that most of the 'city' was subterranean. There was a wide ledge that surrounded a vast, square hole in the planet's crust. Tom estimated the rock layer at twenty metres thick and, although clearly worked, the edges were still rough-hewn and craggy. Access down through the hole was by wide steps that were much steeper than the gentle incline of the pyramid's walkway and Paul counted 300 of them before they reached the main level. Turning slowly he cast the brilliant, penetrating beam in a wide circle; its effect revealed to Tom the true scale of this forgotten civilisation. In the direction of the plaza and towards the other three pyramids, the level was endless. And the roof of the cavern was some thirty metres above them. It was astonishing, beyond belief, and Tom felt his heart thumping. He drew a deep breath.

"This is a common level throughout the entire complex," informed Paul, using Tom's flashlight to examine the wall next to him. "And look at this Commander," he continued, shining the light into the corner between the outside wall and the ground. "There's a deep trough cut into the stone." Paul walked to the edge and leaned out. "A couple of metres deep and one and a half across, and there's still some moisture in the bottom. It runs directly beneath the outside walls of the pyramid and seems to collect . . . this is an irrigation system, sir! No question about that."

"Let's walk to the area beneath the plaza, Paul. I'll take the pistol; it might be a good time to have the notebook ready."

"I'm on it," replied Paul and he handed over the weapon and withdrew the tablet-sized computer from his leg pocket and energised it.

Pistol in one hand and the Illuminac in the other, Tom led the way. Although the edges of the cavern were rough and in the main simply worked, and in some areas the ceiling curved down to the ground in a cave-like fashion, the ground was perfectly smooth. They walked for 300 metres or more through a wide expanse. To the left and right they could see openings and small doorways that led from the main thoroughfare like catacombs; there, eerie shadows played inside the adjacent rooms as the two men passed. Away from the effects of the wandering beams of light, the blackness was absolute.

After walking for several minutes, a wide doorway loomed from obscurity in front of them. As they approached, Tom and Paul could see it had a heavy stone lintel set just a metre above head height. The powerful beam from the Illuminac enhanced an area behind; funnelled through the opening, the light became narrow and condensed. Some way in the distance, the bright beam finally petered to nothing. Tom sensed a cavern even bigger than the one they were in. When the two men arrived at the doorway, Paul ran the more user-friendly beam from the flashlight along the lintel – for at close quarters, the Illuminac made their eyes smart. Immediately apparent were a number of inscriptions. Tom recognised them as similar to those on the main door.

"Paul," he started, "take an image of those hieroglyphs, there by the representation of the comet or asteroid or whatever it is. Load it into the translation programme . . ."

Paul focused the built-in imager in the notebook and took the picture; then it was a simple matter of transferring the information to the translator. "'Driven again are we the Atleans. Even before the despair of Homer has faded,'" he quoted. "What the hell does that mean?"

"If I remember correctly from my brief, it said that 'Homer' was the name the colonists called their planet of origin. And 'Atleans' were mentioned as the builders of the Ancient Egyptian pyramids on Earth. 'Driven again are we the Atleans' . . . to me it's referring to their fate . . . first their home planet, and then here, their adopted one."

Paul turned his flashlight beam onto the inscription again and then the stellar object alongside. "That's the cause of it, Commander, that comet," he said. "Have you ever seen a picture of the Bayeux Tapestry? It's that famous relic telling the story of William the Conqueror invading England in ten sixty-six."

"Heard of it, not seen it," replied Tom.

"Well I studied it during my school days – I had an interest in the History of Art. There is a depiction of a comet sewn into the storyline, believed to be Halley's Comet – always stuck in my mind. That carving is remarkably similar. The people who built this place clearly did so for a good reason. I think it was a refuge, and water has something to do with it. This place would have taken decades to excavate and with building those four pyramids . . . God only knows. It would have supported thousands of people and I'd say they had some notice as to the impending catastrophe. I mean forty, fifty, sixty years – maybe more."

Tom could see Paul's face in the ambiance of the Illuminac, despite pointing it at the ground. "We know that Mars had a lot of surface water at one time. Craters forming vast seas, and networks of huge rivers, too . . . We know of the associated erosion and the classic geological features. We also know that there was an abrupt and calamitous shift in the planet's magnetic field at some time in its history – some astronomers say by as much as forty-five degrees. It's long been speculated that the close flyby of a large stellar object, such as a comet, would have been responsible. What if this event happened far more recently than believed – I mean as recent as ten or twenty thousand years ago . . . while there was a civilisation here. A shift in the magnetic field like that could easily have torn a hole in the atmosphere . . ."

"Yes . . . the atmospheric gases would have leaked into space, the reduction in pressure would have caused the oceans to evaporate and over a period of time all the surface water would be lost, and then finally the breatheable atmosphere, too?"

"If it was a relatively small tear, they might have had, well, maybe a century – they would have known what was happening . . ."

"But it's cold down here, Commander; they would have required a power source . . . and what about food? Surface production would have dwindled to nothing. They would need to grow a variety of crops and in sustainable quantities. Biodomes may have been the answer, but nothing has ever been found. That leads us here – underground." Paul shook his head. "Growing sufficient quantities would have been just one of many insurmountable problems . . ."

"Underground . . . here!"

Tom lifted the Illuminac and darted through the opening. Paul was so close on his heels that he ran into the back of him, pushing Tom forward a few paces.

"Sorry . . . I thought . . . huh!"

Both men stood bolt upright, completely still, and they stared. Tom shone his light down a central avenue that seemed to have no ending. Motionless, they stood for more than a minute, until Tom broke the heavy silence by saying: "There's your answer!"

Paul seemed transfixed, unable to reply – as if words could elucidate in any case.

What lay before them were two rows of huge glass domes. On each side of the avenue – itself at least twenty metres wide – one after the other, the domes circled high to the roof of the cavern. They resembled rows of eggs in a long egg box. In the powerful light of the Illuminac, the glass structures appeared to have a slight reddish hue. Tom and Paul could see the first five or six domes on each side, but after that their number faded into the murky distance.

The two men stepped forward and Tom illuminated the first dome on the left-hand side. There was a blanketed reflection of light because of a thin layer of dust but the primary beam penetrated the dome to reveal a number of tall and spindly trees, their variety and shape being very peculiar. In the lofty edifice the beam from Paul's flashlight was overwhelmed and almost useless.

The trees in the first dome assumed a ghostly air and not all were upright; some had fallen and lay at irregular angles, being propped by other, sturdier, examples. All were frozen still, lifeless and distressed.

Tom walked the thirty or so paces to the first dome and irresponsibly knocked on the glass material with the butt of his revolver. The deep thud reflected the thickness of the material and an accompanying reverberation echoed through the cavern for some time. The sound eventually faded in the distance, giving Tom an indication of the extent of the place.

"There's that feeling . . . like a heavy burden of despair is pressing down on your shoulders – just like outside," Paul said, turning full circle and stretching up to take a good look at the roof, "a spirit world, haunted by memories."

With a head gesture, Tom indicated for Paul to follow him and the two men walked for some way along the avenue. Neither spoke. The powerful beam from the Illuminac pierced the darkness in all directions, drilling into hidden corners and bouncing off the curved glass, causing sparkling shards, like dancing fairy lights. The domes contained the remnants of various plant species and not all were tree-like, as some looked to have bushy outlines, and one dome had nothing inside except for a short, blackened field of moss or perhaps grass that had been heavily grazed. Tom noticed that several domes were damaged. Some were cracked, and one, to the right, had a long split and some material had partially fallen in, as if subsidence had created unacceptable stress. Tom checked his chronometer and looked back the way that they had come.

"We've been down here an hour and twenty, Paul," he said. "I've seen enough. We had better get back; otherwise we'll miss the 'ops normal' call."

"Check."

The two men turned to retrace their steps. "Talking about when you were at school," continued Tom reflectively, "when I was a kid I read a book about a space colony. There was a place called Subterrania – on some lost planet. Funny how things stick in your mind from that time in your life . . . this place reminds me of there . . . incredible . . . the Petrified Forests of Subterrania . . ."

"I've got a theory, Commander. Would you like to hear it?" Paul responded, only half-listening.

"Go on."

"It's taken these . . . people . . . a few decades to build this place. By that time the surface water has all but evaporated. The atmosphere is dissipating, too, and ground temperatures are starting to drop. They need water. All that remains, apart from some limited subterranean supplies that are difficult to extract, is vapour in atmosphere. So you build condensing towers that reach up as high as your technology will allow. It's been done many times on Earth. The moisture in the air condenses on the cold stone and runs down to the base and then into that moat we saw back there, below the outside edge of this pyramid. It's water capture on a massive scale, and Zeta One and Two are almost three times larger than this pyramid."

"Yeah, sounds feasible, until the atmosphere has bled away completely, and then what . . . and they would still need an energy source?"

"Then it's the end of days, as they say – not unless

someone out there could have helped. That clearly wasn't the case."

"No, maybe you're right, maybe that's what happened."

Paul took a number of images as the two men retraced their steps through the first cavern. As they approached the steps Tom replaced the revolver into his leg pocket. He felt more relaxed and was pleased that his idea with the key had come to fruition.

"We will make a detailed report on the way back to Osiris, Paul, and formulate a plan for a full survey . . . Wait! What the hell!"

Suddenly a tall figure loomed in the shadows. "Stop!" the shape screeched.

Tom pulled up short and put a restraining hand on Paul's arm, who was instinctively reaching for his static baton.

"Drop your weapons . . . everything!" The words were synthetic and high pitched.

"Do what it says, Paul. No rash moves."

"Comply! Now!"

The figure remained in the shadows, but by its apparent physical dimensions there was no doubt in Tom's mind what confronted them. Tom cast a wary eye behind him – there was no sign of another machine.

Paul's static baton clattered to the ground.

"And the grenades!"

"Better do what it says."

Paul unclipped the two grenades from his belt and threw them onto the ground.

The shape twitched towards Tom.

Tom held his arms up. "I'm unarmed," he said.

In the murkiness Tom saw a tiny red light moving left and right where the figure's head would be. *It's running a scan,* he thought, *but what kind . . . X-ray, infrared . . . contour?* Tom decided to take a chance and keep quiet about the pistol. Imperceptibly he turned his right side towards the figure in order to shield his left leg. In the silent stillness, the purr of tiny motivators seemed amplified.

"What do you want . . . there is nothing here for you!"

"I seek information. You will tell me how you opened the stone door. You will tell me what you have found here."

"That's not going to happen."

"Tell me or die!"

Paul looked sideways at Tom and wondered if this was the right course of action.

"Who programmed you?" continued Tom. "Who's controlling you?"

"I am autonomous!"

"No machine is autonomous; you have a controller."

"Silence!"

Tom surreptitiously pushed Paul to the side, and then pressed on him again with the back of his hand, indicating for them to spread apart. "Move," he whispered over the intercom.

"Stop!"

With that, the machine stepped from the shadows. Tom raised the Illuminac to waist height. It was evidently a Humatron, but Tom instantly noticed its facial features, and the width of its shoulders, two factors that indicated it being another upgraded model. In its right hand it held a Lurzengard pistol and it was pointing directly at Tom.

"You are an HU50 model. Who programmed you?"

The 'X'-shaped head with its flat screen face seemed to look Tom up and down. With the apparent lack of any discernable facial features, Tom knew that the machine was using another system to 'see'; he surmised that it was an infrared system, or at least in combination with synthetic retinas, as the robot appeared to shy away from the light.

"You will tell me how you gained entrance to this pyramid. You will tell me now," it said, and then it stepped towards Paul and stood above him in a most intimidating way.

Paul held his ground and looked up at the screen face. The robot was much bigger than him, wider, probably twice his weight and with a shoulder height halfway up Paul's helmet. But it was the long flexible neck of interlocking metal rings that afforded another metre in height that made the machine look both frightening and menacing. The machine hinged its face down and peered intently into Paul's visor. It stared at him for several seconds in the dim light, and then its face screen morphed into a hideous shape, becoming a skull shape first and then an exact replica of Paul's – as if he was looking in the mirror. Tom's eyes widened in amazement. And then the machine's plasmoltec ability allowed subtle changes to take place, as if Paul was ageing before their very eyes. Finally, his skin peeled from his face and there was a skull again. Paul stumbled backwards, clearly shocked.

The robot slowly pointed its revolver at Paul's chest and Tom saw its finger tighten on the trigger.

"Wait!" Tom barked. "Give it the notebook . . . Paul, give it the notebook now!"

Paul looked hesitantly at Tom – he had no clue as to Tom's intentions, but he pulled the small computer from his pocket and offered it to the Humatron.

"The information is in this computer," Tom said. "You can download it." Tom recalled the technology in the robot's landing vehicle; he knew of their USD port compatibility. "There's a USD port in the side; you can plug in there."

The machine turned its head slowly towards Tom and then back to Paul, and then it looked down at the notebook. It was impossible not to be unnerved by such a malicious creation.

"Where is the outlet? Hold the computer!" it screeched.

Paul hesitated. He didn't know where this course of action was going. But he offered the Humatron the computer with the connection port uppermost as directed. The robot pushed the tip of its right, claw-like little finger into the port. Instantly it began reading the data stored in the notebook and an accompanying red light flashed in the corner of its screen face, which had by now returned to a flat screen with two bulging, red, teardrop-shaped eyes.

Suddenly the machine pulled its hand away and turned the gun on Tom. "There is no relevant data here, only images!" it shouted, clearly demonstrating anger.

"Sorry . . . sorry, wrong computer. It's this one. There was a mix-up. It's this one," replied Tom with a pleading tone, and he pointed to his thigh pocket.

"Get it!" demanded the robot, changing weight impatiently from one leg to the other.

Tom unzipped the pocket and slid his hand inside. He grasped the handle of the revolver and flipped off the safety catch – there was a click! The robot's head twitched in response and it extended its neck towards Tom in an ungainly movement and then studied him suspiciously.

*It's now or never,* Tom thought, and in a calculated response he withdrew the weapon, dived to the ground, took aim and fired. The short volley took the Humatron by complete surprise as armour-piercing sublets pummelled a hole in its chest. The machine fired back but the sublets went high as it stumbled backward. Paul dived forwards as Tom opened fire again with a sustained volley that had the machine's chest cavity breaking open and components shattering. A line of sublets tore into the celluloid material of its leg and electrolytic oil immediately spurted out under pressure. Instinctively, Tom rolled two or three turns to his right just as the robot aimed a counterattack – the stream of sublets narrowly missed him. Tom scrambled to his feet but Paul was up first and rushed for his baton. Tom put three more shots into the face screen; the robot squirmed on the ground and fired blind shots into the air. Tom was about to empty his magazine into the beast but then Paul shouted, "*Clear!*" and simultaneously he dove forward and rammed the baton into the hole in the robot's chest and delivered the high voltage static charge. In a wild involuntary jerk, Paul's arm immediately recoiled from the charge and spun him onto his back, but the robot's body coursed with electricity. At first it shuddered, as if feeling the effects of a defibrillator machine, and then it quivered and vibrated as its motivators shorted and burnt. And then, as a thin column of smoke rose from its power pack, it fell back, paralysed. The hand holding the Lurzengard slid from its body and fell limply onto the ground. Silence descended on the cavern again.

Tom crouched and tentatively made ready to fire by holding the weapon in both hands and at arm's length. Paul, rubbing his arm, climbed to his feet. He adjusted his helmet position and recovered his flashlight. He glanced at Tom, who seeing that the Humatron was completely deactivated, lowered the revolver. They both stood for a moment in silence, simply staring at the machine. And then, as their heart rates subsided and their breathing rhythm settled, they both became aware of a quiet whistle of escaping gas. Tom checked himself over and so did Paul, but it was only on turning his back towards Paul that they realised that Tom had been hit. An examination quickly revealed a tiny stream of condensing oxygen. It leaked from a hole in Tom's backpack – the internal tank had been perforated. Tom immediately checked his life support panel. On the screen, the pictorial representation of a gauge indicated twenty-one per cent and edging into the amber zone, but the red, decimal place digits were counting down quickly.

"Better get going," said Tom, casting a final eye over the Humatron and picking up the notebook.

"How quickly is it going down, Commander?"

"Enough . . . come on!"

Controlling his breathing as best he could, Tom and Paul covered two stone steps in each stride until they reached ground level. On the inclined walkway the going was easier but Tom was using his oxygen quickly. Paul called the PTSV, but to no avail; there would be no trace of his signal outside the thick walls of the pyramid.

"How much have you got left?" asked Paul, as they hurried side by side up the ramp.

Tom checked his forearm. Between pants he said, "Nine per cent . . . I'm breathing hard, so there's a high demand."

The two men retraced their steps to the entrance. The steady incline made the distance seem more than a kilometre; they half-walked, half-ran. When he was behind, Paul could clearly see the tiny spout of milky-coloured gas escaping from Tom's backpack and he was visibly relieved when they dashed through the gaping hole in the stone wall and into a flood of natural light. Outside, the far off sun was lower in the sky and there was a constant barrage of windblown sand. Tom dashed to the head of the steps while Paul quickly crossed the platform to its edge so that he could see the PTSV and be sure of a radio signal. The vehicle was momentarily obscured by a turbulent cloud of reddish-brown sand, but the strong wind soon blew it away, revealing the PTSV's stained, elongated tube – with its antennae and protrusions. In the reduced visibility it resembled a spiny caterpillar. It was then that Paul saw the shattered remains of another Humatron. The carcass was burnt and blackened, two limbs were missing and the head was severed. Blowing sand was already building against it, and he caught sight of a forearm and hand that was nearly covered. *Clearly it had suffered a direct hit from the pulse cannon,* thought Paul, but he had no time to loiter and Tom had disappeared down the steps.

"Open up, Lesley, emergency oxygen situation!" called Paul over the radio.

"You're back . . . thank goodness – say again . . . emergency?"

"Oxygen! Oxygen! The boss's oxygen is nearly out . . . open up for God's sake!"

There was a pause of realisation. "Copied . . . Emergency Code Red – deactivating hull electrification, discharging airlock and opening portal . . . Veronica is suiting up!"

Tom hurtled down the steep external flight of steps with Paul in hot pursuit. It was a headlong dash and one slip could bring disaster. Halfway down Tom checked his gauge – it read one per cent.

"I'm out!" he called to Paul. There was desperation in his tone.

After another few metres Tom started to wheeze. He was out of breath and breathing hard. Moments later he heard his helmet's shuttle valve squeak – he was drawing on the dregs of his cylinder. After a further few breaths the squeaking stopped and his chest suddenly felt restricted. All that remained now was the gas in his helmet and soon that would be predominantly carbon dioxide.

With ten metres to the ground and with his chest feeling tight, Tom made a wayward leap to the side and skidded down the smooth face of the pyramid on his back, only to finish seconds later in a heap on a soft sand dune. With the momentum he continued to roll, tumbling over the dune until he landed on the hard paving. He felt himself becoming light-headed, but he stood and quickened his pace towards the PTSV. He saw the rear portal rotating upwards and then locking into position. He saw an astronaut coming to his aid. A flurry of sand passed and Tom heard the grains raining on the side of his helmet.

More than halfway, but struggling, Tom held onto each breath as long as he could. He staggered a few more steps but fell to his knees – now his head was spinning.

Exerting his self-control, he moderated his breathing to avoid this effect of asphyxiation; he tried short, sharp, pants, but the level of carbon dioxide inside his helmet was becoming poisonous.

Tom climbed to his feet and managed to stagger forward another few paces. A strong gust of wind blew him off balance and he fell to his knees again. He became disorientated and unsure as to the correct direction. His lungs were bursting.

Then Tom felt someone pull at his arm and suddenly he was standing. Paul tucked a shoulder under his and dragged him the last few metres. Veronica was there to operate the airlock and no sooner were the three of them inside than the portal began to close. The twelve seconds felt like an hour. Tom was on his back, and Veronica could see he was turning blue.

The portal locked into position and there was a violent inrush of air. Paul went for the visor first, releasing the safety clips and then pressing the two side buttons simultaneously. The visor flipped open and Veronica pressed an oxygen mask over Tom's nose and mouth; the flow was under pressure and it helped Tom to suck his lungs full. His chest filled. Three or four rapid breaths followed and Tom held onto each for longer than normal. Then his head began to clear. His breathing settled and he tried to nod his recovery within the confines of his helmet and under the mask; eventually he raised a hand and gripped Veronica's forearm to indicate it, as the inner door opened. Paul released the helmet clips, rotated it and pulled it clear of Tom's head, who then sat up and leaned forward against the weight of his pack and rubbed his brow.

Lesley, Anna and Veronica looked on apprehensively. Paul stood, offered a hand and then pulled Tom to his feet. Tom gestured his thanks to Veronica and with his fist prodded Paul on his shoulder in a friendly way. "A successful day then," he said and smiled.

# CHAPTER 28

# TAKING STOCK

**Andromeda – The Fresnel Lunar Hospital**
**4 January – 13:12 Lunar Corrected Time**

Richard looked out through a circular porthole window and peered in a north-westerly direction across the drab, undulating plain. In the far distance he could see the high rim of a giant crater and for a moment he reflected on the memory of Diomedes: was it fate or pure coincidence that this impressive geographical feature be called by the same name? *The old man certainly had an impact on me,* Richard thought, as he smiled to himself. Closer, he thought he could see the smoke haze that still loitered above the Freight Terminal.

Outside the hospital wing, on the surface, it was a mess. In fact the entire area was trashed. Abandoned equipment, broken antenna masts, a vehicle overturned, the carcasses of two Humatrons, some mechanical body parts, the countless spent sublet cartridges he could see close to an observation point, and near the airlock to his left there was a dark violet coloured stain in the grey sand that Richard knew was blood. He breathed a sigh and scanned the area to his right. The low hills that rose from the plain in a northerly direction were much closer – not more than twenty Ks – and there was the pass through which a platoon of robots had streamed and attacked the main complex.

By all accounts they were still retrieving dead troopers from the 1st Regiment in that area, and also from other outlying areas and assessing the wounded – the ward outside which he stood had been allocated to less serious cases. Elsewhere, the hospital was overflowing.

Richard walked across the corridor and peered out through a window that was orientated south. He craned his neck in order to catch a glimpse of the Earth. It hung in Space as a white reflective crescent; silent, even serene, but without any blue. He didn't like the thought of living there any more, and today he didn't like the Moon either. Just then a stretcher appeared from around the corner. He shuffled closer to the sidewall as it passed and acknowledged the orderly – who was dressed in hospital whites – with a nod. On the stretcher there was a young man with his head in bandages. He lay staring blankly at the ceiling. As he watched the two green swing doors close behind the orderly, Richard took stock of his war. Miraculously they had all survived the battle, and relatively unscathed, although Mayard had broken his arm during his ejection, Tardier had been quite seriously concussed by crash landing his Delta and then skidding off into a building, and Chris Quarrie had been burnt after he was brought down. Richard had heard that Tardier was already out of hospital and booked on a shuttle flight home. There was a queue of people waiting for a lift home and a priority list. As a result, the two remaining S2 shuttles were on continuous turnaround. Although well equipped, the Lunar Hospital lacked specialist facilities in some fields and so injuries with difficult complications, such as severed limbs, would be treated on Earth.

Only one of the S2s was fitted with a MEDEVAC Pod. The other ship, the LSS *Ares*, retained its Assault Pod, but that pod's twenty seats were good for the walking wounded. Unfortunately, Richard had ordered that the *Ares* be pulled from the programme for a few hours in order to have an area of blast damage repaired.

Richard checked the time; his duty day would start at eight o'clock, which gave him plenty of time to visit Chris and John and finalise his report – he would mention all of his team in dispatches – and then get back to his Unit for a shower, a bite to eat with Rachel and a change of clothes. He was expecting to fly two round trips to Earth.

Richard had also decided to recommend all the pilots of Black Formation for permanent residency in the colony as a result of their actions – should they wish to move from Earth – and he knew Chris would be very interested in an appointment to Andromeda's Shuttle Wing. Certainly he would be glad to have him in the squadron.

Disturbed from his thoughts as one of the automatic swing doors opened with a whoosh, Richard turned and looked back at the middle-aged nurse who was now standing in the doorway. She looked tired. Richard smiled at her.

"You can come in now, Commander," she said, her Scottish accent pronounced.

# CHAPTER 29

## AUTOMATED EVIL

**Squadron Offices – Shuttle Wing**
**15:54 Lunar Corrected Time**

"Yes . . . Richard Reece here!"

"Richard . . . Peter Rothschild. I'm back in Whitehall – have you heard?"

"Good afternoon, Peter. I'm being told a lot of things at the moment, mostly to do with the rebuild. There is a lot of work to be done; re-equipping my squadron is just one job – it's going to take months."

"I mean about the *Enigma*."

"Nothing specific."

"She successfully entered a high Earth orbit at 12:04, and has now descended to a seventy-five per cent elliopheric holding orbit . . . She's come home, and there are a lot of relieved faces in the Federation, I can tell you."

"Any damage?"

"The Federation are still trying to establish communications – so far nothing at all from EMILY. However, the approach and entry procedures were executed in a textbook fashion apparently, so people are relaxing here."

"What's the next move?"

"She will be prepared for future Space flights, as funding will allow. Professor Nieve is arranging a visit. The Federation will use a servicing vehicle to take him and a number of other scientists and engineers."

"Any idea where she's been the last four years or so?"

"Yes, as a matter of fact. Staff on Osiris Base made the initial calculations a few days ago and the Science Council has just verified their results."

"And?"

"She's been to the star duo known collectively as Sirius . . . and that's official. To be more precise, she had a close encounter with a planet that orbits Sirius B."

Richard's eyes widened with surprise. He immediately thought of the Great Pyramid on the Giza Plateau and its association with that star by way of a precisely aligned shaft that runs from the central Queen's Chamber to the extremity of the structure.

"But that's impossible," he said. "The Sirius pairing is eight point six light years away; that's a round trip of more than seventeen light years!"

"It appears that the *Enigma* has been travelling in time – by slipping into another dimension. Scientists here are very excited by that. I'm not a scientist myself, as you know, but the thought of time travel is somewhat enlivening."

Richard nodded knowingly; he knew well enough of Hayden's Second Law. But he felt awkward about the news. His natural distrust of robots made him highly sceptical, and EMILY was certainly no exception. "The Federation should put their heads before their hearts on this, Peter . . . or their coffers, for that matter – that's my advice."

"Always one to put a damper on things, Richard. I'll have you know that there is a lot of optimism here regarding EMILY and where she has been."

Richard reflected on Rothschild's news for a few moments. "All the evidence that I have accrued – and it is substantial – points to the 'old people' arriving here from a planet in the Sirius system. Don't you think that's a bit of a coincidence?"

"Let's not go there again, Richard. We both know the Federation's scepticism on that matter."

"The colonialist theory is well documented and the Sirius system *is* the axis. I've never understood why the Federation has taken the line it has."

"Because of the implications, Richard! You know that as well as I do. The Vatican has never budged and never will – it's the fundamental belief. We are going over old ground again."

"History repeating itself again more like . . . It's like going back to the time of Copernicus and Galileo, when the Church refused to believe that our Solar System was sun-centred and not Earth-centred. The colonist theory was brushed under the carpet, so to speak, by the religious communities, more particularly by the creationalist movements. No . . . it's too much of a coincidence that EMILY should choose to revisit the Sirius B system. What if it is our ancestral home? Have you thought about that?"

"Personally, I always thought the colonialist theory was a bit far-fetched. All the same, I thought that you would appreciate the information."

"I do, Peter – thanks very much." Richard paused; he knew there was no point in pressing his concerns – nobody seemed to share them. "Anyway," he said, in a resigned tone, "while I've got you on the phone, did Madame Vallogia and Asharf Makkoum make it back to Cairo without undue inconvenience?"

"They are on their way. I believe their flight lands a little later this evening. I informed Professor Mubarakar as a matter of course and he insisted on providing a suitable vehicle to meet them at the airport."

"Very good . . . thanks. Well, keep in touch, Peter, and I'll do the same." With that Richard replaced the receiver.

Richard drew a deep breath and leaned back in his chair thoughtfully. He was suspicious of the coincidence. The Sirius system . . . more particularly Sirius B. *If EMILY wanted to travel to a star, why not Alpha Centauri – that one was half the distance,* he thought. He considered the

'Sirius shaft', engineered within the Great Pyramid, and he recalled the wooden trap, some way along that shaft that was installed by the builders of that monument for a specific purpose. It had remained closed for thousands of years, but he had deciphered an inscription during his search for the Ark of the Light that had allowed Naomi, Asharf and him to open the door – albeit temporarily. Indeed, they had escaped through it after being attacked by Humatrons inside the pyramid.

After a few moments of deliberation, Richard checked the time, re-read the last paragraph of his report, and then dismissed all thoughts of history and the colonies, and the old people.

## CHAPTER 30

# PREVIOUS PANDEMIC

Richard was in the squadron's maintenance facility inspecting an extensive skin repair on the Lunar Space Ship *Ares* when a woman's voice echoed around the domed, hanger building; she called for his immediate attention.

"Commander Reece is requested to take an urgent video call in his office. Urgent call for Commander Reece, please."

"Dammed PA," said Richard to his Chief Engineer. "Never any time . . . Listen Chief, it looks good to me. Ask the Duty Officer to nominate two pilots for the test flight – I want experienced pilots, none of the new guys. Initially, limit their altitude to ninety thousand feet until you can analyse the stress data. After that, and if all's well, they can complete the test schedule – let me know the results. We are due to resume the medical evacuation programme at 21:00 hours."

"Yes, Commander – I'm onto it," responded the engineer.

Richard quickened his step towards a communications point in the hangar. He picked up the receiver and pushed a key on the pad. "Commander Reece here," he said. "Apparently I've got a call coming in. Who is it?"

"It's a conference call, sir. Set up by London. I understand the Space Federation is also participating. I've patched it through to your office at the request of Mr Peter Rothschild in Whitehall. The signal is scrambled, sir – highest security directive. I've taken the liberty of posting two security officers outside your door."

Richard shook his head and then growled: "What the hell is it this time! Okay . . . I'm on my way, tell them."

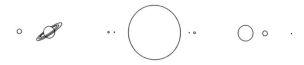

Richard arrived promptly at his office and returned a salute from the two uniformed and armed security guards; they stood ominously on either side of his door.

*Seems a bit of overkill,* he thought, as one of the men closed the door behind him. He strode over to his desk and collapsed into his high-backed swivel chair and simultaneously pressed a button on his desktop that resulted in a large screen rising up. The screen burst into life and an image of Peter Rothschild quickly sharpened. The words 'Audiovisual Confirmed' and 'Security – President Level Class 1' appeared along the bottom of the screen, along with a number of small, square, live portraits of the people linked to the conference call – one was General Roper in Florida and another was Professor Nieve, with the word 'London' appearing below his head.

"Sorry, everyone . . . been busy in the maintenance department. There's a lot of clearing up to do, as you can imagine." Richard said, realising that he may have appeared a little less respectful than he ought, considering who he was looking at in the other portrait blocks. He settled into his chair as Rothschild spoke.

Peter Rothschild – whose earlier expression of satisfaction and optimism appeared to have completely disappeared – commenced the proceedings. "Richard – bit of a scare on . . . we need information."

"If I can! What is it?"

"You will recall several days ago that you gave me a polythene forensic pouch containing a small amount of dust and sediment that you said came from inside the Ark of the Light. Please can you enlighten us a little on this matter?"

Richard was surprised; he had forgotten about the

pouch and what it contained. His eyes narrowed as he recalled the events. "Er, yes, I suppose so. Madame Vallogia . . . she is a Master of the Antiquities, as you know. When it comes to the processes involved with restoring ancient artefacts she dots every i and crosses every t. As it was described to me, the sediment is what was brushed from the inside of the Ark and scraped from the corners. She did this immediately prior to the renovation programme commencing."

"Could the material sample in the pouch have been contaminated?"

"Unlikely, I'd say. Those pouches are triple sealed – completely airtight by nature. I would imagine that there would be some oxidation of the deposit; after all, it's probably thousands of years old."

"That's what we are concerned about," said Rothschild with a frown. "Please, carry on."

"Well, that's it really . . . nothing was ever placed in the Ark . . . not that I know. Why don't you call Madame Vallogia herself?"

"She's in Cairo somewhere and we can't get in touch with her. Anything else, Richard . . . your thoughts, perhaps?"

"My thoughts . . . ?" Richard shrugged. "The deposit will most probably contain atmospheric elements present at the time that the Ark was constructed; there will be oxidation, particularly with material from the corners, where you tend to get a timely build-up and perhaps a skin forming. There might even be microscopic samples of bacteria or similar. If a gas chromatograph is used it may be possible to isolate some of the elements that made up the atmosphere at the time – learn something of the conditions present when the Ark was made – give a clue to where it actually came from."

"The chromatographic process has already been completed, and so too a microbiological analysis," Professor Nieve interjected. "And that's our problem!"

Richard pressed a button on his control panel that switched Rothschild's image to half screen size and moved it to his left. The current speaker then automatically came into frame on his right. Professor Nieve's concerned expression unnerved Richard.

"What is it, Professor – what's the problem?"

Professor Nieve ignored Richard's question and instead asked one of his own. "Commander, we all know your belief – from your experiences – that the 'old people', the colonists, came from a planet in the Sirius system. I myself am in two minds, but most here remain highly sceptical of the entire hypothesis, as you can understand. However, despite a wash of cynicism from the scientific community, we now have unequivocal evidence that the *Enigma* has visited the Sirius sector, more particularly a lifeless planet that orbits Sirius B."

Richard nodded. "Yes, I have heard about that." He looked at Rothschild.

"Recent research carried out by the Osiris Science Officer on Mars has revealed that the planet in question was at one point in its history very similar to the Earth –

by that I mean the conditions on its surface. It is highly probable that it could have supported life similar to our own. That is before the star Sirius B itself became unstable and expanded to become a red giant. We have analysed the samples from the Ark and discovered remnants of nitrogen, oxygen, argon and carbon dioxide in almost the exact proportions that we find here on Earth . . ."

"This is 'Goldilocks' stuff! With all due respect, Professor, you'd better get on with it," barked General Roper. "We are running out of time. Our ship is due to dock in a few hours!"

Professor Nieve looked to his right and then back at Richard. "Based on our gas analysis, the Ark could have been made here on Earth, Commander, but equally, it could have been made elsewhere."

Richard looked confused. "If you are asking my opinion as to whether the Ark of the Light was constructed here on Earth, or alternatively, before the colonists left their home planet, then I would say the latter. Why would they bring the materials and do the job on a new planet? Why? It makes no sense. They used the Ark to carry their last remaining crystals, the Kalahari crystals – that are essentially unstable. Eridu, Babylon . . . even Atlantis, they were all powered by the crystals."

"Atlantis!" exclaimed an official off-screen. "Let us be serious here, please!"

Richard knew it was a mistake to mention Atlantis; it only served to undermine his credibility. He paused and looked at the row of faces in portrait. "The Ark was constructed elsewhere, on the home planet – that's always been my belief!" he said forcibly.

Professor Nieve addressed a colleague. "Professor Varela, if you would?"

The image of a younger scientist wearing a white laboratory coat appeared on the right-hand split screen. He looked to be in his late thirties and wore a pair of frameless spectacles that clipped into a tiny peg set in the bridge of his nose. His hair was dark and balding. Richard noticed that another three people had joined the conference, making a total of fourteen. The names included prominent members of the ISSF Council, the UK's Health Minister and the World Health Organisation's current president.

"Get on with it . . . goddamn scientists!" General Roper was heard to say. He was off-screen and clearly his words were not meant to be heard.

Professor Varela was in a brightly lit laboratory. The word 'Geneva' appeared beneath his name on the screen. Richard magnified his image to near life size. He looked pale and stressed. He stood behind a white-topped table on which there were numerous instruments and, to his right, Richard recognised a compact Shultzer electron microscope. He looked like a science teacher explaining a classroom experiment with his arms folded in front of him. Occasionally he peered over his spectacles at someone off-screen. He was waiting for a sign.

"Everyone is now seated Matthew, please," said Professor Nieve.

Matthew Varela nodded and looked into his camera. "What we have found in the material sample from the ancient artefact has grave consequences for us all," he said in good English and with a slight Germanic accent. His manner was open but restrained. "Initially, we ran a routine sweep for prokaryote micro-organisms . . . bacteria to the layman. We did not expect to find anything unusual, indeed the sample material was analysed in one of our general, outlying laboratories." Varela paused momentarily. "What we discovered, however, was isolated cells of *Yersinia pestis*." Varela paused again to add weight to his words. His brow furrowed as he stared above his spectacles. "Ladies and gentlemen," he continued, "this is the bacterium that causes bubonic plague."

There was a gasp from the audience.

Varela shifted his weight between legs and for a moment appeared nervous. Then he raised a hand. "We quickly brought the material here to our central facility and ran a much broader check whilst instigating an isolation initiative," he explained. "This sweep revealed viral samples – but not just common examples as one finds in . . . soil, or food, for instance, but samples that specifically cause infectious disease in humans – namely influenza."

There was a flurry of conversation among the audience.

"It could be argued that diseases such as plague and flu have been infecting man for as long as he has been on this planet," continued Varela. "Epidemics and pandemics have raged and waned throughout recorded history – and so we were concerned, but not overly so. After all, current treatments have a broad range and are effective. Nevertheless, we decided to isolate the viral strain and categorise it, and we found that it is related to the H1N1 strain – a subtype of the influenza A virus. Now, this 'Ark of the Light' artefact that has been referred to, it could have been constructed during a local flu outbreak, or even perhaps during an epidemic. However – and this is our problem – we further compared this virus to all current types of influenza virus . . . H1N2, H3N1, H3N2, H2N3, swine influenza virus . . . SIV, but there was no exact match, although we found a common protein, a protein that was also present in the avian flu pandemic of two thousand and twenty-six. So we also referenced the so called Spanish flu pandemic of nineteen eighteen, an unusually severe and deadly strain of avian influenza that killed fifty to one hundred million people worldwide over about twelve months during nineteen eighteen and nineteen nineteen – incidentally, thought to be one of the most deadly pandemics in human history – and again there was a link . . . the same protein!"

"With all due respect, Professor," said General Roper impatiently, "what are you saying here, that the people who built the Ark had colds?"

Professor Varela shrugged. "Quite possibly, General, or at least that examples of the virus and bacteria in question were present in the air – there would be a level of immunity to these infections, though. But *when* they built the Ark, that's the astonishing thing."

"What do you mean?"

"Because we could not find an exact match, we ran a computer-based mutation model – a kind of evolutionary process in reverse. That's when we raised the alarm."

"Tell us, man, for God's sake," said Roper, unable to restrain himself.

Varela sighed and glanced at General Roper, as if to say 'such exacting science cannot be rushed'. "By running the mutation model," he said, "and going back in time, so to speak, we did find a match – an exact match." Varela picked up an electronic tablet reader from the table top and referred to it. "As far as the strains of influenza virus that infects humans are concerned, we think we have found in the sample material the *original* form – the forerunner to the mutation process – the very first influenza A virus!"

"How many years ago?" interjected Richard, sitting up straight in his chair. "As far as the computer programme goes, I mean. How many years ago does this 'exact' match occur . . . ? What I'm asking is how long did the mutation cycle take . . . ?"

"At least ten thousand years!"

"So what you are saying is that the virus and bacteria found in the Ark is a snapshot of their form in what . . . eight thousand BC? And from that form, the influenza A virus and the strains present today have gradually evolved?"

"Yes . . . correct."

Richard looked at Rothschild. This revelation was adding considerable weight to his colonist hypothesis.

"I don't understand what the problem is!" interjected General Roper, who looked away from the screen and then back at Professor Varela.

"It has taken thousands of years and two billion deaths for the human race to acquire the immunity it has against the current strains of virus and bacteria that populate our planet, General," explained Varela. "These basic life forms are continuously changing, mutating, probing our natural defences – we are constantly exposed to them. Those who aren't, those who live in isolation, lose their resistance – not to mention the allergy question. We know that periodically such pathogens get the upper hand. That's when epidemics and pandemics occur. It's been the case throughout our history – the bubonic plague, the flu pandemics of the last four decades, including avian and bovine flu. Drugs are only successful to a point; it's our own immune systems that must evolve. But the pathogens that we have discovered in the sample provided by Commander Reece, and taken from the ancient artefact, are primitive pathogens – in their original form. Such a form would be alien to us here on Earth. We would have no natural protection against it and producing a vaccine would require living specimens and would take at least six weeks."

"But can't you resuscitate viruses, Matthew?" Professor Nieve asked, as microbiology wasn't his field. "Certain strains have been known to survive for millennia and in extremely inhospitable conditions!"

Professor Varela shook his head. "Unfortunately that is no longer possible," he replied. "When we realised what we were dealing with and to prevent any accidents, we radiated the cells with gamma rays to ensure all life processes were terminated."

"To sum this up then," Richard interjected. "The Ark of the Light, before it was recently cleaned and renovated, contained a dormant strain of influenza virus that humankind has no resistance to and also samples of the bacteria that causes bubonic plague?"

Varela nodded. "That is correct," he said.

"Okay . . . let's go further with this." Richard rubbed his brow and then ran his hand over his head. "The Ark was built by the 'old people' . . . we know this because the materials used in its construction are not to be found on planet Earth. The old people were colonists and believed to originate from a planet in the Sirius B system – let's not mention the irrefutable historical evidence at this point – and the *Enigma*, a spacecraft controlled by the malevolent computer EMILY, is now in orbit having returned from a round trip to Homer, the planet referred to by the old people as their home planet." Richard paused at the realisation. "Then you were right to raise the alarm, Professor Varela. I'd say we have a problem alright . . . a big problem . . . one the size of the *Enigma* in fact!"

General Roper raised his hand. "Hold on!" he implored. "Before we press the button on this and cause worldwide panic. We do not know why these 'colonists' left the planet they called Homer." He looked at Professor Nieve.

"We know that Sirius B was a normal star that gradually turned into a red giant. Radiation output from stars undergoing these death throes increases markedly and the physical dimensions of the star similarly. But this does not happen overnight. It is a gradual process taking many thousands of years. However, as we understand it, all life on a planet such as Homer would die quite early in the process."

"How long would a civilisation survive after discovering that their star was becoming a red giant?"

"That is a very difficult question to answer, General, because there are so many variables; much depends on the complexity of the civilisation."

"Make a qualified guess please, Professor."

Professor Nieve thought for a moment. "The atmospheric temperature would increase at a prescribed rate – slowly at first and then accelerating as greenhouse gasses increased. Radiation levels would also increase. Eventually the protective layers, such as the Van Allen belts around our planet, would break down and high energy cosmic radiation would reach the surface. Thereafter everything would die – even at relatively deep subterranean levels."

"So how long?"

Professor Nieve shook his head. "How long is a piece of string?"

"Please Professor," pressed the General, "give us a

ball park figure . . . five hundred years . . . ? More? Less?"

"In the case of the Sirius system, where we have a good deal of astronomical data, I would estimate a century at most."

"So if the civilisation inhabiting such a planet has not already ventured into Space at that point, you would expect there to be a concerted effort to do so."

"We are ourselves living proof of what can be achieved in a mere century, General Roper."

"If it was to take longer than that . . . say, five hundred years," someone else started, "then what would be the first effects?"

"We have run numerous simulations over the years in an effort to ascertain the effects on Earth should the solar radiation output from our sun increase. We found in all cases that there was a blooming of microbiological activity as a result of the initial increase in temperature. An increase of one to five degrees Celsius is all it takes and then the micro-organism populations go viral, so to speak."

"You include bacteria as well as viruses in that group?"

"Yes, of course. Here on Earth, for example, our environment would be swamped by harmful as well as helpful bacteria and viruses. The most deadly strains of pathogens would increase proportionally to other micro-organisms, perhaps more so. The present human population of this planet is more than sixteen billion, infection would spread very quickly."

"Is that why these colonists left their home planet?"

"It is possible, General, yes. But more likely they left because of the temperature and radiation increase. As I said, the viral and bacterial manifestation would be consequential, and this higher concentration is essentially, and probably quite accurately, recorded in the sample from the Ark."

"Could we get back to our specific concern?" asked the UK's Health Minister. She was a woman in her late fifties. "What confronts us has the potential to be more than a pandemic. From your simulation, Professor Varela, should such a pathogen be released in our atmosphere, what would the results be and in what time frame?"

"That's an easy question, Madame," replied Varela. "The entire population of the Earth would be eradicated within a month."

There was a collective gasp.

"Sorry, but that's my position on it," Varela continued. "As I said, there would be no time to acquire immunity or develop a vaccine. As a virulent strain of flu the infection would sweep through the world's population unabated. There would be no place to hide. The subterranean colonies would be incubators."

"And that's it?"

Professor Varela shrugged. "Some small mammals may survive; those who live in isolation – probably on islands. It would be like the end of the dinosaur era, when the meteorite collided with the Earth and formed the Gulf of Mexico. This planet would eventually repopulate with other species that had a natural immunity. In time a new dominant species would evolve – they may be like us, they may not."

That disclosure kicked off numerous conversations – some between members of the panel and some in their vicinity. Gradually, the volume increased. Richard checked the time; it was less than an hour to his planned take-off. He would have no influence on the meeting's outcome. Even if the panel made a decision it would need to go to the Federation Council for final approval. *Damned bureaucracy,* he thought, *unless something was done quickly, EMILY will have her revenge.*

Richard pressed a button on his panel that called Peter Rothschild. Rothschild, in London, gave Richard his attention. "Peter, I've got a humanitarian flight at twenty-one hundred hours," he explained. "Over to the Cityport – patients for specialist treatment in Guy's Hospital. I'm not required here anymore so I'm leaving . . . okay?"

Rothschild nodded his approval and then turned back to his previous conversation.

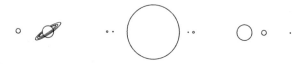

As Richard established a high orbit and reprogrammed the navigation computer with coordinates for the re-entry phase, he suddenly saw the *Enigma* appear on the horizon from behind the Earth. She was an impressive sight; her massive, ominous, dark grey hull and those long, thin, characteristic thrust tubes. She was far too distant for Richard to pick out any detail and with the sun behind her she was primarily in silhouette, but he somehow sensed that EMILY had her laser initiator trained on him and he began to feel decidedly uneasy.

Richard was about to call Canaveral in order to coordinate his re-entry when out of the corner of his eye on the left side of the *Ares,* and way below, he saw a small servicing vessel zoom past. The vessel was on a direct course for the *Enigma.* He was surprised. Clearly no decision had been reached by the Federation as to the contamination issue and a rendezvous was still on the cards. He tracked the small spacecraft as it passed from the Southern Hemisphere to the Northern Hemisphere and sped towards the great hulk. A bright white stroboscopic flash every ten seconds made the vessel stand out against the reflective cloud as it neared the edge of the Earth's disc.

Richard selected the frequency allocated by Space Control to the *Enigma* – a dedicated frequency for orbital coordination and general communications. He listened for a few minutes, but all was silent. He knew how important the *Enigma* was to the Federation for ongoing research and future Space missions, and also there was the prohibitive cost of replacing her, but surely their intentions were not to placate EMILY – or humour her for the sake of her technology and experience. Surely they couldn't ignore the fact that she had swept through the atmosphere of the planet Homer, and may now be contaminated with a deadly virus. *Delaying a move against her – even a precautionary move – is like playing with fire,* he thought. Richard looked at Yannick, his co-pilot, and nodded his approval to commence the re-entry profile. Moments later the autopilot selected five degrees nose down.

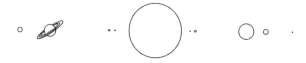

Passing over the East Coast of Iceland at 86,000 feet on a course for London, and with *Enigma*'s Space frequency still selected, Richard was paying attention to his instruments when suddenly there was an anxious radio transmission: *"Terminate Docking Sequence. Initiate Abort Code 666. No contact. Do you copy? No contact."*

Richard knew exactly who that transmission was directed at. Something had happened! *Someone on the Federation Council seeing sense at last,* he speculated. If so they had certainly left it late, as Abort Code 666 was an emergency directive. Richard turned his attention to the approach phase as the *Ares* disappeared into cloud. They would land in fifteen minutes and Richard would call Rothschild.

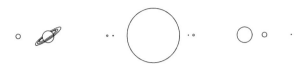

No sooner was Richard in the terminal building when his telepager rang. He pulled it from the breast pocket of his flight suit and looked at the small screen to see Rothschild's name flashing.

"Yes, Peter."

"There's a car waiting for you – outside 'Arrivals'. Come to my office please . . . quickly!"

Richard attracted the attention of his young co-pilot, Yannick Vuylsteke, who was arranging a refuel with the handling agent. Richard pointed to his chronometer and raised a finger indicating one hour. Yannick nodded and Richard promptly left the building.

There were three black sedans outside the Arrivals Hall. As Richard approached them, the hazard lights on the leading vehicle flashed a few times and Richard quickly climbed into the back of it. The sedan's wheels screeched as it pulled away. Richard was settling in for the twenty-minute drive when his pager rang again.

"I'm on my way, Peter . . . What's happening?"

Rothschild seemed uncharacteristically flustered. "The Council decided to abort the rendezvous," he answered. "Until the contamination question could be clarified. The servicing vessel was alongside when it aborted the docking sequence. As it changed course, EMILY vaporised it with her laser."

"What!"

"Nobody could believe it. General Roper has declared it an open act of aggression and launched an attack!"

"Bloody hell! But with what?"

"There's not much available. Sentinel Wing has around five Delta Class fighters remaining; they are already engaging."

Richard closed his eyes and held the bridge of his nose. "Not Doug Winton . . ." he mumbled.

"What did you say?"

"I said it's suicide, Peter. We all know it's suicide."

"And there is something else!" said Rothschild, after a pause of realisation.

"What is it?"

"There had been no answer from EMILY on the radio, despite frequent calls by Space Control on a dedicated frequency – but EMILY spoke a few minutes ago."

"Go on!"

"I've got a recording . . . I'll play it to you."

Richard listened intently.

"*You may now know my intentions, but you cannot stop me. Soon the entire human race will be eradicated.*" EMILY's synthetic voice seemed surreal, but it was also laced with spite and malice.

"That's it?"

"That is all of it. She has said nothing else since. Look, Richard, the Federation are unsure of their next move – we are very poorly placed. Do you have any ideas?"

"Is there another way that she can get the virus to the surface?"

"The Council asked the same question . . . Professor Nieve told them that there are atmospheric sample pods on board."

Richard leaned forward and tapped the driver on the shoulder. When Richard had his attention he turned his finger in a circle and pointed back the way they had come and gestured with his head, and then he flopped back in his seat and thought for a moment.

"Are you there?"

"Yes, Peter, I'm here. I've got a plan. It's a long shot, but it's better than nothing. We are turning around. I'm going back. Call the Handling Agent at the Cityport. Get a message to my co-pilot to prepare the *Ares* for flight. I'll call you back!"

# CHAPTER 31

## POWERLESS

Richard was already halfway out of the door when the sedan screeched to a halt. He ran towards a set of double doors that had a bold sign overhead reading: 'VIP Departures'. He leaped the three sets of stone steps leading up to them in as many strides. A security guard stepped aside as the doors opened automatically and Richard ran into the building. He stopped momentarily to get his bearings but Peter Rothschild had made the requested call and consequently an executive approached Richard immediately.

"This way, sir," she said and pointed to another door on the opposite side of the foyer. It had a sign over it that read: 'Royal Access'.

The route through security and immigration lay wide open and when Richard cleared those departments the woman opened a staff access door that allowed Richard onto the apron. He sprinted towards the shuttle. The auxiliary power unit was already running and Richard knew that Yannick had already commenced the flight prep. *It will be difficult to say no to the young man this time,* Richard thought. He quickly glanced at the structure of the S2 as he approached, checking for any obvious panels left open, or ground equipment still attached, but all seemed in order and he subsequently leapt up the short flight of personnel steps. Turning to press a button that raised the steps, Richard shouted: "Yannick, get onto the tower, we need to start clearance . . . and an unrestricted climb to fifty per cent elliopheric!"

"Aye aye, sir!" was the reply.

Richard checked the door mechanism and the green light that signified its correct closure and then he rushed through a doorway and along the short, narrow, corridor that led into the flight deck. Yannick was in his seat on the right-hand side, fully kitted and with his helmet on the cowling next to him. He turned. Richard knew that expectant expression only too well.

"This is going to be dangerous . . . we may not . . ."

"Prestart checks completed, Commander. All systems green. And I have start clearance . . ."

"Okay, Yannick, you're on – start the engines!" said Richard, nodding his approval. Richard climbed into his seat and began strapping in.

"I'm to call back for take-off clearance, sir."

Richard nodded again. "Copied," he said, and made a selection on his communications panel that opened a satellite telecom link. He pressed a series of keys on the panel and dialled in Mubarakar's mobile telephone number. It rang for several seconds but there was no answer. "Damn it!"

"Starting number two," said Yannick.

Richard pressed another key on the panel and selected "Open speaker". He redialled Mubarakar's number – again there was no answer. This time Richard let it ring. He set about connecting his life support system and checked his oxygen supply. The double ringtone reverberated around the flight deck. To Richard it seemed to grow louder each time, like an assertion of failure. He shook his head. "*Damn it!*" he complained. Yannick looked at him with a troubled expression. Richard quickly dialled another number. After a few ringtones someone picked up.

"Rothschild!"

"Peter, Richard here, lift-off in two minutes but I can't get hold of Mubarakar . . . What's the situation?"

"General Roper has sent what's left of Sentinel Wing against EMILY, but she's destroyed three fighters and sent two home badly damaged. There's not much else . . ."

"For God's sake, why? It's suicide against that laser system, we all know that. It's designed to pinpoint Space debris in the ship's path when she's travelling at light-related speeds; it's the most potent weapon system ever . . ."

all he's done is played our hand . . . and it's a losing one!"

"This is life and death! They will throw everything they have at her."

"Where is the *Enigma* now?"

"Wait a minute . . . I have a monitor linked to mission control in Canaveral and an open line to the General." There was a pause. "Apparently, she is over the United States at seventy-two per cent elliopheric. Her orbital concentricity is decreasing. Roper says that when she reaches fifty-eight per cent she will release whatever it is that contains the pathogens."

"Both engines started and in the green, sir," said Yannick.

"Good, start the retros! Go on, Peter."

"Professor Nieve has recalled the serial numbers of the atmospheric sample pods that *Enigma* carried on her inventory during her maiden voyage. I'm told that they are a Type Four. For such flightless vehicles to reach the surface without overheating there is a specific re-entry profile. However, this type of profile has very narrow parameters. It was originally devised to return satellites to Earth when their power cells were depleted."

"Yes, I know of it . . ."

"Canaveral Centre has recalculated those re-entry coordinates . . ."

"*And* . . ."

"The S2 cannot track a Type Four, Richard, the profile is too steep – your ship would break up."

"What about the laser? Selected to manual?"

Rothschild paused again to check data. "Canaveral has run the simulation. They said it would be a lucky shot – the fate of humankind on a lucky shot!"

Richard shook his head. "Are they sure that's the only delivery system available on the *Enigma*? I mean, EMILY would know the risks associated with that profile, too . . . she's been a long way to get those pathogens . . . it works both ways."

"Professor Nieve has said that there is nothing onboard the *Enigma* that could double as a controllable delivery system and only an astroengineer would have the knowledge and skill to modify one of the sample pods in their inventory. Even if Gregory Searle is alive, he certainly does not have those capabilities."

"So the Professor thinks that EMILY is committed?"

"In more ways than one!"

Richard nodded his understanding – it was clear that the odds were stacked heavily against them. The Dispatcher outside caught Richard's eye; he was waving his arms in a desperate attempt to attract Richard's attention. When Richard looked at him, the man gave an 'away chocks' hand signal. Richard looked down; he had deselected the ground controller's frequency. "Oh shit!" he cursed and with his thumbs rolling outwards he gave the man the signal to go ahead and remove the restrainers. The Dispatcher pressed something in his hand and hydraulic clamps detached from the landing gear struts and descended into the concrete. A light extinguished on the instrument panel.

Undeterred by Rothschild's news, Richard looked across at Yannick and said: "Ask for take-off, will you?" Then he turned his attention back to Rothschild. "Because of that direct attack, Peter, EMILY knows her secret is out. She will be on full alert and expecting more of the same. She also knows that a pod in free-fall is fair game. In other words, she will expect us to target it during re-entry and will use her weapon control and laser system to cover the pod's trajectory until it is low enough to open." Richard tapped the instrument panel cowling nervously. He had another idea, but it would have implications – possibly criminal implications. *I will cross that bridge when I come to it,* he thought. "Listen, Peter, I have an idea, and for it to work the window of opportunity is very limited . . ."

"We have take-off clearance, Commander," interjected Yannick.

"Richard, what is your plan?"

"I haven't time to explain, Peter, sorry. But I need to talk to Mubarakar. Let Roper know that I'm lifting from London Cityport and climbing directly to seventy per cent elliopheric. For this idea to work the *Ares* will be bait . . . I'll call you back!"

Richard glanced at his co-pilot. "Checklist, Yannick!"

"Completed, Commander."

"Copied! Well done! You have control. Vertical climb to the Compton Gate and then join the Dover Four Bravo transition . . ."

"Me, sir?"

"Yes you! Don't forget, we've not much fuel and so we're very light. All the same use eighty per cent combined thrust – forget burning the tarmac. When established in the transition, call London Control for an uninterrupted climb. I need to make another call."

Richard redialled Professor Mubarakar's number and pressed the initiate button. He listened intently to the calling tone and to his dismay the number continued to ring. Feeling distinctly uneasy he cut off the call and tried again.

Suddenly someone answered; Richard's relief was palpable. "Hello," the man said, and Richard instantly recognised Mubarakar's deep, resonant tone.

"Professor, it's Richard, I've been trying to get hold of you . . . Is Naomi with you?"

"Yes, Richard. Madame is here and Asharf, too."

"What about the machine, professor . . . ? Did it work?"

"It is incredible, my young friend. Madame first tried the more modern languages, those that she speaks easily – Arabic and Latin – but to no avail. Then Coptic and Ancient Egyptian where she has less fluency – again it did not respond. But it seems that there is enough commonality between the old language of Atlantis and Ancient Greek for the figure to understand. It moves, my boy . . . it moves!"

"Where are you, exactly?"

"We approach the Plateau of Giza. There is a

religious festival here . . . a national holiday! Today of all days, the way is clear."

"Good! Please, Professor. Be specific. How long until you reach the Great Pyramid?"

"Ten minutes, not more . . . and then another ten to gain entry. Madame has taken me into her confidence. She will take me inside – to see the fabled temple. The machine moves slowly but precisely."

"Okay, now please listen, Professor. The experiment continues. I'll explain later. Do you have a watch?"

"Of course! I have my trusted pocket watch, handed down to me by my father. The mechanism is a century old but it keeps perfect time."

Richard paused. "We have a critical situation but I have an idea. For it to work, everything depends on timing. I cannot emphasise that enough, Professor. There is something I want you to do and you must be absolutely precise in your timing – a second too soon or a second too late and I will fail. But first you must set your watch to Universal Corrected Time."

"Yes, I understand. I adjust it now. What time do you have?"

"On the third mark it will be fourteen zero six. Six minutes after two precisely . . . Now, now, now!"

"I have it!"

"Good. *14:30* . . . that is the critical time. That's when Asharf must open the trap door. The secret lies in the Queen's Chamber – he will remember, and Naomi will, too."

"But there is nothing in the Queen's Chamber. Only the outline of a granite sarcophagus that was broken-up and removed in the eighteenth century!"

"That sarcophagus was placed there more than a thousand years after the pyramid was completed, Professor. You'll have to trust me on this. The chamber has another purpose – the original purpose. It is why it has a volume of precisely nine cubits and the ceiling is 'V'-shaped to concentrate energy, and why the walls and the ceiling are of such thick granite and why they are blackened as if by fire and cannot be cleaned. Go there first. There are inscriptions inside a square shaft . . . and a code to open a trap door inside that shaft. The trapdoor is a valve, Professor, like an old Light Emitting Diode. Only then should you all go to the Temple of Osiris. Tell that to Naomi. She will know what to do with the crystal – but only at fourteen-thirty. You must ensure that the shaft that points to Sirius is opened by fourteen-thirty!"

"Yes! Yes! It will be done. After a lifetime of questions things become clear . . . If I die tomorrow, I will be happy."

Richard smirked to himself at the thought of Mubarakar's enlightenment. He wished that he could see the Professor's beaming face when Naomi placed her hand in the recess and the secret door opened between the King's Chamber and the Great Temple. "I may not speak to you again, Professor," Richard said finally and in a subdued tone. "I wish you good luck."

"We *will* speak again, young friend."

With that, Richard closed the channel.

Richard snapped back to reality. Yannick glanced at him wide eyed. Richard looked up at his instrument panel. The altimeter was passing 10,000 feet and climbing rapidly and the speed was 500 knots. Everything seemed under control. He gave a brief smile to Yannick. "Good flying," he said. "Now, what's the outbound clearance?"

"We are approaching Dover, Commander, and clear to Flight Level Four Three Zero. Supersonic approved after Dover – Mach 5 initially. Then an unrestricted climb to seventy per cent. British Control has opened a corridor for us." Yannick's expression of bewilderment refused to shift.

"Disregard the restriction at Dover – accelerate to Mach 10. Do it now Yannick, and we will not follow the corridor either!"

"But what about the sonic boom over London?"

Richard shook his head dismissively and then reached forward and disconnected the autopilot.

As 'Pilot Flying', Yannick immediately assumed control. Now clearly astonished, he looked across at Richard. "But that is our clearance, sir!"

Richard felt the acceleration through his seat back as Yannick reluctantly opened the thrust levers. He knew an explanation was necessary. "EMILY, the computer controlling the *Enigma* will be monitoring all ATC frequencies," Richard said, skewing in his seat and reaching across the overhead panel to make a switch selection on Yannick's side. "She will have heard that clearance and will be expecting us to follow it. At the moment she doesn't know who we are or what we are doing. But there is very little global air traffic and she will be suspicious of anything launching with orbital capability. She has a very sophisticated sensor system and a laser initiator that can vaporise a pea at ten thousand kilometres. The moment we pass fifty per cent elliopheric she will treat us as a threat. We are going to be a little unorthodox from here on in, Yannick. I have control."

"Er, yes, you have control, sir, you . . ."

"This is British Control calling *Ares* . . . come in *Ares* . . ."

Richard answered: "Five by five, go ahead!"

"Message from Canaveral Centre – the *Enigma* is accelerating. It's not clear why."

"Copied."

Richard looked across at Yannick. "She's on to us," he said, and he rolled the *Ares* – one of the earlier models of the S2 Space Shuttle – into a steep right turn.

Fitted out with an Assault Pod that was all but empty, except for a few items of medical equipment, the *Ares* was unusually light and manoeuvrable. Richard was very familiar with the type and had pushed the edge of the flight envelope once by achieving 120 lutens, but the authorised limit had never been more than 100 lutens and the current limit was 90 – this because most of the fleet was reaching the end of the designed fatigue life. He would need to handle the *Ares* gently and coax every last luten from her if he was to execute his plan successfully *and* avoid EMILY's ruthless aim.

"Sitrep, British!" said Richard.

"She wants a better look at you, currently over Japan and heading west," was the reply over the radio.

"Copied."


As the *Ares* passed 41,000 feet in a rapid climb she punched through the top of the thick, grey and insipid-looking cloud. Above this continuous emulsified layer, which appeared to congeal and cocoon Planet Earth, the brilliance of the sun was merely reflected back into Space. But the light that streamed through the broad, semi-circular windscreen and onto Richard and Yannick was far more welcome. Like an early morning lunar sunrise it filled their artificial microcosm with hope. Richard, however, remained apprehensive. Their southerly course had taken them over Spain, the Straits of Gibraltar and Morocco, and now he would avoid EMILY's interest by turning right over the Atlantic and maintaining his course towards the southern United States and therefore in the opposite hemisphere. He stabilised the speed at a pre-orbital Mach 12. He would delay a further climb for the time being. He checked the ship's chronometer; it read 14:24. He prayed that by now Naomi, Asharf, the Professor and the machine were inside the Temple of Osiris – possibly close to the central altar on which was the chalice.

Richard knew that EMILY had a good idea of where he was and that by nature of his evasive manoeuvres he was now a legitimate target. Her over-the-horizon sensors were effective, but not to the extent of precise tracking in an opposing hemisphere. Nonetheless, she could compute his position fairly accurately by measuring disturbances in the Earth's magnetic field, like whales do when looking for a mate. He could only hope that maliciousness and a lust for revenge against humanity would cloud her thoughts in the final moments of releasing the contaminated pod and allow him to position himself. The radio fell silent because he had left the jurisdiction of Euro Control and had entered that of the North Atlantic region. He flipped to a satellite channel and caught the end of a transmission from Canaveral that called for him to check-in. Yannick's finger hesitated over the transmit button. Richard shook his head. "No more transmissions," he said. "It could compromise us."

Unusually, Richard had decided that he and Yannick should wear their helmets, because in the event of an explosive decompression there would be no time to don them, and if the ship was still flyable it might save their lives. And anyway, in the bright sunlight their visors came in very useful.

"How long do we wait, sir?"

"This is Canaveral Centre transmitting blind. Opposition passing sixty per cent elliopheric – we think this is it – this time over the East Coast. We think November Yankee airspace. I say again . . . this time!"

Richard looked at Yannick with a stern expression. "In order for EMILY to release a Type Four pod and be sure that it does not burn up or even overheat during re-entry, she will need to release it at fifty-eight per cent elliopheric precisely. Then she will cover it's trajectory with her laser weapon until it reaches a suitable level. To disperse incubated micro-organisms most effectively in the current weather conditions the Federation has calculated an opening altitude of seven thousand feet – EMILY will have correlated the same meteorological information and made the same calculation. With the winds as they are at the moment, the East Coast of America is looking most likely – you heard them – they think it will be in New York's Eastern Atlantic region."

Yannick shook his head at the thought of such genocide. "The pod will be in free-fall," he said. "Do you know the parameters? I mean, how do we . . . ?"

Richard raised his hand to quell Yannick's anxiety. "It's a very steep trajectory, I know that. There is a pressure switch and a mechanism that will operate to open the pod at the selected altitude. By the time that happens, it will be over the East Coast. Then the prevailing easterlies will blow the contamination over the remainder of the States. From there, and within a week, the Pacific basin will become infected, and then Asia and then Europe. Within a month everybody is dead from flu or bubonic plague or similar."

Yannick turned pale. "Is anything moving against her?"

Richard shook his head. "Deltas have no chance against her. We went too far with this machine, Yannick, and that's the truth of the matter. I can only hope that the Lunar Senate, having already suffered at the hands of these systems, will ban all systems above Level Six."

"So we are . . ."

"Earth's last hope . . . you got it . . . just you and me against the mighty *Enigma*."

"And you have this plan using the Egyptian pyramids?" Yannick didn't look hopeful.

"The *Great* Pyramid to be precise. Now listen carefully. I've entered the precise coordinates of the pyramid into our navigation computer and, using our stellar database, I've also plotted a back course from the star Sirius B in the Canis Major constellation." Richard pointed at the navigation screen. "You see that line emanating from the pyramid's position?"

Yannick nodded.

"If you extend it, it goes directly to the star."

Yannick sat up straight. "I've got it! You want the *Enigma* to fly through that position." He paused thoughtfully. "Why? What's going to happen to her?"

"Nothing! Not unless she is there at precisely the right time – and even then I'm not sure if anything will come of it."

"But!"

"I'm banking on a communication signal, Yannick. A plasma wave powerful enough to travel over eight light years – don't ask me why."

"At the time you mentioned to your friend . . . fourteen-thirty!"

Richard nodded and checked the chronometer. Yannick's eyes were drawn there, too. The radio crackled.

"This is Canaveral. Be advised, opposition over Tenerife, passing fifty-nine per cent elliopheric. Listen out on coded frequency Theta Four Two Six."

Richard checked his own position. They were close to the mid-Atlantic and heading towards Bermuda. He looked at Yannick and smiled faintly. "She's coming in fast; soon she will have line of sight and fire at us. Now . . . change the frequency as instructed."

Yannick nodded. "Why are we changing the coded frequency again, sir? I don't . . ."

Richard quickly advanced the thrust levers that controlled the S2's two rocket motors and the ship began to accelerate. He checked his instruments as he spoke. "EMILY is an immensely powerful computer. When she was completed around five years ago she was the most powerful terrestrial system ever built. She will be running millions of frequency permutations every second trying to decode our messages. We can't leave anything to chance – Canaveral knows that, too. Check your harness and hold on!" With that, Richard rolled ninety degrees to the left and pulled into a hard turn. Yannick groaned at the unexpected g-force.

When Richard was pointing east, back towards the *Enigma*, he rolled his wings level and began climbing. Within seconds a woman's voice shouted an alarm: "Danger! Danger! Long-range contact! Collision course! Collision Course!"

"Yannick . . . deselect that damned warning system and give me *Enigma*'s range!"

Yannick pressed a button and then checked the sensor array. "Two thousand miles and closing *really fast!*"

Instantly, Richard reversed his manoeuvre and dived, and no sooner had the ship responded when a brilliant red beam of light scorched past the windscreen. "What's the time?" Richard called.

"Fourteen twenty-eight . . . and ten seconds . . . eleven!"

"Got to keep out of her sight for another minute!" Richard screamed.

Richard began a series of high-energy evasive manoeuvres – he threw the ship to the left and then to the right. He started a sudden climb and then rolled inverted and pulled through into a steep dive. Now pencil-thin laser beams rained down on them. He jammed the thrust levers against their stops and the *Ares* shuddered with the increased power.

"Yannick! Quickly! Give me a heading to the 'star line'!"

Heavy vibration permeated the ship as Richard rolled into another evasive manoeuvre. Yannick found it difficult to read the screen. "You need to head west!" he answered. "Two nine zero degrees."

Both men hung in their straps momentarily as Richard pulled the ship inverted again and then pushed the nose to offload the g-force. "How far?"

"Er . . . two hundred miles!"

EMILY's aim was being refined with each laser-burst, and despite a growing frustration with the pathetic craft she would have her day soon. She maintained fifty-eight per cent elliopheric precisely and headed a little north of west.

"You are approaching latitude north zero four zero, longitude east zero four five," said Canaveral's controller over the new coded channel.

Richard knew that Canaveral and the Federation were watching his struggle by satellite link and he also knew that the position he had just heard over the radio was the boundary between Santa Maria Oceanic Control and New York Oceanic Control. *Enigma*'s course was taking her directly towards the release point. He had only seconds remaining. He watched his Mach meter transition from Mach 15 in a near vertical climb to 43 lutens as he entered a suborbital regime and then, as he passed fifty-two per cent elliopheric, he pushed the nose down and dived towards the star line again.

"Eighty miles!" Yannick screamed.

"Say the time!" Richard shouted in response.

And then, just as EMILY's laser initiator had acquired the S2's trajectory, Richard instinctively rolled into a dummy turn; first left and then almost instantaneously a snap-roll to the right. A blinding volley of energy flashed across the sky. The beams were so close to the *Ares* that they illuminated her cockpit as if the sun itself was bursting through. The first volley narrowly missed, but a beam from the second caught their left wingtip and an explosion rocked the ship that snatched the control stick from Richard's hand. Richard fought to recover from the ensuing spin and the *Ares* plummeted.

## Inside the Temple of Osiris – simultaneous

The robot stood motionless on the raised stone plinth close to the altar stone. Professor Mubarakar and Asharf were nearby and gazed wide-eyed as Madame Vallogia opened the square panel on the back of the machine. Then she made ready with the pair of tongs that Richard had left in his helmet box in Mubarakar's house. Completely shielded inside the thick granite walls of the Great Pyramid, the crystal had a milky-white hue that appeared absorbent and lifeless. Carefully she picked it from its recess within the mechanism of the robot and withdrew it through an aperture. Extraction complete, she turned slowly towards the carved stone chalice.

Mubarakar had his pocket watch in his hand and he became fixated on its face as the seconds ticked by. He swayed from one leg to the other, barely able to contain his nerves. "Ten seconds!" he said, without looking up.

Asharf had his hands clasped over his nose and mouth. There was an air of high tension. "Careful, Madame," he uttered, as if suffering excruciating pain, but his words were muffled between his fingers.

Holding the crystal in the tongs and a few centimetres above the inscribed tabletop, Naomi made to drop the crystal into the chalice, which was plainly shaped and approximately ten centimetres in diameter and fifteen high. But over the rim her grip loosened and the crystal fell. It bounced onto the stone and rolled. She gasped. Asharf covered his eyes, but the crystal stopped just short of the edge. Quickly she picked it up again.

"It is time!" said Mubarakar.

Naomi concentrated with a fixed stare as she repeated the task. This time she was careful to lift it over the rim and she placed it down gently inside the chalice.

Almost immediately the crystal responded by changing to a luminescent white. A look of surprise descended over Naomi's face and she could not help but take a step backwards. Then the crystal began to glow from within and then to pulsate. Quickly Naomi turned and, putting her arms up to collect both Professor Mubarakar and Asharf in her sweep across the plinth, they all scurried clear. They did not stop until they were more than twenty metres away and by that time the vast edifice of the interior was bathed in brilliant light.

## Above the North Atlantic – simultaneous

With expert handling, Richard had recovered from the spin but thick black smoke now streamed from the outer section of the left-hand wing. Yannick gave another course correction and Richard, with full throttle and fiery exhaust plumes, threw caution aside in order to achieve the star line. Closing on the position, Richard glanced at the chronometer on the instrument panel. It read: 14:30:02. He was late. His face was flushed within the confines of his helmet and he was sweating. His heart sank, but he held a steady course.

EMILY finally achieved her aim of isolating the coded frequency. "Now I have you!" she called over the radio, her synthetic voice vindictive in triumph. In the low orbit, she flew in the wake of the *Ares* and followed its smoky trail for a few seconds, positioning for an easy kill.

Richard held his breath and waited to die. But there was a delay . . . Unbeknown to him, EMILY's attention was momentarily diverted as she ejected the pod. The conical, capsule-shaped device fired off from beneath the great, grey, bulk of the *Enigma* on a perfect trajectory for re-entry.

Richard checked the navigation display and at that precise moment he noted them passing through the star line. They were flying flat-out, but not, it seemed, fast enough. His eyes were drawn to the chronometer and so too were Yannick's. But they were fourteen seconds late and on the sensor screen he could see that the *Enigma* was perhaps another three or four seconds further behind. They had failed, and a tiny white blip on the screen signified the contaminated pod in free-fall. At that precise instant Richard was in two minds as to whether to continue his evasive tactics and fight for their lives, or let it be, as even if he escaped there was nowhere to go; and EMILY would surely deal with the human colonists on the Moon and on Mars, too – in her own time.

Suddenly, an incredibly brilliant white flash passed over his ship and streamed into Space. It was pencil straight and unbelievably radiant so that even through his darkened visor it made Richard's eyes smart. Had he time to look at the navigation display, Richard would see the flash exactly overlay the 'star line'. The blinding light disappeared for a moment and then reappeared again. And for another five or six seconds it seemed to illuminate the entire hemisphere. And then, as quickly as it had appeared, it disappeared.

Richard didn't wait, but hauled the *Ares* into a hard right-hand turn, all the while waiting to be targeted by the *Enigma*. But nothing happened. He held his breath, kept the turn going until he was pointing in the opposite direction and then flew a collision course – EMILY would not be expecting that manoeuvre and it might destabilise her for a few seconds. Suddenly, Richard closed the thrust levers and the *Ares* started to decelerate. Realising what he was seeing, he reached across and put a hand on Yannick's shoulder. Yannick traced his eye line and a broad smile lightened his features.

Richard measured the *Enigma*'s speed as 31 lutens, but the computation indicated a rapid decrease. Within a few seconds it fell to 29 and then to 28 lutens. Based on that rate she would be drifting in an unstable orbit within the hour. Richard was suspicious; EMILY was devious as well as malevolent. He kept his distance and steered the *Ares* so as to maintain his relative position of five kilometres off her starboard bow.

"Put her on screen and magnify by five, Yannick," Richard ordered. The subsequent picture on the central screen made Richard sit up with surprise. The mighty *Enigma* appeared completely lifeless. There were no lights, no moving scanners, in fact no electromagnetic transmissions of any kind, and the laser initiator appeared locked in an unusual position. Occasionally, flashing streaks of electrical energy crawled over the enormous hulk, like contoured bolts of forked lightning, and Richard pointed out fizzing sheets of blue plasma that played along her thrust tubes – sparking and dancing against the blackness of Space. The *Enigma* had not been destroyed, but the energy beam had effectively electrocuted EMILY, shorting her circuits and burning out her systems.

Richard dropped his shoulders in relief and nodded his approval at Yannick – a gesture that signified much more than just the favourable outcome. He looked up at his instruments and assessed the implications of the numerous flashing lights on the Crew Alert Panel – warnings that prompted him to check the fire extinguisher system and the residual quantities of suppressant – because he had initiated the system in order to dampen the wing fire. Suddenly, he drew a sharp breath. His face turned pale and he stared at Yannick. Immediately, Yannick realised why – they had forgotten the pod. It had completely slipped their minds.

"The bloody pod!" Richard called, and he instantly rammed open the thrust levers and pushed the nose down. Moments later the S2 was in a steep dive. Plummeting towards the Earth, Richard turned west and flew in the direction of New York. "On the sensor display . . . Yannick, can you see it?" he shouted.

In desperation, Yannick adjusted the display's controls, changing the range and the gain and enhancing the clarity of the picture with weather filters. But there was nothing. He had an idea and superimposed a radar picture on the screen and set the range scale to a hundred miles. The scanner swept left and right – still nothing.

He glanced at Richard, shaking his head. "It must be below the scanner's maximum down tilt," he said.

Richard held the full forward stick and checked the pitch angle; the S2 was in a forty-five degree dive and the ship's structure complained at the severity of the manoeuvre by shuddering and bouncing. It felt like flying through heavy turbulence. With their speed still increasing a red light illuminated on the alerting panel. Richard looked up – it was a skin temperature warning.

"We're coming in too steep outside the re-entry profile," Richard screeched, "and we're burning up . . . ! Keep looking for God's sake!"

Yannick made adjustments to the screen as quickly as he could. He tried everything, but still there was no sign of the pod. Richard applied full right rudder in an effort to keep the S2 straight. He glanced at the altimeter to see the digital readout momentarily read 70,000 feet. He knew their rate of descent was well outside the limits. The *Ares* plunged Earthwards with its extremities glowing red-hot. Metal surrounding the damaged left wingtip began pealing backwards as the air density increased and Richard glanced over his left shoulder to see burning shards of metal detaching in that area. He checked the fuel panel to ensure all the fuel had been pumped from that wing into centre and right wing tanks – lest they become a fireball.

Down 65,000 feet . . . 61,000 . . . 59,000 . . . 57,000 feet they plunged. Sunlight reflected from the clouds, grew more intense as they neared their tops.

"Still nothing!" Yannick shouted.

Richard cursed and then abruptly fed in full opposite rudder. The S2 immediately snap-rolled to the left, an effect made more so by the ever-increasing drag from the left wing. Almost instantaneously they were inverted. Richard held that position with rudder and pulled back on the stick increasing their dive. The descent rate increased still further.

Suddenly Yannick pointed to the screen. "I see it! I see it!" Right turn thirty degrees! Turn right thirty degrees!"

Richard responded.

Past 53,000 feet they zoomed . . . 52,000 . . . 50,000. The cloud layer loomed. Then it rushed towards them.

"How far below us?" Richard demanded.

Now the ship was vibrating almost uncontrollably. Heavy shudders ran through her structure. Torrents of sparks flooded past the windscreen and a cacophony of warning lights had illuminated on the panel. To add to the bedlam, a woman's warning voice called: "Rate of descent! Rate of descent! Pull up! Pull up!"

Yannick had to shout to be heard. "Twenty thousand feet below us! Eighteen thousand, seventeen, sixteen . . . A few seconds Commander and you'll be on it!"

Suddenly the *Ares* plunged into the clouds and the brilliance outside was subdued. In the flight deck it quickly grew dark and a smell of burning permeated through the air vents. It was time to make a decision, but what could Richard do? It was too late for the laser; they were well outside its operating parameters even if he could target the pod. They passed 39,000 feet and then 37,000 feet. Richard rolled right-side-up and glanced at the sensor display – the pod was thirty miles ahead and just 5000 feet below. He had to react quickly otherwise he would pass it. Immediately, he closed the thrust levers and pulled back slightly on the nose, arresting the rate of descent. There was only one thing he could do!

"Yannick! Do as I say! No questions . . . ! Get out of your seat, go back and get into the Assault Pod. Strap into the front seat nearest the door – there are controls on the arm rest. If I'm not with you in thirty seconds you eject. Do you understand?"

Yannick nodded; his eyes were afraid.

"Do it!"

Richard wrestled with the controls; he was flying blind. Yannick scrambled from his seat. The pod in free-fall was ten miles ahead of him and 2000 feet below, but *his* altimeter indicated 29,000 feet, then 28,000 feet and then 27,000.

Richard homed in on the pod using the sensor display. At five miles he matched its level, but then checked back precisely on his controls in order to slip just fifty feet below it. Then his higher speed closed the gap. He monitored the skin temperature gauges, but found that the cloud had cooled down the S2's structure sufficiently for the associated warnings to extinguish. In desperation, he glanced at the left wingtip; there was a chance that his plan would work because the contorted metal caused additional friction, and there was still a glow in that area from residual heat.

The altimeter read 20,000 feet at that moment, but the numbers decreased at an alarming rate as Richard chased down the pod. He closed the last few metres and then positioned directly beneath it . . . 18,000 feet! Yannick had been gone for fifteen seconds.

Richard reached up to the fuel control panel and switched on a pump that pressurised the fuel system for delivery back into the left wing tank. He knew that the tank was perforated at its outer extremity and that the surrounding metal was hot enough to ignite the fuel. He engaged the autopilot to hold the ship's parameters . . . 16,000 feet!

Richard unstrapped himself and climbed from his seat. A sudden shudder through the ship threw him off-balance, but he turned and clambered up the back of the co-pilot's seat. The flight path was becoming unstable and he was being thrown from side to side. He looked back for Yannick, who was in his seat in the assault pod and leaning into the aisle staring at him and – with wild hand movements – willing him to come back immediately. The autopilot called 10,000 feet!

Richard reached up to the fuel panel and pressed a button that opened the fuel valve. Now he had but seconds and he turned and hustled back towards Yannick.

"Come on, sir! Come on!" Yannick shouted.

Richard staggered through the doorway and fell into a seat. As the portal closed the woman's voice shouted, "Terrain! Terrain! Pull up! Pull up!" from the flight deck.

Richard had only his lap straps secured as Yannick slammed his fist down on the eject button. Instantaneously, they heard an enormous explosion and the assault pod shook so violently that Richard's arms and legs flailed. Seconds seemed like eternity as the pod was tossed and tumbled. Richard felt the centrifugal force on his body as it spun through the air. He covered his head with his arms and groaned as a small, unsecured item of equipment flew dangerously around the cabin, banging and crashing on the sidewalls and ceiling. His head was a blur. But then, suddenly, the pod's gyroscopic system cut in and it righted itself, and Richard felt a heavy vibration as the noise of retro rockets firing grew louder and louder until it became deafening. For an instant, the g-force pushed him down into his seat and his body was compressed – he felt his face contort and his cheeks sag. Abruptly the noise stopped, and for a second there was silence. He felt his seat harness tense automatically and pull him into his seat with a moment's pain in his shoulders, and then there was an enormous but short-lived thud and a powerful judder.

After a few seconds of nothing, Richard pushed himself up in his seat with his feet and looked across at Yannick. The emergency lights flickered momentarily and strange sloshing noises filtered through the open vents in the ceiling; apart from that, everything was quiet. Richard realised the motion was that of the sea. Yannick smiled back at him, albeit uneasily. He felt sore, but they were both in one piece.

Richard released his harness and the straps fell away. He stood hesitantly but hung on to the seat back because of the wave motion. In the quiet, they heard the repetitive bleeping of the emergency beacon. "I think we can get out now," he said.

# CHAPTER 32

# TIME FOR TURNING

**London – Whitehall**
**6 January – 09:11 Greenwich Mean Time**

"Good morning, I'm Richard Reece."

"Good morning, sir. My name is Sally; I'm Mr Rothschild's new PA."

"Really . . . I didn't know. Things don't usually change around here."

Peter Rothschild walked into the lobby from his office. As usual he looked smart in a dark blue pinstriped suit and a pair of shiny black shoes. "Richard," he said, "good to see you." He raised his left arm in an exaggerated way and made a point of looking at his watch. "Please . . . come in," he said, without reference to the time and without a smile to accompany his welcoming words. With that, he turned and disappeared into his office.

Richard shrugged, gestured his excuses for being late, smiled briefly at the fifty-something woman and followed Rothschild. Inside, Rothschild was waiting by the door and promptly closed it behind Richard. "Please, take a seat," he said, and pointed to the chair by his desk.

Richard sat down and made himself comfortable. Because of his tardiness he tried to conjure a chastised look. Very unusually, Richard was also dressed for 'the city' in a dark, plain suit; but his was a general-sized, government-issue two-piece, and not a Savile Row, made-to-measure three-piece, like Rothschild's.

"Thought I'd get a hero's welcome," Richard said ironically, as Rothschild took his seat on the other side of the desk. "What with *Enigma*'s pod being vaporised just seconds before it was due to open."

Rothschild looked at Richard in a resigned way. "This is MI9, Richard. We are supposed to be a Secret Service department, not a circus – we don't do 'heroes' here – everyone does their job."

Richard raised his eyebrows. There was a moment's silence and then he clicked his tongue and shook his head. "Peter, you are going to have to lighten up you know – or you'll have a heart attack or something."

Barely perceptibly, Rothschild nodded. "You left it rather late, don't you think? That's my only criticism. Canaveral timed the shuttle exploding exactly at the pod's deployment altitude – not much room to manoeuvre, so to speak." A smile flickered but was suppressed and Rothschild nodded again, this time a little more exaggerated. "Anyway, how was your trip?"

"Good thanks, very good in fact. They sent an aircraft carrier, the *Eisenhower*. It's my very own nuclear-powered supercarrier. It was on its way to the Med . . . Yannick and I got off in Gibraltar – nice to see the old place again."

Rothschild looked impressed. "Four days at sea – felt like you were back in the Navy, I expect."

"Certainly did. Perfect for recuperation. Plenty of hot water, good food, good banter, lots of flying stories . . . loved it."

Rothschild nodded emphatically. "Excellent. Well, you don't need me to tell you that you did a good job, a very good job . . . the Prime Minister sends his regards."

"Oh, that's nice."

"You *have* called Rachel, I trust? Am I still the devil reincarnated?"

"It's not all fire and brimstone, Peter. And yes I did – on the ship's SATCOM and again when I got off in Gib. She's fine, looking forward to me getting home – there's a lot to put right over there."

"I expect there is, and I've awarded you two weeks leave . . ."

"Two weeks! I don't think so. I'm having a month off minimum, even if I take some of my holiday allocation."

"You have a squadron to command; let's not forget

713

your responsibilities."

Richard thought for a moment. "The Royal Navy pilot I flew with," he said. "Lieutenant Chris Quarrie . . . He's applied for a resident's permit on the Moon – and his partner, too. I've already written a report recommending the Lunar Senate accept his application. In view of his actions, it's likely to be accepted. He's very competent and has a nice way about him – he will make a Royal Navy Captain, there is no doubt in my mind about that. I'll talk to Eddie Lieven – Andromeda's Chief Operations Officer – into letting him stand in for me for a couple of weeks. It will be good experience."

Rothschild shrugged. "Very well, I don't have a problem with that – I can clear you for a month," he replied.

"Thank you, Peter. I'll do some moon-walking and have a few quiet dinners with Rachel – you understand." Richard paused and looked questioningly at Rothschild. "Anyway, where is Laura Bellingham . . . ? I've never known your office without Laura."

Rothschild glanced at Richard for a moment and then looked down, as if he was put out. He tapped a finger on his desk in a preoccupied way and then he looked Richard in the eye. "Laura was the mole, Richard," he said, straight-faced. "She was passing information to local Spheron agents from right under our noses."

"What!"

Rothschild nodded. "I always thought it was the Americans who were the problem . . . you know that . . .

their SERON interface. But all along the leak was right here in this office."

"How did you find out?"

"Abbey investigated the safe house debacle in Strasbourg. Very few people knew of that house, let alone its address and entry code. Abbey quickly pinned it on Laura, and when confronted she confessed." Rothschild shook his head. "I blame myself for not seeing the signs. All those fifteen- and sixteen-hour days – she was always very conscientious, of course, but those long hours . . . even at the weekends . . . that should have made me suspicious."

"I don't understand."

"She was giving her heating allowance to her ageing mother. Her own apartment was cold and damp, with no hot water and no cooking facilities. It was going on for some time."

Richard's eyes widened – he still didn't get the picture.

"Oldest trick in the book – goes back to the Cold War," enlightened Rothschild. "More than a year ago, Laura's mother needed some expensive hospital treatment. Because of complications and the fact that she had already been treated privately – albeit unsuccessfully – it wasn't covered by the Independent Health Service mandate. Clearly, the conglomerates had their feelers out. She was approached for some information in exchange for the medical expenses – they wanted unclassified information, easily available on the World

Net, actually. Laura didn't see any harm in it. Then her mother's treatment became involved, more expensive. Spheron asked for additional information, only this time a little more 'useful' shall we say." Rothschild tapped his fingers on the deck again. "They were clever, took their time . . . nothing too sensitive. Laura obliged. Then, of course, came the sting. Oil supplies were non-existent and they offered to fill her mother's oil tank up when she left hospital. This time they wanted restricted information. After that she was hooked and it quickly became blackmail; that was a year ago." Rothschild shook his head.

"Is she being charged?"

"I reported the matter to General Roper and apologised for my persistent challenges to their security model. He understood. A similar thing had happened to his friend – you will recall General Buchanan when you retrieved the first batch of crystals?"

Richard nodded.

"Anyway, in answer to your question, no . . . we have managed to keep a lid on it – she didn't do it for herself, for God's sake. And in a roundabout fashion she may well have helped – by us bagging Karl Rhinefeld, you understand." Rothschild looked disappointed. "The Prime Minister sanctioned my recommendation in view of her service."

"And . . . ?"

"Laura has gone to the 'typing pool'; she will never be trusted with confidential information again. We have avoided detention and she remains employed – such a waste of talent." He shook his head again.

Richard was saddened by the news.

"There is, however, some rather good news," continued Rothschild, forcing a smile. "Humatrons extracted a forty-eight kilogram consignment of raw crystal from the same seam that the *Hera*'s crew were working – on the surface of Io, you understand. Their space vehicle was bound for the Moon. Had the attack on Andromeda been successful they would have landed there and the conglomerates would have had the best bargaining commodity in history. Instead, their failsafe plan was to hide in the asteroid belt." Rothschild sat back in his chair. "I must say the Chinese Government has been extremely cooperative here. Their Special Forces moved quickly and decisively against Tongsei, effectively overrunning the Huang Hai Industrial State. They confiscated Tongsei's entire computer network and found a great deal of very useful information – not least the coordinates where the said vehicle was hiding. The Humatron pilots have been instructed to continue their mission. In a few weeks they will be intercepted when adjacent to Mars. The Space Federation Council has agreed that a five kilogram consignment will be allocated to Osiris. Commander Race will reinstate the Petrified Forests of Elysium." Rothschild's expression brightened.

"Yes. Tom copied me in on his report to the Federation. It's amazing what he found inside Zeta Three – such a civilisation; such a loss. And Zeta One and Two are much bigger."

Rothschild nodded. "Using the translation programme that you helped devise a few years ago, the Osiris Science Department was able to interpret the records that were found. The results have certainly changed the way the Federation views Mars."

"So we have come full circle," said Richard, staring out of the window thoughtfully. "Reached the reason why Admiral Dirkot Urket left Earth in the *Star of Hope*. A resurrected ship . . . forgotten skills; it was to take a crystal to that dying civilisation. What must have been going through the survivors' minds that day – when they realised that they had no way of contacting the subterranean colony and their precious crystal was shattered." Richard shook his head. "And the rest, as they say, is history . . . and how sad is that?"

Rothschild agreed. "I have to say that I did not know that the core of Mars is inert. It was in Commander Race's report. The subterranean colonies here on Earth have the heat from our molten core to support their endeavours. It's something that I had not considered, but Commander Race wrote that after their crystal burnt out, the Martian colony chilled very quickly." He paused reflectively. "Anyway, with a new crystal soon to be installed the future is looking bright for the proposed expansion of Osiris."

"You're right, Peter, that's good news. And what have the authorities done about Epsilon Rio and their cyber-technology?"

"Epsilon Rio is also being broken up. Like Spheron and Tongsei, most of their senior management have been arrested. There will be some long sentences I can assure you, and I certainly wouldn't want to be in a high security prison in China or Brazil these days. And some more good news is that the Lunar Senate has requested high level talks with the Federation Council ASAP. It's a move to develop closer ties and instigate mutual defence planning – it seems that their extreme isolationist policies may be a thing of the past. You might find that there is a good deal more cooperation between respective flight operation departments and defence directorates."

Richard nodded his approval. "And what about the main reason for our meeting today, Peter?" Richard said. There was an edge of unease in his tone.

Rothschild stared at Richard for a moment. "Yes, of course," he said, and looked thoughtful. "Listen. Whatever happened inside the Great Pyramid on the day EMILY was paralysed is not my concern. I don't want to know what generated that solar flash, if indeed it was generated. To my mind it could have been anything – a meteorite, a reflection from a solar flare, even a piece of Space junk re-entering the atmosphere. God knows there's enough of it in orbit. You will not find any mention of another crystal in my report, and outside this department nobody is any the wiser."

Richard breathed a deep sigh. "Thank you, Peter."

"No need," replied Rothschild, matter-of-factly.

"And what about the Ark of the Light?"

"It appears to be lost . . . The conglomerates must have disposed of it. Dropped into the South China Sea or something similar, I expect – that's what's written in my report. I don't think we are likely to see that relic again . . . do you?"

Richard smiled faintly. "No," he said. "Gone forever." Richard checked his chronometer. "Well, it's time for my flight. A shuttle to fly me to the Moon – like the song." Richard's smile widened. "I'll be seeing you, Peter – and thanks again."

Richard stood and offered his hand. The two men shook hands over the table.

"I'll be in touch," was Peter Rothschild's passing comment as Richard left the room.

# CHAPTER 33

# MEMORIES OF A TROPICAL PARADISE

**Moon Base Andromeda – Residential Unit 103**
**15 December 2055 – 11 months later**

"Richard, there's an eDiction from the Veloudis Fertility Clinic in Paris, asking if you would consider joining their donor programme again next year. I remember you mentioned something about this but you never told me that you had been there." Rachel was speaking from the kitchen.

"Didn't I? I thought I did," replied Richard from the lounge, where he was playfully bouncing a young child on his knee.

"Well you didn't. So tell me about it." Rachel put her

head around the door.

"When I attended the joint debrief and wash-up in the ISSF Headquarters – last January, towards the end of the month, if I remember correctly. It seemed an ideal opportunity. I took the train from Strasbourg to Paris. I was there for the afternoon along with forty other volunteers. There was a lengthy screening process and they eventually selected twenty-one of us for the donation programme. The advice I received was helpful to us, too, Rachel – if you recall. They told me that there were no physical problems as far as I was concerned. We had to relax . . . try at the time they specified in your cycle . . . it worked, didn't it?"

Rachel stepped into the doorway and shrugged. "I recall something of it I suppose." She walked across to the sofa, sat down next to Richard and smiled at the baby between sips of green tea taken from a white plastic mug. Richard put a hand gently on hers.

"By nature, the programme is completely anonymous," he said in a reassuring way. "The donors' identities are coded; the names are not available – let alone ever used. The samples are frozen; apparently they can last for a few months. The selection process is entirely random. You know that. Anyway, I was happy to do it – I felt I was helping someone in some way – as much as I possibly could within the constraints of our . . . . Well, anyway, I'm unlikely to participate again – the logistics of it are too difficult."

Rachel shrugged. "I understand; let's not talk about

it again – okay?"

"Forgotten . . ." replied Richard.

## Andromeda Flight HQ – the next day
## 10:37 Lunar Corrected Time

"Richard! Peter Rothschild here . . . caught you in your office for once."

"I like to be hands-on, Peter, as you know – not stuck behind a desk all day."

"Yes, quite."

"Anyway, how is London?"

"Much as always. No improvement in the weather, I'm afraid, and the exodus to subsurface living continues apace. At least we have enough electricity for everyone these days."

"The new consignment of crystals – I heard about them."

"Operating well above expectation – very good news I have to say. They seem to have a great deal more latent energy than the originals."

"I don't think that's surprising, Peter. Not if you consider the role the original crystals played in our history . . . Eridu, Babylon, Atlantis, the Colossus of Rhodes, powering the *Star of Hope* . . ."

"Good point! Yes!" Rothschild paused thoughtfully. "Listen, I have some news for you. The planned expansion of the Martian colony has finally been approved by the ISSF Council. They expect to quadruple the Osiris Base real estate in the next three years and the expansion will continue from there. They are planning a population of ten-thousand by the end of the decade and one-hundred-thousand by twenty-seventy. With the rejuvenation of the Elysium plantations, food production appears limitless – they are even talking of aerating the atmosphere again. Perhaps we all might move there one day."

"Nice thought, Peter, but I know you only too well. You wouldn't call just to tell me that. There's something else, isn't there?"

"Yes indeed," said Rothschild after a silent pause. "The Space Federation has already started recruiting. Your name has been mentioned – as a preferred candidate no less. I'm to inform you that there is a managerial position on the first wave – if you want it, of course."

"Go on."

"As Director of Surveying and Land Acquisition – you always wanted your old job back and so did Rachel. The position of Chief Medical Officer is coming up, too. I know Rachel has never really settled over there. There is nothing for her on the Moon, she told me that only recently."

Richard shrugged. "Land acquisition . . . so it starts all over again – will we ever learn?"

"Hopefully we will do it better this time."

"Another nice thought."

"The Prime Minister has agreed to release you from your reserve duties with MI9, and the Federation has made it clear to me that you are their first choice. No one else with your level of experience it seems. The job's there if you want it. Two months to pack."

"What about Thomas?"

"That's just it – part of the deal. They want families with young children – babies over fourteen weeks can travel."

Richard paused and considered the implications. "Is it a one-way ticket, Peter? Be honest."

"They want permanent colonists, and that's the reality of it. I suspect it is, Richard, yes."

"Then we will take it!"

**Later the same morning**

"Commander Reece . . . Lieutenant Oliver here. I'm the Duty Officer on the front desk. You've another call from Earth – this time it's on the private net."

"Okay, thanks Peter, I can take it now. Who is it, do you know?"

"Didn't say, sir."

"Okay, put it through . . . Hello there, Richard Reece."

"*Effendi*, it is I, Asharf Makkoum. I call from Cairo."

"Asharf! What a surprise. Are you well . . . ? Madame Vallogia?"

"All is well, *Effendi*, very well. I have news!"

"News! What news? Go on!"

"I know Madame Vallogia would never call you, not even with such joy. Her pride and dignity would not allow it. So I call to tell you myself – it is our secret, *Effendi*."

"Yes, of course. What is it Asharf . . . ?"

"The fertility treatment Madame was undergoing in Paris – it was a success. This morning Madame had a child . . . all is well . . . and there are no marks. *Effendi* . . . she has a beautiful baby."

Richard leaned back in his chair and stared blankly at the wall. He could hardly believe what he was hearing.

"*Effendi* . . . ? Are you there . . . ? There is more!"

"Yes, sorry . . . I'm here . . ."

"*Effendi*, it is a girl! Madame Vallogia has a daughter!"

## THE END

An image of Queen Nefertiti
taken from the famous bust by
the Egyptian sculptor Thutmose

An image of Queen Cleopatra

# THE MOON

# PALUS PUTREDINIS
### (LATIN FOR 'MARSH OF DECAY')

ANDROMEDA
SPACE CENTRE COORDINATES
26˚ 39 40.37˝ N 02˚20 08.82˝ E
ELEVATION -1900 M

RIMA FRESNEL

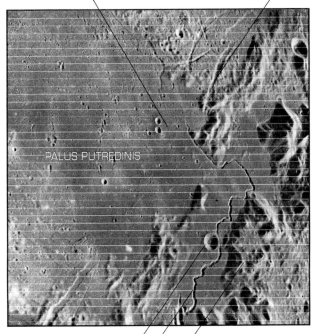

PALUS PUTREDINIS

HADLEY CRATER

APENNINE MOUNTAINS

RIMA HADLEY

# GLOSSARY

The list of special or technical words used in
*Rouge Command*

**Abrive** – Abbreviated digital text message.

**Accelercom** – Accelerated Communication System
– Referenced to light speed i.e. approximately 186,282
miles per second or 300,000 kilometres per second.

**ARPS** – Atomic Reaction Propulsion System –
Propulsion utilising a physical law of motion i.e. 'for
every action there is an equal and opposite reaction'.

**Bulkhead** – Upright partition, usually structural, in a
ship or aircraft.

**CIB** – Central Intelligence Bureau – Specialised
intelligence operation, derived from the two principal
American intelligence and investigation agencies.

**Click(s)** – Colloquial for kilometre.

**CMO** – Chief Medical Officer.

**CMPC** – Cyan Magnetic Pulse Cannon – Close defence
system using high-energy magnetic pulses.

**Comms State** – Communication Security State –
Refers to state of security protection and readiness.

**Cosmic Chronometer** – Extremely accurate clock,
time computations based on the expansion rate of the
universe – "Big Bang" Theory.

**Deck** – Floor/platform/walking surface on ship or
aircraft.

**Deckhead** – Ceiling in ship or aircraft.

**DP Check** – Depressurization Check – Medical check on personnel who have experienced space suit problems on the "outside".

**Elliopherical Orbit** – A precise orbital trajectory related in percentage terms to the radius of a planet – Gravitational attraction decreases with increasing distance/percentage, from the planet's core.

*Enigma* – The most advanced spacecraft ever conceived – Utilises matter-stream propulsion. Capable of speeds referenced to that of light. Controlled by an autonomous self-aware computer called EMILY.

**ESSA** – European Space & Science Agency.

**Frequency** – Number of complete cycles per second, or the rate per second of a vibration constituting a wave, e.g. sound, light or radio waves.

**Gamma Radiation** – Short wave electromagnetic radiation given off by the sun, usually very penetrating and dangerous to humans.

**Greenwich Mean Time** – The mean solar time at the Greenwich meridian, used as the standard time in a zone that includes the British Isles.

**Hatch** – Personnel door in bulkhead: usually structural, airtight, hinged and lockable.

**HOD** – Head of Department.

**Humatron** – Advanced robot series incorporating Level Seven Programming.

**ID** – Identity – Usually in the form of an electronic tag or card.

**ISSF** – International Space and Science Federation –

Multinational/Global body made up of regional Space and Science Agencies.

**Ks** – Colloquial term for kilometres.

**Light Year** – Distance travelled by light in one year.

**LCT** – Lunar Corrected time – local moon time, referenced to earth time and more particularly, Greenwich Mean Time.

**LS** – Life Support – Essential equipment or processes used for sustaining life.

**MCT** – Martian Corrected Time – Time dictated by the Martian hour, day, month and year but referenced to earth time, and more particularly, Greenwich Mean Time.

**NCO** – Non Commissioned Officer.

**Portal** – Door, Entry/exit point: an opening for personnel and usually associated with space vehicles.

**PTSV** – Personnel Transport and Service Vehicle – Multi-wheeled surface support vehicle.

**R&R** – Rest and Recuperation.

**Radio waves** – Electromagnetic waves usually less than 10 centimetres in wavelength.

**RIPS** – Rockwell Illinois Plateau System – System for measuring the degree of complexity and memory capacity of a cybernetic system – has become the internationally recognised reference system.

**Roger** – Form of acknowledgement, usually meaning that an order or statement has been understood.

**SATCOM** – Satellite Communications

**Sickbay** – A term for a medical department or small

medical facility, having military origins.

**Sitrep** – Situation Report – Details of an event or happening.

**_Spartacus_** – Space station that holds its position between earth and Mars by "sailing the solar wind" – Utilises a giant, square sail that is also a photoelectric screen.

**SSA** – Space and Science Agency – Multinational but regional body i.e. European Space and Science Agency or Asian Space and Science Agency.

**SSC** – Special Security Contingent – Specialist security team.

**SWAT Team** – Security, Weapons and Tactical Team.

**TES** – Target Enhancement System – Tracking and lock-on system for weaponry.

**Thrust Levers** – Levers in cockpit controlling the thrust of an engine or rocket motor.

**Sonic Pistol** – Hand held weapon utilising a massively condensed pulse of sound energy. Depending on its severity, when the pulse hits a target it destabilises the atomic structure of the target, usually resulting in severe damage.

**Static Discharge** – Discharge of static electricity.

**Wrist LS Controller** – Wrist mounted life support control and display instrument.

**U-Semini Case** – Transportable containment system, briefcase sized and constructed to carry the Kalahari Crystals - Utilises a magnetron suspension system and enhanced Celestite protective sheath.

# FIRST COLONY
## EVOLUTION

AJ Marshall

**M*Press* Books**

## About the series

The science fiction work *First Colony* is a series containing five novels. Together, the books span the century immediately after the first human 'off planet' birth. By 2050, Moon base Andromeda had expanded from its initial, tentative portacabin-like modules into a sprawling labyrinth of double and triple storied architectural units built from materials mined on the Moon's surface.

After the Proclamation of Independence in May 2050, the new 'Senate of Lunar Colonisation' removed the military-like regime under which Andromeda's two thousand inhabitants lived and worked and implemented a self-governing, self-sustainable democracy based on the charter of the American Declaration of Independence. Those who would return to earth amid its energy calamity and climatic strife did so, but those who remained formed the populous of the *First Colony*. The strict rules governing male and female fraternisation in Andromeda and the immediate return to earth of women falling 'illegally' pregnant whilst on space duties was abolished. Cohabitation was allowed, even encouraged, and the first baby was born nine months to the day after lunar independence. His name was Aaron Wu, born of a British mother and a Chinese father.

*First Colony* charts the life and legacy of this first so-called 'Luman' – a human born in the lunar colonies. Aaron Wu's life begins innocently enough – the result of unique events entwined with fate. Each of the five books then covers two decades in his life, ending with his death in 2153. The novels will set out the trials and tribulations of this character as he rises to becoming the first elected president of an independent space colony.

## BOOK 1: EVOLUTION

Lumens are essentially the same as the humans that preceded them; however, by nature of the changed environment in which they live, minor genetic anomalies are to be expected. When the first of their kind – some say 'subspecies' – visit Earth in 2069, their welcome is euphoric. Such elation is, however, short lived. Suppressed racial intolerance rises again, bolstered by hardship and food shortages. Born on the same day as Aaron, but in a small American town in Arizona, a young woman closely studies a one-metre diameter hologram of the Moon in her bedroom. A little above the floor, the surreal image slowly rotates and the young woman encircles it transfixed. In her nineteen years of life – mainly below the earth's surface – Jessie Parker has never seen the Moon with her own eyes. This because the dense suffocating layer of contaminated cloud that surrounds the Earth has neither lifted nor dispersed in her lifetime. However, she knows that her destiny lies on that neighbouring planetoid, where immigration is illegal and political accord with Earth's teetering governments is strained at best.

# AUTHOR'S COMMENT

*First Colony* is a futuristic novel about man colonising the Moon. As our neighbour and partner in the vastness of space, the Moon's close proximity dictates much more than just the rising and ebbing of our ocean tides. Since time began, the Moon has influenced the very fabric of our existence. Indeed, without the presence of this apparently inert body, the Earth would not have become an oasis for any species, least of all ours. The predictable and eternal passage of the Moon through the night sky has etched its form into the subconscious of each and every generation that has preceded us. And so too, whether in desperation or not, it was just a matter of time before man viewed this familiar place as an achievable goal, with a frontier to be crossed like any other and subsequently a new land to be settled. Like the Americas centuries before, a new world beckoning, with new opportunities and with new dreams over a distant horizon. However, as is often the case, the old lessons learned are quickly forgotten as humankind rushes to stake its claim – except that the irradiated cold of space and the desolate Moon are far less forgiving than any frontier that has beckoned before.

The novel *First Colony* is a work composed of five volumes and the storyline, by nature of being set in the future is essentially science fiction. However, fantasy it is not, as the science described in the books is either fact or based on fact. Indeed, the author's style and his previous works reflect highly believable scenarios.

*First Colony* is about man's inevitable pursuit of the unknown and his innate necessity to colonise; driven in this case as much by environmental calamity as by instinct. It is about the relentless advance of technology and the misuse of knowledge.

*First Colony* is about high adventure and love, about deceit, greed and the unexpected. It is about the dissolving power of governments and the emergence of the all-consuming 'Corporation'. It is an intelligent crime thriller as well as an emotional rollercoaster. It is about Neil Armstrong's legacy and the immortal words he spoke as he stepped from the landing craft *Eagle* on 20 July 1969 as mankind held its breath.

**The *First Colony* Series:**
**Availability:**

# PROLOGUE

Everyone experiences grief at some point in their lives, although its intensity, I now know, is subjective. My first recollection of this debilitating emotion was not my own, but my mother's, and I remember exactly when it occurred. At that precise moment in time, and because of an accident, this 'melancholy' flooded into our lives like water through a breached dam, and for years after I fought to shore up the damage. It was an emotion I tried enormously to forget – to relegate to the recesses of my mind. Perhaps that's why my primary school teacher reported me as hyperactive, amongst other things.

The day before my fifth birthday started innocuously enough, but by midday we knew that my father was dead and thereafter the hell that contains all the sadness, all the wretchedness, all the misery of people, opened beneath our house. My mother immediately fell into that fiery underworld and soon she had dragged me down with her. I didn't kick and scream – at the time I had no idea where I was going. Hindsight is a wonderful thing, but I can't help feeling that even at five I should have flailed my arms and grasped something – that I should have held on for dear life, seizing any and all opportunities before we both vanished into that pit. A purple tree . . . that man Jesus from Earth . . . my pet robot . . . anything – or at least shouted for help or left a trail, like Hansel and Gretel did in the Brothers Grimm story. For longer than I care to remember we floundered beneath that house, or 'module', as it really was. Looking back, it was three years before I climbed high enough to get a hand-hold on the edge of the precipice. At eight years old, I felt like fifteen.

My father died in a mining accident. I'll fill you in on the details later, but he was thirty-eight years old – as was my mother at the time. In fact their birthdays were just a week apart. An Earth week, I mean, not a lunar week – because, unlike me, they were both born on the Earth. They were both sixty seconds in a minute, sixty minutes in an hour, twenty-four hours in a day, three hundred and sixty five days in a year, and so on and so on, type people – again, unlike me. Because I grew up in a different time reference; although my mother would never admit to it.

My early life was disorientating, and not because of my father's absence – although that didn't help – but because life revolved around 'Earth' time from as early as I can remember. Of all the clocks in our home, only one was on lunar time. That was the school clock, and even then it was one of those antique, twin-faced, battery-powered models, with the other face always set on Greenwich Mean Time – always!

GMT, it was at odds with Lunar Corrected Time, creating a sort of bio antagonism, and it served to confuse. All of my friends at school were so young when their parents transitioned that they never experienced the 'terrestrial effect', that was only for the 'oldies'. Retrospectively, however, one helpful thing did result from all those years of disturbed biorhythms – at the age of eighteen, when I first visited the Earth to start my university education, I didn't suffer from lunoxia – not once, never: no dizziness, no diarrhoea, no insomnia. And believe me, with all the other things going on at the time, that was a great help.

To explain further: my parents were human and their bio-clocks were fixed. Indeed, even after thirty-three years as a colonist – and in her last twenty she never left the Moon– my mother's biorhythms hardly changed. She was subconsciously tied to the terrestrial calendar, as with most of the 'oldies' . . . the First Generation. There were a few who adapted, I recall – those who were still in their teens when they came across – but they were the minority. Most FGs arrived when they were in their thirties, were in stable relationships – with their partners back on Earth – and they had had their intended quota of children prior to taking up a lunar appointment. In those days an 'appointment' meant three years. *Maturity* and *stability* – they were the key words when recruiting the lunar workforce. In reality of course, back then, in the First Decade, it was NASA's call as to who was accepted into the programme and who was not, and they, NASA I mean, were shit scared of being sued over excessive radiation exposure. Body defects, early death, child deformities – radiation had a lot to answer for. Of course, it was never the problem they believed it would be. Yes, hindsight is a wonderful thing.

The lunar colony claimed its independence on 21 May 2050, and on that same day, after the old rules had been 'dispatched' back to Earth on the 'last' shuttle – banished, along with any sentiment for the home planet, all the brewing, brooding relationships surfaced like bubbling lava from a volcano. The strict, military-style regulations on cohabitation, the segregated accommodation, the threat of being sent home the moment a pregnancy was detected – and a hormone check was compulsory every month – the no-fraternising and no-touching rules, the authority's obsession and anxiety regarding birth defects, everything, it all simply dissolved into oblivion. There was a lot of bed-hopping that first night by all accounts, and my mother and father were no exception: free love, like the hippy movement on Earth almost a century earlier. Apparently it was mayhem – total chaos: a twenty-four hour party. Nine months later, to the day, I was the first out. Others soon followed, but I was the first. They called me a Luman – a human born in the lunar colony. I was the first Luman. A fact that would enhance and haunt in varying measures each and every day of my life (so far). There were twenty-eight of us, I remember. We all knew each other, but Stefanie was my best friend. I loved her even then, I think. She lived in the module next door for a while, before her family moved to the new Insularum Estate, over on the east side of Andromeda.

We all arrived for our first day of primary school in pristine white uniforms, like thinly padded spacesuits, and saying goodbye set my mother crying again. I was used to it and I could deal with it like a nonchalant teenager would, even though I was only six years old. But I wasn't immune. I would always put an arm around her and provide some comfort – as best I could as an infant; perhaps a little better later, as a junior. The earlier years of pre-school, three of them, lower, middle and upper, were more a playgroup affair and half days. I remember always wanting to stay longer. Just to be out of that module was a joy, but to me Stefanie made each day there seem like the one before Christmas.

The day before Christmas . . . ah yes . . . that day. A happy time for me; always was, and always will be. Why? Because my mother was too – happy, open, sharing and talkative. Actually, it was more the anticipation of the following day that excited my mother and she would smile freely and communicate – make calls, invite people over.

Christmas Day itself, on the other hand, was a particular and peculiar 'Earth Day', and I learnt early that such Earth Days had the opposite effect on her. Christmas Day was, in fact, that 'special day' they tried to slot into a niche in the lunar calendar – 'they' being the Lunar Senate. Of course, there was no niche, in fact there was no place for it at all – never has been, and in my view, never will be – except, perhaps, as a remembrance day. To remind me of it, however, so that it stands out like a radiation burn, my mother *always* cried on that day – perhaps more than on any other. As my mother was essentially a Christian and I was bought up with their beliefs and values – beneath that somewhat misplaced 'planetary umbrella' so to speak – these were our days, but there were similar, equally significant days for the other great 'terrestrial' religions. And there were also other days they also tried to integrate. These were deemed less important and so didn't warrant 'Colony Day' status, which was a day off, like a bank holiday on Earth. Easter Day, Boxing Day, Shrove Tuesday, Palm Sunday. Clearly they meant something to the Oldies, but to us Lumans . . . me . . . they were just annotations on the first calendars that gradually vanished over the years. Scientology had a niche, however, if you could call its brief popularity that. For our neighbours in Module 101 it was important. I remember heated discussions over the dinner table between my mother and her friends and articles in the *Lunar Times*. But again, by the Second Decade that too had petered out.

After my mother had sent me to university on Earth – in her home town of Oxford in the Dual Kingdom

(England and Wales) and against my wishes, I might add – I found forgetting my mother's ever-lasting grief much easier. Upon reflection, it was just because other types of grief took the place of my missing father. I'll come to the story of Stefanie in a moment. But for now, at the age of twenty-one, and as I recount my life to this point, I can honestly say that I understand what my mother went through when my Dad died.

## CHAPTER 1

# FIRST AMONG EQUALS

To my dying day, I will never know if calamitous things happen for a reason. If events, particularly tragic ones, are dictated by a 'higher power' – like some kind of divine interference in our lives – or if an invisible fate line of universal proportions that links the innumerable solar systems and galaxies, directs these occurrences. I mean, why it was that she . . .

To be continued . . .

# FIRST COLONY
## EVOLUTION

ISBN: 978-0-9565077-2-3

CW00406123

# Comedic Arthurian Bundle
Books 1 - 3
The Queen Arthur Adventures

**Published by**: Crimson Myth Press
(www.CrimsonMyth.com)
**Edited by:** Lorelei Logsdon
(www.LoreleiLogsdon.com)
**Cover art**: Amy P. Simmonds
(www.AmyPSimmonds.com)
**Cover Text:** Jake T. Logsdon
(www.JakeLogsdon.com)

# THE RING OF VEILING
## BOOK 1
## THE ADVENTURES OF QUEEN ARTHUR

# THE ARGUMENT

"ARTHUR," SAID GUINEVERE as she walked into the room, "I have had the most trying of days."

"Sorry to hear that, my love."

"Yes, I am feeling quite vexed indeed." She moved to the center of the room. "Come over here, Arthur."

Arthur moved to his beloved with haste.

"Arthur," she said with her hands on her hips, looking quite serious, "I want you to take off my boots."

"As you wish, dear," he replied attentively and then did as she had asked.

"Now, remove my skirt." Without a word, Arthur complied with her desire. "And my blouse," she commanded pointedly.

Arthur was now rather getting into the spirit of things.

Guinevere took a gingerly step backward. "Remove my panties, Arthur." He was quick to oblige. "And, lastly, my brassiere."

Though it took a bit of doing, Arthur complied

with that request as well.

"And Arthur?"

"Yes, my dearest?"

"Don't let me catch you wearing my clothes again!"

Arthur grabbed a robe, one of his own, and took a seat in his high-backed leather chair as his beloved paced before him.

"And I say it again," Guinevere said tersely, "I do not wish to catch you wearing my clothes!"

"Yes, dear," Arthur replied with a nod. "I promise that you shall never catch me."

"Exactly and…no, wait. That's not what I mean when I say that."

"Pardon?"

"It's not the *catching you* part of my demand that you should be focused on, Arthur. It's the *stop wearing my damn clothes* part!"

"Oh, I see."

"It's not how a king should act."

"That's a tad unfair, is it not?" Arthur said, jutting his chin out in defiance. "Was it not you that I saw wearing my full mail outfit just the other night?"

"You saw that?"

"Ah hah!" Arthur pointed at Guinevere. "No, I did not see that, but I find it odd that my suit of armor always seems out of sorts whenever I come back from a…uh…night out." He coughed. "At first I thought maybe it was just due to the servants polishing the metal, but seeing as how it is just as scruffy-looking as always, I can only assume there was some other nefarious action going on. And are you not wearing pants even now?"

Guinevere's face went pale. She looked down at her pantaloons and groaned. Then she opened and closed her mouth multiple times, pointing at Arthur once or twice as if she had something to say. Finally, looking somewhat defeated, she sat down across the room in her pink-cloth chair.

"I wouldn't classify it as nefarious," she murmured.

"Nor would I consider my wearing of your clothes as such."

There was a moment of silence as they both stared purposefully away from each other. Arthur felt a bit embarrassed by the entire ordeal, but he was also tired of hiding who he was.

"What are we to do, Arthur?"

"First," he said conspiratorially, "we could switch chairs."

"Truthfully," Guinevere replied, "I would quite like that."

They each jumped up and crossed the room, looking instantly more at ease in their newfound seating arrangements.

"Second," offered Arthur, "we could keep this our little secret. A lover's mystery that only we two share."

"This would be wise, I think," said Guinevere, "except for the fact that you tend to dress as you do under your suit of armor all the time."

"I've never done such a thing!"

"Come now, Arthur," Guinevere said melodramatically, "be truthful with me."

"Okay, possibly once or twice—"

"Arthur?"

"—a week," he finished. "But nobody is the wiser

of that."

"And if you get injured? Then what? They'll have to remove your outfit to tend to your wounds. They will all learn of your secret at that moment."

Arthur stood up, adjusted his robe, and looked to be irritated. "So what if they come to find out? I am what I am, am I not? I am their king, no?"

"More like their queen…"

"What's that?"

"Nothing," Guinevere said quickly. "Do go on."

He squinted at her momentarily. "I grow tired of hiding anyway, my dear, even if there is a bit of thrill to that as well. Yes, while I know it's most sensible to keep this, as I had said before, our little secret, I'm just…tired of hiding."

"*I* understand, my love. My worry is that your men will not."

"The knights are very accepting, my cherished one. Well, except for—"

"Sir Lance-A-Lot."

"Screweth him!" Arthur slammed his fist on the furry chair's arm.

"If you insist."

"What?" Arthur looked at her irritably. "I actually quite forbid it."

"The fact is that he's a man's man," said Guinevere smoothly. "Much like me."

"Right, but I'm still his king."

"Qu…I mean, that's true, yes."

Another squint. "I need no man's approval."

"Sadly, that's not true, Arthur, and you know it. The people look up to you. They need to know that you are a man of honor and integrity—and you ring true on both items splendidly—but they also need to know that you are a man who is into wearing clothing that befits societal norms."

"It is patently unfair!"

"I agree wholeheartedly," said Guinevere as she adjusted the sock that was stuffed down the front of her pants. "Sadly, it is our current state of affairs."

"I grumble at the angst that it brings."

"As do I, Arthur."

Arthur moved to the window and peeked outside. It was a rather calm evening in Camelot. People were moving about on the streets in small patches, demonstrating far less foot traffic than during the morning hours. Guards stood on the parapets and Arthur was certain that the knights were all preparing for their nightly bender.

"When I was younger," Guinevere said as Arthur continued his gazing, "there was a story about a magical item that allowed a person to be seen however they wished. A weak man could appear strong and muscular; a heavyset man could seem thin and fit; and a flat-chested woman could look to have an enormous set of jugs."

"Jugs?"

"Sorry, I tend to speak differently when I wear pants."

"Ah."

"I just wonder if this magical item truly exists," she said with a sigh. "It sure would solve our problems."

"That would indeed be something," Arthur mused. "I suppose it can't hurt to check with Merlin on the subject."

"Yes," Guinevere said earnestly. "Please do, Arthur. It may be nothing, but it may also be everything."

"Then I shall do so posthaste." Arthur threw off his robe and began putting on his kingly garb. "First, though, I must meet with the knights."

"Oh? Is there something wrong?"

"Lance-A-Lot claims that they are growing bored with all the sitting around. It seems that they are in need of an adventure."

"I see," she said. "Maybe when you speak with Merlin regarding that magical charm you can ask him if he has any suggestions for an adventure. He does seem to have a good deal of ideas."

"No arguing that."

# MERLIN'S NOTEBOOK: THE KNIGHTS OF THE ROUND TABLE

*LITTLE HAS BEEN told of the Knights of the Round Table because little is known about them.*

*The first thing of note is that they are the best sword players in the land. Each, except Sir Gareth, was trained by the master of cling-cling himself, Sir Challasby Lichen, who sadly died in a training incident a few years ago.*

*The second point is that they are quite non-judgmental. They don't care what a man or a woman does with themselves, or others for that matter, as long as it is consensual...which would hopefully always be the case in the event of one doing whatever it was they were doing to themselves.*

*Finally, all of them are of the same mind, except for their leader, Sir Lance-A-Lot.*

*Lance-A-Lot, whose real name is Mitch Bowenkawski, felt that the knights should have some sort of code; a standard of measurement (that only he could measure up to, but that's a different story) to live by. He has no issue with some level of debauchery—the name "Lance-A-Lot" was given to him due to the size of his tallywacker and the frequency with which he employs it, after all. But he expected them to set an example when examples needed to be set, and as he got older this became more important to him.*

# BORED KNIGHTS

ARTHUR STEPPED INTO the main Round Table room and found all the men were fully engaged in merriment.

The fire was roaring under the thick-beamed hearth, ale was sloshing this way and that, haunches of meat lay half-eaten on pewter plates, and wenches danced and laughed as the knights frolicked and cheered. If these men were truly as bored as Sir Lance-A-Lot had claimed, they sure had a funny way of showing it.

Sir Bors de Ganis was standing under one of the archways with one arm held high while he bellowed out lines from what sounded like a play of some sort. Sir Kay looked on, appraisingly. Of all of his knights, Bors and Kay were the only ones that were cultured. They participated in the local theater and sponsored many artistic galas. Whenever high-ranking officials came to Camelot, Bors and Kay, along with their equally snooty wives, were put in charge of the festivities. Though they supported the arts like nobody's business, they could be a bit uppity at times.

Lance-A-Lot stood against one of the walls, appearing to be deep in thought. That had been the case more and more as of late with him.

"Sir Lance-A-Lot," Arthur said as he approached his main knight, "are you feeling ill?"

Lance-A-Lot jolted off the wall. "No, sire. I am well. Why do you ask?"

"I've not seen you participating in the partying very much as of late, so I assumed that you weren't your normal self."

"I guess I've just grown tired of the same routine, sire."

"You mean you're not conquering the ladies anymore?"

"Oh, no," Lance-A-Lot said with a start, "nothing like that. I've just grown bored with all the sitting around."

"I see. And the other men?"

"It doesn't bother me that they sit around, sire."

"No, I mean do they still feel the same way as you had said before?"

"You mean during our one-on-one meeting?" Lance-A-Lot said. "You wouldn't know it by looking at them, but when the alcohol wears off they seem less chipper. We need something to resharpen our skills, sire."

"Indeed," Arthur said while noting that even his own mid-section was growing a tad soggy of late. "A quest would be just the thing."

"Or battle, sire."

"Or both."

"Both would be ideal," Lance-A-Lot agreed. "Honestly, I'd settle for just going on a caravan ride somewhere at this point, sire."

"Fresh ladies to conquer, eh?"

Lance-A-Lot looked despondent. "I *do* miss the initial shocked looks on their faces, sire. The lasses around Camelot no longer guffaw at the sight of me. They merely ask me to go easy on them."

"More than I needed to know," Arthur said with a grimace. "Anyway, I must put serious thought to this, Sir Lance-A-Lot. Actually, as part of that I'm about to visit the wizard this very night."

"Merlin?"

"Unless you know of another wizard?"

"No, sire. I just—"

"You don't trust him," Arthur said, looking back at the men. He ran his fingers through his beard. "You've said this many times."

"He can see things that others cannot. It worries me."

"He's on our side, Sir Lance-A-Lot," Arthur pointed out. Then he paused, thinking. "You know, calling you 'Sir Lance-A-Lot' takes a long time. It's not like 'Sir Kay' or even 'Sir Gareth.' Though, it's better than 'Sir Bors de Ganis,' I'll admit. Would you mind if I called you 'Mitch' instead? I mean, it *is* your real name."

Lance-A-Lot returned to his brooding look for a moment before answering. "I understand your position, sire," he said, "but I fear that the men may find it odd. I wouldn't want them to feel that they can start using that name with me. It would make for too much familiarity in the ranks, if you take my meaning."

"Fair enough, fair enough. How about just 'Lance,' then?"

"Still very informal, sire."

"What about 'Sal?'"

"Sal?"

"Basically, we're using the Sir bit and then your last name."

"But that would be Sbowenkawski, sire."

"No, not your *real* last name. Look, it's kind of a play on your initials, right? 'S' for 'Sir,' leave out the 'Lance' part, and use the 'A' from, well, 'A,' and the 'L' from 'Lot.' From that you get SAL, but we would lowercase the 'A' and the 'L,' of course."

"Oh, yes, I see now," Lance-A-Lot said with a look of uncertainty. "While I *do* admit that I rather like the name Sal, I would have to argue that it's as equally informal as Mitch or Lance."

"But your current name is the most informal of all!" Arthur nearly shrieked. "I mean, it's not even a real name, is it? It's basically a description of your manhood and the rate at which you employ it."

"Well, yes, but—"

"And you want to talk to me about informality?"

"I see your point, but—"

"Everyone calls you by your sexual prowess nickname, man!"

"It kind of stuck, sire," Lance-A-Lot said sheepishly.

"Very many times, I'd say, which is how you got the name in the first place."

"No, I meant—"

"I know what you meant," Arthur said with a grunt. "Forget it. I'll just call you by your sex-inspired name like everyone else does."

"Thank you, sire."

By now Arthur had his arms crossed over his chest and his face had grown stern. He understood the need for formality, obviously, especially when it came to the military, but this was lunacy. He harrumphed more than once as Lance-A-Lot stood stoically beside him.

"You wouldn't much like it if I demanded that you called me 'King Arthur, Ruler of the Realm of Camelot' every time you addressed me, now would you?"

"Probably not, sire."

"Exactly," Arthur stated. "Makes me wonder who really is in charge around here, it does."

"Yes, sire," Lance-A-Lot said in a way that sounded almost sarcastic.

Arthur squinted at him for a moment, but Lance-A-Lot's face didn't betray him in the slightest.

"Well, as I said, I'm going to meet with Merlin and I shall see if he has any thoughts regarding quests whilst I'm there."

"I hope the meeting proves fruitful, sire."

"I'll bet you do," Arthur said snidely as he stormed out of the Round Table room.

# MERLIN'S NOTEBOOK: MERLIN THE WIZARD

PEOPLE CONSIDER ME the greatest wizard in the land, and from their perspective I can understand why they would think that.

Truth is that magic hasn't been practiced in the world for many generations. There was a time when magic was as prolific as swordplay, but that was ages ago. There are still many talismans and artifacts infused with the old magic, but nothing new has been created in quite some time.

Then why do they consider me a wizard? Because I have knowledge that they do not understand. It's the same concept as showing a lantern to a caveman...it's not magic, but they'd think it was.

What the people of my day don't know is that I just happened to get lucky on three fronts:

*1 - I was born with an inquisitive mind.*

*2 - I happen to learn more quickly and more easily than others.*

*3 - Most importantly, I strolled into a cave one day many years ago that was being occupied by Allison, a woman from the future who was well-versed in science and technology.*

*It could arguably be stated that were it not for Allison, I would be nothing more to society than a bean-counter. On the flip side, it could be debated that had someone else stumbled into that cave on that day—who hadn't my capacity for intellectual pursuits, mind you—that Allison would have been taken away and burned at the stake for being a witch.*

*Side note: It's unfair, but society will burn a witch but they won't burn me. I think that it's because the men are afraid of having a woman in their midst who has the upper-hand in one way or another.*

*Well, Allison introduced me to science, showing me things I could not have learned in my era. On top of that, she gave me deep insights into technology, including a rudimentary computational device she called a "Heathkit." Since then I have graduated to a small computing device known as a "laptop."*

*Based on my learnings, I have carefully created tools for my personal growth and craft, and will, at some point, take on an apprentice and show him or her the way as well. For now, though, I keep my knowledge secretive so as not to jeopardize my personal existence.*

*Sadly, society is not ready for the full brunt of my knowledge; nor, in my lifetime, will it likely be.*

# CONSULTING A WIZARD

THE DOOR TO the wizard's lair was small and unadorned. It was pressed into the side of a mountain that sat just outside the main city, roughly a quarter of a mile to the west. While Arthur had visited on numerous occasions, it was different each time. The outside remained similar, except that it rolled along with the changing of the seasons, but the inside was always a surprise.

Arthur took a deep breath and steadied himself. King or not, dealing with a wizard was never much fun. Not because he was more powerful than any man alive, and not because he dabbled in things that should not be dabbled in, but because he was often terse and opinionated. Plus, as Lance-A-Lot had put it, the man knew things that he shouldn't know.

Forcing his resolve, Arthur started to knock on the door when he noticed a little sign that said, "press the button." He followed the arrow and saw a little gold button to the left of the handle. Pressing it, he heard a little musical sequence of bells play.

The door opened.

Peeking out was a man who looked to be in his mid-fifties. He was short, thin, and had long, gray, straggly hair that his beard matched perfectly. He wore a shirt with an image of a man who appeared to be a bard. Above the bard were the words "Elvis lives!" Arthur's first thought was to ask who this Elvis was, but when it came to asking Merlin things, one had to pick one's battles.

"Arthur?" Merlin said in his deep-timbered voice as he looked at a silver bracelet that contained glowing blue numbers. "It's ten o'clock at night. What are you doing here so late?"

"This is how you welcome your king?" Arthur said, trying to gain the upper hand.

"Bah," Merlin said. "You know I don't give a rat's ass about political hooplah, so don't even go there."

Arthur looked around. "Go where?"

"It's just a saying," Merlin replied with a roll of his eyes. "Come on in. I'm assuming that you've got something wacky going on or you wouldn't be here so late. So spill it."

"Spill what?" Arthur said, confused. "I have nothing to spill. And, though it goes against my better judgment to ask this…what does 'wacky' mean?"

Merlin frowned. "It's so trying to go back and forth between eras." Merlin started walking toward the rear of the cave. "Give me a moment, Arthur. I need to get my head straight."

Arthur felt nervous standing alone in the wizard's main room. The items stacked around made little sense to him. There were flameless torches on the wall; mechanical items zipping along tracks, looking like horseless carriages; tons of oddly shaped glasses that contained all sorts of colored liquids, some bubbling and releasing smoke; stacks of books on various desks or just piled up on the floor; and a plethora of drawings of lines and numbers that lacked any artistic substance that Arthur had ever seen.

But in the center of it all sat something miraculous. There were two metal posts sitting on a platform. They were spaced about a hand's width apart. Between them a blue light was moving back and forth, sliding up and down as it went. It was mesmerizing. Of all the things that Arthur had seen in the wizard's den over the years, this one won the prize.

Incapable of holding his curiosity at bay, Arthur reached out to touch the light.

"No!" Merlin raced over to where Arthur was standing and pushed his hand away. "You don't want to touch that, Arthur."

Arthur continued staring at the bolts with a stupefied look. They were dazzling. They called to him. Then, in the recesses of his brain, he began to realize that he'd just been admonished by the wizard. That did not sit well with his subconscious and he soon regained his wits, feeling provoked.

"I daresay that I may touch whatever I wish," he retaliated with a gasp. "I am your king, whether you like it or not, Merlin. That means that everything within this province is, in one way or another, mine should I so choose it to be."

"Actually," Merlin replied with a purse of his lips, "not really. But, hey, if you're going to be all pissy about it, go ahead and touch it. Just don't blame me when it kills you."

"Kills me?" Arthur said hotly. "Are you threatening me?"

"Of course not, you dolt," Merlin said with a laugh. Then he pointed at the device that Arthur had nearly touched. "What do you see when you look at that?"

"It looks like lightning."

"Well done. Now, have you ever seen what lightning can do to a tree?"

"Obviously, I have."

"Imagine yourself as a tree, Arthur," Merlin said. "Imagine that"—he pointed to the device—"as lightning. Now, what do you suppose would happen if you put your finger in there?"

"Oh, I uh—"

"You would be shocked something fierce. Badly enough that your heart would likely stop." Merlin stood there tapping his foot for a moment before he finally softened. "Now, I know there are a lot of things in here that look innocuous, and most probably are, but not all, and I would hate for you to become injured out of ignorance."

"Are you calling me ignorant, Merlin?"

"Ignorance is not the same thing as stupidity, Arthur," Merlin said with a groan. "What I said was not an insult."

"Hmmm."

"Look, why don't you tell me the reason for your

visit so we can move along with things?"

Arthur wanted to hang on to the argument. He despised being on the losing end of debates, even though it happened to him all the time. For now he needed the wizard to help him, so he decided to take the high road.

"Fine, fine," he said, stepping back away from the miniature lightning bolt. He wanted to jump straight to the topic of the magical item that Guinevere had mentioned, but he felt concern over the prospect of letting the wizard know about his fetish. He tried to work his resolve up, but eventually he simply said, "It seems that the knights have been suffering from boredom as of late and I need to find a quest that is worthy of them."

"Okay," Merlin said suspiciously, "and you're seeking *my* advice on this?"

"I just thought that maybe..." He trailed off.

"Something tells me that you didn't come all the way out here just to ask me for ideas, Arthur, especially not this late at night."

"Not exactly, no," Arthur said as his blood pressure began to rise. He loathed the thought of saying anything, but if there was any one man in the world who could help him and his beloved, that man was Merlin. "You see," he started slowly, "I was speaking with Guinevere earlier today and she mentioned that you might know something about a particular item that, well, uh—"

"Something magical, Arthur? A talisman, maybe?"

"I guess," Arthur replied. "I don't know. Maybe things like that don't truly exist. It could be nothing."

Arthur shook his head and bolted for the door. "I'm probably just wasting your time, Merlin. I should go."

"Magical talismans *do* exist, Arthur," Merlin said. "Most are harmless, but some can be quite useful while others can be very dangerous."

"I see," Arthur said, only hearing every other word. "Okay, well, thanks for the information. I'll see you some other time."

"Arthur," Merlin said with concern, "you're acting stranger than usual. Why don't you tell me what's really going on?"

"Stranger than usual?"

"Arthur, I'm probably the most progressive man in the world." He motioned around his room to drive home the point. "You have no fear confiding in me."

Arthur slowly let go of the handle and turned back toward the wizard. It was now or never. If the item spoken of during Guinevere's childhood did exist, it would allow a freedom that he desperately needed; if not, then his secret would be in the mind of not only his beloved, but also that of the elderly wizard before him.

"Guinevere said that there might be an item that I could wear that would make people see me as they expect to see me and not as I really am."

"Ah, I see," said Merlin with a slow nod. "So this is about the fact that you're a cross-dresser?"

"Yes, correct, and…wait, what?"

"A cross-dresser, Arthur," Merlin stated as if it were nothing to him. He then shrugged. "You like the feel of the frilly against your willy."

"I…what?"

"You like wearing women's clothing, Arthur."

"I do no such thing!" Arthur yelped. "The nerve! I could have you flayed alive for talking to me as thus. You could be drawn and quartered. Why, I—"

"Arthur, please remember that I can see things that others cannot. The panties beneath your pants, for example."

Arthur blanched. "You can see them?"

"No, but I had a feeling." Merlin walked over and poured a couple of drinks. "I'm not judging you, Arthur," he said as he handed a glass over. "It doesn't bother me what people do as long as they're not hurting anyone."

"That's basically the knights' credo."

"Indeed, and a good one at that. Your problem, though, is that the general populace doesn't share in that sentiment. Your knights would find your desire odd, but they'd eventually accept it. The people, though? That's a tougher sell."

"Yes," Arthur said, defeated.

"So what you're looking for are the Nipple Rings of Veiling."

"Rings, as in more than one?"

"Correct."

"But, wait…rings for your nipples? Wouldn't they fall off?"

"Why would they fall off?" Merlin said and then he gave a small laugh. "Oh, I see what you're thinking. They're not rings like you put on your fingers, Arthur. They pierce through your nipples, like an earring pierces through the earlobe."

"That sounds terrible," said Arthur, unconsciously

moving both hands to cover his breasts.

"Some talismans are made to be more permanent."

"So, then Guinevere was right? It does exist?"

"*They* do," Merlin emphasized. "There are two of them, Arthur, which is perfect since the other one can be worn by your lovely wife."

"You know about her, too?"

Merlin shrugged and took a seat on one of the rickety stools by the lightning-bolt table.

"Remember when you thought there was an assassin out to get you and you'd asked me to cast a spell on your dwellings to protect things?"

"Yes."

"Well, what I did was install motion sensitive cameras in the top corners of your room, and some motion detectors outside of your room as well. Those cameras caught a lot on tape that I would rather not have seen, but fortunately for you I'm a professional."

"I see," Arthur said, though he didn't. Again, his curiosity got the better of him. "Merlin, what are cameras and motion detectors? And, also, what is tape?"

"You're missing the important part, Arthur. I know why you want the talisman and I know where it is."

Arthur paused to consider things. He was both excited and disturbed.

"I have to admit that I'm not comfortable with you knowing what you know about me and my beloved, Merlin," Arthur said heavily, "but seeing that you know what will happen to you if you betray my trust —"

"Patently nothing," Merlin stated.

"—I shall choose to overlook it," Arthur finished. "Now, you said that you know where this talisman is, yes?"

"Scotland."

"Damn," Arthur said with a frown. "I hate Scotland."

"I know."

# A QUEST PRESENTED

"SILENCE, LADS," SIR Lance-A-Lot yelled above the din. "Your king wishes to address you."

"He wants to un…un…undress us?" Sir Bedivere said, sounding more plastered than he looked.

"He said 'address,' you imbecile," Sir Gawain said in his trademarked snooty tone.

"Oh," Bedivere said with a hurt look. "Not worth…worthy of calling me names."

Sir Gawain drooped his head for a moment. "You are most correct, Sir Bedivere. I offer my heartfelt apologies. May I be caught standing behind an angry steed at the edge of a cliff only to be kicked to my plummeting death."

"Consider it…*hic*…accepted," Bedivere said with a glassy smile.

As this exchange finished up, Arthur patiently waited for Sir Bors de Ganis to finish his scene. The man was lost in another world. He pointed this way and that, clutched his chest dramatically more than once, and even whipped off his hat, all while reciting phrases in his operatic voice. After a good thirty seconds, Arthur nodded at Lance-A-Lot.

"Sir Bors," Lance-A-Lot called out, "would you join us, please?"

There was no response. The play continued.

"Sir Galahad," Lance-A-Lot said to the one knight among the crew who somehow managed to look sour even in the best of times, "would you please—"

"Borsy," Galahad hollered, stopping the actor mid-sentence, "the king wants to yap at us about something or other. Sit yer ass down, yeah?"

Sir Bors moved with haste toward the nearest chair. "My apologies," he said between breaths. "I was just going through the lines of the *Glass Moon* play that that's coming up. It's about a knight who fights a werewolf who turns out to be the king's son." He looked up. Everyone was grimacing. "You all may actually enjoy this one. There's bloodshed."

"Hear, hear!" the knights cried in unison, clanking their mugs.

"Are the men still play...playing the lady's roles?" asked Bedivere.

Sir Kay seemed confused. "Why would there be actual ladies in plays?"

"Makes little sense to me," agreed Bors with a shrug as he dabbed his brow.

Bedivere rolled his eyes and belched.

Arthur nodded toward Lance-A-Lot, indicating that he should take a seat as well. Then Arthur stepped to the head of the main table and looked over the lot. They were a strong bunch. Some educated, most not, but they were good, sturdy men who had a strong desire to do what was right, no matter the cost. These were his knights, and they were the best in the land.

"It has come to my attention that you men have become bored."

"I'm not bored," said Sir Kay.

"Sorry?"

"Sire," Sir Kay said, "you know how it is when you're deep in your work. You have no time to think and reflect. Even when you get a couple of days off, you're so busy recovering and preparing for work to resume that the mind has no time to wander."

Arthur noted that everyone was nodding.

"Go on."

"Well, we've had quite some time during this dry spell, and that's given me time to dream again."

"Is that so?"

"It is, sire," Sir Kay confirmed. "Just the other day, as Sir Bors de Ganis and I were working on a new play—*A Knight to Remember*—we were thinking how wonderful it would be to tour all of Europe, bringing culture to the remotest of regions."

"Culture?"

"The arts," Sir Kay amended. "You see, our feeling is that if we improve the minds of the people, their status would improve along as well."

"Are you saying that you no longer wish to be a knight, Sir Kay?"

Sir Kay had the look of a man who was suddenly in the spotlight. "No, sire, not at all. If anything I would argue that the spread of culture is a very knightly thing indeed."

"I see," Arthur replied understandingly. "Not a bad idea, actually."

"Thank you, sire," Sir Kay said while raising his wine glass.

"And what of you, Sir Bors?"

"Sire?"

"Do you wish to the leave the knighthood?"

Sir Bors appeared taken aback. "I wouldn't hear of it, sire. Nearly all of my plays are based upon incidences that occur herewith."

"Good to hear, Sir Bors," Arthur said. "Anyone else have something to say?" Nobody did. "Well, I have just come from speaking with Merlin—"

"The wizard?"

"Unless you know of another Merlin, Sir Galahad?"

"Well, no."

"Is it a problem that I spoke with him?"

"Besides him being a wizard, you mean?" said Galahad after a moment. "There's just something that rings wrong about that man, is all."

Arthur sighed and leaned forward, placing both hands on the strong wooden table.

"I think you gentlemen need to remember that Merlin helped us through many a pickle over the years." He paused for dramatic effect. "He's on our side, gentlemen."

"Until he's not," Galahad said.

"Why would he not be on our side?"

"Might get a better offer, I suppose." Galahad began scratching on the table. "Could happen to any of us."

"What's that supposed to mean?"

Sir Galahad raised his head. "Just that, as far as kingdoms go, we're all paid under the going rate. So I'm assuming the wizard is, too."

Arthur pushed back off of the table and crossed his arms.

"Is that so?"

Sir Galahad reached down into his pack and pulled out a number of papers. He shuffled through them for a few moments, finally pulling forth the one he was looking for.

"That's the latest edition of *Knights Journal*," he said, sliding it across the table. "It shows the standard pay scale for all knights throughout Europe. We're the lowest paid of the bunch. Even the Scots make twenty-five shillings more a month than we do."

"I see," Arthur said at length while looking down at the paper.

"But don't the Scots have to pay for their own insurance, Sir Galahad?"

"That they do, Sir Lance-A-Lot," Galahad replied as a man who was clearly an expert on the subject, "but they also get their own choice of doctors, and the lines are much shorter."

"Only because there are fewer people who can afford doctoring, I would imagine."

"Survival of the fittest, sire."

"Well," Arthur said, pushing the paper back across the table, "I'm sure that we can discuss an equitable pay increase during the annual meeting next month."

"That'd be appreciated," said Galahad with resolve, "but I don't think it'd solve the wizard changing sides, unless his raise is substantial. There's only one of him and he's in demand."

"By whom?"

"Everyone," Galahad replied, holding up another paper. "Says so in *Wizards Quarterly*."

"You subscribe to *Wizards Quarterly*?"

"No, I buy it off the shelf."

"Why?"

"It's the only one of the bunch that costs less on the stand than by subscription," Galahad said with a shake of his head. "Makes no sense to me. Would be better to get a list of names, I'd think, but he's a wizard so I guess he's got some reason for—"

"No," Arthur interrupted, "I mean why do you read that publication?"

Galahad seemed surprised by the question. "I like to keep up with the times, sire. Doesn't everyone?"

The other knights were busily studying their fingernails.

"Apparently not, Sir Galahad." Arthur pointed at the paper. "Who even writes *Wizards Quarterly*?"

"Merlin does, of course."

"So he writes a paper for himself?" said Sir Gareth. "That makes little sense."

"You know what," Arthur said, waving his hands about, "I'm not worried about Merlin leaving our service. He's happy here. If he weren't, I'm certain he would let me know."

Galahad flipped a couple of pages on the publication and said, "Page seven of the latest *Wizards Quarterly* has an article entitled 'I'm not sure I'm still happy in Camelot.'"

"Truly?" Why hadn't Merlin mentioned anything? They'd had plenty of meetings over the last year. The man could have voiced his dismay on any number of occasions. "I suppose I will need to speak with him on the subject. For now, let's get to the matter at hand, shall we?"

"Hear, hear!"

"We are going on a quest to retrieve a magical talisman."

"A talisman, eh?" said Sir Purcivale, one of the younger knights. "That sounds right fancy. What say you, Tristy?"

"It's a round-and-round from my take, Percy," Sir Tristan replied, tapping his mug of ale to Purcivale's. They looked like a couple of twins to Arthur's eyes. Both young, both short—compared to the other knights—and both with curly blond hair. "Do it got the shimmer, guv?"

Arthur furrowed his brow. "The shimmer?"

"You know," said Purcivale, "is there a bling on the ring?"

"Bling?"

"Glitteries and that, guv," Tristan explained.

Lance-A-Lot spoke up: "He's asking if the ring has a magical field, sire. Something that makes it shine fancifully? Or maybe it gives off a glowing light?"

"Ah," Arthur said. "Honestly, I don't know. Merlin wasn't that specific."

"Would be right set fit if it had the sun's blister," Tristan said thoughtfully.

"No grievance there, Tristy," agreed Purcivale.

"Right," said Arthur with a shrug. "Anyway, I fear

that this quest may be trying at times. It will require your exacting skills if we are to succeed."

"Which skills would those be, sire?" asked Sir Gareth with a look of worry.

"Just knightly things, Sir Gareth."

Gareth's shoulders slumped. "Sire, everyone knows that I'm not all that gifted in knightly things. My hand-to-hand combat is terrible, my swordplay is sub-par at best, and my deftness with the bow is only slightly worse than my prowess with the pike."

"'Tis right true, lad," Sir Lamorak chimed in before Arthur could reply, "but you're the best cook this group has ever had."

"Hear, hear!"

Arthur decided to let Sir Lamorak say his piece. He was the only knight in the bunch who did his best to see the mug as half-full, after all. He was also the only one who kept his uniform shined and pressed. Lamorak had a confidence about him. His main trouble was that he brought this positiveness to battle with him, often helping his foe to improve their fighting tactics before finally doing them in. It was a bit creepy.

"And your gift with song," Lamorak continued, "has carried us through many a trying event."

"Hear, hear!"

"On top of that, your skill with mending our wounds has no equal."

"Hear, hear!"

"And let's not forget the speed with which you are able to sew up rips in our boots and leather-wear. Why, I'd wager that your skills in that alone could rival the best seamstresses in the land."

"Hear, hear!"

Arthur thought about that last testament for a moment. "That could prove useful if my bustier were to become torn."

"Hear...huh?"

"Sorry, I meant my tunic," Arthur said, recovering. "I was just recalling seeing my dearest Guinevere this morning while she was wearing her bustier, is all."

"Ahhh...hear, hear!"

"Hear, hear, indeed," said Lance-A-Lot with a faraway look.

"Settle down," Arthur said warningly. Everyone did. "Now, are there any further questions? I think we've all had our say, yes?" He glanced around the table. The only person who hadn't said anything was Sir Gaheris. He was often the quietest in the bunch, not to mention the most gruff of them all. Big, too. Arthur had once seen him engaged in fisticuffs with five brutes at a pub. They hadn't had a chance. His scarred face was imposing enough, but the eyepatch made it all the more so. "Sir Gaheris, we've not heard from you."

Gaheris set down his mug and looked at Arthur. "I go as I go."

Arthur couldn't help but shudder.

"Good," he said quickly. "Now, not all of you will be making this trip. Some will need to stay back and protect Camelot. I'll leave that up to Mitch...erm, Sir Lance-A-Lot to get sorted."

"I'd like to volunteer to stay, sire," offered Sir Bors. "Our play opens tomorrow night and I'm headlining this one."

"And I've been directing the play," Sir Kay stated. "If either of us are absent, we'll have to postpone."

"I don't have no…no…*hic*…innerest in going to Tallahassee neither," slurred Sir Bedivere.

"Tallahassee?" said Arthur. "What's that?"

"Ain't that where you was going?"

"He said 'talisman,' you deaf idiot," Sir Gawain said with a grunt.

"Oh…a tali…sman," Sir Bedivere said before frowning at Sir Gawain. "Ain't no reason to ca…call me…*hic*…names."

"I chastise myself in the name of the mother," Sir Gawain said sincerely. "May maggots infest my brain upon my death, or even slightly before."

"Good heavens, man," said Sir Kay with a look of disgust. "Can't you just say 'I'm Sorry' like everyone else?"

"I could, but there is so little substance in those words these days, Sir Kay." Sir Gawain turned back toward Arthur. "Sire, I too would like to stay. My day with the therapist is tomorrow and I'm finally making strides."

"If I could stay as well, it would be most appreciated," Sir Lamorak called out. "I'm slated to give a speech at a luncheon tomorrow. It's about how people can use their personal power to achieve wonderful things. I would surely hate to disappoint those who have signed up for the event, sire."

Arthur waited a moment to see if anyone else was going to back out. So much for all that talk from Lance-A-Lot about them all being bored.

"Well, that should make things easier on Sir Lance-A-Lot," he said finally. "Looks like we'll be taking Sirs Galahad, Gareth, Gaheris, Purcivale, and Tristan."

"And me," noted Lance-A-Lot.

"That was assumed," Arthur stated. "Now, men, lend me your ears for this I decree: tonight you are to drink up and be merry, and then get plenty of rest because tomorrow our quest begins."

"Hear, hear!"

"Oh, and Sir Gareth, do bring your instrument along as I'm sure the men would revel in your songs if things become discouraging."

"Hear, hear!"

# SPOONING

ARTHUR FELT A bit self-conscious as he walked into the bedroom. He was wearing a pink robe, stockings, and slippers. The moment he saw Guinevere, though, his mind was set to rest. She was wearing a pair of boxers and a sullied T-shirt.

He stepped out of the slippers and climbed in next to her.

Seeing that it was the night before a quest, there would be no fun-time between them. That was a rule they'd agreed upon many years before. Some people believed that they should engage in coitus before a battle or quest because it may be their last chance, but Arthur and Guinevere felt that it was better to postpone it until Arthur arrived back from the front lines because it would give him a stronger desire to return in one piece.

"So everything is a go?"

"Yes, my love," Arthur said while gazing into her emerald eyes. "We shall pack our supplies in the morning and begin our journey."

"And where is it that you will find the talisman, Arthur?"

"Scotland."

"That's rather vague," she said with a smirk. "Scotland is large."

"I've been there more times than you, my sweet. I'm aware of its enormity."

"No need to get snippy, Arthur," she replied. "Scotland, then."

"Scotland."

"But do you know the *specific* whereabouts of the talisman?"

"Scotland." This time it was said less confidently.

"So you don't know," said Guinevere with a sigh.

"What's to know? I'm the king, right? I'll just walk up to the nearest man, tell him to bring me to his local historian or what have you, and that person will tell me the whereabouts of the Nipple Rings of Veiling."

"I don't believe it will work as you say, Arthur."

Arthur pushed himself up on one elbow. "Do you suddenly doubt me, my cherished?"

"Suddenly?" She pursed her lips for a moment. "No, not suddenly."

"Good," Arthur started and then recognized the dig she'd just given him. "Hey, wait a second. Are you —"

"The problem is that you're not thinking properly, Arthur. I don't know if it's just because you're wearing my goodies or what, but your rationality is lax at present."

"Do my ears deceive me?" Arthur was feeling a bit

hot under the blouse. "Are you honestly speaking to me thusly? I daresay that you should soon find yourself sleeping on the couch."

"That's it," Guinevere said firmly as she sat up. "Listen to me, Arthur, and listen good. I'm the one currently wearing the pantaloons in this relationship, right?"

"Well—"

"Tomorrow morning you're going to get up and go to Merlin's hovel. And—"

"I can't believe—"

"*And* you're going to insist that he join you on this quest so that you can find the rings more simply. Are we clear, Arthur?"

Arthur slumped. It wasn't often that she talked with him like this, so when she did he ended up acquiescing most of the time.

"But Merlin makes everyone feel uncomfortable," he whined.

"Don't whine, Arthur. You know how it irritates me."

"But I don't want him to—"

"It's settled, then," Guinevere stated. "Unless, of course, you want to remove my stockings this instant."

"But it's cold," complained Arthur.

"Then I guess we have an agreement?"

Arthur groaned and lay back down, pulling the blankets up.

"Yes, dear."

"Good," Guinevere said. "Now, turn away from me so we can spoon."

Arthur complied happily, but instantly noticed something was awry.

"Please tell me that's a sock."

# MERLIN'S NOTEBOOK: FILMING

*IF THERE IS any one thing that could be construed as magic, it's the transference of light, color, and shadow onto a thin piece of plastic. While Allison never got into the details of how it works, I have read up on the process and have learned a fair bit. Unfortunately, I still don't understand what light-sensitive emulsion is.*

*Regardless, I have taken photographs and movies using the motion camera on many occasions. I have also used cameras for surveillance at the castle and have even set up night-vision cameras (with something called infrared) to try and spot the creature that continues to steal the apples from the fruit tree beyond my cave. Nothing on that yet, though.*

*What I have yet to do is to take on a full cinematic event, something Allison referred to as a "movie." I truly believe that I am what she calls a "director," at least at heart. But in order to find out I need something that spans the course of hours, days, or even weeks to bring to the camera. I have considered creating a documentary, but I'm not sure what I would pursue that any of my countrymen—or, frankly, anyone from my era —would find interesting. Truth be told, they would probably run away in terror.*

# THE MORNING RUSH

ANYONE WHO KNEW Guinevere understood that she was not an early riser. Once her head hit the pillow and her eyes shut down for the night, it would be near noon before she was back in the land of the living.

Arthur, however, was up at the first calling of the rooster in town.

He donned a nice pair of blue lace panties and then pulled on the rest of his normal gear. It wasn't exactly what he wanted to wear, but with any luck his choice of garb wouldn't be an issue for much longer.

Guinevere was still snoring when Arthur made his way out onto the main street in town.

People were bustling along the sunlit cobblestones, making their way to work or going to buy their wares for the day. Merchants were all set up, calling out for people to check their latest offerings.

It was exhilarating to be among his subjects.

Most of their faces were cheerful as he walked past. Some not so much, but he assumed that had to do with a prior evening's bout with booze. It was one of the many reasons that he avoided alcohol, except from time to time when an event called for him to participate.

The smell of baking bread made him salivate, but he tended to stay away from what Merlin called "carbs." Arthur tried to keep his figure, after all.

"Good morning, m'lord," said one passerby, smiling. It was nice to see that she had all of her teeth.

"Beautiful day," Arthur replied with a wink and they both continued along their separate paths.

"Nice to see his lordship out and about," said a middle-aged man who was wearing a fine green hat.

"Nice to be out and about on such a fine morning," Arthur agreed.

"You're a worm and everyone knows it," said a grimacing old woman.

"It sure is a beaut—" Arthur stopped and looked back for the woman, but she had disappeared into the crowd. "Well, I'll be!"

Just then, another peasant stopped in front of him. This one was wearing a veil, meaning that she was mourning the loss of someone. Arthur tried to see her face, but he could not.

"You're an awful ruler," she said tightly. "I hope that a swarm of leeches attach themselves to your nethers and drain the life from them so you can't possibly produce an heir."

"Hey now," Arthur said in shock, "you can't speak…where are you going?"

She had turned and folded herself into the crowd

as well. Arthur considered chasing after her, but he was now caught up in the tide of those coming toward him. His beautiful day was growing dark indeed.

"Poor excuse for a king, you are," said a sour-looking man.

"This is ridiculous," Arthur said angrily before lowering his head in the hopes that nobody else would recognize him.

"G'day, Mr. King," said a pleasant voice.

"Whatever," replied Arthur.

He picked up his pace until he was free of the main street, resolving to go around the back way when he returned to the castle.

# JOINING THE QUEST

ANYONE WHO KNEW Merlin understood that Guinevere seemed to be an early riser compared to him. Arthur, though, tended not to remember these things about the wizard.

He rang the bell and waited.

Nothing.

He rang the bell again and then took a step back and glanced around to see if maybe the wizard was outside toiling in his garden. He was nowhere to be seen. Clearly the man was at home.

Arthur decided to go the old-fashioned route and started to bang on the door. Just as he was about to give up, the wizard whipped open the door and caught Arthur's fist in his hand.

"What the hell is so damned important that you felt the need to wake me up at this time of day? Is the kingdom on fire?"

"Well, no."

"Are we at war?"

"No."

"Did someone release a plague on the people?"

"Not that I'm aware of."

"Then?" Merlin said with his eyebrows up.

Obviously Merlin was irritated at being awoken, but this was no way to talk to a king.

"Honestly, man," Arthur said with a stern look, "you should show some respect."

"I could say the same, Arthur. Who in their right mind shows up at a wizard's house at the crack of dawn expecting him to be chipper and pleasant?"

"But it's morning," Arthur exclaimed. "The streets below are filled with people. Work is underway and has been for the better part of an hour."

"In your world, maybe, but my house has electricity. I stay up most of the night."

"I don't understand."

"I like the night life, Arthur," Merlin said. "I like to boogie."

"Boogie?"

"It's just a saying."

"I've never heard of it."

"I'm not surprised. Listen, Arthur, was there a reason that you came beating the hell out of my door or were you just bored and looking for someone to torment?"

"As to that," Arthur said with some cheer in his voice, "I will need you to join in this quest."

"Not gonna happen," Merlin said without pause.

"Please don't make things difficult, Merlin."

"I'm not," Merlin said matter-of-factly. "I'm making it quite simple. I'm not going."

"I could order you to go."

"No, you couldn't. I mean, yes, you could, but it wouldn't matter since you have no real authority over me."

"I am your king, man!"

Merlin shut his eyes and took a deep breath. Arthur was livid. The insolence this man showed held no bounds. Even the peasants in town knew better than to stick around after speaking their minds.

"Arthur," Merlin said as if speaking to a child, which only incensed Arthur further, "I get that you're the king and all that, but you're *not* my king. I'm from a different cut than everyone else and you know it." By now he had the door fully open and he was using hand gestures. "When they zig, I zag. I'm the yan to their ying...or is it the other way around? Either way, it's nonsensical to expect me to act as a typical subject when I'm the only one of my kind." He leaned on the door frame. "You can't find another wizard, Arthur, and many countries are clamoring to take me away from you as it is."

"Are you threatening to leave me, Merlin?"

"Yep."

"Oh."

Arthur let the angst go. The fact was that the wizard was right, though as long as he remained in Arthur's employ the king would continue demanding respect, even if those demands continued to fall on deaf ears. This was *his* kingdom, after all.

"Why do you need me to come along with you, anyway?"

"Because we don't know where the talisman is, Merlin."

"Scotland."

"That's what I said," said Arthur, nodding fervently, "but Guinevere pointed out that Scotland is a large country."

"I suppose it is at that."

"Come now, Merlin," Arthur said, "we are in need of your skills. When was the last time I asked you to leave your home for anything?"

"Yeah, yeah, yeah," Merlin said with a groan. Then, suddenly he snapped his fingers and pointed at Arthur. "Hey, wait a snip. I've been thinking about making a full-length film for the last few months now, but I've not had any ideas on what to cover. This could be the perfect gig."

"That sounds exciting," Arthur said supportively.

"Doesn't it?"

"Honestly, I don't know because I haven't the foggiest idea what a full-length film is, or a gig for that matter, but if it will get you out of your door and on the road with us then that's exciting enough for me."

Merlin gave a small laugh and then looked at his feet thoughtfully. "I'll have to bring Allison," he said softly, as though talking to himself.

"Who?" asked Arthur.

"Oh, you don't know her. She's my…uh… apprentice."

"Oh, that's nice," said Arthur. "I didn't know you had an apprentice."

"There are many things you don't know about me, Arthur," Merlin replied offhandedly. "That's just the way of things."

"I have secrets too, you know."

"Not from me," Merlin stated. He tapped his chin for a few moments, looking to be deep in thought. "All right," he said finally, "I'll go. Allison has been struggling to come up with a topic for her doctoral thesis anyway, so I might finally be able to pay her back for all of her help."

"Paying back your apprentice?"

"Huh?" Merlin said, clearly realizing again that he wasn't alone. "Just ignore that. Wizards are an odd bunch, Arthur."

"I shant argue that point," Arthur said, feeling as if he'd gotten a bit of an upper hand. "Good, then. We shall leave once the sun strikes noon."

"Noon is too early," Merlin objected. "We'll go around two or three this afternoon. I've got things to pack up and such."

Arthur turned around to look down over the main street again. He certainly had no intention of heading back through that pit of people. It was pathetic that he actually had to consider cutting through the back alley in order to avoid being criticized, but such was the life of a king, he supposed.

"Don't bring too much, Merlin..." he started as he turned back, only to find that the wizard had shut his door, leaving Arthur alone. "We need to be able to maintain our pace," he finished in a defeated tone.

# MERLIN'S NOTEBOOK: TIME TRAVEL

*THERE'S NOT MUCH known about the full impact of traveling through time. But there is a worry that by having Allison interact with the knights, the world in her future may be drastically altered by the smallest of things.*

*According to Allison, it's only a one-way street. Her learning about us and sharing that information doesn't impact her era, but our learning about her time* would *impact both eras. Or something like that. I'm still fuzzy on the details.*

*It's already bad enough that she and I have discussed many things. Fortunately, I'm a very private person. Even more fortunate is the fact that people tend to fear me and my technology. In other words, I don't share enough for the timeline to be overly abused. I hope.*

# KICKING OFF

THE KNIGHTS WHO were slated to join the quest were all in the courtyard waiting to start the journey.

With the afternoon sun beating down on his gear, Arthur couldn't help but wish he was wearing something more dainty, such as a sundress. Soon enough, he thought hopefully. Until then, he would have to manage the same way he'd done for all of his adult life: begrudgingly.

A couple of the castle helpers brought out the king's crate. It was probably overkill in packing, but with the potentiality of being able to wear anything he wanted after getting a hold of the ring, he couldn't resist.

"Sire," Lance-A-Lot said while staring at the overlarge crate, "I fear that something of that size is going to slow us down immeasurably."

"I could say the same about you," Arthur said under his breath.

"What's that, sire?"

"Nothing, Sir Lance-A-Lot. The items in here are

important. Besides, it's only one crate."

"Yes, sire, but it's nearly the size of a man and it probably weighs about as much as one, too."

"These things are necessities," Arthur said. "And before you admonish me, maybe you should think about the size of the thing that you're carrying."

"It's attached to me, sire," Lance-A-Lot said apologetically.

"What? No, not that! I mean your backpack."

"Oh, yes." Lance-A-Lot slipped the pack off his shoulder. "Do recall, sire, that I have the duty of carrying your documents and decrees whenever we travel."

That was true, but there was undoubtedly more in that pack than mere papers. Of course, Arthur had made a lot of decrees over the years. He peered around to find the other men had packs with them that were also rather sizable. Granted, none of them had a crate, but still.

"Arthur," Guinevere called out from the doorway, "may I have a word, please?" She then smiled at Lance-A-Lot and said, "Oh, hello, Mitch."

"M'lady," Lance-A-Lot replied with a bow.

"No," Arthur said, giving Lance-A-Lot a dirty look, "*my* lady." Arthur stormed over to Guinevere and stepped into the shadow of the doorway. "You know I dislike it when you intrude during the knights' get-togethers."

"Couldn't be helped," she replied calmly. "You are bringing far too much, Arthur. Is it not up to you to set an example for your men?"

"It's only a few things, apple of my eye. Once I

secure the talisman I want to free myself of these dreadful clothes."

"There will be plenty of time for that when you return. Do you not think I'd rather be wearing trousers right about now?"

"But—"

"Arthur," she said in a low voice.

"Oh fine," he replied in a huff, "I'll pare down a little."

"No need," Guinevere said with a wink while handing him a satchel. "I packed everything you should need right here. And worry you not, for I included something delicious in there for when the time is right. It's wrapped and carefully placed at the bottom, where it should stay until the right time."

"Oh?" Arthur said, moving to open the pack.

"Now is not the right time, Arthur," Guinevere said with a sinister grin. "You must wait." She lifted his chin and kissed him gently. "Promise me?"

"Okay, okay, I promise." He then kissed her again. "I shall miss you, my persimmon."

"And I you. Now, scoot along and bring us back those talismans."

Arthur returned back to Lance-A-Lot as the housemen struggled to carry his crate back into the castle. Guinevere, as usual, was right. He didn't need all of the items that he'd brought. His mind raced at what she could have placed in the satchel for him as a surprise, but he was a man of honor. He would not look until the time was right.

"Ah," Lance-A-Lot said, nodding at the satchel, "that is much more sensible, sire."

"Well, I thought it through and came to the conclusion that we needn't have anything to hold us back."

"Wise, sire."

"Make sure the others pare down too, will you? Each shall have a satchel such as mine. If an item doesn't fit, they don't bring it."

"I shall speak with them at once, sire."

Moments later Arthur heard the groaning of men as they began emptying their packs. Bottles were the primary items being set aside, which was a good thing as far as Arthur was concerned. One never knew what to expect when journeying. The last thing he needed was to have a bunch of drunkards at a most inopportune time.

That's when Merlin came through the gates, towing along a young woman who was dressed funnily. More than that, though, was the carriage that sat just beyond the gate. It had a number of odd-looking devices in it, and the wizard was carrying a few more on his person.

"Hey now," Sir Galahad complained, "why's the wizard get to bring all that fluff? I just wanted to have a few periodicals along to feed my mind, but I had to put it all aside."

"And a few bottles too," Lance-A-Lot said, pointing.

"Well, yeah, that too."

Sirs Purcivale and Tristan stepped up and stood on their toes to look out past the gate.

"He's got loads of bits and bobbles," said Purcivale.

"It looks as heavy as a bevy, guv," agreed Tristan.

"I daresay, Mr. Merlin," started Sir Gawain, who wasn't even slated to join on with this journey, "you must be some kind of dullard to think that level of carry along is passable."

Merlin stopped and looked at Gawain with a frown. "First off, Gawain, I don't need any of the knight's horses. I have my own. Secondly, you can stuff your insults up your ass and keep them plugged in with a titanium cork."

"My most humble apologies to you, Mr. Merlin," Sir Gawain said as his initial shock seemed to fade. "It seems as though I'm speaking out of turn again. I *am* working on that, but I've clearly failed again. May the gods strike me with leprosy for speaking to you as thus. And here I am not even joining the trip. I was just looking into lend assistance."

"You're doing a swell job so far," Merlin said with a grunt.

"Mr. Merlin, may I ask what a titanium cork is?"

"Sure, go head," Merlin answered with a shrug before turning toward Arthur. "This is Allision Smith. Allison, this is King Arthur of Camelot."

"Lovely to make your acquaintance, Allison Smith."

"Just Allison," she replied. "No reason to use my full name."

"That's a nice diversion," Arthur said with a sideways glance toward Lance-A-Lot.

Merlin then began pointing at each of the other knights, in turn. "And this is Lance-A-Lot and Galahad and Gareth and Gaheris and Purcivale and Tristan." Then he pointed over his shoulder with his thumb and added, "And that's Gawain. He's staying behind."

"It's a pleasure to meet you all," Allison said with a beaming smile.

"I've never been with a witch before," said Lance-A-Lot in a hungry voice.

"Keep it tucked away, Lance," Merlin warned, "or I'll turn it into something a bit more average."

Lance-A-Lot blanched. "Consider it tucked."

"Now that we've finished with our introductions," Merlin announced, "I must insist that you all treat Allison as if she's not truly here. I know it sounds cruel, but it is the way of my…uh…well, order I suppose. Are we clear?"

Nods all around.

"She may ask you questions now and again, and you may answer them, of course, but just be wary of getting too close to her as she learns magic." He paused and grew dark. "I wouldn't want any of you to get inadvertently transformed into a frog."

The knights all looked at Allison and slowly took a step backward.

Even Arthur found himself moving away from the lovely young lady. Magic was a scary thing, or could be anyway.

"Merlin," Arthur said after a few moments had passed, "do you honestly need to bring all of that? It seems a bit overkill, yes?"

"I saw them dragging your crate away, Arthur," Merlin said. "Could see that monstrosity from all the way up the hill."

"Ah, but they *did* drag it away and now I merely

have this satchel. We are all paring down, after all."

"Sadly," Merlin retorted, "I cannot. I need all of this. I've got cameras, mikes, booms, video editing software, and my laptop. It's all necessary."

Arthur wanted to question what those things were. The confused looks on all his knights' faces spelled that they, too, were curious. But there was no point in asking since the wizard would just claim them to be magical or something.

"Thing is, Merlin, that you'll just slow us all down."

"No, I won't," Merlin replied. "I have a carriage and two horses. The speed at which we scoot should not be affected." He smiled convincingly. "If, however, I do slow us down then we'll just get there when we get there."

"Hmmm," said Arthur.

"Seems unfair, if you ask me."

"Fortunately, Galahad," Merlin replied with a sneer, "we didn't."

"Sir Gaheris," Arthur said, noticing that the man had no carry-on at all, "do you not have a bag?"

"Don't need one."

"No? Not even a hairbrush or possibly a change of clothes?"

"I'm good."

It looked like Arthur was going to have to have his annual "cleanliness" talk with the burly man again. Every year it was the same thing: Gaheris would start out well enough, combing his hair and having his clothes washed once a week. Then it would slowly degrade into monthly washings and then every two months. Finally it would stop altogether and they would discuss it because the other men would begin to complain.

"Shall we get moving, sire?" Lance-A-Lot suggested. "I would imagine we could at least get in a number of miles before dark."

"Indeed, we shall," Arthur said. "Ready your steeds, men."

"Wait, wait," Merlin said.

The wizard motioned Allison to stand next to him. She did and then pulled out a long pole that had a shorter pole hanging from it. On the tip of the shorter pole was a fuzzy-looking top. Merlin then set something that looked like a box on his own shoulder. It had a circular piece of glass in its center and a little red light was blinking above it.

"What is this all about?" Arthur asked.

"I'm filming this adventure, remember?"

"I do," Arthur said, "but I still have no idea what that means."

"Just tell everyone again that it's time to depart," Merlin directed.

"Okay. Everyone, it's—"

"Wait until I say, 'action!'"

"Why?"

"It's just how it's done, Arthur," Merlin said as if Arthur should have known this already. "Okay, take one, and…action!"

Arthur felt confused. "Everyone…let's go."

"Cut!" Merlin yelled and then lowered the box. "Arthur, you have to be more regal than that. You're a king, right?"

"Well, yes, of course I am."

"Then *act* like one," Merlin said. "Let's try this again, everyone. Oh, and Lance, could you move over to the right a couple of steps? Good. Now, turn and face us so that bulge of your whatsitwhosit isn't casting a shadow on Arthur."

"Always seems to," Arthur murmured.

"There," Merlin said as Lance-A-Lot got into place, "that's perfect. Don't move. Okay, Arthur, let's try this again. Take two, and…action!"

Arthur puffed out his chest and put on his best kingly performance.

"We shall commence on our journey straightaway. To your steeds, my knights. Our quest awaits."

"Annnd…cut," Merlin said with a smile. "That was dead-on, Arthur. Top-notch stuff."

"What? Something died? I thought I did it well that time."

"No, 'dead-on' means that you did it perfectly."

"Oh," Arthur said, blinking. "Good. I guess."

# MERLIN'S NOTEBOOK: JOURNEYS

THERE ARE FEW things in this world less appealing than journeys. Packing alone is a pain, but that's not the worst of it.

Riding on a horse gives you bruises and hemorrhoids; the elements are constantly bombarding you during your trek; the food typically consists of dried meat and cheese, if you're lucky; camping out brings bugs, snakes, and all manner of creatures into your little world; most inns are run by money-grabbing fools who sell watered-down beer and mysteriously-flavored stews; and there's a constant risk of being jumped by highwaymen along the way.

Allison says that travel is arduous in the future, too, but she does admit that it has improved greatly over my era, except, she says, when flights are delayed, or worse, canceled...though I have no clue what that means.

# THE ROAD TO SCOTLAND

THE CARAVAN MOVED at a brisk pace. Even Merlin's carriage had kept up without a fuss. Arthur assumed that the items tucked away in the back were not as heavy as they appeared.

Allison seemed like a nice girl. From watching her sitting on the seat at the reins with the wizard, you'd have thought she'd never ridden with horses before. Why anyone would want to sit up on the bench and not in the back carriage was beyond Arthur, but she truly seemed to love it and the king couldn't help but smile at her giddiness.

Arthur adjusted in his saddle, suddenly wishing he'd not gone with the lace panties. Something softer would have made for an easier ride, especially when they were galloping.

At least the weather had calmed a bit. The mid-afternoon heat had been replaced with a mildness that was pleasing. A nice cool breeze picked up as the sun was making its descent toward the horizon. Unfortunately, there was the smell of rain in the air. He glanced up at the sky and saw dark clouds off in the distance. From his experience, they still had a couple of hours before that became a worry, but he wanted to be smartly tucked into an inn before the first drops hit.

He slowed his pace until he was trotting alongside of Merlin's carriage. If anyone knew how far out they were, it would be the wizard.

"We've been traveling for a few hours now," Arthur said, "what does your intuition tell you regarding our progress?"

"My intuition?" Merlin replied quizzically. "Oh, right. Uh, well, let's see." He stuck his finger in his mouth and then held it up in the air for a few moments. Then he looked both left and right and then pushed himself up slightly and glanced toward their rear. "I'd say were roughly a few hours away from Camelot."

"Good, good," said Arthur with a satisfied nod. "Well, that's progress, then."

"Beats spinning our wheels," Merlin replied.

Arthur looked down at the spinning wheels on the carriage. He shrugged. "Are we tracking toward the proper location in Scotland?"

"Should be," said Merlin. "I mean, we'll likely have to make some course corrections once we get to the border, but for now it's looking good."

The king tapped the sides of his horse with his boots and sped back up to rejoin the knights. He didn't want to have a long conversation with Merlin about, well, anything, and he was certain that the wizard felt the same way.

"What did the wizard say?" asked Lance-A-Lot.

"We're going the right direction," Arthur replied while adjusting himself slightly.

"Everything okay?"

"Huh? Oh, yes, Lance-A-Lot, I'm fine. Just a case of saddle-seat, I guess."

"Ah."

"Of course we're going in the right direction," Galahad said. "Don't need a wizard to tell us that. Just look at that big sign right there."

Galahad was pointing at a large wooden sign that sat on the side of the road. It stood a good twenty feet high and had large text that read, "This way to Scotland." Directly under that was a smaller sign that read "Pick up some Buzzard's Ale today!"

"Hmmm," said Arthur while peering back at Merlin, who was whistling, "I wonder if he saw that."

"Probably," Lance-A-Lot answered. "Makes you wonder if he really knows where this magical talisman is."

"Doubt it," Galahad said. "Probably just wanted to get his tail out of that cave of his for a spell."

"A spell?"

"Not that kind, Lance-A-Lot. I meant that he wanted to get away for a while."

"Somehow I doubt that," Arthur said. "He's rather a homebody, after all."

"Well," Lance-A-Lot said doubtfully, "I hope his skills come to play as we approach the border."

"Got bigger problems than that," Galahad said in a

monotone voice as they turned through a clearing of trees.

Up ahead Arthur saw two men wearing black outfits and masks. They were sitting on the back of angry-looking horses and they had their swords at the ready.

"Highwaymen?"

"Yes, sire," said Lance-A-Lot.

"But there are only two of them."

"There'll be more in the woods," Galahad stated while looking up into the hills. "Archers, likely."

"I shall rally the other knights, sire."

"I'll tell Merlin to stay back," Arthur said as he dropped back again to the carriage. Once he was again in-line with the wizard, he said, "Merlin, we have trouble up ahead. It would be best if you and Miss Allison stopped here and took cover inside of the coach."

"Nothing doing," said Merlin. "I came out here to film this adventure and that's precisely what I'm going to do."

"I'm sorry, Merlin, but I must insist."

"You do realize I'm a wizard, right?"

"Of course, but—"

"And you know that means that I can turn you all into a bunch of blathering chickens with a snap of my fingers, yes?"

"It was on your resume when you interviewed for the job," Arthur recalled.

"So why are you worried for my safety, then?" Merlin asked. "If anything, I should be worried for yours."

Merlin snapped the reins and sped up near the front before pulling the carriage to a stop on the side of the path. Arthur found the entire ordeal irritating, but the fact was that the wizard *could* handle himself just fine. Still, if anything did happen to the man, even if just by chance, that would be a blow to Camelot.

As Arthur stepped down from his horse, he noted that Merlin was pulling out a few boxes and setting things up. Allison was at his side helping.

"What's he doing?" asked Lance-A-Lot.

"He's 'filming it'," answered Arthur. "Whatever that means."

One of the highwaymen called out, "Ready your arrows, men."

Arthur looked up into the hills, trying to spot movement. They were obviously well concealed.

The knights had drawn their swords and were walking toward the two highwaymen when the bellowing voice of Merlin froze them all in their tracks.

"You there, knights and brigands alike, I command you to hold!"

Both sides looked questioningly at the wizard.

"You," Merlin pointed at Sir Gareth, "you're pointless in fighting, right?"

"Well—"

"Grab me the tripod."

"You mean Sir Lance-A-Lot?"

"Hmmm? Oh, no," Merlin pointed across the grass, "I mean that stand over there by my carriage. It's to help hold the camera still."

Merlin walked briskly up to the space between the two parties with Allison on his heel. He started setting his items in place while everyone waited in disbelief.

"What in blazes are you doing, man?" Sir Gaheris asked with a grumble. "Can't you see we're about to engage in fisticuffs?"

"As part of my agreement with King Arthur," Merlin said as he continued his work, "I am filming everything that I deem holds merit, and that includes the skirmish that's about to unfold."

"Excuse me," said the dark-haired highwayman, "did you just say King Arthur?"

"Yes."

"So you're saying that we're robbing the king?"

Merlin looked up and then motioned back toward Arthur. "Did you not see the oversized plume on his helmet?"

"Well, of course," answered the man, "but I thought it was some kind of carnival thing."

"How dare you?" said Arthur with a start. "I'll have you flayed alive for that."

"Look," said the highwayman as he put his sword back in its scabbard, "I think we're just going to go. Sorry if we put the scare in you or anything. Just trying to make a living, is all."

"You're not going anywhere," Merlin said.

"Except to hades," agreed Sir Gaheris.

The highwayman frowned at the knight for a moment. "That's a little dramatic, isn't it?" he said. Sir Gaheris did not reply, so the highwayman turned his attention back toward Merlin. "Who are you supposed to be, anyway?"

"I'm Merlin."

"Merlin the Wizard?" the highwayman said with a choke.

"Honestly?" said Arthur with his hands in the air. "Why do people keep having to clarify that? Of course he's the wizard. I mean, seriously, how many people in this world are named Merlin? Nobody is. It's an odd name."

"That was intentional," stated Merlin.

"I would hope so."

The highwayman turned to his partner in crime and said, "I thought you said you'd scouted this bunch out."

"It was dark," the smaller fellow said.

"It was only an hour ago," exclaimed the main highwayman. "The sun ain't even down now."

"Right, but I had forgotten to take me mask off during the scouting. I'd just heard voices."

After a few moments of staring in disbelief at his comrade, the main thief turned toward Arthur and the knights and said, "It appears that we have a misunderstanding here, gents."

"What's there to misunderstand?" Sir Gaheris replied, gripping the hilt of his sword with both hands. "You're a bunch of scum-sucking leeches who need to be shown the blade. Seems pretty clear to me."

"Ouch," said the smaller highwayman. "That hurts, you know."

"Ouch, indeed," agreed his partner. "It's not like we want to be doing this for a living. I'd rather be working an honorable job. But the economy ain't what it used to be. Gotta figure out some way to feed our children."

Sir Gaheris lowered his blade and softened slightly. "The economy is bad?"

"Ever since the brick hut market crashed last year," explained Sir Galahad, "the shilling lost a lot of its value." Everyone was looking at him. "What? There was a big writeup about it in *CFM...Castle Finance Magazine*."

"I didn't know about that," Sir Gaheris said apologetically. "I'm sorry for what I said."

"Don't fret over it," the highwayman said with a wave of his hand. "If I were being truthful, I'd say we've been called worse, and rightfully so. It's just such a challenge to make an honest living in this day and age."

"I'm sorry you feel that way," Arthur chimed in snootily. "Maybe you would be happier living in some other kingdom."

"Been honestly thinking about, m'lord. Pretty much every other country is in a better state of affairs at current. For example, did you know that Scotland has a private healthcare system?"

"So I've heard," answered Arthur with a sigh.

"Okay," Merlin stated, "I'm done. That means we're done talking." He moved to sit in a chair that said "Director" on it. "Now, here's how it's going to work. I'm going to call out 'action' and everyone is going to start kicking each other's asses. Got it?"

"What's he talking about?" the highwayman asked Arthur

"It's best to just do as he says. He *is* a wizard, after

all."

"Right."

"Annnd….action!"

The knights and the brigands began running after each other, trying desperately to kick each other in the rump. Arthur found the scene completely pointless, thinking that it would have been far more interesting to have watched an actual fight.

"Cut, cut, cut!" Merlin got up and looked them all over."What the hell are you all doing?"

"Doing the old 'boot in the britches'," Purcivale said between ragged breaths. "Just like you said, guv."

"Yeah, tappin' the tail with the toe," Tristan agreed.

"I didn't mean it literally, you morons," Merlin said. "I meant that you have to fight. Really get into it."

"But we're no match for the Knights of the Round Table," the highwayman said.

"And they're no match for me," Merlin countered. "Get it?"

"Got it."

"Good." Merlin returned from his chair. "To your point, though, two of you won't do against the skills of these men. Call down the rest of your flock from the hills."

"The what? Oh, I see what you mean. That's just a ruse. There's nobody in the hills. We just say that because it makes people surrender more easily."

"Clever," said Merlin with a nod of his head. "Well, I guess I'll just have to zoom in on you two and somehow make it look like you've got a group of men. I'll handle that in editing."

"Zoom into me?"

"Don't bother asking," Arthur said to the highwayman, "the explanations are often more confusing than the questions."

"Hey," Merlin said after a second, "I have an idea. Gareth, since you stink with the blade anyway, why don't you take your helmet off, turn your shirt inside out, and pretend to be one of the highwaymen?"

"Uh, but—"

"Do it, man," Merlin commanded. "The light is waning."

"I don't want to be a brigand," Sir Gareth complained.

"Would you prefer to be a toad?"

Sir Gareth removed his helmet and set about flipping his shirt inside out. A few moments later he was standing next to the highwaymen, looking almost as if he actually belonged with them.

"Now, I want everyone to do their best in this scene," Merlin said. "Make it count because we only have a few minutes of decent light left. Annnd… action!"

Swords were flashing about. The men were leaping and rolling all over the place. Sir Gareth was mostly running away from Sir Tristan and Sir Purcivale. The main highwayman was putting up a decent effort against Sir Gaheris, which was not an easy thing to do. The smaller highwayman was staving off hit after hit from Sir Lance-A-Lot. All in all, they were faring pretty well, which Arthur knew was only because his knights were going easy on them.

"Okay, okay," Merlin said after a time. "Cut. I've got enough here to piece something together, no thanks to you Sir Gareth. Poor excuse for a knight." He mumbled a few choice words that Arthur could not make out. "Besides, I wouldn't want anyone to get mortally wounded during filming."

"Unless it adds to the dramatic prose, of course," noted Allison.

"Well, yeah, then it's okay."

"Are we finished here?" asked Arthur.

"For now," Merlin replied, stuffing items back into the box he'd brought with him. "It's a lot of work, but I'm confident it will be worth it. Next time I'll need to employ some helpers. Carrying everything around on my own is simply too taxing."

Arthur climbed back on to his horse and said, "We should find a place to stay for the evening. Those clouds are growing ever closer and I'd rather not get soaked."

"After turning these criminals over to the local magistrate, of course," said Sir Gaheris.

"Most certainly."

"Hey now," said the main highwayman, "that's not fair. We never actually got anything from you all, and we even played along with your wizard's game of fighting."

"I've even got a cut on me thumb from it, I do," said his comrade. "And a bloody nose, at that."

"Yeah, look at his poor face."

"I daresay it's an improvement over how it looked before."

"That's a downright awful thing to say to a fella," the smaller highwayman said with the look that he was about to well up.

"Man can't rightly help his genetics," agreed the main highwayman. "And to think that we're supposed to look up to you types. We may be criminals, but at least we're not mean."

"I'd expect such talk from riffraff like us, but not from a Knight of the Round Table."

"Well said, my ugly friend," the larger highwayman said while patting his friend's shoulder, "well said."

Sir Gaheris seemed at a loss for words. Arthur did find the dig a little too pronounced. He'd had a few discussions with Sir Gaheris over the years regarding his gruffness. Yet one more thing to put on his annual review to talk about.

"Don't feel bad," Sir Gareth said, moving toward the highwaymen, "he treats everyone that way. And I know how you both feel, too. I was once down on my luck, struggling to make ends meet. I ended up as a knight out of pure luck. I was singing a song at a pub one evening, a tune about war and bravery, when suddenly a group of these fellows"—he pointed at the knights—"dragged me out and stuck a sword in my hand and a helmet on my head. They said I was one of them." He looked down at the sword. "I don't even know how to use it all that well. I just know that the pointy end is supposed to end up in the other guy."

"So you're a bard?" asked the main brigand.

"And a cook, yes."

"Haven't heard me a good tavern song in years," said the smaller highwayman. "Most of our bards is working in the same field as us these days. They don't feel much like singing."

"Let me ask you men something," Arthur said, pulling his horse close to them, "what would it take to get you to stop your thieving ways?"

"A steady job, I suppose. Or maybe winning the lottery."

"Lottery?" said Arthur.

"Oh, right. Sorry, sire, another Scotland thing."

The smaller highwayman looked up at Arthur. "I don't need riches, m'lord. I just want something that puts food on the table for me wife and kids."

"*You* have a wife and kids?" said Sir Gaheris.

"Sir Gaheris," Arthur admonished, "stay your tongue."

"Well, look at him."

"Indeed," Arthur said, motioning for Gaheris to vacate the immediate area. "Now, where was I? Oh, yes, jobs. Sir Lance-A-Lot, is there truly no work available for honest folk in my land?"

"I, uh, I'm really not sure, sire. That's not my area of expertise."

"The economy stinks," Sir Galahad offered. "Farmers have been tugged around by their short hairs for the last few seasons because of that new tax you put into law regarding grains. That and the aforementioned brick hut market crash, of course."

"But my advisers told me that the tax was a wise thing to enact."

"And for your advisers, it was," replied Galahad. "It gave each of them a cutting share of the dividends."

"Oh."

"For standard folk, though, it resulted in less money for hiring helping hands. You can read all about it in *Investments, Inc.* magazine."

"Seems I don't need to, Sir Galahad," Arthur said while chewing the inside of his cheek. "When we get back, I shall have to put you in a room with my advisers so that we can get things fixed. I shant have my subjects roaming around and attacking convoys because of some silly tax that only benefits the wealthiest in the land."

"But that's the way it's done, sire," Galahad said with a look of confusion.

"Is it?"

"Seems the norm to me," said the main highwayman.

"Aye," agreed his partner.

"Yep," the rest of the knights and Merlin said in unison.

"Well, I think it's time that gets changed," Arthur concluded after a few moments. "For now, what say we treat these gentlemen to a pint of ale and some stew?"

"That would be most excellent, sire."

"I haven't had me a decent stew in months."

"Lance-A-Lot," Arthur commanded, "give these men a few coins from my coffer. I want them to each have enough to feed their families for a month." The two highwaymen were all smiles at this. "I assume that you men have names?"

"Chauncey McDermott," said the larger of the two.

"Leatherton Felhue III," said the other.

"Of the famous Felhue clan in the Southwest?" asked an astonished Arthur.

"No, sire," responded Leatherton, "from the not-so-famous group in the Northeast."

# MERLIN'S NOTEBOOK: INNS

*WHILE IT CAN certainly be argued that staying at any one of the inns in all of Britain is better than sleeping under a wet sky, I would state that the benefit is marginal.*

*Most innkeepers spend the majority of their lives looking for the quick buck, doing as little as possible to keep their lodgings in proper repair. It's rare to find a place that has all the boxes checked. There are a few, to be sure, but those are often in the wealthier districts, and they attract clientele capable of spending a king's ransom to garner a fanciful stay.*

*During my younger years, I learned the horrors of staying at the wrong inn. Bedbugs, watery ale, week-old stew, moldy bread, damp rooms, and exorbitant prices were the norm, and that was for the* nicer *places. The more seedy joints also had rats, lice, leaking roofs, and hired thieves that were given keys to all rooms in return for a cut of the profits from whatever the thieves picked up.*

# SADO'S TAVERN

SADO'S TAVERN WAS certainly large enough to hold them all, and there did appear to be plenty of stables available for the horses, but it wasn't exactly a place befitting a king. The landscaping was shoddy, the grass stood nearly waist-high, the siding looked rotted in most places, and the roof was holier than a friar. But with the clouds growing darker and the wind picking up, it was better than staying out in the open.

"It appears a tad rundown," said Arthur with one eye on the coming storm.

"That it does," Lance-A-Lot replied sourly.

"I assure you, sire," said Chauncey, "that it's the nicest place within ten miles."

"Which doesn't mean all that much," noted Merlin.

"And my cousin owns it," Chauncey added, "so I'm sure we'll get a good rate."

"Well," Arthur said resignedly as a single drop of rain hit his nose, "I don't expect we have much choice at this point. I wouldn't want to sleep in the rain."

"Looking at that roof," said Merlin, pointing, "I'd wager we'll be sleeping in the rain either way."

"They've a decent ale, sire," Leatherton said, "and their stew has been known to have spices from time-to-time."

"Then I guess we shall have to make it our home for the night. Lance-A-Lot, please go have a word with the innkeeper and get everyone rooms."

Lance-A-Lot dismounted and began wading through the high grass.

"Be careful with the innkeeper's main negotiator," said Chauncey. "She's a wily one."

"She's got nice knockers, though," Leatherton was quick to point out.

"Oh, no doubt of that," agreed Chauncey. "Made of wrought iron, they are."

"Her breasts are made of wrought iron?" Sir Gareth asked.

"Not now, Sir Gareth," Arthur said, interrupting the discussion, "we have to focus on preparations. Sirs Purcivale and Tristian, would you be so kind as to work with the inn's stable boy to get all of our horses fed and stored up for the night?"

"O'course, sire," said Purcivale, hopping down from his steed. "We'll be right to it, won't we, Tristy?"

"Like too bugs havin' a nibble, I'd say."

"Maybe a couple of pigs basking in the mud, yeah?"

"Nah," Tristan said with a start, "that's Gaheris, that is!"

The two men laughed at that as everyone else stood waiting for Geheris to pummel them.

"What's this you're saying about me?" asked Gaheris.

Purcivale shrugged and said, "That ye bathe about as much as a squealer, is all. Ain't nothin' wrong with it, guv…unless I'm downwind, that is."

"Yeah," Tristan added in support of his friend, "dirt's got nothing on you, in a manner of speakin'. Somethin' to be proud of, I'd wager."

"Are you two implying that I stink?" said Gaheris with a squint of his only eye.

"Implying it?" said Purcivale. "Wouldn't dream of implying it. Would I, Tristy?"

"Would be downright criminal to *imply* that he stinks, Purcy."

"Hmmm," said Gaheris, looking unsure. Finally, he said, "You're both idiots."

The rain was starting to pick up now. If there was any one thing that Arthur despised, it was being caught in the rain. Worse, he hated it when all of the gear and such became damp. It was uncomfortable.

"Enough of this," he said. "We need those horses tended to quickly."

"Right, right," Purcivale replied, reaching out for the king's reins, "we're on it. No need to get your panties in a bind, sire."

"My what?" Arthur said, looking down at himself worriedly.

"Yer lady-britches, guv," Tristan explained.

"I…uh…"

"It's just a sayin', sire. Nothing to get all worked up about."

"Yeah," said Tristan, "ain't like we was sayin' your

bra strap was showin'."

Arthur looked at his shoulders.

"Oh, for the love of…" Merlin started and then pointed at the two knights. "You two get to work before I turn you into a couple of goats."

"Nay doin' that, Mr. Wizard," said Purcivale with a look of horror. "We don't want to be goats, do we Tristy?"

"Not with Sir Gareth around, Purcy."

"What's that supposed to mean?" said Gareth while blinking rapidly.

Tristan pursed his lips for a second. "Just sayin' that I'm ever surprised that there ain't little Gareth's jumpin' around your yard with horns and bucked teeth, I am."

"My point exactly, Tristy."

"Wait a second here," Gareth argued, "are you two idiots trying to say that I f—"

"That's it," Merlin said in a loud voice as he grabbed both Tristan and Purcivale by the fronts of their tunics. "Go! Now!"

The two knights scrambled off, pulling a few of the horses along while the stable boy took the others. Everyone watched them go. Arthur felt generally wrong with everything that they had said, wondering how much of it was true.

Lance-A-Lot stepped out of the inn with a smirk on his face and lipstick on his collar.

"Told you she had nice knockers," Leatherton said with a knowing nod.

"Wrought iron ones, too," said Lance-A-Lot with a faraway look.

"Odd, ain't it?"

"Indeed, especially the way—" He stopped himself and then turned quickly to Arthur. "Sorry, sire. It was just, well…anyway, I have secured the rooms for the night. They're on the first floor so we won't have issues with rain."

"Good, good. How much did she take, Sir Lance-A-Lot?"

"Almost all of it."

"I'm talking about the money."

"Oh, right. It was twenty-five shillings."

"That's robbery!"

"It was originally fifty shillings, but after I—"

"Never mind, Lance-A-Lot," Arthur said quickly, slamming his eyes shut and grimacing. "I neither need nor want the details."

"I wouldn't mind hearing them," said Allison.

Merlin stared at her in shock.

"Right," Arthur said. "Look, let's just get in there and get some stew and ale before we get drenched."

# QUESTIONS

MERLIN WASN'T ONE who enjoyed partying. At least not in the traditional sense. Booze and babes just weren't his thing. His idea of getting down was playing music from the future—specifically disco—while tinkering with various forms of technology. But he knew that Allison was more into the nightlife than he was and that worried him. She wouldn't divulge any information to hurt the time line when sober, but she was partaking in the consumption of alcohol and that left Merlin uneasy.

"Allison," he said, tapping her on the shoulder, "may I have a word?"

"Sure, what's up?"

"I just want to make sure you know what you're doing," he said as they moved away from the main table. "Fraternizing with this bunch could cause you to have loose lips. You said that you had to be careful or it could screw up the future…though I'm still not a hundred percent sure what that means."

"Chill, Merl," Allison said. "I'm just asking

questions and having a few brews. It's not like I'm filling anyone in on technology or recent scientific breakthroughs. Of course," she added thoughtfully, "I share information with you all the time."

"True, but you know I don't speak to anyone about anything."

"Fair enough," she said between sips, "but what happens if you get hit by a bus? That cave of yours has a lot of goodies in it."

"What's a bus?"

"My point is that your knowledge of my era is far more risky than my questioning of these boobs."

Merlin furrowed his brow and looked at her chest in confusion.

"Don't take that literally, Merl," she said, lifting his chin back up. "I was being derogatory."

"Oh, I see. Well, just be careful."

"You worry too much, Merl," she said before walking back to the party.

Merlin didn't feel that he worried *too* much. It was just the right amount. Truth be told, he didn't care if the future got sullied due to her making a mistake; he was more concerned about her saying something that gave away the fact that he didn't really know how to do magic.

Most of his lifestyle was allowed due to the general populace's lack of understand regarding what precisely magic was, after all. Without that, he was nothing but a middle-aged, scrawny guy with long hair. Or, as Allison had put it, a "hippie."

"You look troubled, wizard," Galahad said as Merlin grabbed a chair at the next table over.

Merlin nodded. "Always one problem or another in my profession."

"Seems to be. A lot of inconsistencies, too."

"Oh?"

Galahad leaned back in his chair and crossed his arms. "I'm still trying to wrap my head around how you managed to water all those fields at the same time up north, during the drought."

"You know about that?"

"It was in *Wizards' Quarterly.*"

"I thought I was the only one who read *WQ?*"

"I thought you were the one who wrote it, Merlin?"

"Exactly," Merlin said. "Anyway, that job was just a case of simple physics. Take water from a source that's at a higher elevation and…" He paused and cleared his throat. "I mean, I just cast a spell of… uh…watering. Yes, watering."

"Right," Galahad said slowly. "Always sounds pretty easy when you say it's just magic."

"It's not that easy," Merlin replied with a tired look. "Believe me."

"The interesting thing is that it seems to take you a while to do this supposed magic. More interesting, though, is that nobody ever sees you actually doing it."

"Supposed?" Merlin said with a huff. "Look, you, it's not like doing magic happens with a mere flick of the wrist if, that's what you're thinking. That only happens at the cinema. Doing proper magic takes time, planning, and concentration."

"What's a cinema?"

"A place where wizards do magic."

"Hmmm."

"Look, Galahad, it's hard to explain these things to non-wizards."

"Maybe you just need to try harder."

"I really don't," Merlin stated.

Galahad grunted and pushed himself back, grasping his mug and draining the contents of his ale. After releasing a hearty belch, he said, "There's something odd about you, wizard."

"I could say the same about you."

"No, no, I mean your 'magic'."

"Of course it would seem odd to you, Galahad. You're not a wizard. And did you just use air quotes?"

"I find it all interesting," said Galahad, ignoring Merlin's question. "You see, I read *Architectural Digest*, *Engineering Times*, and *Project Periodical*. They all talk about similar things that your magazine talks about. In each installment, they have almost identical situations that *Wizards' Quarterly* does, but they use something they call *science* to solve each problem. And yet each time there is always some wealthy guy involved that ain't never named."

Merlin pulled on his collar to relieve a little steam. "That *is* interesting," he said. "I'll have to look into those journals you mentioned. It would be nice to not have to resort to magic all the time. It's very trying on the mind, you know."

"And the wallet, I'd bet."

"Huh?" said Merlin as he looked over at King Arthur. He pretended as if Arthur were calling him over. Pointing to himself as if saying, "Me?" Then he turned back to Galahad. "Looks like Arthur needs me for something. Kings," Merlin said with a shrug. "What are you gonna do?"

"Uh huh."

# THE BLADES OF POWER

"AND I JUST think that we need to be more conscientious regarding how others feel, Sir Gaheris," Arthur said to the gruff man.

"I say that those that ain't with us is against us."

"That's a little harsh, don't you think?"

"Nope."

"That's not a very knightly way of thinking, I'm afraid."

Sir Gaheris grunted and shook his head. "Liberals," he said as if spitting.

"Pardon?"

"I need a drink," Gaheris answered and moved away from the table.

Though the man was a top-notch fighter, he wasn't exactly knightly material. Then again, none of them really were, except for possibly Lamorak. Arthur knew that his knights were the best swordsmen in the land—not considering Sir Gareth in that calculation, of course. But he'd envisioned something more from them. Honor, morality, strength of character. Each of them had this in measure, obviously, but Arthur had hoped they would all be of the same caliber.

Merlin sat down heavily, taking a look over his shoulder. Arthur wasn't sure which was worse, speaking with Gaheris or dealing with Merlin. At least Merlin had some tact.

"How are you fairing with all of this travel, Merlin? You seem concerned about something."

"I'm good, I guess. I worry about the cameras and equipment getting wet, and I could do without Galahad's constant scrutiny. Other than that I've got no complaints. You?"

"Shouldn't have gone with the lace," Arthur said.

"Hmmm?"

"Song, song, song!" the knights cheered, interrupting Arthur and Merlin's conversation.

"I couldn't," Sir Gareth said in what was obviously mock protest. "I'm not properly warmed up."

"Come on, give us a jingle, guv," said Tristan.

"Here's your strings, Gary," Purcivale said, handing him the instrument.

"Okay, fine," Sir Gareth said as he set about tuning up, clearly loving the attention. "Shall I play *Blades of Power* or *Dainty Little Flower*?"

"*Blades of Power*," chimed the knights.

"*Dainty Little Flower*," said Arthur.

Everyone turned to look at him.

"I mean, obviously *Blades of Power*. I was just wondering why you had a song called *Dainty Little Flower* in your repertoire."

"For the ladies, sire."

"Ah, yes. Right."

Sir Gareth began to strum as the knights all settled down and craned their ears. As poor as Gareth was with the sword and the pike and...well, everything that pertained to fighting, he was one of the best bards that Arthur had ever heard. His voice was like a smooth flowing river and his playing was melodic and powerful.

> *The Blades of Power, they sing their song*
> *They slash and smash, all the deathly night long*
> *Their strength is stronger than the strongest of strong*

The knights raised their mugs and sang, "The Blades of Power ring on!"

> *During battle the sinister foe is shattered*
> *The Blades of Power leave cloth torn and tattered*
> *Rain bounces off steel with pitter-patter*

> *The Blades of Power ring on!*

Sir Gareth yelled out, "Everyone!"

> *Slash, bash! The Blades of Power!*
> *Destroying the bad while protecting our towers*
> *Slash, bash! The Blades of Power!*
> *Cutting their way right through our foes*

He continued his strumming for a few bars as the knights swayed back and forth to the rhythm.

> *Struggling and fighting across the land*

*The Blades of Power seek out holy hands*
*No question nor wonder of dastardly plan*

*The Blades of Power ring on!*

*Slash, bash! The Blades of Power!*
*Destroying the bad while protecting our towers*
*Slash, bash! The Blades of Power!*
*Cutting their way right through our foes*

The strumming grew quieter now and Arthur couldn't help but feel pulled in. He even leaned forward on his elbows and noted that Merlin was doing the same. All eyes were upon the bard at this point of the song.

*Now it's been told on a deathly night*
*The Blades of Power shine an unearthly light*
*They brighten the darkness, prepared for a fight*
*Their strength is ever involved*

"Loudly, now!"

*Slash, bash! The Blades of Power!*
*Destroying the bad while protecting our towers*
*Slash, bash! The Blades of Power!*
*Cutting their way right through our foes*

"Let's wrap this up!"

*The Blades of Power, they sing their song*
*They slash and smash, all the deathly night long*

*Their strength is stronger than the strongest of strong!*
*Their strength is stronger than the strongest of strong!*

Gareth stopped his strumming and sang the last line alone.

*Their strength is as strong as Sir Lance-A-Lot's dong!*

Everyone laughed and cheered. Everyone except for Lance-A-Lot, anyway. He simply sighed and shook his head.

Sir Gareth bowed and then placed the instrument back into its case.

Arthur noted that Allison was sitting among the knights, keeping up with them drink for drink. That was quite a feat considering their seemingly insatiable need for ale. Merlin appeared to be antsy regarding this as well.

"Your apprentice looks to be getting along nicely," Arthur said.

"Yes," Merlin replied with a sigh. "I forgot to add her to my list of worries when you'd asked about them before."

"A word of advice from one leader to another," Arthur said as Allison jumped up and began dancing around one of the poles in the room, "sometimes you must let the men play."

Merlin scoffed. "I'm not letting them play with her, Arthur."

"What? Oh, no, I was being metaphorical."

"Oh, right. Lost me there for a second."

Arthur adjusted again. Next time he was going to

go with cotton or silk. Lace was nice for a little while, but not while on a journey such as this. It just ended up cutting in.

"Thong riding up on you?" asked Merlin, though he didn't really seem to be paying much attention to Arthur.

"What's a thong?"

"Just something I saw in a catalog," Merlin replied.

"Catalog?"

"It's a booklet from the futur…ches…" He coughed. "Yeah, that's it, just something I saw in a, um, few churches I've been to over the years."

"Ah, so a thong is a religious item?"

"Probably would be for you," Merlin answered with a look of relief. "Anyway, we are still planning to leave first thing in the morning, right?"

"Preferably just as the sun clears the horizon. I'd like to get to Scotland before nightfall."

"I can't wait," Merlin said. "It's going to be great footage. I'm sure it will make Allison's report shine."

"Oh?"

"It's her doctoral thesis. Gonna blow their socks off."

"I have no idea what any of that just meant," said Arthur while thinking maybe he should have an ale or two.

"More magic stuff."

"So I assumed. I must say that you are a tiring person to be around, Merlin."

"Tell me about it," Merlin said with a nod.

"Well, you are constantly talking about things that make little sense; you complain a lot; you have a funny smell that I can only assume is magically-inspired; and you can be rather obstinate."

Merlin blinked repeatedly. "I was being rhetorical, Arthur."

"Oh," Arthur said with a grimace. "Well, then as Sir Gawain might say, 'may a thousand bees sting my genitals'."

"I could probably arrange that," Merlin stated before looking over his shoulder again at Galahad. "Anyway, I should get going. Early mornings are not my thing, as you know, so I'd better try to get to sleep now or I'll be miserable all day."

"We wouldn't want that," said Arthur sincerely.

"You really wouldn't."

# APPROACHING SCOTLAND

THE CARAVAN LEFT early the next morning, after ensuring that Chauncey and Leatherton had their coins as promised. Arthur also asked them both to speak with other highwaymen about the plans of the crown to make things better in the land.

Arthur, remembering that he was not supposed to look in the deep sections of the satchel was saddened to find that Guinevere had only set him up with another set of lace panties. That meant one more day of discomfort and chafing. At least they were a nice yellow.

It was closing in on evening by the time they'd crossed the final hill to the border of Scotland.

A small building sat at the bottom of the ravine with a couple of red-haired Scots standing guard.

"Halt," called out Merlin.

"But we're almost there," said Arthur.

"Exactly. I need need to catch this on film." Merlin

then set about getting everything ready. "Gareth, snatch that tripod…and no jokes about it. Purcivale and Tristan, you're going to handle the microphones. Allison's got camera two and I'll take camera one."

Suddenly there was a flurry of movement as everyone jumped to their duties. Arthur groaned as Lance-A-Lot moved alongside of him.

"It was part of our agreement," said Arthur resignedly.

"His magic worries me," Lance-A-Lot said quietly, "and I'm sure it's not going to go over well with the Scots."

"Who cares what they think?"

"Typically not I," admitted Lance-A-Lot, "but they do hold this talisman that we are questing after, sire."

"Valid point," Arthur mused while adjusting in his seat. "We'll just have to use diplomacy where we can and swords where we must."

"Still have a sore bottom, sire?"

"It's just these damn lace panties," Arthur said unwittingly. "Even canvas would have been more comfortable, I think."

"Lace, sire?"

Arthur gulped. "Did I say lace?" His heart was racing. "I must be thinking of Guinevere again. You know how I get when we're apart."

"Ah, yes," said Lance-A-Lot with a dreamy look in his eyes, "she's quite the—"

"Watch yourself," Arthur warned, silencing his first knight. "Why don't you go and prepare whatever papers you have in that pack of yours?"

"Straight away, sire."

Merlin came up to Arthur after Lance-A-Lot trotted safely away.

"Okay, Arthur," Merlin said, "listen up. I'm going to need you to be very kingly in this scene."

"Scene?"

"You're going to ride up at the front and meet with the Scots," Merlin said. "You have to show power and guts. You'll have to let them see your machismo."

"With this outfit on?" Arthur said with a scoff. "It'd take ten minutes just to pull it out."

"What are you talking about?" Merlin said and then sighed and shook his head. "Machismo means your manliness, man."

"I understand that, Merlin," Arthur replied evenly. "Frankly, though—and believe me when I tell you that I hate to admit this—it'd probably be more impressive if Lance-A-Lot showed his machismo to them."

"Oh, for the love of…" Merlin took a deep breath and steadied himself. "I'm not talking about your *actual* manliness, Arthur. I'm talking about your personal power. Your inner-strength. Your damned kinglyness!"

"Okay, okay," said Arthur defensively. "No need to…what was it they said? Oh, yes, that's it. No need to get your panties in a bunch."

"That's *your* thing, Arthur," Merlin stated. "Now, let's get to the front and start this show. Remember, don't say anything to them until I say 'action'."

# KING OF SCOTLAND

THE KING OF Scotland's name, too, was Arthur, but he looked a fair bit different than the king of England. This Arthur had fiery red hair and a beard to match, eyes that were bright green, and his normal disposition was one of irritation. The two kings did have a few things in common, though. For example, both of them had a queen who was English.

"Are you just about ready, Arthur?" said his wife, Agnes.

"Aye," Arthur replied, "just getting me britches on."

Just as he had gotten them up to his knees, a knock came at the door. He grunted. Was two minutes of peace so much to ask for? It seemed that every little detail in his kingdom needed his opinion. Everything from the cost of potatoes to the color that people should paint their houses was laid before him. What did he care what people paid for potatoes?

The knock came again, this time more insistent.

"Aye?" he said as he shuffled to the door.

"Got word from the border, me lord," the muffled voice said.

Arthur rolled his eyes and cracked open the door, looking through the slat since his pants were still wrapped around his ankles.

"We're hitchin' up for dindin," Arthur explained. "Canne it wait?"

"It's the English, me lord."

"At me border?" Arthur said, eyes wide.

"Aye, me lord."

"Hold it, hold it," said Arthur seriously, "is we talkin' just a few laddies here or is there after being a contingency?"

"It's their king, me lord."

"What?"

"And his knights, too."

"His knets are with him?"

"Knights, me lord."

"Right, knets."

"Knights."

"Knets."

"It's pronounced 'knights,' me lord. Much like the word that's used for when the moon is out."

"Net."

"Night, me lord. Nye-eeet."

Arthur stood there staring at the man for a few moments. "How long before they're actually at me border?"

"Like I said, me lord, they're already there."

"Then why am I only hearin' of it right nooo?"

"Word just came in, me lord," the man said apologetically.

"Dinnae we have scouts about?"

"Aye, me lord," the messenger replied. "That's how we knew they was comin'."

"And this king and his knets—don't correct me again—is already at me border?" Arthur asked again. "What's the point of havin' scouts if they ain't after finding things out until it's too late?"

"Sorry, me lord. It was Fergus the Fearful's shift. You know that he doesn't stray very far from the gate."

Arthur sighed and dropped his shoulders. Tonight they were having lamb in the main hall, which only happened once a week. Usually it was vegetables and tough meat. Sometimes he had to wonder if there was some sort of conspiracy against him actually having a meal of his liking.

"Fine," he said irritably. "I'll be down soon. Get the men at the ready." He then snaked a hand out through the crack in the door and grabbed the messenger by the tunic. "And save me a slice of that lamb or I'll have your testicles put in molten ore."

"Aye, me lord," the man replied with a terrified look.

The king shut the door, grumbling to himself.

What the hell was the king of England doing at his border anyway? Things had been relatively quiet between the two kingdoms for quite some time now. In truth, Arthur assumed that they'd finally had peace. Not in the way of an accord or anything, just in that both sides stopped fighting. Couldn't last forever, he supposed.

"Arthur," said Agnes, jolting the king from his

thoughts, "did I just hear correctly that the the English king is here?"

"Aye, me love. That ye did."

"Arthur," she said.

"Aye?"

"No, I meant the English king. His name is Arthur, too."

"Ah," said Arthur. "I sometimes forget that you're an Englishman."

"Englishwoman."

"Aye, that too."

She strolled across the room and began adjusting Arthur's garb. "You do realize that if he has brought his knights along, that he likely has—"

"Lance-A-Lot," Arthur said, his voice sounding of dread.

"Indeed," Agnes replied with a mischievous wink.

"Now, now, me love, ye know I'm all about us being free with our sexness, but not with an Englishman."

"You have relations with an Englishwoman, Arthur."

"Aye, but not an Englishman, me sweet."

Agnes looked him sternly in the eye. "I know how you feel about the English, Arthur. It's precisely how *I* feel about the French. But that didn't stop you from sleeping with the French queen during your last visit, now did it?"

"Ye knew about that?" Arthur said in shock.

"I do now."

"Damn."

"I think this Lance-A-Lot fellow," Agnes said while

twisting her hair with her fingers, "would be the perfect bedfellow to even our score, don't you?"

"If the stories about the man are after being true," Arthur said in a defeated tone, "then the next time I'm with ye it'll be like throwing a twig into a cave."

"Let's hope."

"I forbehd it!" Arthur said instantly.

Agnes' stare grew sinister. "Must I remind you who it was that got all of your men to believe that the skirts they're wearing are helpful in battle?"

"Well—"

"And wasn't it me who came up with the name 'kilt,' hmmm?"

"Yes, but—"

"And why was it that I did that for you, Arthur?"

His shoulders fell. "Because ye know I like wearin' yer dallies."

"Precisely," Agnes stated as she walked to the window. "To this day your men don't question it, do they?"

"Some do, but—"

"And it turned out that those skirts were actually quite helpful in battle, as you've said."

"That they are."

"Now," Agnes said without looking back, "you wouldn't want it to get out that the entire kilt craze was truly just a guise so that you could dress, shall we say, more freely, would you?"

"Ye wouldn't," Arthur said hoarsely as he looked at her in disbelief.

"The French queen, Arthur," Agnes said, turning back to face him. "You shouldn't have, but you did.

Time for me to even the score…one way or another."

"Damn."

# ANNND...ACTION!

THE SCOTTISH GUARDS were standing at their post as Arthur, Lance-A-Lot, and Gaheris watched the rest of the men helping Merlin to set up. Arthur could only see the Scots from the waist up, but they looked like a rugged bunch. They'd certainly be more difficult to bypass than Chauncey and Leatherton had been. Fortunately, just like the highwaymen, there were only two of them.

Once everything was in place, Merlin began positioning all of the men, putting Arthur in the front. He ran about adjusting the placement of swords and making the knights correct their helmets and tunics. This was about the only part of Merlin's tinkerings that Arthur found appealing.

"Are you nearly ready, Merlin?" asked Arthur. "The light looks to be waning."

"Don't I know it?" Merlin said as he pushed Arthur's boot farther into the stirrup. "This is the best time of day for this type of shoot. I'm working as quickly as I can." He ran back to his camera.

"Purcivale, move back slightly in your saddle. Perfect. Stay put. Okay," Merlin said after having one last glance around, "is everyone ready?"

Arthur nodded along with the rest of the men.

"Annnd…action!"

"You there," Arthur said in his most kingly voice as he pointed at the closest Scot, "I am King Arthur of England, holder of the throne in Camelot, and I demand entrance into this land."

The guards looked back and forth at each other for a moment, whispering.

"Nay," came the eventual reply.

"That's correct," said Arthur and then he stopped. "Sorry, what?"

"Nay."

Arthur looked over at Lance-A-Lot. "He wants me to nay? Like a horse?"

"I believe he's saying 'no,' sire."

"Pardon me," Arthur asked, "but are you saying 'nay' like what a horse does or are you saying 'no?'"

"Nay."

"So the horse one, then?"

"Nay, the other one."

"Ah, good," Arthur said, feeling as though he'd accomplished something. "Look, I don't wish to have a skirmish with you, but we need to get into your land. As you can well see, my knights can easily overpower you two."

"Aye, were it just we."

"Pardon?"

The guard pulled out a horn from the pack on his shoulder and blew into it. It made a deep sound that grew until it held a note that rang for a good twenty seconds. Moments after he had tucked the horn away, a large group of men, all wearing skirts, crested the hill behind the guard station.

"Well, that changes things," noted Arthur.

"Aye."

"Sorry, but I have to ask," said Arthur after allowing a few moments of silence, "are all your men wearing skirts?"

"They's kilts."

"What's a kilt?"

"It's a, uh, battle…skirt."

"I see," said Arthur. "Are they effective in battle?"

"Aye," the guard replied with a nod, "mostly because the enemy ain't all that fond of gettin' too close to us."

"Ah." Arthur turned to Lance-A-Lot. "We should consider this prospect, don't you think?"

"I'd rather not, sire. I don't believe those things hang low enough to contain me, for one; secondly, the draft must be terrible."

"Ye get used to it," said the main guard. "Kind of freeing, too."

"Look like a bunch of pansies, don't they, Tristy?"

"Hairy-legged wenches at best, Purcy."

"Stay your tongue, you two," commanded Lance-A-Lot. "'Tis not well to speak of soldiers as such. It takes strength of character for a man to dress as his king decrees. Are we not encumbered and set to the point of boiling within our sheets of metal? Yet do we argue and fuss?" Purcivale and Tristy looked downtrodden. "Now, these men wear their skirts—"

"Kilts."

"—sorry, kilts, because their king demands it of them. They are naught but good soldiers for doing so."

"Well put, Sir Lance-A-Lot," said Arthur before turning back toward the guard. "May I ask if you wear anything under those…kilts?"

"Some aye; some nay," the guard said, looking uncomfortable. "Can we get after changin' the subject?"

"Yes, of course. Sorry." Arthur softened his stance, trying a different tactic. "We need to gain entrance to this land for a quest we're on. I would hate for it to turn into anything political, but if that's what needs to be done, then so be it."

"I canne let ye pass."

Just then a rousing came about all of the Scottish soldiers. Arthur pressed up in his stirrups to see what was going on. Finally, he saw a middle-aged, red-haired man riding up with a number of soldiers flanking him. He was kingly looking and he had a sneer on his face of a man who had missed dinner.

"Yer that English king, eh?" said the new arrival.

"Arthur is my name," said Arthur proudly. "And you are?"

"Arthur."

"Yes, that's what I said. And your name?"

"Arthur," the man repeated with a squint. "Are ye daft?"

"I am not daft, thank you very much, and I frankly resent the accusation." Arthur stared down the other man for a few moments. "Now, if you'd so kindly give me your—"

"My name is Arthur, ye twit!"

"Oh, I see. Right, that…uh…well, I wasn't expecting that."

"Why is ye here, laddie?"

"I'm not a lady!"

"He said, 'laddie,' sire. As in 'lad'."

"Oh, sorry. We're on a quest for a talisman."

"A what?"

"A trinket," said English Arthur. "It's magical."

"Magical, eh?" Scottish Arthur replied while glancing over the bunch, landing his eyes on Merlin and Allison. "What are these ones after doing?"

"They're filming the adventure."

"Filmin'?"

"I don't quite understand it myself," said English Arthur. "It's probably best explained by knowing that the man behind that camera is Merlin."

Merlin waved.

"The wizard?"

"Seriously?" said English Arthur with a shriek. "And you're calling *me* daft? How is it that everyone finds that a shock? It's Merlin, man. He's the *only* wizard in existence."

"Nay like wizards," Scottish Arthur said, seemingly ignoring English Arthur's outburst.

"That seems to be a common theme."

"What is it that this magical item ye're after supposed to be for?"

"As to that," English Arthur said, "I would need to speak with you in private."

"I hold no secrets from me men."

"I believe you hold at least one," Merlin claimed, peeking out from behind his camera.

"What are ye after sayin', wizard?"

"I'm certain you don't want me to announce what I know right now, dude," Merlin replied, nodding toward the Scottish army. "Let's just say that those kilts are…interesting."

Scottish Arthur blanched. "Aye," he said in a drawn out way. "Fine. I'm wondering after what a 'dude' is, but King of England, I'll meet with ye."

"What's it about our kilts, me lord?" asked one of the guards.

"Uh…the wizard's after knowing a tactic to defeat them, I'm guessin'."

"Canne trust them wizards, me lord."

"Aye."

"We shall meet, then?" asked English Arthur.

"Aye," replied Scottish Arthur. Then, he slumped a little and said, "Which of yer men is after being Lance-A-Lot?"

"I am he."

"Me queen, Agnes, says that she knows yer ma. Wants a word with ye. Me guards will take ye to her while yer king and me talk."

"Not sure if that's a wise move, King of Scotland."

"Neither is questionin' after me wisdom, King of England."

"I'd like to film this meeting," announced Merlin.

"Sorry, Merlin," English Arthur said, "agreement or no, this meeting will remain private."

"Fine, then I'll film the discussion between Lance-A-Lot and Agnes. Not quite as interesting, but better than nothing."

"Uh…what's he talkin' about?"

"I don't rightly understand the details," said English Arthur, "but it has something to do with him being able to capture an event and then play it back for many to see at a later time."

"Think of it like a series of hand-drawn pictures that move from one position to the next," explained Merlin.

"Aye, one of me court jesters does something like that. Makes it look like things is moving about on the paper."

"Correct," Merlin said with a surprised look. "These devices do something like that, but in full color and they capture everything, including the sound."

"I see," said Scottish Arthur. "Then there's no way I'm lettin' ye film that, uh, discussion between me queen and yer knight."

"But—"

"Ain't gonna happen, wizard," Scottish Arthur stated flatly. "If yer truly as keen as they say, ye'll get the real reason."

Merlin glanced over at Lance-A-Lot. "Ah, I see. Hmmm." Then he snapped his fingers. "Ah ha! I know, we'll set up another mock battle and film that. Don't worry, nobody with be seriously injured."

The two Arthurs looked at each other and shrugged.

# THE MEETING

THE TENT WAS small by kingly standards, but it at least guaranteed a measure of privacy that they would not get out in the open.

Arthur was hopeful that he wouldn't have to get into too much detail regarding the Nipple Ring of Veiling, but he was prepared if it came to that. He would claim that he was losing his hair and that he didn't want the people to feel that they had a bald king. It was flimsy, but royalty tended to understand these things about each other.

"Ye're takin' a big risk comin' into me lands and makin' demands," said Scottish Arthur.

"Scotland will soon be under my rule anyway," said English Arthur with a shrug. "It's inevitable."

"Not by my way of thinkin'."

"We have more men than you."

"You mean knets."

"I suppose we have a good number of nets, too," English Arthur said while mentally trying to draw a correlation, "but I think our knights are more apt to be effective in battle."

Scottish Arthur grimaced and shook his head. "Just tell me of this magical gem yer after findin'."

"You wouldn't understand."

"Try me."

"It's called the Ring of Veiling and—" English Arthur stopped, noting that Scottish Arthur's eyes had widened considerably. "Wait, you know of this item?"

"I'm aware of it," Scottish Arthur said guardedly. "What are ye needin' it fer?"

"There are things I must hide from my people."

"Such as?"

"My, uh, hairline isn't what it used to be," English Arthur said as he adjusted uncomfortably in the rickety chair. The lace was killing him.

"I know that grimace," Scottish Arthur said, pointing at English Arthur. "Nay, it canne be."

"What are you talking about?"

"Tell me, are ye after wearin' ladies dallies?"

"Dallies?" English Arthur said, fearing the worst.

"Aye, lace and flowery underbritches."

Arthur put on his best affronted look. "Talk like that can lead to war, King of Scotland."

"Yer winces tell a different tale, King of England."

"That's simply the result of having a sore bottom due to riding in a saddle these many miles to get here."

He winced again.

"I've a feelin' yer wearing lace right nooo," the Scottish king said. "Takes one to know one, as they're after sayin'."

"You mean—"

"Aye, ever since I was a lad."

English Arthur's jaw had dropped. "I've never met another."

"Nay have I."

"Are you...I mean...well, do you like other men?"

"Nay, I'm just into the dallies. Ye?"

"No," English Arthur answered. "I just like to feel —"

"Pretty."

"Yes."

"Aye."

The two men sat in silence for a few moments. Arthur couldn't believe the odds of this occurrence. He was certain that there were many a man in the general populace who had worn a pair of silky socks now and again, but for his arch rival to be so inclined was unfathomable.

"I guess we have a lot more in common than we thought."

"Seems it."

"I have to ask," English Arthur said, "now that this is in the open between us, how did you get your men to wear skirts?"

"Agnes managed that one," Scottish Arthur said with a grin. "She's a clever one."

"Brilliant."

"Nay gonna argue that." Suddenly Scottish Arthur turned serious again. "Speaking of me queen. Is it after being true what they say about your main knet?"

"Net?"

"Kny-eet," said Scottish Arthur while rolling his

eyes.

"Oh, you mean Lance-A-Lot?"

"Aye. Is his man-nub like they say?"

"His what?"

"Ye know, his bag-o-tricks."

"Uh?"

"His water hose."

"Still not following you."

"The man's albino cave diver."

"Sorry?"

"Beef whistle."

"Still not getting it."

"Beaver basher, boomstick, cranny axe, flesh tower, love muscle, middle stump, nether rod, pork sword, spawn hammer, tan banana, winkie—"

"Honestly," English Arthur said, "I have no idea what you're talking about."

"His Excalibur, man!"

"Oh! You mean his twig and berries!"

"Never heard of it called that before," Scottish Arthur said with a raised eyebrow, "but aye."

"Well," English Arthur said, leaning in, "I've not seen it myself, but I've heard stories that the man can fish with it."

"Not good."

"Worried about Agnes?"

"That I am."

"You're right to be," English Arthur said. "Lance-A-Lot also knew my queen, Guinevere."

"How'd that fare?"

"It took a few months before she could feel my rowboat again," English Arthur admitted, "and I've never felt quite ample enough since."

"Ugh."

"You could stop him."

"Nay," Scottish Arthur said, shaking his head. "I poked the French queen."

"Ah, revenge bang, then."

"Aye." He tapped his finger on the little table. "Anyhoo, seems to me that yer quest is one that I'm after understanding."

"You have no idea how relieved that makes me feel," English Arthur said after taking a deep breath.

"I've even better news for ye."

"Oh?"

"I'm after having it with me." Scottish Arthur pulled off his shirt to reveal two shiny rings pierced through his nipples. "I'm only after needin' the one," he said as he set about unfastening one of them. "I think me brother in garb can have the other."

"Honestly?"

"Aye," said Scottish Arthur with a grimace as he freed the ring, "tis nary a man that understands me fetish such as ye. Wouldn't be right to deny ye as such."

"I don't know what to say, King of Scotland," English Arthur said in amazement.

"Bah, ye'd have done the same," Scottish Arthur said. "And call me Arty when there ain't others about, will ye?"

"Arty?" English Arthur said with his eyebrows up. "I like that. You may call me Art."

"Succinct. I gotta tell ye that putting this thing on ain't exactly like drinkin' tea."

"How do you mean?" Arthur said as he examined the talisman.

"It hurts like hell."

"Oh."

"Worth it, though." Arty removed the second ring and the image of the man changed drastically. No more was he a thick-bearded man in a kilt. He was now wearing a pink teddy, had on full eye makeup, and his face was cleanly shaved.

"Wow," Arthur said in shock.

"Like I said, worth it."

"That's incredible," Arthur said. "Your eye makeup is excellent."

"Agnes."

"She knows, then?"

"Found out a couple of years back."

English Arthur was amazed as the Scottish king stuck the ring back and again transformed into his kingly looking self.

"I feel I should at least give you something in return," English Arthur said.

Then a thought hit him. He reached into the bottom of the satchel and pulled out the wrapped item that Guinevere had dropped in for him. Unwrapping it, he found that it was a one-piece leopard-print leotard.

"Oh my," said Scottish Arthur.

English Arthur handed it over, hoping that Guinevere would be able to secure another one at some point.

# THE PARTY

THE KNIGHTS AND the Scots got along splendidly. There was something about drink and women that seemed to mend otherwise poor relations. Add into that a bit of song, which Gareth would undoubtedly be called upon to do in short order, and it would put a cap on the entirety of the party.

Arthur even had to admit that the inside of the main hall was pretty remarkable. It had the standard high ceilings, of course, but where Arthur's was made primarily of brick and mortar, this one added on a fair amount of handcrafted wood.

Queen Agnes appeared worn out, though oddly satisfied at the same time. She had a glow about her. Sir Lance-A-Lot did not look any worse for wear, though he never did.

"How's it after feelin'?" asked Scottish Arthur.

"Hurts a lot, actually," Arthur said, trying to keep his mind off the piercing.

"Aye. It'll take a while to heal, but I canne see that

pink blush we put on ye."

"You can?" Arthur said with a start.

"Nay, I canne."

"Sorry. I'm not used to the accent."

"What accent?"

"Song, song!" called out the knights. Moments later the Scots joined in on the chant.

"I only know English songs," said Sir Gareth as he began tuning up. Nobody seemed to care. "I suppose I could just make something up."

"Hear, hear!"

Gareth began to strum as the men and women quieted down. The Scottish king was thumping his foot in rhythm. Even Arthur, with his newfound freedom, felt himself swaying along.

> *Weeyeeyee met them at the border*
> *Weeyeeyee told them our tale*
> *Weeyeeyee are drinking together*
> *Our newfound alliance, it never can fail*

> *The English and Scottish shall stand side-by-side*
> *The Scottish and English in each other confide*
> *Two nations as one, united in purpose...*

Scottish Arthur leaned over and whispered, "Art, ye know that what's he's singing about is after being bullsheht."

"Sadly," English Arthur agreed.

"Aye."

"Everyone!" called out Sir Gareth.

*Weeyeeyee met them at the border*
*Weeyeeyee told them our tale*
*Weeyeeyee are drinking together*
*Our newfound alliance, it never can fail*

# BACK AT CAMELOT

TWO DAYS LATER they had returned to Camelot. The trip was uneventful and there was promise of better relations with the Scots, if only for the time-being. Once new kings were in place, things would deteriorate again. Arthur had little doubt of that.

"And they were incredibly welcoming," Arthur excitedly explained to Guinevere. "Honestly, I could see going to parties with that fellow."

"That's lovely to hear, Arthur," she said sadly.

"I just wish that Arty would have been able to part with both rings."

"It's okay, Arthur."

"Again, I offer it freely to you, my cherished."

"It's more important that you have it than I."

"But I feel like such a heel."

"You're the face of the kingdom, dearest. I'm not."

"Still."

Merlin came scrambling up to them. He was looking all over the place for something. Arthur assumed it was one of his cameras or booms or what have you.

"Have either of you seen Allison?"

"She was here earlier," said Arthur, glancing around.

"Yes, I know, but—"

"Wizard," Galahad said, stepping up to them, "I did a little more looking into that watering mess you spoke of before. Are you *sure* you used magic for that?"

"I don't have time for this right now, Galahad," replied Merlin, "but why don't you come to my cave later tonight and I'll tell you everything you want to know."

"Seriously?"

"Yes," Arthur said, equally shocked at Merlin's offer, "seriously?"

"I give you my word," answered Merlin. "I can assure you, however, that you're not going to like it."

"I don't like most things," said Galahad with a shrug.

Guinevere pointed across the courtyard toward a small shed. "Isn't that your Allison…" She paused because directly behind Allison was Sir Lance-A-Lot. "Oh my."

"He sure does get around, doesn't he?" said Galahad.

"Not good," moaned Merlin.

"Merlin," Arthur said, placing his hand on the wizard's shoulder, "I know she's your apprentice, but she's also an adult. She should have the right to make up her own mind, no?"

"Not in our time period," Galahad pointed out.

"I have to hand it to you, Arthur," Merlin said while keeping his eyes on Allison, "you are the most liberal king I've ever met."

"Thank you?"

"Believe me, it's a rare thing, and it's probably the biggest reason I stick around these parts. I get a lot of offers to leave, you know."

"Hmmm."

Merlin then took Arthur aside and said, "As for having only one Nipple Ring of Veiling, may I make a suggestion?"

"Of course."

"Use the law, Arthur," Merlin said earnestly. "You do hold the pen that writes it, after all."

# MERLIN'S NOTEBOOK: LAW

*LAW IS A fickle thing. It works wonders in certain areas and creates mayhem in others. Worded properly, it can be as strong as iron; worded improperly and it can be twisted and fashioned in ways that make it seem like dough.*

*But when a king makes a decree, he has the ability to interpret it however he so chooses. Any of those who try and wiggle around it are often found dangling from the end of a rope.*

*That's the thing about law. Those who follow it are subjected to it, but those who set it in motion have it as their subject. They are above it, in a manner of speaking. Sure, some of them will fall to its horrible embrace if the need arises, but that's simply the way of things.*

# THE DECREE

A HUGE CROWD had gathered at the base of the balcony that hung out from Arthur and Guinevere's room in the castle. It was where he always stood to make announcements as it was the best place for him to be heard throughout the majority of Camelot.

He was full of nerves. The king of Scotland was correct that the first time he ventured out using only the ring's protection, he would be worried regarding its power.

"And you honestly can't see anything?"

"The only thing I notice is that your metal is shining a little brighter than usual. You look fine, Arthur."

Arthur glanced across the room to see himself in the full-length mirror.

"But you know that I'm wearing a purple bra and panties combination along with that wonderful eye makeup you applied."

"And the lipstick."

"Absolutely."

"I *know* you're wearing that, yes, but right now I can see none of it." She grabbed his hand. "I believe that you have finally garnered your freedom, Arthur."

"And now, my sweet, it's time for you to have *your* freedom."

He stepped out to the cheers of his subjects. He noted many sneers as well, but you couldn't please all of the people all of the time. The full complement of knights was standing at the base of the castle looking out toward the crowd. They were there to make sure the people stayed in check.

"People of England, hear my words," he began. "Today I shall make a decree that will seem strange to some and freeing to others."

The people cheered.

"My knights and I have just returned from the border at Scotland. Whilst there we saw things that made it apparent we have fallen behind the times."

The people were murmuring.

"The men there, for example, wear skirts!"

The murmuring grew louder and there were a lot of confused faces.

"Now I'm not suggesting that we do that," Arthur said as a large sigh covered the crowd. "However, I think that we can do them one better."

Faces changed from confused to intrigued.

"You would like to do one better than the Scots, wouldn't you?"

Cheers rang up for a few moments.

"Then we shall!"

The cheers were even louder. Arthur let it go on briefly before motioning them to settle down.

"On this day," Arthur stated, "I, King Arthur, ruler of England, declare that all women in my land may choose to wear pantaloons!"

Cheers rang out again and then suddenly stopped. As one, the people said, "What?"

"Pantaloons," answered Arthur and then cleared his throat. "I said pantaloons. No more having to toil in the fields while wearing dresses, unless you want to, of course. You can wear pants and boots instead, and even a regular shirt if you'd want."

As one, they said, "Why?"

"Because," Arthur replied as if they were all being silly, "we're doing one better than that Scots."

There was the briefest pause before the cheering welled up louder than before. It was one of those moments where a ruler learns which side of the fence he's about to fall toward. Fortunately for Arthur, he fell to the side of loyalty on this day.

"And just to show you that I'm serious about this," Arthur yelled, "I present to you Queen Guinevere in her new outfit."

He reached back and took her hand. She looked very nervous, and rightfully so for she hadn't the protection of the ring that he wore.

Guinevere stepped out, wearing black pantaloons, a plain white shirt, a gray vest, black boots, and her hair had been cut dreadfully short.

The people gasped. They had been used to seeing their queen wearing beautiful dresses, and they had never seen a woman with such a cropped hairstyle.

"Tell the people how it feels, my queen."

"It feels," she said strongly, "like we're better than

the Scots!"

The cheers returned and were deafening, much to Arthur and Guinevere's delight.

The two embraced and then commenced waving as Sir Gareth struck up his band and got the party started.

# MERLIN'S NOTEBOOK: HUMAN NATURE

PEOPLE ARE GENERALLY *slow to change, but there are certain things that can be done to advance their pace.*

*While it was clear to me that those in my era would be steadfastly against cross-dressing, I also knew that competition between nations would ultimately win out. It's the nature of things. When a desired event is challenging to push through the majority, simply engage a stronger event as reason for doing so. Goats will graze in one spot for as long as possible unless their shepherd comes along wielding a stick—or if Sir Gareth arrives after a few ales...but that's a different story.*

*There is little doubt that Arthur's choice of garb would never be accepted by the people of England—even if the queen of Scotland managed to get the Scots to accept their warriors wearing skirts—but they will more readily accept the women wearing more masculine clothing because of the practicality of it.*

*It follows that if you mix functionally logical ideas along with one's allegiance to one's country, you can get them to believe —and do—just about anything.*

# A NEW APPRENTICE

MERLIN WAS STANDING in the back room of his hovel as Allison finished packing her things. It was time for her to return to her own era. Merlin wished that she could stick around since he learned so many things from her, but he knew that she had obligations in the future as well.

"Do you feel you've gotten enough footage?"

"More than I needed, Merlin," she said, holding up something called a 'thumb drive.' "I'm a sure bet to get my doctorate out of this."

"And you'll keep in touch?"

"Don't I always, Merl?" she said, giving him a quick hug.

They were interrupted by a knock at the door.

"That'll be Galahad," Merlin grunted. "He's about to get a lesson that he doesn't want."

"Be careful, Merl," Allison said, "you know how the information I've given you can affect the time line."

"Not really, no," Merlin said. "And what about all

the information you're bringing forward?"

"Doesn't hurt to bring notes from the past forward."

"Somehow I doubt the accuracy of that," Merlin said, "but what do I know?"

"If anything, Merl, it'll help historians because there has been a lot of controversy over whether King Arthur was from England or from Scotland. Imagine their faces when they learn that there was one from each!"

"That does solve a mystery, I suppose."

"Exactly," she said as she stepped onto the little platform in the wall. "Well, until next time, Merl, keep studying."

She disappeared in a flash, leaving the wizard to the sound of continued pounding on his door. He rolled his eyes and headed out into the main room to let the knight in.

"Galahad," he said as he motioned the man inside.

"Nice place."

"Thanks," Merlin said. "Care for a drink?"

"I'm here to learn, Merlin. Not drink."

"So you want to get right to it, then," Merlin said with a nod. "Fine with me. See that little lightning bolt over there?"

"The one flashing between them two poles?"

"Correct."

"What about it?"

"Touch it."

Galahad squinted. "Why?"

"It's lesson number one."

"It looks dangerous."

Merlin shrugged, daring Galahad to back down. "That's magic for you."

"Hmmm," Galahad said, reaching out gingerly. He stopped. "Yeah, I don't think I will."

"Interesting," said Merlin, looking the knight over. "Maybe there's more to you than meets the eye, Galahad."

"What's that supposed to mean?"

"Let me ask you something," Merlin said. "Can you keep secrets?"

"Yeah."

"I mean like *really* keep secrets?"

"I said I could, didn't I?"

"Tell me, would you like to learn magic?"

"Probably not."

"Seriously?"

"Way I see it," started Galahad, "you do a lot of nothing. Why would I want to do a lot of nothing?"

"You're a knight," Merlin noted. "Your job is essentially to do a lot of nothing."

"We drink and engage in merriment," Galahad countered, "and every now and then there's even fisticuffs."

"And you can still do all of those things, Galahad," Merlin stated, "but you can do even more if you know what I know."

"This ain't some ploy to get me to be like some apprentice that goes about picking up your house and making you tea and biscuits, is it?"

"I assure you it is not."

"What about Allison?" Galahad said, looking around.

"She left."

"Oh, sorry to hear that. Didn't work out, then?"

"It was amicable," Merlin said. "Actually, it's quite fantastical. Honestly, Galahad, if you knew where she really went it would blow your mind."

"Much like touching that lightning bolt, I'm guessing."

"No, it was a metaph...never mind. Look, do you want to learn magic or not?"

Galahad took a deep breath and gazed around the room. "I just want to know how things work, Merlin. Can't help myself. Always been a tinkerer, I have. It's like having an itch that I just can't stab."

"I have all the information you're looking for, Galahad."

"So it seems," he said pointing at the table of beakers and books. "Okay, fine, I'll play along. But if I touch this lightning bolt and it kills me, I'm going to be downright angry."

"No," Merlin said, pushing the knight's arm away, "don't touch that. It *will* kill you."

Galahad's mouth dropped open. "You're honestly telling me that you were going to kill me when I got here?"

"Not precisely," argued Merlin. "You're the one who would have touched the bolt. I wasn't going to *make* you do it. How could I? You're a knight, easily twice my size."

"Hmmm."

"Look, answer my question, Galahad. Do you want to learn 'magic' or not?"

"That time *you* used the air quotes, Merlin."

"I surely did," Merlin replied with a smile. "Aren't you just dying to know why?"

Galahad checked out the lightning bolt again. "Damn it," he said. "It's against my better judgment, but I truly do want to know."

"Good," said Merlin, rubbing his hands together. "Good."

"Somehow I don't think so," Galahad said as Merlin placed a stack of books in his hands, with one on top that was entitled *Science for Dummies*.

"Get started, Galahad," Merlin said. "We've got a lot of work ahead of us."

"Maybe I should just touch the lightning bolt," Galahad said as Merlin went to get them tea.

# KNIGHTS IN THE FUTURE
## BOOK 2
## THE ADVENTURES OF QUEEN ARTHUR

# RADIO SILENCE

MERLIN SAT STARING at the screen of the laptop computer that Allison had given him.

It had been over eight months since they'd last spoken and he was concerned. They'd never gone for more than a week without at least some form of communication.

Yes, she was living in the future, and Merlin had originally assumed that Allison was just busy toiling away with her scientific endeavors. Truth was that were it not for her work, they never would have met those years ago while Merlin was out exploring caves. Life would have been much different. Boring, mostly.

But this was puzzling.

They'd talked without fail up until she'd left from her last visit to Camelot. Since then it had been utter radio silence.

To be fair, Allison had returned from their last get-together with a slew of camera footage from the adventure of helping Arthur find the *Ring of Veiling*. Her intent was to edit the video and build a formal presentation for her doctoral thesis on Arthurian Lore. She'd explained to Merlin how this would be her third doctorate. Her other two were in engineering and physics, which she explained stood as the backbone for building the time machine.

Most of the time Merlin just nodded politely when she described these things. He was still barely coming to terms with electricity, chemistry, and basic technology. Advanced mathematics, physics, celestial spheres, and something called "computer programming" continued to sit just outside of his capacity.

What he *did* know was that it was out of character for Allison to miss even a week of discussions, let alone nearly a year.

Something was most definitely wrong and Merlin decided that it was time to learn precisely what.

He strode out of the back room and into the main study.

Sir Galahad was fast asleep on a pile of books. All in all, Galahad had proved a worthy apprentice. He was cantankerous at times and incorrigible at others, but he challenged Merlin to think. Allison had always said that the best teacher was the student. After a couple of weeks having Galahad as an apprentice, Merlin understood the full breadth of her words. All these months later, Merlin thought certain that his personal knowledge must have grown by leaps and bounds.

"Wake up, man," Merlin said, shaking his apprentice. "There's an issue we must attend to straightaway."

Galahad jolted upright. His eyes were red as he wiped the drool from his chin. Plastered to the side of his face was the indent of the book he'd been sleeping upon.

"Ugh," he said in his raspy voice. "What time is it?"

"I don't know," Merlin said as he looked toward the door, "but based on the lack of light streaming through the windows, I'd have to say nighttime."

"Right. So what's the problem?"

"It's been eight months since we've heard from Allison," Merlin said in such a way as to convey that Galahad already knew what the problem was.

"Ah, that again. You go on about this every month, Merlin. Last month it was seven months since you'd heard from her. The month before it was six months —"

"I am aware of how counting works, Gal."

"Really don't like that nickname, Merl."

"Touché," Merlin said with a bow. "Anyway, I'm worried that something has happened to her and each passing day only makes that worry more pronounced."

Galahad began to yawn as he dug his knuckles into his eyes. He stood up and twisted left and right, and then bent backwards slightly with a groan. Finally, he shook his head quickly as if trying to rattle his brain to life.

"So what do you want to do about it?"

"I think we need to go into the future and find out what's happened," Merlin answered soberly.

"Sounds great," Galahad said, blinking. "Maybe after that, we can go back in time to visit the Roman

Empire. I hear that Caligula was a blast to hang around, in a manner of speaking. A real party animal, that guy." He paused as Merlin stared at him. "Or maybe you should consider having a few drinks instead? That would calm your nerves a bit."

"Don't patronize me, Galahad."

"Well, you are being a bit ridiculous."

Merlin leaned back against the wall and crossed his arms. Galahad was ever the pain, but Merlin had learned a thing or two over the last number of months about how Galahad ticked.

"How has your learning been going, Sir Galahad?"

"Uh oh," said Galahad with a sigh, "you're calling me 'Sir Galahad' now. That can't be good." He scratched his head for a moment. "You've also jumped topics pretty quickly there, which can only mean you're up to something."

"Answer the question."

"Fine. I've learned a fair amount."

"You know how electricity works, yes?"

"Considering how you had originally tried to kill me with it, I'd say I've got a decent handle on it."

Merlin ignored that. "And you understand the basic mechanics on how to solve pulling water up from a river basin and onto land?"

"*Archimedes Screw*," Galahad replied.

"And how radio signals work?"

"Almost."

"What about cameras and film?"

"Still baffling to me," said Galahad with a shrug.

"And—"

"Get to the point, Merlin."

Merlin wasn't fond of being spoken to in such a manner, but he knew what he was getting into when he'd decided to take Galahad on as a student and so he pushed the angst away.

"The point is that without Allison you wouldn't know any of that. She is the reason your brain is full of more than hops and barley."

"Hmmm."

"Worse than that," Merlin said, unfolding his arms while walking toward the window, "I'd be nothing but a pencil-pusher in some remote town, struggling through the daily toil of life while my curious mind suffered endlessly."

Galahad grunted. "Oh, all right. Fine. What do we do, then?"

"I'm going to speak to Arthur," Merlin said distantly.

"Why?"

"Because I don't like the idea of going into the future alone."

"I'd be with you," Galahad pointed out.

Merlin nodded slowly. "Exactly."

# A PARTY?

SCOTTISH ARTHUR WAS not a man who took well to being told what to do, except when the person telling him what to do was his queen.

Agnes wanted to have a party. More of a grand ball, to be exact. They'd had a quick get-together when the king of England came down with his men a number of months back, but nothing in the line of fanciness that Queen Agnes had in mind.

Arty—as he liked to be called by his peers—knew his queen's true intentions, though. She wanted to see Camelot's lead knight again.

The king of Scotland grunted to himself.

This had all been his fault. He'd done the naughty with the queen of France after falling into a drunken stupor at a banquet last year. Alcohol, and the fact that the queen of France was smokin' hot, made it all too easy for Arty to put his person where it ought not to be. This would have been fine and good had Agnes not found out about it. He'd never said a word to her, of course. He wasn't stupid. But Agnes had tricked him by intimating that she knew he'd done it, which tripped him up into inadvertently admitting his guilt.

That had opened the door to Agnes having enough ammunition to get even. Unfortunately, her selected man was none other than the human garden hose known as Sir Lance-A-Lot.

Arty sighed and poked a stick at the campfire that his men had built. They were just over halfway to Camelot. He should have left in the morning instead, but Agnes had been nagging him all afternoon and so he'd decided to get away sooner.

Most of his men had drifted off and were snoring. Those still awake were huddled in groups around fires, talking of women and conquests. It wasn't often these days that Arty got to go on journeys such as this, and technically he hadn't had to go at all, but he wasn't going to allow a messenger to deliver this particular invitation. No, it was Arty's goal to personally speak with the king of England to find a way to circumvent Sir Lance-A-Lot's ability to join the party.

"Ridiculous, it 'tis," Arty said with a sneer.

"Aye, me lord," answered Ceallach, Arty's military adviser.

"To think that I'm gonna invite that Lance-A-Lot back into Scotland after he..." Arty paused. "Erm, I mean, uh…"

"What did he do, me lord?" Ceallach said like a man who was building a strategy for war.

"Let's just say he was after probing into matters that dinnae belong to him, and leave it at that."

"Oh," Ceallach replied as his face relaxed. "Ye

mean he boned the missus?"

Arty frowned. "Anyway, if Agnes thinks I'll be invitin' that one along, she's batty."

"Not sure why we would be invitin' the English to anything other than battle anyway, sire, truth be told."

"I know yer feelin', Calle," Arty said as he twitched on the log where he sat. The selection of lacy underbritches seemed fun when he'd left Scotland, but they were beginning to chafe him now. "Their king is after bein' a decent sort, though."

"Aye, me lord. So ye say."

"You doubt me word, Calle?"

"Nay, sire," Ceallach replied with a touch of gloom. "More a case of thinkin' that you've had the lace pulled over yer eyes, is all."

"Lace?" said Arty with a start.

Ceallach closed his eyes briefly and then said, "Wool."

"Ye said lace."

"Meant wool, sire."

"Then why say lace?"

"Thought it'd be more crafty, is all."

"Crafty?"

"Everyone's always after saying 'wool,' me lord," Ceallach explained, "so I think of it as cliché, I do." He looked sideways at the king. "Somethin' wrong with the term 'lace,' sire?"

"Nay," Arty said defensively. "Just wonderin' why ye picked it."

"Maybe there's something about lace that chafes ye, me lord?"

Arty adjusted himself again. "Actually, it... Uh...

Forget it. Anyhoo, point is that this English Arthur is a decent sort. He's a kindred fella, in a manner of speakin'."

"As ye say, me lord."

"Bah! Go to bed, ye git," Arty commanded. "We're only getting an hour or two before we're back on the steeds. Want to get to Camelot before first light."

# SPEAKING TO ARTHUR

KING ARTHUR RARELY had pleasant dreams. His nighttime visuals were more of the sort where people learned of his particular delight in wearing women's clothing. There were trials, laughter, people pointing at him, name-calling, and a slurry of other atrocities that tended to happen to someone who was deemed different.

In this particular nightmare, the local lords and barons had heard of his tawdry behavior and had called for Arthur to be removed from the throne immediately. Guards were sent into the castle to rip him from his kingly slumber. They were pounding on his door…

"Arthur," came the jolting voice of Guinevere, waking him from his dream, "there is someone at the door."

Arthur was still in twilight as he replied, "I know, my dearest. It is me they've come for. They've learned of my inappropriate fashion sense."

"What the hell are you talking about?"

Slowly Arthur's mind came into focus and he realized that this was no longer a dream.

"Nothing."

The pounding on the door continued.

Arthur angrily threw back the covers and began his purposeful stride toward the door.

"Arthur," said Guinevere, "you may wish to put on a robe first."

"Hmmm?" He looked down at himself to find that he was currently garbed in a purple number made of satin with frilly edges. "Oh, right."

The king snagged a proper covering from the wardrobe and finally swung open the door, half-expecting that it *would* be the guards from his dream.

Standing there was Merlin, and he looked intent on having a conversation.

"Good heavens, man," said Arthur as Merlin pushed into the room, "it's the middle of the night!"

Merlin paused. "Your point?"

"Simply that it's not wise to wake anyone at this time, especially not your king!"

"You knock on my door at first light all the time," scoffed Merlin after giving a nod to Guinevere, who had moved to sit on the edge of the bed.

"Precisely," Arthur stated as if the point were obvious. "First light," he added strongly.

"Which is my night, Arthur."

"That's not my fault."

"No, but it is your fault to not respect my sleeping cycles. The world does not revolve around you, you know."

"I'm the king!"

"How many times…" Merlin stopped and held up his hand. "Can we please discuss my purpose for waking you?"

"Oh, sure," Arthur said dramatically, "when *you're* trying to sleep, you're allowed to give me a bunch of bull dung about how I interrupt your slumber, but whenever you feel like intruding on—"

"Arthur, stop this nonsense," Guinevere said. "Merlin obviously has a dilemma or he would never have come here in such a manner."

Arthur crossed his arms, stomped his foot, and said, "Hmmph!"

Guinevere adjusted the sock that she had stuffed in the front of her boxer shorts and leaned forward.

"Now," she said, "what is this all about, Merlin?"

"It's Allison."

"Your apprentice?" Arthur asked. "I thought she had moved on some time ago."

"Yeah, about that..." Merlin said while rubbing his chin. "She was never really my apprentice, Arthur."

"Oh?" said Guinevere.

Merlin sat down on the stone ledge that surrounded the window. Arthur had not seen the man like this before. He appeared concerned, which was normal, but not in this way. While Arthur still hadn't quite adapted to Merlin's particular personality, he would have guessed that the wizard was afraid of something.

"If anything," Merlin said finally, "*I* was *her* apprentice."

"Well, this is interesting," said Guinevere.

"Indeed, it is, my sweet," said Arthur. "Pray tell,

Merlin."

"She's from the future," Merlin replied.

Arthur nodded. So that's what this was all about. Merlin had gone on a bender and his first destination was Arthur's room in the castle. He would have to give the guards a talking to about this. Not that it was really their fault. If the wizard threatened to turn them into toads, or worse, they'd have little recourse but to let the man pass. Still, a drunken Merlin was not to be tolerated.

"The future," Arthur said dryly.

"Yes."

"How's that, again?" asked Guinevere, clearly coming to the same conclusion about alcohol being involved.

Merlin looked up at the ceiling for a moment.

"She came back in time through a machine of some sort," he explained slowly. "I found her in a cave a number of years back and she began teaching me."

"I see," said Guinevere, not sounding all that convinced.

"I don't wish to be rude," Arthur said a few seconds later, "but have you been drinking?"

"No."

"Bumped your head, maybe?"

"No."

"Did you cast a dullard spell on yourself, per chance?"

Merlin merely sighed and gave Guinevere a would-you-please-help-me-out-here look.

"Enough, Arthur," Guinevere said as she stood up

from the bed. "Forgive him, Merlin, but you must understand that what you're saying is rather fantastical."

"Oh, I'm well aware of that, Gwen. But I assure you that it's all true."

"Maybe you've been experimenting with recreational hallucinogens?" Arthur pressed. "I hear they are the rage these days."

Guinevere turned on Arthur and gave him a stern look. It was the look that she typically reserved for when she was wearing women's clothing and he was in his kingly garb. It was that look that said, "You've had it now, mister."

"Arthur," she said evenly, "if you keep this up I shall take away the key to my wardrobe closet and you'll be stuck wearing boxers for the next two weeks."

"Diabolical," Arthur replied as his shoulder's slumped. "Fine, I shall play along." His heart wasn't in it, but he forced himself to feign sincerity. "Okay, Merlin, so your former non-apprentice has gone missing?"

"That's what I said."

"And you fear she is in trouble?"

"Obviously, you bonehead."

"Careful, wizard," said Arthur, having enough trouble with this entire thing as it was. "Remember that I am still your king."

"More of a queen, really," mused Merlin, "and remember that I don't buy in to all of that royal hoopla."

"I could have you tarred and feathered for—"

"What can we do to help, Merlin?" interrupted Guinevere.

Merlin pushed off the ledge and began to pace back and forth. He'd clasped his hands behind his back as he walked from one end of the room to the other. Arthur wasn't sure if this was for dramatic effect or if the man was really thinking, and Arthur still wasn't certain that booze wasn't involved, but after a few more moments it became clear that what Merlin was truly doing was attempting to summon courage. This took Arthur aback. Usually the little man was direct and unwavering when he wanted something.

"I want to go to the future and find her," Merlin said with a wince.

"What?" said Arthur.

"I see," Guinevere said. "How do you propose to accomplish this?"

"I have a time machine in the back room of my house," he answered.

Arthur squinted. "What?"

"And you believe that this... Sorry, what was it called again?"

"Machine."

"Machine," Guinevere said as though she were tasting the word. "And you believe it will help us find your Allison?"

"I'm not sure, but I hope so."

Guinevere nodded. "What do you need from us?"

"Well," Merlin said hopefully, "it may be dangerous and I'm not exactly what you'd call a fighter."

"Wait a second here," Arthur interjected before

Guinevere could make any decrees. "Are you suggesting that I send knights along on this foolhardy errand?"

Merlin bristled. "Is it any more foolish than the one we went on to get you a blasted ring so you could walk around wearing women's trinkets and gowns without anyone knowing about it, dude?"

"*Dude?*" Arthur harrumphed and turned away.

"We will speak with the knights and shall prepare a contingent," Guinevere said, clearly ignoring Arthur's feelings. "We shall depart at first light."

"What?" said Arthur, blinking.

"Thank you, Gwen," Merlin said with a slight bow. "I sometimes wish that you were king. The world would be a better place for it."

"Hey," said Arthur.

"Seeing how he dresses, Merlin," she said and then looked down at herself, "and, honestly, how I do as well, I think the world has already been granted your wish."

"Hey!"

# SELECTING THE KNIGHTS

ARTHUR STOOD AT the same spot he always stood when addressing the Knights of the Round Table. Looking at their surroundings, a better descriptor would probably be Knights of the Pub Table. There wasn't a *round* table to speak of, though he knew that wasn't quite the point.

To his left stood Sir Lance-A-Lot, whose real name was Mitch Bowenkawski. He had gotten the Lance-A-Lot moniker from the rest of the knights because his man-nub was the size of a lance and he employed its use with the ladies a lot.

The rest of the knights sat along each side of the table, each holding either food, tankards, or both.

Going around he saw Sir Bedivere, the knight who imbibed a steady supply of spirits. Should there ever come a time where Camelot had need to fight a war that consisted of winning drinking contests, Sir Bedivere would rule the day.

Beside him were Sir Purcivale and Sir Tristan. They were of the same make and personality. Anyone who didn't know better would assume they were twins. Brothers, at least. They spoke funnily, were rather sarcastic, and they had no qualms saying what they thought. This, of course, could have been due to the fact that very few people could understand them.

Sir Gareth was the company bard. He was slight, and horrible at fighting, but he could sing like an angel and his deftness with musical instruments was untouched. Gareth could also put together a fine meal when in the field, and his ability to stitch up wounds and repair clothing tears stood up there with the best seamstresses.

Another two who were cut by the same jib were Sir Bors de Ganis and Sir Kay. They didn't look like each other, but they were both actors, writers, and directors in the local theater. Any time Camelot was to hold a party, it was these two, along with their wives, who were in charge of planning and execution (not that kind). Sir Bors was tall and bold with a bald head and a tight goatee. Sir Kay was a little shorter and he had neatly cropped hair and a finely trimmed beard. Had Arthur not known better, he would have assumed that they were more than merely friends, but theater people seem to suffer that reputation, which most likely stemmed from the fact that they only allow men to play all roles, and more often than not those roles include dressing the part of a woman. Arthur, of course, did this constantly, though not in a play, as it were, and he knew well that he was *not* interested in other fellows, which allowed him to assume that Bors and Kay were not either.

Sir Gawain was a paradoxical sort. He was big and strong, yet gentle and caring. At the same time, he had a tendency to speak his mind in a very blunt and often hurtful manner. But once he realized his mistake—which often required that someone point it out to him—he would vehemently apologize in the most peculiar of ways.

Sir Lamorak was one of the more positive knights. Actually, he was positively positive, to the point of it being sugary and unrealistic. When they had first met, Arthur assumed that this was due to some form of overcompensation, but it had turned out that Lamorak was honestly just a very glass-half-full kind of guy. He also had those steely blue eyes that you read about in romances. Frankly, of all the knights—except Sir Lance-A-Lot, of course—Lamorak's square jaw and long dark hair made him the most handsome man that Arthur had ever seen.

Arthur quickly looked away, blinking a few times.

Sir Gaheris leaned against the wall beyond the end of the table. He was the tallest of all the knights, and probably the strongest as well. He had mussy brown hair and a full beard to match, and he wore a permanent look of a man who had become a master at grumbling. He was gruff and often irritable, but his skill in fighting was a thing of legend. Arthur had seen him single-handedly skewer five seasoned fighters who were all attacking at once, and the overgrown oaf hadn't even broken a sweat. Plus, of all the knights under Arthur's command, Gaheris was one who rarely questioned orders. He would sometimes ignore them, but he seldom questioned them. One of the primary orders that he seemed to find difficult to accept was that of maintaining a proper bath schedule, which made it a point of discussion each year at the knight's annual review. The fact was that cleanliness and Gaheris did not get along.

"Everyone, quiet down," Lance-A-Lot said. "Our king wishes a word."

"Thank you, Sir Lance-a-lot." Arthur gathered his wits and cleared his throat. "Knights, hear me. We have the potential of going on a quest that is unlike any we've been on before."

"Is there going—*hic*—to be any fighting this time?" said Sir Bedivere in his drunken way.

"It may come to that, of course."

"I heard—*hic*—that last time there was...was...wasn't any fighting."

Purcivale wiped his nose and turned to Tristan. "We did a bit of a go 'round with a couple of highwaymen, ain't we, Tristy?"

"Wasn't much of a tumble, Percy," Tristan said, "but enough to warrant a touch of battle with the ting-tings."

"The what?" said Bedivere in a half-burp.

"Ting-tings, guv," answered Purcivale.

"Eh?"

"Come now, Beddy," said Tristan. "You know what the ting-tings are. Long butterknives, they is."

"Oversized cutlery," agreed Purcivale.

"Huh?" said Bedivere.

"They're talking about swords, Sir Bedivere,"

offered Lance-A-Lot.

"Well, why don't they say—*hic*—that?"

Purcivale leaned back and crossed his arms. "Where's the fun in that?"

"Right," Arthur jumped in, hoping to curb the conversation before it fell into a massive debate. With Purcivale and Tristan at the helm, the true discussion would never get started. "Well, let's get back to the task at hand, shall we? This will be an arduous journey that will test our will. It will require a strong resolve…" Arthur stopped, noting that the bard had his hand up. "Yes, Sir Gareth?"

"Sire, do you know how long this journey will be?"

Arthur was taken aback by this question. He shouldn't have been, since it was asked almost every time he attempted to put a quest together, but he couldn't help feeling that it was inconsequential. Quests took however long they took. All the knights knew this.

"Uknown at this time," he replied smoothly. "It could be hours, days, or even weeks. Why?"

"It's just that my new band is slated to headline this coming weekend and we've all worked very hard to get here."

"Sorry, your new band?"

"Yes, sire," Gareth said, sitting forward excitedly. "We're called *Death Knight*. We play *Heavy Wood* music."

"*Heavy Wood?*" said Arthur, glancing slightly at Sir Lance-A-Lot.

"Rubbish," Bors said with a snort.

"That it is," agreed Kay.

"Excuse me," Gareth fumed, "but do I put down your silly plays?"

"Silly?" Bors looked serious. "They're *not* silly."

"Agreed," Kay said, "and besides now, of course, I have never heard you say a disparaging word regarding our work."

"And do you know why?"

Sir Kay pondered for a moment. "I'm assuming it has something to do with your desire to keep your head attached to your person."

"No," said Gareth. Then he bit his lip and added, "Well, yes, that's true. But it's also because I respect the both of you."

"*Hic*—Why?" said Bedivere.

"Because of that respect," continued Gareth, "I do not sully the things that you are involved in. What have you to say to that?"

"That your music is rubbish," Bors answered with a shrug.

"Precisely," said Kay. "It's a disturbing cacophony of noises that rival only that of angry tomcats."

Gareth's jaw hung open for a moment. "How rude."

"You see, Sir Gareth," Bors told the smaller man, "we are free to speak our minds on the subject for two reasons. Kay?"

Kay smiled. "We're not afraid of losing our heads at the end of your blade."

"And?" said Bors.

"We have no respect for you."

"Ouch," said Gareth, looking suddenly downtrodden.

"Right," said Arthur, making a mental note to have a word with Sir Lance-A-Lot to have a word with Sir Bors and Sir Kay in the manner with which they treat other artists who don't contain themselves to the interests of the theater. "So Gareth won't be joining our trip. Neither will Bedivere."

"I—*hic*—won't?"

"You won't," affirmed Arthur. "However, if we come across a quest that requires someone to be perpetually sloshed, you'll be top on the list of recruits."

Bedivere raised his mug and gave a solitary, "Hear, hear!"

Arthur knew well that there would only be a few willing to tear themselves away from whatever their personal interests were in the area. They would drop everything to defend Camelot, of course, but when it came to quests, only a few of them seemed to enjoy the concept. Lance-A-Lot had often claimed that the men were bored, but Arthur never spotted supporting evidence for that claim. Regardless, each of them was expected to pull their fair share of the duty, so while a few of them remained behind during the Scotland quest, they would have to step up this time.

Still, he would hear their say.

"Anyone else looking to stay behind?"

"If it's all the same to you, sire," said Lamorak, "I have been supporting young Gareth and his band of noisemakers—"

"Hey!"

"Sorry," Lamorak amended, "I meant instrumentalists. I have a touch of an investment to oversee in their future."

"An investment?" questioned Arthur.

"He's the band's manager, sire," Gareth said with a grumble that relayed he was not fond of Lamorak's description of the band.

"Ah."

"I'm out, too," said Gawain.

"And your reason, Sir Gawain?"

"Mostly that I can't stand hanging around Sirs Purcivale and Tristan," Gawain stated. "I know they'll be going because they always do, and I just can't take it. The both of them are fiercely annoying and they smell of soured cheese."

"Sir Gawain," Lamorak chastised his fellow knight, "what have we said about your blurting issues?"

The blood exited Gawain's face. "I've done it again, haven't I?" His head drooped and he blew out a breath before turning to Sirs Purcivale and Tristan. "I implore you to accept my most profound apologies. May I trip and fall face-first into a puddle of sludge, drowning slowly and with much pain and anguish."

"There," said Lamorak, "that's better. Disturbing, but better."

"What's wrong with smelling like cheese, Tristy?"

"Haven't the foggiest, Percy. Much better than the roses that Borsy and Kay smell like."

"What's that?" said Bors.

"Ignore the cheese twins, Sir Bors," Kay said, placing a restraining hand on the larger man's shoulder. "Simply not worth the effort."

"Enough of this," Arthur demanded as he scanned the faces seated at the table. These were supposed to be the best of the best. Men of honor. Men of integrity. They shouldn't be attacking each other with a constant onslaught of rude quips. "I shall decree who is to attend and that will be that. The names are: Bors, Kay, Gaheris, Galahad, Percivale, Tristan, and Mitch."

"That's Lance-A-Lot, sire."

"Hmmm?" said Arthur and then realized what he had said. "Oh, yes, right. Sorry."

"Don't forget about me, Arthur," came the voice of Guinevere, who had walked out of the shadows.

"Right, and Guinevere..." Arthur started and then stopped. "What are you doing in here, my persimmon? This is not a place for a lady."

"Or someone who dresses the part, I would imagine," she countered.

Arthur's eyes widened. "What's that?"

"Nothing." Guinevere yelped, bringing her hand to her mouth. A moment later, appearing even more uncomfortable, she squared her shoulders and painfully muttered, "My love, I ask that I be allowed to go due to the subject matter at hand. I am in a unique position to understand the ladies."

"Me, too," stated Lance-A-Lot.

"Very true, Sir Lance-A-Lot," Guinevere said, batting her eyes, "but I'm talking beyond mere conquests."

"Ah."

"Fine," Arthur said as if making a decree, "I shall allow it." Guinevere gave him a sharp look, which caused him to quickly say, "Uh, my pudding."

She looked away irritably.

Arthur took a deep breath and glanced around at his knights once more. Everyone was waiting for his final commands, except for Bedivere who had finally succumbed to the effects of alcohol. His head was resting in an almost empty bowl of stew and he was snoring like he'd not slept in weeks.

"Get your packs packed and be at the ready," he commanded. "We leave at daybreak."

# APPROACHING TOWN

THE SUN WAS coming up as Arty and his small contingent of kilt-wearing soldiers approached a large castle.

There was a bunch of hubbub coming from the town ahead, signaling that there were merchants about. Dust was on the rise as carriages headed to and from the castle. The king of England definitely had this place moving.

"That'll be this Camelot place, I'm guessin'," said Arty, feeling somewhat awed at the enormity of the building.

"Considerin' that it's a big castle with the points and whatsits," answered Ceallach, "and considerin' that big sign back a ways read *Camelot - Straight Ahead* on it, I'd wager yer after being correct."

"Yer startin' to pick on me nerves, Calle," Arty said without bothering to look at the man.

"Sorry, sire," Ceallach replied. "It's me way."

"And it's me way to put me foot in the arse of any man who gets on me nerves."

"Aye, me lord. Apologies."

Arty pulled the horses to a stop. Best he could tell, they were far enough away to not be considered a threat. Even if there were a sentry on one of those parapets, seeing a band of less than twenty wouldn't be worth worrying over. Still, Arty wasn't interested in causing a commotion.

"Tell the men to stay back and make camp. I'm not after wantin' the *nets* to come rousin' while thinking we're up fer battle."

"Nets?"

"Aye," Arty affirmed as he jumped down and began fastening the packs on the horse. "Not that I don't think we can take 'em, but no point in testin' the theory."

"I'm pretty sure that even our worst could fend off a net, me lord."

"I've seen their nets, Calle," Arty replied. He was struggling to cinch up one of the packs. The leather was still new, making it tough to bend into place. "Ye'd be well advised to not underestimate 'em."

"We are talkin' 'bout ropey things, yeah?"

Arty stopped and looked at Ceallach. "What are ye, daft? I'm talking about their soldiers with the blades and the silver suits."

"Oh, *knights*."

Arty bit his lip and then finished cinching the strap in place.

"Yer temptin' a foot in the arse, Calle."

"Sorry, sire."

"Get to the men and set up camp. I'm going into town."

Ceallach stepped in front of the king. "Alone, me lord?"

"Aye."

"Shouldn't ye at least have guards?"

Arthur understood where the man was coming from. It *was* his duty to protect the king of Scotland, after all. But the logistics behind it were silly at best.

"Nay. Nobody's gonna know it's me unless I say it's me and even then, what would guards do for me?"

"Protect you from—"

"They'd die tryin', but if they want to take me out, it'd only take a couple of nets." He pointed warningly at Ceallach. "Don't be after correcting me again."

"But—"

"Save it, Calle. Ain't gonna change me mind." Arty took one last look around. "Now, get the camp set up. I'll be back soon."

# READY TO GO

ARTHUR HAD BEEN to Merlin's place of residence numerous times, but he'd never been beyond the main living area.

Currently he was standing on a metallic disk of sorts that was embedded into a carved-out alcove. His selected knights were on the platform as well, along with his lovely Guinevere. Merlin, however, was standing over by one of the tables that housed a silver box, a rectangular device that the wizard was clicking away on, and squarish-looking thing that displayed a bunch of characters that looked to be a poor attempt at proper calligraphy.

The place was surprisingly dry for being a cave. All of the mountain innards that Arthur had explored when he was a lad had a dank smell to them. Their walls were always tattered with wet patches and most had trickles of water dropping every few seconds.

Still, there was a smell in the air that seemed tangy, and it wasn't the soured cheese odor that followed Sirs Purcivale and Tristan, either.

"Okay," Merlin said as he kept his eyes focused on his task, "you are all about to see things that will likely terrify you. These are things that dwell in the world of magic—"

"Well," interrupted Galahad, "in a manner of speaking."

"Silence, apprentice!"

"Apprentice?" said Arthur, feeling rather confused.

Merlin looked up. "You haven't told him?"

"I haven't told anyone," Galahad admitted.

"Why not?"

"Because I wanted to keep my knight job in the event that this magic hoopla—to use your term—didn't work out."

"You have a night job, too?" Arthur was feeling quite vexed at that.

"K-N-I-G-H-T, sire," Galahad corrected. "I mean my normal job as a knight, not a nighttime pursuit."

"Oh, right. Sorry." Arthur took inventory of the thought again, though. Something was assuredly amiss. "Wait a moment, here. Are you saying that you've been moonlighting as a wizard, Sir Galahad?"

"Mostly just been reading trade journals and the like, sire, but I've been doing a bit with electric—"

"He's been studying the basics of magic," Merlin interrupted. He did not seem pleased with Galahad's explanation in the least. "Runes, lines, eyes of newt, bones, hair... Things of that nature."

"Uh, well—"

"And if Galahad wishes to continue his studies, he'll know when it's best to agree with his master's words."

"Right," Galahad murmured. "What he said."

Arthur wasn't sure how comfortable he was with one of his knights learning the ins and outs of magic. On the one hand it could prove rather useful in battle; on the other hand, it could just mean that he'd end up having to deal with the idiosyncrasies of *two* wizards. One was bad enough.

"Anyway," Merlin continued, turning his attention back to the glowing box, "we are going to be entering a domain that is vastly different than our own. There will be horseless carriages, enormous metal birds, and all sorts of wondrous devices that are beyond your wildest imagination."

"Sounds like he's tipped a few, Percy," said Tristan.

"More than a few, I'd wager."

"Maybe it would be best if I showed you all a few pictures," Merlin commented as he clicked away with his fingers.

"No offense, Merlin," Bors said, "but I've seen your drawings and they aren't… Oh my."

The box in front of Merlin lit up with an image that could only have been drawn by the finest artisan. It was colorful, vivid, and crisp. Never in all of his years had Arthur seen such a rendition, except for those launching directly from his own eyes, of course.

"What is that?" Kay asked.

"This is what's called an automobile. It's also known as a car. Some refer to it as an auto, or clunker, or jalopy, or… Well, many things."

"What's it do?"

"As to that, Gwen," Merlin replied kindly, "it acts much like our horse and buggies do. It pulls people around conveniently. Although, I have heard Allison say quite a number of negative things about them, too. 'Gas guzzler' comes to mind, but don't ask me to explain what that means."

He clicked on the little square thing that sat under his right hand. If Arthur recalled correctly, Merlin had said it was a rat. It didn't look anything like the rats Arthur had seen in his years, but the wizard had a way of his own when it came to naming things.

"This is an airplane. It flies through the air like a bird."

"It's a damn dragon," Bors cried, pointing.

"No, it's not," Merlin argued swiftly, "and I don't want any of you getting funny ideas either. The last thing we need is the TSA blocking us from flying, should it come to that."

"The what?" asked Arthur.

"Forget it, Arthur, there isn't time. Just promise me that you'll all keep yourselves in check during this quest."

"Are you suggesting that my knights would be anything less than professional?"

"Obviously, yes."

"Oh."

"This is a waste of time," Gaheris said. While the rest of the knights had looks of awe on their faces, Gaheris remained as impassive as always. "We don't need to know the particulars. We go where we go."

"Well said, Sir Gaheris," Arthur agreed. "Let's just get along with it, shall we, Merlin?"

"Are you sure you don't want to see some of the other items first? It may ease your minds."

"We go where we go," repeated Gaheris.

"As you wish," Merlin said with a shrug. "Okay, you'll all have to be pushed together into the center of that platform." He motioned them all to squeeze in. "We all have to fit, so squash together, nice and tight."

"Ooh, Lance," Guinevere said playfully. "Careful with that thing, will you?"

Arthur jolted while struggling to look over his shoulder. "What thing?"

"His sword, Arthur. That's all I meant."

"Ah, yes. Sorry."

"I wouldn't have complained about the *other* thing," Guinevere hinted.

"Pardon?"

"Nothing, dear. You were saying, Merlin?"

"Let me adjust these dials and I'll jump in with you." Merlin was clicking and tapping and moving things around on the picture screen. Sometimes the things that the wizard did were downright terrifying. "Make sure to leave me a small space up there or you'll be on your own."

"Gaheris smells of wee," Purcivale announced.

"And they say we're the rotted bunch, eh Percy?"

Gaheris did not appear bothered by this comment. He merely said, "I go where I go."

"Everyone out," yelled Arthur as he pulled Guinevere away from the knight's vicinity. Gaheris was the only one left on the platform. "Honestly, man, tell me that you didn't just soil your trousers."

"I did not do as such, sire," Gaheris replied evenly.

"Okay, then." Arthur waved at the group.

"Everyone back in."

They resumed their positions on the platform.

"I soiled them right before we walked into Merlin's house," Gaheris stated, clearing up the situation.

"Everyone out!" Arthur was tired of having this talk with Sir Gaheris. "Did you bring a change of clothes with you?"

"No," Gaheris replied.

"Turn and face the wall, then."

"Why?"

"Do as you're told, Sir Gaheris," commanded Lance-A-Lot, "or you shall be left behind."

He did so, which resulted in Sir Purcivale pointing and saying, "The stains on the back are worse than the ones on the front, Tristy."

"I feel like a prime diamond compared to him, I do," commented Tristan.

Arthur dropped his head for a moment and groaned.

"Does anyone have a change of pants handy?"

"I do," said Guinevere. She reached into her pack and pulled out a set of men's trousers. When she looked back up, everyone was staring at her. "What? I'm a lady. We prepare for things like this." She quickly handed the pants to Gaheris. "Go and put these on."

"But—"

"No buts, Sir Gaheris," she said in a tone that relayed she meant business. "You are making us late. The pants are all man, I assure you. Now go and change out of that lot you're wearing."

"Yes, my lady."

"And don't even think about leaving your old ones on my floor," Merlin hollered after the departing Gaheris. "Throw them outside!"

Everyone milled about as they waited. Merlin kept yelling at Purcivale and Tristan to keep their hands off things, which seemed fruitless. Arthur was curious about a number of items, too, but he'd learned the hard way that it was better to keep one's hands in one's pockets when in the lair of Merlin the Wizard.

"Everyone back in," Arthur said as soon as Gaheris returned. The pants had fit him fine, though they were maybe just slightly short.

"Expecting a flood, gov?" Tristan asked the returning knight.

"What?"

"Cut it out," Arthur warned before Purcivale could chime in.

Merlin took two steps toward the platform, but stopped at the side wall and put his hand on a post that was sticking out a few inches.

"Looks like everyone is set," he said. "I'm flipping the switch now."

He flicked the post and a series of lights began to glow under the floor. There were reds and blues and whites and greens and yellows. They rotated faster and faster until it was all Arthur could do to hold in his breakfast. Soon the floor began to vibrate and he felt a scream begin to well up within his soul. But then, just as quickly as it had all started, it stopped… After first making a pop and whir sound.

"What happened?"

"Not sure," Merlin said, running back to the desk.

"Damn. Says here we've got one too many people in there to launch. Either that or someone is carrying too much bulk."

"Nothing I can do about it," Lance-A-Lot said apologetically.

"No, not that," Merlin replied and then appeared to think about it. "Well, actually, maybe it is that. Not sure. Anyway, somebody needs to stay behind."

Percivale raised his hand. "I vote wee-wee pants."

"Aye, I'm with Percy. *The Patriarch of Soiled Britches* should be the one to go."

"I could crush the both of you with one hand," Gaheris stated.

"And yet you can't manage to give the old pits a scrub?"

"Not to mention—"

"Okay, you two, that's enough," Arthur commanded. They weren't even at their destination and these two were already causing as much of a metaphorical stink as Gaheris was causing a literal one. "I think we're going to leave *two* people behind, instead of just one."

"Who?" asked Merlin, looking up.

"Sirs Purcivale and Tristan, that's who."

"Us?" said Purcivale.

"What did we do?" said Tristan.

Arthur gave them a hard stare. "You're both antagonistic, that's what."

"Just saying it like it is, guv," Tristan said, looking hurt.

"Ain't our fault that Gaheris makes a rotting carcass smell perfumey."

"That's it—"

"Hold yourself in check, Sir Gaheris," said Arthur, putting his arm out. "Tristan and Purcivale, you'll be leaving us now."

"But—"

"If you're not off this platform and out of Merlin's house within thirty seconds, I'll release Sir Gaheris upon the both of you."

Tristan gawked. "Okay, okay!"

"We're going already," agreed Purcivale.

Merlin shook his head while he resumed tapping on the thing on his desk.

"Honestly, the best choice you've made in a while, Arthur. Those two are a pain in the rump."

"Yes, but they can be rather resourceful at times."

"Right, well, looks like they've done us a favor actually."

"How so?"

"I had the wrong data entered in here," Merlin answered. "Had we not had the extra bodies along, magic only knows where we would have ended up."

"That's a scary thought," said Galahad.

"Agreed," Guinevere said.

"Nothing to worry about." Merlin scratched his head. He then obviously realized that he'd not had his hat on. He reached back and grabbed it. "I'd forget my leg if it wasn't attached to me."

"What about your robe?"

"Ah, good point, Galahad. Shouldn't run off to a quest without looking wizardly, eh?"

"Is this going to be much longer?" asked Bors. "I'm not all that fond of tight spaces."

"Just a couple more minutes," Merlin said while chewing his fingernails. "Just a couple more minutes."

# SEEKING ARTHUR

SCOTTISH ARTHUR STRODE into the village surrounding the castle as if he owned the place. It was the kingly way to act, after all.

He found it interesting that none of the guards questioned him or anything. Maybe they knew he was a king and thought better of it. His men were trained to be extra wary of kings, but it could be that the English Arthur was more trusting.

Just as he rounded the corner that brought him past a merchant's cart, he looked up and saw Sirs Purcivale and Tristan. He remembered them specifically from their trip down to Scotland because they were both highly annoying.

"Ah, laddies," he said heartily, feigning good tidings, "great to see ya."

"I think he's just called us a couple of ladies, Tristy."

"By the sounds of it, he has," said Tristan. He gave Arty the once over and added, "Not sure if I should be offended or worried."

"No two shakes on that, Tristy," Purcivale said with a nod. "I've not got on my steel undies."

"Best to keep facin' him, Percy."

Arty wasn't sure, but had the distinct feeling that he should be offended by their discussion.

"What are ye two babblin' aboot?"

"Now he's talkin' footwear," Purcivale said.

"Sounds as much, it does."

"Bah," Arty said. "Yer a waste of me time. Where can I find Arthur?"

Purcivale pointed up the hill at the side of a mountain that seemed to be painted like a tree. In Scotland a mountain was after being a mountain and a tree was after being a damn tree. Yet again, it didn't appear that England held to the same rules.

"He's in the wizard's spot," said Purcivale, "but you don't want go in there."

"Do ye know who yer talkin' to, boy?" Arty said firmly.

"At least he got the gender right that time, eh Percy?"

"Mild relief comes along with that, I'll safely say."

Arty bristled and studied the two men harshly. "Is this any way to talk to a king?"

"As long as the king ain't ours," quipped Purcivale.

"And mostly even when he is," added Tristan.

His first thought was to smack them both on the noggin, but this wasn't his roost and he held no jurisdiction here. Still, he was planning to have a word with their king about the way they treated royalty. Based on the way they had acted when in Scotland, though, Arty had a feeling that Arthur didn't fare much better when in their presence. They had to offer up some skill to make them worthy of being in the higher levels of military. Alas, Arty's visual due diligence couldn't spot it.

"Well, I need to speak with yer king."

"Like I said, he's in there."

"Yer after tellin' me he's in that mountain? Or is it a tree?"

"It's the wizard's hut."

"Ah. Makes sense."

"Not to us," said Purcivale, "but we're not cut from the same lace as you lot."

Arty looked at him. "Lace?"

"Cloth."

"But you said lace."

"Meant cloth."

"Then why say lace?"

"He's trying not to be cliché," Tristan offered.

"But why'd ye say lace specifically?" Arty asked and then waved his hand. "Ye know what, never you mind. I'll be takin' me leave of ye."

"Pretty touchy about the lace, eh Percy?"

"Must be a kingly thing, Tristy."

Arty merely squinted at them and then walked away while shaking his head.

# TRANSPORT

ARTHUR STOOD PATIENTLY as Merlin finished up his work. He had made a number of observations about picking proper points in the space-time continuum, dealing with chronology protection conjecture issues, targeting a proper world line, and something about avoiding becoming quantum foam.

Galahad was the only one who looked to understand the entire ordeal.

"Okay," Merlin said finally, "I have set everything up. With Percy and Tristy gone, we now have room for two, including me, and that means we should be all set. Let me just hit this and we'll have ten seconds."

The wizard flipped the switch and jumped onto the platform. The lights began their dance again, as did the vibration of the floor. A flurry of noises had been added to the mix this time.

"Ah, there ye are," said a Scottish voice.

Arthur opened his eyes and found himself staring right into the face of the king of Scotland.

"Arty?"

"Aye," he said while looking around. "What the shet is this thing we're after bein' on? It's awful cramped on this bit-o-metal."

Merlin spun around in the cramped quarters and bellowed, "No, get off the platform!"

The scrawny wizard was pushing Scottish Arthur with all of his might, but the larger man didn't budge.

"Do ye know who yer talkin'—"

# THE FUTURE

THE VIBRATION STOPPED and the flash of light that had nearly blinded him subsided, but it still took a few moments for Arthur to gain his bearings. He reached out for Guinevere. She nodded. At least she was okay.

They were standing in a very strange room. It had smatterings of similarity to what he'd seen in Merlin's house before the platform sent them to this new place, but there were also many differences.

The oil lamps were now all up in the ceiling and the people of this time had somehow managed to stop the flickering. His first thought was that having them up there was a decent enough idea. It gave the room a consistent lighting as opposed to little pockets of light. But how did they go about firing them up on a daily basis? He assumed there was some sort of access that he couldn't see.

He also liked the way the walls were not of brick. Or maybe it was some new type of brick that was flat? How many times had he walked too close to the wall in the middle of the night and scraped his elbow? This was a grand solution to that problem. Plus, these walls had a touch of color. He'd seen painted brick many times, but the way this was done was just as smooth as the surface looked.

The thing that confused him was the tables. "Desks," Merlin had called them. Well, Arthur knew what a desk was, but the ones he'd seen were simple. Four legs, a top, a well for your quill, and a place for the paper you were writing on. He'd seen ones with drawers, too, of course, but these desks had "trays" for something called a "keyboard;" they had "paper clip" containers; they had "monitors" and "speakers;" and one of them even had the ability to grow taller, which Arthur still thought could have just been Merlin using magic to further strike awe into the questing party. Of all these desk items, Arthur thought the chairs most practical. They had wheels and cushions that could change height based on the size of the user. Fantastical!

The only one who hadn't seemed fazed by all of these miracles was Galahad. That made sense being that the man was Merlin's apprentice, something that Arthur was still coming to terms with.

It was a lot to take in, but primary on Arthur's mind was the look that he was being given by Sirs Lance-A-Lot, Bors de Ganis, Kay, Galahad, and Gaheris. Something was clearly awry. He, Guinevere, and the king of Scotland were the only three still on the platform. Everyone else, except for Merlin, who was standing between both sides, had jumped away from the transporter when they'd arrived.

"Why are you all staring at me like that?"

"What the shet just happened?" Arty said while rubbing his eyes.

Galahad pointed at Arthur. "You've got the frilly on your willy."

"What's that?"

"Damn," bemoaned Merlin. "Your ring is gone, or at least its power is."

"What?" Arthur said, reaching up under his gown to check. "Nope, it's still there."

Scottish Arthur looked to be holding back a sneeze. "I feel like someone should be explainin' somethin' to me at the moment."

"Why are you wearing lady's gear?" Gaheris asked with a squint.

"Well, uh—Merlin?"

"Uh, right," Merlin said quickly. "It must be something to do with the time travel. The magic somehow swapped Arthur's normal clothes with Gwen's. Yes, that's it."

"Could it be that yer not after bein' able to hear me?" Arty said, waving his hands around.

"Nobody else's clothes got swapped," noted Galahad. "Why just those two?"

"Maybe because he's closest to her?" Merlin suggested.

"Technically," Lance-A-Lot said, "I was closest to her during the last few moments."

"Indeed," Guinevere purred.

Arthur jolted at that. "What?"

"No, I mean closest as in married to her," explained Merlin.

"Ah, right."

"Helloooo," Arty's voice was getting a bit higher. "Anyone?"

"And what about him?" Galahad said, pointing at Scottish Arthur. "He looks to be wearing a similar getup."

"Maybe it's because they're both kings?" Merlin didn't sound too convincing.

"So ye *can* see me, then." Arty let out a relieved breath. "That's good. Wait... Ye can see me wearin', uh—"

"That explains the clothes," said Bors, "but what about the makeup?"

"Precisely what I was thinking, Borsy," said Kay. "Looks like it's been put on meticulously, too."

"Magic?" Merlin attempted, sounding even less convincing than before.

Guinevere turned to Arthur and gave him a look that he was rather familiar with. It was the look that she gave him whenever she wanted him to do something he didn't feel comfortable doing. Usually this look was accompanied with leather tie-downs and a safe-word, but she wouldn't be expecting something like that now. He hoped.

"Maybe it's time to be honest, dear."

"About what?"

"You know about what," she answered gently.

"No, I don't."

"Yes, you do."

"I really don't," Arthur said, his eyes imploring her to keep her lips sealed.

Arthur couldn't believe his dearest was seriously

considering opening the purse—so to speak—on his situation. If word of this spread through Camelot, he'd be laughed out of power, just like in his nightmares. And wasn't it Guinevere who insisted on keeping all of this private in the first place? She'd been right, of course. Nearly always was. So what in the Seven Hundred and Nineteen Hells was she doing?

"Are we still after bein' in the tree?" whispered Arty.

"Arthur," Guinevere said with her hand on one hip, "either you tell them or I shall."

"Have you lost your senses? This is not—"

"Fine," she said, cutting him off as she turned to the rest of the troop. "Arthur enjoys wearing women's clothes."

"What?" said Galahad.

"Eh?" said Gaheris.

"Pardon?" said Bors.

"Honestly?" said Kay.

Arty coughed and looked around sheepishly. "He does?"

"Now, listen to me," Merlin began, "this is just a magical—"

"No, Merlin," Arthur interrupted. He felt defeated and more than a bit embarrassed, but there was no hiding things now. His beloved had just spoken. They wouldn't believe the wizard over her. "She's right. It's out of the bag anyway."

"I think it's considered *out of the closet* in today's world, Arthur," Merlin muttered.

"Either way," Arthur said as firmly as he could, "it's

true. Yes, I like to wear women's clothes."

A bunch of hands went up.

"And before you ask, no, I'm not interested in sexing with other men."

All their hands went back down.

"Arthur," said Merlin, "in this day and age the term for it is 'gay.'"

"As in happy and skipping around for no apparent reason?" asked Bors.

"No, as in…" Merlin appeared to think about this for a minute. "Well, I suppose they do skip around a fair bit, sure, but I mean it as men sexing with men and women sexing with women."

"That second one is what I call wondrous," Gaheris said dreamily. "Watching that would make me feel gay."

Merlin cocked his head to the side. "You need to think about the first part of how I described that word, Gaheris."

"While I normally go where I go," Gaheris said while scrunching his face, "I don't go there."

"Why have we never seen this before?" Galahad said.

Arthur shrugged. "Because I've hidden it from you, obviously."

"How?" asked Lance-A-Lot.

Arthur wanted to sit down at this point, but his robe wasn't one that left much to the imagination.

"Up until our last quest, I did it very carefully. Since then, when Arty here gave me the ring I was seeking, the magic of said ring made it so everyone saw me the way they expected to see me."

"That explains the donkey ears," noted Bors.

"And the hooves," agreed Kay.

Arthur grimaced. "What's that?"

"So *that's* why ye wanted the ring," said Scottish Arthur, pointing accusingly.

"They can see you, too, Arty," Arthur replied while shaking his head.

"Yer point?"

"They know you like wearing women's clothes, also."

"Nay, I don't." Arty ruffled and made a fist. "Them's words that causes wars, they is."

"Come now, Arty," Arthur said, but Arty didn't budge. Arthur rolled his eyes and motioned to the knights. "It's well known at this point. No sense in hiding it."

"I've no idea what yer talkin' 'bout," Arty replied while crossing his arms.

"We're out of the… What was it again, Merlin?"

"Closet."

"Ah, yes. Thank you, Merlin. We're out of the closet now, Arty."

"What closet?" Arty whined. "I thought we were in a damn tree. Well, a mountain painted like one anyhoo." He looked around for a second. "I'm wantin' to go home now."

"Just own up and be done with it," suggested Arthur. "Honestly, I feel better for doing it."

"I've nay clue what yer yammerin' on aboot, King of England."

"I'm not speaking to a boot, Arty." Arthur looked Arty up and down. "We can all see you're wearing that leopard skin one piece that Guinevere and I gave to you."

"And rosy red cheeks," said Bors.

"And blue eye makeup," noted Kay.

"And black eyeliner," said Galahad.

"And crimson lipstick," Guinevere added.

"What?" Arty said with a wince. "How'd all that be after gettin' there?"

"Seriously, Arty. It's out of the bag."

"It's a mixup! Something happened when we... Actually, what exactly was after happenin'?"

Merlin had taken off his hat and was twirling it around in his hands. "We transported into the future."

"Ah, right," Arty said with a nod. He then peered over at Guinevere and said, "Do all English drink this heavily before noooon?"

"We actually are in the future, Arty," she replied.

"Uh huh."

"She's being truthful."

"Yer in league with them, Lady Guinevere? And why are ye wearing pantaloons?"

"She's one of us, Arty," Arthur answered.

Guinevere's eyebrows went up. "I am not."

"What?" Arthur said as if slapped. "Wait a second here—you're saying that Arty and I can be… Uh…"

"Outed," Merlin offered.

"Outed, but you're going to try and play the innocent card? I don't think so."

"Fine, go ahead," she said angrily.

"What are ye talkin' about?" asked Arty.

"She likes wearing men's clothing."

Arty groaned as his eyes grew as large as Gwen's

thingums. "Say it ain't so."

"Are you honestly judging me, King of Scotland?"

"Uh, well…" He dropped his head. "Nay, I suppose I'm not."

Merlin stopped twirling his hat and slapped it firmly back on his head. He then spun and slowly cast his gaze upon everyone in the room.

"Okay, enough of this," he said. "The point is that these three have a particular need and that's that."

Galahad nodded for a moment as he thoughtfully studied the three who were still on the platform.

"Could be worse," he said with a nod. "Could have claimed to be liberals."

"What's wrong with being a liberal?" Bors asked.

"Yes," agreed Kay, "I'd fancy to know as well."

"Heh," Galahad replied derisively. "Even with a time machine, we haven't enough hours to list all of the things."

"The real tragedy," Bors retorted venomously, "would be if they'd claimed to have been conservatives!"

"I'm a conservative," Gaheris stated.

"And with that admission," said Kay, "we rest our case."

Arthur stepped down from the platform and eyed them all. He could just order them to accept the situation as it was and swear them to silence, but that wasn't his style. He was one who allowed his soldiers the freedom to make up their own minds, assuming their ultimate resolution landed on the same side as his anyway.

"So you're all okay with this?" he asked. "I mean,

again, it's not like any of us are gay—not that there's anything wrong with that," he was quick to amend.

"There is back in our time," Merlin said.

"Right. Well, I need to know your thoughts on this because if it impacts my ability to reign in Camelot then I shall have to take drastic measures."

Everyone spent a few minutes staring at their own boots as Arthur thought back to something his uncle had told him when he was young. "Boy," the old man had said, "there will be times in your life when people will doubt you. During those times is when you'll know who your true followers are. For example," he'd added while pointing to each of the men in the room with him, "these are the most loyal bunch you will ever find." His uncle had been killed in his sleep by those trusted men that very night.

"Uh, well, Kay and I are in the theater, sire," said Bors, breaking the ice. "We see this sort of thing all the time."

"Usually there's a play in process," said Kay, "and the fellow is wearing stockings to play the part of a queen or princess, but to each his own."

"Good. And you, Galahad?"

"Honestly, I don't give a damn what you wear, sire."

"Lance?"

"Wouldn't be my first choice, my King... Erm, Queen?"

"King will do, thank you."

"Sorry, sire," Lance-A-Lot said, bowing slightly. "We all have our issues. Mine is my endowment and yours is, well, that."

"Right." Arthur sighed. "And what of you, Gaheris? Are you okay with my dressing in such a fashion?"

"No."

"Expected," said Arthur. "But you'll be quiet and you'll keep your place. It's beyond your comprehension to do otherwise."

"What?" said Gaheris with a frown.

"See?" Arthur turned to Guinevere. "My petunia, would you have any additional trousers for me, per chance?"

"And me, if ye would," added Arty.

"I don't, but I'm sure that a couple of your knights wouldn't mind lending you their long coats."

Galahad and Lance-A-Lot both handed theirs over. Arthur snagged Lance-A-Lot's, knowing that it was better taken care of. It was also longer, as was most everything with the man.

"What are we supposed to do now, Merlin?"

"Find Allison."

"Allison?" asked Arty.

"Long story," said Arthur. "I'll fill you in later."

Bors tilted his head. "I thought you said you weren't gay?"

"He means he'll tell him the story of Allison and why we're here," Merlin corrected, "you mound of dirt."

"Ah, my apologies."

"Pardon me," Lance-A-Lot said, searching his person. "I just noticed that my sword is missing."

"About time."

"I believe he means his actual sword, Arthur,"

Merlin said. "It looks like everyone is without weapons."

Arthur held out his sword. "I have Excalibur."

"Which points to it being saved due to it's magicalness."

"Then what happened to the rings? They were magical."

"Just because it's magic doesn't mean the magic lasts forever," Merlin answered. "On something like that ring, it's obviously already died out. The sword was infused with something more powerful, and let's not forget that it's further sustained by its owner."

"Me."

"Unless someone else owns it, yes."

"Right."

"My guess," Merlin continued, "is that all weapons are stripped during transport."

"Why do we still have our armor?" Galahad asked.

Merlin checked over the knights. "Because armor isn't a weapon, dude."

"It is the way I use it," corrected Gaheris.

"There's another problem," said Bors, holding up his personal carrying bag. "Our change purses are empty. Last I checked, coins aren't weapons."

"Depends on your perspective," said Galahad.

"Which means we're broke," said Merlin, his right hand pushing the palm of his left.

Guinevere put her arm on Merlin's shoulder. "Maybe we should go back?"

"Aye," declared Arty, "I'm with her."

"Thought of that, too, Gwen," said Merlin. "Problem is that I've not a clue how to use the machine from this side of the time gate."

Gaheris pointed at one of the boxes. "Maybe just punch that square eye-looking thing?"

"Much like you, Gaheris, that square eye-looking thing is not sentient. It's what's known as a monitor."

"Hmmm."

"We can't get back and we have no money," Arthur said, coming to the defense of his less-than-intelligent knight. "It could well be that we are in over our heads."

"Ya think?" Merlin said sarcastically.

"But *you* brought us to this place, Merlin," Arthur replied icily, "and so I shall leave it in *your* capable hands to decide where we go from here."

Merlin swallowed hard. "Right."

# ESCORTED OUT

AS SOON AS Gwen had wiped all of the makeup from Arthur and Arty, they moved out.

Arthur's feet felt cushioned, like there was a little bounce with each step. It wasn't overly bouncy or anything, but it also wasn't the hard floor he was used to back in his time. This floor had a nice dark gray color, too. He liked the slate look and the wooden-plank look that buildings in his day offered, of course, but he could imagine all sorts of options with the spongy material he was currently floating upon.

Merlin turned the handle on a door and it opened slowly without the obligatory creaking that doors in Camelot made. The little wizard peered from side-to-side and then waved everyone along. The troop followed out behind, mimicking his creeping.

They turned the corner and walked directly into the path of a man who was wearing a blue uniform. He was roughly Arthur's height, though he may have held the edge in that department due to the interestingly brimmed hat that he was wearing. His face was cleanly shaved, which accentuated his pudgy cheeks. From the roundness of the fellow's belly, Arthur would have pinned him to be a merchant, but he couldn't spot any wares.

"Excuse me," said the man as he studied the group, "do you all work here?"

Merlin glanced around at the rest of them, obviously hoping someone else would answer. Arthur gave him a look to remind the little man that this was *his* quest.

"No," Merlin answered finally. "We're just here to meet someone."

"Dressed like that?"

"What's wrong with how we're dressed?" Arthur said, checking his person to make sure that his robe wasn't still showing through.

"Nothing," the guard replied, "assuming you're from the dinner theater down the street; otherwise, you look a bit crazy is all."

"Says the fellow with the blue pants and star-shaped badge," noted Bors.

"I like the black truncheon, personally," confessed Kay. "Gives a flair to the rest of the getup." Kay appraised the man for a moment more. "Are you an actor, too?"

"What are they talking about?" the guard asked Merlin.

"We usually don't know," replied the wizard. "We're seeking Allison Smith."

"Dr. Smith, eh?"

Merlin brightened at this. "You know of her?"

"Everyone in this building knows her, mister. She's

the brains of this place, if you know what I mean."

Gaheris ducked and held his hand up. He began looking frantically around. Arthur glanced up to see what Gaheris was shying away from, but everything appeared normal to him. Well, relatively speaking anyway.

"Are you saying we're inside of her head?" Gaheris stammered.

"Honestly?" said Galahad, slapping the larger knight on his arm.

"It's a saying, Sir Geheris," Bors pointed out. "Not to be taken literally."

"Anyway," Merlin said, "we'd like to see Dr. Smith, please."

The guard looked around as if making sure nobody else was within earshot. "She's not here, mister. She's on sabbatical."

"So she's after bein' Jewish?" Arty asked. "Why'd that make her not be here? Last I checked it wasn't after being Saturday."

"Not Sabbath, King of... Erm, I mean, uh Arty," Galahad corrected. "He said sabbatical. It means—"

"Explain it to him later, Galahad," said Merlin before turning back to the guard. "Do you know where she's gone, by chance?"

The guard swiveled his head from side-to-side again. Obviously the man was uncomfortable talking about Allison Smith. Maybe he had a thing for Allison? It was normal for a fellow to be protective of his love. Wasn't Arthur constantly striving to keep his Guinevere safe?

"You really *do* know her, right?" the guard said.

"I've known her for more years than you can imagine, young man," Merlin replied with a smile.

"Well, okay." The man still seemed unsure, but he took a deep breath and said, "I shouldn't be telling you this, but she's down at the local hospital."

"Oh? What's she studying there?"

"Well, that's the other thing I shouldn't be telling you. You see, we're just informing the press and such that's she's on sabbatical." He looked up suddenly. "Hey, wait, you're not the press, are you?"

"I don't believe so," Merlin replied thoughtfully.

"If we are," agreed Galahad, "nobody told us."

"What's the press?" asked Gaheris.

"Was just gonna ask that," said Arty.

"All right, then. She's actually *in* the hospital."

Merlin squinted. "So you said."

"No, I mean that she's a patient."

"Makes sense to me," stated Galahad a couple of moments later. "She's had to put up with Merlin for years. I've only been an apprentice to him for around eight months and I've learned a great deal of patience."

"The boy means that's she's a *patient* in the hospital, you dope," Merlin said over his shoulder.

"Oh, yes, that makes more sense."

"Why is she in the hospital?" Merlin asked.

The guard shrugged. "That's one thing they wouldn't tell us. Asked us not to snoop around about it either."

"What's this snoopin' thing yer after talkin' aboot?" said Arty.

"I wasn't talking about any boots, sir."

"But you did anyway, right?" Merlin said, clearly ignoring Arty's question.

"Talked about boots?" asked the guard with a confused look.

"No," Merlin said. "I mean you snooped around anyway, right?"

"No, sir." The guard was shaking his head furiously. He'd also stood up straight and adjusted his belt. "I would with most people, but Dr. Smith is too much of a bigwig. I could lose my job over something like that."

Arthur was glad to hear the man speak thusly. It was rare to find people who understood their place in the scheme of things. Most thought they were of a higher station than they truly were. Merlin, for example. To find one who was comfortable with their personal situation was refreshing.

"How do we find this hospital you speak of?" Arthur said in a kingly way.

"It's two blocks down on Fifth and West, sir," replied the guard. "Can't miss it."

"Sorry, Fifth and West?"

"Yeah."

"Young man," Guinevere said sweetly, "we're somewhat new to the area. Could you maybe point us toward this place?"

This caused the guard to tilt his head suspiciously. "I thought you worked at the dinner theater."

"Well, yes," Guinevere recovered, "but we've only recently begun that job."

"Follow me, then," the man said as he turned on his heel and walked through the building.

It was all Arthur could do to try and mentally catalog the wonders he was seeing in the place. Large glass windows and doors; little camera-things like the one that Merlin had brought with him on their last adventure were up in the corners of the ceilings; and, most interestingly, big bubbles that appeared to be holding water. There were people standing around those water tanks. They pointed at Arthur and the knights as they walked past, and they were all giggling. Arthur wasn't sure what was so funny. If anything, the fact that they all had nooses hanging from their necks—the men anyway—was what they should be laughing at, even if Arthur couldn't help but admit that those decorative neck ropes were somewhat fashionable.

They walked outside a set of doors and onto a piece of hard ground that was made up of white squares. It felt more like the floors that Arthur was used to walking on inside of buildings.

When Arthur looked up, he could barely breathe due to the wonders he was seeing. Buildings that dwarfed his beloved Camelot surrounded them. They were everywhere. Were it not for his ability to see the sky, he'd have thought that they'd just moved from one building to a much larger building.

Foreign sounds filled the air as well. Hums, horns, clomping of feet, and people chattering as they walked through the area. It wasn't vastly different from Camelot's marketplace as far as the crowds went, but their choice of garb, the surrounding constructions, the lack of dirt, and the fact that there were no merchants that he could make out, made him wonder what precisely all of these people were doing. There seemed to be no purpose to their wanderings.

The smells were also unfamiliar. In Merchant Square, he could smell breads and corn and meats and cheese. And horses. Lots of horses. The smell here was more like that of a blacksmith's workshop.

"Now," the guard said while pointing, "you go up there about two blocks, turn left, and you'll see the hospital on the right."

"Thank you, fine sir," said Guinevere, clearly trying to maintain her composure. She was doing a better job of it than Arthur.

"Have a nice day, folks."

"Nice lad," Arthur said as the guard walked back into the building. "Good to see that people in the future are as kind and cordial as they are in our time."

"Out of the way, you bunch of idiots," said a gruff man who was wearing a long coat and hat. He was portly and pushy. Definitely a merchant.

"Pardon me?" said Arthur haughtily.

The guy stopped, looked Arthur over and mockingly said, "Pardon me." Then he snorted. "You actors. Always thinking you're something special. Go to your stupid dinner house and get off the sidewalk, yeah?" Nobody replied, likely being in too much of a shock to do so. "Idiots," the man said with a shake of his head as he walked away.

Arty stepped forward. "Shouldn't we be after killin' him? A fella sullies me name like that in me land and he's strung up, he is."

"This isn't your land," Merlin was quick to point out.

"Nor is it mine," Arthur agreed. "We're in the future, remember?"

"Still," said Gaheris, his voice carrying a chill, "the man should know his place. Shall I gut him, sire?"

"You shall not," Merlin answered for Arthur. "Keep your wits about you. All of you. You're here to help me in the event that help is needed. We don't know the ways of those who live in this age, but common sense will tell us that we are no longer a part of the ruling class. Therefore, we must use our brains."

Arthur blinked. "Are you implying that we don't use them in our own time?"

"I am saying precisely that," Merlin stated. "You're always jumping at each other and at every—"

The sound of a roaring beast split the air. Everyone jolted as the boxy thing zoomed past. Arthur stood his ground. Lance-A-Lot, Gaheris, Bors, and Kay all moved to protect their king. Merlin, however, leaped into the air and landed in Gaheris's arms. Galahad merely stood there shaking his head.

"What in the Seven Hundred and Nineteen Hells was that?" said Arthur, fighting to maintain his resolve.

"What the shet?" Arty swore, visibly trembling. "It's the devil's magic, it is!" Then he glanced over at Arthur. "That's a lot of hells."

"I imagine it to be one of those horseless carriages you spoke of," said Gaheris as he looked down at Merlin. "Would you let go of me now, please?"

"Right," said Merlin sheepishly as he dropped out of the knight's arms.

"Horseless what?" Arty said.

"You weren't there for the pictures," Guinevere said. "Don't worry, though, I'll explain it to you as we go on."

"Anyway," Merlin said as Guinevere relayed some of the things she'd seen on Merlin's computer, "that security fellow thought we were part of the dinner theater. Bors and Kay, you are both actors of a sort, yes?"

"Of course we are," Bors yelped. "We have written, directed, produced, and starred in countless plays."

"How could you not know this?" Kay lamented.

"I *did* know it," Merlin said with a snicker. "I just enjoy riling up egotistical pricks."

"Heh heh." Gaheris was not one who put too much effort into laughing.

"I didn't know you could laugh, Gaheris," said Merlin.

"There are a lot of things you don't know, wizard."

"Hmmm." Merlin studied the big man for a moment. "Can you act, too?"

"No."

"Well, you're about to learn how. You'll be joining Bors and Kay as they go to that dinner theater and get us some money."

"Heh heh."

"I wasn't joking."

"Oh."

Bors and Kay gave each other serious looks.

"Hold on a moment here, Merlin," Bors said. "We don't even know—"

"Right there, across this expanse," Merlin said,

pointing up the street at a castle that was nestled between two larger buildings. "That's the place. Go there and get a job."

"How do you know that's the right location?" asked Kay.

"First off, it's a castle, and not even a good one. Secondly, look at everyone milling around outside. Notice anything familiar about their choice of garb?"

"So?"

"So, Kay, unless there are a lot of time-travelers out and about today, that's the place!"

"I don't know about this," Bors said wearily. "It just doesn't feel right."

Merlin rolled his eyes and turned to Arthur. "I can only do so much here."

"Merlin is correct, my knights. You have special skills that we don't share."

"He doesn't," said Bors, nodding at Gaheris, who was busily picking his nose.

"Sir Gaheris," Arthur chastised, "what have we said about picking our noses in public?"

"Sorry."

"And to the third-knuckle even."

"Ye've got odd rules, King of England," said Arty. "Ye'll all scratch yer arses in public without a flinch, but diggin' out a fresh nugget is a nay say, eh?"

Arthur went to retaliate, but found himself caught up in trying to unravel what the king of Scotland had actually said.

"Either way, Sir Bors, you've said that you wanted to share culture with the world. Now is your chance. And we need whatever coin you may garner in the process. We haven't a clue how long we'll be stuck in this time."

"You can count on us, sire," said Kay. He put a hand on his fellow actor's shoulder. "It could be fun, Borsy. Just imagine our ability to share with these actors of the day what true knights are like?"

"Well," Bors said, relaxing a bit, "there is truth to that, I'll say."

It got quiet for a few moments. Everyone was taking in the scene of the future.

The horseless carriages kept zipping past, which made everyone in the troop shudder uncontrollably. Arthur had to admit that those would prove quite useful in traveling long distances. They were certainly moving more deftly than any steed he'd ever seen, and since they were enclosed it would protect the inhabitants from the elements.

"I've got to piddle," Gaheris announced.

"Not in those pants I gave you, you don't," Guinevere warned. "I'll tan your hide if you do."

Gaheris held up his hands. "All right, all right." Then he moved over to one of the small trees that stuck up from the walkway.

"No, no," yelled Merlin. "Keep your pants on. I'm sure there is a public restroom of some sort that you can utilize to relieve yourself. Bors and Kay will help you find something."

"Off with you three before he makes a public nuisance of himself," commanded Arthur.

"Yes, sire," Bors and Kay replied in unison as they pulled Gaheris along with them.

Arthur watched as the three knights crossed the

street. It was apparent that things were not the same here as in Camelot because the moment they stepped onto the road, horns sounded all around. There were screeches and people were hanging out of their cars yelling all manner of obscenities at Bors, Kay, and Gaheris.

Gaheris had tried to challenge one of the larger cars—something Merlin had called a truck. The huge knight stood before it, slamming its front with his fists. In response, the thing bellowed a loud honk that caused Gaheris to jump backwards.

"Hit my truck again," yelled the man inside the truck, "and I'll kick your ass."

Kicking someone in the rump seemed like an odd way to do battle, even though Merlin had mentioned it as a form of fighting back in Scotland, but the fellow seemed serious about his promise to do so.

Bors and Kay struggled to pull Gaheris from the fight with the truck, nearly getting run over multiple times in the process.

Finally they got to the other side and leaned against a wall to catch their collective breath.

Arthur decided that he would do his best to avoid crossing into the path of any cars or trucks, if at all possible.

"Well, that just leaves the six of us," said Merlin, bringing Arthur's attention back.

Arthur had to take control of this situation. While this was Merlin's quest, and while he was great at pointing out faults and issues, he wasn't the best when it came to management. Unless, of course, one considered calling people names and constantly berating them as solid managerial skills.

"I would say that you should go to that hospital with your…"—Arthur frowned at Galahad—"apprentice, so you can learn what you can of your Ms. Allison Smith."

"Just call her Allison, Arthur," Merlin said, displaying his management style.

"Gwen, Arty, Lance, and I shall seek additional means of income down that road there."

"We will?" said Arty, but must have caught the look in Arthur's eye. "Ah, yeah, okay."

# THE INTERVIEW

WILHELM MORGANSTERN PRANCED around the room in front of the three knights. Gaheris was not used to this type of behavior. He assumed it had something to do with the man being an actor, but Gaheris had no recollection of Bors or Kay acting in such a manner. Another strangeness was the frilly pink shirt that the man wore under his neatly pressed jacket. The high-leather boots would have been somewhat normal, were it not for the roses engraved on them.

Gaheris wanted to ask questions, but he held himself in check, thinking that he would one day have the opportunity to discuss such things with King Arthur.

"I think this is the first time that I've ever interviewed three people at once," Wilhelm said in a soprano pitch that was impressively operatic.

"Is that so?" asked Bors.

"And I know it's the first time interviewees were wearing their own costumes."

"These ain't costumes," Gaheris said, feeling confused.

"What Sir..." Kay started and then coughed. "Sorry. I mean what Mr. Gaheris is trying to say is that we take our craft seriously."

"Some of the most authentic pieces I've ever seen," Wilhelm said as he studied Kay's sleeve. "Well, except for the trousers on Mr. Gilfarris there," he added with a flick of his wrist.

"It's Gaheris."

"Yeah, whatever. Anyway, so you've impressed me with an authentic look." He stepped back away and rubbed his chin while pursing his lips. "Then again, who's to say that you didn't just pick these up at a Renaissance fair someplace?"

"I am," Gaheris answered.

"What I really need to know is if you can act or not."

"Absolutely," Bors said almost reverently.

"Most definitely," agreed Kay.

"No," stated Gaheris.

"Ha ha ha," Bors said, glancing sideways at Gaheris. "He's our comic relief."

"Indeed, he is," Kay said, joining the merriment. "Isn't that *right*, Mr. Gaheris?"

"No."

"Ha! He does it again."

"Idiots."

"Right," said Wilhelm. "Well, let's get on out in the sand pit and see what you boys have got."

"Sorry," Kay said as Wilhelm headed for the door, "but did you say sand pit?"

"Of course. Follow me."

Gaheris had been on many fields of battle, and he had also been a party to tournaments where spectators lined seats in wooden bleachers, but he'd never seen a place quite like this. It was indoors, which was a novel idea that would have been most welcome during tournaments that were held when it was raining. Gaheris was not fond of getting wet.

He still wasn't certain what it was they were doing here anyway. Acting was all Bors and Kay said, but Gaheris was unfamiliar with such things. Was he to protect them as they did their acting? Was he to act along with them? He hoped it wasn't the second option because he had no intention of skipping around like Wilhelm.

"Let's see what you've got," Wilhelm said after spinning around and crossing his arms in dramatic fashion. "The scene is that the Dark Knight is threatening to take over the castle."

Gaheris felt his mind race. "You mean Batman?"

"Who?" said Bors.

"What?" said Kay.

"Batman is a fellow that Galahad spoke of a couple of months ago," Gaheris explained. "He called him the Dark Knight, but as I recall he is one of the good guys."

"Right," said Wilhelm sourly. "Joking again, I see. The Dark Knight I'm speaking of is a knight who has turned to evil. It's not Batman. Technically, we call ours the Evil Knight, but I just prefer to use the term Dark Knight."

"He means it's a bad knight, Mr. Gaheris,"

explained Bors.

"I have a feeling he's right about that," Gaheris said in agreement.

"No, not that the night is… never mind."

"Anyway," interrupted Wilhelm, "any questions?"

"What is my motivation?" Bors said studiously.

Kay's hand went up a moment later. "Is there a script?"

"Where is a sword that I can use to stab this Evil Knight bastard in his nethers?" Gaheris asked, feeling that his was the only sensible question.

Wilhelm erupted in laughter, including a snort or two. "You *are* humorous, Mr. Gayharryass."

"It's Gaheris."

"Mr. Bors," Wilhelm said without acknowledging Gaheris's correction, "your motivation is to protect your king."

"Ah yes," Bors said, nodding. "Of course."

"Mr. Kay, there is no formal script. We simply have cues that we use. The rest is improvisation."

"We thrive on improvisation," said Kay with a grin.

"Swords, Mr. Gayhyena…"

"Not even close," Gaheris mumbled.

"…will be handed out before the show if we feel your particular character requires one."

"Can't kill Batman without a sword, or a gun I suppose, though I still don't fully understand what a gun is." Gaheris fished around in his mind for a moment before shrugging. "Sir Galahad has funny ideas sometimes."

"Mr. Bors," Wilhelm directed, "you stand over there. Mr. Kay, that's your position. Mr. Gaheris, you'll come walking up behind them and overhear their conversation."

"Why?"

"And action..." Wilhelm said and then halted. "Wait, what?"

"I can hear them right where I am," stated Gaheris. "Why would I walk up behind them?"

"Because that's the scene."

"Besides," continued Gaheris, "it's not honorable to eavesdrop on fellow knights as they're—"

Bors stepped over and grabbed Gaheris by the arm. "May I have a moment with Mr. Gaheris, Mr. Morganstern?"

"I think you should."

Bors pushed Gaheris into the shadows. This concerned Gaheris at first, but not as much as it would have had Wilhelm done the same.

"Gaheris," Bors said seriously, "you need to focus here. We're trying to get this job so we can bring money to King Arthur, yes?"

"Yes."

"So you have to play along. Just do what Mr. Morganstern says."

"But I don't understand it," complained Gaheris.

"That will make you appear more authentic."

"Right."

They returned to Wilhelm and Kay. Gaheris didn't feel much better, but he was a knight and he got that knights didn't always comprehend the full desires of their king. This was especially true after seeing King Arthur wearing ladies clothing.

"Okay, Mr. Morganstern," announced Bors, "I

believe we are prepared."

At that moment a man walked out of a side door and across the sand. He took a straight route that didn't cross paths with the knights, but Gaheris was able to make out his pitch-black outfit with its reflective metal armor.

"Who is that?" he grumbled.

"He's the Dark Knight," Wilhelm said. Then, he added, "No, not Batman. Sorry, I meant the Evil Knight."

This was too much for Gaheris. "Why don't we just kill him now and be done with it?"

"Ha ha," Kay said with a laugh that appeared genuine. "Again with the jokes."

Bors leaned over and hissed, "Will you keep your mouth shut, please!"

"And I thought people in our time were stupid," Gaheris replied with a growl as the Evil Knight exited the area.

# SEEKING ALLISON

MERLIN AND GALAHAD walked into the large sterile building known as a hospital. They had both seen pictures of places like this, but it was always different seeing something in person.

There was an echo to the main room, which likely came from general murmur of the people walking around. Merlin somewhat understood the mechanics of sound, and seeing that there were hard, glossy floors and a wide open space, his brain churned up thoughts of something called reverberation. Galahad would likely know—the man *was* a quick study, after all—but Merlin wasn't in the mood for a lengthy discourse on the subject.

They walked up to a grand desk where a young lady sat. Her hair was up in a bun and she wore thick-framed, red spectacles. From the look on her face, Merlin assumed she was confused by their outfits.

"Nice outfits," she said in a deadpan voice.

"Thank you," Merlin replied, unsure if she was being serious or sarcastic. Considering the young man next to her was snickering, Merlin assumed the latter. He chose to ignore it. "I am seeking Dr. Smith."

"There are eleven Dr. Smiths on site. You'll need to be more specific."

"Ah, yes. My apologies. Dr. *Allison* Smith."

The clerk typed away as an elderly man stepped up next to them. He gave both Galahad and Merlin the once-over, shook his head, and began talking with the young man across the counter.

"Nobody here by that name, mister," said the clerk who was helping them. "We have a Dr. Albert Smith. Maybe that's who you mean?"

"Not unless she's made a number of changes to her anatomy, no," Merlin said, scratching his left eyebrow.

"Happens a lot these days."

"I imagine it does."

"Well, again, there are no doctors on duty by the name of Allison Smith."

"She's a patient," Galahad pointed out.

"Ah, yes. True. Good man, Galahad."

"Galahad?" the clerk said. "You guys are really taking this acting stuff seriously, aren't you?"

"Indeed." Merlin shrugged at Galahad. "So, yes, Allison Smith, who happens to be a doctor, though not of the healing profession, is a patient."

"Right. Well, we have an Allison Smith on the third floor. Room 327."

"Excellent!" Merlin rubbed his hands together, feeling pleased that he would be seeing Allison soon. He had been rather worried about her over these last months after all. But there was a problem. He had no clue how he was to get to this Room 327 the young lady had mentioned. "Um—"

The clerk pointed across the room. "Take the elevator."

"Oh, right, of course," said Merlin with a smile, and then added, "Sorry, the what?"

"Come with me, Merlin," said Galahad with a huff.

"Merlin?" said the clerk, laughing. "You look nothing like what I'd imagine Merlin to look like."

Merlin frowned. "I beg your pardon?"

"No offense. You're just rather short is all, and you don't seem very wizardly."

"I'll have you know that—"

"We should really be going," Galahad said, dragging Merlin along.

"Yes, well, yes." They took a few steps toward the elevator when Merlin yanked his arm away from Galahad. He turned back to the clerk. "Excuse me, miss, but what is your name?"

"Katy," she replied.

"Well, you look nothing like a Katy to me," Merlin said, his nose turned up.

"Good one, Merlin," Galahad said. "Can we go now?"

"The nerve of some people. Telling me that I look nothing like, well, me. Who does that?"

"Apparently a clerk named Katy. Let's turn our attention back to the task at hand." Galahad motioned to the elevator. "We have to get into that silver-looking box."

"The elevator, yes."

"You're familiar with how to use it?" Galahad

asked. "I've seen pictures, but I've never looked at any videos on MeTube."

"YouTube."

"Right, that one."

"And, no, I don't," Merlin said at length. "Honestly wouldn't have even recognized it as an elevator if 'Katy' back there hadn't called it one."

"Why did you use air quotes?"

"Never mind that. Just follow everyone else into that box and let's see what happens."

An elderly lady with a pleasant hat was standing between Merlin and Galahad. She was just a wisp of a woman, barely reaching Galahad's shoulder. Of course, this made her only slightly shorter than Merlin.

"Could you press two please?" she asked.

"Uh—"

"Right there in front of you, young man."

"I..." Galahad looked straight ahead and then down. There sat a series of buttons that all had numbers etched on them. "Oh, right. There you go. Hey, it lit up like those lights back home."

"Yes, it does that," the old woman said with a giggle. "Are you going to floor two as well?"

"No, ma'am. We are going to three."

"Then you had better press that number, too."

"Ah, yes, right. Thank you."

Merlin was still stewing as the box jolted and began lifting. It was somewhat frightening, but he was more set in a fit of irritation and so his subconscious mind decided not to bother him with the fear.

"Telling me that I don't look like Merlin," he

grumbled. "Hah!"

The woman looked up at him. "*You're* supposed to be Merlin?"

"I *am* Merlin."

"Shouldn't you be a little taller, then?" she said and then raised her eyebrows at Galahad. "I think you two should be looking for floor seven."

"Oh? The lady at the front said Ms. Smith was on floor three."

The elevator stopped and dinged. Then the doors split open and the old lady scurried out. She stopped and looked back at the two men, giggled again, shook her head, and said, "Merlin? Please."

The doors closed.

"This is ridiculous. What does a man need to do to prove he's Merlin?"

"Based on the observations, my guess would be to grow a little taller."

Level three looked just like level two had, from inside the elevator anyway.

The two men took a gingerly step out and looked around. Everything was white and looked sterile. There was no color pop from paint or anything of the sort. The only pieces that had any color to them were the machines that were sitting in various locations throughout the area. What the machines were for, Merlin couldn't say. Obviously they had something to do with doctorly pursuits, unless they were robots of some sort. Allison had mentioned a fair deal about robots, though these seemed a little too stationary to fit her description of them.

"May I help you?" asked a woman who was dressed

in white.

"My name is Merlin and this is Galahad—"

"Merlin? You?"

Merlin squinted, but bit his tongue. "We're seeking Allison Smith in room 327, if you please."

"Right behind you there," she said. A moment later she snickered and added, "Merlin."

"This is very unnerving," said Merlin as they walked to room 327.

"I'd say it's quite telling of how history has built you up into something you're obviously not."

"Wait out here," Merlin demanded. His apprentice was clearly enjoying seeing his master's humbling moments far too much. "Sit in one of those chairs and read a magazine. You *are* fond of those, after all."

"I'd rather just come along with you," Galahad replied.

"And I'd rather you didn't. Sit, read, and stay. I'll be back."

"Whatever you say, 'Merlin.'"

"Did you just air-quote me?"

"Everyone else does."

# YOUR PANTS, PLEASE

"I'D RATHER NOT have to order you to do it, Mitch," Arthur said as they stood at the corner of an intersection.

Cars were zooming this way and that along the main road. How anyone could get used to such mayhem was beyond Arthur. He had enough difficulty managing two horse-drawn carriages in the middle of town. Of course those were rather a bit larger and the roads in Camelot were also more narrow. Still, the fumes that these car-things made were offensive to the nose. Then again, so were the fumes the horses were known to make.

"Who's Mitch?" asked Arty.

"Sir Lance-A-Lot's actual name is Mitch," Guinevere answered.

"No foolin'?"

"He prefers to be called Sir Lance-A-Lot when we're around the men, though," said Arthur.

"Ah, you mean the nets."

"I doubt he'd care what I called him around nets."

"Bah."

"Anyway, Mitch," Arthur continued, pointing at Scottish Arthur's legs, "his gown is obviously showing and so he'll need to wear your pants."

"But, sire, I only have tights on under these."

"Yer after wearin' tights?"

"You wear a gown, sire," Lance-A-Lot replied tightly.

"Fair enough. I just didn't know you were after being of the same ilk, is all."

"He's not," Arthur explained. "All of the knights wear tights under their suits of armor."

Arty furrowed his brow at that. "Why?"

"Um…" Arthur began, but hesitated just enough that it was clear he'd fallen under the moniker of "suspicious."

"Oh, no way," Lance-A-Lot said with a gasp. "You mean that you ordered tights as part of the standard garb because of your interest in wearing, well, tights?"

Arthur cringed. He knew he shouldn't have done it back in the day, and the knights had all staunchly protested, except for Bors and Kay, of course. But everyone else had complained for quite some time. It had required a decree before they finally gave in.

"Seemed harmless enough at the time," Arthur answered finally, "and you have to admit that it does help protect against chafing."

"As you say, sire."

"Oh, come on, Mitch, you of all people have to appreciate that tights are useful in holding certain parts of your person in check."

Lance-A-Lot looked like he wanted to reply tersely,

but he controlled himself.

"I would be derelict in my honesty were I to state that as a falsehood, but I'm still not pleased that it was imposed via trickery."

"Well," Guinevere noted, "the side benefit is that it makes your particular situation even more appealing."

"Is that so?"

"I'm standing right here, turtle dove," Arthur said, waving his hand in front of his lady's eyes.

"Sorry, dear."

"Yer all talkin' about his girth pickle, eh?" asked Arty.

"Sorry?" said Arthur.

"What's that?" said Guinevere.

Lance-A-Lot frowned. "My what?"

Arty rubbed his eyes and shook his head.

"His McDingy," he said, as if trying to clarify the situation.

"Hmmm?" said Arthur.

"The man's chubby buddy."

"Not following you," said Guinevere.

"His dragon flask."

"What is it you're speaking of, King of Scotland?" Lance-A-Lot demanded.

Arty took a deep breath. "His jimmy, love banana, pink oboe, whiz whistle, ham javelin, slippery love dolphin, chicksickle, danglin' fury." They all just stared at him. "His blasted Cock-A-Saurus Rex!"

"Do you mean his lady dagger?" said Guinevere hesitantly.

"Never heard it called that before," Arty admitted.

"Goodness, my sweet," Arthur said, trying to hide

his distaste. "Such language is not becoming of you."

"It's the trousers, Arthur. They make me speak out of the male side of my mind."

"Ah, yes. Anyway, where were we?"

"Ye were after trying to get Captain Stiffy here to give me his pants," Arty said.

"That's right." Arthur turned back to Lance-A-Lot. "Mitch?"

"As you wish, sire."

Lance-A-Lot turned away and removed his britches. Underneath them were a long set of white tights. They were opaque, but they did little to hide outlines. From this angle, things weren't that bad, but Arthur was not looking forward to his knight turning back to face them.

And when he finally did, Arthur couldn't help but do a double-take.

"Great Scott, man," Arty yelped. "How do ye not suffer from chronic back pain?"

"He has a big booty to help compensate," Guinevere said dreamily.

Arthur glanced at her. "Booty?"

"The trousers again, dear."

"Hmmm."

Arty studied Lance-A-Lot's member from various angles, looking similar to Merlin when the wizard was studying something out of the ordinary. To be fair, this was *definitely* out of the ordinary.

"Are you saying that's what was in me Agnes?"

"My booty?"

"No, yer yard-o-beef."

"Sorry, sire," Lance-A-Lot replied calmly, "but a

gentleman doesn't kiss and tell."

"Kissin' I can come to terms with, but that thing?" Arty pointed and then sighed. "Nay." He then turned to look at Arthur. "Explains why I was hearing an echo when I was... Uh, never mind."

"I'm familiar with said echo, Arty."

"Can we change the subject, please?" Lance-A-Lot begged.

"I agree with Lance-A-Lot," Guinevere said, coming to the knight's defense. "You've heard that it's not the size that matters, but rather how you use it, I assume?"

"Yes."

"Aye."

"There you go, then," Guinevere said with a firm nod.

"So yer saying that's after bein' true, then?" Arty asked hopefully.

"Not in the least, no," Guinevere replied. "Honestly, I was hoping there wouldn't be a follow-up question."

"Oh."

Arthur sighed and looked away. The sun was out and there was a shadow of Lance-A-Lot's thing casting its way over Arthur's midsection. Fitting.

"Anyway, I'm sure that will garner some glances from people, so do your best to hide it wherever you can."

"I have an idea or two," Guinevere said.

"Careful, *my* queen!"

# CONSPIRACY

GAHERIS HAD BEEN left alone for a while as Bors and Kay spent their time building friendships with the other actors. They were all sharing techniques and the like. These were items that Gaheris did not understand.

What he *did* understand was that there was an evil knight amongst them.

Gaheris had met a few of these nefarious sorts in his lifetime. They were men without honor; they attacked when you weren't looking; they struck fear into the timid and the weak; they drafted massive diabolical plans that were almost always too difficult to follow; they made sure to fully reveal the details of their plan before sending the targeted king to his demise; and they always wore black.

But this particular man was breaking one of the cardinal rules. He was allowing himself to be seen.

Bors and Kay claimed that the man was just another actor, but Gaheris didn't buy it. From his perspective, this was the first bad egg of a knight he'd met who actually had a chance at succeeding.

This fellow was using trickery so that everyone would accept him as one of their own, but at the right moment, the man would strike, and the attack would be so unexpected that he would likely taste victory.

Gaheris shook his head at the idiocy of it all as he set about checking each of the swords that were set out for the knights in this "play."

Not a single one of them was sharp.

"So that's how it'll be, eh?" he said gruffly.

# THE NEWS

MERLIN WALKED INTO the room and found Allison sitting up in bed. The window blinds were open and the sunlight was streaming in, making the room feel warm.

"Merlin?" Allison said. "Is that you or am I hallucinating?"

"Depends on who you ask," he answered with a snort, thinking of how everyone in this time had been treating him.

"What?"

"Nothing. Are you ill?"

"First things first," said Allison. "How did you get here?"

"The time machine, obviously."

"Obviously," she said quickly. "Let me ask a different question: *Why* are you here?"

"Because I've spent the last number of years talking to you on a weekly basis and then suddenly there was radio silence for eight months."

"Ah, yes, sorry about that."

"I assumed you were in grave danger, or worse... dead." He sat down on the edge of the bed, finding it bouncy. "I had to come and find out."

"You do realize that this could seriously jeopardize all of history?"

"So you say, though I don't see how." Merlin had put a lot of thought to this, actually. He could see that someone going backwards in time could mess things up, but how could going forward impact anything? He shrugged. "Fact is that I still haven't come to terms with all of the particulars."

"You'll just have to be careful to avoid interaction wherever possible."

"Right," Merlin said, avoiding eye contact.

"At least you're in here and not out on the town somewhere. That would be very bad."

"Hmmm."

"What is it?" Allison asked.

"What's what?"

"Merlin, tell me."

"I'd rather not."

"Merlin?" Her tone was a little more forceful this time.

"Oh, fine. I brought Arthur and Gwen along, too."

Allison breathed out heavily. "Ill advised, but not horrible."

"And Bors, Kay, and Gaheris," Merlin added quickly.

"What?"

"Just in case."

"Is that all?"

"Not exactly," admitted Merlin. "Galahad is sitting

outside of the door there reading a magazine."

"Oh, Merlin. This is... Wait, he's the only one sitting outside this room?" It was almost a shriek, and Merlin had never heard her sound so irritable before. "Where are the rest of them?"

"Bors, Kay, and Gaheris are trying to find work at the Medieval dinner theater, and Arthur, Gwen, Arty, and Mitch are looking elsewhere for money-making ventures."

"This is bad. Very bad." She had put her hands over her face now. Slowly she opened them. "Who are Arty and Mitch?"

"Arty is the king of Scotland."

"What?" she barked.

He cringed. "And you know Mitch as Sir Lance-A-Lot."

"You... I can't believe... I mean... What were you thinking?"

Merlin was not one who turned away from a deserved spanking, and, no, he wasn't *that* type of fellow, but he wouldn't take the full brunt of the blame for something he wasn't fully responsible for. Allison was just as much at fault for all of this as he was. She was the one who disappeared. A simple call could have solved everything, right?

"I was thinking about how *you* didn't reply to me for eight months," he said defensively. "Don't put all of this on me, little lady."

"Okay, okay," she said, putting her arms up in surrender. "Well, hopefully it won't hurt anything. I mean, the reality is that you've not gone *back* in time, you've come forward."

"Exactly," Merlin affirmed, feeling justified in his thoughts on the subject of impacting the timeline.

"The worry is that you'll all now have visions of the future in your heads when you inevitably *do* go back to your own era. That's where my concern is."

It was an angle that Merlin hadn't considered. In essence, all of the things that everyone saw here could be relayed to those living in the past. How often had even *he* shared things that he shouldn't have? Granted, everyone considered it "magic," but now that a contingency of people knew the truth behind things, the Camelot of past days may indeed be in jeopardy. Worse, now that Arthur knew that magic was a crock of hooey, Merlin could be looking at a long road ahead.

"I'll figure something out on that," he said. "For now, why are you in here?"

"Because, my friend," Allison said with a grin as she pulled away a large pillow she'd been hugging, "I'm about to have a baby."

# ADULT FUN

THE FOUR OF them walked into a place that was called *The Adult Wonderland.*

From the outside it looked as though there would be some racy fashions that both Arthur and Arty would find most appealing. On the inside, though, it was far more than that. How a place like this was allowed to exist was unfathomable to Arthur. There were hidden shops in the deep recesses of the town just outside of Camelot that carried a few juicy items, but this was well beyond what even the most perverse of minds in his era could imagine.

"This place is horrendous," he whispered, almost afraid.

"I find it rather appealing, personally," Guinevere said. Her smile was glowing.

"You would," Arthur said in an accusatory tone.

"Pardon me?"

"Sorry," he said quickly. "It's the gown."

"Ah, yes."

"I've never seen such a den of debauchery," Arty

said, not bothering to keep his voice to a respectful hush.

Lance-A-Lot smiled almost as big as Guinevere did. "Nor have I," he said.

Guinevere pointed to a row across the room. It contained a number of phallic items that were of all shapes and sizes. Arthur groaned.

"Are those what I think they are?" said Guinevere.

"If you mean are those things that look like they're after being fake uterus unicorns," Arty answered, "I think it is."

Arthur eyes widened farther with each step they took toward the man-part-shaped objects.

"They're enormous," he said. "No man could possibly measure up to those things."

"Well—" began Lance-A-Lot.

"Quiet, you."

When Arthur turned back he gaped in horror at the vision of his precious petunia holding one of the beasts as if it were her best friend. Worse yet, she was holding it rather low on her person as if seeing how she might look if she'd been built in such a way. Arthur gave her a sour look, so she quickly moved it back up near eye level.

"It feels so lifelike, Arthur," she said, handing it over to him.

Without thinking, he reached out and touched it. "My, it truly does."

"Bah!" Arty said. "Why are ye after touchin' the thing?"

"What?" Arthur retaliated. "It's not like it's real."

"Nay, but it's after pretending to be."

"Oh, quit being so prudish, Arty," Guinevere said with a laugh as she threw it at him. "Here, see for yourself."

"I don't want ter touch..." He stopped as it landed in his hands. "Oh, that does feel real, don't it?"

"See?"

"The blasted thing even bends all about," Arty added, flexing the item in different directions.

"That could come in handy."

"Aye, lass," Arty agreed. "Even the danglies are proportioned like a real set." He then turned it around and squinted. "What's with the cup on the back?"

Guinevere pointed at a few others that were hanging off the wall. "Seems that it makes it so you can stick it on a wall."

"The wonders of this future ye've brought me to are vast," Arty stated almost reverently.

"Best of all," Guinevere said, snatching the toy back from the king of Scotland, before running her fingers over it, "no splinters!"

By now the proprietor of the establishment had come over. She was roughly Merlin's height, if Arthur was a proper judge, and her beauty was intoxicating. Arthur was careful to keep himself in check so as not to offend Guinevere.

"Excuse me, but may I help you find something?" the lady said with a voice that Arthur imagined could make some of these toys come to life.

"Aye," Arty said without missing a beat. "How much fer the phony zipper rippers?"

"Sorry, the what?"

"He wants to know how much these false man-items cost," said Arthur before Arty could go on another excursion of names.

"Ah, I see. Well, they're all different. It depends on a number of factors, such as material, length, width, vibration capabilities—"

"Vibration?" Guinevere interrupted.

"Of course."

"Sorry, but what's the purpose of that?"

"Seriously, honey?"

"Yes," Guinevere replied with a bit of angst.

"Are you from the Middle Ages or something?" the clerk said. Then she laughed and added, "Just making a joke because of the outfits."

"Good one," Arthur replied, trying to use the vernacular that he'd heard Merlin employ a few times. "Could you please just explain? We are not from the, uh, city."

"I *could* explain," the clerk replied, "but it'd be easier to just suggest that you put this on your special spot and press that button."

Guinevere took the toy with a confused look. The clerk pushed Guinevere's arms down a fair bit, and then pressed the aforementioned button.

"Oh, holy hell," Guinevere said as her face flushed faster than Arthur had ever seen. "How much is this thing?"

"Forty-five."

"I'll take one hundred of them," Guinevere said.

"Ohhhkay," the clerk replied with another laugh.

"Dear," Arthur said, leaning in, "please remember that we have no money at the moment."

"Find some," Guinevere stated flatly. Her face was a fit of sinister determination. "Now!"

"Uh—"

"Whoa," the clerk said as she stared down at Lance-A-Lot. "Are you guys trying to shoplift or something?"

Arthur said, "What?"

The clerk pointed at Lance-A-Lot's lump. "That."

"Sorry," Lance-A-Lot said, turning away. "I didn't want to walk around wearing only tights, but Arty needed my trousers."

"Wait, are you saying that thing is real?"

"Oh, it's real, sister," Guinevere replied. "It doesn't vibrate, but, then again, it doesn't need to."

"Hey," said Arthur.

"Did you say you don't have money?" the clerk said as if struck with inspiration. They all shook their heads. "How do you feel about being on film?"

"Well, I was on it before," Lance-A-Lot said. "When we went down to Scotland last summer. Merlin said he filmed us. Basically just looked like he was holding a box with glass on it and yelling 'action' a lot."

"Right. Well, want to make a couple hundred bucks?"

Lance-A-Lot excitedly said, "That would be wonderful, yes."

"Follow me."

The clerk led the knight through a few racks of clothing. They were headed toward a back room that had a brightly lit sign above it. The sign said, "Employees only. Filming in Progress."

"Uh, lass," Arty called out, "a quick question, if I might?"

"Yeah?"

"That really big one up on the top there. What's it after costin'?"

"One hundred and twenty."

"Pricey," Arty said, scratching his beard, "but I think me Agnes would consider it a consolation prize."

"A what?" Arthur asked.

"Nothing. Just talkin' to meself. Uh, lassy, one more question."

"Go on."

"Again, that big one up there," he pointed at it again. "Are ye after havin' it in white?"

# REHEARSAL

SIR GAHERIS STEPPED out from the shadows and stood next to Sirs Bors and Kay. They were having a discussion with the other actors. Gaheris didn't really care about the majority of the conversation, but he was hopeful that he could glean more information regarding this evil knight.

It seemed, though, that Bors was intent on debating the finer points of why actors should consist of men only.

"But a lady in a play?" he was saying. "I've not heard of such a thing before."

"Everyone knows that the ladies are excellent for throwing after-show parties," agreed Kay, "but they're not of much use *in* the show."

"Well said, Sir Kay."

"You two are joking, I hope?" said the actress.

"Not that we're aware of, dearest Leslie."

"Certainly not I."

"Then you're a couple of sexist pigs," she said as if spitting venom.

"Is that a bad thing?" Bors asked.

"She said it as though it were."

"Of course it's a bad thing, you chauvinists. This is the 2020s! Women have been acting for hundreds of years."

"Is that so?" said Bors, pursing his lips.

"Obviously. I'm playing the queen in tonight's show and you two are nothing but a couple of bumbling underlings." She jutted her chin out defiantly. "Deal with it."

"Never have I been treated thusly," Sir Kay said in shock.

"It's a downright outrage, my lady."

"Okay, okay," Wilhelm chimed in, "everyone calm down. I'm sure this is just a misunderstanding. Now, Bors and Kay are new to our area. From the sound of their accents I'd say they're from the U.K., yes?"

"No," Bors corrected, "we're from England."

"Oh, I see," said Wilhelm. "And is that also true of G. Harry Ass—"

"It's pronounced Gah-Hair-Ess," Gaheris said irritably.

"Ah, that does sound better, doesn't it?"

"Hmmph."

"You're also from England?"

"Where else?" Gaheris replied. "I've never heard of a place called OOK."

"It's U-K," noted Leslie, saying each letter separately.

"What did I say?" asked Gaheris, though there came no reply.

"So, as you can see, Leslie," Wilhelm said to the

actress, "this is just a case of people from England not knowing our ways."

Leslie placed her hands on her hips. "*I'm* from England, you dolt."

"No, you're from the U.K."

"England is in the U.K.!"

"It is?" said Wilhelm. "Who knew?"

"Everyone," Leslie was quick to point out.

"I didn't," said Bors.

Kay shrugged. "Nor I."

"Anyway," Wilhelm carried on as if it didn't really matter in the grand scheme of things, "the point is that they obviously think differently than you do, but that's okay. Just prove to them that you're the top of the peaches and that'll put them in their comfy zone."

"Fine, I'll do just that."

"No offense, my lady," Bors said, holding a hand up to shield his eyes, "but I've a wife and she would not appreciate you showing me your peaches."

"Same for me, I'm afraid," Kay concurred, also hiding his eyes.

"You may convince me whenever you're ready," Gaheris stated, finally having a solid reason to not be married. "I've no wife to contend with."

Leslie shook her head in disgust. "You three are getting dumber by the minute."

"You injure me, madam," Bors replied

"Simply appalling behavior, my lady," Kay said.

"Does this mean you're not going to show your peaches?" asked Gaheris.

"That's enough of this," Wilhelm yelled. "Everyone has their lines and their duties, so break it up and go study. We only have a few hours before the show starts."

# DOCTOR GALAHAD

GALAHAD GREW BORED of reading the athletics magazine. Some of the sports made very little sense to him, and even those that did weren't very exciting.

There was the one with the ball where everyone kicked it around. That seemed interesting enough, but the pictures made it look as though the field was far too large. He could imagine a lot of running and not a lot of scoring.

The game with the men all dressed up in gear was more his style, but even that seemed to be a little on the slow side. It also wasn't exactly clear why they were all crushing each other when they didn't even have the ball. He assumed that the one side was trying to hit the guy with the ball while the other side tried to stop them from doing so. That made sense to a degree, but did there really have to be that many of them?

And he wasn't even going to dignify the one where they were all on ice. He had firsthand experience with combat on ice. To make a sport of it was insanity.

Galahad got up and started to walk the hallways. People gave him funny looks, but that was expected in this new era. In his own time they looked at him with respect. Here, it was more like disdain. He noticed that everyone showed respect to the people who were wearing the long white jackets, though. There was obviously something about that coat because even he found himself impressed with those donning it.

His eye caught a small room on the left and he pushed inside. There were many white jackets in here.

He took a look around to make sure the area was clear and then took one off the wall to try it on. It took a few tries to find the right size, but as soon as he did it just felt right. Galahad hearkened it to the feeling of wearing his full knight garb. He felt strong and confident in this getup.

Just as he was admiring himself in the mirror, a nurse stopped at the door.

"Oh, thank goodness," she said. "We have an emergency situation and need your help."

"Uh…"

"Come on, Dr… Sorry, what's your name?"

"My name is Sir Galahad," he replied uncertainly.

"Of course it is," the nurse said with a frown. "You doctors really like carrying a joke along, don't you?"

"Um…"

"Ever since we went to the medieval dinner theater, you've all been acting strangely. Anyway, we have a problem with one of the patients."

"Why tell me?"

"Because you're a doctor, of course."

She didn't bother to let him clarify the situation. She merely grabbed him by the arm and began dragging him down the hallway. Honestly, he was rather impressed with her strength.

"Wait," he said desperately, "I can't do anything to help with—"

"Okay," she interrupted as they approached a young woman who was lying on the floor, "now, this lady is only a few months pregnant—"

"I can guarantee that the baby is not mine," Galahad said as he wrenched his arm away from the nurse.

The young woman on the floor gave him a disturbed once-over. "So can I," she said.

"Right," said the nurse, grimacing. "Look, Doctor, she's fallen down and we think her leg may be injured."

"No thinking about it," said the fallen woman. "I know it's injured. I'm the one who can feel it."

"Sorry, ma'am," the nurse amended. "I mean we're not sure how serious it is."

"Hmmm," Galahad said, trying to slowly disappear.

The nurse pulled him back. "Can you help her, Doctor?"

They were both looking at him expectantly. He knew nothing about today's medicine, other than it was far more advanced than what was available in his time. He wanted to just run away, but there was a lady in distress here and his training as a knight began to kick in.

"You're not a princess by chance, are you?"

"What?" the young woman on the floor said

incredulously.

"Uh, nothing, was just…" He took a deep breath to calm himself. "Most of my training is in the field of battle, but let's see what can be done." He cleared his throat and brought his hand to his chin, putting himself in a thoughtful stance. "I don't suppose you have any arrows sticking in you? I'm good with extracting those."

"What the hell are you talking about?"

The nurse came to his aid. "He's just joking," she said before turning her face toward him. Her eyes were like cinders. "I hope."

Galahad knew that his methodology was wrong, but it was all he had to work with. He crouched down and, keeping his hands to himself, began studying the woman's leg.

"No blade or knife wounds that I can see," he continued. "No oil burns either. Those are rather painful."

"Please get to it, Doctor," the nurse pleaded.

Galahad stood up. Her leg was possibly broken, unless people in this era were capable of bending their legs in odd directions. He'd not seen anything in the journals about this, though.

"Have you tried bloodletting?"

"What?" the nurse said with a look that spelled doom.

"Right. Well, we can check her humours."

"Her what?"

"Yeah, my what?"

"Her fluids," clarified Galahad. While he wasn't a doctor, everyone knew that checking fluids was the base of all medicine. "There's black bile, phlegm, blood, and yellow bile. It was all written up in last month's Medieval Doctor magazine."

The nurse put her hand on her hip. This could not be good. It was the same stance that he'd seen Lady Guinevere take when she was irritated with King Arthur. "Enough is enough. I'm sorry, ma'am, but this one has obviously lost it. Let me find another doctor."

"Shall I come with you?" Galahad called out as the nurse shoved past him.

She stopped and pointed. "Just go back to the room that I found you in."

"Ah, yes," he said, relieved, "that would probably be best. Good luck to you, my lady," he added to the fallen woman before leaving with haste.

Just as he was about to return the coat, another hand snagged his arm and stopped him. He didn't want to look because he thought certain it would be another nurse. Wearing this jacket obviously came with a lot of responsibility. Wearing a knight's outfit did, too, but at least in that one you didn't have to diagnose people. Well, you kind of did, but it was of the easier dead-or-not-dead sort of judgment.

"Where the devil have you been?" said the familiar voice of Merlin. "And why are you wearing that white coat?"

Galahad felt a sense of relief that it wasn't another nurse.

"Uh, I was doctoring in the other room."

"What? You're not a doctor."

"I tried to explain that," Galahad said in a

distraught voice, "but they wouldn't listen to me."

"It's because of that silly coat, you imbecile. Take it off and put it back before you get us in trouble."

Galahad wanted to retaliate at being called an imbecile, but he sort of felt like one at the moment.

# THE DONE DEAL

IT HAD BEEN nearly an hour since Lance-A-Lot disappeared into the back room. Arthur was about to ask what was taking so long when his lead knight pushed through the velvet curtains with a young lady on each arm. They were both glowing.

"I am honored to have serviced you both," Lance-A-Lot said in his charming way.

"How was he?" asked the clerk.

The two young lasses didn't say a word, but they didn't have to. The looks on their faces spoke volumes about Lance-A-Lot's, well, volume.

"Excellent," the clerk said with a nod. "Well, that scene will be a hit for sure! Honestly, I'm not sure how you managed him, but I wouldn't mind finding out."

"Are we almost done here?" asked Arthur irritably.

"Aye," Arty agreed. "I'm with him. I'd like to be gettin' outta this place. Makes my willy feel dainty when compared to the floppers on the walls."

"Exactly."

The clerk rolled her eyes at the two kings before turning back to Lance-A-Lot. "Your pay is five hundred," she said. "Now, if we take out the money for the items that your friends here have set aside, that leaves you with twenty-five."

"Twenty-five? That's it?"

"Sorry, sweetie," answered the clerk, "but they're buying a lot."

Lance-A-Lot frowned at them. "Anything made of metal?"

"Most everything."

"Remember that you can't take metal through when we return," Lance-A-Lot stated as he looked them over.

"Those things aren't weapons," Guinevere pointed out.

Lance-A-Lot picked up one of the larger devices and gave her a funny look. "Are you sure of that, my lady?"

Guinevere slumped.

"Damn," said Arthur.

"Shet," agreed Arty.

Lance-A-Lot shook his head at them. Arthur would have to have a discussion with the man about this at some point. Who was he to condemn them? Especially after he'd just spent the last hour getting paid to pleasure women!

"Okay," the clerk said as she separated out the items containing metal, "that leaves you with three hundred."

"Is that good?" asked Lance-A-Lot.

"It's not chump change," replied the clerk.

"What kind of change is it?" asked Arthur.

"I think we'll be okay from here," Guinevere said while stepping up and pulling Arthur aside. "Thank you for your assistance today. It was very eye-opening."

"Sure thing," the clerk replied with a slow nod. Then she shrugged and added to Lance-A-Lot, "Come back and see us again, big fella. We'll keep you busy and paid, I guarantee it."

"I shall remember that." Lance-A-Lot appeared to be in his element. "Thank you."

They stepped back outside and onto the sidewalk. A car sped by, causing them all to jump slightly. It would obviously take some time to get used to things, but Arthur had no intention of staying long enough for that. He wanted to get things wrapped up and get back to his castle.

"I can't believe they pay me to do that here," Lance-A-Lot said. He was beaming. "The future is brilliant."

"Don't get used to it," Arthur commanded. "We've got to return at some point and getting paid in our time to do that is against the law."

"It's not against the law for the women to charge for it," Guinevere said.

"I don't understand your point," Arthur replied, confused.

"We'll talk about it later," Guinevere said darkly. "For now, we should find Merlin and let him know that we've secured some coins."

"My tummy's also after grumblin'," Arty pouted.

"I've worked up quite an appetite myself," Lance-

A-Lot agreed.

Guinevere swooned.

"All right, all right," warned Arthur, seeing that his beloved was again making googly eyes at his lead knight. "Keep your sock in your pants, my queen."

"Excuse me?" she said, snapping her head up.

"The gown again," Arthur said apologetically.

"I'm beginning to wonder, Arthur."

"Shall I question your pantaloons excuse?"

"Are they always after bickerin' like this?" Arty asked Lance-A-Lot.

"Only when I'm around."

"Aye, I can understand that."

And that gave Arthur an idea. Keeping everyone together at this point made little sense, especially since he wanted to have a word with Guinevere alone. Enough was enough and he was about to lay down the law… Assuming she let him, of course. But he wasn't about to make an attempt like that unless he was alone with her.

"Why don't you two go and find Merlin and then meet us at the dinner theater?" he said.

"Yes, sire," Lance-A-Lot replied without a fuss.

"Wait a second," Arty said, nodding at Lance-A-Lot. "Ye want me to go with him?"

"Yes, why not?"

"Just that he's still got on the tights—"

"Would you rather he took them off?" Arthur asked with a raised eyebrow.

"I would," Guinevere said in a knee-jerk fashion.

"Honestly," Arthur yelped, giving her a what-the-hell kind of look.

"Sorry, it's the pantaloo—"

"It is not, either," Arthur said strongly. "Reel it in, woman!" Then he pointed at her firmly and added, "And no wisecracks about that statement either."

"Forget it," Arty said, waving at Arthur and Guinevere dismissively. "I'll go with the Lance-A-Log."

"That's Lance-A-Lot, sire."

"Eh? Oh, right, sorry. Anyhoo, goin' with him is better than hearin' you two bickerin'.'"

# LEARNING LINES

THE TIME WAS closing in on the show and the knights were practicing their lines.

Gaheris didn't understand why all of this preparation was needed. To him it was simple. You pick up the sword and shove the pointy end into the enemy soldier. It wasn't what Merlin would call "Rocker Science," which Gaheris assumed had something to do with rocking chairs, but he wasn't sure and he had never felt compelled to ask for clarification.

"Now, Sir Gaheris—" Bors began.

"I thought we were calling him 'Gary' now?" Kay interrupted.

Gaheris looked around. "Who is Gary?"

"Well, sure, in public," Bors explained without answering Gaheris.

"It may be well that we do it always," said Kay, "so we do not lose sight of the name by accident."

"If we slip up and neglect to call him Gary," Bors noted while pointing at Gaheris, "we can just state that we are staying in character."

"Why do you point at me when you say Gary?"

Kay nodded. "I suppose that makes sense."

"What does?" asked Gaheris.

"Good," Bors said. "Now that we have that settled, we need you to work on your lines, Gary."

"Am I supposed to be Gary?"

"I would say that's rather obvious, wouldn't you?" Kay asked.

"But my name is Gaheris."

Bors sighed and placed his hand on Gaheris's shoulder. "Remember that we are acting here, Sir... Erm, Gary."

"So you say," Gaheris replied sullenly. He was honestly trying, but things were still a bit fuzzy to him. He decided to ask questions like Galahad would. "What's the play about?"

"Our era," answered Bors.

"Yes," chimed in Kay, "it's about the Knights of the Round Table."

"Then why are you calling me Gary?"

"Because, man..." Bors started, almost in a rage. Then he stopped himself and glanced at Kay. "Actually, he has a point there."

"That he does, but I have the solution."

"Do tell, Kay."

"We are acting on two fronts here, Gary," Kay said slowly. "One of them is the act that we belong in this future that Merlin has brought us to, yes?"

"I'm listening."

"That means that in this future your name is Gary. Understand?"

"No."

"Excellent," Kay said. "While we're in this play, you're going to be playing the part of yourself, and that is why we're calling you Gary, Gary."

Gaheris felt his head throb. "Uh—"

"Well explained, Sir Kay."

"Thank you, Borsy."

"Let me try to understand," Gaheris said with the feeling that he was not going to get things straight. "I am to pretend to be someone named Gary because we are in the future?"

"Well done," said Kay.

"And this Gary," Gaheris continued, "*is* truly pretend, yes? I am not actually attempting to change who I *actually* am, right?"

"So far so good."

"Now, the Gary from the future—who is actually me pretending—has to pretend to be the real me from the past?"

"Top job, lad," Bors said with a firm smack on Gaheris's back.

"When, pray tell, do I get to be who I really am again?"

"When we return to our time," answered Kay.

"Correct," Bors said with a nod. "Now, is everything clear, Gary?"

"No."

"Good," said Kay.

"Nicely done."

"Right." Gaheris needed a nap. "Whilst I act as this fellow Gary who is pretending to be me, are you two pretending to be yourselves as well?"

"Not exactly," Bors answered while moving his foot in the sand.

Kay sighed heavily. "Dreadfully, no."

"Who then?"

"I'm portraying Sir Purcivale," Bors stated.

"And I am Sir Tristan."

Gaheris grunted. "But they're both idiots."

"Not the way this is written," Bors said, smacking the script with the back of his hand.

"If anything," agreed Kay, "they are most worthy in this play."

"So this really *is* make believe, then," Gaheris said.

"Right. Now, Gary, let's go over the script, shall we?"

There was really no point in arguing. King Arthur had commanded that they do this play and so Gaheris would comply. His was a life of simplicity, even if his current situation was complicated indeed. He would have to get back to his mantra of "I go where I go," which could have many meanings, depending on the context.

Still, even if the idea of this being a play was becoming more and more actualized in his mind, he couldn't help but feel that the Evil Knight was a reality. There was just too much evidence supporting it. The dull swords, the man's outfit, the fact that everyone referred to him as "The Evil Knight" every time the man was near. Add to that the additional evidence that this show was portraying Purcivale and Tristan in a positive light, and it just made Gaheris quite suspicious.

Someone was definitely up to no good.

"It says here that Kay and I will be fighting with the other knights in a tournament of sorts," announced Bors.

Yet another dagger in the side, thought Gaheris as his head snapped up.

"We don't fight other knights."

"It's acting, Gary, remember?" Bors said.

"We're allowed to fight other knights when we're acting?" asked Gaheris.

"Hence the term *acting*," said Kay.

"So you'll come out and grab a blade," said Bors while studying the script.

"*That* I can understand."

"And you'll start attacking the Evil Knight."

"Now we are in league with each other."

"Just before you attack," Bors said, pointing at the document, "you'll yell, 'I am Sir Gaheris, feel the steel of my mighty blade!' and then you'll start swinging."

"What?"

"That's your line," Kay pointed out.

"And that's supposed to be me? I mean, the *real* me?"

"Yes."

"Correct."

"But that's ridiculous. I would never say such a thing."

"Hmmm?" said Bors.

"What you just said that I'm supposed to say. I wouldn't speak those words. They're silly."

"Well," said Kay, "it's in the script, so you have to say it."

"But it's incorrect," Gaheris replied strongly. "I'd

say what I say, not what that says I'd say."

"It's not about what's right, you imbecile!" Bors was clearly at his wit's end. "It's—"

"Borsy," Kay said, again calming his fellow knight, "let me try."

"Hmmmph!"

"Okay, Gary," Kay said as if he were speaking to a child, "what *would* you say in a situation where you were about to attack?"

"As Gary, as Gary pretending to be me, or as the true me?"

"The real you."

Gaheris had been in battle situations many times over his life, actually. He had a set routine for it. One of the tenets he'd learned in his years of warring was that you needed to follow a pattern. If you didn't, you'd begin to second-guess yourself. Do that and you died.

"I wouldn't say anything," he stated. "I'd soil my britches and then I'd walk up and begin cutting down my enemy."

"Sorry, did you say you'd soil your britches?" said Kay with a look of disgust.

"Always do before a fight," Gaheris replied.

Bors held the look of a man who had just eaten a sour peanut. "Why?"

"So I don't do it when I'm in the fight."

"That's gross," said Kay.

"Pre-fight jitters," Gaheris said with a shrug. "Can't help it."

"Couldn't you just go into the woods or maybe the outhouse?" asked Bors.

"I go where I go," Gaheris replied, happy that he was able to further center himself.

"So you say," Kay replied, "but a little tact never hurts anyone, you know?"

"What am I to do, Sir Kay?" Gaheris felt that he was the one teaching now. "Shall I tell the enemy to hold their position whilst I relieve myself in the nearest bush?"

"I'm sure they'd appreciate it," Bors commented.

"Anyway, Sir Gah... Gary," Kay said, waving away the entire conversation, "you'd not say anything before the battle?"

"You've both been to battle with me. When have you heard me say anything?"

"Come to think of it, that's true," Bors said as he scratched his head. "You always make noises, like *guh* and *gah* a number of times before the battle..." He paused and looked up. "Unfortunately, I now understand why."

"I don't understand..." said Kay and then he looked at the ground. "Oh, no, wait, I get it now."

"See?" Gaheris said, feeling vindicated. "So this line you have given me makes no sense. I shall not comply."

"You *must* comply. It's the king's orders."

"Damn the eroding beaches."

"Why would you damn the eroding beaches?"

"I damn what I damn."

"That's really annoying, you know?" said Kay.

"I annoy what I—"

"Just try out your line, man!"

"As you wish, Sir Kay," Gaheris said and then eyed

Bors. "What is it again?"

Bors held the script out at arm's length. "I am Sir Gaheris, feel the steel of my mighty blade!"

"*Gah, guh*," started Gaheris.

Kay jumped back. "Are you soiling your britches?"

"No, I am clearing my throat."

"Oh, okay, it's just that those are the same sounds you... Never mind. Go on."

Gaheris rolled his eyes and told himself, "I am Gary. I am Gary." He then took a deep breath and fought to calm down.

"I am Sir Gaheris, feel my dirty sword!"

"No, no, no," Bors shrieked. "It's 'I am Sir Gaheris, feel the steel of my mighty blade!'"

"What difference does it make?"

"Well," stated Kay, "for one, a 'dirty sword' sounds rather racy, and somewhat vulgar."

"That it does," Bors agreed with a nod.

"Secondly, it's not the line."

"Ugh." Gaheris took another breath. "I am Sir Gaheris and my dirk is ready to stick in you!"

"Honestly, man," Bors said, throwing the script to the ground. "That's not even close!"

"You did say 'dirk,' right?"

"Yes," Gaheris grumbled at Kay through clenched teeth. "And Sir Bors, that is precisely what you instructed me to say."

"I most certainly did not."

"Did too."

"It's right here in black and white, man," Bors said, snatching the script back off the ground.

"More of a bluish color," Gaheris noted, looking at

the ink.

Sir Kay leaned back against the wall and rubbed his eyes. "This is going to take some work, I fear."

"Indeed," Bors agreed with a huff.

# MAKING A FUSS

THIS WAS NOT a discussion that Arthur wanted to have, but enough was enough. He had to make a stand or he would just continue to hold his feelings in until the day he exploded. Still, he understood the importance of not speaking to Guinevere too harshly.

"I'm just saying that the constant references to the man's deftness in the sack is hurtful."

"Are you jealous, Arthur?" Guinevere said with a wink.

"Of the man? No. Of his chauncey? Absolutely. Who in their right mind wouldn't be?"

"I saw a few fellows on the boxes in that store who wouldn't be."

"True," Arthur agreed, "and a couple of the ladies, too, which I'm still trying to wrap my head around."

"So to speak."

"Pardon?"

"Pantaloons."

"Ah, right. Anyway, it's just not kind of you to constantly swoon over the man in front of me."

"I had no idea you were so sensitive about things like this, Arthur." Again, she was saying it in a teasing way.

"It's not sensitivity!" He didn't want to lose his temper, but his resolve had all but failed him. "It's... It's..." He stopped. "Okay, maybe it is sensitivity. But how would you like it if I brought up Cybil all the time?"

Guinevere looked at him with eyes of rage. The teasing was gone now.

"You mean that slut with the gigantic bazangas?"

"Bazangas?" Arthur said, furrowing his brow. "I know, I know, it's the pantaloons. Anyway, yes, her."

"Honestly never understood what you saw in her, Arthur."

"Myself, for one," he said, deciding it was *his* turn to tease.

"Arthur!"

"Doesn't feel so good, does it?" he said defiantly.

"Depends," she said, looking momentarily confused. "What are we talking about?"

"My teasing you, dear."

"Oh, right." She walked a few more paces in silence. "No, I suppose it doesn't."

"Well, that's how it feels to me when you talk about Mitch all the time."

"Okay, okay, I get it," she said and then took his hand. "I'm sorry, Arthur. I guess I just didn't realize how it made you feel."

They looked up to find that Merlin and Galahad were approaching. The timing wasn't the best, but when was there a good time for a king and queen to be alone? Night, sure, but only because they were sleeping in the same bed. They *had* been together a long time, after all, which meant that a place to sleep was their bed's primary purpose these days.

"Hello, Merlin," Arthur said. "Galahad."

"Sire."

Merlin gave them both a dubious glance. "Are we interrupting something?"

"No, Merlin," Guinevere said. "I believe we've finished our discussion. Yes, Arthur?"

"We have, my turtle dove."

"Good, good." Merlin looked back at the hospital. "We found Allison. She's doing fine."

"Was she struck ill?" Guinevere asked.

"In a manner of speaking, I suppose."

"Out with it, man! What's the matter with her?"

"She's pregnant," Merlin answered.

"How wonderful," Arthur said while bringing his hands to his chest.

"Sweet," said Guinevere, adjusting her sock.

Merlin squinted at them both, as did Galahad.

"Anyway," said Merlin, "I suppose it is, sure."

"Is there something wrong with her being with child, Merlin?"

"Yes," Guinevere said, "what's the matter?"

Galahad cracked his neck from side-to-side and said, "You might want to sit down for this."

# I'M A WHAT?

LANCE-A-LOT was not a fan of walking around in public while wearing only tights. It got him far too many looks. The glances of awe from the women were great, but the sneers from the men made him uncomfortable. The winks from some of the men made him even more uncomfortable.

It was also clear that Arty was unhappy to be seen with him, but that wasn't Lance-A-Lot's fault. King Arthur had decreed that the two men would work together to seek out Merlin.

They walked up to the desk that had a sign above it that read "Information."

"Here to get that tumor removed from your leg?" asked the woman behind the counter.

"Sorry?" said Lance-A-Lot.

"That massive lump," she replied, pointing at his tights.

"Oh, uh—"

"That's the man's nether saber," Arty said with a grunt.

"His what?"

"Don't get him started," Lance-A-Lot said quickly. "We're looking for an Allison Smith."

"Ah, yes," the clerk said. "Should have known from the clothes. Take the elevator to floor three. She's in room 327."

"Right, the elevator."

"What the shet's an elevator?" asked Arty.

"You guys really like staying in character, don't you?"

Arty looked around. "What kind of establishment is this, anyhoo?"

"Sorry, we have a... Uh... Show tonight."

"Right, I get it. The other guys who were here earlier were acting funny, too. Just go over there, get inside, and press the number three."

"Thank you."

They approached the elevator and watched it for a few minutes. People walked in and it would close up. Then they'd see through the glass as those folks were lifted or dropped. The box would stop and the people would disappear, only to be replaced by other people. On their level, different people would walk out than those who had originally walked in.

"I'm not gettin' in that thing," Arty said with a gulp.

Lance-A-Lot stood strong. "Come along, sire. I'm sure it will be fine."

"Nay. I'm not doin' it," Arty said as the doors opened again. "Looks like a damn crypt, it does. And ye see how it goes up. Ye think it's after takin' ye to the angels?"

"I don't think it does, sire."

"What if we get in it and it goes down? Could be demons we'd be fed to."

"We have to do our duty, my lord."

"Ye may have," Arty said, sniffing, "but I report to no man but meself."

Lance-A-Lot had little time to mess about with the fears of the king. He didn't know much about Scotland, but he'd battled with enough of them to gauge that they were fierce warriors. Recalling the look of Arty in his full gown and makeup didn't bring forth a vision of a man to be feared, but deep down Lance-A-Lot felt certain that Arty was not a weak-willed warrior. He just needed the right motivation.

"Well," said Lance-A-Lot, "I guess we'll just have to let it be known that the king of Scotland was too timid to join a mere knight in a quest that required the entrance into a silver box."

Arty slumped. "Yer a right bastard, ye know?"

"Sorry, sire."

The doors opened again and Lance-A-Lot strode inside. A moment later, while grasping on to the walls for dear life, Arty followed.

"Bad enough ye got that thing in yer pants what looks like an elephant's trunk holdin' a damn coconut, but ye ain't gotta be a shethead, too."

"She said to press three, right?" Lance-A-Lot said, unfazed. He was used to being spoken to derisively.

"Aye."

The doors closed.

"Oh, me heavens! We're doomed!"

Lance-A-Lot grabbed the king by the shoulder and

spun him around. "If you look out the side, sire, you can see where we just were."

"The world is sinkin' away from us," Arty said hoarsely. "I'll never see me Agnes again."

"Now that's a dreary thought."

"Aye, and..." Arty stood up straight and spun around. "What's that supposed to be after meanin'?" The doors opened, causing Arty to cower again. "Is there angels out there?"

"Come on, will you?" Lance-A-Lot said, looking back at the terrified king.

"Aye, all right." He took a step out just as the doors were closing. They clipped his leg and reopened. The Scottish king jumped into a fighting stance. "Shet! It tried to eat me, it did!"

The doors closed again as Arty slowly stood back up. Lance-A-Lot hoped that the king was starting to grasp how foolish he looked. Something told Lance-A-Lot that probably wasn't the case, though.

"Blimey, they *are* angels," Arty said, pointing at the people wearing white outfits.

"Hard to argue that, but I think we're still in the realm of the living, sire."

"Yer certain?"

"It's just a different era, my lord. I'm sure it's all fine."

Arty blinked a few times. "Are all nets this calm?"

"I would imagine all nets are calm, yes."

"Knyeeeeets," Arty said in exasperation.

"Ah, right. We are trained to be relaxed in the face of adversity, sire."

"Hmmm. I'll have to have a think on that."

"May I help you?" asked one of the nurses as she walked by. She then glanced down at Lance-A-Lot's situation. "Oh, you're on the wrong floor, sweetie. You need to be in Oncology on floor six in order to get that removed."

"It's his boy-melon, lass," Arty said tiredly.

"His what?"

"Nothing, ma'am," Lance-A-Lot said. "I'm sorry if my outfit is too revealing. I am looking for an Allison Smith? She should be here with Merlin."

"Oh, yeah," she snickered. "Merlin. Last I saw him, he was in room 327."

"Thank you. Let's go, sire."

"I'm gonna wait out here and look at the angels," Arty said while taking a seat. "I don't know this Allison person."

"She was Merlin's helper when we came to see you in Scotland."

"The young lass?"

"Yes, sire."

"Ah, right. Well, I think I'd rather keep feastin' me eyes on all the angels."

"As you wish, sire."

Lance-A-Lot took one last look around. He was somewhat worried about leaving the king of Scotland alone, but King Arthur had never put the man's safety in Lance-A-Lot's hands. Besides, a king of Arty's stature should be able to handle himself, even if he was terrified of elevators.

He opened the door and peeked around the corner. "Merlin? Hello?"

"Mitch?" said a voice that Lance-A-Lot had not

heard in many months.

"Oh, hello, Miss Allison. It's Sir Lance-A-Lot."

"I know. That's why I called you Mitch."

"Oh, right." He felt uncomfortable with that, but it wasn't like she was in the military. "Have you seen Merlin?"

"He left a little while ago. Said he was going to catch up with you and Arthur."

"Must have missed him in the hallway."

"So you don't know, then?" Allison said.

"Know what?"

"I'm pregnant," she said.

"How wonderful," Lance-A-Lot said, feeling genuinely happy for her. "My most merry congratulations to you and your husband."

"I have no husband, Mitch."

He felt an instant pang of guilt. "Ah, my apologies, my lady."

"None required. I need no husband. I'm an independent woman."

"Again," he said, thinking this was a bad thing, "my apologies."

"Hmmm."

"Wait," he added at the sudden thought that this young woman had been put in a dastardly situation. "Are you saying that the father of this child of yours has gone derelict? If so, I shall hunt the man down and force him to do the right thing!"

"As to that, Mitch," she explained, "*you* are the father."

"A man should take responsibility for his... What?"

"When I was back in Camelot, you were the only

one I had relations with." She looked out the window. "Frankly, prior to that it had been a few years."

"What?"

"Years," she repeated, "and having you as my first in such a long time wasn't the best of ideas. Took me two weeks to walk normal again."

"I'm confused."

"It's your baby, Mitch. You're the father."

Lance-A-Lot's legs nearly gave out. He moved to the chair and sat down.

"Me?"

"Yes."

"But... how?"

"You of all people should know the answer to that, Mitch."

"Right, sorry." He shook his head, trying to clear out the fog. "I don't know what to say."

"Don't worry, Mitch. I don't expect anything from you. You couldn't have known, and had Merlin not come along, you never would have known."

"So, I'm going to be a father?"

"Well, biologically-speaking, yes."

He sat up straight. "Then I must do what I can to contribute—"

"No, Mitch," Allison interrupted, holding up her hand. "It's not necessary. Really. I can handle it."

"What do you mean?"

"Like I said, I'm an independent woman. I don't need, nor do I want, a husband."

"Oh."

"Besides, you couldn't possibly make any money in this day and age." Then she looked him over. "Well, maybe a little at the dinner theater, I suppose."

"Actually, I was just paid…" He looked up and thought better of continuing his sentence. "Forget it."

"Oooh," Allison said, her face cringing as she leaned forward.

"What is it?" Lance-A-Lot said, fearing the worst.

"Just having some contractions is all. Oooh! *Ouch!*"

Lance-A-Lot rushed to her side. "What do I do?"

"They'll subside shortly," she said through ragged breaths. "*Oooh!*"

# THE GATE

A SMALLISH MAN with a clothing style that fit Arthur's personal taste came out to meet the four Camelotians as they approached the medieval dinner theater.

"You're late," the little fellow hissed. "Everyone is already getting into position. The curtain goes up in thirty minutes."

"Pardon me?" Arthur replied, surprised at the man's demeanor.

"At least you have your outfits on," said the man. He then eyed them carefully. "I don't recall you being on the actors list, though, especially the little guy with the pointy hat. Are you supposed to be a wizard? A stunt double maybe?"

"What?"

"Either way, you need to get down to the rooms and finish up with your makeup."

Arthur smiled. "That sounds lovely."

"Wait, young man," Merlin said. "We're not who you think we are."

"You're actors, right?"

"No. Our friends are acting. We are merely spectators."

"Then why are you dressed like that?"

Galahad stepped up and said, "We are looking to sell a sword."

"We are?" said Merlin.

"What?" said Arthur, knowing that the only sword they had in their possession was Excalibur.

"I'm assuming that the owner of this establishment collects items from the elder age?" Galahad pressed on.

"Mrs. Levstall is a huge collector of Medieval paraphernalia, yes."

Merlin glanced at Galahad. "How the blazes did you know that?"

Galahad motioned to all of the pieces encased in glass on the sides of the building. There were knights' outfits, swords, maces, shields, crossbows, and a number of other items that were related to battle. There were also dresses, barons' outfits, jester hats, and so on.

"Could just be replicas," mused Merlin.

"Look at the notches on that red-tinted one, Merlin," Galahad whispered, just within earshot of Arthur. "That's what Bedivere does. Nobody would know about that. And look at those metal pants with the increased package handler in the mid-section."

"Lance-a-Lot," Merlin and Arthur said simultaneously.

"Exactly."

"Sorry," the small man said. "You're selling a

sword?"

"Correct," answered Galahad.

"I believe we are, yes," Merlin agreed. "And a fine one at that."

"What is the sword?"

"The genuine Excalibur, of course," Merlin replied, pointing at the weapon hanging on Arthur's back.

Arthur merely whimpered.

# TALKING TO THE ANGELS

"HOW LONG HAVE ye been an angel?" Arty asked a particularly pretty red-haired lass who was standing at the counter.

"We're called nurses, sir."

"Nurses?" Arty fished around in his mind for a second. "Ye mean like the people who help the seck?"

"You *are* in a hospital, sir." She then looked him over. "Actually, maybe you're on the wrong floor?"

"I dinnae think so."

"What's your name?"

"I'm Arthur, King of Scotland," he said proudly, "but ye can call me Arty."

"Ah, yes," she replied with a nod. "I think you're on the wrong floor. And is that a gown you're wearing under that coat?"

"Ye can see that?" He looked down at himself. "I thought I had it tucked into Sir Lance-A-Lot's trousers."

"Definitely on the wrong floor," she said gently. "Let me find someone to take you back up to floor number seven, sir."

Arty swallowed hard. "What's up there?"

"People just like you."

"Ye've got people from me homeland on floor seven?" He brightened a bit at the possibility.

"I'm sure there are a few, and there are also others there who you'd certainly be happy to meet. I think there's even one lady who swears she's from another planet."

"She sounds a bit batty, I'd say."

"Exactly. I'll just have an orderly come down to bring you back upstairs."

"I've never been upstairs," he said. "I came from the metal box, ye know?"

"The elevator, you mean?"

"Aye, that's what they were after callin' it," he said with a wink. "Before that we was walking around the city. Before that we was in a building where we had come from the past. I'd like to get back, if I could. Dinnae like it in the future, as they say."

"Riiiight," said the nurse nervously. "Let me get that orderly for you, sir." As if on cue, an orderly walked by. "Ah, you there. Would you please take, uh, the king of Scotland back to floor seven?"

The orderly smiled and checked out Arty. "King of Scotland, eh?"

"Got somethin' to say about it, lad?" replied Arty, pushing his chest out.

"Oh, no, not at all. Just never met anyone from royalty before."

Arty softened. "I like the blue outfit ye've got on. Kind of nursely, but just enough of a difference to make it not questionable."

"Right, thanks. Want to follow me?"

He waved at the pretty nurse before walking over to the elevator. He was not fond of another trip in the thing, but seeing that everyone else was using it as if it were commonplace, he forced his resolve.

"Not fond of this metal box thing."

"It's called an elevator."

"Aye, that's what everyone keeps sayin'."

The door shut again. This time he kept his composure. If his people were up on this level 7, as the nurse had claimed, he didn't want them to see his fear.

The bell chimed and the doors opened again.

"Here we are," said the orderly, leading Arty out and into the main area.

"Looks the same as floor three," noted Arty.

"True, but the people here are, well… let's just say that they're different."

"Obviously," Arty grunted. "What do ye think I am, daft?"

Arty glanced around and took in the scene. There were people wearing all sorts of outfits.

One woman had on a greenish costume with a sun-shaped hat. She was carrying a flameless torch, too. And the sash that ran from shoulder to hip had the word "Liberty" written on it.

Another fellow wore an all-white outfit that was similar to the ones that the nurses were wearing, except that this one came with a glass bubble that was affixed to his head. He also wore heavy white boots with matching gloves, and there was a patch on his chest that had the letters "NASA" embroidered on it.

A number of people were dressed normally enough, but most were sitting by the windows drooling. Others were having conversations with the wall, and one lady was dancing to a symphony that was obvious only she could hear.

The future was becoming more odd with each passing moment.

"The nurse on level three said some of me subjects were after being up here."

"She did?" said the orderly as they approached the main desk.

"Aye, maybe ye've got Feargus the Fearful?"

"I don't think so."

"Doonan the Doolittle?"

"Doesn't sound familiar."

"Ninean the Noisome?"

"No, sorry."

"Couldn't miss him, unless ye were after wearin' a nose clip." He chewed his lip as a thought hit him. "Well, ye better not have Calle here. I told the man to stay put outside of Camelot until I got back."

The orderly glanced over at him. "Have you had your medications today, sir?"

"Had a bit of cumin and anise for me gas," Arty answered. "Do that every mornin'. If I don't, I get the wind somethin' fierce."

"Okay." They reached the main desk and the orderly picked up the sign-in sheet and looked it over. "Excuse me, nurse, but I believe one of your patients escaped."

The nurse studied Arty for a second. "Don't recognize him."

"Claims to be the king of Scotland," the orderly said, setting the sheet back down.

"Claims?" said Arty.

"You do realize that the dinner theater is right down the street, yes?" said the nurse. "We get method actors in here all the time."

The orderly looked up at her and then back over at Arty. He then began to laugh while shaking his head.

"So that's what this is all about?"

"What what is all about?" asked Arty.

"I have to hand it to you, sir, you're quite an impressive actor." The orderly slapped Arty on the shoulder. "Feargus the Fearful, indeed!"

"So he *is* here?"

"They do this for marketing," the nurse said to the orderly.

"Ahh, yes. That makes sense."

"You new around here or something?"

"First week," said the fellow. "Sorry, didn't know. One of the nurses down on three said to bring him up."

"He must be new, too."

"It was a she," the orderly corrected.

"Ah."

"Anyway, sorry about that." The orderly turned to Arty and made his voice sound as regal as he could. "Okay, King of Scotland, it appears that you have earned yourself a patron come the weekend."

"I have? And what's happened to your voice?"

"Incredible how they stay in character," he said, laughing again.

"Annoying if you ask me," replied the nurse.

"What?"

"Just take the elevator back down, if you would, sir," said the orderly as he walked away, still laughing.

Arty took one more look around the room. There were definitely none of his men here, that was for certain.

"That damned metal box again," he said, knowing that he had to go back down to level three.

With nobody to help him this time, he truly had to stand steadfastly against his fear. He pressed the down button and waited for the doors to open. Once inside, he pressed on the number three and held his breath as the doors shut. Once they opened again, he released the air and jumped out into the hallway.

"You're back?" said the nurse who had set him up with the orderly.

"Aye. None of me men were up there."

"Let me get another orderly," she said sweetly.

"They said I was just here marketing for the dinner theater," Arty said, not paying much attention to her.

She stopped. "Ahhh... So that's what this is all about? Only my second week on the job. I suppose I should have known, though. Where would a loony bird get an outfit like that?"

"What?"

An instant later, a light above the room where Allison was staying went off, accompanied by a buzzing sound.

"Uh oh," said the nurse. She ran into the room as

Arty stood there, trying to piece together what had been going on. The nurse dashed back out and called to a fellow behind the desk, "Steve, you'd better get Dr. Carry on the horn. Looks like Allison Smith is going into labor."

Arty grabbed the woman by the arm and pointed. "Is that Steve fellow after being a male nurse?"

"Of course he is," she said with a frown.

"What's the world comin' to?" Then he remembered he was wearing lace undies.

Lance-A-Lot bolted from the room and slapped his hands on Arty's shoulder. "She's going into labor, sire. I'm going to be a father."

"My goodness, lad," Arty said, shocked. "I know yer after havin' a massive tallyhoosit, but I dinnae think even ye can get a lass knocked up that quick and then off to labor."

# THE PLAY BEGINS

GAHERIS LOOKED OUT beyond the curtains and saw that people were filling the stands. They were still being ushered in, but the attack from the Evil Knight was clearly imminent. Whether under the guise of a play or not, it was happening soon. He only hoped that the innocents would be saved. Gaheris was known as a man with a cold heart, but he held a soft place in it for civilians. It was never their role to pit sword against sword.

"Now remember, Gary," Bors warned, "you're in a play."

"I don't think it's as you say," Gaheris replied, keeping his eye on the incoming crowd. "I've checked the swords again just now. They're still not sharp."

"That's because, again, it's a play."

"Yet there is the Evil Knight—"

"He's an actor."

"You *do* understand that, right?" Kay said, spinning Gaheris around. "Just when I think you get it, you say things that make me believe that you don't."

"I understand that the king is in danger," Gaheris replied evenly.

"Who is also an actor," Bors pointed out.

"And even if he weren't, he's not our king."

"A king is a king," Gaheris replied, taking a small detour from his normal saying. "Even that damn Scottish fellow."

"That makes zero sense, Gaheris," Bors said. "You wouldn't just defend any king, right?"

Gaheris held his fellow knight's gaze. "I defend as I defend."

"So you're saying that if we were at war with France, you'd defend their king?" asked Kay.

"Well, no."

"Then?"

"We were instructed to do this thing," Gaheris said.

"It's a *play*, you buffoon," yelled Bors just as Wilhelm rushed into the room.

"Are you all ready?" he said, looking anxiously from face to face.

"Gaheris?" said Kay.

"Who?" asked Wilhelm.

"He's just trying to stay in character," Bors quickly replied.

"Oh, right."

"Gary?" Kay attempted again, "are you ready?"

Gaheris felt his heart rate increase. "I am always ready."

"Excellent," Wilhelm said. "I'll check on the others."

"I have a bad feeling about this," Bors said to Kay.

"Indeed."

# SELLING EXCALIBUR

"WHERE DID YOU get this?" said Mrs. Levstall, an elderly woman who wore an outstanding ensemble of clothing that was accompanied with jewelry and a fashionably pink hat. Arthur was smitten with her immediately. Not because he found her attractive, of course, but rather because he loved her choice of garb.

"I pulled it from a rock," Arthur declared.

"Ha ha," said Mrs. Levstall. "Funny. Seriously, though. Where?"

"Uh, well—"

"We are collectors as well, madam," Merlin interjected. "This was pulled from an archaeological dig a long time ago."

"Where?" she asked thoughtfully.

"May I suggest that it doesn't matter where?" Galahad said, coming to Merlin's aid. "The point is that it's here now."

"Yes, yes," Merlin said. "He's correct."

"What's an archaeological dig?" asked Arthur.

Galahad leaned over. "You truly need to pick up some periodicals, sire."

"Did you just call him sire?"

"No, ma'am," Galahad lied, "I called him 'sir.'"

"Ah, yes," she said, resuming her study of the sword. "Well, I have to say that this is an incredible specimen. I'm willing to pay a great deal of money for this, assuming it's not hot, of course."

"Hot?" Guinevere said, reaching out to touch the blade.

"She means stolen, Gwen," Merlin said and then looked again at Mrs. Levstall. "I assure you that it is not, madam."

"How can I know that for certain?"

"Have you seen this item in any of your journals as of late?" asked Galahad.

"Well, no."

Galahad nodded. "Have you heard rumblings of its existence in recent years?"

"I have not."

"Then the only deduction one could make, madam," stated Galahad, "would be that it has not been availed to the public eye."

Mrs. Levstall leaned back in her chair and crossed her arms. She appeared to be weighing Galahad's words. Arthur couldn't blame her. He'd always known that Galahad was one of his more clever knights, but his looks betrayed his intellect and that often meant that he got questioned when he spoke smartly.

"Or it's been kept in quiet circles," the older lady countered.

"I would assume that one with your collection

would belong to such circles, no?"

"That's true," she said to Galahad. "I must say that you seem to be a well-educated man in the realm of business and collectibles."

"And finance, I might add." Galahad puffed out his chest slightly. "Plus, I've recently started to study electricity."

This didn't seem to impress Mrs. Levstall.

"Well," Merlin said with a cough, "should we assume that you're interested in making a purchase?"

"I believe I am. What are you asking for it?"

At this, Merlin turned back to Galahad, who merely sat staring.

"Gal?" said Merlin.

"Merl?" replied Galahad snarkily.

Merlin sighed. "You said you were well versed in finance."

"Ah, yes, sorry. I would think that something of this rarity would fetch at least one thousand horses."

"Sorry, did you say one thousand horses?"

"I'm up for negotiation, of course."

Mrs. Levstall smiled and said, "You people are quite humorous." Though she didn't actually laugh. "Let's just say that I'm willing to offer you ten million for it."

"Ten million horses?" Galahad replied in shock. "Where would we put them all?"

"I didn't even know there *were* that many horses," agreed Arthur.

"You all love keeping a joke running, don't you?"

Guinevere held up her hand to silence Galahad, Arthur, and Merlin. She then turned to Mrs. Levstall and gave her what appeared to be a look that said, "Men." Mrs. Levstall returned a look that Arthur construed to mean, "I know, right?"

"Could we have a moment, please, Mrs. Levstall?" said Guinevere.

"Of course, dear."

After she walked out, Guinevere said, "While you two were in the hospital, we got a bit of information on money. Mitch was paid in something called dollars."

"Ah, yes," Arthur said, nodding, "forgot about that."

"I've seen these dollars in magazines that Allison brought back," Merlin said with a snap of his fingers.

"And you didn't think that information would prove useful to me?" asked Galahad.

Merlin glanced at him. "You said you were well versed in finance!"

"Of our era, you twit."

"You don't call your master a twit," Merlin admonished.

"I do if he fits the part."

"And why would you ask for one thousand horses anyway?" Merlin spat. "How the hell did you expect us to get them back to Camelot?"

"One at a time, twit."

"Okay, okay," Arthur said. "Calm down, the both of you. We need to keep our heads in the game." He looked back at Guinevere. "These dollars, do you think ten million of them to be a good amount?"

"I'd say it would be simply based on how much Mitch got paid for swinging his sword around."

"I thought his sword disappeared..." started Galahad. "Oh wait, that's not what you meant."

"She always talks like that when she's wearing pantaloons."

"Strange."

"Tell me about it."

"Anyway," Guinevere said, "I'd say that we should take it."

Merlin nodded. "I trust your judgment more than either of these two."

"Hey!"

Guinevere waved Mrs. Levstall back into the room.

"We shall accept this offer you have given us."

"Excellent," she said while resuming her seat. "I'll just need your bank information and I'll make the transfer immediately."

"Hmmm," said Merlin while looking over at Arthur.

Trumpets sounded, jolting them all but Mrs. Levstall, who had gone back to her study of Excalibur. She merely said, "Oh good, the play is beginning."

"Play?" said Arthur, forgetting momentarily where he was. "Ah yes, of course! That's the one that Bors, Kay, and Gaheris are in."

"You mean Gary?" said Mrs. Levstall with a giggle. "Odd bird, that."

"Right...Gary. That's who I meant."

"The other two are actors through and through," the elderly woman added, "but that Gary is so strange."

"No arguing that," agreed Galahad.

"Most convincing form of method-acting I've ever seen, truth be told. High hopes for his performance, I'll say."

Arthur was surprised by this revelation. "Truly?"

"Didn't know you were familiar with the new actors, though," she said, looking up. "Where did you say you were from again?"

"Camel—" began Arthur.

"Toe," finished Merlin, spouting the first word that came to mind.

"What?"

"We're from, uh, Cameltoe," Merlin said after a moment, knowing that it sounded wrong.

"Never heard of it. Well, I mean I've heard it used as a boorish reference, but not as a place where people lived."

She looked to be volleying up another round of questions when a booming voice sounded all around them.

*My lords and ladies, I invite you to a night of wonder. A night full of jousting, skill competitions, and battles not seen since the days of King Arthur!*

The crowd cheered.

"We didn't battle all that much," said Arthur to Galahad, "and what is jousting?"

*There will be kings, queens, knights, and villains.*

The crowd cheered again.

"Definitely had all of those."

"Arthur," said Merlin, giving him a look, "quiet, please."

"Excuse me?"

Guinevere patted his arm. "Mrs. Levstall is trying to think, dear."

"I don't see how... Oh, right. Sorry."

*While cheering and applause is fully expected, and appreciated, we do ask that everyone refrain from banging their mugs and silverware. This noise scares the horses and may cause them to rear and drop the rider.*

"Now that's a battle tactic I hadn't considered," said Galahad.

"What do you mean?"

"Just that in addition to carrying swords, sire... Erm, *sir*, we could also have footman carry along mugs, plates, and metal utensils."

Arthur pursed his lips. "Go on."

"When the enemy riders come toward us, we have the men bang the plates, silverware, and mugs."

"Interesting," Arthur said while looking down at the field of sand. "Make note of it and we'll test the idea when we get back."

"You honestly are the strangest bunch of people I've ever met," said Mrs. Levstall as she looked around the room.

"You have no idea," Merlin agreed.

# THE BATTLE

GAHERIS WATCHED AS Sir Bors de Ganis stood at the base of the faux castle wall, looking up at the overweight king who was sitting on a throne that Gaheris considered tiny. The queen, known to Gaheris as "Leslie," sat on an even smaller chair.

"My lord," Bors called up in his powerful voice, "doeth not the righteousness of thine words summon the truth and goodness of all mankind?"

"Well said, Sir Purcivale," called the king, holding forth his wine. "Well said, indeed."

§ § §

Arthur glanced over at Merlin. "Did he say 'Sir Purcivale?'"

"It's a play, remember?"

"History truly does represent things the way it wants to, doesn't it?"

Merlin frowned. "Tell me about it."

§ § §

"The flowing of words are akin to the seeds of the divine wine when spoken from the lips of a king as worthy as you, sire," Kay said at full volume.

"You honor me, Sir Tristan," the king replied strongly.

§ § §

"Seriously?"

"Arthur," Guinevere said warningly, "keep yourself in check, dear."

"But, come on," said Arthur, motioning toward the sandy pit.

§ § §

"Are you ready for this?" said the man who was dressed in all black as he stepped up beside Gaheris, who was standing by the curtain.

"Aye, I'm ready," Gaheris replied icily. "I don't understand why we don't just kill you now, though. Makes no sense to me."

"You're a funny guy, pal," the man replied, slapping Gaheris on the back.

"And they call me uneducated."

The Evil Knight smiled. "Way to stay in character."

"It's about my time," said another, larger man whom Geheris had not seen before.

He was wearing a black robe that sported a hood. He also had a large, gnarled walking stick and, if

Gaheris wasn't imagining things, he appeared to be carrying a glass ball.

"Who are you supposed to be?"

"I'm Merlin, obviously," the fellow replied.

"You're way too tall to be Merlin," Gaheris scoffed. "And you're fat, too. Merlin is not fat."

"Screw you, pal."

From outside the room, the king exclaimed, "The realm shall ever remain in peace!"

The crowd roared at the proclamation.

"Well, that's my cue," said the fellow claiming to be Merlin as he walked out into the arena.

Fog began to fill the area and the lights dimmed. A hush came across the spectators as a deep, resonating grumble shook the walls.

"Merlin," the king said, "is that you?"

"It is I, my king," said a voice that was far too deep to belong to the fellow who had just walked out.

"Why are you here?"

"I bring dark tidings."

"What of?"

"The most treacherous kind, my sovereign." He lifted the crystal ball and waved his hand over it. "There is one who has betrayed your highness and is threatening to tear this land from your most worthy hands."

§ § §

"I kind of like the way he talks," noted Arthur.

"Ridiculous," said Merlin as he chewed his fingernails.

"Your turn to relax, Merl," said Galahad.

"Up yours, Gal."

§  §  §

"Who is this traitor you speak of?" demanded the king.

"The crystal ball does not reveal all of its secrets, sire, but I can say that his tidings are heinous indeed."

"What shall we do, Merlin?" the king asked. "Is there nothing that your magic can tell us?"

"Prepare yourselves for battle, ye of the most high, for tonight there comes darkness."

The fog returned along with the *oohs* and *ahhs* of the crowd.

"That was fun," said the man who was portraying Merlin. "Good luck, guys."

"Thanks, pal," the Evil Knight said a little too jovially.

"What shall we do, Sirs Purcivale and Tristan?" the king cried. "Have I not just promised the people peace and prosperity?"

"We shall prevail, my king," Bors answered in his operatic way.

"Our knights are the finest in the land, sire." Kay had dropped to one knee dramatically. "Let this Evil Knight bring his worst!"

The crowd roared.

"My turn," the Evil Knight said, grinning ear-to-ear. "Break a leg, buddy."

"I plan to break more than just that," Gaheris said, gripping the hilt of his sword firmly.

"Sure, okay."

The Evil Knight strode purposefully out into the open after pulling down the lid of his helm. Gaheris had to admit that the man looked impressive in his armor, but as a Knight of the Round Table, Gaheris had faced worse. This fellow, evil or not, was young and likely untested in the realm of battle. Still, Gaheris would be careful. He'd been fooled before.

The crowd booed and hissed at the Evil Knight as he arrived at the center of the sandy pit. This did well for Gaheris's faith in these people. At least they were not fooled, even if his fellow knights had been.

"What is this all about?" demanded the king.

"It's the Evil Knight, sire," exclaimed Bors. "I shall summon the guard immediately."

"Your knights are no match for me," said the Evil Knight in a wretched voice that made Gaheris's skin crawl.

"Stay your tongue, man," commanded Kay as he reached for his sword. "Your villainous ways will underline the reasons of your demise."

"The linings of your opprobrious soul shall cower in fear at the ferocity with which our knights wield their blades," yelled Bors.

§ § §

"Honestly," Arthur said while crossing his arms, "whoever wrote this has absolutely no idea how Purcivale and Tristan truly speak. And what in the Seven Hundred and Nineteen Hells does 'opprobrious' mean anyway?"

"Let it go, will you?" Merlin said.

Mrs. Levstall laughed heartily as Guinevere kicked Arthur's leg.

"Ouch!"

§ § §

"Knights of the realm," hollered Bors, "hear me. We have need of you now!"

That was the call that Gaheris had heard many times over his years. It made his heart race and his blood flow. It brought on a mix of excitement and terror that nothing else could ever provide. It was fear personified, and it made his tummy unstable.

"*Gah… Guh…*"

"What are you doing?" said an unfamiliar knight who was standing next to him.

"*Gah… Guh…*"

Another one said, "And what is that smell?" just as they were all pushed out into the pit.

The crowd was cheering at full volume now. It was all Gaheris could do to keep his calm. He was amazed that the horses had been able to hold it together with all of this ruckus. It also made him understand the demand that the crowd not bang their plates and mugs, for if they had started doing that at the moment he feared that he may have to do a second round of *Gahs* and *Guhs*.

"This man has challenged the throne and threatens to send our righteous kingdom into darkness," said Bors.

"His are the ways of the abyss," added Kay. "We

shall not bow to this foe. We shall prevail."

"Strong words," said the Evil Knight, "but I am no fool. I have yet another surprise for you." With that he turned toward the soldiers and commanded, "Knights, come to me!"

In all of his years at battle, Gaheris had never witnessed the likes of this. Maybe this was what *true* magic was like? He'd seen Merlin turn on flameless lamps and even do a few fascinating card tricks, but to flip a regiment of knights from loyalty? Never. One or two men, sure, but not this many.

"What is this devilry?" the king asked, looking genuinely shocked. "Have you men lost your loyalties?"

"They know when a battle is already lost," stated the Evil Knight.

Gaheris pulled forth his sword, knowing that his time was now. Whether this man was *his* king or not was irrelevant. He was commanded by the *true* king of England to defend this fellow, and defend him he shall. Tyranny would never stand as long as a man like Gaheris drew breath.

The crowd silenced as all eyes turned toward him. This startled Gaheris. Had he done something wrong?

Bors hissed, "Say your line, man!"

"Hmmm? Ah, yes. Sorry." He cleared his throat. "I am Sir Gary, and I shall prod you with my rusty dagger!"

The crowd broke into laughter.

"Ridiculous," said Bors, throwing his sword to the ground.

Kay followed suit and said, "Embarrassing."

The Evil Knight started to speak, but then stopped and looked in Gaheris's general direction as the crowd continued laughing.

Finally, he said, "Uh... I shall destroy you all with the true power. The power of darkness!" Then, he stopped and pointed at Sir Gaheris's trousers and added, "My goodness, man, have you soiled your britches?"

"I go where I go," Gaheris replied grimly.

The crowd laughed even harder than before.

"Honestly," said Bors, "I'm about to walk off the set."

"Keep your composure, Borsy."

The king leaned out and yelled, "Attack, my knights! The fate of the realm is in your hands."

# IT'S A BOY!

"IT'S A BOY," said Lance-A-Lot as he burst from Allison's room.

"Congratulations, laddy," said Arty with a wide smile.

"I'm not a lady."

"Nay, I meant… Forget it. Have ye picked a name for the wee lad?"

Lance-A-Lot looked away. "It's not my place."

"Since when?"

"I guess since we came to the future. Besides, sire, Allison already has a name planned."

"Ah," Arty said, understanding how quickly a man could fall under the watchful eye of a lady.

"Mitch Bowenkowski, Jr.," said Lance-A-Lot almost proudly.

"So it *ain't* after bein' yer kid?" Arty asked.

"Yes, he is."

"But ye said Junior, eh?"

"My *real* name is Mitch Bowenkowski, sire."

"No shet? I knew about the Mitch part, but not the

Bowenkowski bit."

The doctor walked out and shook Lance-A-Lot's hand and then walked off. A moment later, the nurse followed, explaining that he could go back in now.

"Do you want to see him?" Lance-A-Lot asked Arty.

"It'd be me honor."

The room was bigger than most spaces that Arty had in his castle back in Medieval Scotland, but it was just as bland as the rest of the hospital. Allison was in a bed that had her angled up slightly. There was a baby lying next to her in its own little bed.

"Hello, Arty," said Allison tiredly.

"Yer after rememberin' me, lass?"

"Of course."

Arty beamed at this. He wasn't considered the most memorable king, after all.

He knelt down and studied the wee baby for a moment.

"Fine lookin' lad." Then he coughed slightly and added, "Sorry about the boy's defect, though." He straightened up. "Things like this happen, though. Nothing to worry about."

"Defect?" Allison said, jerking her head toward the boy.

"What?" said Lance-A-Lot, stepping over.

Arty pointed. "He's got three legs."

"Oh," Lance-A-Lot said with relief. "That's not a leg, sire."

"Sure it is. Ye can see it right... Oh, wait, forgot he was *your* boy."

"Indeed," Allison said, smiling.

"Ah dinnae ken," Arthur said as he rubbed his beard, "but I think they'll be needin' an axe to circumcise the lad."

# IMPROVISE

MRS. LEVSTALL HAD walked over to the ledge of the window and was pointing down at Gaheris.

"What's Gary doing?"

"Fighting," answered Arthur proudly as he looked on.

For a large man, Gaheris was swift on his feet and deft with the blade. His strokes landed in huge arcs, knocking the other actors to the ground with each blow, as he hewed his way across the field toward the man wearing black.

The Evil Knight had dropped his sword and was steadily backing away from the monstrous madman pursuing him, reminding Arthur why Gaheris, faults and all, was worthy to be called a Knight of the Round Table.

"A little too well," said Guinevere, standing next to Arthur, "don't you think?"

"Hmmm?" Arthur said. "Oh, yes, maybe so."

"I don't think he gets that this is a play," said Merlin.

"I'm all about realism," said Mrs. Levstall, "but I fear that man is going to seriously injure someone."

"It's the one thing he thrives at," Galahad stated.

"That and soiling himself," said Arthur.

"Ah, yes, that too."

"Someone needs to stop him," Mrs. Levstall said in a huff.

Arthur stood up and walked to the door. "Don't worry, fair lady. I shall take care of it."

He stepped out of the door, bringing his kingly nature to bear. There were times when a king could be a queen, but right now was not one of those times. No, now was the time for Arthur to stand tall.

There was a tug on his coat as he exited the room, but his mind was focused and he just let his arms go so that the coat fell to the floor.

"Halt," he bellowed above the clamoring of swords and the roar of the crowd.

Everyone stopped and the room filled with silence. When a king spoke, people listened.

A bright light shone directly on Arthur, but he did nothing to shield his eyes. He had to look strong.

The crowd said, "ooh," and then "ahh," and then "huh?"

"Sir Gaheris," he yelled, "I command you to lower your sword this instant!"

Gaheris dropped his sword immediately as Arthur continued his walk toward the main field.

The man playing the part of the king yelled out, "Who are you?"

"I am the *true* king of Camelot," answered Arthur.

"More like queen," the king in the tower said with a

snort.

"What's that?" said Arthur. Then he looked down at himself and realized that he *should* have paid attention to his coat being ripped from his person. He stood now in full sight of the crowd and the actors while wearing his womanly garb. Well, there was no turning back now. "Ah, nothing but a ruse," he said, feeling inspired. "I am dressed as thus to fool the Evil Knight."

"It's working," said the Evil Knight.

Bors turned to Kay and said, "Did you know he could act?"

"Hadn't a clue."

"And again," said Arthur, "let it be known that *I* am the true king of Camelot."

"Are you challenging my throne?" said the actor in the tower.

"Stay your tongue, you wretched fool," Arthur said, really getting into things now. "The throne you sit upon belongs to me and I am the only one who is capable of taming the sword of Gaheris."

The crowd laughed.

"Well, that sounded wrong," said Bors.

The actor portraying the king looked over at Leslie. "Is this in the script?"

She shrugged. "First I've seen it."

"What the hell is going on?" said the Evil Knight.

"Quiet, you," Gaheris warned while taking a step toward the man.

"All right, all right," the Evil Knight replied, holding his hands up in surrender. "Chill out, will ya, pal?"

Arthur lifted his robe, careful to avoid letting everyone see his undergarments, and climbed the railing. He leaped down to the sand and walked purposefully to Sirs Bors, Kay, and Gaheris.

"You have fought bravely today, my knights, but the battle is done. This Evil Knight fellow will give up now, yes?"

"Damn straight," the man said without hesitation.

"Right," said Arthur and then looked down at his pants. "Did you soil your britches again?"

"I go where I go," said Gaheris, shrugging. "You know that, sire."

The crowd laughed again. It clearly didn't take much to entertain a group of people who were filled with ale.

"Gwen is not going to be pleased with you. Those were her—"

"Sire?" interrupted Bors, eying the crowd.

"Oh, yes, sorry." He cleared his throat. "Other knights, arrest the Evil Knight and have him executed!"

"Come with us, you treacherous fool," said Bors, taking the man by his arm.

"You shall suffer the wrath of Camelot," agreed Kay, grabbing the other arm.

"Honestly," Arthur said to Gaheris, "Purcivale and Tristan *do not* speak so eloquently."

"Tell me about it," said Gaheris.

The Evil Knight waited until he was out of Gaheris's reach before shouting, "I shall get you if it takes my dying breath, King Arthur!"

"We shall see," Arthur said, shaking his head.

"Now, Sir Gaheris, you may leave the battlefield knowing that you have served your king well."

"Again," noted the actor in the throne above them, "more like queen."

The crowd laughed and began to clap heartily, even to the point of a standing ovation. Arthur felt elated at this response, finally coming to understand why Bors and Kay enjoyed this acting thing as much as they did.

§ § §

"That's the loudest I've ever seen them cheer in all my years owning this place," said Mrs. Levstall proudly.

"Arthur does carry himself well, doesn't he?" Guinevere said proudly.

"The gown could go, but his instincts are incredible."

Merlin nodded. "He does have a way about him."

"No arguing that," said Galahad. "Makes one hell of a queen."

# BACKSTAGE

WILHELM CAME RUNNING into the room. He was all smiles as he stopped in front of the actors.

"That was simply amazing," he said.

Arthur waved his hand humbly. "It was nothing."

"You're not even on the cast list," said Wilhelm, "but you were incredible. You simply must join the show. We'll do rewrites to fit your part, of course."

"It *was* an inspired performance, sire," Bors said strongly.

"That it was," agreed Kay. "You have excellent instincts."

"Idiots," said Gaheris.

"Thanks for the bruises, asshole," one of the other actors said as he pushed past Gaheris.

Gaheris frowned. "What did he call me?"

"You busted my lip, shit-for-brains," said the Evil Knight before scurrying away, looking terrified.

"Did that evildoer just call me a—"

"For the love of the heavens, Gary," screamed Bors, "it's a play. P. L. A. Y."

"I don't think he can spell, Borsy."

"They were all just actors," finished Bors so loudly that Arthur nearly covered his ears.

"Get it through your fat head, man," Kay agreed.

"They had swords and they were threatening the king," Gaheris said defensively.

"But you can obviously see that it wasn't real, Sir... Erm, Gary," said Arthur, more gently.

Gaheris looked from man to man. "The blade I was given was purposefully dulled, sire."

"All the swords are blunted and dulled," Wilhelm explained, still smiling. "We don't want anyone to become seriously injured."

"Think of the crowds and the food, Gary."

"Yes, sire?"

"Would they be here if this were a true battle?"

Gaheris stepped back and crossed his arms. He looked to be weighing things, or he was possibly soiling his britches again... or maybe both. Finally, he lifted his head.

"So all of this was fake?"

"Of course it was, you needle-headed baboon," said Bors, obviously tired.

"Well, why didn't you say so?" Gaheris asked.

"We *did* say so," Kay said, holding Bors at bay. "We said so repeatedly. At one point, you even agreed that you had to pretend to be yourself and all of that."

"I see it now," Gaheris said with a slow nod. "I offer my apologies, sire, and I believe I should also ask forgiveness from the fellow pretending to be the Evil Knight." He paused and looked up at them all. "He *was* pretending, too, right?"

Bors groaned.

"Moron," said Kay.

"Look, fellas," said Wilhelm, "I don't know what you're all talking about, but Gary has a line of people out there who are begging for his autograph."

"Ah," Bors said, shaking the life back into himself, "we should probably get to the signings, Kay."

"Uh, sorry," Wilhelm said with his hands up, "they didn't ask for either of you."

"Say this isn't true," said Kay.

"You *must* be jesting," Bors added.

"Sorry. They *did* request the autograph of the Arthur wearing the gown, though."

"Dastardly," Kay said to Bors.

Bors just shook his head and whispered, "The fates are truly unfair."

# GOING HOME

TWO WEEKS HAD passed since the night of the show. Everyone had done a few encores, though they couldn't quite replicate the magic of Gaheris not knowing that it was a play. He tried, but it just wasn't the same.

"And so, sire," explained Lance-A-Lot as they stood in the office where the time machine was housed, "I've decided to stay and help raise the child."

Knight or not, Arthur knew that he had no right to come between a man and his family.

"Are you certain of this? Maybe Allison could return to our time?"

"She can't," answered Merlin. "It would mess up the timeline."

"What's a timeline, again?

"I'm still shaky on the details, Arthur."

"My life is here anyway," Allison said as she continued working on the thing called a "computer." Arthur was impressed at the speed with which her fingers moved on the little buttons. "I have no interest in living back in those days," she continued, "and I certainly don't want little Mitchy to have to deal with the medicine of your time."

"No arguing that," said Guinevere.

"Then you are resigning as head of the order?" Arthur asked Lance-A-Lot.

"That depends on you, sire," replied the knight. "I was thinking that we could adopt something I saw that today's military does."

"Oh?"

"We could start up a Knights Reserve."

Arthur furrowed his brow. "What's that?"

"Essentially, you go through all of the training and then you just have to report to do one weekend a month to keep your skills intact."

"Interesting idea, actually."

"So I would come back to Camelot every month for a weekend, train with the lads, and then return here."

"Ye all have strange thoughts," said Arty with a shake of his head.

Arthur ignored him. "And what if there's a war?"

"Then I report for duty as expected."

"I'll have to consider this," Arthur stated.

"I'd love to stay here as well, truth be told," Bors said as he glanced around the room, "but I don't think my lovely Penelope would abide."

"Nor my sweet Beatrice," agreed Kay.

Gaheris grunted. "I wanna go home."

"Aye," said Arty, "I'm with potty-pants."

"Watch yourself," warned Gaheris.

"What? It's just a nickname I've got for ye."

"I don't like that nickname."

"Why not?" Arty asked, seemingly serious. "Ye pee yer pants, don't ye?"

"I go where—"

"Yeah, yeah," Arty said, shushing the man. "We know ye do, and ye've got no qualms with that, have ye?"

"No," answered Gaheris with a sideways look.

"So what's wrong with bein' known by it, then? Own up to who ye are, man." Arty nodded strongly and gave Gaheris a serious look. "Calling ye potty-pants is not a slight, it's a testament to your wee-will! In a manner of speakin' anyhoo."

"Oh, that's different, then." Gaheris looked about thoughtfully. "Thanks for pointing that out, Gay Arty."

"What? I'm not gay!"

"Okay," said Merlin as Arty argued his case with Galahad, "so we're all set to return to Camelot?"

"I have everything input," answered Allison before slapping Galahad's hand. "Could you please not touch those dials?"

"Sorry," he said, rubbing his fingers. "What do they do?"

"They determine the year that you return home."

"Ah."

"You didn't spin them, did you?" she said, glancing at them.

"I don't think so."

"Good," she said. "We should be all set, then. Been having some software issues as of late, but I'm pretty sure all the kinks are out."

"What?" asked Arty.

"Nothing to worry about," she replied as she directed everyone back onto the platform. "Now, everyone get ready to go. Not you, Lance."

"Oh, right."

"I'll put thought to your request, Sir Lance-A-Lot," Arthur said as he shook the man's hand.

"Call me Mitch, sire. At least while we're here."

"Right," Arthur replied with a smile.

"See you soon, Merlin," said Allison, giving the man a hug. "And thanks to you all for caring enough about my well-being to come and seek me out."

"What are friends for?" said Merlin.

"Right." She moved back to the computer and pressed a button. "And three ... two... one…"

The world spun again in that cacophony of lights and noise until they struck the other side of the timeline.

§ § §

Ceallach stood at the edge of the campsite with Doonan. They were both looking at Camelot as the sun began its evening descent.

"It's been too long," Ceallach said.

"Aye," agreed Doonan.

"I'm after thinkin' somethin' nefarious has happened to our king."

"Aye."

"And I want *you* to sneak into town and find out what exactly that is."

"Aye," said Doonan and then choked. "I?"

"Why're you after sayin' yes twice for?"

"Nah, meant me."

"What?"

"Yer wantin' me to go in there alone?" said Doonan worriedly.

"Aye."

§ § §

The disorientation took a few minutes to wear off, which Arthur hoped explained the fact that they appeared to be standing in the middle of the desert. Also, he hoped that it explained why there were soldiers standing around with leather outfits and swords.

"Is it just me or are we not after bein' back in the tree?" asked Arty.

"Uh oh," said Merlin.

"Uh oh?" said Arthur. "Why uh oh?"

"Yeah, Merlin," said Galahad as he rose slowly to his feet, "why uh oh?"

"You didn't spin those dials, right Galahad?"

"Maybe a little."

"Argh!"

Guinevere brushed off her knees. "This is definitely *not* Camelot."

"And those are definitely not our soldiers," noted Bors.

"Agreed, Borsy," said Kay. "The outfits are all wrong."

"Merlin?" said Arthur sternly, "what's going on?

"If I'm correct in what I'm seeing," Merlin said, "at

least judging by the outfits and the swords, and pikes, and those helms, and the buildings in the background, and the fact that *Galahad the Goober* can't keep his hands off things when I've explicitly told him on numerous occasions that—"

"Merlin?" interrupted Arthur.

"Sorry." The wizard gulped. "I think we've been transported back to ancient Rome."

"Yer after jokin', yeah?" said Arty hopefully.

"Sorry, Arty," Merlin replied as the soldiers drew their swords and surrounded the group, "but I'm really not."

"Shet."

Suddenly everyone stopped as they heard a familiar sound from behind them. As one, they all spun around and glanced up at Gaheris. He had a look of sheer determination on his face as he stared past the group and at the Roman soldiers.

"Uh oh," said Bors.

"Indeed," said Kay.

"I'm after knowin' that look," Arty stated.

"Not now, man," hissed Galahad.

"What's he doing?" asked Guinevere.

"Yes, what?" said Merlin.

"Preparing for battle," Arthur replied with a sigh while Gaheris's right eye twitched slightly and his face reddened.

"Gah … Guh …"

# KNIGHTS IN THE PAST
## BOOK 3
## THE ADVENTURES OF QUEEN ARTHUR

# THE PAST IS PRESENT

ARTHUR, GUINEVERE, ARTY, Merlin, Galahad, Bors de Ganis, Kay, and Gaheris all stood in front of a couple of Roman guards who were wielding swords.

The landscape around them signaled that Merlin had been correct in his assumption regarding where they'd landed. This was definitely Ancient Rome. At least according to the descriptions Arthur had read when in school as a lad. There were large buildings in the distance with columns and grand architecture, the grounds were immaculately manicured, people wore little white outfits called "two goes" or something like that, and the guard uniforms were made of that dark leather that Arthur had always found to be fashionable.

While he was certain his knights could easily overpower the two men, especially since one was a bit old and somewhat portly and the other was so thin it was amazing he could hold the sword up at all, Arthur recognized this wasn't Camelot. That meant a skirmish with these two would likely result in bringing the full bore of the Roman guards down upon their heads.

But Sir Gaheris had already started making his trademarked "Gah" and "Guh" sounds that signaled he was readying for battle. And even if you missed the sounds, it wouldn't be long before you caught wind of his preparations.

"Calm yourself, Gaheris," Arthur commanded.

Gaheris grimaced. "But I'm already halfway prepared, sire. I can't easily stop now."

"Well, go over behind that boulder and do what you must."

Gaheris began to carefully pad off to the rock as Arthur shook his head at the man.

Guinevere sighed at Arthur in her way. This was a common thing with his beloved as Arthur seemed to always be doing the wrong thing in one fashion or another, at least in her eyes. But she was his radiant lady... even though she was currently wearing a green top that was cut like one belonging to a ranger and a pair of brown pantaloons that were unheard of for a lady to wear in royal circles. To be fair, though, Arthur had on a green gown and a fresh round of makeup that he'd put on when in Allison's restroom in the future.

"Where does he think he's going?" asked the thin guard, pointing his sword at the departing Gaheris.

"Oh, sorry," Arthur said, remembering their current predicament. "He's gone to relieve some pressure."

"You mean he's taking a—"

Arthur nodded. "Yes."

"I believe there's a fine for that," announced the portly man.

The two guards looked at each other for a moment and nodded.

To Arthur, this clearly indicated there wasn't likely a fine, which was a good thing since they didn't have any currency for this day and age. They hadn't had any in the future either, but they were able to get by using their ingenuity, along with Sir Lance-A-Lot's extra appendage, of course. Unfortunately, Lance wasn't here. Arthur cringed at the fact that he thought it unfortunate.

"What should we do, Arthur?" said Merlin, leaning in to whisper.

The little wizard—or was it "scientist" now?—had on his purple hat (the one covered in stars and moons), a matching jacket, a white shirt that represented some fellow who appeared to be dancing, and the words "Elvis Lives" stenciled on it, and a pair of pants he referred to as "jeans."

"You're the one who got us into this mess, Merlin," Arthur whispered back.

"Right, but you're the kingly sort." Merlin paused and glanced over Arthur in his current garb. "Well, queenly, I guess, but—"

"Oh, so *now* I'm a king?" Arthur said, his voice on the rise. "All those years I've attempted to treat you like one of my subjects and you did nothing but tell me how you didn't go in for that hoopla. But we face a bit of trouble and suddenly having royalty around is comforting, eh?"

"No, you dullard," replied Merlin, "it's because

these two are guards from a different age. And while they will undoubtedly *not* know the name of Merlin, they should well see that flash of royalty that you carry about as if born with it!"

"Oh, right. Sorry." Arthur looked at his feet for a moment before realizing the full breadth of what Merlin had said. "Hey, wait, I *was* born with it."

"No, you achieved it upon finding *Excalibur*."

"Achieved," Arthur conceded, "but by birth it was my destiny."

Merlin waved his hand. "Semantics."

"Sorry to interrupt this engrossing dialog," said the thin guard, "but who exactly are you people?"

Arthur cleared his throat and stood up tall, puffing his chest out.

"I am King Arthur of Camelot."

The chubby guard leaned over. "What did he say?"

"I think he said he's the king of a lot of camels."

"No," said Arthur, furrowing his brow. "I said the King of Camelot."

"Is that where all the camels come from?" asked the heavy one.

"I..." Arthur began, but then blinked a few times. "What?"

Arty, the king of Scotland, who was wearing a leopard-skin outfit that was barely covered by the jacket he'd had on, pushed through and said, "Let me try, yeah?" He then turned to the guards. "Listen, ye couple of daft peons. I dinnae know what it is ye do in yer army of sorts, but we're after bein' a couple of kings, yeah?"

"You two are a couple, then?" asked the portly

guard.

"What?"

"They are both wearing women's clothes," noted the thin one. Then he glanced back quickly. "Not that I'm judging you."

"Oh, no," agreed the portly one vehemently. "Definitely no judging going on over here. No sirree."

"Ah, that," Arty said as his eyes darted around. "Uh... We were at a costume party is all."

"Sure, sure," the thin guard said with a quick nod.

The fat one squinted. "Anyway, were you summoned by the emperor or something?"

"I dinnae think so," answered Arty.

"Yes!" Merlin yelped. "Yes, we were summoned by the emperor. Exactly that."

The portly guard reacted suspiciously to Merlin's outburst. He lowered his sword slightly, tapping a nearby rock with it. He gave a sideways glance to his partner before setting his eyes back on Merlin.

"What's his name, then?"

"Sorry?"

"The Emperor of Rome," replied the fat one. "What's his name?"

"Uh... Well, it's been a while since we got the invitation." Merlin swallowed and began chewing his lip. "Let's see..." He snapped his fingers. "Ah yes, Bulbus Headus."

"No."

"Flatulate?" offered Merlin.

"That's his brother," replied the fat one.

"*Was* his brother," corrected the thin one.

"Oh yes, true."

"Isn't it close enough that we know his brother's name?" asked Merlin.

The fat one shook his head. "Sure isn't."

"Pardon me," said Galahad, raising his hand. He wore his standard garb, which consisted of plate armor, chainmail, and a crimson tabard that housed the drawing of a lion. It was the exact same garb worn by all of the knights in their party. "What year is it?"

"You don't know what year it is?" said the thin one confusedly.

"We're from a different land than you," explained Galahad. "Our calendars aren't likely the same."

"Oh, that makes sense, I guess. Fine, it's what we call 72AD." The thin one looked up. "No idea what the AD stands for, though. Sorry."

Galahad nodded firmly and declared, "Vespasian is your emperor."

"Nope."

"No?" Galahad replied, shocked. "But I was just reading a periodical on Roman history not two weeks ago—"

"You were?" interrupted Arthur.

"Yes, sire. I thought certain—"

"Vitellius?" announced Sir Gaheris, having come back from his mission on the other side of the boulder.

"Nope."

"Titus?" said Gaheris, scratching his head.

"Not even close."

"Too early for him yet, Sir Gaheris," stated Galahad, "but I'm impressed you know any of these names."

"My father was a history teacher."

Galahad gawked at that. "And he taught you?"

"I learned what I learned."

The thin guard waved his sword around menacingly. "What are you two going on about?"

"Yeah," agreed the portly one. "I'm about to stick my sword in one of you."

"Always sounds funny when you say that, Buttus Facius," the thin guard said with a giggle.

"Grow up, Thumpus Rumpus," retaliated Buttus Facius.

"Your names are Thumpus Rumpus and Buttus Facius?" said Bors de Ganis more loudly than he probably should have.

"Yeah, so?" said Thumpus.

"What of it?" agreed Buttus.

"Nothing," Bors replied, obviously refocusing on the swords in front of him. "Just clarifying, is all."

Just as Arthur was about to speak up again, Merlin reached over and grabbed his arm. The old man took a step forward until the points of the swords were touching his chest. Arthur was no wizard—or scientist, as the case may be—but he knew that pointy blades were quite adept at piercing flesh.

"You know," said Merlin as he clasped his hands behind his back studiously, "I'm starting to wonder why you're asking us for your emperor's name."

"For proof that you were invited," said Buttus.

"Could be," Merlin allowed, "or maybe it has something to do with the fact that you don't know his name yourselves and you're hoping we'll jog your memories."

"It's a conspiracy," Galahad said, obviously catching on to the ruse.

"That's not true," said Thumpus.

"Yeah, we know his name," agreed Buttus.

Merlin scoffed. "Sure you do."

"We do!"

"Most assuredly," Buttus again backed up his partner.

"Uh-huh." By now, Merlin was looking at his fingernails.

"Your lack of faith in our word is trying on my nerves," Thumpus said, his eye twitching.

Buttus grew dark. "And mine as well."

Merlin spun away dramatically, allowing his purple robe to float upward. He took two steps before spinning back and pointing at the guard known as Thumpus Rumpus.

"Prove it, then," demanded Merlin. "What's his name?"

"It's Emperor Flaccidus!"

"Technically," amended Buttus, "it used to be Emperor Longus Dongus, but he's gotten a bit older."

Thumpus calmed slightly. "True. And that bet he lost..." He trailed off and then set his stare back on Merlin. "So, there you go, we have proved to you that we do indeed know our emperor's name. What have you to say to that?"

"My apologies," Merlin answered with a bow. On his way back up he added, "Arthur?"

Without missing a beat, Arthur said, "We'd like to speak with Emperor Flaccidus immediately!"

"So you *do* know his name," Thumpus Rumpus said with a satisfied grin.

"All right, then," Buttus Facius said, replacing his sword in its scabbard, "follow us."

# JUPITER

THE INSIDE OF the spaceship looked precisely like you'd expect the inside of a spaceship to look. It was covered in metallic tones, clean lines, video panels, and stations littered with flashing lights, blue buttons, and black knobs. What you wouldn't have expected was the nice living area with a large couch, shag carpeting, and a wide-screen television.

Jupiter and his current wife, Leto, were seated on said couch, watching their favorite show, *CSI: Alpha Centauri*.

Jupiter was a large man with stark gray hair that was styled in such a way to make him appear to always be running. His skin was tanned, which made little sense being that he was rarely ever out in direct sunlight, and his muscles bulged nearly as much as his belly. He *had* been getting old, after all.

Leto was far younger than Jupiter and she was a real beauty. Long, dark hair, emerald-green eyes, perky coconuts, and her skin was flawless. She looked as gorgeous now as she had the day Jupiter met her on their first date from a match on an intergalactic dating site.

The TV show was just about to the point where the big chase was going to happen. Jupiter loved this part of the show. It made his heart race. Plus, he always liked to guess who the culprit was, and so far he was right nearly eighty percent of the time.

"Yo, Dad," Apollo called from one of the terminals in his slightly feminine voice, "looks like something is going on here."

It happened every time.

"Your mother and I are watching a movie, Apollo."

"But—"

"There's fifteen minutes left, Apollo," Jupiter said more tightly.

"Yes, but—"

"Damn it," Jupiter yelled, pausing the video and throwing the remote across the room. "Why do you always do this, boy? You've never got anything to say until I'm right in the middle of something. If I'm watching TV, you interrupt me right before the best part; if I'm on the phone with one of my cousins, you're constantly nagging me to the point where I have to hang up; and let's not even get into what you do during the Olympics!"

"Sorry, Dad," Apollo replied sheepishly. "Just thought you'd want to know about this. It's, well, unexpected."

Apollo glared at the boy, unable to keep his eye from twitching. One look at Apollo told you that he came from the loins of Jupiter. Same hair, though darker; same build, though without the belly; same eyes, though without the crow's feet; and same ability to allure the ladies, though Apollo preferred the gents.

"Calm yourself, Zeus," Leto said, patting her husband's arm lovingly.

"You know you shouldn't use that name, Leto." Jupiter pushed off the couch and went to retrieve the remote, hoping he hadn't broken it again. "Seriously, how many times do I have to ask you to call me Jupiter?"

"What difference does it make?"

"We're all about the Romans right now, so we have to stick with the program. When we refocus on the Greeks, you can go back to calling me Zeus."

Sure enough, the remote was broken. That was the third one this month. Fortunately he kept a supply of them in the drawer under the television.

"It's all such a pain," complained Leto. "We're the gods, right? Why should we have to change our names to suit them?"

Jupiter dug out a new controller and started putting batteries into it.

"It's easier for us to gain acceptance that way. Just roll with it, okay?"

"If you say so."

"Okay, son," Jupiter said, after snapping the back on the remote, "what's so damned important this time?"

"Forget it," replied Apollo while crossing his arms.

"Oh no, I'm not forgetting it." Jupiter took to wagging his finger. "You interrupted me with something spaceship-shattering in your estimation, so what is it?"

Apollo rolled his eyes and uncrossed his arms. "Fine. It looks like King Arthur from England, King Arthur from Scotland, Guinevere, Merlin, and a number of the Knights of the Round Table have just appeared near one of the walls by Emperor Flaccidus's royal palace."

"What?" said Jupiter, dropping the remote.

Athena, who was sitting in a nearby chair reading a Yogsdon and Lung novel, sat up and said, "Is Lance-A-Lot with them?"

"No," Apollo replied sadly.

Athena frowned and stuck her head back into her reading.

Jupiter had always considered Athena to be his most beautiful daughter. Dark hair, emerald eyes, and that same tanned tone that Jupiter was ingrained with. But she had a sinister streak that made up for that beauty. Of course, most of the gods did.

"Why do you ask that?" said Jupiter and he reached in for another remote.

"No reason," answered Athena.

"No reason, indeed," Leto said with a knowing smirk.

"Sounds to me like there's a reason." Jupiter quickly moved to put the remote in a safe place. "What are you two ladies talking about?"

"Oh, it's nothing, dear," Leto said. "She's obviously heard tales from that *other* daughter of yours."

"Are you referring to Aphrodite again?" said Jupiter with a raised eyebrow. "Whenever you say *other daughter* like that you're always talking about her."

"If we're keeping with the Greek naming

convention, yes."

"If I've told you once, I've told you a million times: She's not mine!"

Leto sniffed. "So you say."

"Okay, here we go again," said Jupiter, who was now pacing in front of the television. "When Cronus castrated Uranus and dumped the parts in the sea, Venus—or Aphrodite, in this case—arose from the sea foam on a giant scallop and walked to the shore in Cyprus."

"Riiiiiight," said Leto with a load of sarcasm lacing her voice, "and, if I recall correctly, Athena here came from your forehead."

"Hey," said Athena, "don't drag me into this."

"That's exactly what happened with Athena," said Jupiter, feeling his ire rising. "I told you already that it all started when I was going to bang Metis, but I felt bad about—"

"Getting caught," Leto interrupted.

Jupiter paused. "What? No! I felt that it was *wrong*. But it was kind of late by then and so I had to swallow her."

"Shouldn't that have been the other way around?" said Apollo.

Athena thought to throw her book at him, but deemed it far too valuable. Instead, she merely said, "Gross."

"Honestly, Zeus," Leto said, standing up and heading for the kitchen.

"It's Jupiter," Jupiter corrected, hot on her heels. "Anyway, as I've told you many times, it turned out that Metis was already preggers."

"And how do you suppose that happened?" Leto said over her shoulder.

"Uh..." Jupiter cursed to himself, but pressed on. "Well, anyway, I swallowed her up, you know? Then my stomach starts to hurt and I got the meanest headache you can imagine. Boy, let me tell you, that was one nasty motherf—"

"Forget about it, Zeus," Leto said, pushing past him and back to the main room while carrying a glass of wine.

"Again, it's Jupiter." He waited for her to sit back down. "Anyway, the next thing I know, she just popped out of my forehead. It was pretty surreal."

Leto took a sip of the wine and swirled the remainder in the glass. "I'm never going to buy these silly stories, Jupiter."

"It's Jupiter!" He blinked a couple of times. "Oh, you said that. Sorry. Anyway, it's true, I tell you. It's all true."

"Sure it is, dear."

"It is, and if you think normal childbirth is painful, try having a full-grown adult—who is wielding an axe, by the way—leap out of your forehead."

Leto took another sip after saying, "Ridiculous."

"It truly was," Jupiter replied, accepting her meaning as *he'd* preferred.

Everything got quiet for a few moments. This was a rarity on the ship, and it usually followed one of these little spats. Jupiter was well aware that he was going to be in the proverbial doghouse yet again, which would have been avoided if only he'd be allowed to watch one of his damned shows in peace.

"What's going on?" said Pluto as he walked into the room.

Jupiter held back a groan. It was bad enough having to live on this tiny ship with Athena and Apollo, but at least they were his children... sort of. Pluto, however, was his brother. In fact, if the two men stood side by side, you'd have a hell of a time telling them apart, aside from the fact that Pluto kept his hair longer and tinted brown. Jupiter grunted. It wasn't that Pluto was a bad guy or anything, at least assuming you were a fellow god, but he had become a bit of a mooch over the last year. The deal was that he was going to stay on the ship for a couple of weeks while he searched for a ship of his own, but weeks turned into months, and now he was just another irritant who consumed a lot of food, fought for the remote, and played loud music in the middle of the normal sleep cycle.

"I was just explaining how Aphrodite is *not* my daughter," answered Jupiter.

"Ah, the old 'giant clam' story, eh?" Pluto said, opening a beer.

"Scallop," corrected Jupiter.

"What?"

"It was a giant scallop, not a clam."

Pluto looked at him. "What's the difference?"

"Mostly how they swim," Jupiter answered with a shrug.

"Oh yeah, that's right." He laughed to himself. "That story is a classic. Almost as good as the one about Athena here coming from your brain."

"It was my forehead, and—"

"Don't go there, Pluto," warned Leto. "It's not worth the effort."

"I'll take your word for it," said Pluto as he lumbered over toward Apollo's station. "Well, what's on the video screen that's so interesting?"

"It looks like—" started Apollo.

"King Arthur and some of his cohorts have arrived in Rome," answered Jupiter, interrupting his son.

"No shit?" said Pluto. "How did they go back in time?"

"Not a clue," said Jupiter, "but I think I shall send Apollo and Athena to go and find out. "

"Really?" Apollo said excitedly.

"I see no other way to peacefully watch the end of this show."

"Sweet."

Athena bolted up and ran down the hall, saying, "I'll go get dressed!"

# JUST NOT THE SAME

EMPEROR FLACCIDUS WAS lying on the comfortable lounge bench with his head propped upon the lap of his wife, Queen Slutius. She was feeding him grapes as he gazed up at her olive skin, large brown eyes, and fluffy lips. Seeing her beauty, though, only depressed him further.

"You seem unhappy again, my love," she said in a voice that the birds of the Tiber river swooned over. "Is it something you'd like to discuss?"

"Same problem as ever, I'm afraid," he said, glancing away as another grape touched his lips.

"Ah."

He rolled up to a seated position, looking at his age-weathered hands. He knew he wasn't the man he once was, but he had assumed there were at least another five or ten years of vigor remaining in his blood.

"We never have relations anymore," he said irritably.

"I do."

Flaccidus glanced at her sharply. "What?"

"Uh..." she said with a cough. "*Sure* we do."

"Oh, right." Flaccidus stood and walked to one of the windows. "Well, not as often as we once did. We do it once a month, if I'm lucky."

"That's by your choice, my love."

"I know, I know. I'm not blaming you. It's just—"

"Dear," Slutius said, rising to walk over to his side, "this all happened when you hit the age of fifty and lost that bet with your brother at your birthday party."

"Don't remind me," he groaned.

The queen scratched the wall next to them. "I still can't believe you had him killed."

"I had no choice."

"You could have refused to follow through on the bet," she argued gently.

"And be seen as a man who doesn't uphold his obligations?" He crossed his arms at that. "Never!"

"Then why kill him?"

"Because *he* could have forgiven me the debt instead of... well... what he did."

"But to die over a name change?" Slutius chastised. "That seems rather petty, even for an emperor."

Flaccidus sniffed and moved his hands to his hips. Nobody understood the plight of a man except for another man. Just as women always stated—rightfully—that childbirth is something a man could never comprehend, the same went for the challenges and competition of manhood.

"Do you have any idea how difficult it's been to go from a manly name like Longus Dongus to a wimpy name like Flaccidus?" he said desperately.

"No, but I do know that it's been ever since then that we've stopped having decent relations."

"Precisely my point," spat Flaccidus. "Brother or not, the man needed to die for doing that to me."

"But he was so good in the sack," she moaned as Flaccidus turned away.

He paused. "What was that?"

"Uh... You didn't have to break his back," Slutius replied hurriedly. "Horrible way to go."

"I poisoned him," said Flaccidus with a frown.

"Oh, that's right. Sorry."

Just as the emperor was about to question his wife further on the subject, there came a knock on the door. It was a rarity to be left alone for very long when running an empire.

"Enter," he called out, returning to the bench and seating himself.

Two of his guards walked in and knelt reverently before him. They were his most trusted men.

Hemorrhoidoclese stood a full head over the emperor and was built like a tank. Were he not so valued as a guard, Flaccidus would have loved to see him fight in the open battles. Next to him stood Suppositorius. Where he wasn't quite the physical specimen that Hemorrhoidoclese was, he was quick with the blade and firm of mind. When these two were around, Flaccidus felt safer... assuming there were no gods in the vicinity, of course.

"Yes?"

"Sorry to interrupt, my lord," rumbled Hemorrhoidoclese, "but some emissaries from a distant land claim to have been invited to visit you."

Flaccidus thought over his schedule. As far as he remembered, there were no planned visitations for at least another week.

"Who are they?" he asked.

"There are a couple of queens," began Suppositorius, "a king—"

"It's the other way around, Suppositorius," corrected Hemorrhoidoclese.

"Huh?"

"There are two kings, a queen, and a bunch of soldiers."

"Oh, yeah, that's right. Thanks, Hemorrhoidoclese."

"You bet."

Suppositorius turned back to Flaccidus, "Also, sire, there's an old guy with a pointy hat and strange clothing."

"Well, they're all wearing weird clothes," noted Hemorrhoidoclese.

"Especially the 'kings,'" said Suppositorius with a grin.

Hemorrhoidoclese smiled. "Haha... Yeah."

Flaccidus was not one who enjoyed being left in the dark. He cleared his throat expectantly.

"Sorry, sire," said Suppositorius, coming back to attention.

"Why did you use air quotes when describing the kings?" asked Flaccidus after a moment.

"You see, sire," said Hemorrhoidoclese, "it's that they're kind of dressed like, well—"

"Women," finished Suppositorius.

Hemorrhoidoclese pointed at his fellow guard and

said, "Right."

"Oh?" said Flaccidus, finding that curious. "Well, send them in."

# YER GOIN'

FAR OUTSIDE THE walls of Camelot, Ceallach stood at the edge of the camp where King Arthur of Scotland left him and the rest of the men a number of days before. It had been too long since his king had entered the English walls and Ceallach was finding himself on edge.

To that end, he had picked one of the men and told him to go into town and see what he could learn about their king's whereabouts.

"Are ye sure yer not wantin' to go yerself?" said a worried-looking soldier by the name of Doonan.

The two men stood side by side, staring out at Camelot. It looked majestic as the morning sun shone upon its walls. No better than their own castle back home, of course, but Ceallach had to admit that the banners hanging down the sides of the parapets were a nice touch.

He glanced at Doonan. The man had reddish hair and a scraggly beard that would mark almost all the men at camp, but Doonan was one of the smallest in the entire Scottish Army. Ceallach knew better than to judge the fighting prowess of a person by size alone. He'd lost many a scuffle while clinging to that prejudice, in fact. But when it came to Doonan, one couldn't help but think the man was better suited to life outside the military.

Ceallach sighed and looked around at the others in camp. Any one of them would be better suited for the task at hand, but Doonan was what you might call "expendable."

"Ye'll be fine," answered Ceallach. "What can they do?"

Doonan gulped. "String me up by me nethers."

"Aye, true. Not likely, though. Our king says he's become friends with the English."

"Then maybe they're just after bein' in a party?" Doonan said hopefully. "Wouldn't want to bother him in that case, yeah?"

"Nay," Ceallach replied, staring off at Camelot. "The king said he'd be back. He's not after bein' back."

"Then maybe they've strung *him* up by *his* nethers," Doonan whispered.

"Hope not, but that's what you'll need to go find out."

"Calle, it's just—"

"Doonan," Ceallach said, turning on the smaller man and giving him a look that spelled doom, "yer goin' and I dinnae wanna here another word on it."

"All right, all right," Doonan said, backing away. "No point in gettin' yer kilt in a bunch." Then, as if trying to find solid footing again, he sternly said, "Just know this, Ceallach: I'm not layin' down me sword for no man."

"Ah, that reminds me," Ceallach said, pointing at Doonan's weapon, "leave yer sword behind."

Doonan's eyebrows jumped. "Didn't ye just hear what I said?"

"Ye still have yer axe," said Ceallach. "Now get on with ye!"

# THE AUDIENCE

ARTHUR WAS IMPRESSED with the palace. The grounds were immaculately kept, the buildings were enormous and beautifully designed, especially all the columns and craftsmanship, and the use of marble was inspired. There were sculptures of people he couldn't have known, but they were made with such care he assumed they were either gods or past rulers.

Everyone else in his party seemed to be just as taken aback by the wonders they were seeing. Even Sir Gaheris appeared awed by the sights.

"Okay," Arthur said, bringing their attention back to the problem at hand, "when we go in there, let me do the talking."

"Why you?" asked Arty.

"Because I'm the king, that's why."

Arty puffed out his chest. "So am I."

"Yes, I know," conceded Arthur, "but none of your men are here, which means that I'm in a better position to claim kingship than you are."

"What the shet kind of logic is that? A king is a

king no matter how many subjects he's after havin'!"

Arthur took a deep breath. "Let me put it this way: Who remains king when one kingdom falls to another kingdom?"

"The one who wins, ye daft Englishman!"

"And how many soldiers do you currently have to stand against mine?"

"Oh." Arty pursed his lips and looked at his feet. "Well, when ye put it that way."

"Harsh," noted Merlin.

The doors opened and a large guard waved them in.

"You may enter."

As if the outer area wasn't amazing enough, Arthur's jaw nearly dropped at the designs contained in this room. He knew it was the room of their emperor, but it was far superior to what Arthur had in his own day. He made a mental note to have a word or two with his designers if they ever got back safely.

In front of them sat an older man who was wearing a white outfit and a thin gold crown. He didn't exactly look kingly, especially with his thinning hair, rounded stomach, and hairy arms, but seeing that the guards were giving him proper respect, Arthur knew the man was indeed their ruler.

"Who is in charge here?" the emperor said.

Merlin spoke up first. "I thought you were."

"Merlin," hissed Arthur.

"Merlin is in charge?" the emperor said.

"No," replied the wizard, "*you* are in charge. It's your kingdom, right?"

Flaccidus stuck his tongue in his teeth and then

made a popping sound with his lips. He cracked his neck from side to side as if trying to relax himself.

"I repeat," he said with a glare. "Who is in charge here?"

"Maybe he wants to play that 'Guess his name' game?" suggested Galahad.

"Ah, yes," agreed Merlin. "Good thinking, Galahad." The wizard cleared his throat and winked at the emperor, saying in a grandiose voice, "Emperor Flaccid Dong is in charge."

"Merlin, quiet," Arthur hissed again.

"It's not Emperor Flaccid Dong, you geriatric peasant," the emperor said hotly. "It's Emperor Flaccidus."

"Oh, that's right," Merlin said, deflated. "My apologies."

"Now, what I want to know is who in *your* group is in charge of *your* group?"

Arthur stepped forward. "That would be me. I am Arthur, King of Camelot."

"You're the king of the camels?" said Flaccidus while scrunching up his face.

"No, I'm the king of Camelot."

"Right, I heard you the first time." Flaccidus tilted his head to the side. "So there are a lot of camels in your kingdom, yes?"

"No, it's just the name of the place." Arthur was beginning to wonder how simple these people truly were. "There are no camels. Lots of horses, but no camels."

"Then why not call it Horsealot?" asked the emperor.

"It has nothing to do with the animals," Arthur said, fighting to keep his cool.

"Obviously a stupid kingdom," Flaccidus said flippantly.

Arthur felt the slap of that insult. "Excuse me?"

"Good thing there weren't a lot of ducks in their kingdom," joked the large guard.

"Well played, Guard Hemorrhoidoclese," said Flaccidus with a chuckle.

"What about those small, stubborn horses?" the smaller guard asked his companion.

Hemorrhoidoclese looked about thoughtfully and then snapped his fingers. "You mean the ass, Suppositorius?"

"Haha!" cried Flaccidus. "Assalot!"

"Ah! Good one." Hemorrhoidoclese laughed and then said, "How about the rooster... You know, cock?"

"One of my favorites," said Slutius from behind the emperor.

"Haha..." Flaccidus started and then quickly looked at the queen. "What?"

"Hmmm?" she replied innocently. "Just love how they wake us up in the morning."

"There's the dik-dik," noted Suppositorius.

"Never heard of it," said the larger guard.

"It's a form of antelope."

"Dik-dikalot," Flaccidus said while laughing almost uncontrollably.

"Wouldn't mind visiting there," said Slutius with a dreamy sigh.

Flaccidus's laughter ceased instantly as he frowned

at Slutius. She glanced away, looking uncomfortable.

"Enough of this," Flaccidus stated while returning his study to Arthur. "So you're a king, eh?"

"Yes."

"More of a queen—" started Suppositorius.

"Silence," Flaccidus said, quieting his guard. Then the emperor said over his shoulder, "Do kings have more power than emperors?"

"I don't believe so," replied Slutius. "Certainly not in your palace, anyway."

Flaccidus nodded at this. "So King Arthur, is it?"

"It is," Arthur replied proudly.

The emperor plucked a grape from the vine that was in the bowl next to him and popped it into his mouth. He chewed for a few moments as if thinking about what to say next.

"I've been told that I invited you to my palace."

"Right, about that—"

"Yet I don't recall inviting anyone to my palace by the name of Arthur."

"Yes, well, you see—"

"And yet you claim that I did."

"That's because—"

Flaccidus slammed his hands on the bench. "Explain yourself, man!"

"I've been trying to," Arthur replied angrily.

"No," countered Flaccidus, "you've been talking over me, and that's rude. When someone is speaking you should remain silent, dutifully listening along the way, and then speak when it is your turn."

Arthur softened. "My apologies. You are absolutely correct. In fact, I have actually had this very conversation with a couple of my own men a number of times."

"Accepted," Flaccidus said with a slow blink. "Now, explain why you lied to my guards."

"Because there was no other way to gain an audience with you," explained Arthur.

Flaccidus stuck another grape in his mouth. "And why do you require an audience?"

"Because we've traveled back in ti—"

"We're lost," Merlin interrupted, smacking Arthur on the arm.

"Ouch. What did you strike me for?" Arthur rubbed his bicep. "That hurt, you know?"

Merlin whispered, "You can't tell him we came back in time, you imbecile."

"Oh, right. Sorry."

Flaccidus stood up and approached them, studying their outfits. Arthur wasn't used to being placed under scrutiny as such, but he remained stoic, as did the others.

"Why are you all dressed so curiously?" Flaccidus asked, staring at the pointy hat on Merlin's head.

"Costume party," Guinevere said quickly. "We went to a costume party."

Flaccidus spun back to Slutius. "There was a costume party?"

"First I've heard of it," she answered.

"Guard Suppositorius, did you hear of a costume party?"

"No, my emperor."

"Nor did I, my liege," Hemorrhoidoclese answered before being asked.

"I see." He spun back to Guinevere. "Who threw this party?"

"You wouldn't know her."

"Try me."

"Okay," she said and then paused for a moment. "Uh, it was... Uh... Allison Smith. Yes, that's it. Allison Smith threw the party."

"Strange name," said Flaccidus as he walked away from them while rubbing his chin thoughtfully.

"What are you doing?" whispered Merlin as he leaned in front of Arthur to speak to Guinevere.

"Hopefully getting us out of trouble," Guinevere replied.

"But you shouldn't use her name."

"How can it hurt?"

Merlin opened his mouth a couple of times before saying, "Valid point."

"Guards," Flaccidus commanded a moment later, "I want this Allison Smith found and brought to me immediately."

"Of course, sire," said Hemorrhoidoclese, snapping his fingers at a few other soldiers who ran out of the room as if on a mission.

"Now, Arthur," Flaccidus said, "who are all these people with you?"

"This is my queen, Guinevere," Arthur replied. "That is Merlin, our uh... Court Jester."

"What?" said Merlin.

"This is King Arthur from Scotland."

"Wait," Flaccidus said, holding up a hand. "There are two kings with the same name?"

"I was as surprised as you," Arthur replied.

Flaccidus shrugged. "Okay, go on."

"The rest of these men are my knights. This is Sirs Kay, Bors De Ganis, Galahad, and Gaheris."

Flaccidus turned his gaze on the knights. To their credit, they remained firmly at attention while being inspected. This was most surprising of Gaheris, but Arthur assumed he was more relaxed since that visit to the boulder.

"You called these men 'nights.' Why is that? Do they only run about in the dark? Maybe they're on different shifts? Do you also have a group you call Dayts?" He looked outside. "No, that can't be it... It's still light out there."

"It's because..." Arthur trailed off. "Actually, I don't know. They're essentially elite soldiers, but I don't know where the term originated. Merlin?"

"Not a clue."

"Galahad?"

"I've never thought to look it up, to be honest, sire."

"Gaheris?"

"What?" said the gruff knight.

"You said your father was a history teacher, right?" asked Arthur.

"Yes, my lord."

"Well, do you have any idea where the term 'knight' originated?"

Gaheris looked uncomfortable, but said, "Depends on who you ask. My old dad never made clear, but he said that the accepted etymology comes from the Old English 'cniht.' That means 'boy' or 'servant.' But he'd also claimed there were other scholars who attributed it to the cognate of the Germanic 'knecht,' which is 'servant' or 'bondsman.'"

Bors gave Kay a surprised stare and said, "Is this honestly the same man who soils himself in public?"

"It's truly baffling," replied Kay in awe.

"Enough," demanded Flaccidus. Then he walked back to Arthur. "So these men are your boy-servants, then?"

"Excuse me?" said Bors.

"That's insulting," chimed Kay.

"Rather makes sense with that outfit you're wearing, Arthur," Flaccidus continued, clearly ignoring the knights.

"What?" Arthur said, looking down at himself. "No, it's—"

"A costume party. Yes, I'm aware." Flaccidus walked back to his bench and sat back down. "Now, King Arthur, tell me: Where precisely is your kingdom?"

"You may not want to say—" started Merlin.

"Britain," Arthur answered proudly.

"Oh boy."

"Is that so?" Flaccidus said with a twinkle in his eye.

"It is," replied Arthur. "Is that of particular interest?"

"Oh, indeed," answered the emperor.

"Why?"

"We've just always had problems with your country. But if you are the actual king, than I'd go as far as to say our problems are solved."

Arthur squinted. "Sorry, but how so?"

"Simple, you fool," Flaccidus said with a laugh. "If I execute you, your beloved Britain will no longer have a king!"

"I shall not stand for this," claimed Bors in a strong voice.

"Sit, then," suggested Flaccidus.

That seemed to confuse Bors. "Hmmm?"

"We'll block your every attempt, to protect our king," announced Kay, stepping forward strongly.

Flaccidus snapped up another grape casually and began to chew it.

"I can have one hundred guards brandishing swords with the snap of my fingers," he stated flatly.

"Me too," Slutius said.

Flaccidus reeled around. "What's that?"

"Uh..." Slutius said, clearly catching herself, "I was just saying that it's true you could have guards in here quickly."

"Right," Flaccidus said at length.

And that's when Arthur heard the telltale sound that marked Sir Gaheris's plan to begin battling.

"Gah, guh."

Apparently his trip to the boulder hadn't been sufficient enough.

"What's that man doing?" Flaccidus said, pointing. Then he sniffed the air with a cringe. "And what is that infernal smell?"

Arthur dropped his shoulders. "You don't want to know."

"Is he soiling himself?"

"Yes."

"That's disgusting."

"Yes."

"Take them to the dungeon," commanded Flaccidus. "Quickly!"

# THE DATA

LANCE-A-LOT was seated on the recliner, watching a spirited bout between two men in an octagonal cage. They were punching, kicking, twisting, and doing their best to bloody up each other. It was making him itch for battle.

That's when he smelled something that reminded him of Sir Gaheris.

His son, Mitch Jr., was making goo-goo noises on his lap, seeming rather pleased with himself. Lance picked up the boy to see if the smell was resonating from him. Sure enough, it was.

"I believe the boy has made another gift," Lance said to Allison.

"'Present,'" she corrected while keeping her face locked to the computer screen she'd been studying.

"Yes," said Lance, confused. "I'm here."

"No, I'm not asking you if you're present," she said, looking over her glasses. "I'm saying that the common vernacular for when a child fills its diaper is that they made a 'present,' not a 'gift.'"

"Ah, yes."

"So change him," she said as if it were nothing.

Lance-A-Lot had been through many challenges in his life. He'd fought down ruffians, saved maidens, laid maidens—often the very same ones he'd previously saved, been stabbed twice—once due to the jealousy of an angry husband over laying a self-proclaimed maiden that he'd previously saved, and even catered a party for fifty aristocrats. He was quite the chef, after all.

But never had he faced the horrors of diaper-changing.

"Uhhh..." he said worriedly.

Allison sighed and crossed her arms. Lance-A-Lot always felt worried when she did that because it meant he'd either done something wrong, was *doing* something wrong, or was *about* to do something wrong.

"Mitch," she said, using his actual name, "you can't just sit around watching sports and soap operas on television all day. You have to pull your own weight around here."

"Done that twice today already," Lance replied proudly.

"I don't mean it like that," she said with a frown. "I mean that you have to do your fair share of the work."

"Oh, right. Sorry, dear."

"Now, you change the boy while I go over some data."

It wasn't a request and so Lance set about to his task. He'd seen both Allison and Mrs. Smith, his new mother-in-law, change the boy on many occasions, so he knew the ins and outs of it. But there was something entirely different between watching such an event and participating in one.

In order to keep his mind off what he was doing, he said, "What is data, dear?"

"You don't know what data is?"

"Well, I know what it means, sure, but I only understand its use when dealing with the knights. They give me reports and I figure things out from it."

"Same thing, just that my reports come from the computer."

"Uh-huh," he said. She never gave him much information.

Allison must have recognized that she wasn't being very forthcoming, because she said, "Okay, I'll give you an example. When we sent Arthur and everyone back in time, the system logged information on it. That's data I can use to look at the efficiency of how many systems are running. From that I can derive if there are any needs for updates, performance enhancements, and so on." She began typing away on her keyboard. "So, I can pull up the information on their transport and…" She paused. "Huh."

"Something the matter?" asked Lance as he tried to keep himself from gagging.

"It's just that something looks…" Allison paused again. "Oh, shit."

"You can say that again."

"I sent them to the wrong time," she whispered.

"You mean like night or something?" said Lance as he powdered the boy's bottom.

"No, I mean like..." She began typing and clicking. "Oh boy. They're in 72AD."

Lance finished changing Mitch, Jr. and smiled at his handiwork. While it hadn't been pleasant, he was proud he'd accomplished something. Actually, the last time he'd felt this good about himself since moving in with Allison was when he'd successfully loaded the dishwasher.

He picked up Mitch, Jr., holding him for Allison to check out the accomplishment, but she was busily carrying a look of dread. That's when Lance replayed her last sentence over in his head.

"Are you saying that my king is in trouble?" he asked, feeling his body temperature instantly rise.

"I don't know," she replied, "but considering *where* they ended up, I'd say there's a strong possibility they are."

"What do you mean?"

"Well, they didn't just go back in time, they also landed in Ancient Rome."

Lance's eyes went wide. "What?"

# TURKEY LEG

DOONAN WALKED UP the path that opened into Camelot. It didn't look all that different to him than his home kingdom, except for the litany of merchant carts lining the streets and pushing their wares. There were large ones, small ones, colorful ones, and plain ones. Some had wheels and some were clearly built for permanency.

He kept his head down, not wanting to engage anyone just yet. With any luck, he'd spot a soldier who would be able to help him find the king.

"You there," called out a merchant as Doonan stepped in a puddle, soaking his foot.

Doonan stopped and looked up at the merchant. It was a middle-aged man with a round face and beady eyes. He was standing behind a cart that had pieces of meat dangling from wires, and he was holding up a gigantic turkey leg.

Feeling rather self-conscious, Doonan pointed to himself questioningly.

"Yes, you in the skirt," said the man. "Come over

here and try a delightful turkey leg."

"It's a kilt," said Doonan, stepping over.

"No," replied the merchant, looking at the haunch of meat, "it's a turkey leg."

"I mean me skirt," explained Doonan. "It's called a kilt."

"Ah, well, glad that's cleared up." The merchant began wrapping up the foodstuff with a batch of brown paper. "Now, that will be three silver pieces for the turkey leg."

"I'm not after wantin' any turkey leg," Doonan said with a grimace. "I'm here on a mission to find me king."

"But you said you wanted the leg and I've gone and wrapped it."

"I've said no such thing, ya batty cart-pusher!"

A large man approached them. He was wearing a soldier's outfit that seemed similar to the one Doonan had seen the knights wearing when the king of England had visited a while back. But something didn't quite fit. This fellow had the look of a man who hadn't slept in many days, and the stench of alcohol that permeated from his being masked the merchant's delicacies in an instant.

"Okay, okay," said the man in a tired voice. "What's going on here?"

"Who're you?" asked Doonan.

"I am Sir Bedivere, a Knight of the Round Table."

"Truly?" Doonan said, appraising him once more.

"Yeah, why?"

"Ye just look like yer after bein' a fella that failed at sleepin' off a hangover."

"Well, that's about right," Bedivere replied with a nod, "but it's too early to start drinking again just yet. Now, what's going on here?"

"This man said he wanted a turkey leg and so I wrapped it up and now he won't pay," claimed the merchant.

"I dinnae want any damn turkey leg," Doonan argued. "Who's after eatin' somethin' like that this early in the morn?"

Bedivere glanced over at the merchant. "He's got you there."

"You're siding with him?" the merchant shrieked. "I'm a tax-paying citizen of this town. I pay your wage, man! This skirt-wearing fool is obviously an out-of-towner."

"Which means he's a tourist," Bedivere said pedantically. "The king always says that we could use more tourists to raise up our income."

"By selling turkey legs, I bring in money for the kingdom," the merchant was quick to note.

"Not if there aren't any tourists to buy your food," countered Bedivere.

"Bah," said the merchant. "Other people buy it all the time. I don't need any stinking tourists to pay me for turkey legs."

"I guess that makes the matter settled, then," Bedivere said with a satisfied smile.

"Damn," said the merchant, unwrapping the turkey leg and putting it back with the others. "I'm going to complain about this, I will."

"You do that," acknowledged Bedivere as he motioned Doonan to walk with him down the path.

As soon as they were away from the grumbling shouts of the disgruntled merchant, Bedivere said, "You're from Scotland, yes?"

"How'd ye know?"

"Aside from the accent, you mean?"

"I have an accent?"

"It was your skirt that originally tipped me off."

"Kilt."

"Ah, right. Sorry." Bedivere rubbed his temples. "As you said, I'm still trying to clear my head from last night's boozing. Why are you here?"

Doonan felt that this man may prove helpful to his cause. He *had* been searching for a soldier, after all, and while this one appeared to be on the wrong-end of a beating, he also seemed decent enough.

"Looking for me king," said Doonan.

"Arthur?"

"It's a good sign that you're after knowin' his name."

"Named the same as ours," said Bedivere. "Hard to forget."

"Oh, aye. Seen him, then?"

"I haven't," admitted Bedivere, "but I recall two of the other knights saying that he was up in the wizard's lair, so chances are he's still there."

"Where's that after bein'?"

"It's up there," said Bedivere, pointing up the path. "I'll take you."

# CHECKING IT OUT

APOLLO LANDED THE shuttle in its normal spot, just outside of town. The platform the Romans built as the landing site had the standard sculptures all around, but it was otherwise unadorned and flat. The view was barren except for straight ahead where the heart of the Roman Empire lay. Even at this distance the cityscape was impressive. For this era, anyway.

They used to land much closer in, but after burning a number of people alive and squashing quite a few others, the emperor had pleaded with the gods to use more caution and offered to build a special place for them to land farther away. They had agreed, not wanting to seem heartless, but warned they would only comply if there were a chariot waiting whenever they arrived.

Athena walked down the ramp ahead of him and stepped up into the chariot.

"Take us to the emperor," Apollo commanded the driver, an unshaved man who was dressed sloppily.

The driver nodded and said, "That'll be five bronze

asses."

"Pardon me?" said Apollo.

"The drive from the Chariot of Fire to the palace costs five bronze asses," said the driver, pointing at a fee sheet that was stuck to the panel in front of them. "Not including tip."

"You realize I'm a god, right?"

"Just doing my job, pal," said the driver.

Athena gave the man a look of disdain. "We could snuff you out of existence without breaking a sweat."

"Better that than getting fired and having my wife nag at me to find another job," the guy said with a shrug.

"That bad, eh?" Apollo questioned.

"You have no idea."

"All right." Apollo reached into his change purse and pulled forth some Roman coins. "I can't let a fellow suffer just on account of me."

Athena's look at Apollo was even worse than she'd given the driver.

"You *do* understand what it means to be a god, right?" she said with a scoff.

"Of course I do, but I've seen Mother nagging Father. I can't have this poor man's suffering through that be on my conscience."

"Fair enough," agreed Athena. "It *is* pretty horrible."

"Here you go," Apollo said as he handed over the coins. "Ten butts."

"Asses, and thanks, pal."

# WHO ARE THEY?

GUARD CLEARLYACHICKUS COULDN'T help but think that the prisoners who had been brought down to the dungeon were on to her. At least the woman was, anyway.

"Psst..." she signaled to her partner, Probius, a very cute guard who had taken her under his wing ever since she'd been accepted into the force. He was easily fifteen years her elder, but he was fit and gentlemanly. Plus, she had rather a thing for older men. "Probius, any idea who they are?"

"No," he said in a whisper, keeping his eyes on the wall in front of him.

"No word from the upper ranks?"

"No."

"Oh, come on. You always hear—"

"Please leave me alone, Clearlyachickus," Probius said pleadingly. "Last time I got into one of these long discussions with you, I ended up getting reprimanded by Dickus Headus."

That was true. Supreme Guard Dickus Headus was

a stickler for duty. There was to be no fraternizing with the prisoners, no discussions amongst the guards, and no women anywhere within eye shot, unless she was a prisoner. It was him that Guard Clearlyachickus always feared because he could have her removed from duty if he ever found out her true gender.

"I think the one woman is on to me," she said and then caught herself, remembering that Probius, too, was unaware of the real situation.

"You're not dragging me into a discussion," he said tightly.

It was a constant struggle for her because she wasn't exactly what you would call uncurvy. In fact, she was quite voluptuous. This made it challenging to tape everything into place each morning and to stuff herself into the standard guard outfit. She also had to keep her hair cropped tightly, not get manicures, and avoid any form of makeup, which was the worst because dark eyeliner really brought out her pale green eyes.

But if that prisoner saw through the disguise, certainly others did too. Right? They must have. Especially since she was the only one playing at this game. Sure, there were a few of the guards who were chubby, but none of them in a feminine way. Well, maybe Guard Dudus Lookuslikealadius, and possibly Guard Manboobius.

"Probius?"

"I'm ignoring you."

Clearlyachickus swallowed hard and then said, "Is there anything in particular that you think that woman may have noticed about me?"

"It's like you just don't care," Probius said with a huff.

"Seriously, we've known each other for quite a while now and I need you to be honest with me."

"I wish you would stop saying things," he said at full voice. "You're going to get me in trouble."

"Guard Probius," Supreme Guard Dickus Headus called down in his haughty voice, "would you come hither, please?"

Probius looked away from the wall and at Clearlyachickus. It was not a happy look. It was the kind of look that conveyed that he was very unhappy. It was the kind of look that made Clearlyachickus tingle.

"Damn it," he said. "Thanks a lot, Guard Clearlyachickus."

"What did I do?" she replied innocently as he stormed up the stairs.

# NOW WHAT?

ARTHUR WAS BEING careful not to let his gown touch anything. He was well aware that dungeons were intended to be untidy and uncomfortable, but this was pathetic. The smell alone made him wonder how the torches that were encased behind latticed metal containers didn't explode. There were rats and bugs, and it was warm and damp. The lighting barely illuminated chains on the walls, a ceiling that was dripping what he could only hope was moisture from the humidity, and a floor that was an uneven mix of dirt and stone.

"This place is disgusting," said Bors, wiping away a drop of water that had landed on his head.

"And it smells terrible," agreed Kay.

Gaheris inhaled deeply. "Reminds me of home."

"Your home smells like urine?" asked Kay with a wince.

"Think of who you're speaking to, Sir Kay," Bors reminded.

"Oh, yes. True."

"Something doesn't add up about all of this," said Merlin as he sat on one of the stone benches. He obviously didn't mind the filth. "That emperor's name…" He trailed off.

"Flaccidus?" said Galahad.

"Yes. It's wrong."

Galahad nodded. "On many levels."

"No, I mean I don't recall there being an emperor with that name."

"Well, his real name was Longus Dongus."

"None by that name in lore either, Sir Galahad," noted Gaheris.

"Exactly." Merlin took off his hat and began twirling it. "I wonder if we've ended up in a parallel universe somehow."

"A what?" Arthur asked, thinking certain he'd never heard this term before.

Merlin plopped his hat back on and stood back up, walking to one of the far walls. "I have to think."

Everyone else stood around, except for Gaheris, who took up Merlin's vacated seat. He, too, didn't mind the grime. To be fair, it was more likely that the grime minded him.

"What the shet is a parakeet university?" Arty said, finally. "I didn't know birds went to school."

"No," corrected Galahad. "It's a parallel universe."

"Oh," Arty said with a look of understanding. "That's different, then."

Arthur was surprised by this. "You know what they're talking about, Arty?"

"Not a clue."

"It's an alternate timeline," explained Galahad with

a sigh.

"Well, that clears it up," said Arty, rolling his eyes. "Thanks fer yer keen explanation."

By now, Guinevere had stepped into the fray and was standing with her arms crossed. She often did this whenever she was irritated, seeking knowledge, or both. Usually when she was irritated, though, she was staring at Arthur. Since she was clearly looking only at Galahad, Arthur assumed she was in a learning mood.

"What exactly does that mean, Sir Galahad?" she asked. "And please use terms we can understand."

"Yes, ma'am. It's kind of difficult to explain, really." He scratched at his beard thoughtfully. "I don't even fully understand it myself. I've just started reading about it recently, truth be told."

"Do your best," instructed Guinevere.

This was another thing she said quite often to Arthur.

Galahad closed his eyes for a few moments while bouncing his head around. It was as though he were rehearsing what he was going to say.

"Imagine that there are two of you in existence," he said, peering out at Guinevere from a squint.

"I like it already," said Arthur.

Nobody laughed.

"You can't see the other one," continued Galahad. Then he began making hand gestures as he spoke. "They can't see you either. But you both exist. Your lives will be the same to a point, but they'll also be vastly different. This is because the other you couldn't have made all of the exact choices you made, nor could all of the people who have influenced your world or your particular life have influenced theirs in precisely the same way."

"Have ye been drinkin', man?" said Arty. "I dinnae see a flask aboot, but if'n ye have some to share—"

"King Arty," admonished Guinevere, "if you don't mind?"

Arty's shoulders dropped. "Sorry, lass."

"Now, Galahad," she said, "how many copies of me exist, exactly?"

"There are likely an unlimited number, my lady. All of them with different lives, different thoughts, different feelings..." He shrugged. "But they're all you, in a manner of speaking."

"Sounds like a pile of horse dung, if you ask me," stated Bors.

"Agreed, Borsy," said Kay, which was not surprising considering he nearly always agreed with Bors. "It goes against all that we've been taught in the church as well."

"That it does," Galahad agreed. "I fully admit that it's quite difficult to believe. I'm merely telling you what I've read."

"You realize that a man could be sentenced to an eternity in hell fire for even imagining such thoughts," said Kay.

"Equally hard to believe," replied Galahad.

"Where did you learn of this, Sir Galahad?" Guinevere asked.

"Just one of Merlin's many books."

Merlin had moseyed back to the group and was listening to the end of Galahad's lecture.

"They were all given to me by Allison," the wizard

said. "The thing that Galahad is discussing is known as *Rope Theory*."

"*String*," Galahad amended.

Merlin looked at him. "Hmmm?"

"*String Theory*."

"Ah, yes, that's it."

Guinevere was nodding slowly. Arthur had little faith that she understood their words any more than he did, but then again she always did have a way with seeing things outside the box.

"And how does this knowledge help us in our current situation?" she asked.

"I don't know that it does, Gwen," answered Merlin. "I'm just worried that if this emperor isn't in our native dimension, there may be many other things that are out of whack."

"If it's not our dimension," said Guinevere, "could our other selves be living here?"

"No," said Galahad. "We are far in their past."

"Oh, that's right."

"Sorry to interrupt," interrupted Arthur, "but if none of this is helpful, why are we discussing it?"

Merlin scoffed at this. "Science is always helpful, Arthur, even if it doesn't solve the particular problem at hand."

"Can I say somethin' now?" asked Arty, raising his hand.

"Yes, Arty?" said Guinevere.

Arty looked from face to face as if building up the courage to spit out what was on his mind. Arthur guessed that it was really Guinevere he was worried about. Clearly he was a man who was also married to a woman who had the upper hand.

"Yer all batshit loony," he bellowed. "Talkin' aboot bunches of people bein' the same and all that. Everyone knows there's only one of ye, unless ye've got a twin or somethin'. Besides, that ain't after helpin' us get out of here, is it? Nay, we need to be after settin' up a plan."

"He's right," said Galahad.

Arty had his finger up and wagging in Galahad's face, but it gradually slowed down its pace and then lowered. Arty was left with a confused look. "I am?"

"Not everything you said, no. Just the part about us needing a plan."

"Oh."

"Anyone have any ideas?" asked Arthur.

"We could do a play for the emperor," suggested Bors, going with his mainstay solution for everything.

"Jolly idea," agreed Kay... of course.

Arthur fought not to sigh. "And how would that help us?"

"Get on his good side, obviously," Bors answered.

"Well, it may help the rest of you," Arthur said, pondering the situation, "but I'm doubtful it will save Arty and me."

Merlin reached out and put his hand on Arthur's shoulder. "Kings make sacrifices all the time."

"For their own lot, yeah," agreed Arty, sniffing. "You ain't me lot."

"True, Arty," Arthur said. "This isn't your fight. I must do this alone."

"No," Guinevere stated. "There has to be another way."

"Actually," Arthur said, gazing into his wife's eyes, "this may be the only way. If I speak with this Flaccidus fellow alone, maybe he'll agree to let you all live."

"What about you, Arthur?"

"As Merlin said, my love, kings must sometime make sacrifices."

"No," Guinevere said as her face lost all color. "You can't do that."

"I'll die by your side, sire," Gaheris announced, standing back up.

Arthur thought certain he heard the stone bench release a breath of relief.

"No, Gaheris," Arthur said gently, "you won't."

Gaheris stood firmly. "I die where I die."

"That's true," noted Merlin.

"This is not up for debate, Gaheris," said Arthur, putting on his most kingly voice. "You'll be needed to protect the others."

"Even Bors and Kay?"

"Of course."

Gaheris appeared downtrodden. "As you command, sire."

As if the air in the room weren't thick enough, their conversation stagnated it. Even the torches seemed subdued by the revelation that Arthur was about to face his demise. But Merlin was right. Kings had the good life for a time, but there was always a moment of truth, or many moments of truth, where the king must stand and face the wrath of another in order to protect his people. This was Arthur's moment. It was odd that it had to happen in an era that wasn't even close to being his own, but a kingdom of six was just as deserving as a kingdom of six thousand.

"I'll not stand for this, my husband," Guinevere said, breaking the silence. "Merlin, you must do something."

"What can I do, Gwen?" Merlin said desperately. "We're in a dungeon. You know my magic is nothing but technology, and I have none of it with me that would aid in this."

"Galahad?" she said. "You've studied!"

"Sorry, my lady."

Guinevere spun towards Arthur. "I won't allow it, do you hear—"

"Dear, listen to me," he said, gripping her shoulders. "We've always known that we must be prepared to give ourselves for our people. It's what we were born to do."

"Ah, damn," said Arty as Arthur and Guinevere embraced. "Why'd ye have to go an' get all honorable?" He groaned for a few moments and then waved his arm in a wide arc and slapped himself on the leg with his hand. "All right, I'll go with ye."

"No, Arty, as you said—"

"Screw what I said. I'm just as kingly as yer after bein'. I can't rightly let ya die alone."

"Honestly, Arty," Arthur said, "I can't ask you to do that."

"Who says ye did? It's me arse, not yers, and I'm after makin' up me own mind as to what it does."

Arthur nodded his head at his fellow king. "You're a good friend, Arty."

"Aye," Arty said, looking away. "Let's get this shet over with."

# MERLIN'S HOUSE

DOONAN WASN'T SURE what to make of this Knight Bedivere fellow. He seemed honorable enough, especially the way he'd handled that merchant who had been trying to force the turkey leg down Doonan's throat, but for a man of such regard to be sloshing through town with a hangover was not very soldierly. Well, at least not as it pertains to the reputation of a Knight of the Round Table, anyway.

They had made their way up a small hill outside town where a cliff face stood. It wasn't the biggest crag Doonan had ever seen, but it was the first one he'd ever sighted that was painted in the fashion of a tree.

Bedivere pushed a little button beside the door a few times. A punchy little song played each time. It was more than a bit unnerving to Doonan as magic was not something he found comforting.

"I wonder why he's not answering?" said Bedivere.

"The wizard?" Doonan said worriedly.

"Yeah. I mean, I guess it is pretty early, but he

usually is going to bed just about now."

"But the sun's up."

"Your point?" said Bedivere, shielding his eyes.

Doonan sighed. "I've got none worth sharin'. You English sure is different."

Bedivere looked at Doonan for a moment and then shrugged while nodding. At least he hadn't tried to argue the point. Fact was, the English *were* different. They wore full battle gear instead of kilts, appeared to stay up all night drinking, and acted nonchalant about things like missing kings.

The knight reached again for the magical button, but instead knocked on the door.

It opened slightly.

"Well, that's odd," said Bedivere.

"It's opened," Doonan said with a gulp.

"You saw that too, eh?"

Doonan couldn't help but think that the knight had said that sarcastically.

"Are ye makin' fun?"

"Absolutely," Bedivere replied and then pushed the door open. "Merlin?" he called out. "Merlin, are you here?" He took a step inside. "It's Bedivere. You here? I sure could use some of those little pills that get rid of hangovers."

"He's after havin' pills to clear the fog after a bout of drinkin'?"

"Just helps with the headaches, really," said Bedivere. He then held his hand out to stop Doonan in place. "Stay here a moment." He took two steps toward the back room and then stopped and looked back. "And trust me when I say that you don't want to touch anything."

Doonan glanced around, seeing all sorts of fascinatingly terrifying items. There were lights with no flames, a ball with miniature bits of lightning bouncing around in it, and a stack of books that had all forms of designs on them.

"I wouldn't dare," he whispered. "Probably has some curse on this place as it is."

"Uh, yeah, sure," said Bedivere as if Doonan were an imbecile. "Well, let me look in the back."

It wasn't right for a man of Doonan's status to be standing in a place like this. The hairs on the back of his neck were standing on end and his throat was dry. He'd faced the blade of an enemy more than once in his life as a soldier, but that was nothing compared to this. A blade was tangible. It was held by another man or woman and it poked at you. Simple. Physical. Reality. Magic was another beast completely. It was run by demons, and there was nothing simple about demons.

"Doonan," Bedivere called, causing Doonan to jump, "come on back here."

"Ye sure?" Doonan called back.

"Yes."

"I'm fine where I'm at, so unless you really need me, I'd rather—"

"You want to find your king or not?"

"Aye," Doonan replied as he started walking, cringing with each step.

He turned the corner and found Bedivere standing by a desk of some sort. On it sat a glowing rectangle that had words and images covering it. To the right was a disk-shaped floor that was connected to a semi-hollowed rock face.

"I'm not likin' this," Doonan said as his heart thumped. "What the shet is that?"

Bedivere glanced over. "Looks like a big circle in the ground to me."

"Aye, I can see that. What's it for, ye think?"

"I don't know but there's this magic flashing panel over here. Has numbers and such on it."

"Yeah, I was after seein' that, too. What are ye doin'? Don't touch it!"

"Why not?" said Bedivere, hesitating.

"'Cause ye've no clue what it'll do, ye daft bastard!"

Bedivere laughed. "Why is everyone so afraid of magic?"

"Hmmm, let's see," replied Doonan, adopting a sarcastic tone of his own. "Maybe it's 'cause it can make yer pee sting, cause her tallywhoosit to itch like something mad before it falls off, and it can give ye a fever ye won't soon forget!"

"I think you just described an STD, not magic," noted Bedivere.

"What's the difference?"

"Right," said Bedivere, blinking. "Well, this bit of the screen clearly says, 'Tap here,' soooo—"

"Nooooooo!"

# WHY ARE WE HERE?

MRS. SMITH, LANCE'S new mother-in-law, had arrived to watch Mitch, Jr. while Allison and Lance headed back to rescue Arthur and the gang. She was a middle-aged woman who gave a clear indication of what Allison may look like as she grew older. Lance was not unpleased. He liked the white hair look, after all.

"I appreciate you watching little Mitchy, Mother," Allison said as she continued typing away at her computer.

"Yes," agreed Lance, "it is most kind of you, Mrs. Smith."

"It's no problem," Mrs. Smith replied with a bit of an edge. "I can always play bingo some other night."

Allison looked up from her screen. "That sounded sarcastic."

"Did it?"

"Mother, what's wrong?"

"Dear," said Mrs. Smith, "it's just that you had many potential suitors who would not have caused a situation requiring you to go back into the Roman era. Yet, you chose one from the Middle Ages." She then looked over at Lance. "No offense."

"I understand, Mrs. Smith."

And he did. The fact was he was out of his element in this future, and it showed. The only things he'd mastered in his brief time in this era were the microwave oven, light switches, the shower, opening and closing blinds, the dishwasher, how to order pizza, and changing a diaper. He'd also learned how to use the television remote, but that seemed more of an innate skill with men... at least that's what Allison had told him.

"I truly doubt you understand, Lance," said Mrs. Smith, though not unkindly.

"We've been through this many times, Mother," interjected Allison. "None of this was planned. It just sort of happened, and Mitch and I felt that it would be best for Mitch, Jr. for us to marry. That's all there is to it."

"And we love each other, too," noted Lance.

"Hmmm?" said Allison, and then, "Oh, yes, that too, of course."

Lance sighed. "I suppose it's true what all of those soap operas say about romance being dead in this day and age."

Mrs. Smith did a quick shake of her head as if surprised. "You watch soap operas?"

"Not much else to do around here during the day."

"Which is your favorite?"

"I'm not good with names," admitted Lance, "but I think it's 'As the Globe Spins' maybe?"

"Close enough. We should compare notes."

"I would like that," said Lance emphatically.

"A lot of my friends have a weekly get-together where we discuss the shows and what we think will happen." She looked him over again. "Maybe you could join?"

"Honestly?"

"Sure, why not?" she said with a shrug. "It would be nice to have a man's point of view." She frowned. "Never thought I'd hear myself say that. Anyway, we go right after doing a bout of mall walking. Good for exercise." She must have noticed Lance was giving her an imploring look, because she rolled her eyes and said, "...yes, you can go with us on that, too."

Lance clapped his hands. "Thank you so much, Mrs. Smith. That would be lovely."

"If you ladies are done planning," said Allison as she walked to the door, "we should really get going."

"Huh?" said Lance, looking up. "Oh... Right."

§ § §

The trip over to the office was quick since they lived only a few blocks away. Lance had gotten used to the sound of cars and the garb of other pedestrians, but he kept to his standard wear of the Camelot Age, which wasn't too far off considering how close they lived to the medieval dinner theater. Allison had mentioned a few times that she would like to take him out for clothes shopping, but she was always caught up in her work.

The portal room was the same as he remembered.

Desks everywhere, lighting in the ceiling behind mostly opaque coverings, and a large platform where they had arrived from the past originally.

"I've already uploaded everything to the computer here and it should be all set," said Allison as she studied the screen and pressed a few buttons. "Hop up on the platform and I'll join you in a second."

A few moments later, they were both on the transporter, waiting for the system to go through its standard processes.

First were the lights glowing on the floor like one of those TV shows Lance had watched from the seventies. It was called *Soul Truck* or something like that. It played music that was definitely not what Lance would have thought he'd enjoy, but he had to admit his foot tapped to the rhythm more than once while viewing. Next, the hairs on the back of his neck began to flutter, and then the hair on his head started lifting up. He looked at Allison and her hair was flying all over the place.

Finally, there was a rush of sound, a massive tingling sensation, and everything disappeared.

An instant later, the sights and sounds came rushing back in and they found themselves standing in Merlin's transporter room with Sir Bedivere and a man Lance did not know. He was a red-haired fellow who was wearing a skirt. Well, it was a kilt, but it looked to Lance like a skirt.

"What happened?" said Allison, looking more irritated than confused.

"Bedivere?" said Lance, feeling a little groggy. "That's you, right?"

"Lance?" replied Bedivere. "I… uh…"

The red-haired man was in a fight-or-flight stance. "What kind of devilry is this?"

"We should be in Rome," Allison said frantically as she hopped off the platform and began reviewing the screen at Merlin's desk.

"Rome?" said Bedivere.

"Get ye back or face me blade," said the kilt-wearing man as he pulled an axe out and held it menacingly.

"Who is this?" Lance asked Bedivere.

"One of King Arthur's guys. From Scotland. His name is Doonan."

"Oh," said Lance, the fog finally clearing from his thoughts. "Nice to meet you, Doonan."

Doonan's eyes blazed. "My steel will meet your demonic loins."

"What?" said Lance, grimacing.

"I don't understand what happened," said Allison, throwing up her hands. She then squinted at Bedivere and pointed. "Did you touch that screen?"

Bedivere pointed, also. "That screen?"

"Yes."

"No."

"Are you sure?"

"Yes."

Allison moved past Bedivere, coming close to Doonan.

"Get ye back, witch! I'm not fond of strikin' the lasses, but I shan't be vexed by your curses!"

Lance reached over and snatched the axe away from Doonan as if it were nothing.

"Calm yourself, man."

"He has the strength of an army," Doonan said with a look of awe, his open hands shaking.

"No," Bedivere said, laughing, "he's just a knight, and you were looking the other way."

"Oh. Well, I still have me knife—"

Allison stood up and put a hand on her hip. This was the universal sign that told a man he was in trouble.

"I'm not a witch and this isn't devilry. It's just technology. Honestly, you're like a caveman."

"I am not," Doonan said, looking hurt.

"Then why all the talk of devilry and witches and demons?" countered Allison.

"Because ye just went after poppin' out of thin air, is why! How are ye after explainin' it without the use of magic?"

"Via a time dilation chamber that drops our bodies to a molecular structure, places them into a convecting oscillator with…" She paused. Doonan's face had gone completely white. "What's the matter?"

"Are ye even speakin' English anymore?" Then he gulped. "Or is that witch-speak?"

Lance, who was now mildly used to the idea of time travel and technology, couldn't help but feel bad for the Scotsman. Bedivere seemed slightly uneasy too, but he was known to hang around with Merlin from time to time, so even he appeared desensitized.

"Right," said Lance. "Any idea what happened?"

"Yes," replied Allison. "Bedivere tapped on the screen here and interrupted our transport."

Bedivere looked affronted.

"I did not."

Allison went to put her hand back on her hip, which caused Bedivere to point at Doonan.

"He did it."

"What?" said Doonan. "I dinnae no such thing!"

"Do you two have a habit of going around and touching other people's things?"

Doonan got a serious look on his face. "Not since I had me therapy."

"I don't believe that's what she meant," said Lance, taking a step away from the Scotsman.

"Oh."

"Why are you here, anyway?" asked Lance.

"That's after bein' a deep question," answered Doonan at length while rubbing his chin and looking up thoughtfully. "The Great Lulach said it's all about findin' yer soul mate. 'Course he spent his days in prison after bein' arrested for pinchin' ladies on the bottom. The Not-So-Great Mac Bethad claimed that we're here to worship the way—"

"I'm asking why you have broken into Merlin's chambers?" Lance interrupted.

"We didn't break in, Sir Lance-A-Lot," stated Bedivere. "The door was open."

"Fine. Why are you in this room?"

"I was lookin' for me king," explained Doonan. "He came here a bit back and he's not returned." He paused and glanced around. "Dinnae wanna come here at all, truth be told, but that damnable Calle commanded it, so here I am."

"I see."

"Are ye after knowin' where me king is?" asked the

Scotsman.

"He's in Rome," answered Allison as she began working the keyboard.

"Rome?" Doonan flinched. "Did he go on a horse or somethin'?"

"Ancient Rome," amended Allison.

"What?"

"It's hard to explain," said Lance, "but let's just say that we're on our way to retrieve both him and *our* King Arthur as well."

With what appeared to be a lot of effort, Doonan announced, "I'm going with ye."

"Sorry, no," said Allison. "You've already seen too much as it is."

"He's *me* king!"

Allison nodded. "So you've said. We'll bring him back to you soon enough."

"Ye can't force me to sit by as me king is off in some faraway land!"

"I'm sure he's fine," Allison said with a dismissive wave. "Just relax."

Doonan stood tall and crossed his arms. "I'm going and that's after bein' final."

"Don't make me put a curse on you," Allison replied nonchalantly as she continued typing.

The Scotsman blanched and gulped. "So we're waitin' here, ye say?"

"Both of you," Lance replied. "Bedivere, stay here and touch nothing. Just go sit on the couch and wait. Keep him there, too."

"Understood."

Lance nodded and then tilted his head at the

knight. "You truly do, right?"

"Said I did."

"Right."

# THE EMPEROR, THE KINGS, AND THE GODS

ARTHUR AND ARTY stood in front of Emperor Flaccidus. Arthur hated to have to do this, as it *was* his life that was coming to an end, but to save his men, and especially his beloved Guinevere, he would do what he had to do. Having Arty next to him proved that the English and the Scottish *could* be comrades… at least if it all started due to the fact that both kings happened to share in the desire to wear women's clothing, anyway.

"So," Flaccidus said with a satisfied smile, "you have come to beg for your lives?"

"We aint' beggin' fer nothin', ye daft—"

"Arty," said Arthur, putting out a hand to stay the man. "Sorry, Emperor Flaccidwilly."

"It's Flaccidus!"

"Ah, yes, that. We are not here to beg for our lives, but rather for the lives of our comrades."

Flaccidus resumed his smugness. "Is that so?"

"It does you no harm to keep them alive," Arthur explained.

"True. We could always use a few more slaves."

Arthur fought to remain calm. It was better for them to be enslaved and alive than to be hanging from the end of a rope, or worse.

"As you say."

"Either way, you two must perish because—"

Hemorrhoidoclese burst into the room, causing the two guards on duty to pull their swords and prepare for an attack. Obviously they noted it was one of their own, though, and therefore returned the blades to their respective sheaths.

"My emperor, I'm sorry to interrupt—"

Flaccidus turned to the two Arthurs and said, "It really is annoying when they do that, isn't it?"

"Happens to me all the time," Arthur commiserated.

"Aye. Rangy bastards."

"Does he always speak so gruffly?" asked Flaccidus while scrunching up his nose.

"Ye think he speaks with angst?"

"Was talking about you."

"Oh. Aye." Arty didn't shrug or bow or make any move to apologize. He just pushed out his chest proudly and said, "It's after bein' a trait of me people."

"Right." Flaccidus glanced at his guard. "What is it, Hemorrhoidoclese?"

"Appolo and Athena have just arrived, sire."

Flaccidus nearly fell over. "Send them in, man!"

"Yes, sire."

Hemorrhoidoclese snapped his fingers and the two guards by the doors opened them.

A muscular man led the way. He had wavy hair and a swagger in his step that said he knew he was powerful. Even had Arthur not just seen the way Flaccidus responded to the knowledge that these two were waiting outside, it would have been clear this fellow was royalty.

The woman who followed him was beyond gorgeous, but she too was built like a finely-tuned machine. Her movements were like that of a snake, and, were Arthur being truthful, it was a snake he'd not mind being bitten by.

Both the new arrivals glanced over Arthur and Arty as if they were subjects, mere peons. Oddly, under their gaze, Arthur felt as though he were.

"Flaccidus," said the man by way of greeting.

His voice was a bit more flamboyant than his body language, which seemed out of place to Arthur. It was a singsong voice that belonged to someone a little less... manly.

"My god," said Flaccidus from a kneeling position. "It is always an honor."

Apollo removed his hand from the top of Flaccidus's head. "You may rise."

The woman, whom Arthur assumed was also a "god," was pacing back and forth in front of him and Arty. She appeared to be sizing them up. If she were truly a god, they would be no match for her, but Arthur had learned over his years that some people just had to demonstrate their superiority wherever possible. This was when Arthur recalled that he, too, was royalty.

He coughed to himself.

"So King Arthur and King, well... Arthur." The side of her top lip lifted. "Interesting that you're here."

"Are we after havin' met before?" asked Arty.

"We're gods," said Apollo. "We know everything."

"Gods, eh?"

"That's right."

"I ain't after rememberin' hearin' about no god named Apple Hole."

"It's 'Apollo,' you dimwit," said Apollo tightly. "This is my sister—kind of. Her name is Athena."

"Kind of?" ventured Arthur.

"She came out of my father's forehead," explained Apollo as if it were a thing that was commonplace.

"What the shet?" said Arty with a tilt of his head.

"It's a long story," replied Athena, stepping in closer to Arthur, "and probably just a myth anyway. So why are you here?"

"They claim they were at a costume party," answered Flaccidus before either of the Arthurs could respond.

"Explains the lady's outfits," said Apollo in a way that came across as interest.

Athena turned away and seductively walked over to the table where the grapes were sitting. She plucked one from its stem and began rolling it between her fingers. Arthur swallowed as she looked back and playfully touched the grape to her lips, gently pulling it into her mouth with a smirk.

Both Arthurs were nearly drooling by now, as were

the two guards standing over by the grapes.

"Is Lance-A-Lot with you?" she said and then bit down.

"Huh…?" Arthur replied dumbly. He shook himself back to reality. "No, why?"

Athena frowned. "Damn. Just heard he has quite a… uh… sword."

"Me word," yelped Arty in disbelief. "The damn thing is so impressive that it's a legend hundreds of years before the man was properly born!"

"How could you possibly know about this?" said Arthur.

"As I said," answered Apollo, "we're gods."

"Right."

Apollo then turned and seductively walked over to the same table as Athena. He snapped up a grape and did the same sensuous play that his kind-of sister had done.

Both Arthurs were wincing at this, as were the two guards standing over by the grapes.

"Flaccidus," said Apollo with a sudden frown, "what is your plan with these men?"

"I'm to have them executed."

"On what grounds?" asked Athena, though Arthur couldn't tell if she actually cared or not.

Flaccidus pointed at Arthur and said, "He's the king of Britain and he's the king of Scotland. Solves our issues regarding conquering them both."

"I see," said Apollo, "but I'm sorry we cannot allow this execution to take place."

"But you must! It's—"

"Don't raise your voice at me, Flaccidus," said

Apollo coldly. "I would hate to strike you down."

"Sorry, my god," Flaccidus said quickly, his voice barely audible.

Athena had her arms crossed as well and was giving Flaccidus a very stern look. They definitely had the royalty thing down better than most. Honestly, it was as if they'd invented it.

"Don't forget that we put you in this palace between the normal emperors because you throw a decent party," she said sternly. "You shouldn't be in here at all, and you're already precluded from having a legacy."

"Exactly," agreed Apollo. "You're what we call a stop-gap solution."

"Yes, I know." Flaccidus sighed heavily. "I'm... worthless."

Apollo nodded. "Correct. Now that we have that cleared up, we expect you'll do as we say?"

"Of course, my god."

It wasn't Arthur's place, but seeing a man berated as such was painful to watch. He had subjects who were sometimes naughty, but he would take them aside quietly and discuss the situation, not publicly flog them. There were many kings and queens who loved to humiliate people, of course, but to Arthur's way of thinking it was dishonorable. It was equally dishonorable to stand idly by while it happened.

"Excuse me," he said, raising his arm, "but while I don't know this man very well and while I'm quite certain that we would be dead were it not for your intervention, do you not think that treating him thusly is a bit vexing?"

"No," said Athena as if it were a stupid question.

Apollo frowned and looked up at the ceiling for a moment. "Not at all."

"Harsh," said Arty.

"Thank you for your concern," Flaccidus whispered as he moved over to stand with Arthur, "but, to the gods, an emperor or a king is naught but a peasant."

"I don't treat my peasants with such disdain," declared Arthur.

"Aye, agreed," said Arty. "They'll stick ye with a blade in your nethers during naptime, if'n ye not after bein' careful."

"Enough of this," said Apollo while stomping his foot with each word. "Where are the others in their party?"

"They're in the dungeon, my god," answered Flaccidus.

"Fetch them all!"

# THE ARRIVAL

THE TRANSPORT WASN'T as jarring for Lance-A-Lot this time. It had all the same whirring and noises and such, but he didn't feel nearly as foggy. A little, sure, but not bad.

Allison hadn't seemed bothered either. She just tapped him on the arm and pointed at the two guards standing in front of them. They were facing away.

The one on the left was short, chubby, and had graying hair that spelled he was the older of the two. The fellow on the right was lanky and a bit taller. He was probably the height of Lance himself.

"Who are they, do you suppose?" Lance whispered.

"Roman soldiers, I'd guess."

The thinner of the two guards glanced back over his shoulder and then spun quickly, pulling his sword out in the process.

"Two more of them, Buttus Facius."

"How are we not seeing them when they arrive, Thumpus Rumpus?"

"My guess is that we're looking the wrong way."

"But Nameous Oneus and Nameous Twous are just over the hill," said Buttus. "They should have spotted them."

"True, but they're both idiots."

§ § §

On the other side of the hill stood two very plain guards. They were both of average height, average build, had brown hair, brown eyes, and stood at their posts in average stances. They were neither good nor bad at their jobs, but rather, again, merely average.

"Do you suppose we will ever get ahead in life, Nameous Twous?"

"I don't hold much hope, Nameous Oneus. Why do you ask?"

"I don't know," Twous said, kicking at the dirt. "Just always felt like I was meant to do something more, you know?"

"Not really."

"Like I have a destiny or something."

"Hmmm."

The two stood staring at the open plain before them. Behind were the palaces and governmental buildings and large gardens, but these two were never placed in areas that overlooked that. They got the barren horizon view.

"Like what?" asked Oneus.

"What do you mean?"

"Well, you said you felt like you have a destiny, right?" Oneus said.

"Yeah, so?"

"So what do you think it is, Nameous Twous?"

"Ah, I see." He wiped his brow before answering. "I can't quite put my finger on it, but I sense it shall be rather important indeed. Maybe I'll be sent to save a princess, or possibly they'll choose me to lead an army. Something of that sort."

"Hmmm," said Oneus again, nodding sagely. "I hate to be the bearer of bad news, Nameous Twous, but my thoughts tell me this could not be the case for either of us."

"Why not?"

"It's basic logic," said Oneus.

"It is?" replied Twous.

"Of course."

Twous looked back off into the distance for a moment, but then said, "I don't understand, Nameous Oneus, why would we not be utilized in some grand way?"

"Because we were not even important enough for the authors to give us proper names, man!"

§ § §

Thumpus pointed the sword at Lance and Allison. "Anyway, who are you two?"

"I'm Allison Smith."

"And I'm Mitch Bowenkawski," said Lance powerfully, "though you may know me as Sir Lance-A-Lot."

Buttus scratched his cheek. "Let me guess: Costume party?"

"I don't think—"

"Yes," interrupted Allison. "That's right. Were there others here from the costume party? We're looking for them."

"Took them to the emperor earlier," answered Thumpus. "They said they had an invitation. You have one, too?"

Allison smiled. "Of course. We were with them."

"Were?" Buttus said.

"We, uh…" She turned away slightly as if hiding a blush. "We stopped off in the woods for a little afternoon delight."

"Heh heh," said Buttus.

Thumpus winked at Lance and said, "Well done, Sir Lick-Her-Spot."

"That's Lance-A-Lot."

"Ah, yeah, sorry."

Buttus Facius grunted and said, "Follow us."

# ALONE TIME

JUPITER AND LETO had finished watching the end of *CSI: Alpha Centauri* and Jupiter was not pleased with the outcome.

"How is it that a Roriorian Nun killed the guy?" Jupiter said, scoffing. "It doesn't make any damn sense. Firstly, it's against their Order to do so; secondly, she wasn't even in the vicinity when it happened; and finally *she was dead before he was*!"

"It's just a show, dear," said Leto as she sat in front of the console to check on the status of things on Earth.

A green light blinked.

"Who is that?" said Jupiter, standing behind Leto.

"*That* is Lance-A-Lot," Leto replied with a grin.

"And who is that with him? She's rather ravenous."

"Probably just some floozy."

"Even better," Jupiter said, grinning himself.

Leto leaned back and glanced coyly up at Jupiter. "You thinking what I'm thinking?"

He was. "Swing party?"

They both began to giggle. It wasn't often that Leto would go in for that sort of thing these days, so whenever she brought up the thought, Jupiter was more than happy to oblige. Obviously there was something about this Lance-A-Lot fellow that revved her warp drive, but if that meant Jupiter would get a roll in the hay with the other woman, he wouldn't complain.

"Whatcha'll looking at?" said Pluto as he walked into the room.

"Nothing!" Jupiter said, spinning away from the console. Then he realized he'd been a little too animated. He leaned back on the desk and scratched on its corner. "Nothing at all."

"Hmmm."

"So," Jupiter said at length, "you going out tonight, by chance, Pluto?"

Pluto looked at him curiously. "Wasn't planning on it. Why?"

"No reason. Right, dear?"

"Nothing I can think of…" Leto trailed off and then held up a finger. "Except maybe judging the dead or something?"

"What?"

"You know they call you Hades and you're supposed to judge the dead?"

"Yeah, I know," he said with a shudder. "Never did like that. Kind of creepy."

Jupiter could see that Pluto needed a little more of a hint. The one thing men shared was the ability to tell when one of their pals had the potential to get lucky. It was an unwritten rule that, when spotted, your duty was to vamoose as deftly as possible.

"Anyway," Jupiter said, giving Pluto a knowing look, "was just thinking it may be a nice night for you to be... somewhere... else."

"Sorry?"

"You know," Jupiter said, more insistently, "*go somewhere else* on this fine evening." Then he winked and added, "Like, away from the ship, for example."

Pluto frowned. "What are you talking about?"

Leto sighed and pushed Jupiter out of the way. She then stood up and put her hand on her hip. Both gods flinched.

"We want to bone," she stated. "So go away."

"Oh!" Pluto nearly choked on his drink. "Well... Wow! Uh…"

Leto pointed at the exit to the landing bays. "Now!"

"Jeez," said Pluto, setting his drink down and walking to the door. "Is she like this during your—"

"Now!"

"I'm going, I'm going!"

# ALL BACK

THE ENTIRE ENTOURAGE from Camelot was back up in the main palace.

Arthur quickly detailed what had transpired between him, Arty, the gods, and Flaccidus. The fact that neither of the kings were going to be executed was a relief for everyone, especially the kings who were planned to be executed.

Things were a bit more relaxed now, too. They were all seated and there were small plates of fruits being passed around. Arthur would have preferred a nice bowl of stew and an ale, truth be told, but he wasn't going to press his luck.

"All of you are from a different time, yes?" asked Apollo.

"Well, uh—" started Merlin, giving Arthur a concerned look.

Apollo waved at the wizard. "Speak, Merlin."

"You know my name?"

"Of course," Apollo replied with a chuckle. "We're gods. Right, Athena?"

"Though it should be abundantly clear by now," she said tiredly, "I shall answer it once again: Yes, we're gods."

"Uh, okay," said Merlin. "Well, are you sure you want me to speak of this in front of Fickleweenus?"

"For the love…" Flaccidus closed his eyes and took a deep breath. "My name is Flaccidus, man! Honestly, how difficult is that to remember? Don't you think it's bad enough of a name as it is?"

"Sorry," said Merlin with his hands up in surrender.

"He's just a temporary emperor," Apollo said dismissively. "Who is he going to tell?"

Galahad leaned forward. "Temporary?"

"Of course," said Athena. "Any of the scholars from your day can tell you there's no Emperor Flaccidus in the history of the Roman Empire."

"I was originally Longus Dongus," Flaccidus put in.

"No one cares," Athena said, clearly getting a good deal of enjoyment from the man's humiliation.

"Harsh."

"Truly, it is," Arthur agreed with Arty. He then set down his bowl of fruit and focused on Athena. It wasn't much of a challenge since her beauty was unfathomable. "What have you against this man?"

"He killed off his brother because of a lost bet," Athena answered.

"Horrible thing to do," spat Apollo.

Flaccidus looked at everyone in turn. "He made me change my name from…" He stopped and put his head in his hands. "Oh, never mind."

Arthur had seen many lives taken during his years in royal circles. There was always some enterprising person who had designs on ruling an empire. They rarely understood that to be the ruler put you square in the crosshairs of a slingshot, bow, crossbow, knife, or sword. And if you were in the future, there were also pistols, sniper rifles, and all sorts of advanced explosives—based on the shows he'd seen on Allison's TV, anyway.

"So," Arthur began, "because he had his brother killed—which is indeed dastardly, unless it was for a solid reason, such as protecting the kingdom—you dislike him?"

Athena raised her eyebrows and said, "His brother was great in the sack."

"So true," said Apollo wistfully.

"Amen," agreed Slutius.

Flaccidus snapped his head towards his queen. "What?"

"Okay," Merlin said, obviously having had time to think things through during the discussion over Flaccidus's, well, predicament. "We came back in a time machine."

Apollo nodded sagely. "Is that so?"

"We saw you arrive," noted Athena, "but we weren't sure how you'd done it."

"Indeed. Did you invent this contraption, Merlin?"

"No, Apollo. I haven't a clue how it works."

"Do any of you know?" asked Athena.

Nobody said anything. They all just shook their heads. Merlin and Galahad probably *did* know something about it, but they were being tight-lipped. Surely the gods could manage time travel. If not, how would they know about Arthur, Merlin, and the rest?

There were no future books. Speculative novels, sure, but nothing like a history book of the future.

Arty grunted finally and said, "All I know is that it involves bein' in a cave that's after lookin' like a tree."

"What?" said Apollo.

"It was in my house," answered Merlin. "I live in a hollowed-out cave. Anyway, apparently something went wrong and we ended up here."

"I see, I see." Apollo flicked a grape into the air and expertly caught it between his teeth. "You do realize that this could jeopardize your timeline, right?"

"I'm all too aware of that," Merlin replied, "but I'm afraid we are rather stuck."

They couldn't have been stuck for too long. Allison would have to notice something was awry the moment that she and Lance came back for a visit. That was some time away, sure, but as long as these gods were about, it seemed that Arthur and his party were safe.

"Flaccidus," commanded Athena as she stood and stretched, "prepare a feast for this evening so that we may discuss this further. Put our guests in proper lodgings and keep a set of guards around to protect them from prying eyes." She began a sensual walk to the main door. "I shall be in the main suite."

"Mine?" said Flaccidus.

"Is that a problem?"

"Uh…" Flaccidus's shoulders drooped. "No, my god."

"Didn't think so."

"And I shall be at the bath house," announced Apollo with a wide smile.

Flaccidus sniffed. "Not surprising."

"What was that?" Apollo said, stopping and looking back at the emperor.

"Uh... Was just thinking about who to invite to the feast."

"Good point," Apollo mused. "Too late to get local royalty roused."

"Invite the lower level guards," Athena said wickedly. "Tell them to dress for a night of fun. Make their superiors walk the walls for once."

"Devious," giggled Apollo. "I like it."

"They'll be furious, my god," Flaccidus yelped, looking weaker with every passing moment.

"Would you prefer the fury of your elite guards," Athena said as her eyes grew cold, "or mine?"

# WHERE'D THEY GO?

AS THUMPUS RUMPUS and Buttus Facius walked Allison and Lance down toward the emperor's palace, Lance took the opportunity to look around.

There were large buildings in most directions with some outcroppings of empty areas splitting amongst them. Each structure was impressively put together with gigantic cylindrical columns, grand steps, and carved artistry that demonstrated the skill of the craftsmen from this age. The people were mostly dressed in white outfits that revealed their legs and arms. They wore thin leather belts that appeared to serve no real purpose besides decoration, and Lance was hard-pressed to spot anyone unadorned with jewelry.

The two guards were walking ahead of them, obviously taking the ruse of Lance and Allison being invited guests to heart. Were Lance in their shoes, he would have followed his quarry so that he could keep an eye on them.

"So how long have you two been guards?" asked

Allison.

Thumpus glanced back over his shoulder and answered, "Going five years now for me."

"I'm just about four myself," said Buttus.

"Enjoy it?"

"Better than when I was a towel-boy at the bath house," replied Thumpus.

"What was wrong with being a towel-boy?"

"I was on the male side."

"Ah."

"My last job was okay," said Buttus as they walked down a few steps. "Was a taskmaster."

"What's that?" Lance asked.

"Like it sounds: I yelled at slaves and hit them with a whip when they didn't work hard enough." Buttus shrugged. "Did that for years, but sort of lost the joy in it. It was fun enough at first, sure. I mean, think about it, I was getting *paid* to yell at people all day and hit them with a whip. But I couldn't help but wonder if there was more to life than that."

"And did you find that 'something' in being a guard?" said Allison.

"Not in the least."

"Dignitaries," Thumpus announced.

They stepped off the path for a few moments as a procession of people marched towards them. Each was wearing a gold-leafed tiara, all of different sizes and shapes, and they all had younger servants bumbling behind them who were carrying scrolls and leather pouches.

As each set walked past, Lance was able to hear brief snippets of their conversations.

"…And the regency is to make this proclamation when?" said one pompous-sounding fellow.

"Third week of the month," answered another.

A chubby fellow was saying, "Did you see the way Scabbus Scratchus was digging at himself during our discussion? I swear the man is unwashed."

Lance quickly scanned the flock of important figures to try and spot who this Scabbus fellow may have been. As fortune would have it, the man was only a few in line behind the chubby man who had been saying derogatory things about him. Lance knew this because the guy was giving his groin a full-on scratch.

"Did you see how Slipus Outicus's hindquarters were showing from his outfit again?" said Scabbus Scratchus. "You'd think he'd feel the breeze."

Lance glanced back up the line. Sure enough, the man known as Slipus Outicus was displaying his derrière for the world to see.

"Let me ask you, Dribblus Mucus," queried a strong-looking brute to another who was busily wiping his chin, "do you honestly think we can have the crops sewed up by the end of the season?"

"It can be done, Uranus Bleedus," answered Dribblus. "We just need to stay focused."

Lance found these names odd, but as he watched them pass, he cringed. Some people should simply *not* wear white.

"How are the kids these days, Fukus Toomuchus?" said a man to one of the few women in the group. "You have, what, fifteen now?"

"Seventeen, Rotundus Posterius," the woman

replied.

The marching paused, giving Lance a good view of the man, making clear that his name fit his persona as well.

"How do you keep track of them all?" asked Rotundus with a chuckle.

"It's all in how you name them."

"What are their names again?"

"The oldest is Vini, and then there's Vini, and Vini." She was counting on her fingers while looking up to the right in thought. "Vini, Vini, and Vini. Then Vini, of course, and Vini, Vini—"

"Wait a moment, Fukus Toomuchus," said Rotundus, "you keep saying the same name over and over again. Did you name all of your children Vini?"

"Ah, yes, sorry I didn't explain that. When I was listing them off just now, I was recalling their faces and not thinking of the actual names. You see, when you have so many children it just doesn't make sense to name them all differently. Doing that means that I'll have to call them all to dinner by each name. With seventeen kids, that's a challenge." Fukus Toomuchus smiled proudly. "For me it's easy. When I want them to all come to dinner, I merely holler out, 'Vini, it's meal time!' and they all come running."

"Brilliant," said Rotundus, to which Lance had to agree. "But, Fukus Toomuchus, it begs the question what do you do when you only wish to speak with one of them?"

"Oh, that's easy," she replied with a dismissive wave as the line began moving again. "If I have need to discuss something with only one, I just call them by their last name."

"Ah," said Rotundus Posterius.

Lance had to think about that one for a minute.

Soon they were back on the path and heading towards the palace again.

The weather was hot, but dry. While he wasn't exactly uncomfortable in his getup, he assumed the guards must have been on fire. That was the life of a soldier though, and one that he'd spent many years serving himself. In their own way, they were undoubtedly proud of the fact that they were suffering with sweat. Plus, it gave them something to complain about at the end of the day.

Lance felt an odd sensation at that moment. A tingling. He glanced over at Allison and saw her hair was sticking up. Something was wrong.

§ § §

"What level did you make as taskmaster, Buttus?" Thumpus asked, feeling somewhat impressed.

"Seven."

"I didn't know that. You were pretty near the top. Upper management." Thumpus studied the gruff, middle-aged man as they continued walking. "I'm impressed."

"Yeah, but they wanted to push me up that final step, running an entire section."

"Seriously? You could have been a Vice Taskmaster?"

"Was within reach," replied Buttus, "but I wasn't interested in doing the hours. I like having my evening and weekends. Plus, giving reports to the emperor isn't exactly my idea of fun."

"I'll bet. Well, anyway, as you can see, we've both been guards since—" Thumpus looked back and paused. "They're gone."

"What?" replied Buttus, spinning around. "Shit."

"Where'd they go?" Thumpus said, scanning the area frantically.

"I don't know," Buttus said, looking equally shocked.

Thumpus pulled forth his blade, not sure what else to do. If Supreme Guard Dickus Headus heard about this, they'd be walking nightshift for a month!

"We have to find them," Thumpus said as he started to walk away.

"Orrrr…" Buttus said, grabbing Thumpus by the arm, "we could go back to our post and act like we never saw them in the first place."

"That would be dishonest," said Thumpus, blinking.

"Would you rather be honest and deal with Dickus Headus, or turn a blind eye, get home on time, and *not* be punished?"

Thumpus felt his jaw drop. "Wow, Buttus, you really *were* in upper management!"

# GOTTA DO SOMETHIN'

SITTING IN THE house of a wizard was not something your average Scottish soldier wanted to do. Aside from the fact that just sitting around was dull, there were also the magical trinkets in the room to contend with.

Doonan was still trying to come to terms with the two people who blinked in and out of existence in the back room. He could see that Bedivere wasn't any better off for having seen the event either. If nothing else, they had that in common. Well, that and being in an army, anyway.

"I can't be after just sittin' around whilst me king is in jeopardy," Doonan said, pushing off the couch and stepping to the window. "It ain't right."

"I'm sure he's fine," Bedivere said. "Merlin goes on these things all the time. Never quite understood how he'd disappeared before today, and still don't really *understand* it, but he's clearly got magic on his side, so I'm not worried."

"Well, I am," stated Doonan. "Magic makes me

short hairs curl."

"Of that we can agree."

Bedivere stood up and started walking around as well.

The view out the window was nice. It was a clear image of the castle and the hills beyond. Doonan wasn't a man who traveled much, at least not in a leisurely way, but now and then he got to see visions like this and it made him wonder if maybe it wouldn't be a good idea to take his wife on a trip. Nah, she'd just ruin it with her incessant nagging. Hell, he'd never have joined up in the army had he not married her. Of course, he could go on a trip and just tell her it was a special mission from his commanding officer. He smiled at the thought.

"I wonder if he has a bottle of spirits around here," said Bedivere.

Doonan felt his bladder threaten to loosen. "Ye mean ghosts?"

"No," Bedivere said, looking at Doonan as if he were stupid. "I mean booze."

"Booze?"

"Yeah, that's what Merlin calls it." The knight suddenly grinned and reached into a cubby on one of the desks. "Ah, here's something!"

"You shouldn't be touchin' things."

Bedivere wiped the bottle and studied it for a second.

"Tequila?" he said with a conspiratorially raised eyebrow.

"Ta kill who?" he replied slowly.

"This stuff is called tequila. I've shared many

bottles of this with Merlin over the years. Really good stuff. Care for some?"

"Is it magical?" said Doonan with a gulp.

Bedivere nodded. "After about the third glass."

# SWINGING WITH THE GODS

A BLINK LATER and Lance was standing inside of an odd place. It wasn't anything that Lance had seen before, but he'd heard descriptions of something like it on the television.

It was cold, had panels and screens everywhere, lots of silver accents, and white floors. The air was conditioned similarly to Allison's apartment, which felt nice compared to the heat of the Roman walkway.

Lance found that he wasn't as freaked out as he should have been. Maybe all of this traveling through time over the last little while had calmed him, or maybe his brain was so fogged from the transports that he was simply incapable of reacting as he once did.

"What just happened?" said Allison in a relaxed voice.

"I don't know," Lance replied, "but I have a feeling we're not in Kansas anymore, Two Toes."

"It's 'Toto' and you really need to stop watching so much TV."

"Actually, wait!" Lance said as a moment of clarity swept over him. "Now that you mention it, I saw something like this on *Ancient Anuses*!"

"Aliens."

"What?"

"The show is about aliens, not anuses."

"That's right. Aliens. Sorry."

Just then a man walked around the corner. He was a big man with gray hair that was set just so. He had steely blue eyes and a nice mid-summer tan. Next to him stood a younger woman who was built pleasingly. She had long, dark hair that accentuated her green eyes beautifully.

"Well, hello there," said the man in a deep, resonating voice.

Lance jumped between his beloved and the fellow, ready to defend her with his life. Truth be told, he would have done that for anyone. It was in his training. But there was something more deep-seated about it with his wife. In other words, it wasn't simply a duty-bound response.

Allison, though, was not like the women of Lance's time. She considered male chivalry to be more of a nuisance than an endearment. She'd told him so many times, in fact. So he wasn't all that surprised when she smacked him on the back of his head and pushed him out of the way.

"I can take care of myself, thank you very much."

"Sorry," Lance replied while rubbing his head.

"Who are you?" Allison asked the gray-haired man.

"The name's Jupiter. And you are?"

Allison's eyes opened widely. "Jupiter?"

"Now that's a coincidence," said Jupiter. "I thought I was the only one with that name. Truly something, don't you think, Leto?"

"She was only verifying your name, dear," said Leto with a commiserating roll of the eyes at Allison. Leto then turned and batted her eyelashes a couple of times before saying, "Hello, Sir Lance-A-Lot."

"What's going on here?" said Allison. "Are you two being for real with the names? I mean…" She paused and looked at Lance. Then she ran over to one of the panels and looked down for a moment. Finally, she turned and walked back slowly. "Holy shit, you *are* being for real."

"Yes, dear," said Leto.

Lance felt smart this time. Usually Allison was way ahead of him on things, but since he had nothing to do but watch TV on most days (and nights), he had learned a ton of things that Allison called "pseudoscience."

"You two are a couple of anuses, right?" he ventured with a proud smile.

"Excuse me?"

"Pardon?"

"Aliens, Mitch," Allison corrected.

"Oh, right, that."

"Who is Mitch?" said Jupiter, glancing around the room.

"That's my real name," said Lance.

"Ah," said Jupiter. "Mine's Zeus."

"No effing way," shrieked Allison.

Lance was not used to seeing her respond like that, except when they were in the bedroom, of course.

"I'm being for realz," said Jupiter.

Allison scrunched her face. "'For realz?'"

"Sorry, it's how the kids talk these days. Was just trying to be cool, you know?"

This had obviously been too much for Allison because she began shaking her head and waving her hands. Her actions made Lance feel as though maybe he *should* have been more apprehensive about the situation.

"Hold the phone," she said. "You two are really the Greek and/or Roman gods?"

"You know it," Jupiter replied with a wink.

"This is unreal!"

"It gets better," added Leto.

"How could it possibly get better?"

Leto began twirling her hair in her fingers. "We've brought you up here to make a bit of a proposition."

"Oh?" said Allison.

Jupiter stepped over and took Allison's hand. He gave it a kiss, which was the gentlemanly way to greet a lady, so Lance held himself in check. Still, the man held that kiss a little longer than was polite, at least to Lance's standards.

Finally, Jupiter resumed his standing position and whispered, "Ever been with a god before?"

"Hey now," said Lance, stepping forward, "I'll kick you square in the stones and—"

And that's when Leto seductively touched his arm. "You've not been with a god either, right, Lance?"

"Uhhh…" He tried to answer, but whenever his

nether region got word that potential action was about, the blood in his brain began to lower, making him far more foggy than what the transporter did to him.

"I'm in," stated Allison without flinching.

Lance's brain quickly reassessed the situation. "What?"

"What, what?" his bride said with a shrug. "How many people can say they've boned a god?"

"Most of the people in ancient Rome right now, actually," admitted Leto.

"True," agreed Jupiter.

"Okay, fair enough," Allison conceded, "but I mean since Ancient Greece and Rome."

Lance was confused. On the one hand, Leto *was* exceedingly hot, and they were obviously in some kind of spaceship, which meant this was one woman —or god, as the case may be—he couldn't possibly conquer—sexually speaking—in either his native era of Camelot or his new one with Allison. Especially not the new one. Still, Allison seemed to have jumped at the chance pretty quickly.

"Are you saying you really want to do this?" he asked.

"Oh, come on, Lance," Allison said as if it were nothing. "Leto is *hot*! Even I can see that. Don't act like you don't want to tag her."

"You're not so bad yourself," Leto said sweetly.

"Ravishing," Jupiter agreed, still holding Allison's hand.

"Lance," Allison said with those puppy-dog eyes she sometimes got, "a god just called me ravishing. I can't walk away from that!"

Lance wasn't very comfortable about all of this, but it wasn't like he could compete with a god, right?

"Well, if you're sure—"

"Sweet," said Allison, smiling at Jupiter. "Let's do this, Zeus."

"Technically, it's Jupiter."

"Right, I get that," Allison said, nodding, "and no offense, but I'd rather screw a god than a planet."

# PREPARING FOR THE FEAST

GUINEVERE WAS FINE with going to a feast, but she had nothing to wear. While she rather liked the feel of the boxers and trousers she had on, she didn't feel it was befitting to represent her kingdom, regardless of the era she was currently in. And she certainly didn't think Arthur's green gown was proper for a king to wear to such an event.

Arthur, of course, was busily looking at the architecture in the room. He seemed to be fascinated by the silliest things.

"You seem distant, my petunia," Arthur said after setting down a carving of a cat.

"I don't have my wardrobe, so I feel poorly about joining a party like this."

"You look fine, my love."

"Fine?" Guinevere said, grimacing. "Whatever happened to the days of 'ravishing' and 'picturesque?'"

"You still are, of course," Arthur said, taking her into his arms and then tilting his lower half away. "It's just rather trying to say that when you've got a sock stuffed in your pantaloons."

She nodded. "Fair enough."

"And what of me?" Arthur said, motioning to himself. "If I go down wearing this same outfit, they'll wonder why when there is clearly no costume party happening."

Guinevere was just about to suggest they check for chests and drawers when a knock came at the door.

"Yes?" said Arthur, answering it.

The two guards who had been stationed with them in the dungeon were standing outside, holding outfits that looked similar to those worn by people in this era.

"Pardon our interruption, sir. I am Guard Probius and this is Guard Clearlyachickus. We have brought a change of clothes for you and your lady."

"Oh?" Arthur stepped aside. "Come right in."

Probius and Clearlyachickus stepped into the room and set the clothes at the edge of the bed. Clearlyachickus glanced over at Guinevere a few times, visibly uncomfortable. Guinevere was surprised by her name, thinking maybe she'd heard it wrong. It *was* a her, obviously… right?

"Excuse me," said Guinevere, signaling the guard over.

"Yes, my lady?"

"You're uh—" Guinevere said, suddenly wondering if it was really a wise thing to bring up.

"Yes?" Clearlyachickus said again.

Guinevere glanced at Probius and lowered her voice. "I noticed you in the dungeon. What's your name again?"

"Guard Clearlyachickus, ma'am."

"Clearlyachickus?"

"Yes, ma'am."

"And yet you're dressed like a man."

Clearlyachickus's eyes looked like something Allison had referred to as "a deer in headlights."

'What are you saying?" said Clearlyachickus.

"You *are* a woman, right?"

At this, the guard swallowed hard. She looked over her shoulder at the other guard. Guinevere gazed past the woman as well. Probius was standing facing the headboard of the bed, obviously doing his best to not hear a thing.

"You can tell?" whispered Clearlyachickus.

"Sorry," answered Guinevere with a nod.

"Is it my knockers? I try to tape them, but they're rather—"

"Enormous, yes," said Guinevere. "And, 'knockers'?"

"It's the outfit," the guard replied. "I speak that way when wearing it for some reason."

"I totally understand." Guinevere spun around slowly. "You'll notice I'm wearing men's garb myself."

"I *did* notice that, but I thought you were at a costume party."

"Right, well, my point is that I find myself saying man-terms as well in this getup."

"Ah." Clearlyachickus had the sudden look of finally meeting another person who could understand her predicament. "I also keep my hair short and I try to wear loose clothing when off-duty, but these leather guard outfits make my booty pop."

"And you clearly shave your legs," noted Guinevere.

"Oh, damn," Clearlyachickus groaned. "Didn't think of that."

"*And* your name is Clearlyachickus."

The girl furrowed her brow. "So?"

"Say it aloud."

"Clearlyachickus," she said. "Sorry, I don't see the problem."

"Seriously?" Guinevere said. "Okay, what is a chick?"

"A baby chicken."

"Ah, yes, I suppose it depends in what time you're in, then," said Guinevere, and then added, "and probably locale. In my time a chick is the same thing, but way in the future, it's a name that men call women."

"The future?"

"Yes, we call men 'dudes' or 'guys' and they call us 'babes' or 'chicks.'" She then tilted her head to the side. "Well, not all of them, but you get the idea."

"Not really."

Guinevere felt for the girl. It was bad enough hundreds of years in the future, but she imagined it was even worse in this time. Then again, from looking around at the people here, it may not have been.

"Do any of the other guards know?"

"I don't think so," she said uncertainly.

Guinevere snapped her fingers at Probius. "You

there: Is there anything different about this guard when compared to other guards?"

"What are you doing?" hissed Clearlyachickus.

Probius stepped over, keeping his eyes firmly ahead, looking at neither of them.

"In what way, ma'am?"

"Let's go with physicality," said Guinevere.

"Guard Clearlyachickus is the same as all guards, as far as I can tell," Probius replied without inflection.

"Is that so?"

"We're taught to see no differences in each other, ma'am."

"So there is *nothing* you've noticed that's out of the ordinary with Guard Clearlyachickus?"

"Except for the large knockers and bouncing booty, you mean?" Probius said, speaking precisely as he was expected to.

"Yes, except…" Guinevere crossed her arms and gave him a duck-look. "No, that's exactly what I mean! Doesn't that strike you as odd?"

"It strikes me as the only reason I tolerate getting sent to Dickus Headus all the time," admitted Probius and then snapped his eyes back to the wall.

"What?" said Clearlyachickus.

"Who?" said Guinevere.

Probius began to sweat. "Uh…"

"Wait a second here," Clearlyachickus said, stepping in front of Probius. "You *were* assigned as my partner, right?"

"Yes, of course… Sort of… I mean…" His shoulders dropped along with his stare. He sighed heavily and said, "Not exactly."

"I'm confused," Clearlyachickus said.

"I asked to be on duty with you whenever possible," Probius admitted.

"You did?"

"I did."

"But why?" Clearlyachickus questioned. "I always get you in trouble. I don't *mean* to, but it seems to happen anyway."

"You honestly don't know?" he asked, staring into her eyes.

"No."

"It's because I'd rather look at your physicality, as she put it, than at the other guys. Besides, you smell nice. The other guards just smell."

"Probius! I never knew you knew I was a woman."

"Seriously? Your name is 'Clearlyachickus.'"

"Right."

"Everyone knows," Probius said after a second. "I'm just the only one who pays Dickus Headus to let me... Uh—"

"You *pay* him?"

"Oh boy," said Probius, wiping the sweat from his forehead.

Arthur broke the tension by walking into the room, parading around in his white outfit. He had a spring in his step as he pirouetted a few times.

"What do you think?"

"That's the female outfit, sir," stated Probius.

"Oh?" Arthur replied innocently.

"Arthur," warned Guinevere while shaking her head, "go and change into the proper one, will you?"

Arthur smiled mischievously. "Sorry, my

persimmon."

"Maybe we should get out of your way," said Probius while turning briskly towards the door.

Clearlyachickus was hot on his heels. "Guard Probius, you and I seem to have a few things to discuss!"

# AFTERGLOW

WHEN LETO AND Lance had finished up their fun-time, they headed back out to the main area of the ship.

Lance couldn't quite pinpoint the way he felt other than excited. Not because he'd just boned a god, though that was pretty fantastic, but because he found the entire concept of being on a ship in space rather incredible. Obviously most people would be thrilled to be in his position—and many would also have loved being in the position that Leto was in less than thirty minutes ago. But others from his era would have been terrified—and, yes, that relates to *either* of the aforementioned positions… Leto was quite adventurous, after all.

"That was amazing," Leto said, swooning as they rounded the corner, "and now I know why they call you Lance-A-Lot." She giggled. "Come to think of it, that's the first time I've called a man 'god.'"

Jupiter and Allison were seated on opposite ends of the couch. Jupiter's face was downcast and Allison had her arms crossed. She was wearing a frown of disappointment.

"Was your tryst as lovely as mine, dear?" Leto said, clearly oblivious to the tension in the room

"It was, um…" Jupiter cleared his throat. "Things didn't quite progress as…" He adjusted in his seat. "You see, I felt a little bit of pressure and—"

"He couldn't get it up," announced Allison.

"Yes," Jupiter said, slumping even farther, "that."

"So why didn't you take your Godagra pills?" asked Leto.

"I can't, ever since starting the blood pressure medications," he replied. "You know that."

"Oh, that's right."

"So you two didn't have relations?" asked Lance.

"Nope," replied Allison. "Seems I wasn't enough of a draw to get a god horny enough."

"Oh, don't think that," Jupiter said desperately. "You're quite attractive for a non-god. I'm just not as young as I used to be."

"A non-god?"

"I feel just terrible about this and…" Jupiter paused and looked at Lance's mid-section. He pointed. "Are you trying to steal something from my ship, you pathetic human?"

Lance looked down. "Excuse me?"

"A ray gun, maybe?" Jupiter said, standing forcefully. "One of our advanced batteries, per chance?"

"Jupiter, will you relax?" said Leto. "That's just his dong."

"Oh, sorry." Jupiter instantly seemed to calm

down. "I'm just a bit overwhelmed at the moment and…" His face contorted again. "*That's his dong?*"

"Part of it, anyway."

Jupiter groaned. "Well, I'm sure *that* won't help my performance issues." He turned to Allison. "Honestly, I don't know what you were expecting, dear, but I don't even think a horse could compete with that."

"So I'm learning," replied Allison.

"You are quite lucky, you know?" said Leto with a forlorn look.

Allison gave Jupiter a sideways glance. "Again, so I'm learning."

There was a chiming sound that reminded Lance of the phone ringing in the future. This one played a tune that he hadn't recognized, though, and it seemed to be sounding throughout the ship.

"I'll get it," said Jupiter as he reached for a small, black circular piece that he then pressed into his ear. "Jupiter here. Oh, yes, Apollo, what is it? A feast? Okay, well, I think your mother and I will stay on the ship. You know we only like to make an appearance during dire times." He nodded a few times. "True, true, but I'd rather you and Athena manage this one on your own. We'll send down the latest two arrivals from the future. Hmmm? Oh yes, Allison Smith and Sir Lance-A-Lot showed up a little while after you left." Another few nods. "Right, well, I must go now."

"What's going on?" asked Allison.

"Your friends are apparently the guests of honor at a feast this evening, so you should really get going."

"The sooner, the better," said Allison as she got up and walked to the place that they'd arrived at earlier.

"Again," Jupiter attempted, "I'm truly sorry that things didn't… work."

"Sure. Right. No problem."

Jupiter groaned miserably.

"I'll transport you down to the main chambers," said Leto. Then she glanced again at Lance's middle-region and sighed wistfully. "I should probably make sure the batteries are at full charge first… on many things."

"What?" said Jupiter.

Another man walked in, saying, "You all done yet?"

"Your timing is as impeccable as ever, Pluto," Jupiter said with a sour look.

"Pluto?" asked Allison, looking him over.

"My lady," Pluto said, kissing her hand.

Allison glanced back at Lance questioningly.

"If you feel you must, dear," Lance said, sighing.

"What's this about?" Pluto asked.

"Ever bone a human before?" Allison said with a wink.

"Many times, yes," Pluto replied, letting go of her hand.

"Well, then?"

"Uh, I mean you no offense when I say this, lady," Pluto said uncomfortably, "but you're not my type."

Allison's face tightened. "Oh, yeah? Well, you're not even considered a planet anymore!"

# CAUGHT

ARTHUR FOUND THE male version of the Roman outfit to be nearly as fun to wear as the female version. It was white, loose-fitting, had a nice rope-style belt, and hung somewhat like a skirt, showing off his legs. The sandals felt a little strange, but he had to admit they complemented the outfit perfectly. His favorite bit, though, was the gold-leafed tiara.

It was also nice to see Guinevere wearing a womanly outfit again, but he wouldn't dare say anything to her about it. He would also have to be careful to avoid words like "ravishing" and "picturesque" so that she didn't get a complex.

"Ready, my sweet?"

"I suppose," Guinevere replied, clearly not as happy in her current outfit as Arthur was in his.

They opened the door to find Guard Probius and Guard Clearlyachickus going at it all hot-and-heavy. The two were so intertwined that it was difficult to tell where one of them started and the other one ended.

"Oh, wow," said Guinevere as the two guards jumped away from each other. "Can't say I expected that."

"Ah!" Probius said in shock. "Sorry, my lady. We were... I mean—"

Clearlyachickus attempted to clarify things. "It's just that, uh—"

"How unprofessional," stated Arthur, feeling quite vexed. In all of his years as a king, he had never witnessed anything like this, not with guards anyway. Sure, Lance-A-Lot had a tendency of boning everything in sight, but not while he was on duty. "I shall have a word with your emperor about this."

"Oh, Arthur," Guinevere said, hushing him. "No, you won't."

"I shall so!"

She hand-on-hipped him again. "If you do, I'll take away the key to my naughty clothes cabinet."

Arthur blanched. "You wouldn't."

"Try me."

"Fine," he said with a pout. "I won't say anything, but if you were my guards, you'd be flogged for this breach of protocol."

"No, they wouldn't," Guinevere noted.

"Well, no, but they'd be whipped, at least!"

"Nope."

"Stuck in the cells for a month?" he said hopefully.

"Not even that."

Arthur squared his shoulders. "A firm talking to, then, with accusatory pointing and everything."

"Okay," Guinevere conceded, "you'd probably do that."

Finally Arthur had gotten the upper-hand... sort of.

"He's actually quite an old softy," Guinevere said as she looked back at the newly formed couple.

"Let's not bring *that* into the discussion," Arthur replied, nearly choking.

"I was talking about your demeanor, dear."

"I know you were talking about da wiener and I don't appreciate—"

"*Demeanor*, dear," Guinevere interrupted, giving him one of her looks.

"Oh, right."

"Anyway," Guinevere said, "why don't you two take our room for the next couple of hours?"

"We're on duty until we deliver you to the party, ma'am," said Probius. "After that we're supposed to be *at* the party."

"Well, it'll take you a few minutes to change, right?" Guinevere then chuckled. "And after all that you two have been holding back over the years, I'm sure a few minutes is all you'll need."

Clearlyachickus arched an eyebrow. "Devious."

"You have no idea," agreed Arthur with a sigh.

# TAKING CHANCES

DOONAN WAS NOT one to take chances, unless you include touching ladies' bottoms without their consent as chancy, which the local authority in Scotland had. He'd not done anything nefarious beyond that, of course. It wasn't in his nature. Even when he had pinched a cushion or two, it had been done as sneakily as possible.

But after having a few glasses of this tequila that Bedivere had given him, he was feeling adventurous.

"Want to go down into town and pinch... hic... some bottoms?"

"What?" said Bedivere.

"Uh, nuthin'."

"I got an... hic... idea," Bedivere said.

"What's that?"

"Why don't we go and use that magic-screen thing in the back?"

"For what?"

"To... hic... to... hic... to see what it does."

It didn't sound as pleasant as pinching a tail or two,

but Doonan was feeling bored. There was something in the back of his mind that told him this wasn't the greatest idea, but the alcohol convinced him otherwise.

"Ooookay," he said, following Bedivere to the back room. "Now what?"

"You stand on that platform… hic," Bedivere said, "and I'll do something on this screen."

"Like what?"

"I dunno." Bedivere giggled as he tapped all over the screen. "There, that should do it!"

"Do what?" asked Doonan.

"I dunno."

He pressed the big red button on the screen and the ground began to flash under Doonan's feet.

*Run, you fool!* his subconscious said, but his conscious mind was so muddled that it heard, *This is fun, it's cool!* and so he stayed in place.

An instant later he found himself standing in a field surrounded by gigantic trees. The sky was blue with wisps of red and it was hot and humid. The grass, where there was grass, appeared to be smashed down in places. It looked as if gigantic footprints had crushed the green stems into the ground.

He heard a snort and spun around to see an enormous lizard standing not two hundred feet away. It stood ten-men high, had teeth the size of Doonan's arms, a head that was easily four times his size, and arms that were tiny and swinging pointlessly at chest-level.

Doonan froze in place as the thing seemed to survey him from afar. It was clearly aware of his presence, but Doonan didn't know what to do, especially since his mind was still swimming from the batch of tequila he'd downed.

He gulped as the air grew still.

Suddenly, the massive creature roared so loudly that Doonan grabbed his ears and shat his pants.

It began running at Doonan with such speed that there was nothing the Scotsman could do but empty his bladder too.

Just as the beast was upon him, its wide jaws closing in on snapping Doonan in two, the world flashed and he was back in Merlin's house.

"What… hic… happened?" said Bedivere. "And… hic… what's that smell?"

Doonan couldn't answer verbally. It was all he could do to breathe.

"Well, what?"

He pulled his hands up to make them look as small as possible and then he bared his teeth fiercely.

"What the hell are you doing?" said Bedivere. "Oh wait… hic … Is this charades?"

Doonan nodded.

"Got it. How many words?"

Doonan held up four fingers.

"Four. Okay… short arms and… hic… vicious teeth," said Bedivere as Doonan resumed his stance. "Hmmm, sounds like some kind of creature, maybe?"

Doonan nodded.

Bedivere stroked his beard thoughtfully. "A kitten?"

Doonan frowned.

"You're right, that makes no sense. Ummm… ooh!" The knight spun and looked at the screen.

"Says here you went back… hic… a couple thousand years." Bedivere turned back with wide eyes. "Dinosaur?"

Doonan nodded.

"Wow." Bedivere gulped and then grimaced. "How is that four words?"

Doonan spun around, lifted his kilt, and showed the seat of his underpants.

"Oh, I see," said Bedivere, nodding. "You were doing… hic… charades to answer my 'What's that smell' question, right?"

Doonan nodded.

"But four words?"

Doonan jumped off the platform and croaked, "I shat me pants."

He then grabbed the bottle of tequila, downed the rest of its contents in one shot, and headed off to clean himself up.

# BACK TO THE GUARDS

LANCE AND ALLISON arrived back at the location they'd originally landed when transporting from Merlin's house. In front of them stood the same two guards as before.

"Hello?" said Allison, jarring the two men.

"Ah," said Thumpus, turning, "there you two are. Now, where'd you run off to? Could have gotten us in a world of trouble, you know?"

"Sorry," said Allison, still having a look of angst. "We were brought up to speak with the gods. Well, we were technically brought up to bone them, but it turns out that—"

"The gods, eh?" interrupted Buttus with a sniff.

"Told ya they were real," Thumpus stated.

"Have you seen one directly, then?" Buttus challenged his partner.

"Well, no, but I've heard stories." Thumpus then motioned to Lance and Allison. "These two just said they were with them, didn't they?"

Buttus shook his head. "You watch too many

hand-puppet plays, Thumpus Rumpus."

"I do not," Thumpus responded. "I just watch the one."

"And what's that one called?"

Thumpus mumbled something.

"Sorry, what was that?"

"*Current Aliens.*"

"Exactly!"

"Sorry to interrupt," said Lance, "but we're still supposed to get to the castle."

"It's called a palace," Buttus said, still displaying his emotional glee at having triumphed over Thumpus in their debate. "Honestly, are you all from a different world or something?"

"I'll bet they are," Thumpus said.

Buttus sighed. "And I thought you were one of the sane guards."

"You did?" Thumpus said, looking surprised. "Thanks!"

# THE FEAST

THE ENTIRE TROOP was back together again, but for some reason only Arthur and Guinevere were wearing the white outfits. The rest had on guard uniforms, sans the helmet, including Arty.

They were standing in a large hall with an arched roof, flourishes of gold, statues and busts of people that Arthur knew nothing of, though he assumed they were past emperors or dignitaries, and people milling about, having discussions and eating delicacies. It wasn't all that different from the parties he and Guinevere hosted in Camelot, apart from the size of the building and the number of inhabitants.

The line down the hall was rather long, but they had been told to wait because it was the royal announcer's duty to inform the entire room of each person who was making an entrance.

"What the shet are they makin' *us* wait in a queue for?" said Arty sourly. "We're after bein' royalty!"

"It's not our kingdom, Arty," Arthur pointed out, yet again.

"Oh, it ain't?" Arty said in a grandiose fashion that was laced with sarcasm. "Don't ye think I know that, ye dopey Englishman?"

"Hey!"

Guinevere pushed an arm between the two men and separated them.

"Enough, boys."

They glared at each other for a few more moments before Arty looked away.

"Bah," he said. "I'm sorry for speakin' outta turn as such. It's just that these britches they gave me are splittin' me mossy marbles in two!"

"I know what you mean," said Guinevere."

"Ye do?"

"Well, not in this outfit," she said, pointing at herself, "but I've worn a few that have had that effect."

"Ye have?"

Trumpets sounded, as they did every minute or so, causing most people to pause their conversations and look up at the royal announcer.

*Hear ye, hear ye! I hereby present Guards Cranius Rectus and Itchus Crotchius.*

Conversations resumed as the two guards walked into the pit of activity, gripping wrists and slapping each other on the back. While it may have irritated the supreme guards, as Emperor Flaccidus had expressed concern over, it was abundantly clear that the lower soldiers were getting quite a boost in morale.

"These names are atrocious," Bors announced.

"I wholeheartedly agree," said Kay, unsurprisingly.

"I'm sure their names are fine to them, you twits," Merlin said, looking rather silly wearing his guard outfit while maintaining the pointy hat.

"Says a man who carries the name 'Merlin,'" countered Bors.

"Better than 'Board Up Myanus!'" Merlin retaliated.

Galahad chuckled heartily at this.

"That's 'Bors De Ganis,' and you know it."

"How rude," said Kay.

Arty, who was clearly ignoring everyone else's conversation, said, "And what's with this footwear, anyway? I don't like having stuff between me toes."

The trumpets burst forth again, jolting Arthur the same as they'd done each time they'd sounded. Why they couldn't have just had a soft bell or maybe a firm clearing of the throat, he could not say. Granted, they used trumpets a lot in his day, too, but he'd decreed that it only be done *outdoors*.

*I hereby present Guard Horatio Harrassyurass and his wife, Giganticus Mamarus.*

"I must use the privy," announced Gaheris.

"You couldn't have gone before?" said Kay.

"I go when I go."

"At least he warned us this time," Galahad said before Kay could argue.

"Oh, come on, then," Bors said, taking Gaheris by the hand as if he were a child. "Kay and I will take him to the loo and come back after all this announcing foolishness is over."

They padded off, dragging Gaheris behind them.

"And don't even get me started on that helmet they were after expectin' us to wear," said the irritable Arty. "As if I'm going to put that blasted thing on me head."

*I hereby present Guards Chokus de Chickenus and Drunkus Askunkus.*

"The food smells good, anyway," Merlin said as he stepped from foot to foot.

Arthur understood the wizard's movements since the sandals provided little support. The soles of his feet were already aching and he had the feeling his heels would be bruised before the day was over.

But Merlin was right: The food *did* smell good. There was a buffet of meats, vegetables, fruits, and desserts that was setting Arthur's stomach to grumbling. He'd never been one to have a sweet tooth, but his mouth salivated at the sight of the large white cake that sat at the end of the table. It was slowly shrinking in size as people partook of its yumminess, though, so Arthur feared he may not have the opportunity to sample its delights.

"The food *is* intoxicating," agreed Galalad, "but a more pressing issue is on my mind."

"What?" said Merlin.

"How do we get back to our time?"

"Oh, that. Definitely a problem."

Arty began to fidget again. "It's like they purposefully want to make sure yer danglers never meet each other again!"

*I hereby announce Guard Tortoise Beats Rabbitus and his escort, Bodacious Bootius.*

"The truth is that we may well be trapped here for a while," Merlin stated as they inched forward.

"At least a month," Galahad said. "Allison assured us they'd visit, but that only happens about once a month, right?"

"Before she had a kid, yeah."

"I'm feelin' a breeze, too," said Arty, spinning around. "Is me crack after showin'?"

*I hereby present Guards Prematuria Jackulus, Hernia Rupturus, and Roidus Ragius.*

"We'll just have to learn to make the best of things until Allison and Lance-A-Lot catch on to what has happened," said Guinevere as she grabbed Arthur's arm and pointed excitedly at one of the flaming dishes.

"Precisely," said Arthur, giving her a nod at the beauty of the dish she'd indicated. "There are many things that we can bring to the table in a world as ancient as this."

"No, we can't," Merlin said soberly. "Remember, anything we do could affect the timeline."

"Exactly," Galahad agreed with a grunt.

"Maybe I've just got this on wrong?" Arty said, wincing. "I'm after gettin' chaffed!"

*I hereby present Hottus Totrottus, Tittus Fascinaticus, and Isconstantly Flashingus.*

"Well, we can't just do nothing while waiting for them to rescue us."

"Arthur is right," said Guinevere. "Hopefully Apollo and Athena will aid us with our plight."

Merlin scratched his beard. "I'm still baffled they truly exist."

"You don't believe they're really gods, right?" said Galahad, seemingly taken aback by Merlin's words.

"Of course not, you square-headed mongrel."

"Ye'd think they could have used something other than leather, yeah?" Arty asked. "Or at least have been after softnin' the edges."

*I hereby present Guards Scratchus Continuous, Sextus Transmitus Disius, Tellus Anotherus, Tinius Weenus, and Hugi Bearus.*

They moved forward a bit more. At least now Arthur was able to see the front of the line. If they didn't get to the tables soon, the food would be all but gone. He could only hope there was more being prepared; otherwise, the caterer sorely underestimated how much sustenance it took to feed soldiers.

"What we'll need to do is lay low until Allison arrives," said Merlin. "Talk to as few people as possible, and don't make any suggestions to the people in this era. Even just a simple act of getting two people to talk to each other who never would have before could be catastrophic."

"Truly?"

"It could change everything, Gwen."

"Oh... Hmmm."

"Gwen," said Merlin with a squint, "why do you look concerned?"

Arty started doing short squats. "Pretty soon I'm just gonna take the damn thing off!"

*Hear ye, hear ye! I hereby present Guard Ballus Hairus, his wife Nippletonia, and their sons, Forskinius, Pubius, and Dave.*

"'Dave'?" said Galahad, looking at the others.

"That's what I heard, too," Arthur said.

"Odd name."

"Not really, Galahad."

"I mean for ancient Rome, sire."

"Ah."

"Gwen," Merlin pressed, "is there something you want to tell us?"

"Not really."

"Okay, is there something you *need* to tell us?"

"I'm sure it's nothing."

"Oh, great," Arty whined. "Now it's startin' ta itch!"

*I hereby present Guard Cornus Holious and his wife, Vaginitus.*

It seemed as though the line was moving more quickly all of a sudden. Arthur had noticed that one of the supreme guards—at least he assumed the man was a supreme guard since he was on duty—had come up and given a message to the announcer.

"Gwen?" said Merlin.

"Well," Gwen said as they shuffled forward, "it's just that these two guards obviously had the hots for each other and, well, I let them use our room."

"Me feet hurt, me soggy sack's gettin' split, and me taint is after itchin' like the devil," stated Arty. "Am I truly the only one feelin' this?"

*I hereby present Guards Muttus Nuttus, Sweetus Parfaitius, Schlongus Longorius, Harrius Palmus, and Rectumus Odiferous.*

"Why did you offer them your room?" Merlin said to Guinevere.

"To have relations, what do you think?"

"Oh boy," said Merlin and Galahad in unison.

"Anyone have a tissue or a bit of cloth?" Arty asked.

*I hereby present Folatio the Philanderer, Dubius Phallaci, Wankus Maximus, Dropa de Turda, and Senilius… What's that? You're at a party, Senilius. Yes? For the guards. Hmmm? Yes, Senilius, you're a guard. Now just move along, will you?*

"Looks like we're up next," said Galahad as they approached the royal announcer, who took the cards they had handwritten their names upon.

*Hear ye, hear ye! I hereby present Art Hurr, Gwen of Ear,*

*Gallonhead, Art Tee, and ... Merlin.*

"Why'd he only get your name right?" said Arthur as they walked past the announcer.

"How am I supposed to know?"

"Gallonhead is not even close," complained Galahad.

"Oh, shet," said Arty pathetically. "We're after havin' to walk down steps now?"

# IT'S A WEAPON!

BORS, KAY, AND Gaheris had returned, lucky to avoid having their names butchered by the royal announcer, and after everyone got their fill of food, they headed over to the table where Emperor Flaccidus, Queen Slutius, Apollo, and Athena sat. There was a group of large guards standing in a semi-circle in front of the table. In front of them were…

"Lance-A-Lot?" said Arthur with a start.

"Allison?" Merlin chimed in.

The guards backed away slightly, allowing the new arrivals to step into the mix.

"Good to see you, sire," Lance said with a nod. He then bowed to Guinevere. "My lady."

"Again," said Arthur tightly, "she's *my* lady."

"Sorry, sire."

"I haven't any idea who these new people are, my love," Slutius was saying to Flaccidus, "but I warn you to be cautious because that one looks to be carrying a club in his pants."

Flaccidus snapped his head back and deftly

pointed. "Guards, seize that man!"

"What is the meaning of this?" said Arthur, jumping between the guards and his knight. The other knights, along with Arty, moved into position as well. "Why are you putting guards after this man?"

"He has clearly got some kind of weapon there," the emperor said, pointing.

"Where?" said Arthur, feeling confused.

Flaccidus pointed. "There!"

"That's not after bein' a weapon, ye moronic emperor," Arty said, still wincing uncomfortably from the garb he was wearing.

"Slayed *me* with it more than once," said Guinevere.

Arthur jolted. "More than once?"

"Well, it was the same night."

"Agh! It was bad enough when I'd thought he'd just done it the one time."

"Oh no, many times," Guinevere said proudly. "Just one night. Took me weeks to recover, though."

"Ew," said Arthur, thinking the food he'd just eaten might make an encore presentation. "I don't want to hear this!"

"I wouldn't mind hearing about it," Athena said with a wicked grin.

"Me either, sister," agreed Apollo.

Athena ignored him. "Would rather experience it, though."

"Oooh, snap," Apollo said while moving his head from side to side.

"Sorry, sire."

The Roman guards and the English knights—and Arty, who was so irritated at his current wardrobe situation that Arthur assumed he could have managed the fight all on his own—were staring each other down. It was clearly a losing proposition for the knights, but it was in their training to fight for right.

"I don't understand what's going on here," Flaccidus said, motioning for his guards to back down. "What are you all discussing?"

Arty did another short squat and scrunched his face as though he'd just caught wind of Sir Gaheris's britches.

"Just that the thing in that one's pants," said the Scottish king, "is a different kind of weapon than yer after thinkin' it is."

"What do you mean?" said Flaccidus.

Arty straightened up. "It's his beef cannon."

"Sorry, his what?" Flaccidus replied with a frown.

"Angry cucumber."

"I don't understand."

"His tummy banana."

"Wait," Flaccidus said, "are you telling me that's a piece of fruit?"

"Nay, it's his dangling spout."

"Huh?"

Arty took a deep breath and answered, "His pointy plug, hefty hose, lap club, love python, soldier sausage, dragon dagger, pocket rope, gnarled trunk, stud stilt—"

"You are making no sense at all to me," Flaccidus interrupted, sitting back in his chair while throwing his hands up in surrender.

"Hmmm," said Arty, and then snapped his fingers. "Ah ha! It's his Veinous Maximus!"

"Veinous Maximus?" said Arthur.

Arty shrugged. "When in Rome, yeah?"

"Are you trying to tell me that *that* lump in his trousers is his praetorian penetrator?" said Flaccidus.

"Uh…" It was Arty's turn to squint. "Maybe?"

"Oh," Slutius said with glee. "I see the outline now. Yes, that's not a weapon. I mean, well, it *does* look dangerous. In a good way. A very, very good—"

"Honestly," Flaccidus cut her off, "it's like you just can't get enough. You should have been named Wantsitalot or something."

"Seriously?" said Guinevere. "Her name is already Slutius."

"So?"

"Never mind."

"Anyway," Flaccidus said, setting his hands on the table, "you obviously know these new people, Arthur?"

"We do," answered Arthur. "This is Sir Lance-A-Lot, another of my knights, and this is his wife, Allison Smith."

"Ah ha," Flaccidus said, pointing sternly at Allison. "So you're the one who had a costume party and didn't invite me?"

"I did?" Allison replied, looking around.

"Just roll with it," Merlin whispered. "We didn't expect you to arrive so soon."

"Oh. Uh, yeah, sure. Sorry about the non-invite." Allison's eyes darted about. "Didn't think you'd be interested."

"Why wouldn't I be?" Flaccidus replied, looking injured by her comment. "I like to dress up and have fun. Just because I'm an emperor doesn't mean I'm a stick-in-the-mud."

"No," agreed Athena. "That would be Apollo."

Apollo sat up. "What?"

"Well," Allison continued, "I'll remember for next time."

"There may not be a next time," said Flaccidus sinisterly.

"All right, all right," Athena said, waving her hands. "Calm down, Flaccidus, and everyone else. These people are under our protection."

That shut everyone up. It was one thing to go against the Roman soldiers, but it was entirely something else to do battle with those whom the Roman soldiers feared.

"I cannae take it anymore," said Arty as he reached under himself and pulled down on the leather strap that had been squishing his nethers.

Everyone cringed at the sight of Arty's junk dangling freely.

"Who the shet made these outfits? This strap is threatenin' to snip off me tenderviddles, it is."

"That's not supposed to go under there," said Athena, giggling. "It's meant for holding a dagger."

"It is after holdin' me dagger!"

"No," she said while pointing around at the other soldiers who had on the same outfit. "See?"

"Damn. I'll be back."

"So what do we do now?" said Arthur as he watched Arty skitter away while reaching under his person to hold the strap down.

"I don't know about the rest of you," said Athena,

"but I could stand a little alone time with Lance-A-Lot."

Slutius cooed, "Me too."

"For the love of…" Flaccidus stopped and then just shrugged. "You know what. Just do it. I've had about enough of you anyway."

"Back off, ladies," Allison said, pulling Lance closer to her. "He's mine."

"Excuse me?" said Athena as though Allison was naught but an antagonistic little fly.

"He's my husband."

"So?"

"And he also slept with your mother," Allison said with a look that said she believed she'd just gotten an edge.

Athena's expression contorted. "He slept with my father's forehead?"

"What?"

"Long story," Apollo interjected, "and nobody believes it anyway."

"Wait," Athena piped up again, "are you saying he slept with Leto?"

"Precisely."

"Ew. Well, that ruins that."

"I'm still okay with it," announced Slutius.

"Of course you are," Flaccidus wailed. "You're a damn slut!" He instantly stopped with a look of eureka. "Oh," he said, turning to Guinevere, "I hear it now."

Guinevere gave him a wan smile.

"Right," said Arthur before this could go any further. "Well, seeing that we've resolved *that* issue—

though it does always seem to be a point of discussion with him around—what do we do now?"

# TIME TO GO

ARTHUR STOOD WITH Arty and Flaccidus near one of the columns. Arty had addressed his wardrobe malfunction, but he was still shifting from side to side and wincing now and then.

Allison and Merlin were busily discussing the transporter technology with Apollo and Athena as Queen Slutius stood over by one of the windows chatting up Sir Lance-A-Lot.

"Don't let him do it," Arty was saying to Flaccidus. "Ye'll be after regretting it for all yer days."

"The way I see it, she'll get it out of her system," Flaccidus replied with a shrug.

"That ain't the problem," Arty replied. "It's the getting it *in to* her system that ye should be worried about."

"Oh."

"He'll not do anything anyway," Arthur said. "Allison is here, and unless she approves of Lance having relations with another woman, he won't partake. He's honorable that way. When he's single, he's a regular horn dog—to borrow a term from Merlin, but when he has a significant other, he wouldn't dare step out on her, unless, again, she approved of such a deed."

As if on cue, Slutius looked suddenly sad. Lance put a hand on her shoulder for a moment before walking back over to Allison.

"See?"

"Aye," said Arty.

"Whew," said Flaccidus.

"Ye don't know the half of it," Arty said, "and ye'll be damn glad yer wife ain't after knowin' the whole of it!"

"Right," said Arthur as he motioned towards Merlin and the gods. "I'm going to start rounding everyone up."

The discussion that he'd entered was full of words he didn't understand. This wasn't uncommon when it came to speaking with the likes of Merlin, but at least he could ask for definitions during those one-on-one talks. With this bunch bandying about words regarding time travel, computers, and other odd-sounding terms, it was akin to standing with a group of people who were all speaking a foreign language.

"Sorry to interrupt," Arthur said at a break in the conversation, "but we should really be getting back."

"True," Merlin agreed. "We've overstayed our welcome as it is."

"Actually, how exactly are we going to get back?" asked Galahad.

"I have a personal transport device," she answered, reaching into her pocket and pulling out a small box.

"I just need you all to join me in one of the rooms or some other location where it's just us. Then I'll transport to Merlin's house, set up the computer, and have you all transported as well."

Merlin raised an eyebrow. "Clever."

"Comes with the territory."

Arthur took one last look around the hall. It was beautiful, to be sure. He'd almost wished Merlin had brought along one of his picture-taking devices so he could permanently capture the moment.

"Well," he said to Apollo and Athena, "it was definitely an interesting stay."

"Sorry about how Flaccidus treated you when you arrived," Athena said with a frown. "Again, he's just a temporary fill-in until we find someone more fitting for the job."

"He wasn't so bad," said Arthur. "Merely trying to protect his land."

"If you say so."

"He's a boob," Apollo stated outright. Everyone looked at him. "What? He is."

"Right, well, then."

Arthur bowed and stepped away.

Guinevere was speaking with Guards Probius and Clearlyachickus by the main door. The two lovebirds looked to be glowing. While Arthur still found their behavior unprofessional, he couldn't help but appreciate that they'd found happiness with each other. This was especially true because he knew how Guinevere so loved playing the role of cupid.

Probius had more of a relieved look than a joyous one, but Arthur understood that relief was akin to happiness when it came to certain soldiers.

"We have to leave, my persimmon," said Arthur, giving a smile to Clearlyachickus.

"Already?"

"Sorry, dear, but it's time."

"Oh, all right."

She gave Clearlyachickus a prolonged hug, which left Arthur feeling as though he should at least shake hands with Probius.

"Was a pleasure meeting you," Arthur said in a cordial tone.

"And you, sire."

Arthur felt as though he should say something more. He was never one for these awkward moments.

"Uh... may you have lots of success in your life."

"Thank you, sire."

"Uh... and may all of your dreams come true."

"That would be wonderful, sire."

"Uh... and may you have lots of children who grow to do great things."

"Most kind, sire."

"Uh... and may your lineage be great and produce kingdoms of splendor." He was really reaching now.

"It would be a dream come true, sire." Probius shifted uncomfortably. "My apologies for the lack of discipline outside of your room. It was just—"

"No, no," Arthur said, seeing that the man was woefully distraught over the situation. A king learned over time when a soldier was just playing the game of sorrow—Purcivale and Tristan came to mind—and when he was genuine. "As the pointy-hat wearing fellow over there would said, 'We're good.'"

"Thank you, sire."

"Right." Arthur cleared his throat. "My love?"

"Don't they make a wonderful couple dear?" Guinevere said, glowing.

Arthur peeked over his shoulder again at Merlin. The wizard would not take kindly to Guinevere having been a part of this union. She clearly understood Arthur's worry, too, as she gave him one of those "oopsie" looks.

"And I'm equally thrilled that you helped me to see the light, my lady," Clearlyachickus said. "I'm going to start an underground movement to improve the well-being of ladies everywhere in Rome."

"That's wonderful," said Guinevere, beaming. "Isn't it, Arthur?"

"Uh… yes, of course. Wonderful."

Arthur quickly locked eyes with Probius, who remained stoic. If he were feeling any concern over the words of his new lover, he was hiding it well. This told Arthur the relationship between these two had a solid chance of success.

"Puddin'," Arthur said again, "we should really be moving along. Merlin is going to start getting—"

"Yes, you're right," she interrupted. "Farewell to you both. I'm sure you'll live happily ever after, as they say."

They padded off to a room where the rest of the troop had gone. It was much smaller than the other rooms Arthur had seen, but it still carried the same style of decor and coloring. Honestly, there wasn't a room he'd seen on this trip that wasn't impressive… aside from the dungeon, of course.

"Good luck to you all," said Athena as she and Apollo stood at the door. "We'll assuredly see some of you soon."

"Looking forward to it," Merlin said, seeming to have changed his mind on the role of these self-proclaimed gods.

The door shut, leaving the original troop, plus Lance-A-Lot and Allison.

"Okay," said Allison. "I'm going to transport to the future and will bring you along shortly. It should only take a couple of minutes." She was about to press a button on a little device she was carrying, but stopped. "Nobody leave this room, understood?"

"I stay where I stay," announced Gaheris.

"We'll be here," affirmed Arthur.

"Aye," Arty agreed. "I'm tired of this shet. I wanna be after gettin' home!"

"Good," said Allison, and then pressed the button.

# BACK TO CAMELOT

THE MOMENT THEY returned to Merlin's house, Arty jumped off the platform and breathed a sigh of relief.

"Never thought I'd be happy to be back in this damn tree."

"It is good to be home," Merlin said with a smile. "Also, you may not have noticed, but you two dudes look like kings again."

Arthur glanced over at Arty, seeing the man in his full Scottish outfit. Arty was looking back, nodding and grinning in a way to let Arthur know that he, too, was seeing only Arthur's English garb. Guinevere was dressed in pantaloons still, but she didn't have one of the Rings of Veiling that Arthur and Arty had.

They heard the sound of song coming from the other room. Well, more precisely, they heard two drunken men singing two different songs as if competing with each other.

When they rounded the corner, they found Sir Bedivere standing face to face with a Scottish soldier, both of whom were drinking, laughing, and singing.

"What's this after bein', then, Doonan?" said Arty.

"Hmmm?" Doonan said, looking as though he were having trouble maintaining his balance. "Ooooh, shet. Sorry... hic... sire! They had tequila."

"Ta kill who?" said Arty.

Merlin held up a bottle and tipped it, showing that the contents had been drained. "Tequila. It's a potent brand of booze."

"It's Sir Bedivere's primary skill," Arthur said in accusation, staring at the bottle.

Arty looked at him. "What?"

"Drinking," Arthur answered.

"Same with Doonan," Arty said, "though he was supposed to have had therapy for that... among other things we shan't rightly mention. Now, tell me, ye rangy soldier, what are ye after doin' here?"

"Calle... hic... told me to come up and find ye, sire." Doonan swallowed hard and shook his head. "I seen some things here that I cannae unsee, but I shan't... hic... say a word ter nobody aboot it. Ever. Hic. Trust me!"

"Well, I'll have Ceallache's head on a platter for that. Told him ta stay put, I did!"

Doonan winked. "Ooookay," he said in sing-song fashion.

"Wait a second here," said Merlin, taking off his hat and setting it aside. "Shouldn't we have come back merely minutes from when we originally left?"

"I didn't think it would matter a few days either way," answered Allison.

"How long have we been gone, then, local time?"

"About a week," she answered.

"Oh," Arty said, lowering his hackles. "Well, that's after bein' different, then."

"Ooookay."

"Actually, Arty," Arthur said curiously, "I never did ask you why you came up to visit me in the first place."

"Oh yeah, aboot that. Me wife is throwin' a bash and wanted me to invite ye and yer Nets."

"My Nets?"

"He means knights," noted Guinevere.

"Aye, and don't get started on that," warned Arty. "It's been a long week, yeah?"

"Sorry," said Arthur. "Couldn't you have just sent a messenger?"

"Aye, and after all that's happened, I'll damn sure be after doin' that next time!" He then leaned in and added, "But I wanted to make sure not *all* of your Nets made it. Me queen still fancies another rumble with the human axe-handle."

"Sorry, sire," said Lance, obviously overhearing.

"Do you sleep with everyone?" said Allison irritably.

"Slept with you," noted Merlin.

"True." She dropped her angst. "Sorry, Mitch."

"Well," said Arthur, "we'd be delighted to join your party. Wouldn't we, dear?"

"Of course!"

Arty nodded. "Good, good. Uh—"

"Tell your wife that Lance and I have other plans," Allison said as Arty glanced at them.

"Aye." He then made a "whew" sound. "Sets me

mind at ease, that."

"Speaking of having other plans," Allison said, glancing at the metal band on her wrist, "we should really be getting back to little Mitchy."

"Yes, dear," agreed Lance before turning to Arthur. "Sire, I shall return again in a few weeks to do my monthly tour of duty."

"That's fine," Arthur said. "Thanks to you both for fetching us from Rome. I wasn't all that excited to stay there for long."

"It was my fault you got put in the wrong time and place anyway," Allison admitted. "Well, technically, it was Galahad's fault because he kept fiddling with things."

Galahad coughed. "Sorry."

"Lesson learned," she said in a kind way. "You'll get better at it, Gal."

"Thanks, Al."

Allison frowned at him. "Touché."

They said their goodbyes and headed off to the transporter. Arthur would be lying if he said he wouldn't miss Lance-A-Lot. The king could do without certain reminders of the man, but Lance wasn't the lead knight due to his third leg. He was a good soldier who was conscientious and duty-bound.

Everyone stepped out into the waning sunlight.

It was quite a vision. The street below was still bustling with activity as guards marched along the parapets and the alleyways. Fresh baked goods and grilled meats could be smelled even from their perch at the top of the hill, and though Arthur had already been filled to the brink with foodstuffs from the

Roman era, he couldn't help but have a craving for a crumpet or two.

"Gah, guh," said Gaheris suddenly.

"What are ye doin', man?" Arty said, stepping away from the large knight. "There's no fight to be had."

"He goes where he goes," Galahad noted before Gaheris could defend himself.

"Vile, it is," claimed Arty.

"Go home and do that, Gaheris!"

"Sorry, sire," Gaheris said to Arthur with a look of shame as he clomped down the hill toward the row of houses that marked the Knights' Quarters.

"Well, we're off to see how the theater is doing," announced Bors.

"Probably falling apart without us," stated Kay happily.

They nodded at each other and then at the rest of the troop before turning to walk down the hill.

"I suppose we should check in on the wives, too," Bors could be heard saying.

"Probably having a blast without us," Kay replied.

Arthur glanced over at the Scottish king. The man looked rather regal with his magical ring hiding his true choice of garb.

"Well, Arty, it was good of you to come. You're welcome to stay longer, if you'd like."

"Nay, I'd best be gettin' back before Calle goes and starts stormin' the walls here."

"Understood."

The two men gripped arms for a moment, needing no words to explain the kinship (and queenship) they shared. It wasn't likely that another reign of two kings from the lands of Scotland and England would ever again exist that could claim to share both a vision of peace and sense of fashion.

"See ye at the party in a few weeks," Arty said with a nod to Guinevere. "Come along, Doonan."

"Ooookay."

"Bye, Doonan," Bedivere called out. "Was fu... hic... fun!"

"Aye, it was," Doonan called back, stumbling as he walked. "Yer after bein' ooookay in... hic... me book."

"Tha...hic...thanks," Bedivere said an instant before his eyes rolled up into his head and he passed out.

After all they'd been through over the last week, Arthur knew things were going to be pretty dull for a while. He needed a break, certainly—they *all* did—but seeing the wonders of both the future and the past made him see the present as mundane. Then again, he had something that neither era had, at least not unless you went inside a medieval dinner theater. He had true knights with true sport and true feasts that none could outdo. Though he did quite fancy the cake from the Roman times.

"I just want to make sure that everyone realizes we can't talk about any of this," Merlin said to nobody in particular.

"Yep," said Galahad.

"Indeed," agreed Arthur.

Guinevere merely nodded, looking off into the distance as a nice breeze blew across the lot of them.

"Off with you, then," Merlin said, shooing them away. "I have to catch some sleep and start figuring out what's falling apart in this area so Galahad and I can fix it."

"Ugh," Galahad said by way of agreement.

As Arthur and Guinevere walked down the path that led to their beloved castle, they held each other's hand. It was nice to know that the peasants couldn't see what he was truly wearing, especially on such a fine evening.

"I think I shall miss that adventure, Arthur."

"Oddly, so shall I, my persimmon."

"Maybe we can do it again sometime?" she said as they turned a corner.

"Never say, 'never,' as they say."

"Indeed," Guinevere said, smiling. "Indeed."

# GENE. E. ALOGY

TWO WEEKS LATER Guinevere had reminded Arthur of the appointment she'd set up with one of the new scholars in town. The man's name was Gene E. Alogy. Arthur hadn't bothered to ask what the "E" stood for. Looking at the squat fellow, with his balding head, ruddy cheeks, and disheveled clothing, Arthur guessed "Egbert" would have been fitting. He only thought this because he had gone to school with an Egbert who looked just like the man, with the exception that the younger Egbert had hair.

Typically these types of meetings would be held in the grand chambers, but Guinevere had told Arthur that he needed to be seen among the people more, so they went to Mr. Alogy's place of business instead.

"Please, please," Mr. Alogy said, motioning to the chairs in front of him, "have a seat. I have a lot to show you today."

"Remember that I have a regency meeting in less than an hour, dear," Arthur reminded his beloved.

"I'll keep that in mind, sire," Mr. Alogy replied with

an odd look.

"No, I was speaking with my wife, good sir."

"Oh! Right."

The man went back to shuffling papers. He was clearly nervous, which was almost always the case with people who met with Arthur and/or Guinevere. Arthur had always tried his best to calm them down, but it rarely worked.

He turned to studying the room. There were stacks of paper everywhere, a tattered map on the wall that was stuck full of pins, and a painting of a walrus that seemed rather out of place.

"Nice office you have here," Arthur said, attempting to put the man at ease.

"Thank you, sire. I apologize for the mess. I've been working night and day to prepare these documents for you."

"That's a kindness," Arthur replied with a smile. "By the way, what precisely are these documents supposed to reveal?"

The man paused and looked up. "Your ancestry, sire."

"Ah."

Arthur looked over at Guinevere and shrugged.

"It's important to know where we come from, dear."

"I suppose," conceded Arthur, "but I think it's more important to know where we're going."

"Without knowledge of the past," Mr. Alogy said as he sat the final stack in place and plopped into his chair, "we're doomed to repeat it. Or so they say."

Arthur found it difficult to argue that tidbit. He

assumed every era held some of the same dynamics. Kings or rulers of some sort, peasants, soldiers, merchants, chefs, artisans, craftsman, and many other professions.

"What have you found, Mr. Alogy?" Guinevere asked, clearly far more interested in this venture down memory lane than Arthur was.

"Your parents were—"

"You know who my parents were?" said Arthur, instantly realizing what this was actually about.

He'd heard "ancestry," sure, but he hadn't put two and two together.

He'd never known his parents in great detail. His earliest memories were of his father being hauled off to fight a battle for the English Army and his mother handing up Arthur and his sister for adoption. Arthur had only been four years old at the time. He'd searched for years and years, but had never found his long-lost sibling.

"Are they alive?"

"I'm sorry," Mr. Alogy said sadly.

"Sorry, my love," Guinevere said while touching his hand. She then turned back to Mr. Alogy. "Let's jump back to the farthest information you found, and work our way forward. My husband must meet with the regents soon, as he said, and I have a class to attend on the finer points of fist-fighting and drinking ale."

"Fist-fighting and ale-drinking?" said Arthur, shocked.

"Let it go, dear."

"Right," said Mr. Alogy, clearing his throat. "Well, I was only able to get back as far as 72AD. There just weren't very many records prior to that."

Arthur and Guinevere glanced at each other.

"Apparently, there were two guards named Probius and Clearlyachickus—odd names, if you ask me," Mr. Alogy said with a chuckle. Then he looked up and coughed. "Sorry. Anyway, they had a young child named Findus Excaliburus who went off on a search for a magical sword. He never found it, but his search took him to Britain where he met and married a woman named Agnes." He peered up for a second.

Guinevere and Arthur looked at each other with mouths agape.

"Merlin was right," said Arthur.

"And you'll never say a word to him about it," warned Guinevere.

Arthur was confused. "Why not?"

"Because he'll hold it over my head forever, that's why not."

"True," mused Arthur. "He'll do the same with me since I was there when it happened." Arthur then gave Mr. Alogy a strong stare. "That information never leaves this room. Do you understand?"

"Of course, my lord," Mr. Alogy replied firmly.

"Good," said Guinevere as her shoulders relaxed. "Now, continue, if you please."

"Right. Right." Mr. Alogy shuffled his papers again. "Well, uh, Probius and Clearlyachickus had another child by the name of Locatus Dadamnswordus, though his mother seemingly called him Billy."

"Billy?" said Arthur.

"Correct. Now, Billy also set off to find this sword, but failed in every attempt." Mr. Alogy flipped the pages. "Now, he finally gave up his search after marrying a Scottish woman named Liza. At this point, they stopped using the odd names, and had a daughter by the name of Igraine. She never hunted for the sword, though. Instead, she set about building a clothing empire. Mostly blouses, negligees, and things of that nature."

Again, the two royals looked at each other.

"Well, she ended up marrying a man named Gorlois—"

"Is he my father?"

"No, sire," Mr. Alogy replied. "Actually, rumor has it that a man named Merlin—"

"Merlin?"

"Different one," Mr. Alogy said quickly.

"There was another man with that name?" Arthur said doubtfully.

"Anyway, he was friends with this fellow named Uther Pendragon and—"

Arthur sat up. "That's *my* last name."

"Yes, sire."

"Go on, go on!"

"Uh… well, Uther was in love with Igraine, so he asked Merlin to help him put on a disguise so that he could look like Gorlois. He was doing this so that he could bone your mom."

"What?"

"Sorry, sire! I mean, uh—"

"Just continue, Mr. Alogy," Guinevere said, again patting Arthur's hand reassuringly.

"Yes, ma'am. Uther's disguise was a success and he ended up, well, scoring with your mother."

"That's disturbing," said Arthur, no longer certain he wanted to know about his parents.

"Shall I continue?"

"Please," urged Guinevere again.

"Gorlois was killed—"

"How?"

"I don't know, sire. I couldn't find information on that." The man swallowed. "Well, as soon as that happened, Uther married Igraine and they had you and your sister."

Arthur looked up. "What is her name?"

"Anna."

"Is she alive?"

"No, sire."

"Damn it all to hell!"

Arthur launched from his chair and began pacing around the room. There was so much information coming in at him that he could barely process it. His earliest ancestors were the two guards that Guinevere had offered their room to back in Ancient Rome; the next in line hunted for the same sword that he'd finally found, which secured him the title of King in England; and his father had apparently gone through the trouble of dressing like another man in order to have relations with his mother. He also assumed that his father had a hand in the death of his mother's original husband, though he could only hope that wasn't the case.

It was so much to digest that he was struggling to keep his emotions in check.

To make matters worse, there were horns sounding from all over the campus. This often happened whenever diplomats arrived, which made sense seeing that this was the day he was to meet with the local regency.

"Is there more?" he said finally.

"Yes, sire," said Mr. Alogy slowly.

"Spit it out, man," demanded Arthur.

"You also had a brother that nobody knew about."

Arthur felt his jaw go slack. "A brother?"

"Yes, sire."

"Is he dead, too?"

"No, sire," said Mr. Alogy. "In fact, I took the liberty of having a courier run all of this paperwork to him a few days ago. My guess is that he will read them and eventually visit you."

At that moment the door burst open and the smiling face of Scottish Arthur stepped into the room. He was holding his arms out in grandiose fashion. In one of his hands was a wad of paper with a stamp that read "Gene E. Alogy."

Arty's face was lit up.

"Me bruddah!"

Arthur turned slowly towards Mr. Alogy.

"You've got to be kidding."

# ACKNOWLEDGEMENTS

## Thanks to *The Ring of Veiling* and *Knights in the Future* launch group!

(listed in alphabetical order by first name)

Adam "Beefy" Pederick, Alex McKenzie, Allen Maltbie, Amy Simmonds, Andrea Tootell, Andy Crank, Annet Davidson, Aragorn Berner, Arto Suokas, Barrie & Muriel Mee, Benny Bennett, Bob Gouldy, Bob Topping, Brian Floyd, Camille Green, Candy Valdez, Catherine Currie, Cher Eaves, Chastity Jackson, Chris Hargrave, Chris Anthony, Chris Wakeham, Christopher Ridgway, Clare Short, Conrad Z-ro, Darrell Northcott, Dave Watson, David P. Ridgway, Diann Pustay, Earl Brown, Eric Hirsch, Eric Ludwig, Erin Mattox, Fergy Ferg, Geoffrey Ackers, Grant Taff Lewis, Gretchen Wickline Carter, Helen Wrenn, Helena Coker, Holly Roth-Nelson, Hugh Davies, Ian Nick Tarry, Igloo Q. Birdbath, J. Ed Baker, Jack Tufford, James Robinson, Jamie Smith, Jan Gray, Jason Mills, Jenna Burns, Jennie Nichols, Jennifer Willison, James Hannah, Jo Freeman, Jodie Stackowiak, Joe Simon, Joel Jackson, John Barbaretti, John Chappell, John "Yiaagaitia" Debnam, John "Murphyfields" Ladbury, John Scott, John Weaver, Julia Taylor, Keith Hall, Kevan Busby, Kim Phelan, Lee Goodrow, Leigh Evans, Les McCandless, Lesley Donnachie, Leslie Grotti Jost, Linda Carter, Lizzie Fletcher,

Madeleine Fenner, Mags Kelly, Mahri McGregor, Mark Brown, Martin Smith, Matthew Wilson, Michael Crosby, Mike Black, Mike Ikirt, Neil Gurling, Neil Lowrie, Nic Jansen, Nick Moon, Nigel Brett, Noah Sturdevant, Paul Deakin, Paul McCarthy, Paul Raymond, Paul Turner-Smithson, Paulette "Elsolel" Kilgore, Phyllis McGrath, Rachel Blakeman, Richard Doubleday, Sammie Elestial, Sandee Lloyd, Scott Ackermann, Sean Ellis, Sharon Ward, Shirley MacDonald, Sion Morris, Stephen A. Smith, Steve Grossman, Steve Hayes, Steve Shamka, Tammy Wilson-Lewallen, Teresa Cattrall Ferguson, Terry Foster, Thomas Mayes, Tony Dawson, Tony Dodds, Tracey Herron, Traci Hoffman, and Yelaerb-Gnortsmra Hag Erialc.

## Thanks to the *Knights in the Past* launch group!
(listed in alphabetical order by first name)

Adam Goldstein, Adam "Beefy" Pederick, Camille E. Green, Carolyn Jean Evans, Christopher Ridgway, Dan Sippel, Debbie Tily, Diann Pustay, Eden England-Woods, Fiona Sanders, Grant Taft Lewis, Helen Day, Ian Nick Tarry, Jackie Spencer, Jamie Smith, Jan Gray, Jodie Stackowiak, John Debnam, Karen Atkinson, Karen Brown, Lizzy Marjot, Lynette Wood, Mark Brown, Matthew Stuart Thomas Wilson, Michael Illingworth, Noah Sturdevant, Pamita Rao, Sandee Lloyd, Sharon Kennedy,

Stephen Bagwell, Teresa Cattrall Ferguson, Ty Seale.

*We'd also like to thank the following people for their contributions in helping to name the Roman guards in* **Knights in the Past...**

(Listed in alphabetical order by first name. Note that there were many names contributed, but these were the ones that received the most votes!)

**Allen Maltbie contributed:** Cranius Rectus, Itchus Crotchius, Roidus Ragius, Drunkus Askunkus, Rotundus Posteriorus, Bodacious Bootius, and Dave.

**Jamie Smith contributed:** Tortoise Beatus Rabbitus, Horatio Harrassyurass, Dubius Phallaci, Dropa de Turda, and Hugi Bearus.

**John Debnam contributed:** Prematuria Jackulus, Hottus Totrottus, and Sextus Transmittus Disius.

**John Ladbury contributed:** Wankus Maximus.

**Joe Simon contributed:** Schlongus Longorius, Harrius Palmus, Rectumus Odiferous, and Chokus de Chickinus.

**Mark Brown contributed:** Slipus Outicus.

**Nigel Brett contributed:** Uranus Bleedus.

**Noah Sturdevant contributed:** Giganticus Mamarus and Isconstantly Flashingus.

**Scott Reid contributed:** Tinius Weenus.

**Steven Palfrey contributed:** Tittus Fascinaticus, Hernia Rupturus, Scratchus Continuous, Scabbus Scratchus, and Dribblus Mucus.

**Teresa Cattrall Ferguson contributed:** Tellus Anotherus, Folatio the Philanderer, and Senilius.

# ABOUT THE AUTHORS

## John P. Logsdon

John was raised in the MD/VA/DC area. Growing up, John had a steady interest in writing stories, playing music, and tinkering with computers. He spent over 20 years working in the video games industry where he acted as designer and producer on many online games. He's written science fiction, fantasy, humor, and even books on game development. While he enjoys writing lighthearted adventures and wacky comedies most, he can't seem to turn down writing darker fiction. John lives with his wife, son, and Chihuahua.

On the web: www.JohnPLogsdon.com

## Christopher P. Young

Chris grew up in the Maryland suburbs. He spent the majority of his childhood reading and writing science fiction and learning the craft of storytelling. He worked as a designer and producer in the video games industry for a number of years as well as working in technology and admin services. He enjoys writing both serious and comedic science fiction and fantasy. Chris lives with his wife and an ever-growing population of critters.

# CRIMSON MYTH PRESS

*Crimson Myth Press* offers more books by this author as well as books from a few other hand-picked authors. From science fiction & fantasy to adventure & mystery, we bring the best stories for adults and kids alike.

Check out our complete book catalog:

www.CrimsonMyth.com

Printed in Great Britain
by Amazon